THE QUE

Philippa Gregory is an established writer and broadcaster for radio and television. She holds a PhD in eighteenth-century literature from the University of Edinburgh. She has been widely praised for her historical novels, including *Earthly Joys, Virgin Earth, A Respectable Trade, The Queen's Fool, The Virgin's Lover, The Constant Princess, The Boleyn Inheritance, The Other Queen,* as well as her works of contemporary suspense. *The Other Boleyn Girl* was adapted for BBC television and is now a major film, starring Scarlett Johansson, Natalie Portman and Eric Bana. Philippa Gregory lives in the North of England with her family and welcomes visitors to her website PhilippaGregory.com

By the same author

PHILIPPA GREGORY

THE QUEEN'S FOOL

HARPER

HarperCollins*Publishers*
77–85 Fulham Palace Road,
Hammersmith, London W6 8JB

www.harpercollins.co.uk

This production 2011
1

First published by in Great Britain by
HarperCollins*Publishers* 2003

ISBN: 978 0 00 791464 7

Typeset in PostScript Linotype Minion
with Medici Script display
by Palimpsest Book Production Limited,
Falkirk, Stirlingshire

Printed and bound in Great Britain by
Clays Ltd, St Ives plc

MIX
Paper from
responsible sources
FSC® C007454

FSC is a non-profit international organisation established to promote the
responsible management of the world's forests. Products carrying the FSC
label are independently certified to assure consumers that they come
from forests that are managed to meet the social, economic and
ecological needs of present and future generations.

Find out more about HarperCollins and the environment at
www.harpercollins.co.uk/green

For Anthony

Summer 1548

The girl, giggling and over-excited, was running in the sunlit garden, running away from her stepfather, but not so fast that he could not catch her. Her stepmother, seated in an arbour with Rosamund roses in bud all around her, caught sight of the fourteen-year-old girl and the handsome man chasing around the broad tree trunks on the smooth turf and smiled, determined to see only the best in both of them: the girl she was bringing up and the man she had adored for years.

He snatched at the hem of the girl's swinging gown and caught her up to him for a moment. 'A forfeit!' he said, his dark face close to her flushed cheeks.

They both knew what the forfeit would be. Like quicksilver she slid from his grasp and dodged away, to the far side of an ornamental fountain with a broad circular bowl. Fat carp were swimming slowly in the water; Elizabeth's excited face was reflected in the surface as she leaned forward to taunt him.

'Can't catch me!'

''Course I can.'

She leaned low so that he could see her small breasts at the top of the square-cut green gown. She felt his eyes on her and the colour in her cheeks deepened. He watched, amused and aroused, as her neck flushed rosy pink.

'I can catch you any time I want to,' he said, thinking of the chase of sex that ends in bed.

'Come on then!' she said, not knowing exactly what she was inviting, but knowing that she wanted to hear his feet pounding the grass behind her, sense his hands outstretched to grab at her; and, more than anything else, to feel his arms around her, pulling her against the fascinating contours of his body, the scratchy embroidery of his doublet against her cheek, the press of his thigh against her legs.

She gave a little scream and dashed away again down an *allée* of yew trees, where the Chelsea garden ran down to the river. The queen, smiling, looked up from her sewing and saw her beloved stepdaughter racing between the trees, her handsome husband a few easy strides behind. She looked down again at her sewing and did not see him catch Elizabeth, whirl her around, put her back to the red papery bark of the yew tree, and clamp his hand over her half-open mouth.

Elizabeth's eyes blazed black with excitement, but she did not struggle. When he realised that she would not scream, he took his hand away and bent his dark head.

Elizabeth felt the smooth sweep of his moustache against her lips, smelled the heady scent of his hair, his skin. She closed her eyes and tipped back her head to offer her lips, her neck, her breasts to his mouth. When she felt his sharp teeth graze her skin, she was no longer a giggling child, she was a young woman in the heat of first desire.

Gently he loosened his grip on her waist, and his hand stole up the firmly boned stomacher to the neck of her gown, where he could slide a finger down inside her linen to touch her breasts. Her nipple was hard and aroused, when he rubbed it she gave a little mew of pleasure that made him laugh at the predictability of female desire, a deep chuckle in the back of his throat.

Elizabeth pressed herself against the length of his body, feeling his thigh push forward between her legs in reply. She had a sensation like an overwhelming curiosity. She longed to know what might happen next.

When he made a movement away from her, as if to release her, she wound her arms around his back and pulled him into her again. She felt rather than saw Tom Seymour's smile of pleasure at her culpability, as his mouth came down on hers again and his tongue licked, as delicate as a cat, against the side of her mouth. Torn between disgust and desire at the extraordinary sensation, she slid her own tongue to meet his and felt the terrible intimacy of a grown man's intrusive kiss.

All at once it was too much for her, and she shrank back from him, but he knew the rhythm of this dance which she had so light-heartedly invoked, and which would now beat through her very veins. He caught at the hem of her brocade skirt and pulled it up and up until he could get at her, sliding his practised hand up her thighs, underneath her linen shift. Instinctively she clamped her legs together against his touch until he brushed, with calculated gentleness, the back of his hand on her hidden sex. At the teasing touch of his knuckles, she melted; he could feel her almost dissolve beneath him. She would have fallen if he had not had a firm arm around her waist, and he knew at that moment that he could have the king's own daughter, Princess Elizabeth, against a tree in the queen's garden. The girl was a virgin in name alone. In reality, she was little more than a whore.

A light step on the path made him quickly turn, dropping Elizabeth's gown and putting her behind him, out of sight. Anyone could read the tranced willingness on the girl's face; she was lost in her desire. He was afraid it was the queen, his wife, whose love for him was insulted every day that he seduced her ward under her very nose: the queen, who had been entrusted with the care of her stepdaughter the princess, Queen Katherine who had sat at Henry VIII's deathbed but dreamed of this man.

But it was not the queen who stood before him on the path. It was only a girl, a little girl of about nine years old, with big solemn dark eyes and a white Spanish cap tied under her chin. She carried two books strapped with bookseller's tape in her hand, and she regarded him with a cool objective interest, as if she had seen and understood everything.

'How now, sweetheart!' he exclaimed, falsely cheerful. 'You gave me a start. I might have thought you a fairy, appearing so suddenly.'

She frowned at his rapid, over-loud speech, and then she replied, very slowly with a strong Spanish accent. 'Forgive me, sir. My father told me to bring these books to Sir Thomas Seymour and they said you were in the garden.'

She proffered the package of books, and Tom Seymour was forced to step forward and take them from her hands. 'You're the bookseller's daughter,' he said cheerfully. 'The bookseller from Spain.'

She bowed her head in assent, not taking her dark scrutiny from his face.

'What are you staring at, child?' he asked, conscious of Elizabeth, hastily rearranging her gown behind him.

'I was looking at you, sir, but I saw something most dreadful.'

'What?' he demanded. For a moment he was afraid she would say that she had seen him with the Princess of England backed up against a tree like a common doxy, her skirt pulled up out of the way and his fingers dabbling at her purse.

'I saw a scaffold behind you,' said the surprising child, and then turned and walked away as if she had completed her errand and there was nothing more for her to do in the sunlit garden.

Tom Seymour whirled back to Elizabeth, who was trying to comb her disordered hair with fingers that were still shaking with desire. At once she stretched out her arms to him, wanting more.

'Did you hear that?'

Elizabeth's eyes were slits of black. 'No,' she said silkily. 'Did she say something?'

'She only said that she saw the scaffold behind me!' He was more shaken than he wanted to reveal. He tried for a bluff laugh, but it came out with a quaver of fear.

At the mention of the scaffold Elizabeth was suddenly alert. 'Why?' she snapped. 'Why should she say such a thing?'

'God knows,' he said. 'Stupid little witch. Probably mistook the word, she's foreign. Probably meant throne! Probably saw the throne behind me!'

But this joke was no more successful than his bluster, since in Elizabeth's imagination the throne and the scaffold were always close neighbours. The colour drained from her face, leaving her sallow with fear.

'Who is she?' Her voice was sharp with nervousness. 'Who is she working for?'

He turned to look for the child but the *allée* was empty. At the distant end of it he could see his wife walking slowly towards them, her back arched to carry the pregnant curve of her belly.

'Not a word,' he said quickly to the girl at his side. 'Not a word of this, sweetheart. You don't want to upset your stepmother.'

He hardly needed to warn her. At the first hint of danger the girl was wary, smoothing her dress, conscious always that she must play a part, that she must survive. He could always rely on Elizabeth's duplicity. She might be only fourteen but she had been trained in deceit every day since the death of her mother, she had been an apprentice cheat for twelve long years. And she was the daughter of a liar – two liars, he thought spitefully. She might feel desire; but she was always more alert to danger or ambition than to lust. He took her cold hand and led her up the *allée* towards his wife Katherine. He tried for a merry smile. 'I caught her at last!' he called out.

He glanced around, he could not see the child anywhere. 'We had such a race!' he cried.

I was that child, and that was the first sight I ever had of the Princess Elizabeth: damp with desire, panting with lust, rubbing herself like a cat against another woman's husband. But it was the first and last time I saw Tom Seymour. Within a year, he was dead on the scaffold charged with treason, and Elizabeth had denied three times having anything more than the most common acquaintance with him.

Winter 1552–53

'I remember this!' I said excitedly to my father, turning from the rail of the Thames barge as we tacked our way upstream. 'Father! I remember this! I remember these gardens running down to the water, and the great houses, and the day you sent me to deliver some books to the lord, the English lord, and I came upon him in the garden with the princess.'

He found a smile for me, though his face was weary from our long journey. 'Do you, child?' he asked quietly. 'That was a happy summer for us. She said . . .' He broke off. We never mentioned my mother's name, even when we were alone. At first it had been a precaution to keep us safe from those who had killed her and would come after us, but now we were hiding from grief as well as from the Inquisition; and grief was an inveterate stalker.

'Will we live here?' I asked hopefully, looking at the beautiful riverside palaces and the level lawns. I was eager for a new home after years of travelling.

'Nowhere as grand as this,' he said gently. 'We will have to start small, Hannah, in just a little shop. We have to make our lives again. And when we are settled then you will come out of boy's clothes, and dress as a girl again, and marry young Daniel Carpenter.'

'And can we stop running?' I asked, very low.

My father hesitated. We had been running from the Inquisition for so long that it was almost impossible to hope that we had reached a safe haven. We ran away the very night that my mother was found guilty of being a Jew – a false Christian, a 'Marrano' – by the church

6

court, and we were long gone when they released her to the civil court to be burned alive at the stake. We ran from her like a pair of Judas Iscariots, desperate to save our own skins, though my father would tell me later, over and over again, with tears in his eyes, that we could never have saved her. If we had stayed in Aragon, they would have come for us too, and then all three of us would have died, instead of two being saved. When I swore that I would rather have died than live without her, he said very slowly and sadly that I would learn that life was the most precious thing of all. One day I would understand that she would have gladly given her life to save mine.

First over the border to Portugal, smuggled out by bandits who took every coin from my father's purse and left him with his manuscripts and books, only because they could find no use for them. By boat to Bordeaux, a stormy crossing when we lived on deck without shelter from the scudding rain and the flying spray, and I thought we would die of the cold or drowning. We hugged the most precious books to our bellies as if they were infants that we should keep warm and dry. Overland to Paris, all the way pretending to be something that we were not: a merchant and his young apprentice-lad, pilgrims on the way to Chartres, itinerant traders, a minor lord and his pageboy travelling for pleasure, a scholar and his tutor going to the great university of Paris; anything rather than admit that we were new Christians, a suspicious couple with the smell of the smoke from the auto-da-fé still clinging to our clothes, and night terrors still clinging to our sleep.

We met my mother's cousins in Paris, and they sent us on to their kin in Amsterdam, where they directed us to London. We were to hide our race under English skies, we were to become Londoners. We were to become Protestant Christians. We would learn to like it. I must learn to like it.

The kin – the People whose name cannot be spoken, whose faith is hidden, the People who are condemned to wander, banned from every country in Christendom – were thriving in secret in London as in Paris, as in Amsterdam. We all lived as Christians and observed the laws of the church, the feast days and fast days and rituals. Many of us, like my mother, believed sincerely in both faiths, kept the Sabbath in secret, a hidden candle burning, the food prepared, the housework done, so that the day could be holy with the scraps of half-remembered

Jewish prayers, and then, the very next day, went to Mass with a clean conscience. My mother taught me the Bible and all of the Torah that she could remember together, as one sacred lesson. She cautioned me that our family connections and our faith were secret, a deep and dangerous secret. We must be discreet and trust in God, in the churches we had so richly endowed, in our friends: the nuns and priests and teachers that we knew so well. When the Inquisition came, we were caught like innocent chickens whose necks should be wrung and not slashed.

Others ran, as we had done; and emerged, as we had done, in the other great cities of Christendom to find their kin, to find refuge and help from distant cousins or loyal friends. Our family helped us to London with letters of introduction to the d'Israeli family, who here went by the name of Carpenter, organised my betrothal to the Carpenter boy, financed my father's purchase of the printing press and found us the rooms over the shop off Fleet Street.

In the months after our arrival I set myself to learn my way around yet another city, as my father set up his print shop with an absolute determination to survive and to provide for me. At once, his stock of texts was much in demand, especially his copies of the gospels that he had brought inside the waistband of his breeches and now translated into English. He bought the books and manuscripts which once belonged to the libraries of religious houses – destroyed by Henry, the king before the young king, Edward. The scholarship of centuries was thrown to the winds by the old king, Henry, and every shop on each corner had a pile of papers that could be bought by the bushel. It was a bibliographer's heaven. My father went out daily and came back with something rare and precious and when he had tidied it, and indexed it, everyone wanted to buy. They were mad for the Holy Word in London. At night, even when he was weary, he set print and ran off short copies of the gospels and simple texts for the faithful to study, all in English, all clear and simple. This was a country determined to read for itself and to live without priests, so at least I could be glad of that.

We sold the texts cheaply, at little more than cost price, to spread the word of God. We let it be known that we believed in giving the Word to the people, because we were convinced Protestants now. We could not have been better Protestants if our lives had depended on it.

Of course, our lives did depend on it.

I ran errands, read proofs, helped with translations, set print, stitched like a saddler with the sharp needle of the binder, read the backwards-writing on the stone of the printing press. On days when I was not busy in the print shop I stood outside to summon passers-by. I still dressed in the boy's clothes I had used for our escape and anyone would have mistaken me for an idle lad, breeches flapping against my bare calves, bare feet crammed into old shoes, cap askew. I lounged against the wall of our shop like a vagrant lad whenever the sun came out, drinking in the weak English sunshine and idly surveying the street. To my right was another bookseller's shop, smaller than ours and with cheaper wares. To the left was a publisher of chap books, poems and tracts for itinerant pedlars and ballad sellers, beyond him a painter of miniatures and maker of dainty toys, and beyond him a portrait painter and limner. We were all workers with paper and ink in this street, and Father told me that I should be grateful for a life which kept my hands soft. I should have been; but I was not.

It was a narrow street, meaner even than our temporary lodgings in Paris. Each house was clamped on to another house, all of them tottering like squat drunkards down to the river, the gable windows overhanging the cobbles below and blocking out the sky, so the pale sunshine striped the earth-plastered walls, like the slashing on a sleeve. The smell of the street was as strong as a farmyard's. Every morning the women threw the contents of the chamber pots and the washing bowls from the overhanging windows and tipped the night-soil buckets into the stream in the middle of the street where it gurgled slowly away, draining sluggishly into the dirty ditch of the River Thames.

I wanted to live somewhere better than this, somewhere like the Princess Elizabeth's garden with trees and flowers and a view down to the river. I wanted to be someone better than this: not a bookseller's ragged apprentice, a hidden girl, a woman heading for betrothal to a stranger.

As I stood there, warming myself like a sulky Spanish cat in the sunshine, I heard the ring of a spur against a cobblestone and I snapped my eyes open and leaped to attention. Before me, casting a long shadow, was a young man. He was richly dressed, a tall hat on his head, a cape swinging from his shoulders, a thin silver sword at his side. He was the most breathtakingly handsome man I had ever seen.

All of this was startling enough, I could feel myself staring at him as if he were a descended angel. But behind him was a second man.

This was an older man, near thirty years of age, with the pale skin of a scholar, and dark deep-set eyes. I had seen his sort before. He was one of those who visited my father's bookshop in Aragon, who came to us in Paris and who would be one of my father's customers and friends here in London. He was a scholar, I could see it in the stoop of his neck and the rounded shoulders. He was a writer, I saw the permanent stain of ink on the third finger of his right hand; and he was something greater even than these: a thinker, a man prepared to seek out what was hidden. He was a dangerous man: a man not afraid of heresies, not afraid of questions, always wanting to know more; a man who would seek the truth behind the truth.

I had known a Jesuit priest like this man. He had come to my father's shop in Spain, and begged him to get manuscripts, old manuscripts, older than the Bible, older even than the Word of God. I had known a Jewish scholar like this man, he too had come to my father's bookstore and asked for the forbidden books, remnants of the Torah, the Law. Jesuit and scholar had come often to buy their books; and one day they had come no more. Ideas are more dangerous than an unsheathed sword in this world, half of them are forbidden, the other half would lead a man to question the very place of the earth itself, safe at the centre of the universe.

I had been so interested in these two, the young man like a god, the older man like a priest, that I had not looked at the third. This third man was all dressed in white, gleaming like enamelled silver, I could hardly see him for the brightness of the sun on his sparkling cloak. I looked for his face and could see only a blaze of silver, I blinked and still I could not see him. Then I came to my senses and realised that whoever they might be, they were all three looking in the doorway of the bookshop next door.

One swift glance at our own dark doorway showed me that my father was in the inside room mixing fresh ink, and had not seen my failure to summon customers. Cursing myself for an idle fool, I jumped forward into their path and said clearly, in my newly acquired English accent, 'Good day to you, sirs. Can we help you? We have the finest collection of pleasing and moral books you will find in London, the most interesting manuscripts at the fairest of prices and drawings wrought with the most artistry and the greatest charm that . . .'

'I am looking for the shop of Oliver Green, the printer,' the young man said.

At the moment his dark eyes flicked to mine, I felt myself freeze, as if all the clocks in London had suddenly stopped still and their pendulums were caught silent. I wanted to hold him: there, in his red slashed doublet in the winter sunshine, forever. I wanted him to look at me and see me, me, as I truly was; not an urchin lad with a dirty face, but a girl, almost a young woman. But his glance flicked indifferently past me to our shop, and I came to my senses and held open the door for the three of them.

'This is the shop of the scholar and bookmaker Oliver Green. Step inside, my lords,' I invited them and I shouted, into the inner dark room: 'Father! Here are three great lords to see you!'

I heard the clatter as he pushed back his high printer's stool and came out, wiping his hands on his apron, the smell of ink and hot pressed paper following him. 'Welcome,' he said. 'Welcome to you both.' He was wearing his usual black suit and his linen at the cuffs was stained with ink. I saw him through their eyes for a moment and saw a man of fifty, his thick hair bleached white from shock, his face deep-furrowed, his height concealed in the scholar's stoop.

He prompted me with a nod, and I pulled forward three stools from under the counter, but the lords did not sit, they stood looking around.

'And how may I serve you?' he asked. Only I could have seen that he was afraid of them, afraid of all three: the handsome younger man who swept off his hat and pushed his dark curled hair back from his face, the quietly dressed older man and, behind them, the silent lord in shining white.

'We are seeking Oliver Green, the bookseller,' the young lord said.

My father nodded his head. 'I am Oliver Green,' he said quietly, his Spanish accent very thick. 'And I will serve you in any way that I can do. Any way that is pleasing to the laws of the land, and the customs . . .'

'Yes, yes,' the young man said sharply. 'We hear that you are just come from Spain, Oliver Green.'

My father nodded again. 'I am just come to England indeed, but we left Spain three years ago, sir.'

'An Englishman?'

'An Englishman now, if you please,' my father said cautiously.

'Your name? It is a very English name?'

'It was Verde,' he said with a wry smile. 'It is easier for Englishmen if we call ourselves Green.'

'And you are a Christian? And a publisher of Christian theology and philosophy?'

I could see the small gulp in my father's throat at the dangerous question, but his voice was steady and strong when he answered. 'Most certainly, sir.'

'And are you of the reformed or the old tradition?' the young man asked, his voice very quiet.

My father did not know what answer they wanted to this, nor could he know what might hang on it. Actually *we* might hang on it, or burn for it, or go to the block for it, however it was that they chose this day to deal with heretics in this country under the young King Edward.

'The reformed,' he said tentatively. 'Though christened into the old faith in Spain, I follow the English church now.' There was a pause. 'Praise be to God,' he offered. 'I am a good servant of King Edward, and I want nothing more than to work my trade and live according to his laws, and worship in his church.'

I could smell the sweat of his terror as acrid as smoke, and it frightened me. I brushed the back of my hand under my cheek, as if to wipe away the smuts from a fire. 'It's all right. I am sure they want our books, not us,' I said in a quick undertone in Spanish.

My father nodded to show he had heard me. But the young lord was on to my whisper at once. 'What did the lad say?'

'I said that you are scholars,' I lied in English.

'Go inside, *querida*,' my father said quickly to me. 'You must forgive the child, my lords. My wife died just three years ago and the child is a fool, only kept to mind the door.'

'The child speaks only the truth,' the older man remarked pleasantly. 'For we have not come to disturb you, there is no need to be afraid. We have only come to see your books. I am a scholar; not an inquisitor. I only wanted to see your library.'

I hovered at the doorway and the older man turned to me. 'But why did you say three lords?' he asked.

My father snapped his fingers to order me to go, but the young lord said: 'Wait. Let the boy answer. What harm is it? There are only two of us, lad. How many can you see?'

I looked from the older man to the handsome young man and saw that there were, indeed, only two of them. The third, the man in white as bright as burnished pewter, had gone as if he had never been there at all.

'I saw a third man behind you, sir,' I said to the older one. 'Out in the street. I am sorry. He is not there now.'

'She is a fool but a good girl,' my father said, waving me away.

'No, wait,' the young man said. 'Wait a minute. I thought this was a lad. A girl? Why d'you have her dressed as a boy?'

'And who was the third man?' his companion asked me.

My father became more and more anxious under the barrage of questions. 'Let her go, my lords,' he said pitifully. 'She is nothing more than a girl, a little maid with a weak mind, still shocked by her mother's death. I can show you my books, and I have some fine manuscripts you may like to see as well. I can show you . . .'

'I want to see them indeed,' the older man said firmly. 'But first, I want to speak with the child. May I?'

My father subsided, unable to refuse such great men. The older man took me by the hand and led me into the centre of the little shop. A glimmer of light through the leaded window fell on my face and he put a hand under my chin and turned my face one way and then the other.

'What was the third man like?' he asked me quietly.

'All in white,' I said through half-closed lips. 'And shining.'

'What did he wear?'

'I could only see a white cape.'

'And on his head?'

'I could only see the whiteness.'

'And his face?'

'I couldn't see his face for the brightness of the light.'

'D'you think he had a name, child?'

13

I could feel the word coming into my mouth though I did not understand it. 'Uriel.'

The hand underneath my chin was very still. The man looked into my face as if he would read me like one of my father's books. 'Uriel?'

'Yes, sir.'

'Have you heard that name before?'

'No, sir.'

'Do you know who Uriel is?'

I shook my head. 'I just thought it was the name of the one who came in with you. But I never heard the name before I just said it.'

The younger man turned to my father. 'When you say she is a fool, d'you mean that she has the Sight?'

'She talks out of turn,' my father said stubbornly. 'Nothing more. She is a good girl, I send her to church every day of her life. She means no offence, she just speaks out. She cannot help it. She is a fool, nothing more.'

'And why d'you keep her dressed like a boy?' he asked.

My father shrugged. 'Oh, my lords, these are troubled times. I had to bring her across Spain and France, and then through the Low Countries without a mother to guard her. I have to send her on errands and have her act as clerk for me. It would have been better for me if she had been a boy. When she is a woman full-grown, I will have to let her have a gown, I suppose, but I won't know how to manage her. I shall be lost with a girl. But a young lad I can manage, as a lad she can be of use.'

'She has the Sight,' the older man breathed. 'Praise God, I come looking for manuscripts and I find a girl who sees Uriel and knows his holy name.' He turned to my father. 'Does she have any knowledge of sacred things? Has she read anything more than the Bible and her catechism? Does she read your books?'

'Before God, no,' my father said earnestly, lying with every sign of conviction. 'I swear to you, my lord, I have brought her up to be a good ignorant girl. She knows nothing, I promise you. Nothing.'

The older man shook his head. 'Please,' he said gently to me and then to my father, 'do not fear me. You can trust me. This girl has the Sight, hasn't she?'

'No,' my father said baldly, denying me for my own safety. 'She's nothing more than a fool and the burden of my life. More worry than

14

she is worth. If I had kin to send her to – I would. She's not worth your attention . . .'

'Peace,' the young man said gently. 'We did not come to distress you. This gentleman is John Dee, my tutor. I am Robert Dudley. You need not fear us.'

At their names my father grew even more anxious, as well he might. The handsome young man was the son of the greatest man in the land: Lord John Dudley, protector of the King of England himself. If they took a liking to my father's library then we could find ourselves supplying books to the king, a scholarly king, and our fortune would be made. But if they found our books seditious or blasphemous or heretical, too questioning, or too filled with the new knowledge, then we could be thrown into prison or into exile again or to our deaths.

'You're very gracious, sir. Shall I bring my books to the palace? The light here is very poor for reading, there is no need to demean yourselves to my little shop . . .'

The older man did not release me. He was still holding my chin and looking into my face.

'I have studies of the Bible,' my father went on rapidly. 'Some very ancient in Latin and Greek and also books in other languages. I have some drawings of Roman temples with their proportions explained, I have a copy of some mathematical tables for numbers which I was given but of course I have not the learning to understand them, I have some drawings of anatomy from the Greek . . .'

Finally the man called John Dee let me go. 'May I see your library?'

I saw my father's reluctance to let the man browse the shelves and drawers of his collection. He was afraid that some of the books might now, under some new ruling, be banned as heretical. I knew that the books of secret wisdom in Greek and Hebrew were always hidden, behind the sliding back of the bookshelf. But even the ones on show might lead us into trouble in these unpredictable times. 'I will bring them out to you here?'

'No, I will come inside.'

'Of course, my lord,' he surrendered. 'It will be an honour to me.'

He led the way into the inner room and John Dee followed him. The young lord, Robert Dudley, took a seat on one of the stools and looked at me with interest.

'Twelve years old?'

'Yes, sir,' I lied promptly, although in truth I was nearly fourteen.

'And a maid, though dressed as a lad.'

'Yes, sir.'

'No marriage arranged for you?'

'Not straight away, sir.'

'But a betrothal in sight?'

'Yes, sir.'

'And who has your father picked out for you?'

'I am to marry a cousin from my mother's family when I am sixteen,' I replied. 'I don't particularly wish it.'

'You're a maid,' he scoffed. 'All young maids say they don't wish it.'

I shot a look at him which showed my resentment too clearly.

'Oho! Have I offended you, Mistress Boy?'

'I know my own mind, sir,' I said quietly. 'And I am not a maid like any other.'

'Clearly. So what is your mind, Mistress Boy?'

'I don't wish to marry.'

'And how shall you eat?'

'I should like to have my own shop, and print my own books.'

'And do you think a girl, even a pretty one in breeches, could manage without a husband?'

'I am sure I could,' I said. 'Widow Worthing has a shop across the lanes.'

'A widow has had a husband to give her a fortune, she didn't have to make her own.'

'A girl can make her own fortune,' I said stoutly. 'I should think a girl could command a shop.'

'And what else can a girl command?' he teased me. 'A ship? An army? A kingdom?'

'You will see a woman run a kingdom, you will see a woman can run a kingdom better than any in the world before,' I fired back, and then checked at the look on his face. I put my hand over my mouth. 'I didn't mean to say that,' I whispered. 'I know that a woman should always be ruled by her father or husband.'

He looked at me as if he would hear more. 'Do you think, Mistress Boy, that I will live to see a woman rule a kingdom?'

'In Spain it was done,' I said weakly. 'Once. Queen Isabella.'

He nodded and let it go, as if drawing us both back from the brink of something dangerous. 'So. D'you know your way to Whitehall Palace, Mistress Boy?'

'Yes, sir.'

'Then when Mr Dee has chosen the books he wants to see, you can bring them there, to my rooms. All right?'

I nodded.

'How is your father's shop prospering?' he asked. 'Selling many books? Many customers coming?'

'Some,' I said cautiously. 'But it is early days for us yet.'

'Your gift does not guide him in his business, then?'

I shook my head. 'It is not a gift. It is more like folly, as he says.'

'You speak out? And you can see what others cannot?'

'Sometimes.'

'And what did you see when you looked at me?'

His voice was pitched very low, as if he would lead me to whisper a reply. I raised my eyes from his boots, his strong legs, his beautiful surcoat, to the soft folds of his white ruff, his sensuous mouth, his half-lidded dark eyes. He was smiling at me, as if he understood that my cheeks, my ears, even my hair felt hot as if he were the sun from Spain on my head. 'When I first saw you, I thought I knew you.'

'From before?' he asked.

'From a time to come,' I said awkwardly. 'I thought that I would know you, in the days ahead.'

'Not if you are a lad!' He smiled to himself at the bawdiness of his thought. 'So what condition will I be in when you know me, Mistress Boy? Am I to be a great man? Am I to command a kingdom while you command a bookshop?'

'Indeed, I hope you will be a great man,' I said stiffly. I would say nothing more, this warm teasing must not lull me into thinking that it was safe to confide in him.

'What d'you think of me?' he asked silkily.

I took a quiet breath. 'I think that you would trouble a young woman who was not in breeches.'

He laughed out loud at that. 'Please God that is a true seeing,' he said. 'But I never fear trouble with girls, it is their fathers who strike me with terror.'

I smiled back, I could not help myself. There was something about the way his eyes danced when he laughed that made me want to laugh too, that made me long to say something extraordinarily witty and grown-up so that he would look at me and see me not as a child but as a young woman.

'And have you ever foretold the future and it came true?' he asked, suddenly serious.

The question itself was dangerous in a country that was always alert for witchcraft. 'I have no powers,' I said quickly.

'But without exerting powers, can you see the future? It is given to some of us, as a holy gift, to know what might be. My friend here, Mr Dee, believes that angels guide the course of mankind and may sometimes warn us against sin, just as the course of the stars can tell a man what his destiny might be.'

I shook my head doltishly at this dangerous talk, determined not to respond to him.

He looked thoughtful. 'Can you dance or play an instrument? Learn a part in a masque and say your lines?'

'Not very well,' I said unhelpfully.

He laughed at my reluctance. 'Well, we shall see, Mistress Boy. We shall see what you can do.'

I gave my little boyish bow and took care to say nothing more

Next day, carrying a parcel of books and a carefully rolled scroll of manuscript, I walked across the town, past the Temple Bar and past the green fields of Covent Garden to Whitehall Palace. It was cold with a sleety rain which forced my head down and made me pull my cap low over my ears. The wind off the river was as icy as if it were coming straight from the Russias, it blew me up King's Street to the very gates of Whitehall Palace.

I had never been inside a royal palace before, and I had thought I would just give the books to the guards on the gate, but when I showed them the note that Lord Robert had scrawled, with the Dudley seal of the bear and staff at the bottom, they bowed me through as though I were a visiting prince, and ordered a man to guide me.

Inside the gates, the palace was like a series of courtyards, each beautifully built, with a great garden in the middle set with apple trees and arbours and seats. The soldier from the gate led me across the first garden and gave me no time to stop and stare at the finely dressed lords and ladies who, wrapped in furs and velvets against the cold, were playing at bowls on the green. Inside the door, swung open by another pair of soldiers, there were more fine people in a great chamber, and behind that great room another, and then another. My guide led me through door after door until we came to a long gallery and Robert Dudley was at the far end of it, and I was so relieved to find him, the only man I knew in the whole palace, that I ran a few steps towards him and called out: 'My lord!'

The guard hesitated, as if he would block me from getting any closer, but Robert Dudley waved him aside. 'Mistress Boy!' he exclaimed. He got to his feet and then I saw his companion. It was the young king, King Edward, fifteen years of age and beautifully dressed in plush blue velvet but with a face the colour of skimmed milk and thinner than any lad I had ever seen before.

I dropped to my knee, holding tight to my father's books and trying to doff my cap at the same time, as Lord Robert remarked: 'This is the girl-boy. Don't you think she would be a wonderful player?'

I did not look up but I heard the king's voice, thinned with pain. 'You take such fancies, Dudley. Why should she be a player?'

'Her voice,' Dudley said. 'Such a voice, very sweet, and that accent, part Spanish and part London, I could listen to her forever. And she holds herself like a princess in beggar's clothes. Don't you think she's a delightful child?'

I kept my head down so that he should not see my delighted beam. I hugged the words to my skinny chest: 'a princess in beggar's clothes', 'a sweet voice', 'delightful'.

The young king returned me to the real world. 'Why, what part should she play? A girl, playing a boy, playing a girl. Besides, it's against Holy Writ for a girl to dress as a boy.' His voice tailed away into a cough which shook him like a bear might shake a dog.

I looked up and saw Dudley make a little gesture towards the young man as if he would hold him. The king took his handkerchief from his mouth and I saw a glimpse of a dark stain, darker than blood. Quickly, he tucked it out of sight.

'It's no sin,' Dudley said soothingly. 'She's no sinner. The girl is a holy fool. She saw an angel walking in Fleet Street. Can you imagine it? I was there, she truly did.'

The younger man turned to me at once, his face brightened with interest. 'You can see angels?'

I kept down on my knee and lowered my gaze. 'My father says I am a fool,' I volunteered. 'I am sorry, Your Grace.'

'But did you see an angel in Fleet Street?'

I nodded, my eyes downcast. I could not deny my gift. 'Yes, sire. I am sorry. I was mistaken. I didn't mean to give offence . . .'

'What can you see for me?' he interrupted.

I looked up. Anyone could have seen the shadow of death on his face, in his waxy skin, in his swollen eyes, in his bony thinness, even without the evidence of the stain on his handkerchief and the tremor of his lips. I tried to tell a lie but I could feel the words coming despite myself. 'I see the gates of heaven opening.'

Again, Robert Dudley made that little gesture, as if he would touch the boy, but his hand fell to his side.

The young king was not angry. He smiled. 'This child tells the truth when everyone else lies to me,' he said. 'All the rest of you run around finding new ways to lie. But this little one . . .' He lost his breath and smiled at me.

'Your Grace, the gates of heaven have been opened since your birth,' Dudley said soothingly. 'As your mother ascended. The girl's saying nothing more than that.' He shot me an angry look. 'Aren't you?'

The young king gestured to me. 'Stay at court. 'You shall be my fool.'

'I have to go home to my father, Your Grace,' I said as quietly and as humbly as I could, ignoring Lord Robert's glare. 'I only came today to bring Lord Robert his books.'

'You shall be my fool and wear my livery,' the young man ruled. 'Robert, I am grateful to you for finding her for me. I shan't forget it.'

It was a dismissal. Robert Dudley bowed and snapped his fingers for me, turned on his heel and went from the room. I hesitated, wanting to refuse the king, but there was nothing to do but bow to him and run after Robert Dudley as he crossed the huge presence chamber, negligently brushing off the couple of men who tried to stop him and ask after the health of the king. 'Not now,' he said.

He went down a long gallery, towards double doors guarded by more soldiers with pikes, who flung them open as we approached. Dudley passed through to their salute and I went after him at a run, like some pet greyhound scampering at its master's heels. Finally we came to a great pair of doors where the soldiers wore the Dudley livery and we went in.

'Father,' Dudley said and dropped to one knee.

There was a man at the fireplace of the great inner hall, looking down into the flames. He turned and made an unemotional blessing over his son's head with two fingers. I dropped to my knee too, and stayed down even when I felt Robert Dudley rise up beside me.

'How's the king this morning?'

'Worse,' Robert said flatly. 'Cough bad, he brought up some black bile, breathless. Can't last, Father.'

'And this is the girl?'

'This is the bookseller's daughter, calls herself twelve, I'd guess older, dresses like a lad but certainly a girl. Has the Sight, according to John Dee. I took her into the king as you ordered, begged her for a fool. She told him that she saw the gates of heaven opened for him. He liked it. She is to be his fool.'

'Good,' the duke said. 'And have you told her of her duties?'

'I brought her straight here.'

'Stand, fool.'

I rose to my feet and took my first look at Robert Dudley's father, the Duke of Northumberland, the greatest man in the kingdom. I took him in: a long bony face like a horse, dark eyes, balding head half-hidden by a rich velvet cap with a big silver brooch of his coat of arms: the bear and staff. A Spanish beard and moustache round a full mouth. I looked into his eyes and saw – nothing. This was a man whose face could hide his thoughts, a man whose very thoughts could conspire to hide his thoughts.

'So?' he asked of me. 'What do you see with those big black eyes of yours, my girl-boy fool?'

21

'Well, I don't see any angels behind you,' I said abruptly and was rewarded by an amused smile from the duke and a crack of laughter from his son.

'Excellent,' he said. 'Well done.' He turned to me. 'Listen, fool – what's your name?'

'Hannah Green, my lord.'

'Listen, Hannah the Fool, you have been begged for a fool and the king has accepted you, according to our laws and customs. D'you know what that means?'

I shook my head.

'You become his, like one of his puppies, like one of his soldiers. Your job, like a puppy and not like a soldier, is to be yourself. Say the first thing that comes into your head, do whatever you wish. It will amuse him. It will amuse us, and it will set before us all the work of the Lord, which will please him. You will tell the truth in this court of liars, you will be our innocent in this wicked world. Understand?'

'How am I to be?' I was absolutely confounded. 'What d'you want of me?'

'You are to be yourself. Speak as your gift commands you. Say whatever you wish. The king has no holy fool at present and he likes an innocent at court. He has commanded you. You are now a royal fool. One of the household. You will be paid to be his fool.'

I waited.

'Do you understand, fool?'

'Yes. But I don't accept.'

'You can't accept or not accept. You've been begged for a fool, you have no legal standing, you have no voice. Your father has handed you over to Lord Robert here, and he has given you to the king. You are now the king's.'

'If I refuse?' I could feel myself trembling.

'You can't refuse.'

'If I run away?'

'Punished according to the king's wishes. Whipped like a puppy. You were your father's property, now you are ours. And we have begged you for a fool to the king. He owns you. D'you understand?'

'My father would not sell me,' I said stubbornly. 'He would not let me go.'

'He cannot stand against us,' Robert said quietly behind me. 'And I promised him that you would be safer here than out on the street. I gave him my word and he accepted. The business was done while we ordered the books, Hannah. It is finished.'

'Now,' continued the duke. 'Not like a puppy, and not like a fool, you have another task to do.'

I waited.

'You are to be our vassal.'

At the strange English word I glanced at Robert Dudley.

'Servant to command, servant for life,' he explained.

'Our vassal. Everything you hear, everything you see, you come and tell me. Anything the king prays for, anything that makes him weep, anything that makes him laugh, you come and tell me, or you tell Robert here. You are our eyes and our ears at his side. Understand?'

'My lord, I have to go home to my father,' I said desperately. 'I cannot be the king's fool nor your vassal. I have work to do at the bookshop.'

The duke raised one eyebrow at his son. Robert leaned towards me and spoke very quietly.

'Mistress Boy, your own father cannot care for you. He said that in your hearing, d'you remember?'

'Yes, but, my lord, he only meant that I am a trouble to him . . .'

'Mistress Boy, I think your father is not a good Christian from a good Christian family at all, but a Jew. I think you came from Spain because you were expelled by the Spanish for the sin of Jewishness, and if your neighbours and the good citizens of London knew that you were Jews, you would not last for very long in your new little home.'

'We are Marranos, our family converted years and years ago,' I whispered. 'I have been baptised, I am betrothed to marry a young man of my father's choosing, a Christian Englishman . . .'

'I wouldn't go in that direction,' Robert Dudley warned bluntly. 'Lead us to that young man and I imagine you lead us to a family of Jews living in the heart of England itself, and from thence to – where did you say? Amsterdam? And then Paris?'

I opened my mouth to deny it, but I could not speak for fear.

'All forbidden Jews, all pretending to be Christians. All lighting a candle on Friday night, all avoiding pork, all living with the noose around their necks.'

'Sir!'

'They all helped and guided you here, didn't they? All Jews, all practising a forbidden religion in secret, all helping one another. A secret network, just as the most fearful of Christians claim.'

'My lord!'

'Do you really want to be the key that leads this most Christian king to seek you out? Don't you know that the reformed church can light a pyre just as bright as the Papists? Do you want to pile your family on it? And all their friends? Have you ever smelled roasting human flesh?'

I was shaking in terror, my throat so dry that I could say nothing. I just looked at him and I knew my eyes were black with fear and he would see the sheen of sweat on my forehead.

'I know. You know. Your father knows he cannot keep you safe. But I can. Enough. I won't say another word.'

He paused. I tried to speak but all I could manage was a little croak of terror. Robert Dudley nodded at the craven depth of my fear. 'Now, luckily for you, your Sight has won you the safest and highest place that you might dream of. Serve the king well, serve our family well and your father is safe. Fail us in any one thing and he is tossed in a blanket till his eyes fall backwards in his head, and you are married to a red-faced chapel-going Luther-reading pig herder. You can choose.'

There was the briefest of moments. Then the Duke of Northumberland waved me away. He did not even wait for me to make my choice. He did not need the Sight to know what my choice would have to be.

'And you are to live at court?' my father confirmed.

We were eating our dinner, a small pie brought in from the bakehouse at the end of the street. The unfamiliar taste of English pastry stuck at the back of my throat, my father forced down gravy that was flavoured with bacon rinds.

'I am to sleep with the maidservants,' I said glumly. 'And wear the livery of the king's pages. I am to be his companion.'

'It's better than I could have provided for you,' my father said, trying to be cheerful. 'We won't make enough money to pay the rent on this house next quarter, unless Lord Robert orders some more books.'

'I can send you my wages,' I offered. 'I am to be paid.'

He patted my hand. 'You're a good girl,' he said. 'Never forget that. Never forget your mother, never forget that you are one of the children of Israel.'

I nodded, saying nothing. I saw him spoon a little of the contaminated gravy and swallow it down.

'I am to go to the palace tomorrow,' I whispered. 'I am to start at once. Father . . .'

'I will come to the gate and see you every evening,' he promised. 'And if you are unhappy or they treat you badly we will run away. We can go back to Amsterdam, we can go to Turkey. We will find somewhere, *querida*. Have courage, daughter. You are one of the Chosen.'

'How will I keep the fast days?' I demanded in sudden grief. 'They will make me work on the Sabbath. How will I say the prayers? They will make me eat pork!'

He met my gaze and then he bowed his head. 'I shall keep the law for you here,' he said. 'God is good. He understands. You remember what that German scholar said? That God allows us to break the laws rather than lose our lives. I will pray for you, Hannah. And even if you are praying on your knees in the Christian chapel God still sees you and hears your prayer.'

'Father, Lord Robert knows who we are. He knows why we left Spain. He knows who we are.'

'He said nothing directly to me.'

'He threatened me. He knows we are Jews and he said that he would keep our secret as long as I obey him. He threatened me.'

'Daughter, we are safe nowhere. And you at least are under his patronage. He swore to me that you would be safe in his household. Nobody would question one of his servants. Nobody would question the king's own fool.'

'Father, how could you let me go? Why did you agree that they could take me away from you?'

'Hannah, how could I stop them?'

In the lime-washed room under the eaves of the palace roof I turned over the pile of my new clothes and read the inventory from the office of the Master of the Household:

> Item: one pageboy livery in yellow.
> Item: one pair of hose, dark red.
> Item: one pair of hose, dark green.
> Item: one surcoat, long.
> Item: two linen shirts for wearing underneath.
> Item: two pairs of sleeves, one pair red, one pair green.
> Item: one black hat.
> Item: one black cloak for riding.
> Item: pair of slippers fit for dancing.
> Item: pair of boots fit for riding.
> Item: pair of boots fit for walking.
> Everything used but clean and darned and delivered to the king's fool, Hannah Green.

'I shall look a fool indeed.'

That night I whispered an account of my day to my father as he stood at the postern gate and I leaned against the doorway, half-in, half-out. 'There are two fools at court already, a dwarf called Thomasina, and a man called Will Somers. He was kind to me, and showed me where I should sit, beside him. He is a witty man, he made everyone laugh.'

'And what do you do?'

'Nothing as yet. I have thought of nothing to say.'

My father glanced around. In the darkness of the garden an owl hooted, almost like a signal.

'Can you think of something? Won't they want you to think of something?'

'Father, I cannot make myself see things, I cannot command the Sight. It just comes or it does not.'

'Did you see Lord Robert?'

'He winked at me.' I leaned back against the cold stone and drew my warm new cloak around my shoulders.

'The king?'

'He was not even at dinner. He was sick, they sent his food to his rooms. They served a great dinner as if he were at the table but they sent a little plate to his rooms for him. The duke took his place at the head of the table, all but sitting on the throne.'

'And does the duke have his eye on you?'

'He did not seem to see me at all.'

'Has he forgotten you?'

'Ah, he doesn't have to look to know who is where, and what they are doing. He will not have forgotten me. He is not a man who forgets anything.'

The duke had decided that there was to be a masque at Candlemas and gave it out as the king's command, so we all had to wear special costumes and learn our lines. Will Somers, the king's fool who had come to court twenty years ago when he was a boy the same age as me, was to introduce the piece and recite a rhyme, the king's choristers were to sing, and I was to recite a poem, specially composed for the occasion. My costume was to be a new livery, specially made for me in the fool's colour of yellow. My hand-me-down livery was too tight on my chest. I was that odd androgynous thing, a girl on the threshold of being a woman. One day, in a certain light, as I turned my head before the mirror I could see the glimpse of a stranger, a beauty. Another day I was as plain as a slate.

The Master of the Revels gave me a little sword and ordered that Will and I should prepare for a fight, which would fit somewhere into the story of the masque.

We met for our first practice in one of the antechambers off the great hall. I was awkward and unwilling, I did not want to learn to fight with swords like a boy, I did not want to be the butt of jokes by taking a public beating. No man at court but Will Somers could have persuaded me to it, but he treated our lesson as if he had been hired to improve my understanding of Greek. He behaved as if it was a skill I needed to learn, and he wanted me to learn well.

He started with my stance. Resting his hands on my shoulders, he gently smoothed them down, took my chin and raised it up. 'Hold your head high, like a princess,' he said. 'Have you ever seen Lady

27

Mary slouch? Ever seen Lady Elizabeth drop her head? No. They walk as if they are princesses born and bred; dainty like a pair of goats.'

'Goats?' I asked, trying to raise my head without hunching up my shoulders.

Will Somers grinned at the laborious unfolding of the jest. 'Up one minute, down the next,' he said. 'Heir one moment, bastard the next. Up the mountain and down again. Princesses and goats, all alike. You must stand like a princess, and dance like a goat.'

'I have seen the Lady Elizabeth,' I volunteered.

'Have you?'

'Once, when I was a little girl. My father brought me on a visit to London and I had to deliver some books to Admiral Lord Seymour.'

Will put a gentle hand on my shoulder. 'Least said, soonest mended,' he advised quietly. Then he slapped his forehead and gave me his merry smile. 'Here am I, telling a woman to mind her tongue! Fool that I am!'

The lesson went on. He showed me the swordsman's stance, hand on my hip for balance, how to slide forward with my leading foot always on the floor so that I should not trip or fall, how to move behind the sword and to let it retreat to me. Then we started on the feints and passes.

Will first commanded me to stab at him. I hesitated. 'What if I hit you?'

'Then I shall take a splinter, not a deadly cut,' he pointed out. 'It's only wood, Hannah.'

'Get ready then,' I said nervously and lunged forward.

To my amazement Will sidestepped me and was at my side, his wooden sword to my throat. 'You're dead,' he said. 'Not so good at foresight after all.'

I giggled. 'I'm no good at this,' I admitted. 'Try again.'

This time I lunged with a good deal more energy and caught the hem of his coat as he flicked to one side.

'Excellent,' he said breathlessly. 'And again.'

We practised until I could make a convincing stab at him and then he started to lunge at me and teach me to drop to one side or the other. Then he rolled out a thick carpet on the floor and showed me how to turn head over heels.

'Comical,' he announced, sitting upright, his legs entwined like a child seated to read a book.

'Not very,' I said.

'Ah, you're a holy fool, not a jester,' he said. 'You have no sense of the laughable.'

'I have,' I said, stung. 'It's just that you are not funny.'

'I have been the most comical man in England for nearly twenty years,' he insisted. 'I came to court when Henry loved Anne Boleyn and once boxed my ears for jesting against her. But the joke was on her, later. I was the funniest man in England before you were born.'

'Why, how old are you?' I asked, looking into his face. The laughter lines were deeply engraved on either side of his mouth, crow's feet by his eyes. But he was lithe and lanky as a boy.

'As old as my tongue and a little older than my teeth,' he said.

'No, really.'

'I am thirty-three. Why, d'you want to marry me?'

'Not at all. Thank you.'

'You would wed the wittiest fool in the world.'

'I would rather not marry a fool.'

'Now that is inevitable. A wise man is a bachelor.'

'Well, you don't make me laugh,' I said provocatively.

'Ah, you're a girl. Women have no sense of the ludicrous.'

'I have,' I insisted.

'It is well known that women, not being in the image of God, can have no sense of what is funny and what is not.'

'I have! I have!'

'Of course women do not!' he triumphed. 'For why else would a woman ever marry a man? Have you ever seen a man when he desires a woman?'

I shook my head. Will put the wooden sword between his legs and made a little rush to one side of the room and then the other. 'He can't think, he can't speak, he can't command his thoughts or his wishes, he runs everywhere behind his cock like a hound behind a scent, all he can do is howl. How-oww-oww-owwl!'

I was laughing out loud as Will raced around the room, straining backwards as if to restrain his wooden sword, leaning back as if to take the weight of it. He broke off and smiled at me. 'Of course women have no wit,' he said. 'Who with any wit would ever have a man?'

'Well, not I,' I said.

'God bless you and keep you a virgin then, Maid-Boy. But how shall you get a husband if you will not have a man?'

'I don't want one.'

'Then you are a fool indeed. For without a husband how shall you have a living?'

'I shall make my own.'

'Then again you are a fool, for the only living you can make is from fooling. That makes you a fool three times over. Once for not wanting a husband, twice for making a living without him, and thrice since the living you make is from fooling. At least I am just a fool, but you are a triple fool.'

'Not at all!' I rejoined, falling in with the rhythm of his speech. 'Because you have been a fool for years, you have been a fool for two generations of kings, and I have only been one for a few weeks.'

He laughed at that and slapped me on the shoulder. 'Take care, Maid-Boy, or you will not be a holy fool but a witty fool and I tell you, clowning and jesting every day is harder work than saying something surprising once a month.'

I laughed at the thought of my work being to say something surprising once a month.

'Up and at it!' Will Somers said, pulling me to my feet. 'We have to plan how you are going to murder me amusingly by Candlemas.'

We had our sword dance planned in good time and it did seem very funny. At least two practices ended in us both having fits of giggles as we mistimed a lunge and cracked heads together, or both feinted at the same time, and fell backwards, and toppled over. But one day the Master of the Revels put his head into the room and said: 'You won't be needed. The king is not having a masque.'

I turned with the play-sword still in my hand. 'But we're all ready!'

'He's sick,' the Master said dourly.

'And is the Lady Mary still coming to court?' Will asked, pulling on his jerkin against the cold draught of air whistling in through the open door.

'Said to be,' the Master said. 'She'll get better rooms and a better cut of the meat this time, don't you think, Will?'

He shut the door before Will could reply, and so I turned and asked, 'What does he mean?'

Will's face was grave. 'He means that those of the court who move towards the heir and away from the king will be making their move now.'

'Because?'

'Because flies swarm to the hottest dung heap. Plop, plop, buzz.'

'Will? What d'you mean?'

'Ah, child. Lady Mary is the heir. She will be queen if we lose the king, God bless him, poor lad.'

'But she's a heret –'

'Of the Catholic faith,' he corrected me smoothly.

'And King Edward . . .'

'His heart will break to leave the kingdom to a Catholic heir but he can do nothing about it. It's how King Henry left it. God bless him, he must be rolling in his shroud to see it come to this. He thought that King Edward would grow to be a strong and merry man and have half a dozen little princes in the nursery. It makes you think, doesn't it? Is England ever to get any peace? Two young lusty kings: Henry's father, Henry himself, handsome as the sun, each of them, lecherous as sparrows, and they leave us with nothing but a lad as weak as a girl, and an old maid to come after him?'

He looked at me and I saw him rub his face, as if to brush off some wetness round his eyes. 'Means nothing to you,' he said gruffly. 'Newly come from Spain, damned black-eyed girl. But if you were English, you'd be a worried man now; if you were a man, and if you were a sensible man instead of being a girl and a fool at that.'

He swung open the door and set off into the great hall on his long legs, nodding at the soldiers who shouted a good-natured greeting to him.

'And what will happen to us?' I demanded in a hissed whisper, trotting after him. 'If the young king dies and his sister takes the throne?'

Will threw me a sideways grin. 'Then we shall be Queen Mary's fools,' he said simply. 'And if I can make her laugh it will be a novelty indeed.'

My father came to the side gate that night and he brought someone with him, a young man dressed in a cape of dark worsted, dark ringlets of hair falling almost to his collar, dark eyes, and a shy boyish smile. It took me a moment to recognise him; he was Daniel Carpenter, my betrothed. It was only the second time I had ever seen him, and I was embarrassed that I failed to recognise him and then utterly shamed to be seen by him in my pageboy livery in golden yellow, the colour of the holy fool. I pulled my cape around me, to hide my breeches, and made him an awkward little bow.

He was a young man of twenty years old, training to be a physician like his father, who had died only last year. His kin had come to England from Portugal eighty years ago as the d'Israeli family. They changed their name to the most English one they could find, hiding their education and their foreign parentage behind the name of a working man. It was typical of their satirical wit to choose the occupation of the most famous Jew of all – Jesus. I had spoken to Daniel only once before, when he and his mother welcomed us to England with a gift of bread and some wine, and I knew next to nothing about him.

He had no more choice in this marriage than I, and I did not know if he resented it as much, or even more. They had chosen him for me because we were sixth cousins, twice removed, and within ten years of each other's age. That was all that was required and it was better than it might have been. There were not enough cousins and uncles and nephews in England for anyone to be very particular as to whom they might marry. There were no more than twenty families of Jewish descent in London, and half as many again scattered around the towns of England. Since we were bound to marry among ourselves we had very little choice. Daniel could have been fifty years of age, half-blind, half-dead even, and I would still have been wedded to him and bedded by my sixteenth birthday. More important than anything else in the world, more important than wealth or fitness for each other, was that we would be bound to each other in secrecy. He knew that my mother had been burned to death as a heretic accused of secret Jewish practices. I knew that beneath his smart English breeches he was circumcised. Whether he had turned to the risen Jesus in his heart and believed the words of the sermons that were preached at his local church every day and twice on Sundays would be something I might discover about him later, as in time he must learn about me. What we knew for certain of each other was that our Christian faith was new, but our race was very old, and that we had been the hated ones of Europe for more than three hundred years and that Jews were still forbidden to set foot in most of the countries of Christendom, including this one, this England, which we would call our home.

'Daniel asked to see you alone,' my father said awkwardly, and he stepped back a little, out of earshot.

'I heard that you had been begged for a fool,' Daniel said. I looked at him and watched his face slowly colour red till even his ears were glowing. He had a young man's face, skin as soft as a girl's, a down of a dark moustache on his upper lip, which matched his silky dark eyebrows over deep-set dark eyes. At first glance he looked more Portuguese than Jewish, but the heavy-lidded eyes would have betrayed him to one who was looking.

I slid my gaze from his face and took in a slight frame with broad shoulders, narrow waist, long legs: a handsome young man.

'Yes,' I said shortly. 'I have a place at court.'

'When you are sixteen you will have to leave court and come home again,' he said.

I raised my eyebrows at this young stranger. 'Who gives this order?'

'I do.'

I allowed a frosty little silence to fall. 'I don't believe you have any command over me.'

'When I am your husband ...'

'Then, yes.'

'I am your betrothed. You are promised to me. I have some rights.'

I showed him a sulky face. 'I am commanded by the king, I am commanded by the Duke of Northumberland, I am commanded by his son Lord Robert Dudley, I am commanded by my father; you might as well join in. Every other man in London seems to think he can order me.'

He gave a little gulp of involuntary laughter and at once his face was lighter, like a boy's. He clipped me gently on my shoulder as if I were his comrade in a gang. I found I was smiling back at him. 'Oh, poor maid,' he said. 'Poor set-upon maid.'

I shook my head. 'Fool indeed.'

'Don't you want to come away from all these commanding men?'

I shrugged. 'I am better living here, than being a burden on my father.'

'You could come home with me.'

'Then I would be a burden on you.'

'When I have served my apprenticeship and I am a physician I will make a home for us.'

'And when will that be?' I asked him with the sharp cruelty of a young girl. Again I watched the slow painful rise of his blush.

'Within two years,' he said stiffly. 'I shall be able to keep a wife by the time you are ready for marriage.'

'Come for me then,' I said unhelpfully. 'Come with your orders then, if I am still here.'

'In the meantime, we are still betrothed,' he insisted.

I tried to read his face. 'As much as we ever have been. The old women seem to have arranged it to their satisfaction if not to ours. Did you want more?'

'I like to know where I am,' he said stubbornly. 'I have waited for you and your father to come from Paris and then from Amsterdam. For months we none of us knew if you were alive or dead. When you finally came to England I thought you would be glad of . . . be glad of . . . a home. And then I hear you and your father are to set up house together, you are not coming to live with Mother and me; and you have not put aside your boy's costume. Then I hear you are working for him like a son. And then I hear you have left the protection of your father's house. And now I find you at court.'

It was not the Sight that helped me through all of this, but the sharp intuition of a girl on the edge of womanhood. 'You thought I would rush to you,' I crowed. 'You thought you would rescue me, that I would be a fearful girl longing to cling to a man, ready to fling myself at you!'

The sudden darkening of his flush and the jerk of his head told me that I had hit the mark.

'Well, learn this, young apprentice physician, I have seen sights and travelled in countries that you cannot imagine. I have been afraid and

34

I have been in danger, and I have never for one moment thought that I would throw myself at a man for his help.'

'You are not . . .' He was lost for words, choking on a young man's indignation. 'You are not . . . maidenly.'

'I thank God for it.'

'You are not . . . a biddable girl.'

'I thank my mother for that.'

'You are not . . .' His temper was getting the better of him. 'You would not be my first choice!'

That silenced me, and we looked at each other in some sort of shock at the distance we had come in so little a time.

'Do you want another girl?' I asked, a little shaken.

'I don't know another girl,' he said sulkily. 'But I don't want a girl who doesn't want me.'

'It's not you I dislike,' I volunteered. 'It's marriage itself. I would not choose marriage at all. What is it but the servitude of women hoping for safety, to men who cannot even keep them safe?'

My father glanced over curiously and saw the two of us, face to face, aghast in silence. Daniel turned away from me and took two paces to one side, I leaned against the cold stone of the doorpost and wondered if he would stride off into the night and that would be the last I would see of him. I wondered how displeased my father would be with me if I lost a good offer through my impertinence, and if we would be able to stay in England at all if Daniel and his family considered themselves insulted by us newcomers. We might be family and entitled to the help of our kin, but the hidden Jews of England were a tight little world and if they decided to exclude us, we would have nowhere to go but on our travels again.

Daniel mastered himself, and came back to me.

'You do wrong to taunt me, Hannah Green,' he said, his voice trembling with his intensity. 'Whatever else, we are promised to one another. You hold my life in your hands and I hold yours in mine. We should not disagree. This is a dangerous world for us. We should cleave together for our own safety.'

'There is no safety,' I said coldly. 'You have lived too long in this quiet country if you think there is ever any safety for such as us.'

'We can make a home here,' he said earnestly. 'You and I can be

35

married and have children who will be English children. They will know nothing but this life, we need not even tell them of your mother, of her faith. Nor of our own.'

'Oh, you'll tell them,' I predicted. 'You say you won't now, but once we have a child you won't be able to resist it. And you'll find ways to light the candle on Friday night and not to work on the Sabbath. You'll be a doctor then, you will circumcise the boys in secret and teach them the prayers. You'll have me teach the girls to make unleavened bread and to keep the milk from the meat and to drain the blood from the beef. The moment you have children of your own you will want to teach them. And so it goes on, like some sickness that we pass on, one to another.'

'It's no sickness,' he whispered passionately. Even in the midst of our quarrel, nothing would make us raise our voices. We were always aware of the shadows in the garden, always alert to the possibility that someone might be listening. 'It is an insult to call it a sickness. It is our gift, we are chosen to keep faith.'

I would have argued for the sake of contradicting him, but it went against the deeper grain of my love for my mother and her faith. 'Yes,' I said, surrendering to the truth. 'It is not a sickness, but it kills us just as if it were. My grandmother and my aunt died of it, my mother too. And this is what you propose to me. A lifetime of fear, not Chosen so much as cursed.'

'If you don't want to marry me, then you can marry a Christian and pretend that you know nothing more,' he pointed out, 'None of us would betray you. I would let you go. You can deny the faith that your mother and your grandmother died for. Just say the word and I shall tell your father that I wish to be released.'

I hesitated. For all that I had bragged of my courage, I did not dare to tell my father that I would overthrow his plans. I did not dare to tell the old women who had arranged all of this, thinking only of my safety and Daniel's future, that I wanted none of it. I wanted to be free; I did not want to be cast out.

'I don't know,' I said, a girl's plea. 'I'm not ready to say . . . I don't know yet.'

'Then be guided by those who do,' he said flatly. He saw me bridle at that. 'Look, you can't fight everyone,' he advised me. 'You have to choose where you belong and rest there.'

'It's too great a cost for me,' I whispered. 'For you it is a good life, the home is made around you, the children come, you sit at the head of the table and lead the prayers. For me it is to lose everything I might be and everything I might do, and become nothing but your helpmeet and your servant.'

'This is not being a Jew, this is being a girl,' he said. 'Whether you married a Christian or a Jew, you would be his servant. What else can a woman be? Would you deny your sex as well as your religion?'

I said nothing.

'You are not a faithful woman,' he said slowly. 'You would betray yourself.'

'That's a dreadful thing to say,' I whispered.

'But true,' he maintained. 'You are a Jew and you are a young woman and you are my betrothed, and all these things you would deny. Who do you work for in the court? The king? The Dudleys? Are you faithful to them?'

I thought of how I had been pledged as a vassal, begged as a fool and appointed as a spy. 'I just want to be free,' I said. 'I don't want to be anybody's anything.'

'In fool's livery?'

I saw my father looking towards us. He could sense that we were far from courtship. I saw him make a little tentative move as if to interrupt us, but then he waited.

'Shall I tell them that we cannot agree and ask you to release me from our betrothal?' Daniel asked tightly.

Wilfully, I was about to agree, but his stillness, his silence, his patient waiting for my reply made me look at this young man, this Daniel Carpenter, more closely. The light was going from the sky and in the half-darkness I could see the man he would become. He would be handsome, he would have a dark mobile face, a quick observing eye, a sensitive mouth, a strong straight nose like mine, thick black hair like mine. And he would be a wise man, he was a wise youth, he had seen me and understood me and contradicted my very core, and yet still he stood waiting. He would give me a chance. He would be a generous husband. He would want to be kind.

'Leave me now,' I said feebly. 'I can't say now. I have said too much already. I am sorry for speaking out. I am sorry if I angered you.'

But his anger had left him as quickly as it had come, and that was another thing that I liked in him.

'Shall I come again?'

'All right.'

'Are we still betrothed?'

I shrugged. There was too much riding on my answer. '*I* haven't broken it,' I said, finding the easiest way out. 'It's not broken yet.'

He nodded. 'I shall need to know,' he warned me. 'If I am not to marry you, then I could marry another. I shall want to marry within two years; you, or another girl.'

'You have so many to choose from?' I taunted him, knowing that he had not.

'There are many girls in London,' he returned. 'I could marry outside our kin, well enough.'

'I can see them allowing that!' I exclaimed. 'You'll have to marry a Jew, there's no escape from that. They will send you a fat Parisian or a girl with skin the colour of mud from Turkey.'

'I would try to be a good husband even to a fat Parisian or to a young girl from Turkey,' he said steadily. 'And it is more important to love and cherish the wife that God gives you than to run after some silly maid who does not know her own mind.'

'Would that be me?' I asked sharply.

I expected his colour to rise but this time he did not blush. He met my eyes frankly and it was I who looked away first. 'I think you are a silly maid if you turn from the love and protection of a man who would be a good husband, to a life of deceit at court.'

My father came up beside Daniel before I could reply, and put a hand on his shoulder.

'And so you two are getting acquainted,' he said hopefully. 'What d'you make of your wife-to-be, Daniel?'

I expected Daniel to complain of me to my father. Most young men would have been all a-prickle with their pride stinging, but he gave me a small rueful smile. 'I think we are coming to know each other,' he said gently. 'We have overleaped being polite strangers and reached disagreement very quickly, don't you think, Hannah?'

'Commendably quick,' I said, and was rewarded by the warmth of his smile.

Lady Mary came to London for the Candlemas feast, as had been planned; it seemed that no-one had told her that her brother was too sick to rise from his bed. She rode in through the palace gate of Whitehall with a great train behind her, and was greeted at the very threshold of the palace by the duke, with his sons, including Lord Robert, at his side, and the council of England bowing low before her. Seated high on her horse, her small determined face looking down at the sea of humbly bowing heads, I thought I saw a smile of pure amusement cross her lips before she put down her hand to be kissed.

I had heard so much about her, the beloved daughter of the king who had been put aside on the word of Anne Boleyn, the whore. The princess who had been humbled to dust, the mourning girl who had been forbidden to see her dying mother. I had expected a figure of tragedy: she had endured a life which would have broken most women; but what I saw was a stocky little fighter with enough wit about her to smile at the court, knocking their noses on their knees because, suddenly, she was the heir with formidable prospects.

The duke treated her as if she were queen already. She was helped from her horse and led in to the banquet. The king was in his chamber, coughing and retching in his little bed; but they had the banquet anyway, and I saw the Lady Mary look round at the beaming faces as if to note that when the heir was in the ascendant, a king could lie sick and alone, and no-one mind at all.

There was dancing after dinner but she did not rise from her seat, though she tapped her foot and seemed to enjoy the music. Will made her laugh a couple of times, and she smiled on him as if he were a familiar face in a dangerous world. She had known him when he was her father's fool and given her brother carry-backs, and sung nonsense songs at her and sworn it was Spanish. When she looked around the court now at the hard faces of the men who had seen her insulted and humiliated by her own baby brother it must have been a small relief to know that Will Somers at least never changed in his unswerving good humour.

She did not drink deeply, and she ate very little; she was not a famous glutton as her father had been. I looked her over, as did the court: this woman who might be my next mistress. She was a woman in her thirty-seventh year, but she still had the pretty colouring of a girl: pale skin and cheeks which readily flushed rosy pink. She wore her hood set back off her square honest face and showed her hair, dark brown with a tinge of Tudor red. Her smile was her great charm; it came slowly, and her eyes were warm. But what struck me most about her was her air of honesty. She did not look at all like my idea of a princess – having spent a few weeks at court I thought everyone there smiled with hard eyes and said one thing and meant the opposite. But this princess looked as if she said nothing that she did not mean, as if she longed to believe that others were honest too, that she wanted to ride a straight road.

She had a grim little face in repose, but it was all redeemed by that smile: the smile of the best-beloved princess, the first of her father's children, born when he was a young man who still adored his wife. She had quick dark eyes, Spanish eyes, from her mother and her rapid appreciation of everything around her. She held herself upright in her chair, the dark collar of her gown framing her shoulders and neck. She had a great jewelled cross at her throat as if to flaunt her religion in this most Protestant court, and I thought that she must be either very brave or very reckless to insist on her faith when her brother's men were burning heretics for less. But then I saw the tremor in her hand when she reached for her golden goblet and I imagined that like many women she had learned to put on a braver face than she might feel.

When there was a break in the dancing, Robert Dudley was at her side, whispering to her, and she glanced over to me and he beckoned me forward.

'I hear you are from Spain, and my brother's new fool,' she said in English.

I bowed low. 'Yes, Your Grace.'

'Speak Spanish,' Lord Robert commanded me, and I bowed again and told her in Spanish that I was glad to be at court.

When I looked up I saw the delight in her face at hearing her mother's language. 'What part of Spain?' she asked eagerly in English.

'Castile, Your Grace,' I lied at once. I did not want any inquiries made of us and of my family's destruction in our home of Aragon.

'And why did you come to England?'

I was prepared for the question. My father and I had discussed the dangers of every answer and settled on the safest. 'My father is a great scholar,' I said. 'He wanted to print books from his library of manuscripts, and he wanted to work in London, which is such a centre of learning.'

At once the smile left her, and her face grew harder. 'I suppose he turns out copies of the Bible to mislead people who cannot begin to understand it,' she said crossly.

My gaze slid to Robert Dudley, who had bought one of my father's Bibles newly translated into English.

'In the Latin only,' he said smoothly. 'A very pure translation, Lady Mary, and with very few errors. I daresay Hannah will bring you one, if you would like.'

'My father would be honoured,' I said.

She nodded. 'And you are my brother's holy fool,' she said. 'D'you have any words of wisdom for me?'

I shook my head helplessly. 'I wish I could see at will, Your Grace. I am much less wise than you, I should think.'

'She told my tutor John Dee that she could see an angel walking with us,' Robert put in.

The Lady Mary looked at me with more respect.

'But then she told my father that she saw no angels behind him.'

Her face at once creased into laughter. 'No! Did she? And what said your father? Was he sorry not to have an angel at his side?'

'I don't think he was very surprised,' Robert said, smiling too. 'But this is a good little maid, and I think she does have a true gift. She has been a great comfort to your brother in his illness. She has a gift of seeing the truth and speaking true, and he likes that.'

'That alone is a rare gift to find at court,' the Lady Mary said. She nodded kindly to me and I stepped back and the music started up again. I kept my eye on Robert Dudley as he led out one young lady and then another to dance before the Lady Mary, and I was rewarded when after some minutes he glanced over to me and gave me a hidden approving smile.

The Lady Mary did not see the king that night but the chambermaids' gossip was that when she went into his room the next day she came out again, white as a winding sheet. She had not known till then that her little brother was so near to his death.

After that, there was no reason for her to stay. She rode out as she had come, with a great retinue following behind, and all the court bowing as low as they could reach, to indicate their new-found loyalty; half of them praying silently that, when the young king died and she came to the throne, she would be blessed with forgetfulness and overlook the priests they had burned at the stake, and the churches they had despoiled.

I was watching this charade of humility from one of the palace windows when I felt a gentle touch on my sleeve. I turned, and there was Lord Robert, smiling down at me.

'My lord, I thought you would be with your father, saying goodbye to the Lady Mary.'

'No, I came to find you.'

'For me?'

'To ask you if you would do me a service?'

I felt my colour rise to my cheeks. 'Anything . . .' I stammered.

He smiled. 'Just one small thing. Would you come with me to my tutor's rooms, and see if you can assist him in one of his experiments?'

I nodded and Lord Robert took my hand and, drawing it into the crook of his arm, led me to the Northumberland private quarters. The great doors were guarded by Northumberland men, and as soon as they saw the favoured son of the house they snapped to attention and swung the double doors open. The great hall beyond was deserted, the retainers and the Northumberland court were in the Whitehall garden demonstrating their immense respect to the departing Lady Mary. Lord Robert led me up the grand stairs, through a gallery, to his own rooms. John Dee was seated in the library overlooking an inner garden.

He raised his head as we came into the room. 'Ah, Hannah Verde.'

It was so odd for me to hear my real name, given in full, that for a moment I did not respond, and then I dipped a little bow. 'Yes, sir.'

'She says she will help. But I have not told her what you want,' Lord Robert said.

Mr Dee rose from the table. 'I have a special mirror,' he said. 'I think it possible that, one with special sight might see rays of light that are not visible to the ordinary eye, d'you understand?'

I did not.

'Just as we cannot see a sound or a scent, but we know that something is there, I think it possible that the planets and the angels send out rays of light, which we might see if we had the right glass to see them in.'

'Oh,' I said blankly.

The tutor broke off with a smile. 'No matter. You need not understand me. I was only thinking that since you saw the angel Uriel that day, you might see such rays in this mirror.'

'I don't mind looking, if Lord Robert wishes it,' I volunteered.

He nodded. 'I have it ready. Come in.' He led the way to an inner chamber. The window was shielded by a thick curtain, all the cold winter light blocked out. A square table was placed before it, the four legs standing on four wax seals. On top of the table was an extraordinary mirror of great beauty, a gold-wrought frame, a bevelled rim, and a golden sheen on the silvering. I stepped up to it and saw myself, reflected in gold, looking not like the boy-girl I was, but like a young woman. For a moment I thought I saw my mother looking back at me, her lovely smile and that gesture when she turned her head. 'Oh!' I exclaimed.

'D'you see anything?' Dee asked, I could hear the excitement in his voice.

'I thought I saw my mother,' I whispered.

He paused for a moment. 'Can you hear her?' he asked, his voice shaking.

I waited for a moment, longing with all my heart that she would come to me. But it was only my own face that looked back at me, my eyes enlarged and darkened by unshed tears.

'She's not here,' I said sadly. 'I would give anything to hear her voice, but I cannot. She has gone from me. I just thought that I saw her for a moment; but it is my own face in the mirror.'

'I want you to close your eyes,' he said, 'and listen carefully to the prayer that I am going to read. When you say "amen" you can open your eyes again and tell me what you see. Are you ready?'

I closed my eyes and I could hear him softly blowing out the few candles illuminating the shadowy room. Behind me I was conscious of Lord Robert sitting quietly on a wooden chair. I wanted only to please him. 'I am ready,' I whispered.

It was a long prayer in Latin, I understood it despite Mr Dee's English pronunciation of the words. It was a prayer for guidance and for the angels to come and protect the work we would do. I whispered 'amen' and then I opened my eyes.

The candles were all out. The mirror was a pool of darkness, black reflected in black, I could see nothing.

'Show us when the king will die,' Mr Dee whispered from behind me.

I watched, waiting for something to happen, my eyes staring into the blackness.

Nothing.

'The day of the king's death,' Dee whispered again.

In truth, I could see nothing. I waited. Nothing came to me. How could it? I was not some sibyl on a Greek hillside, I was not some saint to whom mysteries were revealed. I stared into the darkness until my eyes grew hot and dry and I knew that far from being a holy fool I was a fool pure and simple, looking at nothing, at a reflection of nothing, while the greatest mind in the kingdom waited for my answer.

I had to say something. There was no going back and telling them that the Sight came to me so seldom and so unheralded that they would have done better to leave me leaning against the wall of my father's shop. They knew who I was, they had promised me sanctuary from danger. They had bought me and now they expected some benefit for their bargain. I had to say something.

'July,' I said quietly, as good a reply as any.

'Which year?' Mr Dee prompted me, his voice silky and quiet.

Common sense alone suggested that the young king could not live much longer. 'This year,' I said unwillingly.

'The day?'

'The sixth,' I whispered in reply, and I heard the scratch of Lord Robert's pen as he recorded my mountebank prophecy.

'Tell the name of the next ruler of England,' Mr Dee whispered.

I was about to reply 'Queen Mary', echoing his own tranced tone. 'Jane,' I said simply, surprising myself.

I turned to Lord Robert. 'I don't know why I said that. I am most sorry, my lord. I don't know . . .'

John Dee quickly grasped my jaw, and turned my head back to the mirror. 'Don't talk!' he ordered. 'Just tell us what you see.'

'I see nothing,' I said helplessly. 'I am sorry, I am sorry, my lord. I am sorry, I can't see anything.'

'The king who comes after Jane,' he urged me. 'Look, Hannah. Tell me what you see. Does Jane have a son?'

I would have said 'yes' but my tongue would not move in my dry mouth. 'I cannot see,' I said humbly. 'Truly, I cannot see.'

'A closing prayer,' Mr Dee said, holding me in my chair by a firm grip on my shoulders. He prayed again in Latin that the work should be blessed, that the visions should be true, and that no-one in this world nor in any other should be harmed by our scrying.

'Amen,' I said, more fervently now that I knew this was dangerous work, perhaps even treasonous work.

I felt Lord Robert rise to leave the room and I pulled away from Mr Dee and ran after him.

'Was it what you wanted?' I demanded.

'Did you tell me what you thought I wanted to hear?'

'No! I spoke as it came to me.' That was true of the sudden word 'Jane', I thought.

He looked sharply at me. 'Do you promise? Mistress Boy, you are no use to John Dee nor to me if you choose your words to please me. The only way you can please me is by seeing true and saying true.'

'I am! I did!' My anxiety to please him and my fear of the mirror were together too much for me and I gave a little sob. 'I did, my lord.'

His face did not soften. 'Swear?'

'Yes.'

He rested a hand on my shoulder. My head throbbed so much that I longed to lean my cheek against the coolness of his sleeve but I thought I should not. I stood stock-still like the boy he called me, to face his scrutiny.

'Then you have done very well for me,' he said. 'That was what I wanted.'

Mr Dee came out of the inner chamber, his face alight. 'She has the Sight,' he said. 'She has it indeed.'

Lord Robert looked at his tutor. 'Will this make a great difference to your work?'

The older man shrugged. 'Who knows? We are all children in darkness. But she has the Sight.' He paused, and then turned to me. 'Hannah Verde, I must tell you one thing.'

'Yes, sir?'

'You have the Sight because you are pure in heart. Please, for yourself and for the gift you bear, refuse any offers of marriage, resist any seduction, keep yourself pure.'

Behind me, Lord Robert gave a snort of amusement.

I felt my colour rise slowly from my neck to my ear lobes to my temples. 'I have no carnal desires,' I said in a voice as low as a whisper. I did not dare to look at Lord Robert.

'Then you will see true,' John Dee said.

'But I don't understand,' I protested. 'Who is Jane? It is Lady Mary who will be queen if His Grace dies.'

Lord Robert put his finger on my lips and at once I was silent. 'Sit down,' he said and pressed me into a chair. He drew up a stool and sat beside me, his face close to mine. 'Mistress Boy, you have seen today two things that would have us all hanged if they were known.'

My heart raced with fear. 'My lord?'

'Just by looking in the mirror you put us all in danger.'

My hand went to my cheek as if I would wipe away smuts from a fire. 'My lord?'

'You must say not a word of this. It is treason to cast the horoscope of a king, and the punishment for treason is death. You cast his horoscope today and you foretold the day of his death. D'you want to see me on the scaffold?'

'No! I . . .'

'Do you want to die yourself?'

'No!' I could hear a quaver in my voice. 'My lord, I am afraid.'

'Then never say one word of this to anyone. Not even to your father. As to the Jane of the mirror . . .'

I waited.

'Just forget all you saw, forget I even asked you to look in the mirror. Forget the mirror, forget the room.'

I looked at him solemnly. 'I won't have to do it again?'

'You will never have to do it again unless you consent. But you must forget it now.' He gave me his sweet seductive smile. 'Because I ask it of you,' he whispered. 'Because I ask it of you as your friend, I have put my life in your hands.'

I was lost. 'All right,' I said.

The court moved to Greenwich Palace in February and it was given out that the king was better. But he never asked for me, nor for Will Somers, he did not ask for music nor for company, nor did he ever come to the great hall for dinner. The physicians, who had been in full-blown attendance with their gowns flapping, waiting in every corner of the court, talking amongst themselves and giving carefully guarded replies to all inquiries, seemed to slip away as the days wore on and there was no news of his recovery, and not even their cheerful predictions about leeches cleansing the young man's blood and poison carefully administered killing his disease, seemed to ring very true. Lord Robert's father, the Duke of Northumberland, was all but king in Edward's place, seated at the right hand of an empty throne at dinner, taking the chair at the head of the council table every week, but telling everyone that the king was well, getting better all the time, looking forward to the finer weather, planning a progress this summer.

I said nothing. I was being paid as a fool to say surprising and impertinent things but I could think of nothing more impertinent and surprising than the truth – that the young king was half-prisoner to his protector, that he was dying without companions or nursing, and that this whole court, every great man in the land, was thinking of the crown and not of the boy; and that it was a great cruelty, to a boy only a little older than me and without a mother or a father to care for him, to be left to die alone. I looked around me at the men who assured each other that the young man of fifteen, coughing his lungs out in hiding, would be fit to take a wife this summer, and I thought that I would be a fool indeed if I did not see that they were a bunch of liars and rogues.

While the young king vomited black bile in his chamber, the men outside quietly helped themselves to the pensions, to the fees from offices, to the rents from monasteries that they closed for piety and then robbed for greed, and no-one said one word against it. I would have been a fool indeed to tell the truth in this court of liars, I would have been as incongruous as an angel in Fleet Street. I kept my head down, I sat near Will Somers at dinner, and I kept silent.

I had new work to do. Lord Robert's tutor Mr Dee sought me out and asked if I would read with him. His eyes were tired, he said, and my father had sent him some manuscripts that could be more easily deciphered by young sight.

'I don't read very well,' I said cautiously.

He was pacing ahead of me in one of the sunny galleries overlooking the river, but at my words he turned and smiled.

'You are a very careful young woman,' he said. 'And that is wise in these changing times. But you are safe with me and with Lord Robert. I imagine you can read English and Latin fluently, am I right?'

I nodded.

'And Spanish, of course, and perhaps French?'

I kept my silence. It was obvious that I spoke and read Spanish as my native tongue, and he would guess that I must have picked up some French during our stay in Paris.

Mr Dee came a little closer and bent his head to whisper in my ear. 'Can you read Greek? I need someone who can read Greek for me.'

If I had been older and wiser I would have denied my knowledge. But I was only fourteen and proud of my abilities. My mother herself had taught me to read Greek and Hebrew, and my Father called me his little scholar, as good as any boy.

'Yes,' I said. 'I can read Greek and Hebrew.'

'Hebrew?' he exclaimed, his interest sharpened. 'Dear God, child, what have you seen in Hebrew? Have you seen the Torah?'

At once I knew I should have said nothing. If I said yes, that I had seen the laws of the Jews and the prayers, then I would have identified myself and my father beyond doubt as Jews and practising Jews at that. I thought of my mother telling me that my vanity would get me into trouble. I had always thought that she meant my love of fine clothes and ribbons for my hair. Now, dressed as a boy in a fool's livery I had committed the sin of vanity, I had been prideful of my schooling and the punishment could be extreme.

'Mr Dee . . .' I whispered, aghast.

He smiled at me. 'I guessed you had fled Spain as soon as I saw you,' he said gently. 'I guessed you were Conversos. But it was not for me to say. And it is not in Lord Robert's nature to persecute someone for the faith of their fathers, especially a faith which they have surrendered. You go to church, don't you? And observe feast days? You believe in Jesus Christ and his mercy?'

'Oh yes, my lord. Without fail.' There was no point in telling him that there was no more devout Christian than a Jew trying to be invisible.

Mr Dee paused. 'As for me, I pray for a time when we are beyond such divisions, beyond them to the truth itself. Some men think that there is neither God nor Allah nor Elohim . . .'

At his speaking the sacred name of the only God I gave a little gasp of surprise. 'Mr Dee? Are you one of the Chosen People?'

He shook his head. 'I believe there is a creator, a great creator of the world, but I do not know his name. I know the names that he is given by man. Why should I prefer one name to another? What I want to know is His Holy Nature, what I want is the help of his angels, what I want to do is to further his work, to make gold from base, to make Holy from Vulgar.' He broke off. 'Does any of this mean anything to you?'

I kept my face blank. In my father's library in Spain there had been books that told of the secrets of the making of the world, and there had been the scholar who had come to read them, and the Jesuit who wanted to know the secrets beyond those of his order.

'Alchemy?' I asked, my voice very low.

He nodded. 'The creator has given us a world full of mysteries,' he said. 'But I believe that they will be known to us one day. Now we understand a little, and the church of the Pope, and the church of the king, and the laws of the land all say that we should not question. But I don't believe that it is the law of God that we should not question. I think that he has made this world as a great and glorious mechanical garden, one that works to its own laws and grows to its own laws and that we will one day come to understand it. Alchemy – the art of change – is how we shall come to understand it, and when we know how things are made, we can make them ourselves, we will have the knowledge of God, we ourselves will be transubstantiated, we shall be angels . . .'

He broke off. 'Does your father have many works on alchemy? He showed me only those on religion. Does he have alchemy texts in Hebrew? Will you read them to me?'

'I only know the permitted books,' I said cautiously. 'My father does not keep forbidden books.' Not even this kind man who trusted me with his own secrets could lure me into speaking the truth. I had been raised in utter secrecy, I would never lose the habit of fear-filled duplicity. 'I can read Hebrew, but I don't know the Jewish prayers. My father and I are good Christians. And he has not shown me any books on alchemy, he does not stock them. I am too young to understand books like that. I don't know that he would want me to read Hebrew to you, sir.'

'I will ask him and surely he will allow it,' he said easily. 'Reading Hebrew is a gift of God, a skill with languages is the sign of a pure heart. Hebrew is the language of the angels, it is the closest we mortals can come to speaking to God. Did you not know that?'

I shook my head.

'But of course,' he continued, glowing with enthusiasm. 'God spoke to Adam and Eve in the Garden of Eden before the Fall and they became the first people of earth. They must have spoken Hebrew, they must have understood God in that language. There is a language beyond Hebrew, which is what God speaks with heavenly beings, and it is that language which I hope to discover. And the way to it must be through Hebrew, through Greek and through Persian.' He broke off for a moment. 'You don't speak or read Persian, do you? Or any of the Arab tongues?'

'No,' I said.

'No matter,' he replied. 'You shall come every morning and read with me for an hour and we shall make great progress.'

'If Lord Robert says I may,' I temporised.

Mr Dee smiled at me. 'Young lady, you are going to help me to understand nothing less than the meaning of all things. There is a key to the universe and we are just beginning to grasp at it. There are rules, unchangeable rules, which command the courses of the planets, the tides of the sea, and the affairs of men, and I know, I absolutely know, that all these things are interlinked: the sea, the planets, and the history of man. With God's grace and with the skill we can muster we will discover these laws and when we know them . . .' He paused. 'We will know everything.'

Spring 1553

I was allowed to go home to my father in April and I took him my wages for the quarter. I went in my old boy's clothes that he had bought me when we first came to England and found that my wrists poked out at the sleeves and I could not get my growing feet into the shoes. I had to cut out the heels and go slipshod through the city.

'They will have to put you in gowns soon,' my father remarked. 'You are half a woman already. What news of the court?'

'None,' I said. 'Everyone says that the king is growing stronger with the warmer weather.' I did not add that everyone was speaking a lie.

'God bless him and keep him,' my father said piously. He looked at me, as if he would know more. 'And Lord Robert. Do you see him?'

I felt myself colour. 'Now and then.' I could have told him to the very hour and the minute when I had last seen Lord Robert. He had not spoken to me, perhaps he had not even seen me. He had been mounted on his horse, about to go hawking for herons along the mudflats of the river shore. He was wearing a black cape and a black hat with a dark feather pinned to the ribbon with a jet brooch. He had a beautiful hooded falcon on his wrist and he rode with one hand outstretched to keep the bird steady and his other hand holding the curvetting horse, which was pawing the ground in its eagerness. He looked like a prince in a story book, he was laughing. I had watched him as I might have watched a seagull riding the wind blowing up the Thames: as a thing so beautiful that it illuminated my day. I watched him, not a woman desiring a man; but a girl

51

worshipping an icon, something far beyond reach but perfection in every way.

'There is to be a great wedding,' I said to fill the pause. 'Lord Robert's father has arranged it.'

'Who is to marry?' my father asked with a gossip's curiosity.

I ticked off the three couples on my fingers. 'Lady Katherine Dudley is to marry Lord Henry Hastings, and the two Grey sisters are to marry Lord Guilford Dudley and Lord Henry Herbert.'

'And you know them all!' my father boasted, proud as any parent.

I shook my head. 'Only the Dudleys,' I said. 'And not one of them would know me out of livery. I am a very lowly servant at court, Father.'

He cut a slice of bread for me and one for himself. It was stale bread, yesterday's loaf. He had a small piece of cheese on one plate. On the other side of the room was a piece of meat, which we would eat later, in defiance of the English way of doing things which was to set all of the dinner, meats, breads, puddings as well, on the table at the same time. I thought however much we might pretend, anyone who strolled into the room now would see that we were trying to eat the right way: dairy and meat separate. Anyone looking at my father's vellum skin and my dark eyes would know us for Jews. We might say that we were converted, we might attend church as enthusiastically as Lady Elizabeth herself was loudly praised for doing, but anyone would know us for Jews, and if they wanted an excuse to rob or denounce us, they would have it to their hand.

'Do you not know the Grey sisters?'

'Hardly at all,' I said. 'They are the king's cousins. They say that Lady Jane does not want to marry, she lives only to study her books. But her mother and her father have beaten her till she agreed.'

My father nodded, the forcible ordering of a daughter was no surprise. 'And what else?' he asked. 'What of Lord Robert's father, the Duke of Northumberland?'

'He's very much disliked.' I lowered my voice to a whisper. 'But he is like a king himself. He goes in and out of the king's bedroom and says that this or that is the king's own wish. What can anyone do against him?'

'They took up our neighbour the portrait painter only last week,' my father remarked. 'Mr Tuller. They said he was a Catholic and a heretic. Took him off for questioning, and he has not come back. He had copied a picture of Our Lady some years ago, and someone searched a house and found it hidden, with his name signed at the foot.' My father shook his head. 'It makes no sense in law,' he complained. 'Whatever their conviction, it makes no sense. When he painted the picture it was allowed. Now it is heresy. When he painted the picture it was a work of art. Now it is a crime. The picture has not changed, it is the law which has changed and they apply the law to the years when it did not exist, before it was written. These people are barbarians. They lack all reason.'

We both glanced towards the door. The street was quiet, the door locked.

'D'you think we should leave?' I asked, very low. I realised for the first time that now I wanted to stay.

He chewed his bread, thinking. 'Not yet,' he said cautiously. 'Besides, where could we go that was safe? I'd rather be in Protestant England than Catholic France. We are good reformed Christians now. You go to church, don't you?'

'Twice, sometimes three times a day,' I assured him. 'It's a very observant court.'

'I make sure I am seen to go. And I give to charity, and I pay my parish dues. We can do nothing more. We've both been baptised. What can any man say against us?'

I said nothing. We both knew that anyone could say anything against anyone. In the countries that had turned the ritual of the church into a burning matter no-one could be sure that they would not offend by the way they prayed, even by which direction they faced when they prayed.

'If the king falls ill and dies,' my father whispered, 'then Lady Mary takes the throne, and she is a Roman Catholic. Will she make the whole country become Roman Catholic again?'

'Who knows what will happen?' I asked, thinking of my naming the next heir as 'Jane' and Robert Dudley's lack of surprise. 'I wouldn't put a groat wager on Lady Mary coming to the throne. There are bigger players in this game than you and I, Father. And I don't know what they are planning.'

'If Lady Mary inherits and the country becomes Roman Catholic again then there are some books I shall have to be rid of,' my father said anxiously. 'And we are known as good Lutheran booksellers.'

I put my hand up and rubbed my cheek, as if I would brush smuts away. At once he touched my hand. 'Don't do that, *querida*. Don't worry. Everyone in the country will have to change, not just us. Everyone will be the same.'

I glanced over to where the Sabbath candle burned under the upended pitcher, its light hidden but its flame burning for our God. 'But we're not the same,' I said simply.

John Dee and I read together every morning like devoted scholars. Mostly he commanded me to read the Bible in Greek and then the same passage in Latin so that he might compare the translations. He was working on the oldest parts of the Bible, trying to unravel the secrets of the real making of the world from the flowery speech. He sat with his head resting in his hand, jotting notes as I wrote, sometimes raising his hand to ask me to pause as a thought struck him. It was easy work for me, I could read without comprehension, and when I did not know how to pronounce a word (and there were many such words) I just spelled it out, and Mr Dee would recognise it. I could not help but like him, he was such a kind and gentle man; and I had a growing admiration for his immense ability. He seemed to me to be a man of almost inspired understanding. When he was alone he read mathematics, he played games with codes and numbers, he created acrostics and riddles of intense complexity. He exchanged letters and theories with the greatest thinkers of Christendom, forever staying just ahead of the Papal Inquisitions, which forbade the very questions that everyone's work suggested.

He had invented a game of his own that only Lord Robert and he could play, called Chess on Many Floors, for which Mr Dee had invented a chess board on three levels made of thick bevelled glass, where the players could go up and down as well as along. It made a game of such difficulty that he and Lord Robert would play the same round for weeks at a time. Other times he would retreat into his inner study and be silent for all the afternoon or all the morning and I knew that he was gazing in the scrying mirror and trying to see what might exist in the world just beyond our own, the world of the spirits which he knew must be there, but which he glimpsed only occasionally.

In his inner chamber he had a small stone bench, with a little fireplace hollowed out of the stone. He would light a charcoal fire, and suspend above it great glass vessels filled with herbs in water. A complicated network of glass tubes would drain liquor from one bottle to the other and then would stand and cool. Sometimes he would be in there for hours and all I would hear, as I copied page after page of numbers for him, was the quiet clink of one flask against another as he poured liquid into a vessel, or the hiss of the bellows as he heated the little fire.

In the afternoons Will Somers and I practised our sword fighting, leaving aside the comical tricks and concentrating on proper fighting, until he told me that I was a commendable swordsman for a fool, and that if I ever found myself in trouble I might use a sword to fight my way out: 'Like a proud hidalgo', he said.

Although I was glad to learn a useful skill, we thought that the lessons would have been for nothing since the king continued to be so sick; until in May we were commanded to the great wedding feasts at Durham House in the Strand. The duke wanted a memorable wedding for his family and Will and I were part of an elaborate dinner entertainment.

'You would think it a royal wedding,' Will said slyly to me.

'How, royal?' I asked.

He put his finger to his lips. 'Jane's mother, Frances Brandon, is King Henry's niece, the daughter of his sister. Jane and Katherine are royal cousins.'

'Yes,' I said. 'And so?'

'And Jane is to marry a Dudley.'

'Yes,' I said, following this not at all.

'Who more royal than the Dudleys?' he demanded.

'The king's sisters,' I pointed out. 'Jane's own mother. And others too.'

'Not if you measure in terms of desire,' Will explained sweetly. 'In terms of desire there is no-one more royal than the duke. He loves the throne so much he practically tastes it. He almost gobbles it up.'

55

Will had gone too far for me. I got to my feet. 'I don't understand,' I said flatly.

'You are a wise child to be so dense,' he said and patted my head.

Our sword fight was preceded by dancers and a masque and followed by jugglers, and we acquitted ourselves well. The guests roared with laughter at Will's tumbles and my triumphant skill, and the contrast between our looks: Will so tall and gangling, thrusting his sword wildly this way and that; and me, neat and determined, dancing around him and stabbing with my little sword, and parrying his blows.

The chief bride was as white as the pearls embroidered on her gold gown. Her bridegroom sat closer to his mother than to his new bride and neither bride nor groom spoke so much as one word to each other. Jane's sister had been married to her betrothed in the same ceremony and she and he toasted each other and drank amorously from the same loving cup. But when the shout went up for a toast for Jane and Guilford, I could see that it cost Lady Jane an effort to raise her golden goblet to her new husband. Her eyes were red and raw, and the shadows under her eyes were dark with fatigue; there were marks on either side of her neck that looked like thumbprints. It looked very much as if someone had shaken the bride by the neck till she agreed to take her vows. She barely touched the bridal ale with her lips, I did not see her swallow.

'What d'you think, Hannah the Fool?' the Duke of Northumberland shouted down the hall to me. 'Shall she be a lucky bride?'

My neighbours turned to me, and I felt the old swimming sensation that was a sign of the Sight coming. I tried to fight it off, this court would be the worst place in the world to tell the truth. I could not stop the words coming. 'Never more lucky than today,' I said.

Lord Robert flashed a cautionary look at me but I could not take back the words. I had spoken as I felt, not with the skill of a courtier. My sense was that Jane's luck, at a low ebb when she married with a bruise on her throat, would now run ever more swiftly downhill. But the duke took it as a compliment to his son and laughed at me, and raised his goblet. Guilford, little more than a dolt, beamed at his mother, while

Lord Robert shook his head, and half-closed his eyes, as if he wished he was elsewhere.

There was dancing, and a bride had to dance at her own wedding, though Lady Jane sat in her chair, as stubborn as a white mule. Lord Robert led her gently to the dance floor. I saw him whisper to her and she found a wan little smile and put her hand in his. I wondered what he was saying to cheer her. In the moments when the dancers paused and awaited their turn in the circle his mouth was so close to her ear that I thought she must feel the warmth of his breath on her bare neck. I watched without envy. I did not long to be her, with his long fingers holding my hand, or his dark eyes on my face. I gazed on them as I might look on a pair of beautiful portraits, his face turned to her as sharp as a hawk's beak in profile, her pallor warming under his kindness.

The court danced until late, as if there were great joy from such weddings, and then the three couples were taken to their bedrooms and put to bed with much throwing of rose petals and sprinkling of rose water. But it was all show, no more real than Will and I fighting with wooden swords. None of the marriages was to be consummated yet, and the next day Lady Jane went home with her parents to Suffolk Place, Guilford Dudley went home with his mother, complaining of stomach ache and bloating, and Lord Robert and the duke were up early to return to the king at Greenwich.

'Why does your brother not make a house with his wife?' I asked Lord Robert. I met him at the gateway of the stable-yard, and he waited beside me while they brought out his great horse.

'Well, it is not unusual. I do not live with mine,' he remarked.

I saw the roofs of Durham House tilt against the sky, as I staggered back and held on to the wall till the world steadied again. 'You have a wife?'

'Oho, did you not know that, my little seer? I thought you knew everything?'

'I did not know . . .' I began.

'Oh yes, I have been married since I was a lad. And I thank God for it.'

'Because you like her so much?' I stammered, feeling an odd pain like sickness under my ribs.

'Because if I had not been married already, it would have been me married to Jane Grey and dancing to my father's bidding.'

'Does your wife never come to court?'

'Almost never. She will only live in the country, she has no liking for London, we cannot agree ... and it is easier for me ...' He broke off and glanced towards his father, who was mounting a big black hunter and giving his grooms orders about the rest of the horses. I knew at once that it was easier for Lord Robert to move this way and that, his father's spy, his father's agent, if he was not accompanied by a wife whose face might betray them.

'What's her name?'

'Amy,' he said casually. 'Why?'

I had no answer. Numbly, I shook my head. I could feel an intense discomfort in my belly. For a moment I thought I had taken Guilford Dudley's bloat. It burned me like bile. 'Do you have children?'

If he had said that he had children, if he had said that he had a girl, a beloved daughter, I think I would have doubled up and vomited on the cobbles at his feet.

But he shook his head. 'No,' he said shortly. 'You must tell me one day when I shall get a son and an heir. Can you do that?'

I looked up and tried to smile despite the burning in my throat. 'I don't think I can.'

'Are you afraid of the mirror?'

I shook my head. 'I'm not afraid, if you are there.'

He smiled at that. 'You have all the cunning of a woman, never mind the skills of a holy fool. You seek me out, don't you, Mistress Boy?'

I shook my head. 'No, sir.'

'You didn't like the thought of me married.'

'I was surprised, only.'

Lord Robert put his gloved hand under my chin and turned my face up to him so that I was forced to meet his dark eyes. 'Don't be a woman, a lying woman. Tell me the truth. Are you troubled with the desires of a maid, my little Mistress Boy?'

I was too young to hide it. I felt the tears come into my eyes and I stayed still, letting him hold me.

He saw the tears and knew what they meant. 'Desire? And for me?'

Still I said nothing, looking at him dumbly through my blurred vision.

'I promised your father that I would not let any harm come to you,' he said gently.

'It has come already,' I said, speaking the inescapable truth.

He shook his head, his dark eyes warm. 'Oh, this is nothing. This is young love, green-sickness. The mistake I made in my youth was to marry for such a slim cause. But you, you will survive this and go on to marry your betrothed and have a houseful of black-eyed children.'

I shook my head but my throat was too tight to speak.

'It is not love that matters, Mistress Boy, it is what you choose to do with it. What d'you choose to do with yours?'

'I could serve you.'

He took one of my cold hands and took it up to his lips. Entranced, I felt his mouth touch the tips of my fingers, a touch as intimate as any kiss on the lips. My own mouth softened, in a little pursed shape of longing, as if I would have him kiss me, there, in the courtyard before them all.

'Yes,' he said gently, not raising his head but whispering against my fingers. 'You could serve me. A loving servant is a great gift for any man. Will you be mine, Mistress Boy? Heart and soul? And do whatever I ask of you?'

His moustache brushed against my hand, as soft as the breast feathers of his hawk.

'Yes,' I said, hardly grasping the enormity of my promise.

'Whatever I ask of you?'

'Yes.'

At once he straightened up, suddenly decisive. 'Good. Then I have a new post for you, new work.'

'Not at court?' I asked.

'No.'

'You begged me to the king,' I reminded him. 'I am his fool.'

His mouth twisted in a moment's pity. 'The poor lad won't miss you,' he said. 'I shall tell you all of it. Come to Greenwich tomorrow, with the rest of them, and I'll tell you then.'

He laughed at himself as if the future was an adventure that he wanted to start at once. 'Come to Greenwich tomorrow,' he threw over his shoulder as he strode towards his horse. His groom cupped his hands for his master's boot and Lord Robert vaulted up into the high saddle of his hunter. I watched him turn his horse and clatter out of the stable-yard, into the Strand and then towards the cold English morning sun. His father followed behind at a more sober pace, and I saw that as they passed, although all the men pulled off their hats and bent their heads to show the respect that the duke commanded, their faces were sour.

I clattered into the courtyard of the palace at Greenwich riding astride one of the carthorses pulling the wagon with supplies. It was a beautiful spring day, the fields running down to the river were a sea of gold and silver daffodils, and they reminded me of Mr Dee's desire to turn base metal to gold. As I paused, feeling the warmer breeze against my face, one of the Dudley servants shouted towards me: 'Hannah the Fool?'

'Yes?'

'To go to Lord Robert and his father in their privy rooms at once. At once, lad!'

I nodded and went into the palace at a run, past the royal chambers to the ones that were no less grand, guarded by soldiers in the Dudley livery. They swung open the double doors for me and I was in the presence room where the duke would hear the petitions of common people. I went through another set of doors, and another, the rooms getting smaller and more intimate, until the last double doors opened, and there was Lord Robert leaning over a desk with a manuscript scroll spread out before him, his father looking over his shoulder. I recognised at once that it was Mr Dee's writing, and that it was a map that he had made partly from ancient maps of Britain borrowed from my father, and partly from calculations of his own based on the sailors' charts of the coastline. Mr Dee had prepared the map because he believed that England's greatest fortune were the seas around the coast; but the duke was using it for a different purpose.

He had placed little counters in a crowd at London, and more in the painted blue sea. A set of counters of a different colour was in the north of the country, Scots, I thought, and another little group like Lord Robert's chess pawns in the east of the country. I made a deep bow to Lord Robert and to his father.

'It has to be done at speed,' the duke remarked, scowling. 'If it is done at once, before anyone has a chance to protest, then we can deal with the north, with the Spanish, and with those of her tenants who stay loyal, in our own time.'

'And she?' Lord Robert asked quietly.

'She can do nothing,' the duke said. 'And if she tries to run, your little spy will warn us.' He looked up at me on those words. 'Hannah Green, I am sending you to wait upon the Lady Mary. You are to be her fool until I summon you back to court. My son assures me that you can keep your counsel. Is he right?'

The skin on the back of my neck went cold. 'I can keep a secret,' I said unhelpfully. 'But I don't like to.'

'And you will not go into a trance and speak of foretellings and smoke and crystals and betray everything?'

'You hired me for my trances and foretellings,' I reminded him. 'I can't order the Sight.'

'Does she do it often?' he demanded of his son.

Lord Robert shook his head. 'Rarely, and never out of turn. Her fear is greater than her gift. She is witty enough to turn anything. Besides, who would listen to a fool?'

The duke gave his quick bark of a laugh. 'Another fool,' he suggested.

Robert smiled. 'Hannah will keep our secrets,' he said gently. 'She is mine, heart and soul.'

The duke nodded. 'Well, then. Tell her the rest.'

I shook my head, wanting to block my ears; but Lord Robert came around the table and took my hand. He stood close to me and when I looked up from my study of the floor I met his dark gaze. 'Mistress Boy, I need you to go to the Lady Mary and write to me and tell me what she thinks, and where she goes, and who she meets.'

I blinked. 'Spy on her?'

He hesitated. 'Befriend her.'

'Spy on her. Exactly,' his father said brusquely.

'Will you do this for me?' Lord Robert asked. 'It would be a very great service to me. It is the service I ask of your love.'

'Will I be in danger?' I asked. In my head I could hear the knock of

61

the Inquisition on the heavy wooden door and the trample of their feet over our threshold.

'No,' he promised me. 'I have guaranteed your safety while you are mine. You will be my fool, under my protection. No-one can hurt you if you are a Dudley.'

'What must I do?'

'Watch the Lady Mary and report to me.'

'You want me to write to you? Will I never see you?'

He smiled. 'You shall come to me when I send for you,' he said. 'And if anything happens . . .'

'What?'

He shrugged. 'These are exciting times, Mistress Boy. Who knows what might happen? That's why I need you to tell me what Lady Mary does. Will you do this for me? For love of me, Mistress Boy? To keep me safe?'

I nodded. 'Yes.'

He put his hand into his jacket and brought out a letter. It was from my father to the duke, promising him the delivery of some manuscripts. 'Here is a mystery for you,' Lord Robert said gently. 'See the first twenty-six letters of the first sentence?'

I scanned them. 'Yes.'

'They are to be your alphabet. When you write to me I want you to use these. Where it says "My Lord", that is your ABC. The M for "my" is your A. The Y is your B. And so on, do you understand? When you have a letter which occurs twice you only use it once. You use the first set for your first letter to me and your second set for your second letter, and so on. I have a copy of the letter and when your message comes to me I can translate it.'

He saw my eyes run down the page. There was only one thing I was looking for and it was how long this system would last. There were enough sentences to translate as many as a dozen letters; he was sending me away for weeks.

'I have to write in code?' I asked nervously.

His warm hand covered my cold fingers. 'Only to prevent gossip,' he said reassuringly. 'So that we can write privately to one another.'

'How long do I have to stay away?' I whispered.

'Oh, not for so very long.'

'Will you reply to me?'

He shook his head. 'Only if I need to ask you something, and if I do, I will use this almanac also. My first letter will be the first twenty-six characters, my second the next set. Don't keep my letters to you, burn them as soon as you have read them. And don't make copies of yours to me.'

I nodded.

'If anyone finds this letter it is just something you brought from your father to me and forgot.'

'Yes, sir.'

'Do you promise to do this exactly as I ask?'

'Yes,' I said miserably. 'When do I have to go?'

'Within three days,' the duke said from his place behind the table. 'There's a cart going to the Lady Mary with some goods for her. You can ride alongside that. You shall have one of my ponies, girl, and you can keep her at Lady Mary's house for your return. And if something should happen that you think threatens me or Lord Robert, something very grave indeed, you can ride to warn us at once. Will you do that?'

'Why, what should threaten you?' I asked the man who ruled England.

'I shall be the one that wonders what might threaten me. You shall be the one to warn me if it does. You are to be Robert's eyes and ears at the house of the Lady Mary. He tells me that he can trust you; make sure that he can.'

'Yes, sir,' I said obediently.

Lord Robert said that I might send for my father to say goodbye to him and he came downriver to Greenwich Palace in a fishing smack on the ebbing tide, with Daniel seated beside him.

'You!' I said without any enthusiasm, when I saw him help my father from the bobbing boat.

'Me,' he replied with the glimmer of a smile. 'Constant, aren't I?'

I went to my father and felt his arms come around me. 'Oh, Papa,' I whispered in Spanish. 'I wish we had never come to England at all.'

'*Querida*, has someone hurt you?'

'I have to go to the Lady Mary and I am afraid of the journey, and afraid of living at her house, I am afraid of . . .' I broke off, tasting the many lies on my tongue and realising that I would never be able to tell anyone the truth about myself ever again. 'I am just being foolish, I suppose.'

'Daughter, come home to me. I will ask Lord Robert to release you, we can close the shop, we can leave England. You are not trapped here . . .'

'Lord Robert himself asked me to go,' I said simply. 'And I already said I would.'

His gentle hand caressed my cropped hair. '*Querida*, you are unhappy?'

'I am not unhappy,' I said, finding a smile for him. 'I am being foolish. For look, I am being sent to live with the heir to the throne, and Lord Robert himself has asked me to go.'

He was only partly reassured. 'I shall be here, and if you send for me I shall come to you. Or Daniel will come and fetch you away. Won't you, Daniel?'

I turned in my father's arms to look at my betrothed. He was leaning against the wooden railing that ran around the jetty. He was waiting patiently, but he was pale and he was scowling with anxiety.

'I would rather fetch you away now.'

My father released me and I took a step towards Daniel. Behind him, bobbing at the jetty, their boat was waiting for them. I saw the swirl of water and saw the tide was ready to turn; we could go upstream almost at once. He had timed this moment very carefully.

'I have agreed to go to serve Lady Mary,' I said quietly to him.

'She is a Papist in a Protestant country,' he said. 'You could not have chosen a place where your faith and practices will be more scrutinised. It is me who is named for Daniel, not you. Why should you go into the very den of lions? And what are you to do for Lady Mary?'

He stepped closer to me so we could whisper.

'I am to be her companion, be her fool.' I paused and decided to tell him the truth. 'I am to spy for Lord Robert and his father.'

His head was so close to mine that I could feel the warmth of his cheek against my forehead as he leaned closer to speak into my ear.

'Spy on Lady Mary?'

'Yes.'

'And you have agreed?'

I hesitated. 'They know that Father and I are Jews,' I said.

He was silent for a moment. I felt the solidity of his chest against my shoulder. His arm came around my waist to hold me closer to him and I felt the warmth of his grip. A rare sense of safety came over me as he held me, and for a moment I stood still.

'They are going to act against us?'

'No.'

'But you are a hostage.'

'In a way. It feels more as if Lord Robert knows my secret and trusts me with his. I feel bound to him.'

He nodded for a moment, I craned my neck to look up into his scowling face. For a moment I thought he was angry then I realised that he was thinking hard. 'Does he know my name?' he demanded. 'Of my mother, of my sisters? Are we all at risk?'

'He knows I am betrothed, but not of you by name. And he knows nothing of your family,' I said, with quick pride. 'I have not brought danger to your door.'

'No, you keep it all to yourself,' he said with a brief unhappy smile. 'And if you were questioned you could not keep it secret for long.'

'I would not betray you,' I said quickly.

His face was troubled. 'No-one can remain silent on the rack, Hannah. A pile of stones will crush the truth out of most people.' He looked down the river over my head. 'Hannah, I should forbid you to go.'

He felt my instantaneous move of disagreement. 'Don't quarrel with me for nothing, for clumsy words,' he said quickly. 'I did not mean forbid like a master. I meant I should beg you not to go – is that better? This road leads straight into danger.'

'I am in danger whatever I do,' I said. 'And this way, Lord Robert will protect me.'

'But only while you do his bidding.'

I nodded. I could not tell him that I had volunteered to walk into this danger, and I would have risked worse for love of Lord Robert.

Gently he released me. 'I am sorry you are here, and unprotected,' he said. 'If you had sent for me I would have come sooner. This is a burden that you shouldn't have to bear alone.'

I thought of the terror of my childhood, of my wild apprenticeship in fear on our flight through Europe. 'It is my burden.'

'But you have kin now, you have me,' he said with the pride of a young man made head of his family too young. 'I shall bear your burdens for you.'

'I bear my own,' I said stubbornly.

'Oh yes, you are your own woman. But if you would condescend to send for me if you are in danger, I would come and perhaps be allowed to help you escape.'

I giggled at that. 'I promise that I will.' I held out my hand to him in a gesture which suited my boy's clothing. But he took my hand and drew me close to him again and bent his head. Very gently he kissed me, full on the lips, and I felt the warmth of his mouth on mine.

He released me and stepped back to the boat. I found I was slightly dizzy, as if I had gulped down strong wine. 'Oh, Daniel!' I breathed, but he was climbing into the boat and did not hear me. I turned to my father and caught him hiding his smile.

'God bless you, daughter, and bring you home safe to us,' he said quietly. I knelt on the wooden pier for my father's blessing and felt his hand come down on my head in the familiar, beloved caress. He took my hands and raised me up. 'He *is* an attractive young man, isn't he?' he demanded, a chuckle behind his voice. Then he wrapped his cape around himself and went down the steps to the fishing smack.

They cast off and the little boat travelled swiftly across the darkening water, leaving me alone on the wooden pier. The mist hanging on the river and the gathering dark hid their silhouette, and all I could hear was the splash of the oars and the creak of the rowlocks. Then that sound was gone too and all that was left was the smack and suck of the rising tide and the quiet whistle of the wind.

Summer 1553

Lady Mary was at her house at Hunsdon, in the county of Hertfordshire. It took us three days to get to her, riding northward out of London, on a winding road through muddy valleys and then climbing arduously through hills called the North Weald, journeying some of the way with another band of travellers, and staying overnight on the road, once at an inn, once at a grand house that had been a monastery and was now in the hands of the man who had cleansed it of heresy at some profit to himself. These days they could offer us no rooms better than a hay loft over the stable, and the carter complained that in the old days this had been a generous house of good monks where any traveller might be sure of a good dinner and a comfortable bed, and a prayer to help him on his way. He had stayed here once when his son had been sick nearly to death and the monks had taken him into their care and nursed him back to health with their own herbs and skills. They had charged him not a penny, but said that they were doing the work of God by serving poor men. The same story could have been told up and down the country at every great monastery or abbey on the roads. But now all the religious houses were in the possession of the great lords, the men of court who had made their fortunes by advising that the world would be a better place if wealth was stripped from the English church and poured into their own pockets. Now the feeding of the poor at the monastery gates, the making of free medicines in the nunnery hospitals, the teaching of the children and the care of the old people of the village had gone the way of the beautiful statues, the illuminated manuscripts, and the great libraries.

The carter muttered to me that this was the case all around the country. The great religious houses, which had been the very backbone of England, had been emptied of the men and women who had been called by God to serve in them. The public good had been turned to private profit and there would never be public good again.

'If the poor king dies then Lady Mary will come to the throne and turn it all back,' he said. 'She will be a queen for the people. A queen who returns us to the old ways.'

I reined back my pony. We were on the high road and there was no-one within earshot but I was always fearful of anything that smacked of intrigue.

'And look at these roads,' he went on, turning on the box of the cart to complain over his shoulder. 'Dust in summer and mud in winter, never a pot hole filled in, never a highwayman pursued. D'you know why not?'

'I'll ride ahead, you're right, the dust is dreadful,' I said.

He nodded and motioned me forward. I could hear his litany of complaint receding in the distance behind me:

'Because once the shrines are closed there are no pilgrims, and if there are no pilgrims then there is no-one on the roads but the worst sort of people, and those that prey on them. Never a kind word, never a good house, never a decent road . . .'

I let the mare scramble up a little bank where the ground was softer beneath her small hooves and we ranged ahead of the cart.

Since I had not known the England that he said was lost, I could not feel, as he did, that the country was a lesser place. On that morning in early summer it seemed very fine to me, the roses twining through the hedgerows and a dozen butterflies hovering around the honeysuckle and the beanflowers. The fields were cultivated in prim little stripes, like the bound spine of a book, the sheep ranging on the upper hills, little fluffy dots against the rich damp green. It was a countryside so unlike my own that I could not stop marvelling at it, the open villages with the black-and-white beamed buildings, and the roofs thatched with golden reeds, the rivers that seemed to melt into the roads in glassy slow-moving fords at every corner. It was a country so damp that it was no wonder that every cottage garden was bright green with growth, even the dung hills were topped with waving daisies, even the roofs of the older houses were as green as limes with moss. Compared to my own country, this was a land as sodden as a printer's sponge, damp with life.

At first I noticed the things that were missing. There were no twisted rows of vines, no bent and bowed olive trees. There were no orchards of orange trees, or lemons or limes. The hills were rounded and green, not high and hot and rocky, and above them the sky was dappled with cloud, not the hot unrelieved blue of my home, and there were larks rising, and no circling eagles.

I rode in a state of wonder that a country could be so lush and so green; but even among this fertile wealth there was hunger. I saw it in the faces of some of the villagers, and in the fresh mounds of the graveyards. The carter was right, the balance that had been England at peace for a brief generation had been overthrown under the last king, and the new one continued the work of setting the country into turmoil. The great religious houses had closed and thrown the men and women who served and laboured in them on to the roads. The great libraries were spilled and gone to waste – I had seen enough torn manuscripts at my father's shop to know that centuries of scholarship had been thrown aside in the fear of heresy. The great golden vessels of the wealthy church had been taken by private men and melted down, the beautiful statues and works of art, some with their feet or hands worn smooth by a million kisses of the faithful, had been thrown down and smashed. There had been a great voyage of destruction through a wealthy peaceful country and it would take years before the church could be a safe haven again for the spiritual pilgrim or the weary traveller. If it ever could be made safe again.

It was such an adventure to travel so freely in a strange country that I was sorry when the carter whistled to me and called out, 'Here's Hunsdon now,' and I realised that these carefree days were over, that I had to return to work, and that now I had two tasks: one as a holy fool in a household where belief and faith were key concerns, and the other as a spy in a household where treason and tale-bearing were the greatest occupations.

I swallowed on a throat which was dry from the dust of the road and also from fear, I pulled my horse alongside the cart and we went in through the lodge gates together, as if I would shelter behind the bulk of the four turning wheels, and hide from the scrutiny of those blank windows that stared out over the lane and seemed to watch for our arrival.

Lady Mary was in her chamber sewing blackwork, the famous Spanish embroidery of black thread on white linen, while one of her ladies, standing at a lectern, read aloud to her. The first thing I heard, on reaching her presence, was a Spanish word, mispronounced, and she gave a merry laugh when she saw me wince.

'Ah, at last! A girl who can speak Spanish!' she exclaimed and gave me her hand to kiss. 'If you could only read it!'

I thought for a moment. 'I can read it,' I said, considering it reasonable that the daughter of a bookseller should be able to read her native tongue.

'Oh, can you? And Latin?'

'Not Latin,' I said, having learned of the danger of pride in my education from my encounter with John Dee. 'Just Spanish and now I am learning to read English too.'

Lady Mary turned to her maid in waiting. 'You will be pleased to hear that, Susan! Now you will not need to read to me in the afternoons.'

Susan did not look at all pleased to hear that she was to be supplanted by a fool in livery, but she took a seat on a stool like the other women and took up some sewing.

'You shall tell me all the news of the court,' the Lady Mary invited me. 'Perhaps we should talk alone.'

One nod to the ladies and they took themselves off to the bay window and seated themselves in a circle in the brighter light, talking quietly as if to give us the illusion of privacy. I imagined every one of them was straining to hear what I might say.

'My brother the king?' she asked me, gesturing that I should sit on a cushion at her feet. 'Do you have any messages from him?'

'No, Lady Mary,' I said, and saw her disappointment.

'I was hoping he would have thought of me more kindly, now he is so ill,' she said. 'When he was a little boy I nursed him through half a dozen illnesses, I hoped he would remember that and think that we . . .'

I waited for her to say more but then she tapped her fingertips together as if to draw herself back from memories. 'No matter,' she said. 'Any other messages?'

'The duke sends you some game and some early salad leaves,' I said. 'They came in the cart with the furniture, and have been taken round to your kitchens. And he asked me to give you this letter.'

She took it and broke the seal and smoothed it out. I saw her smile and then I heard her warm chuckle. 'You bring me very good news, Hannah the Fool,' she said. 'This is a payment under the will of my late father which has been owed to me all this long while, since his death. I thought I would never see it, but here it is, a draft on a London goldsmith. I can pay my bills and face the shopkeepers of Ware again.'

'I am glad of it,' I said awkwardly, not knowing what else to say.

'Yes,' she said. 'You would have thought that King Henry's only legitimate daughter would have had her fortune in her own hands by now, but they have delayed and withheld until I thought they wanted me to starve to death here. But now I come into favour.'

She paused, thoughtful. 'The question which remains, is, why I am suddenly to be so well treated.' She looked speculatively at me. 'Is Lady Elizabeth given her inheritance too? Are you to visit her with such a letter?'

I shook my head. 'My lady, how would I know? I am only a messenger.'

'No word of it? She's not at court visiting my brother now?'

'She wasn't there when I left,' I said cautiously.

She nodded. 'And he? My brother? Is he better at all?'

I thought of the quiet disappearance of the physicians who came so full of promises and then left after they had done nothing more than torture him with some new cure. On the morning that I had left Greenwich, the duke had brought in an old woman to nurse the king: an old crone of a midwife, skilled only in the birthing of children and the laying out of the dead. Clearly, he was not going to get any better.

'I don't think so, my lady,' I said. 'They were hoping that the summer would ease his chest but he seems to be as bad as ever.'

She leaned towards me. 'Tell me, child, tell me the truth. Is my little brother dying?'

I hesitated, unsure of whether it was treason to tell of the death of the king.

She took my hand and I looked into her square determined face. Her eyes, dark and honest, met mine. She looked like a woman you could trust, a mistress you could love. 'You can tell me, I can keep a secret,' she said. 'I have kept many many secrets.'

'Since you ask it, I will tell you: I am certain that he is dying,' I admitted quietly. 'But the duke denies it.'

She nodded. 'And this wedding?'

I hesitated. 'What wedding?'

She tutted in brief irritation. 'Of Lady Jane Grey to the duke's son, of course. What do they say about it at court?'

'That she was unwilling, and he not much better.'

'And why did the duke insist?' she asked.

'It was time that Guilford was married?' I hazarded.

She looked at me, as bright as a knife blade. 'They say no more than that?'

I shrugged. 'Not in my hearing, my lady.'

'And what of you?' she asked, apparently abandoning interest in Lady Jane. 'Did you ask to come to this exile? From the royal court at Greenwich? And away from your father?' Her wry smile indicated to me that she did not think it likely.

'Lord Robert told me to come,' I confessed. 'And his father, the duke.'

'Did they tell you why?'

I wanted to bite my lips to hold in the secret. 'No, my lady. Just to keep you company.'

She gave me a look that I had never seen from a woman before. Women in Spain tended to glance sideways, a modest woman always looked away. Women in England kept their eyes on the ground before their feet. One of the many reasons why I was glad of my pageboy clothes was that masquerading as a boy I could hold my head up, and look around. But Lady Mary had the bold look of her father's portrait, the swaggering portrait, fists on hips, the look of someone who has been bred to think that he might rule the world. She had his

72

gaze: a straight look that a man might have, scanning my face, reading my eyes, showing me her own open face and her own clear eyes.

'What are you afraid of?' she asked bluntly.

For a moment I was so taken aback I could have told her. I was afraid of arrest, of the Inquisition, afraid of suspicion, afraid of the torture chamber and the heretic's death with kindling heaped around my bare feet and no way to escape. I was afraid of betraying others to their deaths, afraid of the very air of conspiracy itself. I rubbed my cheek with the back of my hand. 'I am just a little nervous,' I said quietly. 'I am new to this country, and to court life.'

She let the silence run and then she looked at me more kindly. 'Poor child, you are very young to be adrift, all alone in these deep waters.'

'I am Lord Robert's vassal,' I said. 'I am not alone.'

She smiled. 'Perhaps you will be very good company,' she said finally. 'There have been days and months and even years when I would have been very glad of a merry face and an uplifted voice.'

'I am not a witty fool,' I said cautiously. 'I am not supposed to be especially merry.'

Lady Mary laughed aloud at that. 'And I am not supposed to be given especially to laughter,' she said. 'Perhaps you will suit me very well. And now, you must meet my companions.'

She called her ladies over to us and named them to me. One or two were the daughters of determined heretics, holding on to the old faith and serving a Roman Catholic princess for pride, two others had the dismal faces of younger daughters with scanty dowries whose chance of service to an out-of-favour princess was only slightly better than the marriage they would have been forced to undertake if they had been left at home. It was a little court with the smell of desperation, on the edge of the kingdom, on the edge of heresy, on the edge of legitimacy.

After dinner the Lady Mary went to Mass. She was supposed to go alone, it was a crime for anyone else to observe the service; but in practice, she went openly and knelt at the very front of the chapel and the rest of her household crept in at the back.

I followed her ladies to the chapel door and then I hovered in a frenzy of worry as to what I should do. I had assured the king and Lord Robert that my father and I were of the reformed faith, but both the king and Lord Robert knew that Lady Mary's household was an island of illegal

Papist practices in a Protestant kingdom. I could feel myself sweating with fear as the meanest housemaid slipped past me to say her prayers, and I did not know the safest thing for me to do. I was in a terror of being reported to the court for being a Roman Catholic, and yet how could I serve in this household as a steadfast Protestant?

In the end, I compromised, by sitting outside where I could hear the mutter of the priest and the whispered responses, but no-one could actually accuse me of attending the service. All the time that I perched on the draughty window-seat I felt ready to leap up and run away. Constantly my hand was at my face, wiping my cheek as if I could feel the smuts from the fires of the Inquisition sticking to my skin. It made me sick in my belly not to know the safest place to be.

After Mass I was summoned to Lady Mary's room to hear her read from the Bible in Latin. I tried to keep my face blank as if I did not understand the words, and when she handed it to me to put it on its stand at the end of the reading, I had to remind myself not to check the front pages for the printer. I thought it was not such a good edition as my father printed.

She went to bed early, walking with her candle flickering before her, down the long shadowed corridor, past the dark draughty windows of the house, looking out over the darkness of the empty land beyond the tumbling-down castle walls. Everyone else went to bed too, there was nothing to wait up for, nothing was going to happen. There would be no visitors coming to see the popular princess, there would be no mummers or dancers or pedlars drawn by the wealth of the court. I thought that it was no wonder that she was not a merry princess. If the duke had wanted to keep Lady Mary in a place where she would be rarely visited, where her heart and spirits were sure to sink, where she would experience coldness and loneliness every day, he could not have chosen a place more certain to make her unhappy.

The household at Hunsdon turned out to be as I had thought: a melancholy place of outsiders, ruled by an invalid. Lady Mary was plagued with headaches, which often came in the evening, darkening her face as the light drained from the sky. Her ladies would notice her frown; but she never mentioned the pain and never drooped in her wooden chair nor leaned against the carved back, nor rested against the arms. She sat as her mother had taught her, upright like a queen, and she kept her head up, even when her eyes were squinting against dim candles. I remarked on her physical frailty to Jane Dormer, the Lady Mary's closest friend and lady in waiting, and she said briefly that the pains I saw now were nothing. When it was the Lady's time of the month, she would be gripped with cramps as severe as those of childbirth, which nothing could ease.

'What ails her?' I asked.

Jane shrugged. 'She was never a strong child,' she said. 'Always slight and delicate. But when her mother was put aside and her father denied her, it was as if he had poisoned her. She could not stop vomiting and voiding her food, she could not get out of bed but she had to crawl across the floor. There were some who said she had been poisoned indeed, by the witch Boleyn. The princess was near to death and they would not let her see her mother. The queen could not come to her for fear of never being allowed back to her own court. The Boleyn woman and the king destroyed the two of them: mother and daughter. Queen Katherine hung on for as long as she could but illness and heartbreak killed her. Lady Mary should have died too – she suffered so much; but she survived. They made her deny her faith, they made her deny her mother's marriage. Ever since then she has been tormented by these pains.'

'Can't the doctors . . . ?'

'They wouldn't even let her see a doctor for many years,' Jane said irritably. 'She could have died for want of care, not once but several times. The witch Boleyn wanted her dead and more than once I swear she sent poison. She has had a bitter life: half-prisoner, half-saint, always swallowing down grief and anger.'

The mornings were the best times for Lady Mary. After she had been to Mass and broken her fast she liked to walk, and often she chose me to walk with her. One warm day in late June she commanded me to walk at her side and to name the flowers and describe the weather in Spanish. I had to keep my steps short so that I did not stride ahead of her, and she often stopped with her hand to her side, the colour draining from her face. 'Are you not well this morning, my lady?' I asked.

'Just tired,' she said. 'I did not sleep last night.'

She smiled at the concern on my face. 'Oh, it is nothing worse than it has always been. I should learn to have more serenity. But not to know . . . and to have to wait . . . and to know that he is in the hands of advisors who have set their hearts . . .'

'Your brother?' I asked when she fell silent.

'I have thought of him every day from the day he was born!' she burst out passionately. 'Such a tiny boy and so much expected of him. So quick to learn and so – I don't know – so cold in his heart where he should have been warm. Poor boy, poor motherless boy! All three of us, thrown together, and none of us with a mother living, and none of us knowing what would happen next.

'I had more care of Elizabeth than I did of him, of course. And now she is far from me, and I cannot even see him. Of course I worry about him: about what they are doing to his soul, about what they are doing to his body . . . and about what they are doing to his will,' she added very quietly.

'His will?'

'It is my inheritance,' she said fiercely. 'If you report, as I imagine you do, tell them I never forget that. Tell them that it is my inheritance and nothing can change that.'

'I don't report!' I exclaimed, shocked. It was true, I had sent no report, there was nothing in our dull lives and quiet nights to report to Lord Robert or his father. This was a sick princess on a knife blade of watching and waiting, not a traitor spinning plots.

'Whether or no,' she dismissed my defence, 'nothing and no-one can deny me my place. My father himself left it to me. It is me and then it is Elizabeth. I have never plotted against Edward, though there were some who came to me and asked me in my mother's name to stand against him. I know that in her turn Elizabeth will never plot against me. We are three heirs, taking precedence one after another to honour our father. Elizabeth knows that I am the next heir after Edward, he came first as the boy, I come second as the princess, the first legitimate princess. We all three will obey our father and we stand to inherit one after the other as my father commanded. I trust Elizabeth, as Edward trusts me. And since you promise that you don't report, you can make this reply if anyone asks you: tell them that I will keep my inheritance. And tell them that this is my country.'

Her weariness was gone, the colour had flamed into her cheeks. She looked around the small walled garden as if she could see the whole kingdom, the great prosperity which could be restored, and the changes she would make when she held the throne. The monasteries she would restore, the abbeys she would found, the life she could breathe back into it. 'It is mine,' she said. 'And I am an English queen-to-be. No-one can put me aside.'

Her face was illuminated with her sense of destiny. 'It is the purpose of my life,' she said. 'Nobody will pity me ever again. They will see that I have dedicated my life to being the bride of this country. I will be a virgin queen, I shall have no children but the people of this country, I shall be their mother. There shall be no-one to distract me, there shall be no-one to command me. I shall live for them. It is my holy calling. I shall give myself up for them.'

She turned from me and strode back to the house and I followed her at a distance. The morning sun burning off the mist made a lightness in the air all around her, and I had a moment's dizziness as I realised that this woman would be a great queen for England, a queen who had a real vision for this country, who would bring back the richness and beauty and charity that her father had stripped out from the churches and from the daily life. The sun was so bright around her yellow silk hood that it was like a crown, and I stumbled on a tussock of grass and fell.

She turned and saw me on my knees. 'Hannah?'

'You will be queen,' I said simply, the Sight speaking in my voice. 'The king will die within a month. Long live the queen. Poor boy, the poor boy.'

In a second she was by my side, holding me up. 'What did you say?'

'You will be queen,' I said. 'He is sinking fast now.'

I lost my senses for a moment and then I opened my eyes again and she was looking down at me, still holding me closely.

'Can you tell me any more?' she asked me gently.

I shook my head. 'I am sorry, Lady Mary, I barely know what I said. It was not said knowingly.'

She nodded. 'It is the Holy Spirit which moves you to speak, especially to speak such news to me. Will you swear to keep it secret between us?'

For a moment I hesitated, thinking of the complicated webs of loyalties that were interwoven around me: my duty to Lord Robert, my honour for my father and mother and our kin, my promise to Daniel Carpenter, and now this troubled woman asking me to keep a secret for her. I nodded. It was no disloyalty not to tell Lord Robert something he must already know. 'Yes, Lady Mary.'

I tried to rise but I dropped back to my knees with dizziness.

'Wait,' she said. 'Don't get up till your head is clear.'

She sat beside me on the grass and gently put my head in her lap. The morning sunshine was warm, the garden buzzed with the sleepy noise of bees and the distant haunting call of a cuckoo. 'Close your eyes,' she said.

I wanted to sleep as she held me. 'I am not a spy,' I said.

Her finger touched my lips. 'Hush,' she said. 'I know that you work for the Dudleys. And I know you are a good girl. Who better than I to understand a life of complicated loyalties? You need not fear, little Hannah. I understand.'

I felt her soft touch on my hair, she wound my short-cropped curls around her finger. I felt my eyes close and the sinews of my back and neck unknot as I realised I was safe with her.

She, in her turn, was far away in the past. 'I used to sit like this when Elizabeth took her afternoon nap,' she said. 'She would rest her head in my lap and I would plait her hair while she slept. She had hair of bronze and copper and gold, all the colours of gold in one curl. She was such a pretty child, she had that shining innocence of children. And I was only twenty. I used to pretend to myself that she was my baby, and that I was happily married to a man who loved me, and that soon we would have another baby – a son.'

We sat in silence for long moments, and then I heard the door of the house bang open. I sat up and saw one of Lady Mary's ladies burst out of the shadowy interior and look wildly around for her. Lady Mary waved and the girl ran over. It was Lady Margaret. As she came close I felt

Lady Mary's posture rise, her back straighten, she steadied herself for the news I had foretold. She would let her companion find her here, seated simply in the English garden, her fool dozing beside her, and she would greet the news of her inheritance with words from the Psalms that she had prepared. She whispered them now: 'This is the Lord's doing; it is marvellous in our eyes.'

'Lady Mary! Oh!'

The girl was almost speechless with her desire to tell, and breathless from her run. 'At church just now . . .'

'What?'

'They didn't pray for you.'

'Pray for me?'

'No. They prayed for the king and his advisors, same as always, but where the prayer says "and for the king's sisters", they missed you out.'

Lady Mary's bright gaze swept the girl's face. 'Both of us? Elizabeth too?'

'Yes!'

'You are sure?'

'Yes.'

Lady Mary rose to her feet, her eyes narrowed with anxiety. 'Send out Mr Tomlinson into Ware, tell him to go on to Bishop Stortford if need be, tell him to get reports from other churches. See if this is happening everywhere.'

The girl bobbed a curtsey, picked up her skirts and ran back into the house.

'What does it mean?' I asked, scrambling to my feet.

She looked at me without seeing me. 'It means that Northumberland has started to move against me. First, he does not warn me how ill my brother is. Then, he commands the priests to leave Elizabeth and me from the prayers; next, he will command them to mention another, the king's new heir. Then, when my poor brother is dead, they will arrest me, arrest Elizabeth, and put their false prince on the throne.'

'Who?' I asked.

'Edward Courtenay,' she said decisively. 'My cousin. He is the only one Northumberland would choose, since he cannot put himself or his sons on the throne.'

I suddenly saw it. The wedding feast, the white face of Lady Jane Grey, the bruises at her throat as if someone had taken her by the neck to shake their ambition into her. 'Oh, but he can: Lady Jane Grey,' I said.

'Newly wed to Northumberland's son Guilford,' Lady Mary agreed. She paused for a moment. 'I would not have thought they would have dared. Her mother, my cousin, would have to step aside, she would have to resign her claim for her daughter. But Jane is a Protestant, and Dudley's father commands the keys to the kingdom.' She gave a harsh laugh. 'My God! She is *such* a Protestant. She has out-Protestanted Elizabeth, and that must have taken some doing. She has Protestanted her way into my brother's will. She has Protestanted her way into treason, God forgive her, the poor little fool. They will take her and destroy her, poor girl. But first, they will destroy me. They have to. Robbing me of the prayers of my people is only the first thing. Next, they will arrest me, then there will be some charge and I will be executed.'

Her pale face suddenly drained even paler and I saw her stagger. 'My God, what of Elizabeth? He will kill us both,' she whispered. 'He will have to. Otherwise there will be rebellions against him from both Protestant and Catholic. He has to be rid of me to be rid of men of courage of the true faith. But he has to be rid of Elizabeth too. Why would a Protestant follow Queen Jane and a cat's-paw like Guilford Dudley if they could have Elizabeth for queen? If I am dead, she is the next heir, a Protestant heir. He must be planning to forge some charge of treason against us both; one of us is not enough. Elizabeth and I will be dead within three months.'

She strode away from me by a couple of paces, and then she turned and came back again. 'I must save Elizabeth,' she said. 'Whatever else happens. I must warn her not to go to London. She must come here. They shall not take my throne from me. I have not come so far and borne so much for them to rob me of my country, and plunge my country into sin. I will not fail now.'

She turned towards the house. 'Come, Hannah!' she threw over her shoulder. 'Come quickly!'

She wrote to warn Elizabeth, she wrote for advice. I did not see either letter; but that night I took the manuscript Lord Robert had given to me, and using my father's letter as the base of the code I carefully wrote out the message. 'M is much alarmed that she is left out of the prayers.

She believes that Lady J will be named heir. She has written to Eliz to warn her. And to the Sp ambassador for advice.' I paused then. It was arduous work, translating every letter into another, but I wanted to write something, a line, a word, to remind him of me, to prompt him to recall me to court. Some line, some simple thing that he would read and think of me, not as his spy, not as a fool, but as me, myself, a girl who had promised to serve him heart and soul, for love.

'I miss you,' I wrote, and then I scratched it out, not even troubling to translate it into code.

'When can I come home?' went the same way.

'I am frightened,' was the most honest of all the confessions.

In the end I wrote nothing, there was nothing I could think of that would turn Lord Robert's attention to me, while the boy king was dying and his own young white-faced sister-in-law was stepping up to the throne of England and bringing the Dudley family to absolute greatness.

Then there was nothing to do but to wait for news of the death of the king to come from London. Lady Mary had her own private messages coming and going. But every three days or so she received a letter from the duke to tell her that the fine weather was doing its business and the king was on the mend, that his fever had broken, that his chest pains were better, that a new doctor had been appointed who had high hopes that the king would be well by midsummer. I watched Lady Mary read these optimistic notes through once, saw her eyes narrow slightly in disbelief; and then she folded them and put them away in a drawer in her writing desk, and never looked at them again.

Then, in the first days of July, one letter made her snatch her breath and put a hand to her heart.

'How is the king, my Lady?' I asked her. 'Not worse?'

Her colour burned in her cheeks. 'The duke says that he is better, that he has rallied and that he wants to see me.' She rose to her feet and paced to the window. 'Please God he is indeed better,' she said quietly to herself. 'Better, and wanting to restore me to our old affection, better, and seeing through his false advisors. Perhaps God has given him strength to get well and to come to a right understanding at last. Or at least well enough to put a stop to this plot. Oh, Mother of God, guide me in what I should do.'

'Shall we go?' I asked. I was on my feet already at the thought of returning to London, to court, to see Lord Robert again, to see my father, and Daniel, back to the relative safety of the men who would protect me.

I saw her shoulders straighten as she took the decision. 'If he asks for me, of course I have to go. Tell them to get the horses ready. We'll leave tomorrow.'

She went from the room with a rustle of her thick skirts, and I heard her calling to her ladies to pack their clothes, we were all going to London. I heard her run up stairs, her feet pattering on the bare wooden treads like those of a young girl, and then her voice, light and excited, as she called back down to Jane Dormer to take especial care to pack her finest jewels for if the king was indeed well then there would be dancing and feasting at court.

Next day we were on the road, Lady Mary's pennant before us, her soldiers around us, and the country people tumbling out of their houses in the small villages to call out blessings on her name, and holding up their children for them to see her: a real princess, and a pretty smiling princess at that.

Lady Mary on horseback was a different woman from the white-faced half-prisoner that I had first met at Hunsdon. Riding towards London with the people of England cheering her on, she looked like a true princess. She wore a deep red gown and jacket, which made her dark eyes shine. She rode well, one hand in a worn red glove on the bridle, the other waving to everyone who called out to her, the colour blazing in her cheeks, a stray lock of rich brown hair escaping from her hat, her head up, her courage high, her weariness all gone. She sat well in the saddle, proud as a queen, swaying with the pace of the horse as we made our way to the great road to London.

I rode beside her for much of the way, the little bay pony that the duke had given me stepping out to keep pace with Lady Mary's bigger horse. She commanded me to sing the songs of my Spanish childhood, and sometimes she recognised the words or the tune as something her mother had once sung to her, and she would sing with me, a little quaver in her voice at the memory of the mother who had loved her.

We rode hard along the London road, splashing through the fords at their summertime low, cantering where the tracks were soft enough. She was desperate to get to court to discover what was happening. I remembered John Dee's mirror and how I had guessed at the date of the king's death, the sixth of July, but I did not dare to say anything. I had spoken the name of the next Queen of England, and it had not been Queen Mary. The sixth of July had been a guess to please my lord, and the name Jane had come to me from nowhere – both might mean nothing. But as Lady Mary rode to London, hoping that her fears would prove to be unfounded, I rode at her side hoping that my Sight was all the chicanery and nonsense that I thought it must be.

Of all of the nervous train who rode with her I was the most anxious. For if I had seen true, she was riding not to a reconciliation with her brother the king, but to attend the coronation of Lady Jane. She was riding fast towards her own abdication, and we would all share her bad luck.

We rode all the morning and came just after midday into the town of Hoddesdon, weary of the saddle and hoping for a good dinner and a rest before we continued the journey. Without warning, a man stepped out from a doorway and put his hand up to signal to her. Clearly, she recognised him. At once she waved him forward so he could speak to her privately. He stood close to her horse's neck and took her rein familiarly in his arm and she leaned down towards him. He was very brief, and though I strained to hear, he kept his voice low. Then he stepped back and melted away into the mean streets of the little town and Lady Mary snapped an order to halt, and tumbled down from her saddle so fast that her Master of Horse could scarcely catch her. She went into the nearest inn at a run, shouting for paper and pen, and ordering everyone to drink, eat, see to their horses and be ready to leave again within the hour.

'Mother of God, I really can't,' Lady Margaret said pitifully as her royal mistress strode past. 'I'm too tired to go another step.'

'Then stay behind,' snapped Lady Mary, who never snapped. That sharpness of tone warned us that the hopeful ride to London, to visit the young, recovering king, had suddenly gone terribly wrong.

I did not dare to write a note for Lord Robert. There was no easy way to get it to him and the whole mood of the journey had changed. Whatever the man had told her it was not that her brother was well and summoning her to dance at his court. When she came out of the parlour she was pale and her eyes were red, but she was not softened by grief. She was sharp with decision, and she was angry.

She sent one messenger flying south down the road to London to find the Spanish ambassador, to beg for his advice and to alert the Spanish emperor that she would need his help to claim her throne. She took another messenger aside for a verbal message for Lady Elizabeth, she did not dare to write it down, she did not dare to give the impression that the sisters were plotting against their dying brother. 'Speak only to her when you are alone,' she emphasised. 'Tell her not to go to London, it is a trap. Tell her to come at once to me for her own safety.'

She sent a further message to the duke himself, swearing that she was too ill to ride to London, but that she would rest quietly at home at Hunsdon. Then she ordered the main group to stay behind. 'I'll take you, Lady Margaret, and you, Hannah,' she said. She smiled at her favourite, Jane Dormer. 'Follow us,' she said, and she leaned forward to whisper our destination in her ear. 'You must bring this company on behind us. We are going to travel too fast for everyone to keep pace.'

She picked six men to escort us, gave her followers a brief leave-taking and snapped her fingers for her Master of Horse to help her into the saddle. She wheeled her horse round and led us out of Hoddesdon, back the way we had come out of the town. But this time we took the great road north, racing away from London, as the sun slowly wheeled overhead and then set on our left, as the sky lost its colour, and a small silvery moon rose over the dark silhouettes of trees.

'Where are we going, Lady Mary? It's getting dark,' Lady Margaret asked plaintively. 'We can't ride in the dark.'

'Kenninghall,' Lady Mary crisply replied.

'Where's Kenninghall?' I asked, seeing Lady Margaret's aghast face.

'Norfolk,' she said as if it were the end of the world. 'God help us, she's running away.'

'Running away?' I felt my throat tense at the scent of danger.

'It's towards the sea. She'll get a ship out of Lowestoft and run to

Spain. Whatever that man told her must mean that she's in such danger that she has to get out of the country altogether.'

'What danger?' I asked urgently.

Lady Margaret shrugged. 'Who knows? A charge of treason? But what about us? If she goes to Spain I'm riding for home. I'm not going to be stuck with a traitor for a mistress. It's been bad enough in England, I'll not be exiled to Spain.'

I said nothing, I was feverishly racking my brains to think of where I might be safest: at home with my father, with Lady Mary, or taking a horse and trying to get back to Lord Robert.

'What about you?' she pressed me.

I shook my head, my voice quite lost in fear, my hand feverishly rubbing at my cheek. 'I don't know, I don't know. I should go home, I suppose. But I don't know the way on my own. I don't know what my father would want me to do. I don't understand the rights and the wrongs of it.'

She laughed, a bitter laugh for a young woman. 'There are no rights and wrongs,' she said. 'There are only those who are likely to win and those who are likely to lose. And Lady Mary with six men, me and a fool, up against the Duke of Northumberland with his army and the Tower of London and every castle in the kingdom, is going to lose.'

It was a punishing ride. We did not check until it was fully night, when we paused at the home of a gentleman, John Huddlestone, at Sawston Hall. I begged a piece of paper and a pen from the housekeeper and wrote a letter, not to Lord Robert, whose address I did not dare to give, but to John Dee. 'My dear tutor,' I wrote, hoping this would mislead anyone who opened my letter, 'this little riddle may amuse you.' Then underneath I wrote the coded letters in the form of a serpentine circle, hoping to make it look like a game that a girl of my age might send to a kind scholar. It simply read, 'She is going to Kenninghall.' And then I wrote: 'What am I to do?'

The housekeeper promised to send it to Greenwich by the carter who would pass by tomorrow, and I had to hope that it would find its destination and be read by the right man. Then I stepped into a little truckle bed that they had pulled out beside the kitchen fire and despite my exhaustion I lay sleepless in the slowly dimming firelight, wondering where I might find safety.

I woke painfully early, at five in the morning, to find the kitchen lad clattering pails of water and sacks of logs past my head. Lady Mary heard Mass in John Huddlestone's chapel, as if it were not a forbidden ceremony, broke her fast, and was back in the saddle by seven in the morning, riding in the highest of spirits away from Sawston Hall with John Huddlestone at her side to show her the way.

I was riding at the back, the dozen or so horses clattering ahead of me, my little pony too tired to keep pace, when I smelled an old terrible scent on the air. I smelled burning, I smelled smoke. Not the appetising smoke of the roast beef on the spit, not the innocent seasonal smell of burning leaves. I could smell the scent of heresy, a fire lit with ill-will, burning up someone's happiness, burning up someone's faith, burning up someone's house ... I turned in the saddle and saw the glow on the horizon where the house we had just left, Sawston Hall, was being torched.

'My lady!' I called out. She heard me, and turned her head and then reined in her horse, John Huddlestone beside her.

'Your house!' I said simply to him.

He looked beyond me, he squinted his eyes to see. He couldn't tell for sure, he could not smell the smoke as I had done. Lady Mary looked at me. 'Are you sure, Hannah?'

I nodded. 'I can smell it. I can smell smoke.' I heard the quaver of fear in my voice. My hand was at my cheek brushing my face as if the smuts were falling on me. 'I can smell smoke. Your house is being burned out, sir.'

He turned his horse as if he would ride straight home, then he remembered the woman whose visit had cost him his home and his fortune. 'Forgive me, Lady Mary. I must go home ... My wife ...'

'Go,' she said gently. 'And be very well assured that when I come into my own, you shall come into yours. I will give you another house, a bigger and richer house than this one you have lost for your loyalty to me. I shall not forget.'

He nodded, half-deaf with worry, and then set his horse at a gallop to where the blaze of his house glowed on the horizon. His groom rode up beside Lady Mary. 'D'you want me to guide you, my lady?' he asked.

'Yes,' she answered. 'Can you take me to Bury St Edmunds?'

He put his cap back on his head. 'Through Mildenhall and Thetford forest? Yes, m'lady.'

She gave the signal to move on and she rode without once looking back. I thought that she was a princess indeed, if she could see last night's refuge burned to the ground and think only of the struggle ahead of her and not of the ruins left behind.

That night we stayed at Euston Hall near Thetford, and I lay on the floor of Lady Mary's bedroom, wrapped in my cape, still fully dressed, waiting for the alarm that I was sure must come. All night my senses were on the alert for the tramp of muffled feet, for the glimpse of a dipping brand, for the smell of smoke from a torch. I did little more than doze, waiting all the night for a Protestant mob to come and tear down this safe house as they had done Sawston Hall. I had a great horror of being trapped inside the house when they torched the roof and the stairs. I could not close my eyes for fear that I would be wakened by the smell of smoke, so that it was almost a relief near dawn when I heard the sound of a horse's hooves on cobbles and I was up at the window in a second, knowing that my sleepless watch was rewarded, my hand outstretched to her as she woke, cautioning her to be quiet.

'What can you see?' she demanded from the bed, as she pulled back the covers. 'How many men?'

'Only one horse, he looks weary.'

'Go and see who it is.'

I hurried down the wooden stairs to the hall. The porter had the spy hole opened and was arguing with the traveller, who seemed to be demanding admission to stay the night. I touched the porter on the shoulder and he stood aside. I had to stretch up on tiptoes to see through the spy hole in the door.

'And who are you?' I demanded, my voice as gruff as I could make it, acting a confidence that I did not feel.

'Who are you?' he asked back. I heard at once the sharp cadence of London speech.

'You'd better tell me what you want,' I insisted.

He came closer to the spy hole and lowered his quiet voice to a whisper. 'I have important news for a great lady. It is about her brother. D'you understand me?'

There was no way of knowing whether or not he was sent to entrap us. I took the risk, stepped back and nodded to the porter. 'Let him in, and then bar the door behind him again.'

He came in. I wished to God that I could have made the Sight work for me when I demanded it. I would have given anything to know if there were a dozen men behind him, even now encircling the house and striking flints in the hay barns. But I could be sure of nothing except that he was weary and travel-stained and buoyed up by excitement.

'What's the message?'

'I shall tell it to no-one but herself.'

There was a rustle of silken skirts and Lady Mary came down the stairs. 'And you are?' she asked.

It was his response to the sight of her that convinced me that he was on our side, and that the world had changed for us, overnight. Fast as a stooping falcon, he dropped down to one knee, pulled his hat from his head, and bowed to her, as to a queen.

God save her, she did not turn a hair. She extended her hand as if she had been Queen of England for all her life. He kissed it reverently, and then looked up into her face.

'I am Robert Raynes, a goldsmith of London, sent by Sir Nicholas Throckmorton to bring you the news that your brother Edward is dead, Your Grace. You are Queen of England.'

'God bless him,' she said softly. 'God save Edward's precious soul.'

There was a short silence.

'Did he die in faith?' she asked.

He shook his head. 'He died as a Protestant.'

She nodded. 'And I am proclaimed queen?' she demanded in a much sharper tone.

He shook his head. 'Can I speak freely?'

'You have ridden a long way to tell a riddle if you do not,' she observed drily.

'The king died in much pain on the night of the sixth,' he said quietly.

'The *sixth*?' she interrupted.

'Yes. Before his death he changed his father's will.'

'He had no legal right to do so. He cannot have changed the settlement.'

'Nonetheless he did. You are denied the succession, the Lady Elizabeth also. Lady Jane Grey is named as his heir.'

'He never did this willingly,' she said, her face blanched.

The man shrugged. 'It was done in his hand, and the council and the justices all agreed and signed to it.'

'*All* the council?' she asked.

'To a man.'

'And what about me?'

'I am to warn you that you are named as a traitor to the throne. Lord Robert Dudley is on his way now to arrest you and take you to the Tower.'

'Lord Robert is coming?' I asked.

'He will go to Hunsdon first,' Lady Mary reassured me. 'I wrote to his father that I was staying there. He won't know where we are.'

I did not contradict her, but I knew that John Dee would send my note on to him this very day, and that thanks to me, he would know exactly where to look for us.

Her concern was all for her sister. 'And Lady Elizabeth?'

He shrugged. 'I don't know. She may be arrested already. They were going to her home too.'

'Where is Robert Dudley now?'

'I don't know that either. It has taken me the whole day to find you myself. I traced you from Sawston Hall because I heard of the fire and guessed you had been there. I am sorry, my l ... Your Grace.'

'And when was the king's death announced? And Lady Jane falsely proclaimed?'

'Not when I left.'

She took a moment to understand, and then she was angry. 'He has died, and it has not been announced? My brother is lying dead, unwatched? Without the rites of the church? Without any honours done to him at all?'

'His death was still a secret when I left.'

She nodded, her lips biting back anything she might have said, her eyes suddenly veiled and cautious. 'I thank you for coming to me,' she said. 'Thank Sir Nicholas for his services to me which I had no cause to anticipate.'

The sarcasm in this was rather sharp, even for the man on his knees. 'He told me you are the true queen now,' he volunteered. 'And that he and all his household are to serve you.'

'I am the true queen,' she said. 'I always was the true princess. And I will have my kingdom. You can sleep here tonight. The porter will find you a bed. Go back to London in the morning and convey my thanks to him. He has done the right thing to inform me. I am queen, and I will have my throne.'

She turned on her heel and swept up the stair. I hesitated for only one moment.

'Did you say the sixth?' I asked the London man. 'The sixth of July, that the king died?'

'Yes.'

I dropped him a curtsey and followed Lady Mary upstairs. As soon as we got into her room she closed the door behind us, and threw aside her regal dignity. 'Get me the clothes of a serving girl, and wake John Huddlestone's groom,' she said urgently. 'Then go to the stables and get two horses ready, one with a pillion saddle for me and the groom, one for you.'

'My lady?'

'You call me Your Grace now,' she said grimly. 'I am Queen of England. Now hurry.'

'What am I to tell the groom?'

'Tell him that we have to get to Kenninghall today. That I will ride behind him, we will leave the rest of them here. You come with me.'

I nodded and hurried from the room. The serving maid who had waited on us last night was sleeping with half a dozen others in the attic bedrooms. I went up the stairs and peeped in the door. I found her in the half-darkness and shook her awake, put my hand over her mouth and hissed in her ear: 'I've had enough of this, I'm running away. I'll give you a silver shilling for your clothes. You can say I stole them and no-one will be the wiser.'

'Two shillings,' she said instantly.

'Agreed,' I said. 'Give them me, and I'll bring you the money.'

She fumbled under her pillow for her shift and her smock. 'Just the gown and cape,' I ordered, shrinking from the thought of putting the Queen of England in louse-ridden linen. She bundled them up for me with her cap and I went light-footed downstairs to Lady Mary's room.

'Here,' I said. 'They cost me two shillings.'

She found the coins in her purse. 'No boots.'

'Please wear your own boots,' I said fervently. 'I've run away before, I know what it's like. You'll never get anywhere in borrowed boots.'

She smiled at that. 'Hurry,' was all she said.

I ran back upstairs with the two shillings and then I found Tom, John Huddlestone's groom, and sent him down to the stables to get the horses ready. I crept down to the bakery just outside the kitchen door, and found, as I had hoped, a batch of bread rolls baked in the warmth of the oven last night. I stuffed my breeches pockets and my jacket pockets with half a dozen of them so that I looked like a donkey with panniers, and then I went back to the hall.

Lady Mary was there, dressed as a serving maid, her hood pulled over her face. The porter was arguing, reluctant to open the door to the stable-yard for a maidservant. She turned with relief when she heard me approach light-footed on the stone flags.

'Come on,' I said reasonably to the man. 'She is a servant of John Huddlestone, his groom is waiting. He told us to leave at first light. We're to go back to Sawston Hall and we shall be whipped if we are late.'

He complained about visitors in the night disturbing a Christian household's sleep, and then people leaving early; but he opened the door and Lady Mary and I slipped through. Tom was in the yard, holding one big hunter with a pillion saddle on its back and a smaller horse for me. I would have to leave my little pony behind, this was going to be a hard ride.

He got into the saddle and took the hunter to the mounting block. I helped the Lady Mary scramble up behind him, she took a tight grip around his waist and kept her hood pulled forward to hide her face. I had to take my horse to the mounting block too, the stirrup was too high for me to mount without help. When I was up on him, the ground seemed a long way away, he sidestepped nervously and I jerked on the reins too tightly and made him toss his head and sidle. I had never ridden such a big horse before, and I was frightened of him; but no smaller animal could manage the hard ride we must make today.

Tom turned his horse's head and led the way out of the yard. I turned after him and heard my heart pounding and knew that I was on the run, once again, and afraid, once again, and that this time I was perhaps in a worse case than I had been when we had run from Spain, or when we had run from Portugal, even when we had run from France. Because this time I was running with the pretender to the throne of England, with Lord Robert Dudley and his army in pursuit, and I was his vassal sworn; her trusted servant, and a Jew; but a practising Christian, serving a Papist princess in a country sworn to be Protestant. Little wonder that my heart was in my mouth and beating louder than the clopping of the hooves of the big horses as we went down the road to the east, pushing them into a canter towards the rising sun.

When we reached Kenninghall at midday, I saw why we had ridden till the horses foundered to get here. The sun was high in the sky and it made the fortified manor house look squat and indomitable in the flat uncompromising landscape. It was a solid moated house, and as we drew closer I saw that it was no pretty play-castle; this had a drawbridge that could be raised, and a portcullis above it that could be dropped down to seal the only entrance. It was built in warm red brick, a deceptively beautiful house that could nonetheless be held in a siege.

Lady Mary was not expected, and the few servants who lived at the house to keep it in order came tumbling out of the doors in a flurry of surprise and greeting. After a nod from Lady Mary I quickly told them of the astounding news from London as they took our horses into the stable-yard. A ragged cheer went up at the news of her accession to the throne and they pulled me down from the saddle and clapped me on the back like the lad I appeared to be. I let out a yelp of pain. The inner part of my legs from my ankles to my thighs had been skinned raw from three days in the saddle, and my back and shoulders and wrists were locked tight from the jolting ride from Hunsdon to Hoddesdon, to Sawston to Thetford to here.

Lady Mary must have been near-dead with exhaustion, sitting pillion for all that long time, a woman of nearly forty years and in poor health, but only I saw the grimace of pain as they lifted her down to the ground;

92

everyone else saw the tilt of her chin as she heard them shout for her, and the charm of the Tudor smile as she welcomed them all into the great hall and bid them good cheer. She took a moment to pray for the soul of her dead brother and then she raised her head and promised them that just as she had been a fair landlord and mistress to them, she would be a good queen.

That earned her another cheer and the hall started to fill with people, workers from the fields and woods and villagers from their homes, and the servants ran about with flagons of ale and cups of wine and loaves of bread and meat. The Lady Mary took her seat at the head of the hall and smiled on everyone as if she had never been ill in her life, then after an hour of good company, she laughed out loud and said she must get out of this cloak and this poor gown, and went to her rooms.

The few house servants had flung themselves into getting her rooms ready and her bed was made with linen. It was only the second-best bedding, but if she was as weary as I then she would have slept on homespun. They brought in a bath tub, lined it with sheets to protect her from splinters, and filled it with hot water. And they found some old gowns, which she had left behind when she was last at this house, and laid them out on the bed for her to choose.

'You can go,' she said to me, as she threw the servant girl's cloak from her shoulders to the floor, and turned her back to the maid to be unlaced. 'Find something to eat and go straight to bed. You must be tired out.'

'Thank you,' I said, hobbling for the door with my painful bow-legged stride.

'And, Hannah?'

'Yes, lady . . . Yes, Your Grace?'

'Whoever it is who has paid your wages while you have been in my household, and whatever they hoped to gain from that – you have been a good friend to me this day. I will not forget it.'

I paused, thinking of the two letters I had written to Lord Robert that would bring him hard on our heels, thinking what would happen to this determined, ambitious woman when he caught us, thinking that he was certain to catch us here, since I had told him exactly where to come; and then it would be the Tower for her, and probably her death for treason. I had been a spy in her household and the falsest of friends. I had been a byword for dishonour and she had known some of it; but she could not have dreamed of the falseness that had become second nature to me.

If I could have confessed to her then, I would have done. The words were on my tongue, I wanted to tell her that I had been put into her household to work against her; but that now that I knew her, and loved her, I would do anything to serve her. I wanted to tell her that Robert Dudley was my lord and I would always be bound to do anything he asked me. I wanted to tell her that everything I did seemed to be always full of contradictions: black and white, love and fear, all at once.

But I could say nothing, and I had been brought up to hold secrets under my lying tongue, so I just dropped to one knee before her and bowed my head.

She did not give me her hand to kiss, like a queen would have done. She put her hand on my head like my own mother used to do and she said, 'God bless you, Hannah, and keep you safe from sin.'

At that moment, at that particular tenderness, at the very touch of my mother's hand, I felt the tears well up in my eyes; and I got myself out of the room and into my own small attic bedchamber and into my bed without bath or dinner, before anybody should see me cry like the little girl I still was.

We were at Kenninghall for three days on siege alert, but still Lord Robert and his company of cavalry did not come. The gentlemen from the country all around the manor came pouring in with their servants and their kinsmen, some of them armed, some of them bringing blacksmiths to hammer out spears and lances from the pruning hooks, spades and scythes that they brought with them. The Lady Mary proclaimed herself as queen in the great hall, despite the advice of more cautious men, and flying in the face of a pleading letter from the Spanish ambassador. He had written to tell her that her brother was dead, that Northumberland was unbeatable, and that she should set about negotiating with him while her uncle in Spain would do his best to save her from the trumped-up charge of treason and sentence of death which was certain to come. That part of his letter made her look grim, but there was worse.

He warned her that Northumberland had sent warships into the

French seas off Norfolk, specially to prevent the Spanish ships from rescuing her and taking her to safety. There could be no escape for her, the emperor could not even attempt to save her. She must surrender to the duke and give up her claim to the crown, and throw herself on his mercy.

'What can you see, Hannah?' she asked me. It was early morning, and she had just come from Mass, her rosary beads still in her fingers, her forehead still damp with holy water. It was a bad morning for her, her face, sometimes so illuminated and merry with hope, was grey and tired. She looked sick of fear itself.

I shook my head. 'I have only seen for you once, Your Grace, and I was certain then that you would be queen. And now you are. I have seen nothing since.'

'I am queen indeed now,' she said wryly. 'I am proclaimed queen by myself at least. I wish you had told me how long it would last, and if anyone else would agree with me.'

'I wish I could,' I said sincerely. 'What are we going to do?'

'They tell me to surrender,' she said simply. 'The advisors I have trusted all my life, my Spanish kinsmen, my mother's only friends. They all tell me that I will be executed if I continue with this course, that it's a battle I can't win. The duke has the Tower, he has London, he has the country, he has the warships at sea and an army of followers and the royal guard. He has all the coin of the realm at the Mint, he has all the weapons of the nation at the Tower. I have this one castle, this one village, these few loyal men and their pitchforks. And somewhere out there is Lord Robert and his troop coming towards us.'

'Can't we get away?' I asked.

She shook her head. 'Not fast enough, not far enough. If I could have got on a Spanish warship then, perhaps . . . but the duke has the sea between here and France held down by English warships, he was ready for this, and I was unprepared. I am trapped.'

I remembered John Dee's map spread out in the duke's study and the little counters which signified soldiers and sailors on ships all around Norfolk, and Lady Mary trapped in the middle of them.

'Will you have to surrender?' I whispered.

I had thought she was frightened; but at my question the colour rushed into her cheeks, and she smiled as if I had suggested a challenge, a great gamble. 'You know, I'm damned if I will!' she swore. She laughed aloud as if it was a bet for a joust rather than her life on the table. 'I have spent my life running and lying and hiding. Just once, *just once* I should be glad to ride out under my own standard and defy the men who have denied me, and denied my right and denied the authority of the church and God himself.'

I felt my own spirits leap up at her enthusiasm. 'My la . . . Your Grace!' I stumbled.

She turned a brilliant smile on me. 'Why not?' she said. 'Why should I not, just once, fight like a man and defy them?'

'But can you win?' I asked blankly.

She shrugged, an absolutely Spanish gesture. 'Oh! It's not likely!' She smiled at me as if she were truly merry at the desperate choice before her. 'Ah, but Hannah, I have been humbled to dust by these men who would now put a commoner such as Lady Jane before me. They once put Elizabeth before me. They made me wait on her as if I were her maid in her nursery. And now I have my chance. I can fight them instead of bowing to them. I can die fighting them instead of crawling to them, begging for my life. When I see it like this, I have no choice. And I thank God, there *is* no better choice for me than to raise my standard and to fight for my father's throne and my mother's honour, my inheritance. And I have Elizabeth to think of, too. I have her safety to secure. I have her inheritance to pass on to her. She is my sister, she is my responsibility. I have written to her to bid her come here, so that she can be safe. I have promised her a refuge, and I will fight for our inheritance.'

Lady Mary gathered her rosary beads in her short workmanlike fingers, tucked them into the pocket of her gown and strode towards the door of the great hall where her armies of gentlemen and soldiers were breaking their fast. She entered the head of the hall and mounted the dais. 'Today we move out,' she announced, loud and clear enough for the least man at the back of the hall to hear her. 'We go to Framlingham, a day's ride, no more than that. I shall raise my standard there. If we can get there before Lord Robert we can hold him off in a siege. We can hold him off for months. I can fight a battle from there. I can collect troops.'

There was a murmur of surprise and then approbation.

'Trust me!' she commanded them. 'I will not fail you. I am your proclaimed queen and you will see me on the throne, and then I will remember who was here today. I will remember and you will be repaid many times over for doing your duty to the true Queen of England.'

There was a deep low roar, easily given from men who have just eaten well. I found my knees were shaking at the sight of her courage. She swept to the door at the back of the hall and I jumped unsteadily ahead of her and opened it for her.

'And where is he?' I asked. She did not have to be told who I was asking for.

'Oh, not far,' Lady Mary said grimly. 'South of King's Lynn, I am told. Something must have delayed him, he could have taken us here if he had come at once. But I cannot get news of him. I don't know where he is for sure.'

'Will he guess that we are going to Framlingham?' I asked, thinking of the note that had gone to him, naming her destination here, its spiral on the paper like a curled snake.

She paused at the doorway and looked back at me. 'There is bound to be one person in such a gathering who will slip away and tell him. There is always a spy in the camp. Don't you think, Hannah?'

For a moment I thought she had trapped me. I looked up at her, my lies very dry in my throat, my girl's face growing pale.

'A spy?' I quavered. I put my hand to my cheek and rubbed it hard.

She nodded. 'I never trust anyone. I always know that there are spies about me. And if you had been the girl I was, you would have learned the same. After my father sent my mother away from me there was no-one near me who did not try to persuade me that Anne Boleyn was true queen and her bastard child the true heir. The Duke of Norfolk shouted into my face that if he were my father he would bang my head against the wall until my brains fell out. They made me deny my mother, they made me deny my faith, they threatened me with death on the scaffold like Thomas More and Bishop Fisher – men I knew and loved. I was a girl of twenty and they made me proclaim myself a bastard and my faith a heresy.

'Then, all in a summer's day, Anne was dead and all they spoke of was Queen Jane and her child, Edward, and little Elizabeth was no longer my enemy but a motherless child, a forgotten daughter, just like me. Then the other queens . . .' She almost smiled. 'One after another, three other women came to me and I was ordered to curtsey to them as queen and call them Mother, and none of them came close to my heart. In that long time I learned never to trust a word that any man says and never even to listen to a woman. The last woman I loved was my mother. The last man I trusted was my father. And he destroyed her, and she died of heartbreak, so what was I to think? Will I ever be a woman who can trust now?'

She broke off and looked at me. 'My heart broke when I was a little more than twenty years old,' she said wonderingly. 'And d'you know, only now do I begin to think that there might be a life for me.'

She smiled. 'Oh, Hannah!' she sighed and patted me on the cheek. 'Don't look so grave. It was all a long time ago and if we can triumph in this adventure then my story is ended happily. I shall have my mother's throne restored, I shall wear her jewels. I shall see her memory honoured and she will look down from heaven and see her daughter on the throne that she bore me to inherit. I shall think myself a happy woman. Don't you see?'

I smiled uncomfortably.

'What's the matter?' she asked.

I swallowed on my dry throat. 'I am afraid,' I confessed. 'I am sorry.'

She nodded. 'We are all afraid,' she said frankly. 'Me too. Go down and choose a horse from the stable and get a pair of riding boots. We are an army on the march today. God save us that we may make Framlingham without running into Lord Robert and his army.'

Mary raised her standard at Framlingham Castle, a fortress to match any in England, and unbelievably half the world turned up on horseback and on foot to swear allegiance to her and death to the rebels. I walked beside her as she went down the massed ranks of the men and thanked them for coming to her and swore to be a true and honest queen to them.

We had news from London at last. The announcement of King Edward's death had been made shamefully late. After the poor boy had died, the duke had kept the corpse hidden in his room while the ink dried on his will, and the powerful men of the country considered where their best interests lay. Lady Jane Grey had to be dragged on to the throne by her father-in-law. They said she had cried very bitterly and said that she could not be queen, and that the Lady Mary was the rightful heir, as everyone knew. It did not save her from her fate. They unfurled the canopy of state over her bowed head, they served her on bended knee despite her tearful protests, and the Duke of Northumberland proclaimed her as queen and bent his sly head to her.

The country was launched into civil war, directed against us, the traitors. Lady Elizabeth had not replied to the Lady Mary's warnings, nor come to join us at Framlingham. She had taken to her bed when she had heard the news of her brother's death and was too sick even to read her letters. When Lady Mary learned of that, she turned away for a moment to hide the hurt in her face. She had counted on Elizabeth's support, the two princesses together defending their father's will, and she had promised herself that she would keep her young sister safe. To find that Elizabeth was hiding under the bed covers rather than racing to be with her sister, was a blow to Mary's heart as well as to her cause.

We learned that Windsor Castle had been fortified and provisioned for a siege, the guns of the Tower of London were battle-ready and turned to face inland, and Queen Jane had taken up residence in the royal apartments in the Tower and was said to lock the great gate every night to prevent any of her court slipping away: a coerced queen with a coerced court.

Northumberland himself, the battle-hardened veteran, had raised an army and was coming to root out our Lady Mary, who was now officially named as a traitor to Queen Jane. 'Queen Jane indeed!' Jane Dormer exclaimed, irritably. The royal council had ordered Lady Mary's arrest for treason, there was a price on her head as a traitor. She was alone in all of England. She was a rebel against a proclaimed queen, she was beyond the law. Not even her uncle, the Spanish emperor, would support her.

No-one knew how many troops Northumberland had under his command, no-one knew how long we could last at Framlingham. He would join with Lord Robert's company of horse, and then the two men would come against Lady Mary: well-trained, well-paid men, experienced fighting men up against one woman and a chaotic camp of volunteers.

And yet, every day more men arrived from the surrounding country-side, swearing that they would fight for the rightful queen. The sailors from the warships anchored at Yarmouth who had been ordered to set sail to attack any Spanish ships which might be hanging offshore to rescue her, had mutinied against their commanders, and said that she must not leave the country: not because they had blocked her escape, but because she should be mounting the throne. They left their ships and marched inland to support us: a proper troop, accustomed to fighting. They marched into the castle in ranks, quite unlike our own draggle of farm labourers. At once they started teaching the men gathered at the castle how to fight and the rules of battle: the charge, the swerve, the retreat. I watched them arrive, and I watched them settle in, and for the first time I thought that Lady Mary might have a chance to escape capture.

She appointed an almoner to send out carts to bring in food for the makeshift army, which now camped all around the castle. She appointed building teams to repair the great curtain wall. She sent scouring parties out to beg and borrow weapons. She sent out scouts in every direction every dawn and dusk to see if they could find the duke and Lord Robert's army in their stealthy approach.

Every day she reviewed the troops and promised them her thanks and a more solid reward if they would stand by her, hold the line; and every afternoon she walked on the battlements, along the mighty curtain wall which ran around the impenetrable castle, and looked to the London road for the plume of dust which would tell her that the most powerful man in England was riding at the head of his army against her.

There were very many advisors to tell the Lady Mary that she could not win a pitched battle against the duke. I used to listen to their confident predictions and wonder if it would be safer for me to slip away now, before the encounter which must end in defeat. The duke had seen a dozen actions, he had fought and held power on the battlefield and in the council chamber. He forged an alliance with France and he could bring French troops against us if he did not defeat us at once, and then the lives of Englishmen would be taken by Frenchmen, the French would fight on English soil and it would all be her fault. The horror of the Wars of the Roses, with brother against brother, would be re-lived once more if Lady Mary would not see reason and surrender.

But then, in the middle of July, it all fell apart for the duke. His alliances, his treaties, could not hold against the sense that every Englishman had that Mary, Henry's daughter, was the rightful queen. Northumberland was hated by many and it was clear that he would rule through Jane as he had ruled through Edward. The people of England, from lords to commoners, muttered and then declared against him.

The accord he had stitched together to darn Queen Jane into the fabric of England all unravelled. More and more men declared in public for Lady Mary, more and more men secretly slipped away from the duke's cause. Lord Robert himself was defeated by an army of outraged citizens, who just sprang up from the ploughed furrows, swearing that they would protect the rightful queen. Lord Robert declared for the Lady Mary and deserted his father but, despite turning his coat, was captured at Bury by citizens who declared him a traitor. The duke himself, trapped at Cambridge, his army disappearing like mist in the morning, announced suddenly that he too was for Lady Mary and sent her a message explaining that he had only ever tried to do his best for the realm.

'What does this mean?' I asked her, seeing the letter shaking so violently in her hand that she could hardly read it.

'It means I have won,' she said simply. 'Won by right, accepted right and not by battle. I am queen and the people's choice. Despite the duke himself, the people have spoken and I am the queen they want.'

'And what will happen to the duke?' I asked, thinking of his son, Lord Robert, somewhere a prisoner.

'He's a traitor,' she said, her eyes cold. 'What do you think would have happened to me if I had lost?'

I said nothing. I waited for a moment, a heartbeat, a girl's heartbeat. 'And what will happen to Lord Robert?' I asked, my voice very small.

Lady Mary turned. 'He is a traitor and a traitor's son. What do you think will happen to him?'

Lady Mary took her big horse and, riding side saddle, set off on the road to London, a thousand, two thousand men riding behind her, and their men, their tenants and retainers and followers coming on foot behind them. The Lady Mary was at the head of a mighty army with only her ladies and me, her fool, riding with her.

When I looked back I could see the dust from the horses' hooves and the tramping feet drifting like a veil across the ripening fields. When we marched through villages, men came running out of their doors, their sickles or bill hooks in their hands, and fell in with the army and matched their step to the marching men's. The women waved and cheered and some of them ran out with flowers for the Lady Mary or threw roses in the road before her horse. The Lady Mary, in her old red riding habit, with her head held high, rode her big horse like a knight going into battle, a queen going to claim her own. She rode like a princess out of a story book to whom everything, at last, is given. She had won the greatest victory of her life by sheer determination and courage and her reward was the adoration of the people that she would rule.

Everyone thought that her coming to the throne would be the return of the good years, rich harvests, warm weather, and an end to the constant epidemics of plague and sweat and colds. Everyone thought that she would restore the wealth of the church, the beauty of the shrines and the certainty of faith. Everyone remembered the sweetness and beauty of her mother who had been Queen of England for longer than she had been a princess of Spain, who had been the wife that the king had loved the longest and the best, and who had died with a blessing for him, even though he had deserted her. Everyone was glad to see her daughter riding to her mother's throne with her golden cap on her head and her army of men behind her, their bright glad faces showing the world that they were proud to serve such a princess and to bring her to her capital city, which even now declared for her and was ringing the bells in every church tower to make her welcome.

On the road to London I wrote a note for Lord Robert, and translated it into his code. It read: 'You will be tried for treason and executed. Please, my lord, escape. Please, my lord, escape.' I put it into the fire in the hearth of an inn and watched it burn black, and then I took the poker and mashed it into black ash. There was no way that I could get the warning to him, and in truth, he would not need a warning.

He knew the risks he was running and he would have known them when he was defeated and gave himself up at Bury. He would know now, wherever he was, whether in the prison of some small town being taunted by men who would have kissed his shoe a month ago, or already in the Tower, that he was a dead man, a condemned man. He had committed treason against the rightful heir to the throne and the punishment for treason was death, hanging until he lost consciousness, coming back into awareness with the shock of the agony of the executioner slicing his stomach open and pulling his guts out of his slit belly before his face so that his last sight would be his own pulsing entrails, and then they would quarter him: first slashing his head from his body and then hacking his body into four pieces, setting his handsome head up on a stake as a warning to others, and sending his butchered corpse to the four corners of the city. It was as bad a death as anyone could face, almost as bad as being burned alive and I, of all people, knew how bad that was.

I did not cry for him, as we rode to London. I was a young girl but I had seen enough death and known enough fear to have learned not to cry for grief. But I found I could not sleep at night, not any night, for wondering where Lord Robert was, and whether I would ever see him again, and whether he would ever forgive me for riding into the capital of England, with crowds cheering and crying out blessings, at the side of the woman who had so roundly defeated him, and who would see him and all his family destroyed.

Lady Elizabeth, too sick to rise from her bed during the days of danger, managed to get to London before us. 'That girl is first, everywhere she goes,' Jane Dormer said sourly to me.

Lady Elizabeth came riding out from the city to greet us, at the head of a thousand men, all in the Tudor colours of green and white, riding in her pride as if she had never been sick with terror and hiding in her bed. She came out as if she were Lord Mayor of London, coming to give us the keys to the city, with the cheers of the Londoners ringing like a peal of bells all around her, crying 'God bless!' to the two princesses.

I reined in my horse and fell back a little so that I could see her. I had been longing to see her again ever since Lady Mary had spoken of her with such affection, ever since Will Somers had called her a goat: up one moment and down the next. I remembered the flash of a green skirt, the invitingly tilted red head against the dark bark of the tree, the girl in the garden that I had seen running from her stepfather, and making sure that he caught her. I was desperately curious to see how that girl had changed.

The girl on horseback was far beyond the child of shining innocence that Lady Mary had described, beyond the victim of circumstance that Will had imagined, and yet not the calculating siren that Jane Dormer hated. I saw instead a woman riding towards her destiny with absolute confidence. She was young, only nineteen years old, yet she was imposing. I saw at once that she had arranged this cavalcade – she knew the power of appearances and she had the skill to design them. The green of her livery had been chosen by her to suit the flaming brazen red of her hair which she wore loose beneath her green hood as if to flaunt her youth and maidenhood beside her older spinster sister. Green and white were the Tudor colours of her father, and no-one looking at her high brow and red hair could doubt this girl's paternity. The men riding closest to her as her guards had been picked, without doubt, for their looks. There was not one man beside her who was not remarkably handsome. The dull-looking ones were all scattered, further back in her train. Her ladies were the reverse; there was not one who outshone her, a clever choice, but one which only a coquette would make. She rode a white gelding, a big animal, almost as grand as a man's warhorse, and she sat on it as if she had been born to ride, as if she took joy in mastering the power of the beast. She gleamed with health and youth and vitality, she shone with the glamour of success. Against her radiance, the Lady Mary, drained by the strain of the last two months, faded into second place.

Lady Elizabeth's entourage halted before us and Lady Mary started to dismount as Lady Elizabeth flung herself down from her horse as if she had been waiting all her life for this moment, as if she had never skulked in bed, biting her nails and wondering what would happen next. At the sight of her, the Lady Mary's face lit up, as a mother will smile on seeing her child. Clearly, Elizabeth riding in her pride was a sight that gave her sister a pure unselfish joy. Lady Mary held out her arms, Elizabeth plunged into her embrace and Lady Mary kissed her warmly. They held each other for a moment, scrutinising each other's faces and I knew, as Elizabeth's bright gaze met Mary's honest eyes, that my mistress would not have the skill to see through the fabled Tudor charm to the fabled Tudor duplicity which lay beneath.

Lady Mary turned to Elizabeth's companions, gave them her hand and kissed each of them on the cheek to thank them for bearing Elizabeth company and giving us such a grand welcome into London. Lady Mary folded Elizabeth's hand under her arm, and scanned her face again. She could not have doubted that Elizabeth was well, the girl was radiant with health and energy, but still I heard a few whispered confidences of Elizabeth's faintness, and swelling of her belly, and headache, and the mysterious illness that had confined her to bed, unable to move, while the Lady Mary had stared down her own fear alone, and armed the country and prepared to fight for their father's will.

Elizabeth welcomed her sister to the city and congratulated her on her great victory. 'A victory of hearts,' she said. 'You are queen of the hearts of your people, the only way to rule this country.'

'Our victory,' Mary said generously at once. 'Northumberland would have put us both to death, you as well as me. I have won the right for us both to take our inheritance. You will be an acknowledged princess again, my sister and my heir, and you will ride beside me when I enter London.'

'Your Grace honours me too much,' Elizabeth said sweetly.

'She does indeed,' Jane Dormer said in a hiss of a whisper to me. 'Sly bastard.'

The Lady Mary gave the signal to mount and Elizabeth turned to her horse as her groom helped her into her saddle. She smiled around at us; saw me, riding astride in my pageboy livery, and her gaze went past me, utterly uninterested. She did not recognise me as the child who had seen her with Tom Seymour in the garden, so long ago.

But I was interested in her. From the first glimpse I had of her, up against a tree like a common whore, she had haunted my memory. There was something about her that absolutely fascinated me. The first sight I had of her was that of a foolish girl, a flirt, a disloyal daughter, but there was always more to her than that. She had survived the execution of her lover, she had avoided the danger of a dozen plots. She had controlled her desire, she had played the game of a courtier like an expert, not like a girl. She had become her brother's favourite sister, the Protestant princess. She had stood outside the conspiracies of the court and yet known to a penny the price of every man. Her smile was utterly carefree, her laugh as light as birdsong; but her eyes were as sharp as a black-eyed cat that misses nothing.

I wanted to know every single thing about her, to discover everything she did, and said, and thought. I wanted to know if she hemmed her own linen, I wanted to know who starched her ruff. I wanted to know how often she washed her great mane of red hair. As soon as I saw her, in her green gown at the head of such a troop of men and women on that huge white horse, I saw a woman that I could one day wish to be. A woman who was proud of her beauty and beautiful in her pride; and I longed to grow into a woman like that. The Lady Elizabeth seemed to me to be something that Hannah the Fool might become. I had been an unhappy girl for so long, and then a boy for so long, and a fool for so long that I had no idea how to be a woman – the very idea baffled me. But when I saw the Lady Elizabeth, high on her horse, blazing with beauty and confidence, I thought that this was the sort of woman that I might be. I had never seen such a thing in my life before. This was a woman who gave no quarter to a disabling maidenly modesty, this was a woman who looked as if she could claim the ground she walked on.

But she was not bold in a brazen way, for all of her red hair, and her smiling face, and the energy of her every movement. She deployed all the modesty of a young woman, with a sideways sliding smile at the man who lifted her back into the saddle, and a flirtatious turn of the head as she gathered up the reins. She looked like someone who knew all the pleasures of being a young woman and was not prepared to take the pains. She looked like a young woman who knew her mind.

I looked from her to the Lady Mary, the mistress that I had come to love, and I thought that it would be better for her if she made plans to marry off Lady Elizabeth at once, and send her far away. No household could be at peace with this firebrand in its midst, and no kingdom could settle with such an heir burning so brightly beside an ageing queen.

Autumn 1553

As Lady Mary became established in her new life as the next Queen of England I realised that I must speak to her about my own future. September came and I was paid my wage from the queen's household accounts, just as if I were a musician or a pageboy in very truth, or one of her other servants. Clearly, I had exchanged one master for another, the king to whom I had been begged as a fool was dead, the lord who had sworn me as his vassal was in the Tower, and the Lady Mary on whom I had been battened all this summer was now my mistress. In a move contrary to the spirit of the times – since everyone else in the country seemed to be coming to court with their palm outstretched to assure her that their village would never have declared for her had it not been for their own heroic isolated efforts – I thought that perhaps the moment had come for me to excuse myself from royal service and go back to my father.

I chose my time carefully, just after Mass when the Lady Mary walked back from her chapel at Richmond in a mood of quiet exaltation. The raising of the Host was not an empty piece of theatre to her, it was the presence of the risen God, you could see it in her eyes and in the serenity of her smile. She was uplifted by it in a way I had only ever seen before in those who held to a religious life for conviction. She was more abbess than queen when she walked back from Mass, and it was then that I fell into step beside her.

'Your Grace?'

'Yes, Hannah?' she smiled at me. 'Do you have any words of wisdom for me?'

'I am a most irregular fool,' I said. 'I see that I pronounce very rarely.'

'You told me I would be queen, and I held that to my heart in the days when I was afraid,' she said. 'I can wait for the gift of the Holy Spirit to move you.'

'It was that I wanted to speak to you about,' I said awkwardly. 'I have just been paid by the keeper of your household . . .'

She waited. 'Has he underpaid you?' she asked politely.

'No! Not at all! That is not what I meant!' I exclaimed desperately. 'No, Your Grace. This is the first time that you have paid me. I was paid by the king before. But I came into his service when I was begged as a fool to him by the Duke of Northumberland, who then sent me as a companion to you. I was merely going to say that you, er, you don't have to have me.'

As I spoke, we turned into her private apartments and it was as well, for she gave a most unqueenly gurgle of laughter. 'You are not, as it were, compulsory?'

I found I was smiling too. 'Please, Your Grace. I was taken from my father on the whim of the duke and then begged as a fool to the king. Since then I have been in your household without you ever asking for my company. I just wanted to say that you can release me, I know you never asked for me.'

She sobered at once. 'Do you want to go home, Hannah?'

'Not especially, Your Grace,' I said tentatively. 'I love my father very well but at home I am his clerk and printer. It is more enjoyable and more interesting at court, of course.' I did not add the proviso – if I can be safe here – but that question always dominated me.

'You have a betrothed, don't you?'

'Yes,' I said, disposing of him promptly. 'But we are not to marry for years yet.'

She smiled at the childishness of my reply. 'Hannah, would you like to stay with me?' she asked sweetly.

I knelt at her feet, and spoke from my heart. 'I would,' I said. I trusted her, I thought I might be safe with her. 'But I cannot promise to have the Sight.'

'I know that,' she said gently. 'It is the gift of the Holy Spirit, which blows where it lists, I don't expect you to be my astrologer. I want you to be my little maid, my little friend. Will you be that?'

'Yes, Your Grace, I should like that,' I said, and felt the touch of her hand on my head.

She was silent for a moment, her hand resting gently as I knelt before her. 'It is very rare to find one that I can trust,' she said quietly. 'I know that you came into my household paid by my enemies; but I think your gift comes from God, and I believe that you came to me from God. And you love me now, don't you, Hannah?'

'Yes, Your Grace,' I said simply. 'I don't think anyone could serve you and not come to love you.'

She smiled a little sadly. 'Oh, it is possible,' she said, and I knew she was thinking of the women who had been employed in the royal nursery and paid to love the Princess Elizabeth and to humiliate the older child. She took her hand from my head and I felt her step away, and I looked up to see her going towards the window to look out at the garden. 'You can come with me now, and bear me company,' she said quietly. 'I have to talk with my sister.'

I followed her as she walked through her private rooms to the gallery which ran looking out over the river. The fields were all shaven bare and yellow. But it had not been a good harvest. It had rained at harvest time, and if they could not dry the wheat then the grains would rot and there would not be enough to last through the winter, and there would be hunger in the land. And after hunger came illness. To be a good queen in England under these wet skies you had to command the weather itself; and not even Lady Mary, on her knees to her God for hours every day, could manage that.

There was a rustle of a silk underskirt and I peeped around and saw the Lady Elizabeth had entered the gallery from the other end. The young woman took in my presence and she gave me her mischievous smile, as if we were somehow allies. I felt like one of a pair of schoolmates summoned before a severe teacher and I found that I was smiling back at her. Elizabeth could always do that; she could enlist your friendship with a turn of her head. Then she directed her attention to her sister.

'Your Grace is well?'

Lady Mary nodded and then spoke coolly. 'You asked to see me.'

At once the beautiful pale face became sober and grave. Lady Elizabeth dropped to her knees, her mane of copper hair tumbled around her shoulders as she dropped her head forward. 'Sister, I am afraid you are displeased with me.'

The Lady Mary was silent for a moment. I saw her check a rapid movement forward to raise up her half-sister. Instead she kept her distance and the cool tone of her voice. 'And so?' she asked.

'I can think of no means where I have displeased you, unless it is that you suspect my religion,' Lady Elizabeth said, her head still penitently bowed.

'You don't come to Mass,' the Lady Mary observed stiffly.

The copper head nodded. 'I know. Is it that which offends you?'

'Of course!' Lady Mary replied. 'How can I love you as my sister if you refuse the church?'

'Oh!' Elizabeth gave a little gasp. 'I feared it was that. But sister, you don't understand me. I want to come to Mass. But I have been afraid. I didn't want to show my ignorance. It's so foolish . . . but you see . . . I don't know how to do it.' Elizabeth raised a tearstained face to her sister. 'Nobody ever taught me what I should do. I was not brought up in the way of the Faith as you were. No-one ever taught me. You remember, I was brought up at Hatfield and then I lived with Katherine Parr and she was a most determined Protestant. How could I ever be taught the things you learned at your mother's knee? Please, sister, please don't blame me for an ignorance which I could not help. When I was a little girl and we lived together, you did not teach me your faith then.'

'I was forbidden to practise it myself!' the Lady Mary exclaimed.

'So you know what it was like for me,' Elizabeth said persuasively. 'Don't blame me for the faults of my upbringing, sister.'

'You can choose now,' the Lady Mary said firmly. 'You live in a free court now. You can choose.'

Elizabeth hesitated. 'Can I have instruction?' she asked. 'Can you recommend things that I should read, perhaps I could talk with your confessor? I am conscious of so many things that I don't understand. Your Grace will help me? Your Grace will guide me in the right ways?'

It was impossible not to believe her. The tears on her cheeks were real enough, the colour had flushed into her face. Gently Lady Mary went forward, gently she outstretched her hand and put it on Elizabeth's bowed head. The young woman trembled under her touch. 'Please don't be angry with me, sister,' I heard her breathe. 'I am all alone in the world now; but for you.'

Mary put her hands on her sister's shoulders and raised her up. Elizabeth was normally half a head higher than the Lady Mary but she drooped in her sadness so that she had to look up at her older sister.

'Oh, Elizabeth,' Mary whispered. 'If you would confess your sins and turn to the true church I would be so very happy. All I want, all I have ever wanted, is to see this country in the true faith. And if I never marry, and if you come after me as another virgin queen, as another Catholic princess, what a kingdom we could build here together. I shall bring the country back to the true faith and you shall come after me and keep it under the rule of God.'

'Amen to that, Amen,' Elizabeth whispered, and at the joyful sincerity in her voice I thought of how often I had stood in church or at Mass and whispered 'Amen', and that, however sweet the sound was, it could always mean nothing.

These were not easy days for the Lady Mary. She was preparing for her coronation but the Tower, where the Kings of England usually spent their coronation night, was filled with traitors who had armed against her only a few months before.

Her advisors, especially the Spanish ambassador, told her that she should execute at once everyone who had been involved in the rebellion. Left alive, they would only become a focus of discontent; dead they would be soon forgotten.

'I will not have the blood of that foolish girl on my hands,' the Lady Mary said.

Lady Jane had written to her cousin and confessed that she had been wrong to take the throne but that she had acted under duress.

'I know Cousin Jane,' the Lady Mary said quietly to Jane Dormer one evening, while the musicians plucked away at their strings and the court yawned and waited for their beds. 'I have known her since she was a girl, I know her almost as well as I know Elizabeth. She is a most determined Protestant, and she has spent her life at her studies. She is more scholar than girl, awkward as a colt and rude as a Franciscan in her conviction. She and I cannot agree about matters of religion; but she has no worldly ambition at all. She would never have put herself before one of my father's named heirs. She knew I was to be queen, she would never have denied me. The sin was done by the Duke of Northumberland and by Jane's father between them.'

'You can't pardon everyone,' Jane Dormer said bluntly. 'And she was proclaimed queen and sat beneath the canopy of state. You can't pretend it did not happen.'

Lady Mary nodded. 'The duke had to die,' she agreed. 'But there it can end. I shall release Jane's father, the Duke of Suffolk, and Jane and her husband Guilford can stay in the Tower until after my coronation.'

'And Robert Dudley?' I asked in as small a voice as I could make.

She looked around and saw me, seated on the steps before her throne, her greyhound beside me. 'Oh are you there, little fool?' she said gently. 'Yes, your old master shall be tried for treason but held, not executed, until it is safe to release him. Does that content you?'

'Whatever Your Grace wishes,' I said obediently, but my heart leaped at the thought of his survival.

'It won't content those who want your safety,' Jane Dormer pointed out bluntly. 'How can you live in peace when those who would have destroyed you are still walking on this earth? How will you make them stop their plotting? D'you think they would have pardoned and released *you* if they had won?'

The Lady Mary smiled and put her hand over the hand of her best friend. 'Jane, this throne was given to me by God. No-one thought that I would survive Kenninghall, no-one thought that I would ride out of Framlingham without a shot being fired. And yet I rode into London with the blessing of the people. God has sent me to be queen. I shall show His mercy whenever I can. Even to those who know it not.'

I sent a note to my father that I would come on Michaelmas Day, and I collected my wages and walked through the darkening streets to him. I strode out without fear in new good-fitting boots and with a little sword at my side. I wore the livery of a beloved queen, no-one would molest me, and if they did, thanks to Will Somers, I could defend myself.

The door of the bookshop was closed, candlelight showing through the shutters, the street secure and quiet. I tapped on the door and he opened it cautiously. It was Friday night and the Sabbath candle was hidden under a pitcher beneath the counter, burning its holy light into the darkness.

He was pale as I came into the room and I knew, with the quick understanding of a fellow refugee, that the knock on the door had startled him. Even when he was expecting me, even when there was no cause to fear, his heart missed a beat at the knock in the night. I knew this for him, because it was true for me.

'Father, it is only me,' I said gently and I knelt before him, and he blessed me and raised me up.

'So, you are in service to the royal court again,' he said, smiling. 'How your fortunes do rise, my daughter.'

'She is a wonderful woman,' I said. 'So it is no thanks to me that my fortunes have risen. I would have escaped her service at the beginning if I could have done, and yet now I would rather serve her than anyone else in the land.'

'Rather than Lord Robert?'

I glanced towards the closed door. 'There is no serving him,' I said. 'Only the Tower guards can serve him and I pray that they do it well.'

My father shook his head. 'I remember him coming here that day, a man you would think who would command half the world, and now . . .'

'She won't execute him,' I said. 'She will be merciful to all now that the duke himself is dead.'

My father nodded. 'Dangerous times,' he said. 'Mr Dee remarked the other day that dangerous times are a crucible for change.'

'You have seen him?'

My father nodded. 'He came to see if I had the last pages of a manuscript in his possession, or if I could find another copy for him. It is a most troubling loss. He bought the book and it is a prescription for an alchemical process, but the last three pages are missing.'

I smiled. 'Was it a recipe for gold? And somehow incomplete?'

My father smiled back. It was a family joke that we could live like

Spanish grandees on the proceeds of the alchemist books that promised to deliver the recipe for the philosopher's stone: the instructions to change base metal into gold, the elixir of eternal life. My father had dozens of books on the subject and when I was young I had begged him to show me them, so that we might create the stone and become rich. But he had showed me a dazzling collection of mysteries, pictures and poems and spells and prayers, and in the end, no man any the wiser or the richer. Many men, brilliant men, had bought book after book trying to translate the riddles that were traditionally used to hide the secret of alchemy, and none of them had ever come back to us to say that they had found the secret and now would live forever.

'If any man ever finds it, and can make gold, it will be John Dee,' my father said. 'He is a most profound student and thinker.'

'I know that,' I said, thinking of the afternoons when I had sat on his high stool and read passage after passage of Greek or Latin while he translated as swiftly as I spoke, surrounded by the tools of his craft. 'But do you think he can see into the future?'

'Hannah, this man can see around corners! He has created a machine that can see over buildings or around them. He can predict the course of the stars, he can measure and predict the movements of the tides, he is creating a map of the country that a man can use to navigate the whole coastline.'

'Yes, I have seen that,' I concurred, thinking that I last saw it on the desk of the queen's enemies. 'He should have a care who uses his work.'

'His work is pure study,' my father said firmly. 'He cannot be blamed for the use that men make of his inventions. This is a great man, the death of his patron means nothing. He will be remembered long after the duke and all of his family are forgotten.'

'Not Lord Robert,' I stipulated.

'Even him,' my father asserted. 'I tell you, child, I have never met a man who could read and understand words, tables, mechanical diagrams, even codes, more quickly than this John Dee. Oh! And I nearly forgot. He has ordered some books to be delivered to Lord Robert in the Tower.'

'Has he?' I said, my attention suddenly sharpened. 'Shall I take them to Lord Robert for him?'

'As soon as they arrive,' my father said gently. 'And, Hannah, if you see Lord Robert . . .'

'Yes?'

'*Querida*, you must ask him to release you from your service to him and bid him farewell. He is a traitor sentenced to death. It is time that you said farewell.'

I would have argued but my father raised his hand. 'I command it, daughter,' he insisted. 'We live in this country as toads beneath the ploughshare. We cannot increase the risk to our lives. You have to bid him farewell. He is a named traitor. We cannot be associated with him.'

I bowed my head.

'Daniel wishes it too.'

My head came up at that. 'Why, whatever would he know about it?'

My father smiled. 'He is not an ignorant boy, Hannah.'

'He is not at court. He does not know the way of that world.'

'He is going to be a very great physician,' my father said gently. 'Many nights he comes here and reads the books on herbs and medicines. He is studying the Greek texts on health and illness. You should not think that just because he is not a Spaniard, he is ignorant.'

'But he can know nothing of the skills of the Moorish doctors,' I said. 'And you yourself told me that they were the wisest in the world. That they had learned all the Greeks had to teach and gone further.'

'Yes,' my father conceded. 'But he is a thoughtful young man, and a hard worker, and he has a gift for study. He comes here twice a week to read. And he always asks for you.'

'Does he?'

My father nodded. 'He calls you his princess,' he said.

I was so surprised for a moment that I could not speak. 'His princess?'

'Yes,' my father said, smiling at my incomprehension. 'He speaks like a young man in love. He comes to see me and he asks me, "How is my Princess?" – and he means you, Hannah.'

The coronation of my mistress, Lady Mary was set for the first day of

October and the whole court, the whole city of London, and the whole country had spent much of the summer preparing for the celebration which would bring Henry's daughter to his throne at last. There were faces missing from the crowds that lined the London streets. Devoted Protestants, mistrusting the queen's sincere promise of tolerance, had already frightened themselves into exile, and fled overseas. They found a friendly reception in France; the traditional enemy of England was arming against England again. There were faces missing from the queen's council; the queen's father would have wondered where some of his favourites were now. Some were ashamed of their past treatment of her, some Protestants would not serve her, and some had the grace to stay home in their converted abbeys. But the rest of the court, city and country turned out in their thousands to greet the new queen, the queen whose rights they had defended against other, Protestant claimants, the Catholic queen whose enthusiastic faith they knew, and that, nonetheless, they preferred to all others.

It was a fairy-tale coronation, the first I had ever seen. It was a spectacle like something out of one of my father's story books. A princess in a golden chariot, wearing blue velvet trimmed with white ermine, riding through the streets of her city, which were hung with tapestries, past fountains running with wine so that the very air was heady with the warm scent of it, past crowds who screamed with delight at the sight of their princess, their virgin queen, and pausing by groups of children who sang hymns in praise of the woman who had fought to be queen and was bringing the old religion back home again.

In the second carriage was the Protestant princess, but the cheers for her were nothing compared to the roar that greeted the diminutive queen every time her chariot rounded a corner. With Princess Elizabeth rode Henry's neglected queen, Anne of Cleves, fatter than ever, with a ready smile for the crowd, the knowing gleam, I thought, of one survivor to another. And behind that chariot came forty-six ladies of the court and country, on foot and dressed in their best, and flagging a little by the time we had processed from Whitehall to the Tower.

Behind them, in the procession of officers of the court, came all the minor gentry and officials, me amongst them. Ever since I had come to England I had known myself to be a stranger, a refugee from a terror that I had to pretend I did not fear. But when I walked in the queen's

116

coronation procession with Will Somers, the witty fool, beside me, and my yellow cap on my head and my fool's bell on a stick in my hand, I had a sense of coming into my own. I was the queen's fool, my destiny had led me to be there with her from the first moment of her betrayal, through her flight and to her courageous proclamation. She had earned her throne and I had earned my place at her side.

I did not care that I was named as a fool. I was the holy fool, known to have the Sight, known to have predicted this day when the queen would come to her own. Some even crossed themselves as I went by, acknowledging the power that was vested in me. So I marched with my head up and I did not fear that all those eyes upon me would see my olive skin and my dark hair and name me for a Spaniard or worse. I thought myself an Englishwoman that day, and a loyal Englishwoman at that, with a proven love for my queen and for my adopted country; and I was glad to be one.

We slept that night in the Tower and the next day Lady Mary was crowned Queen of England, with her sister Elizabeth carrying her train, and the first to kneel to her and to swear allegiance. I could hardly see the two of them, I was crammed at the back of the Abbey, peering around a gentleman of the court, and in any case, my sight was blinded with tears at the knowledge that my Lady Mary had come to her throne, her sister beside her, and her lifelong battle for recognition and justice was over at last. God (whatever His name might be) had finally blessed her; she had won.

However united the queen and her sister had appeared when Elizabeth had kneeled before her, the Lady Elizabeth continued to carry her brother's prayer book on a little chain at her waist, was never seen except in the soberest of gowns, and rarely appeared at Mass. She could not have shown the world more plainly that she was the Protestant alternative to the queen to whom she had just sworn lifelong loyalty. As ever, with Elizabeth, there was nothing that the queen could specifically criticise, it was the very air of her: the way she always set herself slightly apart, the way she always seemed to carry herself as if she, regretfully, could not wholly agree.

After several days of this the queen sent a brisk message to Elizabeth that she was expected to attend Mass, with the rest of the court, in the morning. A reply came as we were preparing to leave the queen's presence chamber. The queen, putting out her hand for her missal, turned her head to see one of Elizabeth's ladies in waiting standing in the doorway with a message from Lady Elizabeth.

'She begs to be excused today, and says she is not well.'

'Why, what is the matter with her?' the queen asked a little sharply. 'She was well enough yesterday.'

'She is sick in her stomach, she is in much pain,' the lady replied. 'Her lady in waiting, Mrs Ashley, says she is not well enough to go to Mass.'

'Tell Lady Elizabeth that I expect her at my chapel this morning, without fail,' the Lady Mary said calmly as she turned back to her lady in waiting and took her missal; but I saw her hands shaking as she turned the pages to find the place.

We were on the threshold of the Lady Mary's apartments, the guard just about to fling open the door so that we could walk along the gallery filled with well-wishers, spectators and petitioners, when one of Elizabeth's other ladies slipped in through a side door.

'Your Grace,' she whispered, poised with a message.

The queen did not even turn her head. 'Tell Lady Elizabeth that I expect to see her at Mass,' she said and nodded to the guard. He flung open the door and we heard the little gasp of awe that greeted the queen wherever she went. The people dropped into curtseys and bows and she went through them, her cheeks blazing with two spots of red which meant that she was angry, and the hand which held her coral rosary beads trembling.

Lady Elizabeth came late into Mass, we heard her sigh as she crept through the crowded gallery, almost doubled-up with discomfort. There was a mutter of concern for the young girl, crippled with pain. She slipped into the pew behind the queen and we heard her loud whisper to one of her ladies: 'Martha, if I faint, can you hold me up?'

The queen's attention was on the priest who celebrated the Mass with his back to her, his entire attention focused on the bread and wine before him. To Mary, as to the priest, it was the only moment of the day that had any true significance; all the rest was worldly show.

Of course, the rest of us sinners could hardly wait for the worldly show to recommence.

Lady Elizabeth left the church in the queen's train, holding her belly and groaning. She could hardly walk, her face was as deathly white as if she had powdered it with rice powder. The queen stalked ahead, her expression grim. When she reached her apartments she ordered the doors shut on the public gallery to close out the murmurs of concern at Lady Elizabeth's pallor and her enfeebled progress and the cruelty of the queen insisting on such an invalid attending Mass when she was so very ill.

'That poor girl should be abed,' one woman said clearly to the closing door.

'Indeed,' the queen said to herself.

Winter 1553

It was as dark as midnight, though it was still only six in the evening, the mist peeling like a black shroud off the corpse of the cold river. The smell in my nostrils was the scent of despair from the massive wet weeping walls of the Tower of London, surely the most gloomy palace that any monarch ever built. I presented myself to the postern gate and the guard held up a flaming torch to see my white face.

'A young lad,' he concluded.

'I've got books to deliver to Lord Robert,' I said.

He withdrew the torch and the darkness flooded over me, then the creak of the hinges warned me that he was opening the gate outward and I stepped back to let the big wet timbers swing open, and then I stepped forward to go in.

'Let me see them,' he said.

I proffered the books readily enough. They were works of theology defending the Papist point of view, licensed by the Vatican and authorised by the queen's own council.

'Go through,' the guard said.

I walked on the slippery cobblestones to the guardhouse, and from there along a causeway, the rank mud shining in the moonlight on either side, and then up a flight of wooden steps to the high door-way in the fortress wall of the white tower. If there was an attack or a rescue attempt, the soldiers inside could just kick the outside steps away, and they were unreachable. No-one could get my lord out.

Another soldier was waiting in the doorway. He led me inside and then rapped at an inner door and swung it open to admit me.

At last I saw him, my Lord Robert, leaning over his papers, a candle at his elbow, the golden light shining on his dark head, on his pale skin, and then the slow-dawning radiance of his smile.

'Mistress Boy! Oh! My Mistress Boy!'

I dropped to one knee. 'My lord!' was all I could say before I burst into tears.

He laughed, pulled me to my feet, put his arm around my shoulders, wiped my face, all in one dizzying caress. 'Come now, child, come now. What's wrong?'

'It's you!' I gulped. 'You being here. And you look so . . .' I could not bear to say 'pale', 'ill', 'tired', 'defeated', but all those words were true. 'Imprisoned,' I found at last. 'And your lovely clothes! And . . . and what's going to happen now?'

He laughed as if none of it mattered, and led me over to the fire, seated himself on a chair and pulled up a stool so that I was facing him, like a favourite nephew. Timidly, I reached forward and put my hands on his knees. I wanted to touch him to be sure that he was real. I had dreamed of him so often, and now he was here before me; unchanged but for the deep lines scored on his face by defeat and disappointment.

'Lord Robert . . .' I whispered.

He met my gaze. 'Yes, little one,' he said softly. 'It was a great gamble and we lost, and the price we will pay is a heavy one. But you're not a child; you know that it's not an easy world. I will pay the price when I have to.'

'Will they . . . ?' I could not bear to ask him if it was his own death that he was facing with this indomitable smile.

'Oh, I should think so,' he said cheerfully. 'Very soon. I would, if I were the queen. Now tell me the news. We don't have much time.'

I pulled my stool a little closer, marshalling my thoughts. I did not want to tell him the news, which was all bad, I wanted to look into his drawn face, and touch his hand. I wanted to tell him that I had longed to see him, and that I had written him letter after letter in the code which I knew he would have lost, and sent them all into the flames of the fire.

'Come on,' he said eagerly. 'Tell me everything.'

'The queen is considering if she should marry, you'll know that, I suppose,' I said, low-voiced. 'And she has been ill. They have proposed one man after another. The best choice is Philip of Spain. The Spanish ambassador tells her that it will be a good marriage but she is afraid. She knows she cannot rule alone but she is afraid of a man ruling over her.'

'But she will go ahead?'

'She might withdraw. I can't tell. She is half-sick with fear at the thought of it. She is afraid of having a man in her bed, and afraid for her throne without one.'

'And Lady Elizabeth?'

I glanced at the thick wooden door and dropped my low voice to an even quieter murmur. 'She and the queen cannot agree these days,' I said. 'They started very warmly, Lady Mary wanted Elizabeth at her side all the time, acknowledged her as her heir; but they cannot live happily together now. Lady Elizabeth is no longer the little girl of the queen's teaching, and in debate she is her master. She is as quick-witted as an alchemist. The queen hates argument about sacred things and Lady Elizabeth has ready arguments for everything and accepts nothing. She looks at everything with hard eyes . . .' I broke off.

'Hard eyes?' he queried. 'She has beautiful eyes.'

'I mean she looks hard at things,' I explained. 'She has no faith, she never closes her eyes in awe. She is not like my lady, you never see her amazed at the raising of the Host. She wants to know everything as a fact, she trusts nothing.'

Lord Robert nodded at the accuracy of the description. 'Aye. She was always one to take nothing on trust.'

'The queen forced her to Mass and Lady Elizabeth went with her hand on her belly, sighing for pain. Then, when the queen pressed her again, she said that she had converted. The queen wanted the truth from her. She asked her to tell the secrets of her heart: if she believed in the Holy Sacrament or no.'

'The secrets of Elizabeth's heart!' he exclaimed, laughing. 'What can the queen be thinking of? Elizabeth allows no-one near the secrets of her heart. Even when she was a child in the nursery she would barely whisper them to herself.'

'Well, she said she would give out in public that she is convinced of the merits of the old religion,' I said. 'But she doesn't do so. And she goes to Mass only when she has to. And everyone says . . .'

'What do they say, my little spy?'

'That she is sending out letters to true Protestants, that she has a network of supporters. That the French will pay for an uprising against the queen. And that, at the very least, she only has to wait until the queen dies and then the throne is all hers anyway, and she can throw off all disguise and be a Protestant queen as she is now a Protestant princess.'

'Oho.' He paused, taking all this in. 'And the queen believes all this slander?'

I looked up at him, hoping that he would understand. 'She thought that Elizabeth would be a sister to her,' I said. 'She went with her into London at the very moment of her greatest triumph. She took Elizabeth at her side then, and again at the day of her coronation. What more could she do to show that she loved her and trusted her and saw her as the next heir? And since then, every day, she hears that Elizabeth has done this, or said that, and she sees Elizabeth avoiding Mass, and pretending that she will go, and sliding in her conscience forward and back as she wishes. And Elizabeth . . .' I broke off.

'Elizabeth what?'

'She was there at the coronation, she was placed second only to the queen at the queen's own request. She rode in a chariot behind the queen's,' I said in a fierce whisper. 'She carried her train at the coronation, she was first to kneel before the new queen and put her hands in hers and swear to be a true and faithful subject. She swore fidelity before God. How can she now plot against her?'

He sat back in his chair and observed my heat with interest. 'Is the queen angry with Elizabeth?'

I shook my head. 'No. It's worse than anger. She is disappointed in her. She is lonely, Lord Robert. She wanted her little sister at her side. She singled her out for love and respect. She can hardly believe now that Elizabeth does not love her; to find that Elizabeth would plot against her is very painful. And she is assured that she is plotting. Someone comes with a new story every day.'

'Do they bring any evidence?'

'Enough to have her arrested a dozen times over, I think. There are too many rumours for her to be as innocent as she looks.'

'And still the queen does nothing against her?'

'She wants to bring peace,' I said. 'She won't act against Elizabeth unless she has to. She says that she won't execute Lady Jane, or your brother . . .' I did not say 'or you' but we were both thinking of the sentence of death hanging over him. 'She wants to bring peace to this country.'

'Well, amen to that,' Lord Robert said. 'And will Elizabeth stay at court for Christmas?'

'She has asked to leave. She says she is ill again and needs the peace of the country.'

'And is she ill?'

I shrugged. 'Who can say? She was very bloated and ill-looking when I saw her the other day. But nobody ever really sees her. She keeps to her rooms. She comes out only when she has to. No-one speaks to her, the women are unkind to her. Everyone says there is nothing wrong with her but envy.'

He shook his head at the petty spite of women. 'All this and the poor girl has to carry a rosary and a missal and go to Mass!'

'She's not a poor girl,' I said, stung. 'She is poorly treated by the ladies of the queen's court, but she can blame herself for that. It is only when there are people to see that she speaks very softly and walks with her head drooping. And as for Mass, everyone has to go, all the time. They sing a Mass in the queen's chapel seven times a day. Everyone goes at least twice a day.'

He half-smiled at the rapid turn of the court to piety. 'And Lady Jane? Is she truly not to die for her treason?'

'The queen will never kill her own cousin, a young woman,' I assured him. 'She's to live here for a while as a prisoner in the Tower, and then be released, when the country is quiet.'

He made a little grimace. 'A great risk for the queen. If I were her advisor I would tell her to make an end of it, to make an end of all of us.'

'She knows it was not Lady Jane's choice. It would be cruel of the queen to punish Lady Jane; and she is never cruel.'

'And the girl was only sixteen,' he said, half to himself. He rose to his feet, hardly aware of me. 'I should have stopped it,' he said. 'I should have kept Jane safely out of it, whatever plots my father made . . .'

He looked out of the window at the dark courtyard below where his own father had been executed, begging for mercy, offering evidence against Jane, against his sons, anyone, if he could be spared. When he had knelt before the block, the blindfold over his eyes had slipped down and he had pulled it up and then groped about on his hands and knees, pleading with the headsman to wait until he was ready. It was a miserable end; but not as miserable as the death he had given to the young king in his charge, who had been innocent of everything.

'I was a fool,' Robert said bitterly. 'Blinded by my own ambition. I am surprised you did not foresee it, child, I would have thought the heavens would have been rocking with laughter over the Dudley hubris. I wish to God you had warned me in time.'

I stood, my back to the fire. 'I wish I had done,' I said sadly. 'I would have done anything to save you from being here.'

'And shall I stay here till I rot?' he asked quietly. 'Can you foresee that for me? Some nights I hear the rats skitter on the floor and I think, this is all I will ever hear, this square of blue sky through the window will be all I ever see. She will not behead me, but she will cut off my youth.'

In silence, I shook my head. 'I listen and listen, and once I asked her directly. She said that she wanted no blood spilt that could be spared. She won't execute you and she must let you go free when Lady Jane goes free.'

'I wouldn't if I were her,' he said quietly. 'If I were her, I would rid myself of Elizabeth, of Jane, of my brother and of me; and name Mary Stuart as the next heir, French or not. One clean cut. That's the only way to get this country back into the Papist church and keep it there, and soon she will realise it. She has to wipe us out, this generation of Protestant plotters. If she does not she will have to cut off one head after another and watch others rise.'

I crossed the room and stood behind him. Timidly I put my hand on his shoulder. He turned and looked at me as if he had forgotten my presence. 'And you?' he asked gently. 'Safe in royal service now?'

'I am never safe,' I said in a low voice. 'You know why. I never can be safe. I never can feel safe. I love the queen and no-one questions who I am or where I have come from. I am known as her fool, as if I had been with her all my life. I should feel safe, but I always feel as if I am creeping across thin ice.'

He nodded. 'I'll take your secret with me to the scaffold if I go that way,' he promised. 'You have nothing to fear from me, child. And I have told no-one who you were or where you came from.'

I nodded. When I looked up he was watching me, his dark eyes warm. 'You've grown, Mistress Boy,' he remarked. 'Soon be a woman. I shall be sorry not to see it.'

I had nothing to say. I stood dumbly before him. He smiled as if he knew only too well the churn of my emotions. 'Ah, little fool. I should have left you in your father's shop that day, and not drawn you into this.'

'My father told me to bid you farewell.'

'Aye, he is right. You can leave me now. I will release you from your promise to love me. You are no longer my vassal. I let you go.'

It was little more than a joke to him. He knew as well as I did that you cannot release a girl from her promise to love a man. She either gets herself free or she is bound for life.

'I'm not free,' I whispered. 'My father told me to come to see you and to say goodbye. But I am not free. I never will be.'

'Would you serve me still?'

I nodded.

Lord Robert smiled and leaned forward, his mouth so close to my ear that I could feel the warmth of his breath. 'Then do this one last thing for me. Go to Lady Elizabeth. Bid her be of good cheer. Tell her to study with my old tutor, John Dee. Tell her to seek him out, and study with him, without fail. Then find John Dee and tell him two things. One: I think he should make contact with his old master, Sir William Pickering. Got that?'

'Yes,' I said. 'Sir William. I know of him.'

'And two: tell him to meet also with James Crofts and Tom Wyatt. I think they are engaged in an alchemical experiment that is near to John Dee's heart. Edward Courtenay can make a chemical wedding. Can you remember all of that?'

'Yes,' I said. 'But I don't know what it means.'

'All the better. They are to make gold from the basest of metal, and cast down silver to ash. Tell him that. He'll know what I mean. And tell him that I will play my part in the alchemy, if he will get me there.'

'Where?' I asked.

'Just remember the message,' he said. 'Tell it back to me.'

I repeated it, word for word, and he nodded. 'And finally, come back to me just once, for one last time, and tell me what you can see in John Dee's mirror. I need to know. Whatever becomes of me, I need to know what will happen to England.'

I nodded, but he did not let me go at once. He put his lips to my neck, just below my ear, a little brush of a kiss, a little breath of a kiss. 'You're a good girl,' he said. 'And I thank you.'

He let me go then, and I stepped back, backwards and backwards from him as if I could not bear to turn away. I tapped on the door behind me, and the guard swung it open. 'God bless you and keep you safe, my lord,' I said. Lord Robert turned his head and gave me a smile which was so sweet that it broke my heart even as the door closed and hid him from me.

'God speed, lad,' he replied evenly, to the closing door, and then it was shut and I was in the darkness and the cold and without him once more.

In the street outside I took to my heels and started to run home. A shadow suddenly stepped out of a doorway and blocked my way. I gasped in alarm.

'Hush, it's me, Daniel.'

'How did you know I was here?'

'I went to your father's shop and he told me you were taking books into the Tower for Lord Robert.'

'Oh.'

He fell into step beside me. 'Surely you don't need to serve him now.'

'No,' I said. 'He has released me.' I very much wished that Daniel would go away so that I could think of the kiss on my neck and the warmth of Lord Robert's breath against my ear.

'So you won't serve him again,' he said pedantically.

'I just said,' I snapped. 'I am not serving him now. I am delivering books for my father. It just happened to be to Lord Robert. I did not even see him. I just took them in and gave them to a guard.'

'Then when did he release you from his service?'

'Months ago,' I lied, trying to recover.

'When he was arrested?'

I rounded on him. 'What does it matter to you? I am released from his service, I serve Queen Mary now. What more d'you need to know?'

His temper rose with mine. 'I have a right to know everything that you do. You are to be my wife, your name will be mine. And while you insist on running from court to Tower, you put yourself into danger, and the rest of us into danger too.'

'You're in no danger,' I retorted. 'What would you know of it? You've never done anything or been anywhere. The world has turned upside down and back again while you have stayed safe at home. Why should you be in danger?'

'I've not played off one master against another, and shown a false face and spied and given false witness, if that's what you mean,' he said sharply. 'I did not ever think those were great and admirable acts. I have kept my faith and buried my father according to my faith. I have supported my mother and my sisters, and I have saved money against the day of my marriage. Our marriage. While you run around the dark streets, dressed as a pageboy, serve in a Papist court, visit a condemned traitor, and reproach me for having done nothing.'

I pulled my hand away from him. 'Don't you see he's going to die?' I shouted, and then I was aware that the tears were streaming down my face. Angrily, I rubbed them away with my sleeve. 'Don't you know that they're going to execute him and no-one can save him? Or at best they'll leave him in there to wait and wait and wait and die of waiting? He can't even save himself? Don't you see that everyone I love seems to be taken from me, for no crime? With no way of saving them? Don't you think I miss my mother every day of my life? Don't you think I smell smoke every night in my dreams and now this man . . . this man . . .' I broke off in tears.

Daniel caught me by the shoulders, not in an embrace, but with a firm grip to hold me at arm's length so that he could read my face with a long impartial measuring glance. 'This man is nothing to do with the death of your mother,' he said flatly. 'Nothing to do with someone dying for their faith. So don't dress up your lust as sorrow. You have been serving two masters, sworn enemies. One of them was bound to end up in there. If it was not Lord Robert then it would have been Queen Mary. One of them was bound to triumph, one of them was bound to die.'

I wrenched myself from his grip, pulling away from his hard

unsympathetic eyes, and started to trudge for home. After a few moments I heard him come after me.

'Would you be weeping like this if it had been Queen Mary in there, with her head on the block?' he asked.

'Ssshhh,' I said, always cautious. 'Yes.'

He said nothing, but his silence showed his great scepticism.

'I have done nothing dishonourable,' I said flatly.

'I doubt you,' he said, as coldly as me. 'If you have been honourable it has only been for lack of opportunity.'

'Whoreson,' I said under my breath so he could not hear, and he marched me home in silence and we parted at my doorway with a handshake which was neither cousinly nor loving. I let him go, I would have been glad to throw a large volume at his retreating upright head. Then I went in to my father and wondered how long it would before Daniel came to see him to say that he wanted to be released from our betrothal, and what would happen to me then.

As Fool to the queen I was expected to be in her chambers every day, at her side. But as soon as I could be absent for an hour without attracting notice, I took a chance, and went to the old Dudley rooms to look for John Dee. I tapped on the door and a man in strange livery opened it and looked suspiciously at me.

'I thought the Dudley household lived here,' I said timidly.

'Not any more,' he said smartly.

'Where will I find them?'

He shrugged. 'The duchess has rooms near the queen. Her sons are in the Tower. Her husband is in hell.'

'The tutor?'

He shrugged. 'Gone away. Back to his father's house, I should think.'

I nodded and took myself back to the queen's rooms, and sat by her feet on a small cushion. Her little dog, a greyhound, had a cushion that matched mine; and dog and I sat, noses parallel, watching with the same brown-eyed incomprehension, while the courtiers came and made their bows and applied for land and places and favours of grants of money, and sometimes the queen patted the dog and sometimes she patted me;

and dog and I stayed mum, and never said what we thought of these pious Catholics who had kept the flame of their faith so wonderfully hidden for so long. Well-hidden while they proclaimed the Protestant religion, hidden while they saw Catholics burned, waiting till this moment, like daffodils at Easter, to burst forth and flower. To think that there were so many believers in the country, and nobody knew them till now!

When they were all gone she walked up to a window embrasure where no-one could hear us and beckoned for me. 'Hannah?'

'Yes, Your Grace?' I went to her side at once.

'Isn't it time you were out of your pageboy livery? You will be a woman soon.'

I hesitated. 'If you will allow it, Your Grace, I would rather go on dressed as a pageboy.'

She looked at me curiously. 'Don't you long for a pretty gown, and to grow your hair, child? Don't you want to be a young woman? I thought I would give you a gown for Christmas.'

I thought of my mother plaiting my thick black hair and winding the plaits around her fingers and telling me I would become a beauty, a famously beautiful woman. I thought of her chiding me for my love of rich cloth, and how I had begged for a green velvet gown for Hanukah.

'I lost my love of finery when I lost my mother,' I said quietly. 'There's no pleasure in it for me without her to choose and fit the dresses on me, and tell me that they suit me. I don't even want long hair without her here to plait it for me.'

Her face became tender. 'When did she die?'

'When I was eleven years old,' I lied. 'She took the plague.' I would never risk revealing the truth that she had been burned as a heretic, not even with this queen who looked so gravely and sorrowfully into my face.

'Poor child,' she said gently. 'It is a loss that you never forget. You can learn to bear it, but you never forget it.'

'Every time something good happens to me I want to tell her. Every time something bad happens I want her help.'

She nodded. 'I used to write to my mother, even when I knew that they would never allow me to send my letters to her. Even though there was nothing in them that they could have objected to, no secrets, just my need for her and my sorrow that she was far from me. But they would not let me write to her. I just wanted to tell her that I loved her and I missed her. And then she died and I was not allowed to go to her. I could not even hold her hand and close her eyes.'

She put her hand to her eyes and pressed her cool fingertips against her eyelids, as if to hold back old tears.

She cleared her throat. 'But this cannot mean that you never wear a gown,' she said lightly. 'Life goes on, Hannah. Your mother would not want you to grieve. She would want you to grow to be a woman, a beautiful young woman. She would not want her little girl to wear boy's clothes forever.'

'I don't want to be a woman,' I said simply. 'My father has arranged a marriage for me, but I know I am not yet ready to be a woman and a wife.'

'You can't want to be a virgin like me,' she said with a wry smile. 'It's not a course many women would choose.'

'No,' I said. 'Not a virgin queen like you, I have not dedicated myself to being a single woman; but it's as if . . .' I broke off. 'As if I don't know how to be a woman,' I said uncomfortably. 'I watch you, and I watch the ladies of the court.' Tactfully I did not add that of them all, I watched the Lady Elizabeth, who seemed to me to be the epitome of the grace of a girl and the dignity of a princess. 'I watch everyone, and I think I will learn it in time. But not yet.'

She nodded. 'I understand exactly. I don't know how to be a queen without a husband at my side. I have never known of a queen without a man to guide her. And yet I am so afraid of marrying . . .' She paused. 'I don't think a man could ever understand the dread that a woman might feel at the thought of marriage. Especially a woman like me, not a young woman, not a woman given to the pleasures of the flesh, not a woman who is even very desirable . . .' She put a hand out to prevent me from contradicting her. 'I know it, Hannah, you needn't flatter me.

'And worse than all of these things, I am not a woman who finds it easy to trust men. I hate having to sit with the men of power. When they argue in council, my heart thumps in my chest, and I am afraid that my voice will shake when I have to speak.

'And yet I despise men who are weak. When I look at my cousin Edward Courtenay that the Lord Chancellor would have me marry, I could laugh out loud at the thought of it. The boy is a puppy and a vain fool and I could never, never debase myself to lie under such a one as him.

'But if one married a man who was accustomed to command . . .' She paused. 'What a terror it would be,' she said quietly. 'To put your heart in the keeping of a stranger! What a terror to promise to obey a man who might order you to do anything! And to promise to love a man till death . . .' She broke off. 'After all, men do not always consider themselves bound by such promises. And what happens then to a good wife?'

'Did you think you would live and die a virgin?' I asked.

She nodded. 'When I was a princess I was betrothed over and over again. But when my father denied me and called me his bastard, I knew that there would be no offers of marriage. I set away all thoughts of it then, and all thoughts of my own children too.'

'Your father denied you?'

'Yes,' the queen said shortly. 'They made me swear on the Bible to my own bastardy.' Her voice shook, she drew a breath. 'No prince in Europe would have married me after that. To tell you the truth, I was so ashamed I would not have wanted a husband. I could not have looked an honourable man in the face. And when my father died and my brother became king, I thought I could be like a dowager, like a favourite old godmother, his older sister who might advise him, and I thought he would have children that I might care for. But now everything has changed and I am queen, and even though I am queen I find I still cannot make my own choices.' She paused. 'They have offered me Philip of Spain, you know.'

I waited.

She turned to me as if I had more sense than her greyhound, as if I could advise her. 'Hannah, I am less than a man and less than a woman. I cannot rule as a man, and I cannot give the country the heir that it has a right to desire. I am a half-prince. Neither queen nor king.'

'Surely, the country only needs a ruler it can respect,' I said tentatively. 'And it needs years of peace. I am new-come to this land but even I can see that men don't know what is right and wrong any more. The church has changed and changed again within their lifetimes and they have had to change and change with it. And there is much poverty in the city, and hunger in the country. Can't you just wait? Can't you just feed the poor and restore the lands to the landless, set men back to work and get the beggars and the thieves off the roads? Bring back the beauty to the church and give the monasteries back their lands?'

'And when I have done that?' Queen Mary asked, a strange shaking intensity in her voice. 'What then? When the country is safe inside the church again, when everyone is well fed, when the barns are full and the monasteries and nunneries are prosperous? When the priests are pure in their living and the Bible is read to the people as it should be? When the Mass is celebrated in every village, and the matins bells ring out over all the fields every morning as they should do, as they always have done? What then?'

'Then you will have done the task that God called you to, won't you? . . .' I stammered.

She shook her head. 'I will tell you, what then. Then illness or accident befalls me and I die childless. And the bastard of Anne Boleyn and the lute player Mark Smeaton steps up to claim the throne: Elizabeth. And the moment she is on the throne she throws off her mask and shows herself for what she is.'

I could hardly recognise the hiss of her voice, the hatred in her face. 'Why, what is she? What has she done to upset you so?'

'She has betrayed me,' she said flatly. 'When I was fighting for our inheritance, hers as well as mine, she was writing to the man who was marching against me. I know that now. While I was fighting for her as well as for myself she was making an agreement with him for when I was dead. She would have signed it on my execution block.

'When I took her into London at my side they cheered the Protestant princess, and she smiled at the cheers. When I sent her teachers and scholars to explain to her the errors of her faith she smiled at them, her mother's sly smile, and told them that now she understood, now she would receive the blessing of Mass.

'And then she comes to Mass like a woman forced against her conscience. Hannah! When I was no older than her I had the greatest men of England curse me to my face and threaten me with death if I did not conform to the new religion. They took my mother from me and she died ill and heartbroken and alone, but she never bowed the knee to them. They threatened me with the scaffold for treason! They threatened me with fire for heresy! They were burning men and women for less than I was saying. I had to cling to my faith with all my courage and I did not renounce it until the Emperor of Spain himself told me that I should do so, that I must renounce it, because to keep it was my death sentence. He knew they would kill me if I did not renounce my faith. But all I have done to Elizabeth is to beg her to save her own soul and be my little sister once more!'

'Your Grace . . .' I whispered. 'She's only young, she will learn.'

'She's not that young.'

'She will learn . . .'

'If she is going to learn then she chooses the wrong tutors. She conspires with the kingdom of France against me, she has a band of men who would stop at nothing to see her inherit. Every day someone tells me of another foul plot, and always, the tendrils come back to her. Every time I look at her now, I see a woman steeped in sin, just like her mother, the poisoner. I can almost see her flesh going black from the sin from her heart. I see her turning her back on the Holy Church, I see her turning her back on my love, I see her rushing towards treason and sin.'

'You said she was your little sister,' I reminded her. 'You said you loved her as if she was your own child.'

'I did love her,' the queen said bitterly. 'More than she remembers. More than I should have done, knowing what her mother did to mine. I did love her. But she is not the child that I loved any more. She is not the little girl that I taught to write and read. She has gone wrong. She has been corrupted. She is steeped in sin. I cannot save her; she is a witch and the daughter of a witch.'

'She's a young woman,' I protested quietly. 'Not a witch.'

'Worse than a witch,' she accused. 'A heretic. A hypocrite. A whore. I know her for all these. A heretic because she takes the Mass; but I know her to be a Protestant, and she is forsworn with her eyes on the Host. A hypocrite because she does not even own to her faith. There are brave men and women in this land who would go to the stake for their error; but she is not one of them. When my brother Edward was on the throne she was then a shining light of the reformed religion. She was the Protestant princess in her dark gowns and her white ruffs and her eyes turned down and no gold or jewels in her ears or on her fingers. Now he is dead she kneels beside me to see the raising of the Host, and crosses herself, and curtsies to the altar, but I know it is all false. It is an insult to me, which is nothing; but it is an insult to my mother who was pushed aside for her mother, and it is an insult to the Holy Church, which is a sin against God himself.

'And, God forgive her, she is a whore because of what she did with Thomas Seymour. The whole world would know it; but that other great Protestant whore hid the two of them, and died in hiding it.'

'Who?' I asked. I was appalled and fascinated, all at once, remembering the girl in the sunlit garden and the man who held her against a tree and put his hand up her skirt.

'Katherine Parr,' Queen Mary said through her teeth. 'She knew that her husband Thomas Seymour had been seduced by Elizabeth. She caught them at it in Elizabeth's chamber, Elizabeth in her shift, Lord Thomas all over her. Katherine Parr bundled Elizabeth off to the country, out of the way. She faced down the gossip, she denied everything. She protected the girl – well, she had to, the child was in her house. She protected her husband, and then she died giving birth to his child. Fool. Foolish woman.'

She shook her head. 'Poor woman. She loved him so much that she married him before my father was cold in the ground. She scandalised the court, and she risked her place in the world. And he rewarded her by tickling a fourteen-year-old girl in her house, under her supervision. And that girl, my Elizabeth, my little sister, wriggled under his caresses and protested that she would die if he touched her again, but never locked her bedroom door, never complained to her stepmother and never found a better lodging.

'I knew of it. Good God, there was such gossip even I, hidden away in the country, heard of it. I wrote to her and said she should come to me, I had a home, I could provide for us both. She wrote me very sweetly, very fair. She wrote to me that nothing was happening to her and that she did not need to move house. And all the time she was letting him into her chamber in the morning, and letting him lift the hem of her gown to see her shift, and one time, God help her, letting him cut her gown off her, so that she was all but naked before him.

'She never sent to me for help, though she knew I would have taken her away within the day. A little whore then, and a whore now, and I knew it, God forgive me, and hoped that she might be bettered. I thought if I gave her a place at my side, and the honour which would be hers, then she would grow into being a princess. I thought that a young whore in the making could be unmade, could be made anew, could be taught to be a princess. But she cannot. She will not. You will see how she behaves in the future when she has the chance of a tickling once again.'

'Your Grace . . .' I was overwhelmed by the spilling out of her spite.

She took a breath and turned to the window. She rested her forehead against the thick pane of glass and I saw how the heat from her hair misted the glass. It was cold outside, the unbearable English winter, and the Thames was iron-grey beyond the stone-coloured garden beneath the pewter sky. I could see the queen's reflected face in the thick glass like a cameo drowned in water, I could see the feverish energy pulsing through her body.

'I must be free of this hatred,' she said quietly. 'I must be free of the pain that her mother brought me. I must disown her.'

'Your Grace . . .' I said again, more gently.

She turned back to me.

'She will come after me if I die without heir,' she said flatly. 'That lying whore. Anything I achieve will be overturned by her, will be spoiled by her. Everything in my life has always been despoiled by her. I was England's only princess and the great joy of my mother's heart. A moment, an eyelid blink, and I was serving in Elizabeth's nursery as her maid, and my mother was deserted and then dead. Elizabeth, the whore's daughter, is corruption itself. I have to have a child to put between her and the throne. It is the greatest duty I owe to this country, to my mother and to myself.'

'You will have to marry Philip of Spain?'

She nodded. 'He, as well as any other,' she said. 'I can make a treaty with him that will hold. He knows, his father knows, what this country is like. I can be queen and wife with a man like him. He has his own land, his own fortune, he does not need little England. And then I can be queen of my own country and wife to him, and a mother.'

There was something in the way she said 'mother' that alerted me. I had felt her touch on my head, I had seen her with the children that tumbled out from dirty cottages.

'Why, you long for a child for yourself,' I exclaimed.

I saw the need in her eyes and then she turned away from me to the window and the view of the cold river again. 'Oh yes,' she said quietly to

136

the cold garden outside. 'I have longed for a child of my own for twenty years. That was why I loved my poor brother so much. In the hunger of my heart I even loved Elizabeth when she was a baby. Perhaps God in his goodness will give me a son of my own now.' She looked at me. 'You have the Sight. Will I have a child, Hannah? Will I have a child of my own, to hold in my arms and to love? A child who will grow and inherit my throne and make England a great country?'

I waited for a moment, in case anything came to me. All I had was a sense of great despair and hopelessness, nothing more. I dropped my gaze to the floor and I knelt before her. 'I am sorry, Your Grace,' I said. 'The Sight cannot be commanded. I can't tell you the answer to that question, nor any other. My vision comes and goes as it wishes. I cannot say if you will have a child.'

'Then I will predict for you,' she said grimly. 'I will tell you this. I will marry this Philip of Spain without love, without desire, but with a very true sense that it is what this country needs. He will bring us the wealth and the power of Spain, he will make this country a part of the empire, which we need so much. He will help me restore this country to the discipline of the true church, and he will give me a child to be a godly Christian heir to keep this country in the right ways.' She paused. 'You should say Amen,' she prompted me.

'Amen.' It was easily said. I was a Christian Jew, a girl dressed as a boy, a young woman in love with one man and betrothed to another. A girl grieving for her mother and never mentioning her name. I spent all my life in feigned agreement. 'Amen,' I said.

The door opened and Jane Dormer beckoned two porters into the room, carrying a frame between them, swathed in linen cloth. 'Something for you, Your Grace!' she said with a roguish smile. 'Something you will like to see.'

The queen was slow to throw off her thoughtful mood. 'What is it, Jane? I am weary now.'

In answer, Mistress Dormer waited till the men had leaned their burden against the wall, and then took the hem of the cloth and turned to her royal mistress. 'Are you ready?'

The queen was persuaded into smiling. 'Is this the portrait of Philip?' she asked. 'I won't be cozened by it. You forget, I am old enough to remember when my father married a portrait but divorced the sitter. He said that it was the worst trick that had ever been played upon a man. A portrait is always handsome. I won't be taken in by a portrait.'

In answer, Jane Dormer swept the cloth aside. I heard the queen's indrawn breath, saw her colour come and go in her pale cheeks, and then heard her little girlish giggle. 'My God, Jane, this is a man!' she whispered.

Jane Dormer collapsed with laughter, dropped the cloth and dashed across the room to stand back to admire the portrait.

He was indeed a handsome man. He was young, he must have been in his mid-twenties to the queen's forty years, brown-bearded with dark smiling eyes, a full sensual mouth, a good figure, broad shoulders and slim strong legs. He was wearing dark red with a dark red cap at a rakish angle on his curly brown hair. He looked like a man who would whisper lovemaking in a woman's ear until she was weak at the knees. He looked like a handsome rogue, but there was a firmness about his mouth and a set to his shoulders which suggested that he might nonetheless be capable of honest dealing.

'What d'you think, Your Grace?' Jane demanded.

The queen said nothing. I looked from the portrait back to her face again. She was gazing at him. For a moment I could not think what she reminded me of, then I knew it. It was my own face in the looking glass when I thought of Robert Dudley. It was that same awakening, widening of the eyes, the same unaware dawning of a smile.

'He's very . . . pleasing,' she said

Jane Dormer met my eyes and smiled at me.

I wanted to smile back but my head was ringing with a strange noise, a tingling noise like little bells.

'What dark eyes he has,' Jane pointed out.

'Yes,' the queen breathed.

'He wears his collar very high, that must be the fashion in Spain. He'll bring the newest fashions to court.'

The noise in my head was getting louder. I put my hands over my ears but the sound echoed louder inside my head, it was a jangling noise now.

'Yes,' the queen said.

'And see? A gold cross on a chain,' Jane cooed. 'Thank God, there will be a Catholic Christian prince for England once more.'

It was too much to bear now. It was like being in a bell tower at full peal. I bowed over and twisted round, trying to shake the terrible ringing out of my ears. Then I burst out, 'Your Grace! Your heart will break!' and at once the noise was cut off short and there was silence, a silence somehow even louder than the ringing bells had been, and the queen was looking at me, and Jane Dormer was looking at me, and I realised I had spoken out of turn, shouted out as a fool.

'What did you say?' Jane Dormer challenged me to repeat my words, defying me to spoil the happy mood of the afternoon, of two women examining a portrait of a handsome man.

'I said, "Your Grace, your heart will break",' I repeated. 'But I can't say why.'

'If you can't say why, you had better not have spoken at all,' Jane Dormer flared up, always passionately loyal to her mistress.

'I know,' I said numbly. 'I can't help it.'

'Scant wisdom to tell a woman that her heart will break but not how or why!'

'I know,' I said again. 'I am sorry.'

Jane turned to the queen. 'Your Grace, pay no heed to the fool.'

The queen's face, which had been so bright and so animated, suddenly turned sulky. 'You can both leave,' she said flatly. She hunched her shoulders and turned away. In that quintessential gesture of a stubborn woman I knew that she had made her choice and that no wise words would change her mind. No fool's words either. 'You can go,' she said. Jane made a move to shroud the portrait with its cloth. 'You can leave that there,' she said. 'I might look at it again.'

While the long negotiations about the marriage went on between the queen's council, sick with apprehension at the thought of a Spaniard on the throne of England, and the Spanish representatives, eager to add another kingdom to their sprawling empire, I found my way to the home of John Dee's father. It was a small house near the river in the city. I tapped on the door and for a moment no-one answered. Then a window above the front door opened and someone shouted down: 'Who is it?'

'I seek Roland Dee,' I called up. The little roof over the front door concealed me; he could hear my voice, but not see me.

'He's not here,' John Dee called back.

'Mr Dee, it is me. Hannah the Fool,' I called up. 'I was looking for you.'

'Hush,' he said quickly and slammed the casement window shut. I heard his feet echoing on the wooden stairs inside the house and the noise of the bolts being drawn, and then the door opened inward to a dark hall. 'Come in quickly,' he said.

I squeezed through the gap and he slammed the door shut and bolted it. We stood face to face inside the dark hallway in silence. I was about to speak but he put a hand on my arm to caution me to be silent. At once I froze. Outside I could hear the normal noises of the London street, people walking by, a few tradesmen calling out, street sellers offering their wares, the distant shout from someone unloading at the river.

'Did anyone follow you? Did you tell anyone you were looking for me?'

My heart thudded at the question. I felt my hand go to my cheek as if to rub off a smut. 'Why? What has happened?'

'Could anyone have followed you?'

I tried to think, but I was aware only of the thudding of my frightened heart. 'No, sir. I don't think so.'

John Dee nodded, and then he turned and went upstairs without a word to me. I hesitated, and then I followed him. For a groat I would have slipped out of the back door and run to my father's house and never seen him again.

At the top of the stairs the door was open and he beckoned me into his room. At the window was his desk with a beautiful strange brass instrument in pride of place. To the side was a big scrubbed oak table, spread with his papers, rulers, pencils, pens, ink pots and scrolls of paper covered with minute writing and many numbers.

I could not satisfy my curiosity until I knew that I was safe. 'Are you a wanted man, Mr Dee? Should I go?'

He smiled and shook his head. 'I'm over-cautious,' he said frankly. 'My father was taken up for questioning but he is a known member of a reading group – Protestant thinkers. No-one has anything against me. I was just startled when I saw you.'

'You are sure?' I pressed him.

He gave a little laugh. 'Hannah, you are like a young doe on the edge of flight. Be calm. You are safe here.'

I steadied myself and started to look around. He saw my gaze go back to the instrument at the window.

'What d'you think that is?' he asked.

I shook my head. It was a beautiful thing, not an instrument I could recognise. It was made in brass, a ball as big as a pigeon's egg in the centre on a stalk, around it a brass ring cunningly supported by two other stalks which meant it could swing and move, a ball sliding around on it. Outside there was another ring and another ball, outside that, another. They were a series of rings and balls and the furthest from the centre was the smallest.

'This,' he said softly, 'is a model of the world. This is how the creator, the great master carpenter of the heavens, made the world and then set it in motion. This holds the secret of how God's mind works.' He leaned forward and gently touched the first ring. As if by magic they all started to move slowly, each going at its own pace, each following its own orbit, sometimes passing, sometimes overtaking each other. Only the little gold egg in the centre did not move, everything else swung around it.

'Where is our world?' I asked.

He smiled at me. 'Here,' he said, pointing to the golden egg at the very centre of all the others. He pointed to the next ring with the slowly circling ball. 'This the moon.' He pointed to the next. 'This the sun.' He pointed to the next few. 'These are the planets, and beyond them, these are the stars, and this –' he gestured to a ring that was unlike all the others, a ring made of silver, which had moved at his first touch and made all the others move in time. 'This is the *primum mobile*. It is God's touch on the world symbolised by this ring that started the movement of everything, that made the world begin. This is the Word. This is the manifestation of "Let there be light".'

'Light,' I repeated softly.

He nodded. '"Let there be light". If I knew what made this move, I would know the secret of all the movement of the heavens,' he said. 'In this model I can play the part of God. But in the real heavens, what is the force that makes the planets swing around, that makes the sun circle the earth?'

He was waiting for me to answer, knowing that I could not, since nobody knew the answer. I shook my head, dizzied by the movement of the golden balls on their golden rings.

He put a hand on it to steady it and I watched it slow and stop. 'My friend, Gerard Mercator, made this for me when we were both students together. He will be a great map-maker one day, I know it. And I –' He broke off. 'I shall follow my path,' he said. 'Wherever it leads me. I have to be clear in my head and free from ambition and live in a country which is clear and free. I have to walk a clear path.'

He paused for a moment and then, as if he suddenly remembered me, 'And you? What did you come here for?' he asked in quite a different tone of voice. 'Why did you call for my father?'

'I didn't want him. I was looking for you. I only wanted to ask him where you were,' I said. 'They told me at the court that you had gone home to your father. I was seeking you. I have a message.'

He was suddenly alight with eagerness. 'A message? From who?'

'From Lord Robert.'

His face fell. 'For a moment I thought an angel might have come to you with a message for me. What does Lord Robert want?'

'He wants to know what will come to pass. He gave me two tasks. One, to tell Lady Elizabeth to seek you out and ask you to be her tutor, and the other to tell you to meet with some men.'

'What men?'

'Sir William Pickering, Tom Wyatt, and James Croft,' I recited. 'And he said to tell you this: that they are engaged in an alchemical experiment to make gold from base metal and to refine silver back to ash and you should help them with this. Edward Courtenay can make a chemical wedding. And I am to go back to him and tell him what will come to pass.'

Mr Dee glanced at the window as if he feared eavesdroppers on the very sill outside. 'These are not good times for me to serve a suspect princess and a man in the Tower for treason, and three others whose names I may already know, whose plans I may already doubt.'

I gave him a steady look. 'As you wish, sir.'

'And you could be more safely employed, young woman,' he said. 'What is he thinking of, exposing you to such danger?'

'I am his to command,' I said firmly. 'I have given my word.'

'He should release you,' he said gently. 'He cannot command anything from the Tower.'

'He has released me. I am to see him only once more,' I said. 'When I go back and tell him what you have foreseen for England.'

'Shall we look in the mirror and see now?' he asked.

I hesitated. I was afraid of the dark mirror and the darkened room, afraid of the things that might come through the darkness to haunt us. 'Mr Dee, last time I did not have a true seeing,' I confessed awkwardly.

'When you said the date of the death of the king?'

I nodded.

'When you predicted that the next queen would be Jane?'

'Yes.'

'Your answers were true,' he observed.

'They were nothing more than guesses,' I said. 'I plucked them from the air. I am sorry.'

He smiled. 'Then just do that again,' he said. 'Just guess for me. Just guess for Lord Robert. Since he asks it?'

I was caught and I knew it. 'Very well.'

'We'll do it now,' he said. 'Sit down, close your eyes, try to think of nothing. I will get the room ready for you.'

I did as he told me and sat on a stool. I could hear him moving quietly in the next room, the swish of a closing curtain, and the little spitting noise of flame as he carried a taper from a fire to light the candles. Then he said quietly: 'It is ready. Come, and may the good angels guide us.'

He took my hand and led me into a small box room. The same mirror we had used before was leaning against a wall, a table before it supported a wax tablet printed with strange signs. A candle was burning before the mirror and he had put another opposite, so that they seemed like innumerable candles disappearing into infinite distance, beyond the world, beyond the sun and the moon and the planets as he had showed them to me on his swinging circular model; not all the way to heaven but into absolute darkness where finally there would be more darkness than candle-flame and it would be nothing but dark.

I drew a long breath to ward off my fear and seated myself before the mirror. I heard his muttered prayer and I repeated: 'Amen'. Then I gazed into the darkness of the mirror.

I could hear myself speaking but I could hardly make out the words. I could hear the scratching of his pen as he wrote down what I was saying. I could hear myself reciting a string of numbers, and then strange words, like a wild poetry which had a rhythm and a beauty of its own; but no meaning that I could tell. Then I heard my voice say very clearly in English: 'There will be a child, but no child. There will be a king but no king. There will be a virgin queen all-forgotten. There will be a queen but no virgin.'

'And Lord Robert Dudley?' he whispered.

'He will have the making of a prince who will change the history of the world,' I whispered in reply. 'And he will die, beloved by a queen, safe in his bed.'

When I recovered my senses John Dee was standing by me with a drink which tasted of fruit with a tang behind it of metal.

'Are you all right?' he asked me.

I nodded. 'Yes. A little sleepy.'

'You had better go back to court,' he said. 'You will be missed.'

'Will you not come, and see Lady Elizabeth?'

He looked thoughtful. 'Yes, when I am sure it is safe. You can tell Lord Robert that I will serve him, and I will serve the cause, and that I too think the time is ripe now. I'll advise her and be her intelligencer during these days of change. But I have to take care.'

'Are you not afraid?' I asked, thinking of my own terror of being observed, my own fear of the knock on the door in darkness.

'Not very,' he said slowly. 'I have friends in powerful places. I have plans to complete. The queen is restoring the monasteries and their libraries must be restored too. It is my God-given duty to find and restore the books to their shelves, the manuscripts and the scholarship. And I hope to see base metal turn to gold.'

'The philosopher's stone?' I asked.

He smiled. 'This time it is a riddle.'

'What shall I tell Lord Robert when I go back to see him in the Tower?' I asked.

John Dee looked thoughtful. 'Tell him nothing more than he will die in his bed beloved of a queen,' he said. 'You saw it, though you did not know what you could see. That's the truth, though it seems impossible now.'

'And are you sure?' I asked. 'Are you sure that he will not be executed?'

He nodded. 'I'm sure. There is much for him to do, and the time of a queen of gold will come. Lord Robert is not a man to die young with his work unfinished. And I foresee a great love for him, the greatest love he has ever known.'

I waited, hardly breathing. 'Do you know who he will love?' I whispered.

Not for a moment did I think it would be me. How could it be? I was his vassal, he called me Mistress Boy, he laughed at the girl's adoration that he saw in my face and offered to release me. Not even at that moment when John Dee predicted a great love for him did I think that it would be me.

'A queen will love him,' John Dee said. 'He will be the greatest love of her life.'

'But she is to marry Philip of Spain,' I observed.

He shook his head. 'I can't see a Spaniard on the throne of England,' he predicted. 'And neither can many others.'

It was hard to find a way to speak with the Lady Elizabeth without half the court remarking on it. Although she had no friends at court and only a small circle of her own household, she seemed to be continually surrounded by apparently casual passers-by, half of whom were paid to spy on her. The French king had his spies in England, the Spanish emperor had his network. All the great men had maids and men in other households to keep watch for any signs of change or of treason, and the queen herself was creating and paying a network of informers. For all I knew, someone was paid to report on me, and the very thought of it made me sick with fear. It was a tense world of continual suspicion and pretend friendship. I was reminded of John Dee's model of the earth with all the planets going around it. This princess was like the earth, at the very centre of everything, except all the stars in her firmament watched her with envious eyes and wished her ill. I thought it no wonder that she was paler and paler and the shadows under her eyes were turning from the blue to the dark violet of bruises, as the Christmas feast approached and there was no goodwill from anyone for her.

The queen's enmity grew every day that Elizabeth walked through the court with her head high, and her nose in the air, every time she turned away from the statue of Our Lady in the chapel, every time she left off her rosary and wore instead a miniature prayer book on a chain at her waist. Everyone knew that the prayer book contained her brother's dying prayer: 'Oh my lord God, defend this realm from Papistry and maintain thy true religion'. To wear this, in preference to the coral rosary that the queen had given her, was more than a public act of defiance, it was a living tableau of disobedience.

To Elizabeth, it was perhaps little more than a showy rebellion; but to our queen it was an insult that went straight to her heart. When Elizabeth rode out dressed in rich colours and smiling and waving, people would cheer her and doff their hats for her; when she stayed home in plain black and white people came to Whitehall Palace to see her dine at the queen's table and remark on her fragile beauty and the plain Protestant piety of her dress.

The queen could see that although Elizabeth never openly defied her, she continually gave the gossip mongers material to take outside the court and to spread among those who kept to their Protestant ways:

'The Protestant princess was pale today, and did not touch the stoop of holy water.'

'The Protestant princess begged to be excused from evening Mass because she was unwell again.'

'The Protestant princess, all but prisoner in the Papist court, is keeping to her faith as best as she can, and biding her time in the very jaws of the Antichrist.'

'The Protestant princess is a very martyr to her faith and her plain-faced sister is as dogged as a pack of bear-baiters, hounding the young woman's pure conscience.'

The queen, resplendent in rich gowns and delighting in her mother's jewels, looked tawdry beside the blaze of Elizabeth's hair, the martyr whiteness of her pallor and the extreme modesty of her black dress. However the queen dressed, whatever she wore, Elizabeth, the Protestant princess, gleamed with the radiance of a girl on the edge of womanhood.

The queen beside her, old enough to be her mother, looked weary, and overwhelmed by the task she had inherited.

So I could not simply go to Elizabeth's rooms and ask to see her. I might as well have announced myself to the ambassador from Spain who watched Elizabeth's every step, and reported everything to the queen. But one day, as I was walking behind her in the gallery, she stumbled for a moment. I went to help her, and she took my arm.

'I have broken the heel on my shoe, I must send it to the cobbler,' she said.

'Let me help you to your rooms,' I offered, and added in a whisper, 'I have a message for you, from Lord Robert Dudley.'

She did not even flicker a sideways glance at me, and in that absolute control I saw at once that she was a consummate plotter and that the queen was right to fear her.

'I can receive no messages without my sister's blessing,' Elizabeth said sweetly. 'But I would be very glad if you would help me to my chamber, I wrenched my foot when the heel broke.'

She bent down and took off her shoe. I could not help but notice the pretty embroidery on her stocking, but I thought it was not the time to ask her for the pattern. Always, everything she owned, everything she did, fascinated me. I gave her my arm. A courtier passing looked at us both. 'The princess has broken the heel of her shoe,' I explained. He nodded, and went on. He, for one, was not going to trouble himself to help her.

Elizabeth kept her eyes straight ahead, she limped slightly on her stockinged foot and it made her walk slowly. She gave me plenty of time to deliver the message that she had said she could not hear without permission.

'Lord Robert asks you to summon John Dee as your tutor,' I said quietly. 'He said, "without fail".'

Still, she did not look at me.

'Can I tell him you will do so?'

'You can tell him that I will not do anything that would displease my sister the queen,' she said easily. 'But I have long wanted to study with Mr Dee and I was going to ask him to read with me. I am particularly interested in reading the teaching of the early fathers of the Holy Church.'

She shot one veiled glance at me.

'I am trying to learn about the Roman Catholic church,' she said. 'My education has been much neglected until now.'

We were at the door of her rooms. A guard stood to attention as we approached and swung the door open. Elizabeth released me. 'Thank you for your help,' she said coolly, and went inside. As the door shut behind her I saw her bend down and put her shoe back on. The heel was, of course, perfectly sound.

John Dee's prediction that the men of England would rise up to prevent the queen marrying a Spaniard was proved every day in dozens of incidents. There were ballads sung against the marriage, the braver preachers thundered against a match so dangerous to the independence of the country. Crude drawings appeared on every lime-washed wall in the city, chap books were handed out slandering the Spanish prince, abusing the queen for even considering him. It was no help that the Spanish ambassador assured every nobleman at court that his prince had no interest in taking power in England, that the prince had been persuaded to the match by his father, that indeed Prince Philip, a desirable man of under thirty years might well have sought a bride to bring him more pleasure and profit than the Queen of England, eleven years his senior. Any suggestion that he wanted the match was proof of Spanish greed, any hint that he might have looked elsewhere was an insult.

The queen herself nearly collapsed under the weight of conflicting advice, under her great fear that she would lose the love of the people of England without gaining the support of Spain.

'Why did you say my heart would break?' she feverishly demanded of me, one day. 'Was it because you could foresee it would be like this? With all my councillors telling me to refuse the match, and yet all of them telling me to marry and have a child without delay? With all the country dancing at my coronation and then, minutes later, all of them cursing the news of my wedding?'

'No,' I said. 'I could not have foretold this. I think no-one could have foretold such a turn-around in such a little time.'

'I have to guard against them,' she said, more to herself than to me.

'At every turn I have to keep them at my beck and call. The great lords, and every man under them, have to be my loyal servants; but all the time they whisper in corners and set themselves up to judge me.'

She rose from her chair and walked the eight steps to the window, turned and walked back again. I remembered the first time I had seen her at Hunsdon, in the little court where she rarely laughed, where she was little more than a prisoner. Now she was Queen of England and still she was imprisoned by the will of the people, and still she did not laugh.

'And the council are worse than the ladies of my chamber!' she exclaimed. 'They argue ceaselessly in my very presence, there are dozens of them but I cannot get a single sensible word of advice, they all desire something different, and they all – all of them! – lie to me. My spies bring me one set of stories, and the Spanish ambassador tells me others. And all the time I know that they are massing against me. They will pull me down from the throne and push Elizabeth on to it out of sheer madness. They will snatch themselves from the certainty of heaven and throw themselves into hell because they have studied heresy, and now they cannot hear the true word when it is given to them.'

'People like to think for themselves . . .' I suggested.

She rounded on me. 'No, they don't. They like to follow a man who is prepared to think for them. And now they think they have found him. They have found Thomas Wyatt. Oh yes, I know of him. The son of Anne Boleyn's lover, whose side d'you think he is on? They have men like Robert Dudley, waiting on his chance in the Tower, and they have a princess like Elizabeth: a foolish girl, too young to know her own mind, too vain to take care, and too greedy to wait, as I had to wait, as I had to wait honourably, for all those long testing years. I waited in a wilderness, Hannah. But she will not wait at all.'

'You need not fear Robert Dudley,' I said quickly. 'D'you not remember that he declared for you? Against his own father? But who is this Wyatt?'

She walked to the wall and back to the window again. 'He has sworn he will be faithful to me but deny me my husband,' she said. 'As if such a thing could be done! He says he will pull me from the throne, and then put me back again.'

'Does he have many on his side?'

'Half of Kent,' she whispered. 'And that sly devil Edward Courtenay as king in waiting, if I know him, and Elizabeth hoping to be his queen. And there will be money coming from somewhere to pay him for his crime, I don't doubt.'

'Money?'

Her voice was bitter. 'Francs. The enemies of England are always paid in francs.'

'Can't you arrest him?'

'When I find him, I can,' she said. 'He's a traitor ten times over. But I don't know where he is nor when he plans to make his move.' She walked to the window and looked out, as if she would see beyond the garden at the foot of the palace walls, over the silver Thames, cold in the winter sunlight, all the way to Kent and the men who kept their plans hidden.

I was struck by the contrast between our hopes on the road to London and how it was, now that she was queen crowned. 'D'you know, I thought when we rode into London that all your struggles would be over.'

The look she turned to me was haunted, her eyes shadowed with brown, her skin as thick as candle-wax. She looked years older than she had done that day when we had ridden in to cheering crowds at the head of a cheering army. 'I thought so too,' she said. 'I thought that my unhappiness was over. The fear that I felt all through my childhood: the nightmares at night, and the terrible waking every day to find that they were true. I thought that if I was proclaimed queen and crowned queen then I would feel safe. But now it is worse than before. Every day I hear of another plot against me, every day I see someone look askance when I go to Mass, every day I hear someone admire Lady Elizabeth's learning or her dignity or her grace. Every day I know that another man has whispered with the French ambassador, spread a little gossip, told a little lie, suggested that I would throw my kingdom into the lap of Spain; as if I had not spent my life, my whole life, waiting for the throne! As if my mother did not sacrifice herself, refuse any agreement with the king so that she might keep me as the heir! She died without me at her side, without a kind word from him, in a cold damp ruin, far away from her friends, so that I might one day be queen. As though I would throw away her inheritance for a mere fancy for a portrait! Are they mad that they think I might so forget myself?

'There is nothing, *nothing*, more precious to me than this throne. There

150

is nothing more precious to me than these people; and yet they cannot see it and they will not trust me!'

She was shaking, I had never seen her so distressed. 'Your Grace,' I said. 'You must be calm. You have to seem serene, even when you are not.'

'I have to have someone on my side,' she whispered, as if she had not heard me. 'Someone who cares about me, someone who understands the danger I am in. Someone to protect me.'

'Prince Philip of Spain will not . . .' I began but she raised her hand to silence me.

'Hannah, I have nothing else to hope for but him. I hope that he comes to me, despite all the wicked slander against him, despite the danger to us both. Despite the threats that they will kill him the moment he sets foot in this kingdom. I hope to God that he has the courage to come to me and make me his wife and keep me safe. For as God is my witness, I cannot rule this kingdom without him.'

'You said you would be a virgin queen,' I reminded her. 'You said you would live as a nun for your people and have no husband but them and no children but them.'

She turned away from the window, from the view of the cold river and the iron sky. 'I said it,' she concurred. 'But I did not know then what it would be like. I did not know then that being a queen would bring me even more pain than being a princess. I did not know that to be a virgin queen, as I am, means to be forever in danger, forever haunted by the fear of the future, and forever alone. And worse than everything else: forever knowing that nothing I do will last.'

The queen's dark mood lasted till dinner time and she took her seat with her head bowed and her face grim. A deadened silence fell over the great hall, no-one could be merry with the queen under a cloud, and everyone had their own fears. If the queen could not hold her throne, who could be sure of the safety of his house? If she were to be thrown down and Elizabeth to take her place then the men who had just restored their chapels and were paying for Masses to be sung would have to turn their coats again. It was a quiet anxious court, everyone looking around, and then there was a ripple of interest as Will Somers rose up from his seat, straightened his doublet with a foppish flick of his wrists and approached the queen's table. When he knew that all eyes were upon him he dropped elegantly to one knee and flourished a kerchief in a bow.

'What is it, Will?' she asked absently.

'I have come to proposaloh matrimonioh,' Will said, as solemn as a bishop, with a ridiculous pronunciation of the words. The whole court held its breath.

The queen looked up, the glimmer of a smile in her eyes. 'Matrimony? Will?'

'I am a proclaimed bacheloroh,' he said, from the back of the hall there was a suppressed giggle. 'As everybody knowsohs. But I am prepared to overlookoh it, on this occasionoh.'

'What occasion?' The queen's voice trembled with laughter.

'On the occasion of my proposaloh,' he said. 'To Your Grace, of matrimonioh.'

It was dangerous ground, even for Will.

'I am not seeking a husband,' the queen said primly.

'Then I will withdraw,' he said with immense dignity. He rose to his feet and stepped backwards from the throne. The court held its breath for the jest, the queen too. He paused; his timing was that of a musician, a composer of laughter. He turned. 'But don't you go thinkingoh,' he waved a long bony forefinger at her in warning, 'don't you go thinkingoh that you have to throw yourself away on the son of a mere emperororoh. Now you know you could have me, you know.'

The court collapsed into a gale of laughter, even the queen laughed as Will, with his comical gangling gait, went back to his seat and poured himself an extra large bumper of wine. I looked across at him and he raised it to me, one fool to another. He had done exactly what he was supposed to do: to take the most difficult and most painful thing and turn it into a jest. But Will could always do more than that, he could take the sting from it, he could make a jest that hurt no-one, so that even the queen, who knew that she was tearing her country apart over her determination to be married, could smile and eat her dinner and forget the forces massing against her for at least one evening.

I went home to my father leaving a court humming with gossip, walking through a city seething with rebellion. The rumours of a secret army mustering to wage war against the queen were everywhere. Everyone knew of one man or another missing from his home, run off to join the rebels. Lady Elizabeth was said to be ready and willing to marry a good Englishman – Edward Courtenay – and had promised to take the throne as soon as her sister was deposed. The men of Kent would not allow a Spanish prince to conquer and subdue them. England was not some dowry which a princess, a half-Spanish princess, could hand over to Spain. There were good Englishmen that the queen should take if she had a mind to marry. There was handsome young Edward Courtenay with a kinship to the royal line on his own account. There were Protestant princelings all over Europe, there were gentlemen of breeding and education who would make a good king-consort to the queen. Assuredly she must marry, and marry at once, for no woman in the world could rule a household, much less a kingdom, without the guidance of a man; a woman's nature was not fitted to the work, her intelligence could not stretch to the decisions, her courage was not great enough for the difficulties, she had no steadfastness in her nature for the long haul. Of course the queen must marry, and give the kingdom a son and heir. But she should not marry, she should never even have *thought* of marrying a Spanish prince. The very notion was treason to England and she must be mad for love of him, as everyone was saying, even to think of it. And a queen who could set aside common sense for her lust was not fit to rule. Better to overthrow a queen maddened by desire in her old age than suffer a Spanish tyrant.

My father had company in the bookshop. Daniel Carpenter's mother was perched on one of the stools at the counter, her son beside her. I knelt for my father's blessing, and then made a little bow to Mrs Carpenter and to my husband-to-be. The two parents looked at Daniel and I, as prickly as cats on a garden wall, and tried, without success, to hide their worldly-wise amusement at the irritability of a young couple during courtship.

'I waited to see you and hear the news from court,' Mrs Carpenter said. 'And Daniel wanted to see you, of course.'

The glance that Daniel shot at her made it clear that he did not wish her to explain his doings to me.

'Is the queen's marriage to go ahead?' my father asked. He poured me a glass of good Spanish red wine and pulled up a stool for me at the counter of the shop. I noted with wry amusement that my work as fool had made me a personage worthy of respect, with a seat and my own glass of wine.

'Without doubt,' I said. 'The queen is desperate for a helper and a companion, and it is natural she should want a Spanish prince.'

I said nothing about the portrait which she had hung in her privy chamber, on the opposite wall from the prie-dieu, and which she consulted with a glance at every difficult moment, turning her head from a statue of God to a picture of her husband-to-be and back again.

My father glanced at Mrs Carpenter. 'Please God it makes no difference to us,' he said. 'Please God she does not bring in Spanish ways.'

She nodded, but she failed to cross herself as she should have done. Instead she leaned forward and patted my father's hand. 'Forget the past,' she said reassuringly. 'We have lived in England for three generations. Nobody can think that we are anything but good Christians and good Englishmen.'

'I cannot stay if it is to become another Spain,' my father said in a low voice. 'You know, every Sunday, every saint's day, they burned heretics, sometimes hundreds at a time. And those of us who had practised Christianity for years were put on trial alongside those who had hardly pretended to it. And no-one could prove their innocence! Old women who had missed Mass because they were sick, young women who had been seen to look away when they raised the Host, any excuse, any reason, and you could be informed against. And always, always, it was those who had made money, or those who had advanced in the world and made enemies. And with my books and my business and my reputation for scholarship, I knew they would come for me, and I started to prepare. But I did not think they would take my parents, my wife's sister, my wife before me . . .' He broke off. 'I should have thought of it, we should have gone earlier.'

'Papa, we couldn't save her,' I said, comforting him with the same words that he had used to me when I had cried that we should have stayed and died beside her.

'Old times,' Mrs Carpenter said briskly. 'And they won't come here. Not the Holy Inquisition, not in England.'

'Oh yes, they will,' Daniel asserted.

It was as if he had said a foul word. A silence fell at once; his mother and my father both turned to look at him.

'A Spanish prince, a half-Spanish queen, she must be determined to restore the church. How better to do it than to bring in the Inquisition to root out heresy? And Prince Philip has long been an enthusiast for the Inquisition.'

'She's too merciful to do it,' I said. 'She has not even executed Lady Jane, though all her advisors say that she should. Lady Elizabeth drags her feet to Mass and misses it whenever she can and no-one says anything. If the Inquisition were to be called in to judge then Elizabeth would be found guilty a dozen times over. But the queen believes that the truth of Holy Writ will become apparent, of its own accord. She will never burn heretics. She knows what it is like to be afraid for her life. She knows what it is like to be wrongly accused.

'She will marry Philip of Spain but she will not hand over the country to him. She will never be his cipher. She wants to be a good queen, as her mother was. I think she will restore this country to the true faith by gentle means; already, half the country is glad to return to the Mass, the others will follow later.'

'I hope so,' Daniel said. 'But I say again – we should be prepared. I don't want to hear a knock on the door one night and know that we are too late to save ourselves. I won't be taken unawares, I won't go without a fight.'

'Why, where would we go?' I asked. I could feel that old feeling of terror in the pit of my belly, the feeling that nowhere would ever be safe for me, that forever I would be waiting for the noise of feet on the stairs, and smelling smoke on the air.

'First Amsterdam, and then Italy,' he said firmly. 'You and I will marry as soon as we get to Amsterdam and then continue overland. We will travel all together. Your father and my mother and my sisters with us. I can complete my training as a physician in Italy and there are Italian cities that are tolerant of Jews, where we could live openly in our faith. Your father can sell his books, and my sisters could find work. We will live as a family.'

'See how he plans ahead,' Mrs Carpenter said in an approving whisper to my father. He too was smiling at Daniel as if this young man was the answer to every question.

'We are not promised to marry till next year,' I said. 'I'm not ready to marry yet.'

'Oh, not again,' said my father.

'All girls think that,' said Mrs Carpenter.

Daniel said nothing.

I slid down from my stool. 'May we talk privately?' I asked.

'Go into the printing room,' my father recommended Daniel. 'Your mother and I will take a glass of wine out here.'

He poured more wine for her and I caught her amused smile as Daniel and I went into the inside room where the big press stood.

'Mr Dee tells me that I will lose the Sight if I marry,' I said earnestly. 'He believes it is a gift from God, I cannot throw it away.'

'It is guesswork and waking dreams,' Daniel said roundly.

It was so close to my own opinion that I could hardly argue. 'It is beyond our understanding,' I said stoutly. 'Mr Dee wants me to be his scryer. He is an alchemist and he says . . .'

'It sounds like witchcraft. When Prince Philip of Spain comes to England, John Dee will be tried for a witch.'

'He won't. It's holy work. He prays before and after scrying. It's a holy spiritual task.'

'And what have you learned, so far?' he asked sarcastically.

I thought of all the secrets I had known already, the child who would not be a child, the virgin but not queen, the queen but no virgin, and the safety and glory which would come to my lord. 'There are secrets I cannot tell you,' I said, and then I added: 'And that is another reason that I cannot be your wife. There should not be secrets between man and wife.'

He turned away with an exclamation of irritation. 'Don't be clever with me,' he said. 'You have insulted me before my mother and before your father by saying you don't want to marry at all. Don't come in here with me and try to be clever about going back on your word. You are so full of trickery that you will talk yourself out of happiness and into heartbreak.'

'How should I be happy if I have to be a nothing?' I asked. 'I am the favourite of Queen Mary, I am highly paid. I could take bribes and favours to the value of hundreds of pounds. I am trusted by the queen herself. The greatest philosopher in the land thinks I have a gift from God to foretell the future. And you think my happiness lies in walking away from all this to marry an apprentice physician!'

He caught my hands, which were twisting together, and pulled me towards him. His breath was coming as quickly as my own. 'Enough,' he said angrily. 'You have insulted me enough, I think. You need not marry an apprentice physician. You can be Robert Dudley's whore or his tutor's adept. You can think yourself the queen's companion but everyone knows you as the fool. You make yourself less than what I would offer you. You could be the wife of an honourable man who would love you and instead you throw yourself into the gutter for any passerby to pick up.'

'I do not!' I gasped, trying to pull my hands away.

Suddenly he pulled me towards him and wrapped his arms around my waist. His dark head came down, his mouth close to mine. I could smell the pomade in his hair and the heat of the skin of his cheek. I shrank back even as I felt the desire to go forward.

'Do you love another man?' he demanded urgently.

'No,' I lied.

'Do you swear, on all you believe, whatever that is, that you are free to marry me?'

'I am free to marry you,' I said, honestly enough, for God knew as well as I did that no-one else wanted me.

'With honour,' he specified.

I felt my lips part, I could have spat at him in my temper. 'Of course, with honour,' I said. 'Have I not told you that my gift is dependent on my virginity? Have I not said that I will not risk that?' I pulled away from him but his grip on me tightened. Despite myself, my body took in the sense of him: the strength of his arms, the power of his thighs which pressed against me, the scent of him, and for some odd reason, the feeling of absolute safety that he gave me. I had to pull away from him to stop myself from yielding. I realised that I wanted to mould myself around him, put my head on his shoulder, let him hold me against him and know that I was safe – if only I would let him love me, if only I would let myself love him.

'If they bring in the Inquisition, we will have to leave, you know that.'

His grip was as hard as ever, I felt his hips against my belly and had to stop myself rising on my toes to lean against him.

'Yes, I know that,' I said, only half-hearing him, feeling him with every inch of my body.

'If we leave, you will have to come with me as my wife, I will take you and your father to safety under no other condition.'

'Yes.'

'Then we are agreed?'

'If we have to leave England then I will marry you,' I said.

'And in any case we will marry when you are sixteen.'

I nodded, my eyes closed. Then I felt his mouth come down on to mine and I felt his kiss melt every argument away.

He released me and I leaned back against the printing press to steady myself. He smiled as if he knew that I was dizzy with desire. 'As to Lord Robert, it is my request that you serve him no longer,' he said. 'He is a convicted traitor, he is imprisoned, and you endanger yourself and us all by seeking his company.' His look darkened. 'And he is not a man I would trust with my betrothed.'

'He thinks of me as a child and a fool,' I corrected him.

'You are neither,' he said gently. 'And neither am I. You are half in love with him, Hannah, and I won't tolerate it.'

I hesitated, ready to argue, and then I felt the most curious sensation of my life: the desire to tell the truth to someone. I had never before felt the desire to be honest, I had spent all my life enmeshed in lies: a Jew in a Christian country, a girl in boy's clothing, a passionate young woman dressed as a Holy Fool, and now a young woman betrothed to one man and in love with another.

'If I tell you the truth about something, will you help me?' I asked.

'I will give you the best help I can,' he said.

'Daniel, talking with you is like bargaining with a Pharisee.'

'Hannah, talking with you is like catching fish in the Sea of Galilee. What is it you would tell me?'

I would have turned away but he caught me and drew me back close to him. His body pressed against me, I felt his hardness and I suddenly understood – an older girl would have understood long before – that this was the currency of desire. He was my betrothed. He desired me. I desired him. All I had to do was to tell him the truth.

'Daniel, this is the truth. I saw that the king would die, I named the day. I saw that Jane would be crowned queen. I saw that Queen Mary would be queen, and I have seen a glimpse of her future, which is heartbreak, and the future of England, which is unclear to me. John Dee says I have a gift of Sight. He tells me it comes in part from me being a virgin and I want to honour the gift. And I want to marry you. And I desire you. And I cannot help but love Lord Robert. All those things. All at once.' I had my forehead pressed against his chest, I could feel the buttons of his jerkin against my forehead and I had the uncomfortable thought that when I looked up he would see the mark of his buttons printed on my skin and I would look, not desirable, but foolish. Nonetheless I stayed, holding him close, while he considered the rush of truths I had told him. Moments later he eased me back from him and looked into my eyes.

'Is it an honourable love, as a servant to a master?' he asked.

He saw my eyes shift away from his serious gaze and he put his hand under my chin to hold my face up to him. 'Tell me, Hannah. You are to be my wife. I have a right to know. Is it an honourable love?'

I felt my lip quiver and the tears come to my eyes. 'It's all muddled up,' I said weakly. 'I love him for what he is . . .' I was silenced by the impossibility of conveying to Daniel the desirability of Robert Dudley; his looks, his clothes, his wealth, his boots, his horses were all beyond my vocabulary. 'He is . . . wonderful.' I did not dare look into his eyes. 'I love him for what he might become – he will be freed, he will be a great man, a great man, Daniel. He will be the maker of a Prince of England. And tonight he is in the Tower, waiting for the sentence of death, and I think of him, and I think of my mother waiting, like he is waiting, for the morning when they took her out . . .' I lost my voice, I shook my head. 'He is a prisoner as she was. He is on the edge of death, as she was. Of course I love him.'

He held me for a few more seconds and then he coldly put me from him. I could almost feel the icy air of the quiet printing room rush between us. 'This is not your mother. He is not a prisoner of faith,' he said quietly. 'He is not being tried by the Inquisition but by a queen whom you assure me is merciful and wise. There is no reason to love a man who has plotted and intrigued his way to treason. He would have put Lady Jane on the throne and beheaded the mistress that you say you love: Queen Mary. He is not an honourable man.'

I opened my mouth to argue but there was nothing I could say.

'And you are all mixed up with him, with his train, with his treasonous plans, and with your feeling for him. I won't call it love because if I thought for one moment it was anything more than a girl's fancy I would go out now to your father and break our betrothal. But I tell you this. You have to leave the service of Robert Dudley, whatever future you have seen for him. You have to avoid John Dee and you have to surrender your gift. You can serve the queen until you are sixteen but you have to be my betrothed in word and in every act you take. And in eighteen months' time from now, when you are sixteen, we will marry and you will leave court.'

'Eighteen months?' I said, very low.

He took my hand to his mouth and he bit the fat mons veneris at the root of my thumb, where the plumpness of the flesh tells hucksters and fairground fortune-tellers that the woman is ready for love.

'Eighteen months,' he said flatly. 'Or I swear I will take another girl to be my wife and throw you away to whatever future the soothsayer, the traitor, and the queen make up for you.'

It was a cold winter, and not even Christmas brought any joy to the people. Every day brought the queen news of more petty complainings and uprisings in every county in the land. Every incident was small, hardly worth regarding, snowballs were thrown at the Spanish ambassador, a dead cat was slung into the aisle of a church, there were some insulting words scrawled on a wall, a woman prophesied doom in a churchyard – nothing to frighten the priests or the lords of the counties individually; but put together, they were unmistakeable signs of widespread unease.

The queen held Christmas at Whitehall and appointed a Lord of Misrule and demanded a merry court in the old ways, but it was no good. The missing places at the Christmas feast told their own story: Lady Elizabeth did not even visit her sister, but stayed at Ashridge, her house on the great north road, ideally placed to advance on London as soon as someone gave the word. Half a dozen of the queen's council were unaccountably missing; the French ambassador was busier than any good Christian should be at Christmastide. It was clear that there was trouble brewing right up to the very throne, and the queen knew it, we all of us knew it.

She was advised by her Lord Chancellor, Bishop Gardiner, and by the Spanish ambassador that she should move to the Tower and put the country on a war footing, or move right away from London and prepare Windsor Castle for a siege. But the grit I had seen in her in the days when she and I had ridden cross-country with only a stable groom to guide us came to her again, and she swore that she would not run from her palace in the very first Christmas of her reign. She had been England's anointed queen for less than three months, was she to be another queen as Jane? Should she too lock herself and her dwindling court into the Tower, as another more popular princess gathered her army about her and prepared to march on London? Mary swore she would stay in Whitehall from Christmas until Easter and defy the rumours of her own defeat.

'But it's not very merry, is it, Hannah?' she asked me sadly. 'I have waited for this Christmas all my life, and now it seems that people have forgotten how to be happy.'

We were all but alone in her rooms. Jane Dormer was seated in the bay window to catch the last of the grey unhelpful afternoon light on her sewing. One lady was playing at a lute, a mournful wail of a song, and another was laying out embroidery threads and winding them off the skein. It was anything but merry. You would have thought that this was the court of a queen on the brink of death, not one about to marry.

'Next year it will be better,' I said. 'When you are married and Prince Philip is here.'

At the very mention of his name the colour rose up in her pale cheeks. 'Hush,' she said, gleaming. 'I would be wrong to expect it of him. He will have to be often in his other kingdoms. There is no greater empire in the world than the one he will inherit, you know.'

'Yes,' I said, thinking of the fires of the auto-da-fé. 'I know how powerful the Spanish empire is.'

'Of course you do,' she said, recalling my nationality. 'And we must speak Spanish all the time to improve my accent. We'll speak Spanish now.'

Jane Dormer looked up and laughed. 'Ah, we must all speak Spanish soon.'

'He won't impose it,' the queen said quickly, always conscious of spies even here, in her private rooms. 'He wants nothing but what is best for Englishmen.'

'I know that,' Jane said soothingly. 'I was only joking, Your Grace.'

The queen nodded, but the frown did not leave her face. 'I have written to Lady Elizabeth to tell her to return to court,' she said. 'She must come back for the Christmas feast, I should not have allowed her to leave.'

'Well, it's not as if she adds much to the merriment,' Jane remarked comfortably.

'I do not require her presence for the merriment she brings me,' the queen said sharply, 'but for the greater pleasure of knowing where she is.'

'You may have to excuse her, if she is too ill to travel ...' Jane remarked.

'Yes,' said the queen. 'If she is. But, if she is too ill to travel, then why would she move from Ashridge to Donnington Castle? Why would a sick girl, too ill to come to London where she might be cared for, instead plan a journey to a castle ideally placed for siege, at the very heart of England?'

There was a diplomatic silence.

'The country will come round to Prince Philip,' Jane Dormer said gently. 'And all this worry will be forgotten.'

Suddenly, there was a sharp knock from the guards outside and the double doors were thrown open. The noise startled me and I was on my feet in an instant, my heart pounding. A messenger stood in the doorway, the Lord Chancellor with him, and the veteran soldier Thomas Howard, Duke of Norfolk beside him, their faces grim.

I fell back, as if I would hide behind her. I had an immediate certainty that they had come for me, they somehow had discovered who I was, and had a warrant for my arrest as a heretic Jew.

Then I saw they were not looking at me. They were looking at the queen and their jaws were set and their eyes cold.

'Oh, no,' I whispered.

She must have thought it was the end for her, as she rose slowly to her feet and looked from one stern face to another. She knew that the duke could turn his coat in a moment, the council could have mustered a swift plot; they had done it before against Jane, they could do it again. But she did not blench, the face she turned to them was as serene as if they had come to invite her to dine. In that moment I loved her for her courage, for her absolute queenly determination never to show fear. 'How now, my lords?' she said pleasantly, her voice steady though they walked into the centre of the room and looked at her with hard eyes. 'I hope you bring me good news for all you seem so severe.'

'Your Grace, it is not good news,' Bishop Gardiner said flatly. 'The rebels are marching against you. My young friend Edward Courtenay has seen the wisdom to confess to me and throw himself on your mercy.'

I saw her eyes flicker away, to one side, as her swift intelligence assessed this information; but her expression did not otherwise alter at all, she was still smiling. 'And Edward tells you?'

'That a plot is in train to march on London, to put you in the Tower and to set the Lady Elizabeth on the throne in your place. We have the names of some of them: Sir William Pickering, Sir Peter Carew in Devon, Sir Thomas Wyatt in Kent, and Sir James Crofts.'

For the first time she looked shaken. 'Peter Carew, who turned out for me in my time of need, in the autumn? Who raised the men of Devon for me?'

'Yes.'

'And Sir James Crofts, my good friend?'

'Yes, Your Grace.'

I kept back behind her. These were the very men that my lord had named to me, that he had asked me to name to John Dee. These were the men who were to make a chemical wedding and to pull down silver and replace it with gold. Now I thought I knew what he meant. I thought I knew which queen was silver and which was gold in his metaphor. And I thought that I had again betrayed the queen while taking her wage, and that it would not be long before someone discovered who had been the catalyst in this plot.

She took a breath to steady herself. 'Any others?'

Bishop Gardiner looked at me. I flinched back from his gaze but it went on past me. He did not even see me, he had to give her the worst news. 'The Duke of Suffolk is not at his house in Sheen, and no-one knows where he has gone.'

I saw Jane Dormer stiffen in the window-seat. If the Duke of Suffolk had disappeared then it could mean only one thing: he was raising his hundreds of tenants and retainers to restore the throne to his daughter

Jane. We were faced with an uprising for Elizabeth and a rebellion for Queen Jane. Those two names could turn out more than half of the country, and all the courage and determination that Queen Mary had shown before could come to nothing now.

'And Lady Elizabeth? Does she know of this? Is she at Ashridge still?'

'Courtenay says that she was on the brink of marriage with him, and the two of them were to take your throne and rule together. Thank God the lad has seen sense and come over to us in time. She knows of everything, she is waiting in readiness. The King of France will support her claim and send a French army to put her on the throne. She may even now be riding to head the rebel army.'

I saw the queen's colour drain from her face. 'Are you sure of this? My Elizabeth would have marched to my execution?'

'Yes,' the duke said flatly. 'She is up to her pretty ears in it.'

'Thank God Courtenay has told us of this now,' the bishop interrupted. 'There may still be time for us to get you safely away.'

'I would have thanked Courtenay more if he had the sense never to engage in it,' my queen countered sharply. 'Your young friend is a fool, my lord, and a weak disloyal fool at that.' She did not wait for his defence. 'So what must we do?'

The duke stepped forward. 'You must go to Framlingham at once, Your Grace. And we will put a warship on standby to take you out of the country to Spain. This is a battle you cannot win. Once you're safe in Spain perhaps you can regroup, perhaps Prince Philip . . .'

I saw her grip on the back of her chair tighten. 'It is a mere six months since I rode into London *from* Framlingham,' she said. 'The people wanted me as queen then.'

'You were their choice in preference to the Duke of Northumberland with Queen Jane as his puppet,' he brutally reminded her. 'Not instead of Elizabeth. The people want the Protestant religion and the Protestant princess. Indeed, they may be prepared to die for it. They won't have you with Prince Philip of Spain as king.'

'I won't leave London,' she said. 'I have waited all my life for my mother's throne, I shan't abandon it now.'

'You have no choice,' he warned her. 'They will be at the gates of the city within days.'

'I will wait till that moment.'

'Your Grace,' Bishop Gardiner said. 'You could withdraw to Windsor at least . . .'

Queen Mary rounded on him. 'Not to Windsor, not to the Tower, not to anywhere but here! I am England's princess and I will stay here in my palace until they tell me that they want me as England's princess no more. Don't speak to me of leaving, my lords, for I will not consider it.'

The bishop retreated from her passion. 'As you wish, Your Grace. But these are troubled times and you are risking your life . . .'

'The times may be troubled, but I am not troubled,' she said fiercely.

'You are gambling with your life as well as your throne,' the duke almost shouted at her.

'I know that!' she exclaimed.

He took a breath. 'Do I have your command to muster the royal guard, and the city's trained bands and lead them out against Wyatt in Kent?' he asked.

'Yes,' she said. 'But there must be no sieges of towns and no sacking of villages.'

'It cannot be done!' he protested. 'In battle, one cannot protect the battle ground.'

'These are your orders,' she insisted icily. 'I will not have a civil war fought over my wheat fields, especially in these starving times. These rebels must be put down like vermin. I won't have innocent people hurt by the hunt.'

For a moment he looked as if he would argue. Then she leaned towards him. 'Trust me in this,' she said persuasively. 'I know. I am a virgin queen, my only children are my people. They have to see that I love them and care for them. I cannot get married on a tide of their innocent blood. This has to be gently done, and firmly done, and done only once. Can you do it for me?'

He shook his head. 'No,' he said. He was too afraid to waste time in flattery. 'Nobody can do it. They are gathering in their hundreds, in their thousands. These people understand only one thing and that is force. They understand gibbets at the cross-roads and heads on pikes. You cannot rule Englishmen and be merciful, Your Grace.'

'You are mistaken,' she said, going head to head with him, as determined as he was. 'I came to this throne by a miracle and God does not

165

change his mind. We will win these men back by the love of God. You have to do it as I command. It has to be done as God would have it, or His miracle cannot take place.'

The duke looked as if he would have argued.

'It is my command,' she said flatly.

He shrugged and bowed. 'As you command then,' he said. 'Whatever the consequences.'

She looked over his head to me, her face quizzical, as if to ask what I thought. I made a little bow, I did not want her to know the sense of immense dread that I felt.

Winter 1554

I came to wish that I had warned her in that moment. The Duke of Norfolk took the apprentice boys from London and the queen's own guard, and marched them down to Kent to meet Wyatt's force in a set-piece battle, which should have routed the men from Kent in a day. But the moment the royal army faced Wyatt's men and saw their honest faces and their determination, our forces, who had sworn to protect the queen, threw their caps in the air and shouted 'We are all Englishmen!'

Not a shot was fired. They embraced each other as brothers and turned against their commander, united against the queen. The duke, desperate to escape with his life, hared back to London, having done nothing but add a trained force to Wyatt's raggle-taggle army who came onward, even more quickly, even more determined than they were before, right up to the gates of London.

The sailors on the warships on the Medway, always a powerful bellwether of opinion, deserted to Wyatt in a body, abandoning the queen's cause, united by their hatred of Spain, and determined to have a Protestant English queen. They took the small arms from the ships, the stores, and their skill as fighting men. I remembered how the arrival of the ships' companies from Yarmouth had changed everything for us at Framlingham. We had known then, when the sailors had joined us to fight on land, that it was a battle by the people, and that the people united could not be defeated. Now they were united once more, but this time against us. When she heard the news from the Medway, I thought that the queen must realise she had lost.

She sat down with a much diminished council in a room filled with the acrid smell of fear.

'Half of them have fled to their homes in the country,' she told Jane Dormer as she looked at the empty seats around the table. 'And they will be writing letters to Elizabeth now, trying to balance their scales, trying to join the winning side.'

She was harassed by advice. Those who had stayed at court were divided between men who said that she should cancel the marriage, and promise to choose a Protestant prince for a husband, and those who were begging her to call in the Spanish to help put down the rebellion with exemplary savagery.

'And thus prove to everyone that I cannot rule alone!' the queen exclaimed.

Thomas Wyatt's army, swelled by recruits from every village on the London road, reached the south bank of the Thames on a wave of enthusiasm, and found London Bridge raised against them, and the guns of the Tower trained on the southern bank ready for them.

'They are not to open fire,' the queen ruled.

'Your Grace, for the love of God . . .'

She shook her head. 'You want me to open fire on Southwark, a village that greeted me so kindly as queen? I will not fire on the people of London.'

'The rebels are encamped within range now. We could open fire and destroy them in one cannonade.'

'They will have to stay there until we can raise an army to drive them away.'

'Your Grace, you have no army. There are no men who will fight for you.'

She was pale but she did not waver for a moment. 'I have no army *yet*,' she emphasised. 'But I will raise one from the good men of London.'

Against her council's advice, and with the enemy force growing stronger every day that they camped, unchallenged, on the south bank of the city, the queen put on her great gown of state and went to the Guildhall to meet the Mayor and the people. Jane Dormer, her other ladies and I went in her train, dressed as grandly as we could and looking confident, though we knew we were proceeding to disaster.

'I don't know why *you* are coming,' one of the old men of the council said pointedly to me. 'There are fools enough in her train already.'

'But I am a holy fool, an innocent fool,' I said pertly. 'And there are few enough innocent here. You would not be one, I reckon.'

'I am a fool to be here at all,' he said sourly.

Of all of the queen's council and certainly of all of her ladies in waiting, only Jane and I had any hopes of getting out of London alive; but Jane and I had seen her at Framlingham, and we knew that this was a queen to back against all odds. We saw the sharpness in her dark eyes and the pride in her carriage. We had seen her put her crown on her small dark head and smile at herself in the looking glass. We had seen a queen, not filled with fear of an unbeatable enemy, but playing for her life as if it were a game of quoits. She was at her very best when she and her God stood against disaster; with an enemy at the very gates of London you would want no other queen.

But despite all this, I was afraid. I had seen men and women put to violent death, I had smelled the smoke from the burnings of heretics. I knew, as few of her ladies knew, what death meant.

'Are you coming with me, Hannah?' she asked pleasantly as she mounted the steps to the Guildhall.

'Oh yes, Your Grace,' I said through cold lips.

They had set up a throne for her in the Guildhall and half of London came from sheer curiosity, crowding to hear the queen argue for her life. When she stood, a small figure under the weighty golden crown, draped in the heavy robes of state, I thought for a moment that she would not be able to convince them to keep their faith with her. She looked too frail, she looked too much like a woman who would indeed be ruled by her husband. She looked like a woman you could not trust.

She opened her mouth to speak and there was no sound. 'Dear God, let her speak.' I thought she had lost her voice from fear itself, and Wyatt might as well march into the hall now and claim the throne for the Lady Elizabeth, for the queen could not defend herself. But then her voice boomed out, as loud as if she were shouting every word, but as clear and sweet as if she were singing like a chorister in the chapel on Christmas Day.

She told them everything, it was as simple as that. She told them the story of her inheritance: that she was a king's daughter and she claimed her father's power, and their fealty. She reminded them that she was a virgin without a child of her own and that she loved the people of the country as only a mother can love her child, that she loved them as a mistress, and that, loving them so intensely, she could not doubt but that they loved her in return.

She was seductive. Our Mary, whom we had seen ill, beleaguered, pitifully alone under virtual house arrest, and only once as a commander; stood before them and she blazed with passion until they caught her fire and were part of it. She swore to them that she was marrying for their benefit, solely to give them an heir, and if they did not think it was the best choice then she would live and die a virgin for them; that she was their queen – it meant nothing to her whether she had a man or not. What was important was the throne, which was hers, and the inheritance, which should come to her son. Nothing else mattered more. Nothing else could ever matter more. She would be guided by them in her marriage, as in everything else. She would rule them as a queen on her own, whether married or not. She was theirs, they were hers, there was nothing that could change it.

Looking around the hall I saw the people begin to smile, and then nod. These were men who wanted to love a queen, who wanted a sense that the world could be held fast, that a woman could hold her desires, that a country could be made safe, that change could be held back. She swore to them that if they would stay true to her, she would be true to them and then she smiled at them, as if it was all a game. I knew that smile and I knew that tone; it was the same as at Framlingham when she had demanded why should she not take an army out against tremendous odds? Why should she not fight for her throne? And now, once again, there were tremendous odds against her: a popular army encamped at Southwark, a popular princess on the move against her, the greatest power in Europe mobilising, and her allies nowhere to be seen. Mary tossed her head under the heavy crown and the rays from the diamonds shot around the room in arrows of light. She smiled at the huge crowd of Londoners as if every one of them adored her – and at that moment they did.

'And now, good subjects, pluck up your hearts and like true men face up against these rebels and fear them not, for I assure you, I fear them nothing at all!'

She was tremendous. They threw their caps in the air, they cheered her as if she were the Virgin Mary herself. And they raced outside and took the news to all those who had not been able to get into the Guildhall, until the whole city was humming with the words of the queen who had sworn that she would be a mother to them, a mistress to them, and that she loved them so much she would marry or not as they pleased, as long as they would love her in return.

London went mad for Mary. The men volunteered to march against the rebels, the women tore up their best linen into bandages and baked bread for the volunteer soldiers to take in their knapsacks. In their hundreds, the men volunteered; in their thousands, and the battle was won; not when Wyatt's army was cornered and defeated just a few days later, but in that single afternoon, by Mary, standing on her own two feet, head held high, blazing with courage and telling them that as a virgin queen she demanded their love for her as she gave them hers.

Once again the queen learned that holding the throne was harder than winning it. She spent the days after the uprising struggling with her conscience, faced with the agonising question of what should be done with the rebels who had come against her and been so dramatically defeated. Clearly, God would protect this Mary on her throne, but God was not to be mocked. Mary must also protect herself.

Every advisor that she consulted was insistent that the realm would never be at peace until the network of trouble-makers was arrested, tried with treason and executed. There could be no more mercy from a tender-hearted queen. Even those who in the past had praised the queen for holding Lady Jane and the Dudley brothers in the Tower for safe-keeping were now urging her to make an end to it, and send them to the block. It did not matter that Jane had not led this rebellion, just as it did not matter that she had not commanded the rebellion that had put her on the throne. Hers was the head that they would crown, and so hers was the head that must be struck off the body.

'She would do the same to you, Your Grace,' they murmured to her.

'She is a girl of sixteen,' the queen replied, her fingers pressed against her aching temples.

'Her father joined the rebels for her cause. The others joined for the Princess Elizabeth. Both young women are your darkest shadows. Both young women were born to be your enemies. Their existence means that your life is in perpetual danger. Both of them must be destroyed.'

The queen took their hard-hearted advice to her prie-dieu. 'Jane is guilty of nothing but her lineage,' the queen whispered, looking up at the statue of the crucified Christ.

She waited, as if hoping for the miracle of a reply.

'And You know, as I do, that Elizabeth is guilty indeed,' she said, very low. 'But how can I send my cousin and my sister to the scaffold?'

Jane Dormer shot me a look and the two of us moved our stools so as to block the view and the hearing of the other ladies in waiting. The queen on her knees should not be overheard. She was consulting the only advisor she truly trusted. She was bringing to the naked stabbed feet of her God the choices she had to make.

The council looked for evidence of Elizabeth's conspiracy with the rebels and they found enough to hang her a dozen times over. She had met with both Thomas Wyatt and with Sir William Pickering, even as the rebellion had been launched. On my own account, I knew that she had taken a message from me with all the ease of a practised conspirator. There was no doubt in my mind, there was no doubt in the queen's mind, that if the rebellion had succeeded – as it would have done but for the folly of Edward Courtenay – that it would now be Queen Elizabeth sitting at the head of the council and wondering whether she should sign the death warrant for her half-sister and her cousin. There was not a doubt in my mind that Queen Elizabeth too would spend hours on her knees. But Elizabeth would sign.

A guard tapped on the door, and looked into the quiet room.

'What is it?' Jane Dormer asked very softly.

'Message for the fool, at the side gate,' the young man said.

I nodded and crept from the room, crossed the great presence chamber where there was a flurry of interest in the small crowd as I opened the door from the queen's private apartments, and came out. They were all petitioners, up from the country: from Wales and from Devon and from Kent, the places which had risen against the queen.

They would be asking for mercy now, mercy from a queen that they would have destroyed. I saw their hopeful faces as the door opened for me, and did not wonder that she spent hours on her knees, trying to discover the will of God. The queen had been merciful to those who had taken the throne from her once; was she now to show mercy again? And what about the next time, and the time after that?

I did not have to show these traitors any courtly politeness. I scowled at them and elbowed my way through. I felt absolute uncompromising hatred of them, that they should have set themselves up to destroy the queen not once, but twice, and now came to court with their caps twisted in their hands and their heads bowed down to ask for the chance to go home and plot against her again.

I pushed past them and down the twisting stone stair to the gate. I found I was hoping that Daniel would be there, and so I was disappointed when I saw a pageboy, a lad I did not know, in homespun, wearing no livery and bearing no badge.

'What d'you want with me?' I asked, instantly alert.

'I bring you these to take to Lord Robert,' he said simply and thrust two books, one a book of prayers, one a testament, into my arms.

'From who?'

He shook his head. 'He wants them,' he said. 'I was told you would be glad to take them to him.' Without waiting for my reply he faded away into the darkness, running half-stooped along the shelter of the wall, leaving me with the two books in my arms.

Before I went back into the palace I turned both books upside down, and checked the endpapers for any hidden messages. There was nothing. I could take them to him if I wished. All I did not know was whether or not I wanted to go.

I chose to go to the Tower in the morning, in broad daylight, as if I had nothing to hide. I showed the guard the books at the door and this time he riffled the pages and looked at the spine as if to make sure that there was nothing hidden. He stared at the print. 'What's this?'

'Greek,' I said. 'And the other is Latin.'

He looked me up and down. 'Show me the inside of your jacket. Turn out your pockets.'

I did as I was bid. 'Are you a lad or a lass then, or something in between?'

'I am the queen's fool,' I said. 'And it would be better for you if you let me pass.'

'God bless her Grace!' he said with sudden enthusiasm. 'And whatever oddities she chooses to amuse herself with!' He led the way to a new building, walking across the green. I followed him, keeping my head turned from the place where they usually built the scaffold.

We went in a handsome double door and up the twisting stone stairs. The guard at the top stood to one side and unlocked the door to let me in.

Lord Robert was standing by the window, breathing the cold air which blew in from the river. He turned his head at the opening of the door and his pleasure at seeing me was obvious. 'Mistress Boy!' he said. 'At last!'

This room was a bigger and better one than he had been in before. It looked out over the dark yard outside, the White Tower glowering against the sky. A big fireplace dominated the room, carved horribly with crests and initials and names of men who had been kept there so long that they had the time to put their names into stone with pocket knives. His own crest was there, carved by his brother and his father, who had worked the stone while waiting for their sentence, and had scratched their names while the scaffold was built outside their window.

The months in prison were starting to leave a mark on him. His skin was pallid, whiter even than winter-pale, he had not been allowed to walk in the garden since the rebellion. His eyes were set deeper in their sockets than when he had been the favoured son of the most powerful man in England. But his linen was clean and his cheeks were shaved and his hair was shiny and silky, and my heart still turned over at the sight of him, even while I hung back and tried to see him for what he was: a traitor and a man condemned to death, waiting for the day of his execution.

He read my face in one quick glance. 'Displeased with me, Mistress Boy?' he demanded. 'Have I offended you?'

I shook my head. 'No, my lord.'

He came closer and though I could smell the clean leather of his boots and the warm perfume of his velvet jacket, I leaned away from him.

He put his hand under my chin and turned my face up. 'You're unhappy,' he remarked. 'What is it? Not the betrothed, surely?'

'No,' I said.

'What then? Missing Spain?'

'No.'

'Unhappy at court?' he guessed. 'Girls catfighting?'

I shook my head.

'You don't want to be here? You didn't want to come?' Then, quickly spotting the little flicker of emotion that went across my face, he said: 'Oho! Faithless! You have been turned, Mistress Boy, as often spies are. You have been turned around and now you are spying on me.'

'No,' I said flatly. 'Never. I would never spy on you.'

I would have moved away but he put his hands on either side of my face and held me so that I could not get away from him, and he could read my eyes as if I were a broken code.

'You have despaired of my cause and despaired of me and become her servant and not mine,' he accused me. 'You love the queen.'

'Nobody could help loving the queen,' I said defensively. 'She is a most beautiful woman. She is the bravest woman I have ever known and she struggles with her faith and with the world every day. She is halfway to being a saint.'

He smiled at that. 'You're such a girl,' he said, laughing at me. 'You're always in love with somebody. And so you prefer this queen to me, your true lord.'

'No,' I said. 'For here I am, doing your bidding. As I was told. Though it was a stranger who came to me and I did not know if I was safe.'

He shrugged at that. 'And tell me, you did not betray me?'

'When?' I demanded, shocked.

'When I asked you to take a message to Lady Elizabeth and to my tutor?'

He could see the horror in my face at the very thought of such a betrayal. 'Good God, no, my lord. I did both errands and I told no-one.'

'Then how did it all go wrong?' He dropped his hands from my face and turned away. He paced to the window and back to the table that he used for a study desk. He turned at the desk and went to the fireplace. I thought this must be a regular path for him, four steps to his table, four steps to the fireplace, four steps back to the window; no further than this for a man who used to ride out on his horse before he broke his fast, and then hunt all day, and dance with the ladies of the court all night.

'My lord, that's easily answered. It was Edward Courtenay who told Bishop Gardiner and the plot was discovered,' I said very quietly. 'The bishop brought the news to the queen.'

He whirled around. 'They let that spineless puppy out of their sight for a moment?'

'The bishop knew that something was being planned. Everyone knew that something was being planned.'

He nodded. 'Tom Wyatt was always indiscreet.'

'He will pay for it. They are questioning him now.'

'To discover who else is in the plot?'

'To get him to name the Princess Elizabeth.'

Lord Robert pushed his fists on either side of the window frame, as if he would stretch the stone wide and fly free. 'They have evidence against her?'

'Enough,' I said acerbically. 'The queen is on her knees right now, praying for guidance. If she decides that it is God's will that she should sacrifice Elizabeth, she has more than enough evidence.'

'And Jane?'

'The queen is fighting to save her. She has asked Jane to be taught the true faith. She is hoping that she will recant and then she can be forgiven.'

He laughed shortly. 'The true faith is it, Mistress Boy?'

I flushed scarlet. 'My lord, it's only how everyone talks at court now.'

'And you with them, my little *conversa*, my *nueva cristiana*?'

'Yes, my lord,' I said steadily, meeting his eyes.

'What a bargain to put before a sixteen-year-old girl,' he said. 'Poor Jane. Her faith or death. Does the queen want to make a martyr of her cousin?'

'She wants to make converts,' I said. 'She wants to save Jane from death and from damnation.'

'And me?' he asked quietly. 'Am I to be saved, or am I a brand for the burning, d'you think?'

I shook my head. 'I don't know, my lord. But if Queen Mary follows the advice she is given, then every man whose loyalty is questionable will be hanged. Already the soldiers who fought in the rebellion are on the scaffolds at every corner.'

'Then I had better read these books quickly,' he said drily. 'Perhaps a light will dawn for me. What d'you think, Mistress Boy? Did a light dawn for you? You and the true faith, as you call it?'

There was a hammering on the door and the guard swung the door open. 'Is the fool to leave?'

'In a moment,' Lord Robert said hastily. 'I haven't paid him yet. Give me a moment.'

The guard glared at us both suspiciously, shut the door and locked it again. There was a brief painful second of silence.

'My lord,' I burst out, 'do not torment me. I am as I always was. I am yours.'

He took a breath. Then he managed to smile. 'Mistress Boy, I am a dead man,' he said simply. 'You should mourn me and then forget me. Thank God you are not the poorer for knowing me. I have placed you as a favourite in the court of the winning side. I have done you a favour, my little lad. I am glad I did it.'

'My lord,' I whispered earnestly. 'You cannot die. Your tutor and I looked in the mirror and saw your fortune. There was no doubt about it, it cannot end here. He said that you are to die safe in your bed, and that you will have a great love, the love of a queen.'

For a moment he frowned as he heard the words, then he gave a little sigh, as a man tempted by false hope. 'A few days ago I would have begged to hear more. But it is too late now. The guard will come. You have to go. Hear this. I release you from your loyalty to me and to my cause. Your work for me is finished. You can earn a good living at court and then marry your young man. You can be the queen's fool in very truth and forget me.'

I stepped a little closer. 'My lord, I will never be able to forget you.'

Lord Robert smiled. 'I thank you for that, and I will be glad of whatever prayers you offer up at the hour of my death. Unlike most of my countrymen, I don't really mind what prayers they are.

And I know that they will come from the heart, and yours is a loving heart.'

'Shall I carry any message from you?' I asked eagerly. 'To Mr Dee? Or to the Lady Elizabeth?'

He shook his head. 'No messages. It is over. I think that I will see all my fellows in heaven very soon. Or not, depending on which of us is right about the nature of God.'

'You can't die,' I cried, anguished.

'I don't think they will leave me much choice,' he said.

I could hardly bear his bitterness. 'Lord Robert,' I whispered. 'Can I do nothing for you? Nothing at all?'

'Yes,' he said. 'See if you can persuade the queen to forgive Jane and Elizabeth. Jane because she is innocent of everything, and Elizabeth because she is a woman who should live. A woman like her was not born to die young. If I thought I could leave you with that commission and you could succeed, I could die in some peace.'

'And for you?' I asked.

He put his hand under my chin again, bent his dark head and kissed me gently on the lips. 'For me, nothing,' he said softly. 'I am a dead man. And that kiss, Mistress Boy, my dear little vassal, that kiss was the last I will ever give you. That was goodbye.'

He turned away from me and faced the window and shouted: 'Guard!' for the man to unlock the door. Then there was nothing for me to do but to leave him, in that cold room, looking out into the darkness, waiting for the news that his scaffold was built, the axeman was waiting, and that his life was over.

I went back to court in a dazed silence and when we went to Mass four times a day I dropped down to my knees and prayed in earnest that the God who had saved Mary should save my Lord Robert too.

My mood of exhausted pessimism suited the queen. We did not live like a victorious court in a victorious city. It was a court hanging on a thread of its own indecision, sick with worry. Every day, after Mass and breakfast, Queen Mary walked by the side of the river, her cold hands dug deep in her muff, her steps hastened by the cold wind blowing her skirts forward. I walked behind her with my black cape wrapped tightly around my shoulders and my face tucked into the collar. I was glad of the thick hose of my fool's livery and glad of my warm jacket. I would not have dressed as a woman in those wintry days for all the Spanish princes in the empire.

I knew she was troubled and so I kept silent. I dogged her footsteps two steps behind her because I knew she liked the comfort of a companion's tread on the frozen gravel at her back. She had spent so many years alone, she had taken so many lonely walks, that she liked to know that someone was keeping vigil with her.

The wind coming off the river was too cold for her to walk for long, even with a thick cape and a fur collar at her neck. She turned on her heel and I nearly bumped into her as I ploughed forward, my head down.

'I beg pardon, Your Grace,' I said, ducking a little bow and stepping out of her way.

'You can walk beside me,' she said.

I fell into step, saying nothing, but waiting for her to speak. She was silent till we came to the small garden door where the guard swung it open before her. Inside a maid was waiting to take her cloak and to offer her a pair of dry shoes. I swung my cloak over my arm and stamped my feet on the rushes to warm them.

'Come with me,' the queen said over her shoulder and led the way up the winding stone stairs to her apartments. I knew why she had chosen the garden stairs. If we had gone through the main building we would have found the hall, the stairs, and the presence chamber filled with petitioners, half of them come to beg for sons or brothers who were due to follow Tom Wyatt to a death sentence. Queen Mary had to pass through crowds of tearstained women every time she went to Mass, every time she went to dine. They held out their hands to her, palms clasped, they called out her name. Endlessly they begged her for mercy, constantly she had to refuse. No wonder that she preferred to walk alone in the garden and slip up the secret stairs.

The stairs emerged into a little lobby room, which led to the queen's private chamber. Jane Dormer was sewing in the window-seat, half a dozen women working alongside her; one of the queen's ladies was reading from the Book of Psalms. I saw the queen run her eye over the room like a school mistress observing an obedient class and give a little nod of pleasure. Philip of Spain, when he finally came, would find a sober and devout court.

'Come, Hannah,' she said, taking a seat at the fireside and gesturing to me to sit on a stool nearby.

I dropped down, folded my knees under my chin and looked up at her.

'I want you to do me a service,' she said abruptly.

'Of course, Your Grace,' I said. I was about to rise to my feet in case she was sending me on an errand but she put her hand on my shoulder.

'I'm not sending you to run a message,' she said. 'I am sending you to look at something for me.'

'Look at something?'

'Look with your gift, with your inner eye.'

I hesitated. 'Your Grace, I will try, but you know it is not at my command.'

'No, but you have seen the future twice with me; once you spoke of my becoming queen and once you spoke to warn me of heartbreak. Now I want you to warn me again.'

'Warn you against what?' My voice was as low as hers. No-one in the room could have heard us over the crackle of the logs in the fireplace.

'Against Elizabeth,' she breathed.

For a moment I said nothing, my gaze on the red ember caverns under the big applewood logs.

'Your Grace, there are wiser heads than mine to advise you,' I said with difficulty. In the brightness of the fire I could almost see the flame of the princess's hair, the dazzle of her confident smile.

'None I trust more. None who comes with your gift.'

I hesitated. 'Is she coming to court?'

Mary shook her head. 'She won't come. She says she is ill. She says she is near death with sickness, a swelling of the belly and of her limbs. She is too ill to get out of bed. Too ill to be moved. It is an old illness of hers, a real one, I believe. But it always comes on at certain times.'

'Certain times?'

'When she is very afraid,' Mary said quietly, 'and when she has been caught out. The first time she was sick like this was when they executed Thomas Seymour. Now I think she fears being accused of another plot. I am sending my doctors to see her, and I want you to go too.'

'Of course.' I did not know what else I could say.

'Sit with her, read to her, be her companion as you have been mine. If she is well enough to come to court, you can travel with her and keep her spirits up on the journey. If she is dying you can comfort her, send for a priest and try to turn her thoughts to her salvation. It is not too late for her to be forgiven by God. Pray with her.'

'Anything else?' My voice was a thread of sound. The queen had to lean forward to hear me.

'Spy on her,' she said flatly. 'Everything she does, everyone she sees, everyone in that household of hers who are all heretics and liars, every one. Every name you hear mentioned, every friend they hold dear. Write to me every day and tell me what you have learned. I have to know if she is plotting against me. I have to have evidence.'

I clasped my hands tight around my knees and felt the tremble in my legs and the quiver in my fingers. 'I cannot be a spy,' I breathed. 'I cannot betray a young woman to her death.'

'You have no other master now,' she reminded me gently. 'Northumberland is dead and Robert Dudley in the Tower. What else can you do but my bidding?'

'I am a fool, not a spy,' I said. 'I am your fool, not your spy.'

'You are my fool and you shall give me the gift of your counsel,' she ordered. 'And I say, go to Elizabeth, serve her as you serve me, and report to me everything you see and hear, but more importantly wait for your gift to speak. I think you will see through her lies and be able to tell me what is in her heart.'

'But if she is sick and dying . . .'

For a moment the hard lines around her mouth and eyes softened. 'If she dies then I will have lost my only sister,' she said bleakly. 'I will have sent inquisitors to her when I should have gone myself and held her in my arms. I don't forget that she was a baby when I first cared for her, I don't forget that she learned to walk holding on to my fingers.' She paused for a moment, smiling at the thought of those fat little hands clutching at her for support, and then she shook her head, as if she would dismiss the love she had for that little red-headed toddler.

'It comes too pat,' she said simply. 'Tom Wyatt is arrested, his army fails, and Elizabeth takes to her bed too ill to write, too ill to reply to me, too ill to come to London. She is as ill as she was when Jane was put on the throne and I wanted her at my side. She is always ill when there is danger. She has been plotting against me and she has suffered nothing but a reverse; not a change of heart. I have to know if she and I can live together as queen and heir, as sisters; or that the worst has come to me and she is my enemy and will stop at nothing till my death.' She turned her dark honest gaze back to me. 'You can tell me that,' she said. 'It is no dishonour to warn me if she hates me and would have me dead. You can bring her to London, or write to me that she is indeed ill. You shall be my eyes and ears at her bedside and God will guide you.'

I surrendered to her conviction. 'When do I leave?'

'Tomorrow at dawn,' the queen said. 'You can visit your father tonight if you wish, you need not come to dinner.'

I rose to my feet and gave her a little bow. She put out her hand to me. 'Hannah,' she said quietly.

'Yes, Your Grace?'

'I wish you could see into her heart and see that she is able to love me, and able to turn to the true faith.'

'I hope I see that too,' I said fervently.

Her mouth was working, holding back tears. 'But if she is faithless, you must tell me, even though it will break my heart.'

'I will.'

'If she can be saved then we could rule together. She could be my sister at my side, the first of my subjects, the girl who is to come after me.'

'Please God.'

'Amen,' she said quietly. 'I miss her. I want her safe with me. Amen.'

I sent a message to tell my father that I would come to visit him, and that I would bring our dinner. As I tapped on the door I saw that he was working late, the illuminated printing room was bright at the rear of the dark shop. The light poured into the shop when he opened the press room door and came out, holding his candle high.

'Hannah! *Mi querida!*'

In a moment he had the bolt shot aside and I tumbled in, setting down my basket of food to hug him and then kneeling before him for his blessing.

'I brought you dinner from the palace,' I said.

He chuckled. 'A treat! I shall eat like a queen.'

'She eats very badly,' I said. 'She's not a good doer at all. You should eat like a councillor if you want to grow fat.'

He pushed the door shut behind me, turned his head and shouted towards the print room. 'Daniel! She is here!'

'Is Daniel here?' I asked nervously.

'He came to help me set some text for a medical book, and when I said that you were coming, he stayed on,' my father said happily.

'There isn't enough for him,' I said ungraciously. I had not forgotten that we had parted on a quarrel.

My father smiled at my petulance but said nothing as the door of the print room opened and Daniel came out, wearing an apron over his black breeches, the front bib stained with black ink, his hands dirty.

'Good evening,' I said, unsmiling.

'Good evening,' he replied.

'Now!' my father said in pleasurable anticipation of his dinner. He drew three high stools up to the counter as Daniel went out to the yard to wash his hands. I unpacked the basket. A venison pasty, a loaf of manchet bread still warm from the oven, a couple of slices of beef carved from the spit and wrapped in muslin, and half a dozen slender roasted chops of lamb. Two bottles of good red wine had gone into my basket from the queen's own cellar. I had brought no vegetables; but from the sweet kitchen I had stolen a bowl of syllabub. We put the syllabub with cream to one side to eat later, and spread the rest of the feast on the table. My father opened the wine as I fetched three tankards from the cupboard under the counter and a couple of horn-handled knives.

'So, what news?' my father asked as we started to eat.

'I am to go to Princess Elizabeth. She is said to be sick. The queen wants me to be her companion.'

Daniel looked up, but said nothing.

'Where is she?' my father asked.

'At her house at Ashridge.'

'Are you going alone?' he asked with concern.

'No. The queen is sending her doctors and a couple of her councillors. I should think we might be as many as ten in the party.'

He nodded. 'I am glad. I don't think the roads are safe. Many of the rebels got away and are heading back for their homes and they are angry men, and armed.'

'I'll be well guarded,' I said. I gnawed on a chop bone and glanced up to see Daniel watching me. I put it to one side, having quite lost my appetite.

'When will you come back?' Daniel asked quietly.

'When Princess Elizabeth is fit to travel,' I said.

'Have you heard from Lord Robert?' my father asked.

'I am released from his service,' I said stiffly. I kept my eyes on the counter top, I did not want either of them to see my pain. 'He is preparing for his death.'

'It must come,' my father said simply. 'Has the queen signed the warrant for the execution of his brother and Lady Jane?'

'Not yet,' I said. 'But it will be any day now.'

He nodded. 'Hard times,' he said. 'And who would have thought that the queen could have raised the city and defeated the rebels?'

I shook my head.

'She can hold this country,' my father said. 'While she can command the hearts of the people as she does, she can be queen. She might even be a great queen.'

'Have you heard from John Dee?' I asked.

'He's travelling,' my father said. 'Buying manuscripts by the barrel. He sends them back to me here for safe-keeping. He's right to stay far from London, his name was mentioned. Most of the rebels have been his friends before now.'

'They were all men of the court,' I contradicted him. 'They knew everyone. Queen Mary herself befriended Edward Courtenay. At one time they said she would marry him.'

'I heard it was him who named the others?' Daniel asked.

I nodded.

'Neither a good subject nor a good friend,' Daniel ruled.

'A man with temptations we cannot imagine,' I said smartly. Then I thought of the Edward Courtenay I knew: a weak mouth and a flushed complexion. A boy pretending to be a man, and not even a pleasant boy. A braggart hoping to leap higher by courting Queen Mary or Lady Elizabeth, or anyone who would help him rise.

'Forgive me,' I said to my betrothed. 'You are right. He is neither a good subject nor a good friend, he's not even much of a boy.'

His smile warmed his face, and warmed me. I took a piece of bread and felt a sense of ease. 'How is your mother?' I asked politely.

'She has been ill in this cold wet weather, but she is well now.'

'And your sisters?'

'They are well. When you come back from Ashridge I should like you to come to my house to meet them.'

I nodded. I could not imagine meeting Daniel's sisters.

'There will soon come a time when we all live together,' he said. 'It would be better if you meet now, so that you can all become accustomed.'

I said nothing. We had not parted as a betrothed couple but clearly Daniel wanted to ignore that quarrel, as he had overlooked others. Our betrothal was still unbroken, then. I smiled at him. I could not imagine living in his house with his mother ordering things as they had always been done and his sisters fluttering around him as the favoured child: the son.

'Do you think they will admire my breeches?' I asked provocatively.

I saw him flush. 'No, not particularly,' he said shortly. He leaned back on the counter and took a sip of wine. He looked towards my father. 'I think I'll finish that page now,' he said. He stepped down from the stool and reached for his printer's apron.

'Shall I bring your syllabub out later?' I asked.

He looked at me, his eyes dark and hard. 'No,' he said. 'I have no taste for things that are sweet and sour at the same time.'

Will Somers was in the stable-yard while they were saddling up the horses for our journey, cracking jokes with the men.

'Will, are you coming with us?' I asked hopefully.

He shook his head. 'Not I! Too cold for me! I'd have thought it no job for you either, Hannah Green.'

I made a face. 'The queen asked it of me. She asked me to look into Elizabeth's heart.'

'Into her heart?' he repeated comically. 'First find it!'

'What else could I do?' I demanded.

'Nothing but obey.'

'And what should I do now?'

'The same.'

I drew a little closer. 'Will, d'you think she was really plotting to throw down the queen and put herself on the throne?'

He smiled his little world-weary smile. 'Fool, there is not a doubt of it. And you a fool even to question it.'

'Then if I say she is pretending to be ill, if I report that she is a liar, I bring her to her death.'

He nodded.

'Will, I cannot do that to a woman such as the princess. It would be like shooting a lark.'

'Then miss your aim,' he said.

'I should lie to the queen and say that the princess is innocent?'

'You have a gift of Sight, don't you?' he demanded.

'I wish I did not.'

'It is time to cultivate the gift of blindness. If you have no opinion, you cannot be asked to account for it. You are an innnocent fool, be more innocent than fool.'

I nodded, a little cheered. One of the men brought my horse out of the stable and Will cupped his hand to throw me up into the saddle.

'Up you go,' he said. 'Higher and higher. Fool and now councillor. It must be a lonely queen indeed who turns to a fool for counsel.'

It took us three days to travel the thirty miles to Ashridge, struggling, heads bowed through a storm of sleet, always freezing cold. The councillors led by Lady Elizabeth's own cousin, Lord William Howard, were afraid of rebels on the roads and we had to go at the marching pace of our guards while the wind whipped down the rutted track which was all there was of a road, and the sun peeped, a pale wintry yellow, through dark clouds.

We reached the house by noon and we were glad to see the curl of smoke from the tall chimneys. We clattered round to the stable-yard and found no grooms to take the horses, no-one ready to serve us. Lady Elizabeth kept only a small staff, one Master of Horse and half a dozen lads, and none of them was ready to greet a train such as ours. We left the soldiers to make themselves as comfortable as they could be, and trooped round to the front door of the house.

The princess's own cousin hammered on the door and tried the handle. It was bolted and barred from the inside. He stepped back and looked around for the captain of the guard. It was at that moment that I realised his orders were very different from mine. I was here to look into her heart, to restore her to the affection of her sister. He was here to bring her to London, alive or dead.

'Knock again,' he said grimly. 'And then break it down.'

At once the door yielded, swung open to our knock by an unenthusiastic pair of menservants who looked anxiously at the great men, the doctors in their furred coats and the men at arms behind them.

We marched into the great hall like enemies, without invitation. The place was in silence, extra rushes on the floor to muffle the sound of the servants' feet, a strong smell of mint purifying the air. A redoubtable woman, Mrs Kat Ashley, Elizabeth's best servant and protector, was at the head of the hall, her hands clasped together under a solid bosom, her hair scraped back under an imposing hood. She looked the royal train up and down as if we were a pack of pirates.

The councillors delivered their letters of introduction, the physicians theirs. She took them without looking at them.

'I shall tell my lady that you are here but she is too sick to see anyone,' she said flatly. 'I will see that you are served such dinner as we can lay before you; but we have not the rooms to accommodate such a great company as yourselves.'

'We will stay at Hillham Hall, Mrs Ashley,' Sir Thomas Cornwallis said helpfully.

She raised her eyebrow as if she did not think much of his choice and turned to the door at the head of the hall. I fell into step behind her. At once she rounded on me.

'And where d'you think you're going?'

I looked up at her, my face innocent. 'With you, Mrs Ashley. To the Lady Elizabeth.'

'She'll see no-one,' the woman ruled. 'She is too ill.'

'Then let me pray at the foot of her bed,' I said quietly.

'If she is so very ill she will want the fool's prayers,' someone said from the hall. 'That child can see angels.'

Kat Ashley, caught out by her own story, nodded briefly and let me follow her out of the door, through the presence chamber and into Elizabeth's private rooms.

There was a heavy damask curtain over the door to shut out the noise from the presence chamber. There were matching curtains at the window, drawn tight against light and air. Only candles illuminated the room with their flickering light and showed the princess, red hair spread like a haemorrhage on the pillow, her face white.

At once I could see she was ill indeed. Her belly was as swollen as if she were pregnant but her hands as they lay on the embroidered coverlet were swollen too, the fingers fat and thick as if she were a gross old lady and not a girl of twenty. Her lovely face was puffy, even her neck was thick.

'What is the matter with her?' I demanded.

'Dropsy,' Mrs Ashley replied. 'Worse than she has ever had it before. She needs rest and peace.'

'My lady,' I breathed.

She raised her head and peered at me from under swollen eyelids. 'Who?'

'The queen's fool,' I said. 'Hannah.'

She veiled her eyes. 'A message?' she asked, her voice a thread.

'No,' I said quickly. 'I am come to you from Queen Mary. She has sent me to be your companion.'

'I thank her,' she said, her voice a whisper. 'You can tell her that I am sick indeed and need to be alone.'

'She has sent doctors to make you better,' I said. 'They are waiting to see you.'

'I am too sick to travel,' Elizabeth said, speaking strongly for the first time.

I bit my lip to hide my smile. She was ill, no-one could manifest a swelling of the very knuckles of their fingers in order to escape a charge of treason. But she would play her illness as the trump card it was.

'She has sent her councillors to accompany you,' I warned her.

'Who?'

'Your cousin, Lord William Howard, among others.'

I saw her swollen lips twist in a bitter smile. 'She must be very determined against me if she sends my own kin to arrest me,' she remarked.

'May I be your companion during your illness?' I suggested.

She turned her head away. 'I am too tired,' she said. 'You can come back when I am better.'

I rose from my kneeling position by the bed and stepped backwards. Kat Ashley jerked her head towards the door to send me from the room.

'And you can tell those who have come to take her that she is near death!' she said bluntly. 'You can't threaten her with the scaffold, she is slipping away all on her own!' A half-sob escaped her and I saw that she was drawn as tight as a lute string with anxiety for the princess.

'No-one is threatening her,' I said.

She gave a little snort of disbelief. 'They have come to take her, haven't they?'

'Yes,' I said unwillingly. 'But they have no warrant, she is not under arrest.'

'Then she shall not leave,' she said angrily.

'I'll tell them she is too ill to travel,' I said. 'But the physicians will want to see her, whatever I say.'

She made a little irritable puffing noise and stepped closer to the bed to straighten the quilt. I glimpsed a quick bright glance from beneath Elizabeth's swollen eyelids, as I bowed again and let myself out of the room.

Then we waited. Good God, how we waited. She was the absolute mistress of delay. When the physicians said she was well enough to leave she could not choose the gowns she would bring, then her ladies could not pack them in time for us to set off before dusk. Then everything had to be unpacked again since we were staying another day, and then Elizabeth was so exhausted she could see no-one at all the next day, and the merry dance of Elizabeth's waiting began again.

During one of these mornings, when the big trunks were being laboriously loaded into the wagons, I went to the Lady Elizabeth to see if I could assist her. She was lying on a day bed, in an attitude of total exhaustion.

'It is all packed,' she said. 'And I am so tired I do not know I can begin the journey.'

The swelling of her body had reduced but she was clearly still unwell. She would have looked better if she had not powdered her cheeks with rice powder and, I swear, darkened the shadows under her eyes. She looked like a sick woman enacting the part of a sick woman.

'The queen is determined that you shall go to London,' I warned her. 'Her litter arrived for you yesterday, you can travel lying down if you will.'

She bit her lip. 'Do you know if she will accuse me when we get there?' she asked, her voice very low. 'I am innocent of plotting against her, but there are many who would speak against me, slanderers and liars.'

'She loves you,' I reassured her. 'I think she would take you back into her favour and into her heart even now, if you would just accept her faith.'

Elizabeth looked into my eyes, that straight honest Tudor look, like her father, like her sister. 'Are you telling me the truth?' she asked. 'Are you a holy fool or a trickster, Hannah Green?'

'I am neither,' I said, meeting her gaze. 'I was begged for a fool by Robert Dudley, against my wishes. I never wanted to be a fool. I have a gift of Sight which comes to me unbidden, and sometimes shows me things that I cannot even understand. And most of the time it doesn't come at all.'

'You saw an angel behind Robert Dudley,' she reminded me.

I smiled. 'I did.'

'What was it like?'

I giggled, I couldn't help it. 'Lady Elizabeth, I was so taken with Lord Robert that I hardly noticed the angel.'

She sat up, quite forgetting her pose of illness, and laughed with me. 'He is very . . . he is so . . . he is indeed a man you look at.'

'And I only realised it was an angel afterwards,' I said to excuse myself. 'At the time I was just overwhelmed by the three of them, Mr Dee, Lord Robert, and the third.'

'And do your visions come to pass?' she asked keenly. 'You scried for Mr Dee, didn't you?'

I hesitated with a sense of the ground opening into a chasm under my feet. 'Who says so?' I asked cautiously.

She smiled at me, a flash of small white teeth as if she were a bright fox. 'Never mind what I know. I am asking what you know.'

'Some things that I see have come to pass,' I said, honestly enough. 'But sometimes the very things I need to know, the most important things in the world, I cannot tell. Then it is a useless gift. If it had warned me – just once –'

'What warning?' she asked.

'The death of my mother,' I said. I would have bitten back the words as soon as they were spoken. I did not want to tell my past to this sharp-minded princess.

I glanced at her face but she was looking at me with intense sympathy. 'I did not know,' she said gently. 'Did she die in Spain? You came from Spain, did you not?'

'In Spain,' I said. 'Of the plague.' I felt a sharp twist of pain in my belly at lying about my mother, but I did not dare to think of the fires of the Inquisition with this young woman watching me. It was as if she could have seen the flicker of their reflected flames in my eyes.

'I am sorry,' she said, very low. 'It is hard for a young woman to grow up without a mother.'

I knew she was thinking of herself for a moment, and of the mother who had died on the scaffold with the names of witch, adulteress and whore. She put away the thought. 'But what made you come to England?'

'We have kin here. And my father had arranged a marriage for me. We wanted to start again.'

She smiled at my breeches. 'Does your betrothed know that he will be getting a girl who is half-boy?'

I made a little pout. 'He does not like me at court, he does not like me in livery, and he does not like me in breeches.'

'But do you like him?'

'Well enough as a cousin. Not enough for a husband.'

'And do you have any choice in the matter?'

'Not much,' I said shortly.

She nodded. 'It's always the same for all women,' she said, a hint of resentment in her voice. 'The only people who can choose their lives are those in breeches. You do right to wear them.'

'I'll have to put them aside soon,' I said. 'I was allowed to wear them when I was little more than a child but I . . .' I checked myself. I did not want to confide in her. She had a gift, this princess, the Tudor gift, of opening confidences.

'When I was your age, I thought I would never know how to be a young woman,' she said, echoing my thought. 'All I wanted to do was to be a scholar, I could see how to do that. I had a wonderful tutor and he taught me Latin and Greek and all the spoken languages too. I wanted to please my father so much, I thought he would be proud of me if I could be as clever as Edward. I used to write to him in Greek – can you imagine? The greatest dread of my life was that I would be married and sent away from England. The greatest hope of my life was that I might be a great and learned lady and be allowed to stay at court. When my father died I thought I would be always at court: my brother's favourite sister, and aunt to his many children, and together we would see my father's work complete.'

She shook her head. 'Indeed, I should not want your gift of Sight,' she said. 'If I had known that I would come to this, under the shadow of my sister's displeasure, and my beloved brother dead, and my father's legacy thrown away . . .'

Elizabeth broke off and then turned to me, her dark eyes filled with tears. She stretched out her hand palm upwards, and I could see that she was shaking slightly. 'Can you see my future?' she asked. 'Will Mary greet me as a sister and know that I have done no wrong? Will you tell her that I am innocent in my heart?'

'If she can, she will.' I took her hand, but kept my eyes on the pale face which had so suddenly blanched. She leaned back against the richly embroidered pillows. 'Truly, Princess, the queen would be your friend. I know this. She would be very happy to hear of your innocence.'

She pulled her hand away. 'Even if the Vatican named me a saint, she would not be happy,' she said. 'And I will tell you why. It isn't my absence from court, it isn't even my doubts about her religion. It is the rage that lives between sisters. She will never forgive me for what they did to her mother, and for what they did to her. She will never forgive me for being my father's darling and the baby of the court. She will never forgive me for being the best beloved daughter. I remember her as a young woman, sitting at the foot of my bed and staring at me as if she would hold the pillow over my face, though she was singing me a lullaby all the time. She has loves and hates, all mixed up. And the last thing she wants at court is a younger sister to show her up.'

I said nothing; it was too shrewd an assessment.

'A younger sister who is prettier than her,' Elizabeth reminded me. 'A younger sister who looks like a pure Tudor and not like a half-caste Spaniard.'

I turned my head. 'Have a care, Princess.'

Elizabeth laughed, a wild little laugh. 'She sent you here to see into my heart. Didn't she? She has great faith in God working his purpose in her life. Telling her what is to be. But her God is very slow in bringing her joy, I think. That long long wait for the throne and then a rebellious kingdom at the end of it. And now a wedding but a bridegroom who is in no hurry to come, but instead stays at home with his mistress. What do you see for her, fool?'

I shook my head. 'Nothing, Your Grace. I cannot see to command. And in any case, I am afraid to look.'

'Mr Dee believes that you could be a great seer, one who might help him unveil the mysteries of the heavens.'

I turned my head, afraid that my face might show the sudden vivid image I had in my mind's eye, the dark mirror, and the words spilling out of my mouth, telling of the two queens who would rule England. A child, but no child, a king but no king, a virgin queen all-forgotten, a queen but no virgin. I did not know who these might be. 'I have not spoken with Mr Dee for many months,' I said cautiously. 'I hardly know him.'

'You once spoke to me without my invitation, you mentioned his name, and others,' she said, her voice very low.

I did not falter for a second. 'I did not, your ladyship. If you remember, the heel of your shoe broke and I helped you to your room.'

She half-closed her eyes and smiled. 'Not a fool at all then, Hannah.'

'I can tell a hawk from a handsaw,' I said shortly.

There was a silence between us, then she sat up and put her feet to the ground. 'Help me up,' she said.

I took her arm and she leaned her weight against me. She staggered slightly as she got to her feet, this was no pretence. She was a sick girl, and I felt her tremble and knew that she was sick with fear. She took a step towards the window and looked out over the cold garden, each leaf dripping a teardrop of ice.

'I dare not go to London,' she said to me in a soft moan. 'Help me, Hannah. I dare not go. Have you heard from Lord Robert? Have you truly nothing for me from John Dee? From any of the others? Is there no-one there who will help me?'

'Lady Elizabeth, I swear to you, it is over. There is no-one who can rescue you, there is no force that can come against your sister. I have not seen Mr Dee for months, and the last time I saw Lord Robert he was in the Tower awaiting execution. He did not expect to live long. He has released me from his service.' I heard the tiny shake in my voice, and I drew a breath and steadied myself. 'His last words to me were to tell me to ask for mercy for Lady Jane.' I did not add that he had asked for mercy for Elizabeth too. She did not look as if she needed reminding that she was as close to the block as her cousin.

She closed her eyes and leaned against the wooden shutters. 'And did you plead for her? Will she be forgiven?'

'The queen is always merciful,' I said.

She looked at me with eyes that were filled with tears. 'I hope so indeed,' Elizabeth said gravely. 'For what about me?'

The next day she could resist no longer. The wagons with her trunks, furniture, and linens had already gone, swaying south down the great north road. The queen's own litter with cushions and rugs of the warmest wool was standing at the door, four white mules harnessed to it, the muleteer at the ready. At the doorway Elizabeth staggered and seemed to faint but the doctors were at her side and they half-lifted and half-dragged her into the litter and bundled her in. She cried out as if in pain but I thought it was fear that was choking her. She was sick with fear. She knew she was going to her trial for treason, and then death.

We travelled slowly. At every halt the princess delayed, asking for a longer rest, complaining of the jolting pace, unable to put a foot to the ground to step down from the litter, and then unable to climb back in again. Her face, the only part of her exposed to the wintry wind, grew pink from the cold and became more swollen. It was no weather for a journey at all, certainly no weather for an invalid, but the queen's councillors would not be delayed. With Elizabeth's own cousin urging them onward, their determination told Elizabeth as clearly as if they had the warrant in their hand that she was destined for death.

No-one would dare to offend the next heir to the throne as they were daring to treat her. No-one would make the next monarch of England climb into a litter on a dark morning and jolt down a rutted frozen road before it was even light. Anyone who treated Elizabeth in this way must know for sure that she would never become queen.

We were three days into a journey that seemed as if it would last forever as the princess rose later every morning, too pained with her aching joints to face the litter until midday. Whenever we stopped on the road to dine she sat late at the table and was reluctant to get back into the litter. By the time we got to the house where we were spending the night the councillors were swearing at their horses with frustration, and stamping to their chambers, kicking the rushes aside.

'What do you think to gain from this delay, Princess?' I asked her one morning when Lord Howard had sent me into her bedchamber for the tenth time to ask when she would be ready to come. 'The queen is not more likely to forgive you if she is kept waiting.'

She was standing stock-still, while one of her ladies slowly wound a scarf around her throat. 'I gain another day,' she said.

'But to do what?'

She smiled at me, though her eyes were dark with fear. 'Ah, Hannah, you have never longed to live as I long to live if you do not know that another day is the most precious thing. I would do anything right now to gain another day, and tomorrow it will be the same. Every day we do not reach London is another day that I am alive. Every morning that I wake, every night that I sleep is a victory for me.'

On the fourth day into the journey a messenger met us on the road, carrying a letter for Lord William Howard. He read it and tucked it into the front of his doublet, his face suddenly grim. Elizabeth waited till he was looking away and then crooked her swollen finger at me. I drew up my horse beside the litter.

'I would give a good deal to know what was in that letter,' she said. 'Go and listen for me. They won't notice you.'

My opportunity came when we stopped to dine. Lord Howard and the other councillors were watching their horses being taken into the stalls. I saw him pull the letter from inside his doublet and I paused beside him to straighten my riding boot.

'Lady Jane is dead,' he announced baldly. 'Executed two days ago. Guilford Dudley before her.'

'And Robert?' I demanded urgently, bobbing up, my voice cutting through the buzz of comment. 'Robert Dudley?'

Much was always forgiven a fool. He nodded at my interest. 'I have no news of him,' he said. 'I should think he was executed alongside his brother.'

I felt the world become blurred around me and I realised I was about to faint. I plumped down on to the cold step and put my head in my hands. 'Lord Robert,' I whispered into my knees. 'My lord.'

It was impossible that he was dead, that bright dark-eyed vitality gone forever. It was impossible to think that the executioner could slice off his head as if he were an ordinary traitor, that his dark eyes and his sweet smile and his easy charm would not save him at the block. Who could bring themselves to kill bonny Robin? Who could sign such a warrant, what headsman could bear to do it? And it was all the more impossible since I had seen the prophecy in his favour. I had heard the words as they had come out of my mouth, I had smelled the candle smoke, I had seen the flickering bob of the flame and the mirrors which ran reflection into glimmer all the way back into Mr Dee's darkness. I had known then that he would be beloved by a queen, that he would die in his bed. I had been shown it, the words had been told to me. If my Lord Robert was dead then not only was the great love of my life dead, but also I had been taught in the hardest way possible that my gift was a chimera and a delusion. Everything was over in one sweep of the axe.

I got to my feet and staggered back against the stone wall.

'Are you sick, fool?' came the cool voice of one of Lord Howard's men. His Lordship glanced over indifferently.

I gulped down the lump that was in my throat. 'May I tell Lady Elizabeth about Lady Jane?' I asked him. 'She will want to know.'

'You can tell her,' he said. 'And I should think she *would* want to know. Everyone will know within a few days. Jane and the Dudleys died on the block before a crowd of hundreds. It's public business.'

'The charge?' I asked, although I knew the answer.

'Treason,' he said flatly. 'Tell her that. Treason. And pretending to the throne.'

Without another word being said, everyone turned to the litter where Lady Elizabeth, her hand outstretched to Mrs Ashley, the other holding to the side of the door, was laboriously descending.

'So die all traitors,' said her cousin, looking at the white-faced girl, his own kin, who had been a friend to every man who now swung on the gibbet. 'So die all traitors.'

'Amen,' said a voice from the back of the crowd.

I waited till she had dined before I found my way to her side. She was dipping her fingers in the basin of water held out to her by the yeoman of the ewery and then holding them for a pageboy to pat dry.

'The letter?' she asked me, without turning her head.

'It'll be public news within the day,' I said. 'I am sorry to tell you, Lady Elizabeth, that your cousin Lady Jane Grey has been executed and her husband . . . and Lord Robert Dudley too.'

The hands she held out to the pageboy were perfectly steady, but I could see her eyes darken. 'She has done it then,' she observed quietly. 'The queen. She has found the courage to execute her own kin, her own cousin, a young woman she knew from childhood.' She looked at me, her hands as steady as the pageboy's who patted at her fingers with the monogrammed linen. 'The queen has found the power of the axe. No-one will be able to sleep. Thank God I am innocent of any wrongdoing.'

I nodded but I hardly heard the words. I was thinking of Lord Robert going out to his death with his dark head held high.

She took her hands from the towel and turned from the table. 'I am very tired,' she said to her cousin. 'Too tired to travel any further today. I have to rest.'

'Lady Elizabeth, we have to go on,' he said.

She shook her head in absolute refusal. 'I cannot,' she said simply. 'I will rest now and we will leave early tomorrow.'

'As long as it is early,' he conceded. 'At dawn, Your Ladyship.'

She gave him a smile that went no further than her lips. 'Of course,' she said.

However she prolonged the journey it had to end, and ten days after we had first set off we arrived at the house of a private gentleman in Highgate, late in the evening.

I was housed with Lady Elizabeth's ladies, and they were up at dawn preparing for her entry into London. As I saw the white linen and petticoats and the virginal white gown being brushed and pressed and carried into her chamber I remembered the day that she greeted her sister into the city of London, wearing the Tudor colours of white and green. Now she was driven snow, all in white, a martyr-bride. When the litter came to the door she was ready, there was no delaying when there was a crowd collecting to see her.

'You'll want the curtains closed,' Lord Howard said gruffly to her.

'Keep them back,' she said at once. 'The people can see me. They can see what condition I am in when I am forced out of my house for a fortnight's journey in all weathers.'

'Ten days,' he said gruffly. 'And could have been done in five.'

She did not deign to answer him, but lay back on her pillows and lifted her hand to indicate that he could go. I heard him swear briefly under his breath and then swing into the saddle of his horse. I pulled my horse up behind the litter and the little cavalcade turned out of the courtyard to the London road and into the city.

London was stinking of death. At every street corner there were gallows with a dreadful burden swinging from the cross-bar. If you peeped up you could see the dead man, face like a gargoyle, lips pulled back, eyes bulging, glaring down at you. When the wind blew, the stink from the corpses swept down the street and the bodies swayed back and forth, their coats flailing around them as if they were still alive and kicking for their life.

Elizabeth kept her eyes straight to the front and did not look left or right, but she sensed the dangling bodies at every corner; half of them were known to her, and all of them had died in a rebellion that they believed she had summoned. She was as pale as her white dress when she first got into the litter, but she was blanched like skimmed milk by the time we had ridden down King's Street.

A few people called out to her: 'God save Your Grace!' and she was recalled to herself and raised a weak hand to them with a piteous face. She looked like a martyr being dragged to her death and, under this avenue of gallows, no-one could doubt her fear. This was Elizabeth's rebellion and forty-five swinging corpses attested to the fact that it had failed. Now Elizabeth would have to face the justice that had executed them. No-one could doubt she would die too.

At Whitehall they rolled the great gates wide for us at the first sight of our cavalcade walking slowly towards the palace. Elizabeth straightened up in the litter and looked towards the great steps of the palace. Queen Mary was not there to greet her sister, and neither was anyone of the court. She arrived to silent disgrace. A single gentleman-server was on the steps and he spoke to Lord Howard, not to the princess, as if they were her gaolers.

Lord Howard came to the litter and put out his hand for her.

'An apartment has been prepared for you,' he said shortly. 'You may choose two attendants to take with you.'

'My ladies must come with me,' she argued instantly. 'I am not well.'

'The orders are two attendants and no more,' he said briefly. 'Choose.'

The coldness of the voice that he had used with her on the journey was now barbed. We were in London, a hundred eyes and ears were on him. Lord Howard would be very certain that no-one would see him show any kindness to his traitor cousin. 'Choose.'

'Mrs Ashley and . . .' Elizabeth looked around and her eye fell on me.

I stepped back, as anxious as any other turncoat not to be linked with this doomed princess. But she knew through me she had a chance to reach the queen. 'Mrs Ashley and Hannah the Fool,' she said.

Lord Howard laughed. 'Three fools together then,' he said under his breath and waved the gentleman to go ahead of the three of us into Elizabeth's apartments.

I did not wait to see Elizabeth settled in her rooms before I sought out my fellow fool Will Somers. He was dozing in the great hall on one of the benches. Someone had draped a cloak over him as he slept, everyone loved Will.

I sat on the bench beside him, wondering if I might wake him.

Without opening his eyes he remarked: 'A pair of fools we must be; parted for weeks and we don't even speak,' and he sat bolt upright and hugged me around the shoulders.

'I thought you were asleep,' I said.

'I was fooling,' he said with dignity. 'I have decided that a sleeping fool is funnier than one who is awake. Especially in this court.'

'Why?' I asked warily.

'Nobody laughs at my jests,' he said. 'So I tried to see if they would laugh at my silence. And since they prefer a silent fool, they will love a sleeping fool. And if I am asleep I will not know if they are laughing or not. So I can comfort myself that I am very amusing. I dream of my wit and then I wake up laughing. It's a witty thought, is it not?'

'Very,' I said.

He turned to me. 'The princess has come, has she?'

I nodded.

'Ill?'

'Very. Truly ill, I think.'

'The queen could offer her an instant cure for all pain. She has become a surgeon, she specialises in amputations.'

'Please God it does not come to that,' I said quickly. 'But Will, tell me – did Robert Dudley make a good death? Was it quick?'

'Still alive,' he said. 'Against all the odds.'

I felt my heart turn over. 'Dear God, they told me he was beheaded.'

'Steady,' Will said. 'Here, put your head between your knees.'

From a long way off I heard his voice ask me:

'Better now? Swoony little maid?'

I straightened up.

'Blushing now,' Will observed. 'Soon be out of breeches with the blood flowing this fast, my little maid.'

'You are sure he is alive? I thought he was dead. They told me he was dead.'

'He should be dead, God knows. He's seen his father and his brother and his poor sister-in-law all taken out and executed underneath his window and yet he's still there,' Will said. 'Perhaps his hair is white with shock but his head's still on his shoulders.'

'He's alive?' I could still hardly believe it. 'You're sure?'

'For the moment.'

'Could I visit him without trouble?'

He laughed. 'The Dudleys always bring trouble,' he said.

'I mean without being suspected.'

He shook his head. 'This is a court gone dark,' he said sadly. 'Nobody can do anything without being suspected. That is why I sleep. I cannot be accused of plotting in my sleep. I have an innocent sleep. I take care not to dream.'

'I just want to see him,' I said. I could not keep the longing from my voice. 'Just to see him and know that he is alive and will stay alive.'

'He is like any man,' Will said fairly. 'Mortal. I can assure you that he is alive today. But I can't tell you for how long. That will have to satisfy you.'

Spring 1554

In the days that followed I went between the queen's apartments and Lady Elizabeth's, but in neither place could I be comfortable. The queen was tight-lipped and determined. She knew that Elizabeth must die for treason, and yet she could not bear to send the girl to the Tower. The council examined the princess and were certain that she had known everything of the plot, that she had masterminded one half of it, that she would have held Ashridge to the north for the rebels while they took London from the south, and that – and this was the worst – that she had summoned help from France for the rebellion. It was thanks to the loyalty of London that the queen was on the throne and the princess under arrest and not the other way around.

Though everyone urged it on her, the queen was reluctant to try Elizabeth with a charge of treason, because of the uproar it would create in the country. She had been dismayed by the numbers who had come out for Elizabeth's rebellion, no-one could predict how many might come out to save her life. A further thirty men were marched home to Kent to be hanged in their own towns and villages but there could be no doubt that there would be hundreds ready to take their place if they thought that the Protestant princess was to be sent to the scaffold.

And worse than that: Queen Mary could not force her own determination. She had hoped that Elizabeth would come to court a penitent, and they could have reconciled. She had hoped that Elizabeth would have learned that Mary was stronger than her, that she could command the city even if Elizabeth could summon half of Kent. But Elizabeth would not confess, would not beg her sister for mercy. Prideful and unyielding, she continued to swear that she was innocent of anything, and Mary could not bear to see her with the lies on her lips. Hour after hour the queen knelt before her prie-dieu, her chin on her hands, her eyes fixed on the crucifix, praying for guidance as to what she should do with her treacherous sister.

'She would have beheaded you in minutes,' Jane Dormer said bluntly when the queen rose from her knees and walked to the fireside, leaning her head against the stone chimney breast and looking into the flames. 'She would have had your head off your shoulders the moment she put the crown on her own. She would not have cared if you were guilty of envy or rebellion. She would have killed you for simply being the heir.'

'She is my sister,' Mary replied. 'I taught her to walk. I held her hands while she stumbled. Am I now to send her to hell?'

Jane Dormer shrugged her disagreement, and picked up her sewing.

'I shall pray for guidance,' the queen said quietly. 'I must find a way to live with Elizabeth.'

The cold days turned warmer in March and the skies grew pale earlier in the mornings and later at night. The court stayed on tiptoe, watching to see what would happen to the princess. She was examined almost daily by the councillors but the queen would not see her face to face. 'I cannot,' she said shortly, and I knew then that she was nerving herself to send Elizabeth to trial, and from there it would be a short walk to the scaffold.

They had enough evidence to hang her three times over but still the queen waited. Just before Easter I was glad to get a letter from my father asking me if I could absent myself from court for a week and come to the shop. He said he was unwell and needed someone to open and close the shutters for him, but I was not to worry, it was just a passing fever and Daniel came every day.

I was a little irritated at the thought of Daniel in constant attendance, but I took the letter to the queen and when she gave me leave, packed a spare pair of breeches and a new clean linen shirt, and made my way to the princess's apartment.

'I have been given leave to go to my home, to my father,' I said as I knelt before her.

There was a clatter from the room above. The royal cousin Lady Margaret Douglas's kitchen had been moved over Elizabeth's bedroom, and they had not been asked to work quietly. Judging from the noise, they had been given extra pans just to bang together. Lady Margaret, a sour-faced Tudor, would have a strong claim to the throne if Elizabeth were to die and she had every reason to drive the princess into irritable exhaustion.

Elizabeth flinched at the crash. 'Going? When will you return?' she asked.

'Within the week, your ladyship.'

She nodded and to my surprise I saw that her mouth was working, as if she were about to cry. 'Do you have to go, Hannah?' she asked in a small voice.

'I do,' I said. 'He is ill, he has a fever. I have to go to him.'

She turned away and brushed her eyes with the back of her hand. 'Good God, I am weak as a child losing a nursemaid!'

'What's the matter?' I asked. I had never seen her so low. I had seen her swollen and sick on her bed and yet even then I had seen her eyes gleam with bright cunning. 'What is it?'

'I am frozen to my very bones with fear,' Elizabeth said. 'I tell you, Hannah, if fear is cold and darkness I am living in the wastes of the Russias. No-one sees me but to interrogate me, no-one touches me but to position me for questioning. No-one smiles at me, they stare as if they would see my heart. My only friends in the whole world have been exiled, imprisoned or beheaded. I am only twenty years old and I am utterly alone. I am only a young woman and yet I have no-one's love and care. No-one comes near me but Kat and you, and now you tell me you are leaving.'

'I have to see my father,' I said. 'But I'll come back as soon as he is well.'

The face she turned to me was not that of the defiant princess, the hated Protestant enemy at this passionately Catholic court. The face she turned to me was that of a young woman, alone with no mother or father, and no friends. A young woman trying to find the courage to face a death that must come soon. 'You will come back to me, Hannah? I have become accustomed to you. And I have no-one about me but you and Kat. I ask it of you as a friend, not a princess. You will come back?'

'Yes,' I promised. I took her hand. She had not exaggerated about feeling cold, she was as icy as if she were dead already. 'I swear I will come back.'

Her clammy fingers returned my grip. 'You will think me a coward, perhaps,' she said. 'But I swear to you, Hannah, that I cannot keep up my courage without a friendly face by me. And I think soon I shall need all the courage I can summon. Come back to me, please. Come back quick.'

My father's shop had the shutters up though it was only early in the afternoon. I quickened my step as I turned down the street and I felt for the first time a fear clutch at my heart at the thought that he was a mortal man, just like Robert Dudley, and that none of us could say how long we would live.

Daniel was putting the bolt on the last shutter and he turned around at the rapid sound of my footsteps.

'Good,' he said shortly. 'Come inside.'

I put my hand on his arm. 'Daniel, is he very ill?'

He covered my hand briefly with his own. 'Come inside.'

I went into the shop. The counter was bare of books, the printing room quiet. I went up the rickety stairs at the rear of the shop and looked towards the little truckle bed in the corner of the room, fearing that I would see him there, too ill to stand.

The bed was heaped with papers and a small pile of clothes. My father was standing before it. I recognised at once the signs of packing for a long journey.

'Oh, no,' I said.

My father turned to me. 'It's time for us to go,' he said. 'Did they give you permission to come away for a week?'

'Yes,' I said. 'But they expect me back. I came running down here in terror that you were ill.'

'That gives us a week,' he said, disregarding my complaint. 'More than enough time to get to France.'

'Not again,' I said flatly. 'You said we were to stay in England.'

'It's not safe,' Daniel insisted, coming into the room behind me. 'The queen's marriage is to go ahead, and Prince Philip of Spain will bring in the Inquisition. Already the gallows are up on the street corners, and there is an informer in every village. We cannot stay here.'

'You said we would be English.' I appealed past him to my father. 'And the gallows are for traitors, not for heretics.'

'She will hang traitors today and heretics tomorrow,' Daniel said firmly. 'She has discovered that the only way to make herself safe on the throne is through blood. She executed her own cousin, she will execute her own sister. Can you doubt that she would hesitate for a moment to hang you?'

I shook my head. 'She is not executing Elizabeth, she is struggling to show her mercy. It is not about Elizabeth's religion, it is about her obedience. And we are obedient subjects. And she is fond of me.'

Daniel took my hand and led me to the bed, which was covered with rolls of manuscript. 'See these? Every one is now a forbidden book,' he said. 'These are your father's fortune, they are your dowry. When your father came to England these were his library, his great collection, now they would serve only as evidence against him. What are we to do with them? Burn them before they burn us?'

'Keep them safe for better times,' I said, incurably the daughter of a librarian.

He shook his head. 'There is nowhere safe for them, and there is nowhere safe for their owner in a country ruled by Spain. We have to go away and take them with us.'

'But where do we have to go now?' I cried. It was the wail of a child who has been too long travelling.

'Venice,' he said shortly. 'France, then Italy, and then Venice. I shall study at Padua, your father will be able to open a print shop in Venice, and we will be safe there. The Italians have a love of learning, the city is filled with scholars. Your father can buy and sell texts again.'

I waited, I knew what was coming next. 'And we will marry,' he said. 'We will marry as soon as we arrive in France.'

'And your mother and your sisters?' I asked. It was living with them that I dreaded as much as marriage.

'They are packing now,' he said.

'When do we leave?'

'In two days' time, at dawn. Palm Sunday.'

'Why so soon?' I gasped.

'Because they have come asking questions already.'

I stared at Daniel, unable to take in the words, but already filled with horror as my worst fears started to take shape. 'They came for my father?'

'They came to my shop looking for John Dee,' my father said quietly. 'They knew that he sent books to Lord Robert. They knew that he had seen the princess. They knew that he had foretold the young king's death, and that is treason. They wanted to see the books that he asked me to store here.'

I was twisting my hands together. 'Books? What books? Are they hidden?'

'I have them safe in the cellar,' he said. 'But they will find them if they take up the floorboards.'

'Why are you storing forbidden books?' I cried out in frustrated anger. 'Why store John Dee's books for him?'

His face was gentle. 'Because all books are forbidden when a country turns to terror. The scaffolds on the corners, the list of things you may not read. These things always go together. John Dee and Lord Robert and even Daniel here and I, even you, my child, are all scholars steeped in knowledge that has suddenly become against the law. To stop us reading forbidden books they will have to burn every manuscript. But to stop us thinking forbidden thoughts they will have to cut off our heads.'

'We are not guilty of treason,' I said stubbornly. 'Lord Robert is still alive, John Dee too. And the charges are treason, not heretical thinking. The queen is merciful . . .'

'And what happens when Elizabeth confesses?' Daniel snapped at me. 'When she names her fellow traitors, not just Thomas Wyatt but Robert Dudley, John Dee, perhaps even you. Have you never taken a message or run an errand for her? Could you swear to it?'

I hesitated. 'She would never confess. She knows the price of confession.'

'She is a woman.' He dismissed her. 'They will frighten her and then promise her forgiveness, and she will confess to anything.'

'You know nothing about her, you know nothing about this!' I flared up. 'I know her. This is not a young woman who is easily frightened, and more than that, her fear does not lead her to tears. If she is afraid she will fight like a bated cat. She is not a girl who gives up and weeps.'

'She is a woman,' he said again. 'And she is enmeshed with Dudley and Dee and Wyatt and the rest of them. I warned you of this. I told you that if you played a double game at court you would bring danger on yourself and danger to us all, and now you have led danger to our door.'

I was breathless with rage. 'What door?' I demanded. 'We have no door. We have the open road, we have the sea between us and France and then we have to cross France like a family of beggars because you, like a coward, are afraid of your own shadow.'

For a moment I thought Daniel would strike me. His hand flew up and then he froze. 'I am sorry you call me a coward before your father's face.' He spat out the words. 'I am sorry you think so lowly of me, your husband-to-be, and the man trying to save you and your father from a traitor's death. But whatever you think of me, I am commanding you to help your father pack and be ready.'

I took a breath, my heart still hammering with rage. 'I am not coming,' I said flatly.

'Daughter!' my father started.

I turned to him. 'You go, Father, if you wish. But I am not running away from a danger that I don't see. I am a favourite at the palace with the queen and I am in no danger from her, and too small a person to attract the attention of the council. I don't believe you are in any danger either. Please don't throw away what we have started here. Please don't make us run away again.'

My father took me into his arms and held my head against his shoulder. I felt myself rest against him and for a moment I longed to be the little girl who went to him for help, who had known that his judgement was always right. 'You said we would stay here,' I whispered. 'You told me this was to be my home.'

'*Querida*, we have to go,' he said quietly. 'I truly believe they will come: first for the rebels, and then for the Protestants, and then for us.'

I lifted my head and I stepped back from him. 'Father, I cannot spend my life running away. I want a home.'

'My daughter, we are the people who have no home.'

There was a silence. 'I don't want to be one of the people without a home,' I said. 'I have a home at court, and friends at court, and my place there. I don't want to go to France and then Italy.'

He paused. 'I was afraid you would say that. I don't want to force you. You are free to take your own decision, my daughter. But it is my wish that you come with me.'

Daniel walked the few paces to the attic window, then he turned and looked at me. 'Hannah Verde, you are my betrothed wife and I order you to come with me.'

I drew myself up and faced him. 'I will not come.'

'Then our betrothal will be ended.'

My father raised a hand in dissent, but he said nothing.

'So be it,' I said. I felt cold.

'It is your wish that our betrothal is ended?' he asked again, as if he could not believe that I would reject him. That hint of arrogance helped me to my decision.

'It is my wish that our betrothal is ended,' I said, my voice as steady as his own. 'I release you from your promise to me, and I ask you to release me.'

'That's easily done,' he flared. 'I release you, Hannah, and I hope that you never have cause to regret this decision.' He turned on his heel and went to the stair. He paused. 'But nonetheless, you will help your father,' he said, still commanding me, I noticed. 'And if you change your mind you may come with us. I would not be vengeful. You can come as his daughter and as a stranger to me.'

'I shan't change my mind,' I said fiercely. 'And I don't need you to tell me to help my father. I am a good daughter to him and I would be a good wife to the right man.'

'And who would the right man be?' Daniel sneered. 'A married man and a convicted traitor?'

'Now, now,' my father said gently. 'You have agreed to part.'

'I am sorry you think so badly of me,' I said icily. 'I shall care for my father and I will help him leave when you bring the wagon.'

Daniel clattered down the stairs and then we heard the shop door bang, and he was gone.

Over the next two days we worked in an almost unbroken silence. I helped my father tie his books together, the manuscripts we rolled into scrolls and packed in barrels, and pushed them behind the press in the printing room. He could take only the core of his library; the rest of the books would have to follow later.

'I wish you would come too,' he said earnestly. 'You're too young to be left here on your own.'

'I'm under the protection of the queen,' I said. 'And hundreds of people at court are the same age as me.'

'You are one of the chosen to bear witness,' he said in a fierce whisper. 'You should be with your people.'

'Chosen to witness?' I demanded bitterly. 'More like chosen never to have a home. Chosen to be always packing our most precious things and leaving the rest behind? Chosen to be always one skip ahead of the fire or the hangman's noose?'

'Better one skip ahead,' my father said wryly.

We worked all through the last night, and when he would not stop to eat, I knew that he was mourning for me as a daughter that he had lost. At dawn I heard the creaking of wheels in the street and I looked out of the downstairs window, and there was the dark shape of the wagon lumbering towards us with Daniel leading a stocky pair of horses.

'Here they are,' I said quietly to my father, and started to heave the boxes of books through the door. The wagon halted beside me and Daniel gently put me aside. 'I'll do that,' he said. He lifted the boxes into the back of the cart, where I saw the glimpse of four pale faces: his mother and his three sisters. 'Hello,' I said awkwardly, and then went back to the shop.

I felt so wretched I could hardly carry the boxes from the rear of the printing shop out to the cart and hand them over to Daniel. My father did nothing. He stood with his forehead leaning against the wall of the house.

'The press,' he said quietly.

'I will see that it is taken down, sheeted and stored safely,' I promised. 'Along with everything else. And when you decide to come back, it will be here for you and we can start again.'

'We won't come back,' Daniel said. 'This country is going to be a Spanish dominion. How can we be safe here? How can you be safe here? Do you think the Inquisition has no memory? Do you think your names are not on their records as heretics and runaways? They will be here in force, there will be courts in every city up and down the land. Do you think you and your father will escape? Newly arrived from Spain? Named Verde? Do you really think you will pass as an English girl called Hannah Green? With your speech, and your looks?'

I put my hands to my face, I nearly put them over my ears.

'Daughter,' my father said.

It was unbearable.

'All right,' I said furiously, in anger and despair. 'Enough! All right! I'll come.'

Daniel said nothing in his triumph, he did not even smile. My father muttered, 'Praise God,' and picked up a box as if he were a twenty-year-old porter and loaded it on the back of the wagon. Within minutes everything was done and I was locking the front door of the shop with the key.

'We'll pay the rent for the next year,' Daniel decided. 'Then we can fetch the rest of the stuff.'

'You'll carry a printing press across England, France and Italy?' I asked nastily.

'If I have to,' he said. 'Yes.'

My father climbed in the back of the wagon and held out his hand for me. I hesitated. The three white faces of Daniel's sisters turned to me, blank with hostility. 'Is she coming now?' one of them asked.

'You can help me with the horses,' Daniel said quickly and I left the tailgate of the wagon and went to the head of the nearest horse.

We led them, slipping a little clumsily on the cobbles of the side street, until we came out to the solid track of Fleet Street and headed towards the city.

'Where are we going?' I asked.

'To the docks,' he said. 'There is a ship waiting on the tide, I have booked our passage to France.'

'I have money for my own passage,' I said.

He threw me a dark smile. 'I already paid for you. I knew you would come.'

I gritted my teeth at his arrogance and tugged on the reins of the big horse and said, 'Come on then!' as if the horse were to blame, and as it felt the even ground of the street under its hooves it started a steady walk and I swung up on to the driving box of the wagon. A few moments later and Daniel joined me.

'I did not mean to taunt you,' he said stiffly. 'I only meant that I knew you would do the right thing. You could not leave your father and your People, and choose to live among strangers forever.'

I shook my head. In the cold morning light with the fog curling off the Thames I could see the great palaces that faced out over the river, their pleasure gardens running down to the water's edge. All of them were places I had enjoyed, a favoured guest in the queen's train. We entered the city, just stirring to start the day, and I saw the smoke from the ovens uncurling from the bakers' chimneys, past the church of St Paul's scented once more with incense, and then we headed along the familiar route towards the Tower.

Daniel knew I was thinking of Robert Dudley as the shadow of the curtain wall fell over our little wagon. I looked up, past the wall to where the great white tower pointed like a raised fist shaken at the sky as if to say that whoever held the Tower, held London; and justice and mercy had nothing to do with it.

'Perhaps he'll slither free,' Daniel said.

I turned my head away. 'I'm leaving, aren't I?' I said inconsequentially. 'That should be enough for you.'

There was a light at one of the windows, a little candle flame. I thought of Robert Dudley's table drawn up to the window and his chair before it. I thought of him sleepless in the night, trying to prepare for his own death, mourning those he had brought to theirs, fearful for those who still waited, like the Princess Elizabeth, watching for the morning when they would be told that this was their last day. I wondered if he had any sense of me, out here in the darkness, driving away from him, longing to be with him, betraying him with every step of the big horses' hooves.

'Stay,' Daniel said quietly, as if I had shifted in my seat. 'There is nothing you can do.'

I subsided and looked dully at the thickness of the walls and the forbidding gated entrances as we skirted all around the breadth of the Tower and came back to the riverside at the last.

One of Daniel's sisters poked her head up from the back of the wagon. 'Are we nearly there?' she asked, her voice sharp with fear.

'Nearly,' Daniel said gently. 'Greet your new sister, Hannah. This is Mary.'

'Hello, Mary,' I said.

She nodded at me and stared as if I were some freak show at Bartholomew's fair. She took in the richness of my cloak and the fine quality of my linen and then her eyes went down to the shine on my boots and my embroidered hose and breeches. Then without another word she turned and dropped down to the body of the wagon and whispered to her sisters and I heard their muffled laughter.

'She's shy,' Daniel said. 'She doesn't mean to be rude.'

I was absolutely certain that she was determined to be rude but there was no point in telling him. Instead I wrapped the cloak a little closer around myself and watched the dark flow of the water as we plodded down the road to the dockside.

I glanced back upriver and then I saw a sight that made me put my hand out to Daniel. 'Stop!'

He did not tighten the rein. 'Why? What is it?'

'Stop, I say!' I said abruptly. 'I have seen something on the river.'

He paused then, the horses turned a little as they were pulled up, and I could see the royal barge, but with no standard flying. Queen Mary's own barge, but not with the queen on board, the drumbeat keeping the rowers in time, a dark figure at the front of the boat, two hooded men, one at the rear, one at the prow, scanning the banks in case of trouble.

'They must have Elizabeth,' I guessed.

'You can't possibly tell,' Daniel said. He shot a glance at me. 'And if they do have her? It's nothing to do with us. They'd be bound to arrest her now that Wyatt . . .'

'If they turn into the Tower then they have her on board and they are taking her to her death,' I said flatly. 'And Lord Robert will die too.'

He went to flick the reins to make the horse move on, but I clamped my hand on his wrist. 'Let me see, damn you,' I spat at him.

He waited for a moment. As we watched the barge turned, struggled against the onrush of the tide and then headed towards the Tower. The dark watergate – a heavy portcullis, which protected the Tower from the river – rolled up; this visit was pre-arranged to be secret and silent. The barge went in, the watergate came down, there was utter silence except the plash of the dark water running by us. It was as if the hushed barge and the two dark watching men at prow and stern had never been.

I slipped down from the wagon and I leaned back against the forewheel, closing my eyes. I could imagine the scene as brightly as if it were noon, Elizabeth arguing and delaying and struggling for every extra minute, all the way from the watergate to the room they would have prepared for her in the Tower. I could see her fighting for every grain of sand in the hour glass, as she always did, as she always would do. I could see her bartering words for every moment. And finally, I could see her in her room, looking down on the green where her mother had her head swept from her body with the sharpest French sword they could find, and I could see her watching them build the scaffold that would be her own death place.

Daniel was by my side. 'I have to go to her,' I said. I opened my eyes as if I had wakened from a dream. 'I have to go. I promised I would go back to her, and now she is near death. I cannot betray a promise to a dying woman.'

'You will be identified with her and with him,' he whispered passionately. 'When they come to hang the servants you will be among them.'

I did not even answer him, something nagged in my mind. 'What was that you said about Wyatt?'

He flushed, I saw that I had caught him out. 'Nothing.'

'You did. When I saw the barge. You said something about Wyatt. What about him?'

'He has been tried and found guilty and sentenced to death,' Daniel said abruptly. 'They have his confession to convict Elizabeth.'

'You knew this? And kept it from me?'

'Yes.'

I drew my cloak around my dark breeches, and went around to the back of the wagon.

'Where are you going?' He put his hand out and grabbed me at the elbow.

'I am getting my bag, I am going to the Tower, I am going to Elizabeth,' I said simply. 'I will stay with her till her death and then I will come to find you.'

'You can't travel to Italy on your own,' he said in sudden rage. 'You cannot defy me like this. You are my betrothed, I have told you what we are doing. See, my sisters, my mother, all obey me. You have to do the same.'

I gritted my teeth and squared up to him as if I were in truth a young man and not a girl in breeches. 'See, I do not obey you,' I said bluntly. 'See, I am not a girl like your sisters. See, even if I were your wife you would not find me biddable. Now take your hand off my arm. I am not a girl to be bullied. I am a royal servant, it is treason to touch me. Let me go!'

My father climbed out of the wagon and Daniel's sister Mary tumbled out after him, her face bright with excitement.

'What is happening?' my father asked.

'The Lady Elizabeth has just been taken to the Tower,' I explained. 'We saw the royal barge go in by the watergate. I am certain she was on board. I promised I would go back to her. I was going to break that promise to come with you. But now she is in the Tower and under sentence of death. I cannot leave her. I am honour bound to go to her and I will go.'

My father turned to Daniel, waiting for his decision.

'It is nothing to do with Daniel,' I went on, trying to keep the rage from my voice. 'There is no need to look to him. This is my decision.'

'We will go to France as we planned,' Daniel said steadily. 'But we will wait at Calais for you. We will wait for Elizabeth's execution, and then you will come to us.'

I hesitated. Calais was an English town, part of the English settlement which was all that remained of the great English kingdom in France. 'Don't you fear the Inquisition in Calais?' I asked. 'If they come here, their writ will run there too.'

'If it comes we can get away to France,' he said. 'And we should have warning. Do you promise you will join us?'

'Yes,' I said, feeling my rage and my fear roll away from me. 'Yes, I can promise I will come when it is over, when Elizabeth is safe or dead I will come to you.'

'I shall come back for you when I hear that she is dead,' he said. 'And then we can fetch the printing press and the rest of the papers at the same time.'

My father took my hands in his. 'You will come, *querida*?' he asked gently. 'You won't fail?'

'I love you, Father,' I whispered. 'Of course I will come to you. But I love Lady Elizabeth too, and she is afraid, and I promised to stay near her.'

'You love her?' he asked, surprised. 'A Protestant princess?'

'She is the bravest cleverest woman I have ever known, she is like a quick-witted lion,' I said. 'I love the queen, no-one could help loving the queen, but the princess is like a flame of fire, no-one could help wanting to be near her. And now she will be afraid, and facing death, and I must be with her.'

'What is she doing now?' one of Daniel's sisters demanded in a delighted hiss from the rear of the wagon. Mary stepped up to the side, and I heard their scandalised whispers.

'Give me my bag and let me go,' I said shortly to Daniel. I stepped up to the rear of the wagon and said, 'Goodbye,' to the lot of them.

Daniel dropped my bag on the cobbles. 'I will come for you,' he reminded me.

'Yes, I know,' I said, with as little warmth in my voice as his.

My father kissed my forehead, and put his hand on my head to bless me, then he turned without another word and got back into the wagon. Daniel waited till he was seated inside, and then he reached for me. I would have pulled away, but he pulled me close and he kissed me fiercely on the mouth, a kiss so full of desire and anger that I flinched away from him and only realised, when he abruptly let me go and swung on to the driver's box, that I wanted that kiss from him, and that I wanted more. But it was too late to say anything, too late to do anything. Daniel flicked the reins and the wagon rolled past me, and I was left in the cold London morning with nothing but a small bag at my feet, a hot bruised mouth, and a promised duty to a traitor.

Those days and then weeks in the Tower with the princess were the worst ones of my life in England, the worst days for Elizabeth too. She went into a sort of trance of unhappiness and fear which nothing could lift. She knew that she was going to die, and in the very same spot where they had beheaded her mother Anne Boleyn, her aunt Jane Rochford, her cousin Catherine Howard, and her cousin Jane Grey. There was a lot of family blood already soaked into that earth, and soon hers would join it. That spot, unmarked by any stone on the green inside the walls of the Tower, overshadowed by the White Tower, was the dying ground for the women of her family. She felt doomed the moment she came close to it, she was certain that her red-rimmed eyes were looking on the place of her death.

The warder of the Tower, first frightened by the drama of her arrival – which Elizabeth had milked to its utmost, seating herself on the watergate steps and refusing to go in out of the rain – became yet more alarmed when she sank into a fear-filled despair, which was even more convincing than her theatrics. They allowed her to walk in the warder's garden, inside the safety of the great walls, but then a little lad peeped through the gate with a posy of flowers and the second day he was there again. By the third day the queen's councillors in their fear and their malice decided that it was not safe to allow her even the relief of that exercise, and she was returned to her rooms. She prowled up and down like the lion that I had named her for, and then she lay on her bed and looked up at the tester for long dull hours, saying nothing.

I thought she was preparing herself for death and I asked if she would want to see a priest. She gave me a look that had no life in it at all, she looked as if she was dying from her eyes downward. All her sparkle was drained from her, all that was left was dread.

'Did they tell you to ask me?' she whispered. 'Is he to give me extreme unction? Is it to be tomorrow?'

'No!' I said hastily, cursing myself for making matters worse. 'No! I just thought you might want to pray for your safe deliverance from here.'

She turned her head to the arrow-slit window, which showed her a glimpse of grey sky and allowed a breath of cold air. 'No,' she said shortly. 'Not with the priest that she would send me. She tortured Jane with the prospect of forgiveness, didn't she?'

'She hoped she would convert,' I said, trying to be fair.

'She offered her life in return for her faith.' Her mouth twisted in contempt. 'What a bargain to make with a young girl. Serve her right that Jane had the courage to refuse.' Her eyes darkened again and she turned her face to the counterpane on the bed. 'I don't have that courage. I don't think like that. I have to live.'

Twice in the time that she was awaiting her trial I went to court, to collect my clothes and to gather news. The first time I briefly saw the queen, who asked me coldly how the prisoner was faring.

'See if you can bring her to a sense of penitence. Only that can save her. Tell her if she confesses I will pardon her and she will escape the block.'

'I will,' I promised. 'But can you forgive her, Your Grace?'

She raised her eyes to me and they were filled with tears. 'Not in my heart,' she said softly. 'But if I can save her from a traitor's death I will. I would not see my father's daughter die as a criminal. But she has to confess.'

On my second visit to court the queen was engaged with the council, but I found Will petting a dog on a bench in the great hall.

'Are you not asleep?' I asked.

'Are you not beheaded?' he replied.

'I had to go with her,' I said shortly. 'She asked for me.'

'Let's hope you're not her last request,' he said drily. 'Happen she'll eat you for her last meal.'

'Is she to die?' I whispered.

'Certainly,' he said. 'Wyatt denied her guilt from his scaffold, but all the evidence convicts her.'

'But he cleared her?' I asked hopefully.

Will laughed. 'He cleared all of them. Turns out it was a rebellion of one and we must all have imagined the army. He even cleared Courtenay, who had already confessed! I don't think Wyatt's voice will make much odds. And we won't hear it again. He won't be repeating himself.'

'Has the queen decided against her?'

'The evidence has decided against her,' he said. 'She can't hang a hundred men and spare their leader. Elizabeth breeds treason like old meat breeds maggots. Not much point swatting flies and leaving the meat rotting in the open.'

'Soon?' I asked, aghast.

'Ask her yourself –' He broke off and nodded to the door to the presence chamber. It swung open and the queen came out. She gave a genuine smile of pleasure to see me and I went forward and dropped to my knee before her.

'Hannah!'

'Your Grace,' I said. 'I am glad to see you again.'

A shadow crossed her face. 'You have come from the Tower?'

'As you commanded,' I said quickly.

She nodded. 'I do not want to know how she does.'

At the cold look in her face I kept my lips together and bowed my head.

She nodded at my obedience. 'You can come with me. We are going riding.'

I fell in among her train. There were two or three new faces, ladies and gentlemen, but for a queen's court they were very soberly dressed, and for young people out on a ride for pleasure, they were very quiet. This had become an uneasy court.

I waited till we were all mounted and riding out of the city to the north, past the beautiful Southampton House and on to the open country, before I brought my horse up alongside the queen.

'Your Grace, may I stay with Elizabeth until . . .' I broke off. 'Until the end?' I concluded.

'Do you love her so much?' she asked bitterly. 'Are you hers now?'

'No,' I said. 'I pity her, as you would if you would only see her.'

'I won't see her,' she said firmly. 'And I dare not pity her. But yes, you can keep her company. You are a good girl, Hannah, and I don't forget that we rode into London together on that first day.' She glanced back. The streets of London were very different now, a gibbet on every corner, with a traitor hanging by the neck, and the carrion crows on every rooftop growing fat on good pickings. The stink in the city was like a plague wind, the smell of English treason. 'I had great hopes then,' she said shortly. 'They will return, I know it.'

'I am sure of it,' I said: empty words.

'When Philip of Spain comes we shall make many changes,' she assured me. 'You will see then, things will be better.'

'He is to come soon?'

'This month.'

I nodded. It was the date of Elizabeth's death sentence. He had sworn he would not come to England while the Protestant princess was alive. She had no more than two dozen days left to live.

'Your Grace,' I said tentatively. 'My old master, Robert Dudley, is still in the Tower.'

'I know it,' Queen Mary said quietly. 'Along with other traitors. I wish to hear of none of them. Those who have been found guilty must die to keep the country safe.'

'I know you will be just, and I know you will be merciful,' I prompted her.

'I certainly will be just,' she repeated. 'But some, Elizabeth among them, have outworn mercy from me. She had better pray that she can receive it from God.'

And she touched her horse's flank with her whip and the court broke into a canter and there was nothing more to be said.

Summer 1554

In the middle of May, the proposed month of the queen's wedding, as the weather grew warmer, still the scaffold was not built for Elizabeth, still Philip of Spain did not come. Then, one day, there was a sudden change at the Tower. A Norfolk squire and his blue-liveried men marched into the Tower to make it their own. Elizabeth went from door to window, in a frenzy of fear, craning her head at the arrow-slit, peering through the keyhole of the door trying to see what was happening. Finally, she sent me out to ask if he had come to oversee her execution, and she asked the guard on the door if the scaffold was being built on the green. They swore it was not, but she sent me to look. She could trust nobody, she could never be at peace until she saw with her own eyes, and she would not be allowed to see.

'Trust me,' I said briefly.

She caught my hands in her own. 'Swear you won't lie to me,' she said. 'I have to know if it is to be today. I have to prepare, I am not ready.' She bit her lip, which was already chapped and sore from a hundred nips. 'I'm only twenty, Hannah, I am not ready to die tomorrow.'

I nodded, and went out. The green was empty, there were no sawn planks awaiting a carpenter. She was safe for another day. I stopped at the watergate and fell into conversation with one of the blue-liveried men. The gossip he told me sent me flying back to the princess.

'You're saved,' I said briefly, coming in through the door of her cramped room. Kat Ashley looked up and made the sign of a cross, the old habit forced out of her by her fear.

Elizabeth, who had been kneeling up at the window, looking out at the circling seagulls, turned around, her face pale, her eyelids red. 'What?'

'You're to be released to Sir Henry Bedingfield,' I said. 'And to go with him to Woodstock Palace.'

There was no leap of hope in her face. 'And what then?'

'House arrest,' I said.

'I am not declared innocent? I am not received at court?'

'You're not on trial and you're not executed,' I pointed out. 'And you're away from the Tower. There are other prisoners still left here, in a worse state.'

'They will bury me at Woodstock,' she said. 'This is a trick to get me away from the city so I can be forgotten. They will poison me when I am out of sight and bury me far from court.'

'If the queen wanted you dead she could have sent for a swordsman,' I said. 'This is your freedom, or at least a part-freedom. I should have thought you would be glad.'

Elizabeth's face was dull. 'D'you know what my mother did to her mother?' she asked in a whisper. 'She sent her to a house in the country, and then to another – a smaller meaner place, and then to another, even worse – until the poor woman was in a damp ruin at the end of the world and she died ill, without a physician, starving, with no money to buy food, and crying for her daughter who was not allowed to come to her. Queen Katherine died in poverty and hardship while her daughter was a servant in my nursery, waiting on me. Don't you think that daughter remembers that? Isn't that what will happen to me? Don't you see this is Mary's revenge? Don't you see the absolute precision of it?'

'You're young,' I said. 'Anything could happen.'

'You know I get ill, you know that I never sleep. You know that I have lived my life on the edge of a knife ever since they accused me of bastardy when I was just two years old. I can't survive neglect. I can't survive poison, I can't survive the assassin's knife in the night. I don't think I can survive loneliness and fear for much longer.'

'But Lady Elizabeth,' I pleaded with her. 'You said to me, every moment you have is a moment you have won. When you leave here, you have won yourself another moment.'

'When I leave here I go to a secret and shameful death,' she said flatly. She turned from the window and went to her bed and knelt before it, putting her face in her hands against the embroidered coverlet. 'If they killed me here at least I should have a name as a martyred princess, I would be remembered as another greater Jane. But they do not even have the courage to send me to the scaffold. They will come at me in secret and I will die in hiding.'

I knew I could not leave the Tower without trying to see Lord Robert. He was in the same quarters, tucked opposite the tower, with his family crest carved by his father and his brother in the mantelpiece. I thought it a melancholy room for him to live in, overlooking the green where they had been executed, his death place.

His guard had been doubled. I was searched before I was allowed to his door, and for the first time I was not left alone with him. My service to Elizabeth had tainted my reputation of loyalty to the queen.

When they swung open the door he was at his desk at the window, the evening sun was streaming hot in the window. He was reading, the pages of the little book tipped to the light. He turned in his seat as the door opened and looked to see who was coming in. When he saw me he smiled, a world-weary smile. I stepped into the room and took in the difference in him. He was heavier, his face puffed up with fatigue and boredom, his skin pale from his months of imprisonment, but his dark eyes were steady and his mouth twisted upward in what had once been his merry smile.

'It is Mistress Boy,' he said. 'I sent you away for your own good, child. What are you doing disobeying me by coming back?'

'I went away,' I said, coming into the room, awkwardly conscious of the guard behind me. 'But the queen commanded me to bear the Lady Elizabeth company, so I have been in the Tower with you all this time, but they did not allow me to come to you.'

223

His dark glance flared with interest. 'And is she well?' he asked, his voice deliberately neutral.

'She has been ill and very anxious,' I said. 'I came to see you now because tomorrow we leave. She is to be released under house arrest to Sir Henry Bedingfield and we are to go to Woodstock Palace.'

Lord Robert rose from his seat and went to the window to look out. Only I could have guessed that his heart was hammering with hope. 'Released,' he said quietly. 'Why would Mary be merciful?'

I shrugged my shoulders. It was against the queen's interest, but it was typical of her nature. 'She has a tenderness for Elizabeth even now,' I volunteered. 'She thinks of her still as her little sister. Not even to please her new husband can she send her sister to the scaffold.'

'Elizabeth was always lucky,' he said.

'And you, my lord?' I could not keep the love from my voice.

He turned and smiled at me. 'I am more settled,' he said. 'Whether I live or die is beyond my command, and I understand that now. But I have been wondering about my future. You told me once that I should die in my bed. D'you still think so?'

I glanced awkwardly at the guard. 'I do,' I said. 'I think that, and more. I think you will be the beloved of a queen.'

He tried to laugh but there was no joy in that little room. 'Do you, Mistress Boy?'

I nodded. 'And the making of a prince who will change the history of the world.'

He frowned. 'Are you sure? What d'you mean?'

The guard cleared his throat. 'Beg pardon,' he said, embarrassed. 'Nothing in code.'

Lord Robert shook his head at the idiocy of the man but curbed his impatience. 'Well,' he said, smiling at me. 'It's good to know that you think I will not follow my father out there.' He nodded at the green beyond the window. 'And I am becoming reconciled to prison life. I have my books, I have my visitors, I am served well enough, I have learned to mourn my father and my brother.' He reached out to the fireplace and touched their carved crest. 'I regret their treason, but I pray that they are at peace.'

There was a tap on the door behind us. 'I can't go yet!' I exclaimed, turning, but it was not another guard who stood there, it was a woman. She was a pretty brown-haired woman with a creamy lovely skin and soft brown eyes. She was dressed richly, my quick survey took in the embroidery on her gown and the slashing of velvet and silk on her sleeves. She held the ribbons of her hat casually in one hand, and a basket of fresh salad leaves in the other. She took in the scene, me with my cheeks flushed and my eyes filled with tears, my master Lord Robert smiling in his chair, and then she stepped across the room and he rose to greet her. She kissed him coolly on both cheeks, and turned to me with her hand tucked into his arm as if to say: 'Who are you?'

'And who is this?' she asked. 'Ah! You must be the queen's fool.'

There was a moment before I replied. I had never before minded my title. But the way she said it gave me pause. I waited for Lord Robert to say that I was a holy fool, that I saw angels in Fleet Street, that I had been Mr Dee's scryer, but he said nothing.

'And you must be Lady Dudley,' I said bluntly, taking the fool's prerogative since I had to take the name.

She nodded. 'You can go,' she said quietly, and turned to her husband.

He stopped her. 'I have not yet finished my business with Hannah Green.' He seated her in his chair at his desk and drew me to the other window, out of earshot.

'Hannah, I cannot take you back into my service and you are already released from your oath to love me, but I would be glad if you would remember me,' he said quietly.

'I always remember you,' I whispered.

'And put my case before the queen.'

'My lord, I do. She will hear nothing of anyone in the Tower but I will try again. I will never stop trying.'

'And if anything changes between the princess and the queen, if you should chance to meet with our friend John Dee, I should be glad to know of everything.'

I smiled at his touch on my hand, at his words that told me that he was alive and yearning for life again.

'I shall write to you,' I promised him. 'I shall tell you everything that I can. I cannot be disloyal to the queen –'

'Nor now to Elizabeth either?' he suggested with a smile.

'She is a wonderful young woman,' I said. 'You could not be in her service and not admire her.'

He laughed. 'Child, you want to love and be loved so much that you are always on all sides at once.'

I shook my head. 'Nobody could blame me. The queen's servants all love her, and Elizabeth . . . She is Elizabeth.'

'I've known her all her life,' he said. 'I taught her to jump with her first pony. She was then a most impressive child, and when she grew older, a little queen in the making.'

'Princess,' I reminded him.

'Princess,' he corrected himself. 'Give her my best of wishes, my love and my loyalty. Tell her that if I could have dined with her I would have done.'

I nodded.

'She is her father's daughter,' he said fondly. 'By God, I pity Henry Bedingfield. Once she has recovered from her fright she will lead him a merry dance. He's not the man to command Elizabeth, not even with the whole council to support him. She will outwit and outman him and he will be driven to distraction.'

'Husband?' Amy rose from her seat at the table.

'My lady?' He let go my hand and stepped back towards her.

'I would be alone with you,' she said simply.

I had a sudden rush of absolute hatred towards her and with it came a momentary vision so dark that I stepped back and hissed, like a cat will suddenly spit at a strange dog.

'What is it?' Lord Robert asked me.

'Nothing,' I said. I shook my head to dispel the picture. It was nothing: nothing I could see clearly, nothing I could tell. It was Amy thrown down, pushed clear away from Robert Dudley, and I knew it was my vision clouded by jealousy and a woman's spite that gave me a picture of her flung away, pushed into a darkness as black as death. 'Nothing,' I said again.

He looked at me quizzically but he did not challenge me. 'You had better go,' he said quietly. 'Do not forget me, Hannah.'

I nodded, and went to the door. The guard swung it open for me, I bowed to Lady Dudley and she gave me a brief dismissive nod. She was too anxious to be alone with her husband to care for being polite to someone who was little more than a servant.

'Good day to you, your ladyship,' I said, just to force her to speak to me.

I could not make her acknowledge me. She had turned her back to me; as far as she was concerned, I had gone.

Elizabeth's gloom and fear did not lift until the litter came to the gateway of the Tower and she went out under the dark portcullis into the city of London. Once we were through the city I, and a handful of ladies, rode behind, and the further we went west the more the march turned into a triumphal procession. At the small villages when they heard the rattle of the horses' bits and the clatter of the hooves, they came running out and skipped and danced along the road, the children crying to be lifted up to see the Protestant princess. At the little town of Windsor, in the very shadow of the queen's castle, at Eton and then Wycombe, the people poured out of their houses to smile and wave at her, and Elizabeth, who could never resist an audience, had her pillows plumped up so that she could sit up to see and be seen.

They brought her gifts of food and wines and soon we were all laden with cakes and sweetmeats and posies of the roadside flowers. They cut boughs of hawthorn and may and cast them down on the road before her litter. They thrust little nosegays of primroses and daisies towards her. Sir Henry, riding up and down the little train, desperately tried to stop people crowding forward, tried to prevent the calls of love and loyalty, but it was like riding against a rising river. The people adored her, and when he sent soldiers ahead into the village to ban them from coming to their doorways, they leaned out of their windows instead, and called out her name. And Elizabeth, her copper hair brushed down over her shoulders, her pale face flushed, turned to left and right and waved her long-fingered hand and looked – as only Elizabeth could – at one and the same time like a martyr being taken to execution and like a princess rejoicing in the love of her people.

The next day, and the next, word of the princess's progress spread ahead of us, and they were ringing the bells of the parish church in the villages as we passed through. There was many a priest whose bells pealed out for the Protestant princess who wondered what his bishop would make of it, but there were too many bell ringers to be resisted, and all that Sir Henry could do was order his soldiers to ride closer to the litter and ensure that at least no-one attempted a rescue.

All this flattery was meat and drink to Elizabeth. Already her swollen fingers and ankles were returning to their normal size, her face blushed rosy, her eyes came alive, and her wit sharpened. At night she dined and slept in houses where she was welcomed as the heir to the throne, and she laughed and let them entertain her royally. In the day she woke early and was happy enough to travel. The sunshine was like wine to her and her skin soon glowed in the light. She had her hair brushed with hundreds of strokes every morning so that it flowed and crackled around her shoulders, and she wore her hat rakishly to one side with a Tudor green ribbon. Every man at arms had a smile from her, everyone who wished her well had a wave in reply. Elizabeth going through an England ablaze with early summer flowers, even on her way to prison, was in her element.

Woodstock turned out to be a crumbling old palace which had been neglected for years. They had fitted up the gatehouse for Elizabeth in a bodged job that still left draughts howling through the windows and underneath the broken floorboards. It was better than the Tower but she was still undoubtedly a prisoner. At first she was allowed access to only the four rooms of the gatehouse; but then, Elizabeth-like, she extended her parole until she could walk in the gardens, and then into the great orchard.

At first she had to request every piece of paper and pen, one at a time, but as time wore on and she made more and more demands of the harassed Sir Henry she obtained more and more liberties. She insisted on writing to the queen, she demanded the right to appeal to the queen's council. As the weather warmed, she demanded the right to walk out beyond the grounds.

She became increasingly confident that she would not be assassinated by Sir Henry, and instead of fearing him she became utterly contemptuous of him. He, poor man, just as my lord had predicted, was worn grey and thin by the peremptory demands of the queen's most disgraced prisoner, the heir to the throne of England.

Then, one day in early summer, a messenger came from London, with a bundle of business for Elizabeth and a letter for me. It was addressed to 'Hannah Green, with Lady Elizabeth at the Tower of London', and it was not a hand that I recognised.

> *Dear Hannah,*
>
> *This is to tell you that your father is safely arrived in Calais. We have rented a house and a shop and he is buying and selling books and papers. My mother is keeping house for him and my sisters are working, one at a milliner's, one for a glover and one as a housekeeper. I am working for a surgeon, which is hard work but he is a skilled man and I am learning much from him.*
>
> *I am sorry that you did not come with us, and I am sorry that I spoke to you in such a way that did not convince you. You find me abrupt and perhaps demanding. You must remember that I have been the head of my family for some time now and I am accustomed to my sisters and my mother doing as they are bid. You have been the indulged daughter of two parents and are used to having your own way. Your later life gave you dangerous experiences of the world and now you are quite without a master. I understand that you will not do as I command, I understand that you do not see why I should command. It is unmaidenly; but it is the truth of you.*
>
> *Let me try to be clear with you. I cannot become a cat's-paw. I cannot do as you desire and set you up as the master of our home. I have to be man and master at my own bed and board and I cannot imagine any other way, and I believe that I should not imagine any other way. God has given me the rule of your sex. It is up to me to apply that rule with compassion and kindness and to protect you from your mistakes and from mine own. But I am*

ordained to be your master. I cannot hand over the mastery of our family; it is my duty and responsibility, it cannot be yours.

Let me try to make you an offer. I will be a good husband to you. You can ask my sisters – I do not have an ill-kept temper, I am not a man of moods. I have never raised my hand to any of them, I am always kind to them. I can find it in me to be kind to you, far kinder than you imagine at the moment, I think. Indeed, I want to be kind to you, Hannah.

To be brief, I regret that I released you from our betrothal and this letter is to ask you to promise yourself to me once more. I wish to marry you, Hannah.

I think about you all of the time, I want to see you, I want to touch you. When I kissed you goodbye I am afraid I was rough with you and you did not want my kiss. I did not mean to repel you. I felt anger and desire, all mixed up at that moment, and had no care what you might be feeling. I hope to God that the kiss did not frighten you. You see, Hannah, I think I am in love with you.

I tell you this because I don't know what else to do with this hot stir of feelings in my heart and in my body. I cannot sleep and I cannot eat. I am doing everything I should do and yet I cannot settle to anything. Forgive me if this offends you, but what am I to do? Surely I should tell you? If we were married we would share this secret in the marriage bed – but I cannot even think about being wedded and bedded with you, it heats my blood even to think of you as my wife.

Please write back to me as soon as you read this and tell me what you want. I would tear this up rather than have you laugh at it. Perhaps it would be better if I did not send it. It can join the other letters that I have written to you but never sent. There are dozens of them. I cannot tell you what I feel. I cannot tell you in a letter what I want. I cannot tell you how much I feel, how much I want you.

I wish to God you would write to me. I wish to God I could make you understand the fever that I am in.

Daniel

A woman ready for love would have replied at once, a girl ready for womanhood would have at least sent some sort of reply. I read it through very carefully, and then I put it at the back of a fire and burned it, as if I would burn my desire to ashes, along with his letter. At least I had the honesty to recognise my desire. I had felt it when he had held me in the shadowy press room, it had blazed up when he had crushed me to him when we parted at the wagon. But I knew that if I replied to him, he would come to fetch me, and then I would be his wife and a woman tamed. This was a man who believed that God had ordained him to be my natural master. A woman who loved him would have to learn obedience, and I was not yet ready to be an obedient wife.

Besides, I had no time to think about Daniel, or about my future. The messenger from London had brought papers for Elizabeth as well as me. When I entered her rooms I found her wound up to breaking pitch at the prospect of her sister's marriage, and her own disinheritance. She was stalking the room like a furious cat. She had received a cold message from the queen's chamberlain that Philip of Spain had left his country and was sailing for his new home of England, that the court would meet him at Winchester – but Elizabeth herself was not invited. And – as if to add insult to Elizabeth's hurt pride – she was to send me to join the queen and the court at once, on receipt of these orders. The fool was valued more than the princess. My service to Elizabeth was to be put aside, I imagined that it would be forgotten as Elizabeth was currently forgotten.

'This is to insult me,' she spat.

'It will not be the queen's doing,' I said, soothingly. 'It will just be the gathering of her court.'

'I am part of her court!'

I said nothing, diplomatically silent about the numbers of times that Elizabeth had refused to join the court, feigning ill health or demanding a delay, because she had her own reasons to stay at her home.

'She does not dare to meet Philip of Spain with me at her side!' she said crudely. 'She knows he will look from the old queen to the young princess and prefer me!'

I did not correct her. No-one would have looked at Elizabeth with desire at the moment, she was bloated with her illness again, and her eyes were raw and red. Only anger was keeping her on her feet.

'He is betrothed to her,' I said quietly. 'It's not a matter of desire.'

'She cannot leave me here to rot my life away! I will die here, Hannah! I have been sick near to death and there is no-one to care for me, she won't send me doctors, she is hoping I will die!'

'I am sure she will not . . .'

'Then why am I not summoned to court?'

I shook my head. The argument was as circular as Elizabeth's furious pace around the room. Suddenly she stopped, put her hand to her heart.

'I am ill,' she said, her voice very low. 'My heart flutters with anxiety and I have been so sick I cannot get out of bed in the morning. Really, Hannah, even when there is no-one watching. I cannot endure this, I cannot go on like this. Every day I think to have the news that she has decided to have me executed. Every morning I wake thinking that the soldiers will come for me. How long can I live like this, d'you think, Hannah? I am a young woman, I am only twenty! I should be looking forward to a feast at court to celebrate my coming of age, I should have presents and gifts. I should have been betrothed by now! How can I be expected to bear such continuous fear? Nobody knows what it is like.'

I nodded. The only one who could have understood was the queen; for she too had once been the heir that everyone hated. But Elizabeth had thrown away the love of the queen and she would have trouble in finding it again.

'Sit down,' I said gently. 'I will fetch you some small ale.'

'I don't want small ale,' she said crossly, though her legs buckled beneath her. 'I want my place at court. I want my freedom.'

'It will come.' I fetched a jug and a cup from the sideboard and poured her a drink. She sipped it and then looked at me.

'It's all right for you,' she said nastily. 'You're not a prisoner. You're not even my servant. You can come and go as you please. She wants you at her side. You will be able to see all your grand friends again when you meet them at Winchester for the wedding feast. No doubt they will have a new doublet and hose for you – the pet hermaphrodite. No doubt you will be in the queen's train.'

'Perhaps.'

'Hannah, you can't leave me,' she said flatly.

'Lady Elizabeth, I have to go, the queen commands me.'

'She said you were to be my companion.'

'And now she says I am to leave.'

'Hannah!' She broke off, near to tears.

Slowly, I knelt at her feet and looked up into her face. Elizabeth was always such a mixture of raging emotion and calculation that I could rarely take her measure. 'My lady?'

'Hannah, I have no-one here but you and Kat and that idiot Sir Henry. I am a young woman, I am at my peak of beauty and wit and I live alone, a prisoner, with no companion but a nursemaid, a fool and an idiot.'

'Then you will hardly miss the fool,' I said drily.

I meant to make her laugh but when she looked at me her eyes were filled with tears. 'I *will* miss the fool,' she said. 'I have no-one to be my friend, I have no-one to talk to. I have no-one to care for me.'

She rose to her feet. 'Walk with me,' she commanded.

We went through the ramshackle palace and through the door which hung, half off its hinges, into the garden, she leaned on me and I felt her weakness. The grass was sprawled over the path, there were nettles thrusting up in all the ditches. Elizabeth and I made our way through the ruin of the garden like two old women, clinging to each other. For a moment I thought that her fears were true: that this imprisonment would be the death of her, even if the queen did not send for the executioner and his axe. We went through the swinging gate and into the orchard. The petals from the blossom were spilled over the grass like snow, the boughs leaned down with their creamy weight. Elizabeth looked around the orchard before she put her hand in my arm and drew me to her.

'I am ruined,' she said softly. 'If she bears a son to him, I am ruined.' She turned from me and walked across the grass, her shabby black gown brushing the damp petals which clung to the hem. 'A son,' she muttered, cautious even in her chagrin to keep her voice low. 'A damned Spanish son. A damned Catholic Spanish son. And England an outpost of the Spanish empire, England, my England, a cat's-paw of Spanish policy. And the priests back, and the burnings beginning, and my father's faith and my father's legacy torn out of English earth before it has time to flower. Damn her. Damn her to hell and her misconceived child with her.'

'Lady Elizabeth!' I exclaimed. 'Don't say that!'

She rounded on me, her hands up, her fists clenched. If I had been closer, she would have hit me. She was in such a passion she was beyond

233

knowing what she was doing. 'Damn her, and damn you too for standing her friend.'

'You must have thought it might happen,' I started. 'The marriage was agreed, he would not delay for ever . . .'

'Why would I think that she would marry?' she snapped. 'Who would have her? Old and plain, named as a bastard for half her life, half the princes of Europe have refused her already. If it was not for her damned Spanish blood, Philip would never have had her. He must have begged to be excused. He must have gone down on his knees and prayed for any fate rather than to be forced to stick it up that old dried-up virgin.'

'Elizabeth!' I exclaimed, I was genuinely shocked.

'What?' Her eyes were blazing with temper. For a moment I believed that she did not know what she was saying. 'What's wrong with telling the truth? He is a young handsome man who will inherit half of Europe, she is a woman old before her time and old enough anyway. It is disgusting to think of them rutting together like a young piglet on an old sow. It is an abomination. And if she is like her mother she will bear nothing but dead babies.'

I put my hands over my ears. 'You are offensive,' I said frankly.

Elizabeth whirled on me. 'And you are unfaithful!' she shouted. 'You should be my friend, and stand my friend whatever else happens, whatever I say. You were begged to me as a fool, you should be mine. And I say nothing but the truth. I would be ashamed to chase after a young man like her. I would rather die than court a man young enough to be my son. I would rather die now than get to her age and be an unwanted old maid, good for nothing, pleasing to nobody, useless!'

'I am not unfaithful,' I said steadily. 'And I am your companion, she did not beg me as a fool to you. I would be your friend. But I cannot listen to you cursing her like a Billingsgate fishwife.'

She let out a wail at that and dropped to the ground, her face as white as apple blossom, her hair tumbled over her shoulders, her hands clamped over her mouth.

I knelt beside her and took her hands. They were icy, she looked near to collapse. 'Lady Elizabeth,' I said soothingly. 'Be calm. It is a marriage which is bound to take place and there is nothing you can do about it.'

'But not even invited . . .' She gave a little wail.

'Is hard. But she has been merciful to you.' I paused. 'Remember, he would have had you beheaded.'

'And I am to be grateful for that?'

'You could be calm. And wait.'

The face she turned up to me was suddenly glacial. 'If she bears him a son then I will have nothing to wait for but a forced marriage to some Papist prince, or death.'

'You said to me that any day you could stay alive was a victory,' I reminded her.

She did not smile in reply. She shook her head. 'Staying alive is not important,' she said quietly. 'It never was. I was staying alive for England. Staying alive to be England's princess. Staying alive to inherit.'

I did not correct her, the words were true for her now, though I thought I knew Elizabeth too well to see her as a woman only staying alive for her country. But I did not want to launch her into one of her passionate tantrums. 'You must do that,' I said soothingly. 'Stay alive for England. Wait.'

She let me go the next day though her resentment was as powerful as that of a child excluded from a treat. I did not know what upset her more: the gravity of her situation as the only Protestant princess in Roman Catholic England, or not being invited to the greatest event in Christendom since the Field of the Cloth of Gold. When she waved me away without a word and with a sulky turn of her head I thought that missing the party was probably the worst thing for her that morning.

If Sir Henry's men had not known the road to Winchester we could have found it by following the crowds. It seemed that every man, woman and child wanted to see the queen take her husband at last, and the roads were crowded with farmers bringing their produce into the greatest market in the country, entertainers setting up their pitches all along the way, whores and mountebanks and pedlars with cures, goose girls and washerwomen, carters and riders leading strings of spare horses. Then there was all the panoply and organisation of the royal court on the move: the messengers coming and going, the men in livery, the men at arms, the outriders and those galloping desperately to catch up.

Sir Henry's men carried reports of Elizabeth for the queen's council, so we parted at the entrance of Wolvesey Palace, the bishop's great house where the queen was staying. I went straight to the queen's rooms and found a crowd of people at every doorway pushing their way forward with petitions that she might grant. I slid under elbows, between shoulders, sneaking between panelled walls and bulky squires till I reached the guards on the door and stood before their crossed halberds.

'The queen's fool,' I announced myself. One man recognised me. He and his fellow stepped forward and let me dart in behind them and open the door while they held back the weight of the crowd.

Inside the presence chamber it was scarcely less crowded but the clothes were more silks and embroidered leather, and the altercations were taking place in French and Spanish as well as English. Here were the ambitious and rising men and women of the kingdom jockeying for a place and anxious to be seen by the new king who would be creating a court which must – surely to God! – include at least some true-born Englishmen as well as the hundreds of Spaniards he had insisted on bringing over as his personal retinue.

I skirted the perimeter of the hall, overhearing the snatches of conversation, which was mostly scandalous, often speculating on what the handsome young prince would make of the old queen, and I found that my cheeks were blazing with temper and my teeth gritted by the time I got to the door of her private rooms.

The guard let me through with a nod of recognition but even inside the queen's privy chamber there was no peace. There were more ladies and attendants, musicians, singers, escorts and general hangers-on than I had ever seen with her before. I looked around for her, still she was not there, the chair which served as her throne by the fireside was empty. Jane Dormer was in the window-seat sewing, looking as determinedly unimpressed as she had been on the day I had first met her when the queen had been a sick woman, in a court of shadows with no chance of the throne.

'I have come to the queen,' I said to her with a little bow.

'You're among many,' she said dourly.

'I've seen them,' I said. 'Has it been like this since you came from London?'

'Every day there are more people,' she said. 'They must think her soft in the head as well as the heart. If she gave her kingdom away three times over she would not be able to satisfy their demands.'

'Shall I go in?'

'She's praying,' she said. 'But she'll want to see you.'

She rose from the window-seat and I saw that she had positioned herself so that no-one could enter the queen's narrow doorway without first going past Jane. She opened the door and peeped in, then she waved me through.

The queen had been praying before an exquisite gold and mother-of-pearl icon, but now she was sitting back on her heels, her face calm and shining. She radiated joy as she knelt there, so calm and sweet in her happiness that anyone looking at her would have known her for a bride on her wedding day; a woman preparing herself for love.

When she heard the door close behind me she slowly turned her head and smiled. 'Ah, Hannah! How glad I am you have come, you are just in time.'

I crossed the room and knelt before her. 'God bless Your Grace on this most fortunate day.'

She put her hand on my head in blessing in that affectionate familiar gesture. 'It is a fortunate day, isn't it?'

I looked up, the glow around her was shining as brightly as sunshine. 'It is, Your Grace,' I said. I had no doubt of it at all. 'I can see that it is a wonderful day for you.'

'This is the start of my new life,' she said gently. 'The start of my life as a married woman, as a queen with a prince at my side, with my country at peace and the greatest nation in Christendom, my mother's home, as our ally.'

I looked up smiling, I was still on my knees before her.

'And shall I have a child?' she asked in a soft whisper. 'Can you see that for me, Hannah?'

'I am sure of it,' I said in a voice as quiet as her own.

Joy leaped into her face. 'From your heart or from your gift?' she asked me quickly.

'From both,' I said simply. 'I am sure of it, Your Grace.'

She closed her eyes for a moment and I knew she was thanking God for my certainty and for the promise of a future for England where there would be peace and an end to religious faction.

'Now I must get ready,' she said, rising to her feet. 'Ask Jane to send my maids to me, Hannah. I want to get dressed.'

I could not see much of the actual wedding service. I had a glimpse of Prince Philip as he stepped towards the blaze of gold of the altar of Winchester Cathedral but then the person standing before me, a corpulent squire from Somerset, shifted his position and blocked my view and I could only hear the soaring voices of the queen's choristers singing the Wedding Mass and then the soft gasp as Bishop Gardiner raised the couple's clasped hands to show that the wedding was completed and England's virgin queen was now a married woman.

I thought I would see the prince clearly at the wedding feast but as I was hurrying on my way to the hall, I heard the rattle of the weapons of the Spanish guard and I stepped back into a window embrasure as the men at arms marched down and then came the bustle of his court after them, the prince himself at the centre. And then, amid all this hustle of excitement, something happened to me. It was caused by the flurry of silks and velvets, embroidery and diamonds, the dark full richness of the Spanish court. It was caused by the scent of the pomade they wore on their hair and beards, and the perfumed pomander that every man had pinned with a golden buckle to his belt. It was the clink of the priceless inlaid breastplates of the soldiery, the tap of the beautifully forged swords against the stone of the walls. It was the rapid interchange of the language, which was like the coo in a dovecote of home to me who had been a stranger in a strange land for so very long. I smelled the Spaniards and saw them and heard them and sensed them in a way that I had never apprehended anything before, and I stumbled back, feeling for the cold wall behind me to steady me, almost fainting, overwhelmed with a homesickness and a longing for Spain that was so strong that it was almost like a gripe in my belly. I think I even cried out, and one man heard me, one man turned dark familiar eyes and looked towards me.

'What is it, lad?' he asked, seeing my golden pageboy suit.

'It's the queen's holy fool,' one of his men remarked in Spanish. 'Some toy that she affects. A boy-girl, a hermaphrodite.'

'Good God, a wizened old maid served by no maid at all,' someone quipped, his accent Castilian. The prince said 'Hush,' but absent-mindedly, as if he was not defending a new wife but reprimanding a familiar offence.

'Are you sick, child?' he asked me in Spanish.

One of his companions stepped forward and took my hand. 'The prince asks are you sick?' he demanded in careful English.

I felt my hand tremble at his touch, the touch of a Spanish lord on my Spanish skin. I expected him to know me at once, to know that I understood every word he said, that my reply in Spanish was readier on my tongue than my English.

'I am not sick,' I said in English, speaking very quietly and hoping that no-one would hear the vestiges of my accent. 'I was startled by the prince.'

'You startled her only,' he laughed, turning to the prince and speaking in Spanish. 'God grant that you may startle her mistress.'

The prince nodded, indifferent to me, as a servant beneath his notice, and walked on.

'She's more likely to startle him,' someone remarked quietly from the back. 'God save us, how are we to put our prince to bed with such an aged dame?'

'And a virgin,' someone else replied. 'Not even a warm and willing widow who knows what she's been missing. This queen will freeze our lord, he'll wilt at her bedside.'

'And she's so dull,' the first one persisted.

The prince heard that, he halted and looked back at his retinue. 'Enough,' he said clearly, speaking in Spanish, thinking that only they would understand. 'It is done. I have wedded her, and I shall bed her, and if you hear that I cannot do it you can speculate then as to the cause. In the meantime let us have peace. It is not fair dealing to the English to come into the country and insult their queen.'

'They don't deal fair to us . . .' someone started.

'A country of idiots . . .'

'Poor and bad-tempered . . .'

'And grasping!'

239

'Enough,' he said.

I followed them down the gallery to the steps leading to the great chamber. I followed them as if drawn on a chain, I could not have parted from them if my life had depended on it. I was back with my own people, hearing them speak, even though every word they said was a slander against the only woman who had been kind to me, or against England, my second home.

It was Will Somers who caught me out of my trance. He took me by the arm as I was about to follow the Spaniards into the great hall and gave me a little shake. 'How now, maid? In a dream?'

'Will,' I said and grabbed on to his sleeve as if to steady myself. 'Oh, Will!'

'There,' he said, gently patting me on the back as if I were an overwrought pageboy. 'Silly little maid.'

'Will, the Spanish . . .'

He drew me away from the main doors and put a warm arm around my shoulder.

'Take care, little fool,' he warned me. 'The very walls of Winchester have ears and you never know who you are offending.'

'They're so . . .' I could not find the words. 'They're so . . . handsome!' I burst out.

He laughed aloud, released me and clapped his hands. 'Handsome, is it? You, besotted with the señors just like Her Grace, God bless her?'

'It's their . . .' I paused again. 'It's their perfume,' I said simply. 'They smell so wonderful.'

'Oh little maid, it is time you were wed,' he said in mock seriousness. 'If you are running after men and sniffing at their spoor like a little bitch on the hunt then one day you will make your kill and you'll be a holy fool no longer.'

He paused for a moment, measuring me. 'Ah, I had forgot. You were from Spain, weren't you?'

I nodded. There was no point in fooling a fool.

'They make you think of your home,' he predicted. 'Is that it?'

I nodded.

'Ah well,' he said. 'This is a better day for you than for those Englishmen who have spent their lives hating the Spanish. You will have a Spanish master once more. For the rest of us, it's like the end of the world.'

He drew me a little closer. 'And how is the Princess Elizabeth?' he asked softly.

'Angry,' I said. 'Anxious. She was ill in June, you'll have heard that she wanted the queen's physicians, and grieved when they did not come.'

'God keep her,' he said. 'Who'd have thought that she would be there this day, and that we would be here? Who'd have thought that this day would come?'

'Tell me news in return,' I started.

'Lord Robert?'

I nodded.

'Still imprisoned, and there's no-one to speak for him at court, and no-one to listen anyway.'

There was a blast of trumpets, the queen and the prince had entered the hall and taken their seats.

'Time to go,' Will said. He adopted a broad smile and exaggerated his usual gangling gait. 'You will be amazed, child, I have learned to juggle.'

'Do you do it well?' I asked, trotting to keep up with him as he strode towards the great open doors. 'Skilfully?'

'Very badly indeed,' he said with quiet pleasure. 'Very comical.'

There was a roar as he entered the room and I fell back to let him go on.

'You'd not understand being a mere lass,' he said over his shoulder. 'All women laugh very meanly.'

I had not forgotten Daniel Carpenter and his letter to me for all that I had thrown it in the fire after one reading. I might as well have folded it and kept it inside my jerkin, close to my heart, for I remembered every word that he had written, as if I re-read it like a lovesick girl every night.

I found that I was thinking of him more frequently since the arrival

241

of the Spanish court. No-one could have thought badly of marriage who could see the queen; from the morning that she rose from her married bed, she glowed with a warmth that no-one had ever seen in her before. There was a confident serenity about her, she looked like a woman who has found a safe haven at last. She was a woman in love, she was a beloved wife, she had a councillor she could trust, a powerful man devoted to her well being. At last, after a childhood and womanhood filled with anxiety and fear, she could rest in the arms of a man who loved her. I watched her and thought that if a woman as fiercely virginal and as intensely spiritual as the queen could find love, then so perhaps could I. It might be that marriage was not the death of a woman and the end of her true self, but the unfolding of her. It might be that a woman could be a wife without having to cut the pride and the spirit out of herself. A woman might blossom into being a wife, not be trimmed down to fit. And this made me think that Daniel might be the man that I could turn to, that I could trust, Daniel, who loved me, who told me he could not sleep for thinking of me, and whose letter I had read once and then thrust into the fire, but never forgot – indeed, I could recite it word for word.

He also came to my mind for his fears and his cautions, even though I had scoffed at them at the time. Though the Spanish court drew me in like a lodestone swings north, I knew that it was my danger and my death. To be sure, Philip in England was not as he had been in Spain. Philip in England was conciliatory, anxious to bring peace, determined not to give offence to his new kingdom and not to stir up trouble about religion. But Philip nonetheless had been brought up in a land dominated equally by the rule of his father and the demands of the Inquisition. They were Philip's father's laws that had burned my mother at the stake and would have burned me and my father too, if they had caught us. Daniel had been right to be cautious, I even thought he had been right to take his family and my father out of the country. I could hide behind the identity of the queen's fool, a holy child, a companion from her days in the shadows, but anyone who did not have such a provenance could expect to be examined at some time in the future. These were early days, but there were signs that the queen's fabled mercy – so generous to those who challenged her throne – might not extend to those who insulted her faith.

I took great care to go to Mass with the queen and her ladies every day, three times a day, and I was meticulous in those little details of observation that had betrayed so many of my kin in Spain, the turning to the altar at the right moment, the bowing of the head at the raising of the Host, the careful reciting of the prayers. It was not hard for me to do. My belief in the God of my people, the God of the desert and the burning bush, the God of exiles and the oppressed, never very fervent or very strong, was deeply hidden in my heart. I did not think He was forsworn by me performing a little nodding and amening. In truth, I thought that whatever His great purpose in making my people the most miserable outcasts of Christendom, He would forgive the bobbing of such a very unimportant head.

But the attention of the court to such matters made me grateful to Daniel for his caution. In the end, I thought I should write to him, and to my father, and send the letter by some of the many soldiers who were going to Calais to refortify the town against the French, now doubly our enemy since we had a Spanish king. The letter would take some composing: if it fell into the hands of the many spies, English, French, Spanish, Venetian, or even Swedish, it would have to pass as an innocent letter from a lass to her lover. I would have to trust him to read between the lines.

> *Dear Daniel,*
>
> *I did not reply to you earlier because I did not know what to say, besides I have been with the princess at Woodstock and could not have got a letter to you. I am now with the queen at Winchester and we will soon go to London when I can send you this letter.*
>
> *I am very glad that your business took you to Calais, and I propose to join you and my father when matters change here for me, just as we agreed. I think you judged very rightly when you should leave and I am very ready to join you in good time.*
>
> *I read your letter very carefully, Daniel, and I think of you often. To answer you with honesty, I am not eager for marriage as yet, but when you speak to me as you did in your letter, and when you kissed me on parting I felt, not a moment of fear or repulsion, but a delight that I cannot name, not from an affected modesty, but*

because I do not know the name. You did not frighten me, Daniel, I liked your kiss. I would have you as my husband, Daniel, when I am released from court, when the time is right and we are both equally ready. I cannot help be a little apprehensive at the thought of becoming a bride, but having seen the queen's happiness in her marriage it makes me look forward to mine. I accept your proposal that we should be betrothed but I need to see my way clear to marriage.

I do not want to turn you into a cat's-paw in your own home, you are wrong to fear that and to reproach me with a desire I do not have. I do not want to rule over you, but I do not want you to rule over me. I need to be a woman in my own right, and not only a wife. I know that would not be the view of your mother, and maybe not even the view of my father, but, as you said, I am used to having my own way: this is the woman I have become. I have travelled far and lived according to my own means, and I seem to have adopted a lad's pride along with breeches. I don't want to lay aside the pride when I surrender the livery. I hope that your love for me can accommodate the woman that I will grow to be. I would not mislead you in this, Daniel, I cannot be a servant to a husband, I would have to be his friend and comrade. I write to ask you if you could have a wife like this?

I hope this does not distress you, it is so difficult to write these things, but often when we spoke of them we quarrelled – so perhaps letters are a way that we may forge an agreement? And I should want to agree with you, if we are to be betrothed it would have to be on terms that we both could trust.

I enclose a letter for my father, he will tell you the rest of my news. I assure you that I am safe and happy at court and if that ever changes I will come to you as I promised. I do not forget that I went from you only to bear the princess company in the Tower. She is now released from the Tower but she is still a prisoner and to tell you the truth, I still feel that I should honour my service to the queen and to the princess and to bear either of them company as I am commanded. Should things change here, should the queen no longer need me, I will come to you. But these are my obligations. I know if I were an ordinary betrothed girl I

would have no obligations but to you – but Daniel, I am not a girl
like that. I want to complete my service to the queen and then, and
only then, come to you. I hope you can understand this.

 But I should like to be betrothed to you, if we can agree . . .
 Hannah

I re-read the letter and found that even I, the writer, was smiling at
its odd mixture of coming forward and then retreating. I could wish to
write more clearly, but that would only be possible if I could see more
clearly. I folded it up and put it away ready to send to Daniel when the
court moved to London in August.

The queen had planned a triumphant entry for her new husband; and
the city, always a friend to Mary, and now released from the sight and
stench of the gibbets, which had been replaced with triumphal arches,
went mad to see her. A Spaniard at her side could never be a popular
choice, but to see the queen in her golden gown with her happy smile
and to know that at least the deed was done and the country might
now settle down to some stability and peace was to please most of the
great men of the city. Besides, there were advantages to a match that
would open up the Spanish Netherlands to English traders which were
very apparent to the rich men who wanted to increase their fortunes.

The queen and her new husband settled into the Palace of Whitehall
and started to establish the routines of a joint court.

I was in her chamber early one morning, waiting for her to come to
Mass when she emerged in her night gown and knelt in silence before the
prie-dieu. Something in her silence told me that she was deeply moved
and I knelt behind her, bowed my head, and waited. Jane Dormer came
from the queen's bedroom where she slept when the king was not with
his wife and knelt down too, her head bowed. Clearly something very
important had happened. After a good half hour of silent prayer, the
queen still rapt on her knees, I shuffled cautiously towards Jane and
leaned against her shoulder to whisper in a voice so low that it could
not disturb the queen. 'What's happening?'

'She's missed her course,' Jane said, her voice a tiny thread of sound.

'Her course?'

'Her bleeding. She could be with child.'

I felt a lurch in my own belly, like a cold hand laid on the very pit of my stomach. 'Could it be so soon?'

'It only takes once,' Jane said crudely. 'And God bless them, it has been more than once.'

'And she is with child?' I had foretold it, but I could hardly believe it. And I did not feel the joy I would have expected at the prospect of Mary's dreams coming true. 'Really with child?'

She heard the doubt in my voice and turned a hard gaze on me. 'What is it you doubt, fool? My word? Hers? Or d'you think you know something we don't?'

Jane Dormer only ever called me fool when she was angry with me.

'I doubt no-one,' I said quickly. 'Please God it is so. And no-one could want it more than I.'

Jane shook her head. 'No-one could want it more than her,' she said, nodding towards the kneeling queen, 'for she has prayed for this moment for nearly a year. Truth be told, she has prayed to carry a son for England since she was old enough to pray.'

Autumn 1554

The queen said nothing to the king nor to the court, but Jane watched her with the devotion of a mother and next month, in September, when the queen did not bleed, she gave me a small triumphant nod and I grinned back. The queen told the king in secret, but anyone seeing his redoubled tenderness towards her must have guessed that she was carrying his child, and that it was a great hidden joy to them both.

Their happiness illuminated the palace and for the first time I lived at a royal court that was alive with joy and delight in itself. The king's train remained as proud and as glamorous as when they had first entered England, the phrase 'as proud as a Don' became an every day saying. No-one could see the richness of their velvets and the weight of their gold chains and not admire them. When they rode out to hunt they had the very best horses, when they gambled they threw down a small fortune, when they laughed together they made the walls shake and when they danced they showed us the beautiful formal dances of Spain.

The ladies of England flooded to the queen's service and were all lovesick for the Spanish. They all read Spanish poetry, sang Spanish songs, and learned the new Spanish card games. The court was alive with flirtation and music and dancing and parties and in the heart of it all was the queen, serene and smiling, with her young husband always lovingly at her side. We were the most intellectual, the most elegant, the richest court in the whole of Christendom, and we knew it. With Queen Mary glowing at the head of this radiant court we danced at a very pinnacle of self-satisfied pleasure.

In October the queen was informed that Elizabeth was sick again. She asked me to read Sir Henry Bedingfield's report to her as she rested on a day bed. Woodstock, and Elizabeth, and Elizabeth's many ploys for attention seemed far away as the queen gazed dreamily out of the window at the garden where the trees were turning yellow and golden and bronze. 'She can see my doctors if she insists,' she said absently. 'Would you go with them, Hannah? And see if she is as bad as she claims? I don't want to be unkind to her. If she would just admit her part in the plot I would release her, I don't want to be troubled with this, not now.'

It was as if her own happiness was too great not to be shared.

'But if she was to admit a fault, surely the council or the king would want her to face trial?' I suggested.

Queen Mary shook her head. 'She could admit it privately to me, and I would forgive her,' she said. 'Her fellow plotters are dead or gone away, there is no plot left for her any more. And I am carrying an heir to the throne, an heir for England and for the whole Spanish empire, this will be the greatest prince the world has ever known. Elizabeth can admit her fault and I will forgive her. And then she should be married; the king has suggested his cousin, the Duke of Savoy. Tell Elizabeth that this time of waiting and suspicion can be at an end, tell her I am with child. Tell her I shall have my baby in early May. Any hopes she had of the throne will be over by next summer. Make sure she understands, Hannah. There has been bad blood between us but it can be over as soon as she consents.'

I nodded.

'Sir Henry writes that she attends Mass as good daughter of the church,' she said. 'Tell her I am glad of that.' She paused. 'But he tells me that when the time comes in the service to pray for me she never says "amen".' She paused. 'What d'you make of such a thing? She never prays for me, Hannah.'

I was silent. If the queen had been speaking in anger I might have tried to defend Elizabeth, and her pride and her independence of spirit. But the queen was not angry. She looked nothing more than wounded.

'You know, I would pray for her, if our places were reversed,' she said. 'I remember her in my prayers because she is my sister. You could tell her that I pray for her every day, and I have done ever since I cared for her at Hatfield, because she is my sister and because I try to forgive her for plotting against me, and because I try to prepare myself for her release, and to teach myself to deal with her with charity, to judge her mercifully as I hope to be judged. I pray for her well being every day of her life; and then I hear she will not say so much as "amen" to a prayer for me!'

'Your Grace, she is a young woman and very alone,' I said quietly. 'She has no-one to advise her.' To tell the truth I was ashamed of Elizabeth's stubbornness, and meanness of spirit.

'See if you can teach her some of your wisdom, my fool,' the queen suggested with a smile.

I knelt to her and bowed my head. 'I shall miss being with you,' I said honestly. 'Especially now that you are so happy.'

She put her hand on my head. 'I shall miss you too, my little fool,' she said. 'But you shall come back in time for the Christmas feast, and after that you shall bear me company when I am confined.'

'Your Grace, I shall be so pleased to bear you company.'

'A spring baby,' she said dreamily. 'A little spring lamb of God. Won't that be wonderful, Hannah? An heir for England and for Spain.'

It was like travelling to another country to leave Whitehall for Woodstock. I left a happy court, filled with amusements, exulting in optimism, waiting for an heir; and arrived at a small prison, victualled and managed by Elizabeth's old servants who were not even allowed in the ramshackle gatehouse to serve her, but had to do all their business in the tap room of the nearby inn, where they dealt with some very odd customers indeed.

At Woodstock I found Elizabeth very ill. No-one could have doubted her frailty. She was in bed, exhausted and fat, she looked years older than twenty-one. She looked older than her older sister. I thought that her earlier taunts about her youth and beauty and the queen's sterile age had rebounded most cruelly on her this autumn when she was swollen up, as fat as old Anne of Cleves, and the queen was blooming like Ceres. With her jowls bloated by illness Elizabeth bore a startling resemblance to the portraits of her father in his later years. It was a horror to see her girlish prettiness change into his gross features. The clear line of her jaw had disappeared into rolls of fat, her eyes were occluded by the red eyelids, her pretty rosebud mouth was hidden by the fat flesh of her cheeks and the grooved lines running from nose to chin.

Even her beautiful hands were fat. She had laid her rings aside, they would not go on her fingers, the very fingernails were half-hidden by the monstrous growth of the flesh.

I waited till the physicians had seen her and bled her and she had rested before I went into her bed chamber. She threw me one resentful look and lay still on her bed, saying nothing. Kat Ashley flicked out of the door and stood on the outside to guard us from eavesdroppers. 'Don't be too long,' she said as she went past me. 'She's very weak.'

'What is wrong with her?' I whispered.

She shrugged. 'They don't know. They have never known. It is an illness of water, she swells with water and cannot rid herself of it. But she is worse when she is unhappy, and they have made her very unhappy here.'

'Lady Elizabeth,' I said and dropped to my knees by the bed.

'Faithless,' she said, hardly opening her eyes.

I had to choke back a giggle at her irresistible tendency to drama. 'Oh, my lady,' I said reproachfully. 'You know I have to go where I am bid. You must remember that I came to you in the Tower when I need not have come at all.'

'I know you went dancing off to Winchester for the wedding and I have not seen you since.' Her voice rose to match her temper.

'The queen commanded me to go with her to London and now she has sent me to you. And I bring a message.'

She raised herself a little on her pillows. 'I am almost too sick to listen, so tell me briefly. Am I to be released?'

'If you will admit your fault.'

Her dark eyes flared under the puffy eyelids. 'Tell me exactly what she said.'

As precisely as a clerk I recited to her what the queen had offered. I spared her nothing, not the news of the pregnancy, her sister's sadness at Elizabeth's resentment, her willingness to be friends again.

I had thought she would rage when she heard the queen was with child, but she did not even comment. I realised then that she had known the news before I told her. In that case, she had a spy so well positioned that he or she knew a secret I had thought was known only to the king, the queen, Jane Dormer and me. Elizabeth, like a cornered dog, should never be underestimated.

'I will think about what you have told me,' she said, following her usual instinct to buy time. 'Are you to stay with me? Or take an answer back to her?'

'I am not to go back to court until Christmas,' I said. Temptingly, I added: 'If you were to beg her forgiveness perhaps you could be at the court for Christmas. It's very gay now, Princess, the court is filled with handsome grandees and there is dancing every night and the queen is merry.'

She turned her head away from me. 'I should not dance with a Spaniard even if I were to go.' She considered the picture for a moment. 'They could throng around me and beg me to dance and I would not get to my feet.'

'And you would be the only princess,' I reminded her persuasively. 'The only princess in court. If you refused to dance they would all gather round you. And there would be new gowns. You would be the only virgin princess in England, at the greatest court in the world.'

'I'm not a child to tempt with toys,' she said with quiet dignity. 'And I am not a fool. You can go now, Hannah, you have served her and done her bidding. But for the rest of your stay here you shall serve me.'

I nodded and rose to my feet. For a moment I hesitated; she did look so very sick as she lay on her bed facing the prospect of either a confession to treason or an unending imprisonment and disgrace. 'God guide your ladyship,' I said with sudden compassion. 'God guide you, Princess Elizabeth, and bring you safely out of here.'

She closed her eyes and I saw her eyelashes were darkened with tears. 'Amen,' she whispered.

She did not do it. She would not confess. She knew that her stubbornness would condemn her to stay at Woodstock perhaps forever, and she feared that her health would not outlast the queen's resentment. But to confess was to throw herself into the queen's power absolutely, and she would not do that. She mistrusted Mary's mercy, and the relentless Tudor stubbornness drove both sisters. Mary had been named as heir, and then named as bastard, and then made heir again. Exactly the same ordeal had been endured by Elizabeth. Both of them had decided never to surrender, always to claim their birthright, never to despair that the crown would come. Elizabeth would not relinquish the habit of a lifetime, not even for a chance to shine at a wealthy happy court and be received with honour. She might or might not be guilty, but she would never confess.

'What am I to tell the queen?' I asked her at the end of a long week. The physicians had declared her on the way to health once more, they could take a message back to court for me. If Elizabeth continued to mend she could have ridden in triumph to court for Christmas, if only she would confess.

'You can tell her a riddle,' Elizabeth said with feeble malice. She was seated in a chair, a pillow thrust behind her back to support her, a blanket wrapped around a hot brick under her cold feet.

I waited.

'You are a rhyming fool, are you not?'

'No, Princess,' I said quietly. 'As you know. I have no fooling skills.'

'Then I will teach you a rhyme,' she said savagely. 'You can write it to the queen if you wish. You can engrave it on every damned window in this hellhole if you wish.' She smiled grimly at me. 'It goes like this:

> *Much suspected of me*
> *Nothing proved can be*
> *Quoth Elizabeth, prisoner.*

Don't you think that is neat?'

I bowed and went to write my letter to the queen.

Winter 1554–55

We waited, Christmas came and went and there was no joy for me either as I was ordered to stay with Elizabeth until she begged for forgiveness. It was freezing cold at Woodstock, there was not a window that did not direct a draught into the room, there was not a fire that did not smoke. The linen on the beds was always damp, the very floorboards underfoot were wet to the touch. It was a malevolent house in winter. I had been in good health when I arrived, and yet even I could feel myself growing weak from the relentless cold and the darkness, late dawns and early twilights. For Elizabeth, already exhausted by her ordeal in the Tower, always quick to go from anxiety to illness, the house was a killer.

She was too ill to take any pleasure in the festivities, and they were scanty and mean. She was too weak to do more than look out of the window at the mummers who came to the door. She raised her hand to wave at them, Elizabeth would never fail an audience, but after they had gone she sank back on the day bed and lay still. Kat Ashley threw another log on the fire and it hissed as the frost in the grain of the wood started to melt and it smoked most miserably.

I wrote to my father to wish him a merry Christmastide and to tell him that I missed him and hoped to see him soon. I enclosed a note for Daniel in which I sent him my best wishes. A few weeks later, in the cold snows of January when the draughty palace of Woodstock was a nightmare of coldness and darkness from grey dawn to early dusk, I had a letter from each of them. My father's was brief and affectionate, saying that business was good in Calais, and would I please go to check on the shop in London when I was next in the city. Then I opened my letter from Daniel.

> *Dear wife-to-be*
>
> *I am writing to you from the city of Padua to wish you the compliments of the season and hope that this finds you well, as it leaves me. Your father and my family are in good health at Calais and looking for you every day as we hear that matters are quite settled in England now with the queen with child and Lady Elizabeth to leave England and live with queen Mary of Hungary. When she leaves England I trust you will come to Calais where my mother and sisters await you.*
>
> *I am here to study at the great university of medicine. My master suggested that I should come here to learn the art of surgery, at which the Italians and especially the Padua university has excelled, also the pharmacopoeia. I will not trouble you with my studies – but Hannah! These men are unfolding the very secrets of life, they are tracing the flow of the humours around the body and in Venice, which is nearby, they see how the tides and the rivers flow around the body of the world also. I cannot tell you what it is like to be here and to feel that every day we are coming a little closer to understanding everything – from the rise and fall of the tides to the beat of the heart, from the distillation of an essence to the ingredients of the philosopher's stone.*
>
> *You will be surprised to hear that I came upon John Dee in Venice last month when I was listening to a lecture by a very learned friar who is skilled in the use of poisons to kill the disease and yet save the patient. Mr Dee is much respected here for his reputation for learning. He lectured on Euclid and I attended, though I did not understand more than one word in ten. But I think the better of him now that I have seen him in this company with these men who are forging a new sense of the world and one which will transform what we know about everything – from the smallest grain to the greatest planet. He has a most brilliant mind, I understand much better why you think so highly of him.*
>
> *I was glad to get your letter and to know that you think that you will finish your service with the princess soon, I trust then you*

will ask the queen to release you. I am considering now whether we could live away from England for some years. Hannah, my love, Venice is such an exciting city to be in, and the weather so bright and fine, and the men and women so prosperous and the doctors so learned – you cannot blame me for wanting to stay here and for wanting you to share it with me. It is a city of tremendous wealth and beauty, there are no roads at all but canals and the lagoon everywhere, and everyone takes a boat to their doorstep. The study and the scholars here are quite extraordinary and anything can be asked and answered.

I keep your first letter in my doublet against my heart. Now I put your Christmas note beside it and wish you had written more. I think of you daily and dream of you every night.

This is a new world that we are making, with new understandings of the movements of the planets and of the tides. Of course it must be possible that a man and a wife could be married in a new way also. I do not want you as my servant, I want you as my love. I assure you that you shall have the freedom to be your own sweet self. Write to me again and tell me you will come to me soon. I am yours in thought and word and deed and even these studies of mine which fill me with such hope and excitement would mean nothing if I did not think that one day I could share them with you.

Daniel

Daniel's second letter promising love to me went the way of the first, into the fire; but not until I had read it half a dozen times. It had to be destroyed, it was filled with heretical notions that would have trapped me into an inquiry if it had been read by anyone else. But I burned this second letter with regret. I thought that in it I heard the true voice of a young man growing into wisdom, of a betrothed man planning his marriage, of a passionate man looking towards his life with a woman of his choice, of a man I could trust.

It was a long and cold winter and Elizabeth grew no better. The news from the court that the queen was healthy and growing stout did not make her half-sister any merrier as she lay, wrapped in furs, her nose red from cold, looking out of a window of cracked glass over a garden blasted by icy winds and neglect.

We heard that the parliament had restored the Roman Catholic religion and the members had wept for joy to be received once more into the body of the church. There had been a service of thanksgiving that they should once again receive the papal rule that they had once thrown off. On that day Elizabeth looked very bleak as she saw her father's inheritance and her brother's greatest pride thrown away in her sister's victory. From that day on, Elizabeth observed the Mass three times a day with her head obediently bowed. There was no more sliding away from observance. The stakes had gone up.

As the light grew brighter in the morning and the snow melted and drained away into standing puddles of cold water Elizabeth grew a little stronger and started to walk in the garden once more, me running alongside her in my thin-soled riding boots, wrapped against the cold in a blanket, blowing on my icy hands, complaining of the icy wind.

'It would be colder in Hungary,' she said shortly.

I did not remark that everyone seemed to know the queen's private plans for her. 'You would be an honoured guest in Hungary,' I replied. 'There would be a warm fire to come back to.'

'There is only one fire the queen would build for me,' Elizabeth said grimly. 'And if I once went to Hungary you would see it would become such a home for me that I would never be allowed to see England again. I won't go. I won't ever leave England. You can tell her that, when she asks you. I will never leave England willingly, and English men and women will never let me be bundled away as a prisoner. I am not without friends even though I am without a sister.'

I nodded and kept diplomatically silent.

'But if not Hungary, which she has never yet had the courage to propose to me direct, then what?' she asked aloud. 'And God – when?'

Spring 1555

To everyone's surprise the queen weakened first. As the bitter winter melted into a wet spring, Elizabeth was bidden to court, without having to confess, without even writing a word to her sister, and I was ordered to ride in her train, no explanation offered to me for the change of heart and none expected. For Elizabeth it was not the return she might have wanted; she was brought in almost as a prisoner, we travelled early in the morning and late in the afternoon so that we would not be noticed, there was no smiling and waving at any crowds. We skirted the city, the queen had ordered that Elizabeth should not ride down the great roads of London, but as we went through the little lanes I felt my heart skip a beat in terror and I pulled up my horse in the middle of the lane, and made the princess stop.

'Go on, fool,' she said ungraciously. 'Kick him on.'

'God help me, God help me,' I babbled.

'What is it?'

Sir Henry Bedingfield's man saw me stock-still, turned his horse and came back. 'Come on now,' he said roughly. 'Orders are to keep moving.'

'My God,' I said again, it was all I could say.

'She's a holy fool,' Elizabeth said. 'Perhaps she is having a vision.'

'I'll give her a vision,' he said, and took the bridle and pulled my horse forward.

Elizabeth came up alongside. 'Look, she's white as a sheet and shaking,' she said. 'Hannah? What is it?'

I would have fallen from my horse but for her steadying hand on my shoulder. The soldier rode on the other side, dragging my horse onward, his knee pressed against mine, half-holding me in the saddle.

'Hannah!' Elizabeth's voice came again as if from a long way away. 'Are you ill?'

'Smoke,' was all I could say. 'Fire.'

Elizabeth glanced towards the city, where I pointed. 'I can't smell anything,' she said. 'Are you giving a warning, Hannah? Is there going to be a fire?'

Dumbly, I shook my head. My sense of horror was so intense that I could say nothing but, as if from somewhere else, I heard a little mewing sound like that of a child crying from a deep unassuageable distress. 'Fire,' I said softly. 'Fire.'

'Oh, it's the Smithfield fires,' the soldier said. 'That's upset the lass. It's that, isn't it, bairn?'

At Elizabeth's quick look of inquiry he explained. 'New laws. Heretics are put to death by burning. They're burning today in Smithfield. I can't smell it but your little lass here can. It's upset her.' He clapped me on the shoulder with a heavy kindly hand. 'Not surprising,' he said. 'It's a bad business.'

'Burning?' Elizabeth demanded. 'Burning heretics? You mean Protestants? In London? Today?' Her eyes were blazing black with anger but she did not impress the soldier. As far as he was concerned we were little more value than each other. One girl dumb with horror, the other enraged.

'Aye,' he said briefly. 'It's a new world. A new queen on the throne, a new king at her side, and a new law to match. And everyone who was reformed has reformed back again and pretty smartly too. And good thing, I say, and God bless, I say. We've had nothing but foul weather and bad luck since King Henry broke with the Pope. But now the Pope's rule is back and the Holy Father will bless England again and we can have a son and heir and decent weather.'

Elizabeth said not one word. She took her pomander from her belt, put it in my hand and held my hand up to my nose so I could smell the aromatic scent of dried orange and cloves. It did not take away the stink of burning flesh, nothing would ever free me from that memory. I could even hear the cries of those on the stakes, begging their families to fan the flames and to pile on timber so that they might die the quicker and not linger, smelling their own bodies roasting, in a screaming agony of pain.

'Mother,' I choked, and then I was silent.

We rode to Hampton Court in an icy silence and we were greeted as prisoners with a guard. They bundled us in the back door as if they were ashamed to greet us. But once the door of her private rooms was locked behind us Elizabeth turned and took my cold hands in hers.

'I could not smell smoke, nobody could. The soldier only knew that they were burning today, he could not smell it,' she said.

Still I said nothing.

'It was your gift, wasn't it?' she asked curiously.

I cleared my throat, I remembered that curious thick taste at the back of my tongue, the taste of the smoke of human flesh. I brushed a smut from my face, but my hand came away clean.

'Yes,' I admitted.

'You were sent by God to warn me that this was happening,' she said. 'Others might have told me, but you were there; in your face I saw the horror of it.'

I nodded. She could take what she might from it. I knew that it was my own terror she had seen, the horror I had felt as a child when they had dragged my own mother from our house to tie her to a stake and light the fire under her feet on a Sunday afternoon as part of the ritual of every Sunday afternoon, part of the promenade, a pious and pleasurable tradition to everyone else; the death of my mother, the end of my childhood for me.

Princess Elizabeth went to the window, knelt and put her bright head in her hands. 'Dear God, thank you for sending me this messenger with this vision,' I heard her say softly. 'I understand it, I understand my destiny today as I have never done before. Bring me to my throne that I may do my duty for you and for my people. Amen.'

I did not say 'amen', though she glanced around to see if I had joined in her prayer; even in moments of the greatest of spirituality, Elizabeth would always be counting her supporters. But I could not pray to a God who could allow my mother to be burned to death. I could not pray to a God who could be invoked by the torchbearers. I wanted neither God nor His religion. I wanted only to get rid of the smell in my hair, in my skin, in my nostrils. I wanted to rub the smuts from my face.

She rose to her feet. 'I shan't forget this,' she said briefly. 'You have given me a vision today, Hannah. I knew it before, but now I have seen it in your eyes. I have to be queen of this country and put a stop to this horror.'

In the evening, before dinner, I was summoned to the queen's rooms and found her in conference with the king and with the new arrival and greatest favourite: the archbishop and papal legate, Cardinal Reginald Pole. I was in the presence chamber before I saw him, for if I had known he was there I would never have crossed the threshold. I was immediately, instinctively afraid of him. He had sharp piercing eyes, which would look unflinchingly at sinners and saints alike. He had spent a lifetime in exile for his beliefs and he had no doubt that everyone's convictions could and should be tested by fire as his had been. I thought that if he saw me, even for one second, he would smell me out and know me for a Marrano – a converted Jew – and that in this new England of Catholic conviction that he and the king and the queen were making, they would exile me back to my death in Spain at the very least, and execute me in England if they could.

He glanced up as I came into the room and his gaze flicked indifferently over me, but the queen rose from the table and held out her hands in greeting. I ran to her and dropped to my knee at her feet.

'Your Grace!'

'My little fool,' she said tenderly.

I looked up at her and saw at once the changes in her appearance made by her pregnancy. Her colour was good, she was rosy-cheeked, her face plumper and rounder, her eyes brighter from good health. Her belly was a proud curve only partly concealed by the loosened panel of her stomacher and the wider cut of her gown and I thought how proudly she must be letting out the lacing every day to accommodate the growing child. Her breasts were fuller too, her whole face and body proclaimed her happiness and her fertility.

With her hand resting on my head in blessing she turned to the two other men. 'This is my dear little fool Hannah, who has been with me since the death of my brother. She has come a long way with me to share my joy now. She is a faithful loving girl and I use her as my little emissary with Elizabeth, who trusts her too.' She turned to me. 'She is here?'

'Just arrived,' I said.

She tapped my shoulder to bid me rise and I warily got to my feet and looked at the two men.

The king was not glowing like his wife, he looked drawn and tired as if the days of winding his ways through English politics and the long English winter were a strain on a man who was used to the total power and sunny weather of the Alhambra.

The cardinal had the narrow beautiful face of the true ascetic. His gaze, sharp as a knife, went to my eyes, my mouth, and then my pageboy livery. I thought he saw at once, in that one survey, my apostasy, my desires, and my body, growing into womanhood despite my own denial and my borrowed clothes.

'A holy fool?' he asked, his tone neutral.

I bowed my head. 'So they say, Your Excellency.' I flushed with embarrassment, I did not know how he should be addressed in English. We had not had a cardinal legate at court before.

'You see visions?' he asked. 'Hear voices?'

It was clear to me that any grand claims would be greeted with utter scepticism. This was not a man to be taken in with mummer's skills.

'Very rarely,' I said shortly, trying to keep my accent as English as possible. 'And unfortunately, never at times of my choosing.'

'She saw that I would be queen,' Mary said. 'And she foretold my brother's death. And she came to the attention of her first master because she saw an angel in Fleet Street.'

The cardinal smiled and his dark narrow face lit up at once, and I saw that he was a charming man as well as a handsome one. 'An angel?' he queried. 'How did he look? How did you know him for an angel?'

'He was with some gentlemen,' I said uncomfortably. 'And I could hardly see him at all for he was blazing white. And he disappeared. He was just there for a moment and then he was gone. It was the others who named him for an angel. Not me.'

'A most modest soothsayer,' the cardinal smiled. 'From Spain by your accent?'

'My father was Spanish but we live in England now,' I said cautiously. I felt myself take half a step towards the queen and instantly froze. There should be no flinching, these men would detect fear quicker than anything else.

But the cardinal was not much interested in me. He smiled at the king. 'Can you advise us of nothing, holy fool? We are about God's business as it has not been done in England for generations. We are bringing the country back to the church. We are making good what has been bad for so long. And even the voices of the people in the Houses of Parliament are guided by God.'

I hesitated. It was clear to me that this was more rhetoric than a question demanding an answer. But the queen looked to me to speak.

'I would think it should be done gently,' I said. 'But that is my opinion, not the voice of my gift. I just wish that it could be done gently.'

'It should be done quickly and powerfully,' the queen said. 'The longer it takes the more doubts will emerge. Better to be done once and well than with a hundred small changes.'

The two men looked unconvinced. 'One should never offend more men than one can persuade,' her husband, ruler of half of Europe, told her.

I saw her melt at his voice; but she did not change her opinion. 'These are a stubborn people,' she said. 'Given a choice they can never decide. They forced me to execute poor Jane Grey. She offered them a choice and they cannot choose. They are like children who will go from apple to plum and take a bite out of each, and spoil everything.'

The cardinal nodded at the king. 'Her Grace is right,' he said. 'They have suffered change and change about. Best that we should put the whole country on oath, once, and have it all done. Then we would root out heresy, destroy it, and have the country at peace and in the old ways in one move.'

The king looked thoughtful. 'We must do it quickly and clearly, but with mercy,' he said. He turned to the queen. 'I know your passion for the church and I admire it. But you have to be a gentle mother to your people. They have to be persuaded, not forced.'

Sweetly, she put her hand on her swelling belly. 'I want to be a gentle mother indeed,' she said.

He put his hand over her own, as if they would both feel through the hard wall of the stomacher to where their baby stirred and kicked in her womb. 'I know it,' he said. 'Who should know better than I? And together we will make a holy Catholic inheritance for this young man of ours so that when he comes to his throne, here, and in Spain, he will be doubly blessed with the greatest lands in Christendom and the greatest peace the world has ever known.'

Will Somers was clowning at dinner, he gave me a wink as he passed my place. 'Watch this,' he said. He took two small balls from the sleeve of his jerkin and threw them in the air, then added another and another, until all four were spinning at the same time.

'Skilled,' he remarked.

'But not funny,' I said.

In response, he turned his moon face towards me, as if he were completely distracted, ignoring the balls in the air. At once, they clattered down all around us, bouncing off the table, knocking over the pewter goblets, spilling wine everywhere.

The women screamed and leaped up, trying to save their gowns. Will was dumbstruck with amazement at the havoc he had caused: the Spanish grandees shouting with laughter at the sudden consternation released in the English court like a Mayday revel, the queen smiling, her hand on her belly, called out: 'Oh, Will, take care!'

He bowed to her, his nose to his knees, and then came back up, radiant. 'You should blame your holy fool,' he said. 'She distracted me.'

'Oh, did she foresee you causing this uproar?'

'No, Your Grace,' he said sweetly. 'She never foresees anything. In all the time I have known her, in all the time she has been your servant, and eaten remarkably well for a spiritual girl, she has never said one thing of any more insight than any slut might remark.'

I was laughing and protesting at the same time, the queen was laughing out loud, and the king was smiling, trying to follow the jest. 'Oh, Will!' the queen reproached him. 'You know that the child has the Sight!'

'Sight she may have but no speech,' Will said cheerfully. 'For she has never said a word I thought worth hearing. Appetite she has, if you are keeping her for the novelty of that. She is an exceptionally good doer.'

'Why, Will!' I cried out.

'Not one word from her,' he insisted. 'She is a holy fool like your man is king. In name alone.'

It was too far for the Spanish pride. The English roared at the jest but as soon as the Spanish understood it they scowled, and the queen's smile abruptly died.

'Enough,' she said sharply.

Will bowed. 'But also like the king himself, the holy fool has greater gifts than a mere comical fool like me could tell,' he amended quickly.

'Why, what are they?' someone called out.

'The king gives joy to the most gracious lady in the kingdom, as I can only aspire to do,' Will said carefully. 'And the holy fool has brought the queen her heart, as the king has most graciously done.'

The queen nodded at the recovery, and waved Will to his dinner place with the officers. He passed me with a wink. 'Funny,' he said firmly.

'You upset the Spanish,' I said in an undertone. 'And traduced me.'

'I made the court laugh,' he defended himself. 'I am an English fool in an English court. It is my job to upset the Spanish. And you matter not a jot. You are grist, child, grist to the mill of my wit.'

'You grind exceeding small, Will,' I said, still nettled.

'Like God himself,' he said with evident satisfaction.

That night I went to bid goodnight to Lady Elizabeth. She was dressed in her nightgown, a shawl around her shoulders, seated by the fireside. The glowing embers put a warmth in her cheeks and her hair, brushed out over her shoulders, almost sparkled in the light from the dying fire.

'Good night, my lady,' I said quietly, making my bow.

She looked up. 'Ah, the little spy,' she said unpleasantly.

I bowed again, waiting for her permission to leave.

'The queen summoned me, you know,' she said. 'Straight after dinner, for a private chat between loving sisters. It was my last chance to confess. And if I am not mistaken that miserable Spaniard was hidden somewhere in the room, hearing every word. Probably both of them, that turncoat Pole too.'

I waited in case she would say more.

She shrugged her shoulders. 'Well, no matter,' she said bluntly. 'I confessed to nothing, I am innocent of everything. I am the heir and there is nothing they can do about it unless they find some way to murder me. I won't stand trial, I won't marry, and I won't leave the country. I'll just wait.'

I said nothing. Both of us were thinking of the queen's approaching confinement. A healthy baby boy would mean that Elizabeth had waited for nothing. She would do better to marry now while she had the prestige of being heir, or she would end up like her sister: an elderly bride, or worse, a spinster aunt.

'I'd give a lot to know how long I had to wait,' she said frankly.

I bowed again.

'Oh, go away,' she said impatiently. 'If I had known you were bringing me to court for a bedtime lecture from my sister I wouldn't ever have come.'

'I am sorry,' I said. 'But there was a moment when we both thought that court would be better for you than that freezing barn at Woodstock.'

'It wasn't so bad,' Elizabeth said sulkily.

'Princess, it was worse than a pig's hovel.'

She giggled at that, a true girl's giggle. 'Yes,' she admitted. 'And being scolded by Mary is not as bad as being overwatched by that drudge Bedingfield. Yes, I suppose it is better here. It is only . . .' She broke off, and then rose to her feet and pushed the smouldering log with the toe of her slipper. 'I would give a lot to know how long I have to wait,' she repeated.

I visited my father's shop as he had asked me to do in his Christmas letter, to ensure that all was well there. It was a desolate place now; a tile had come from the roof in the winter storms and there was a damp stain down the lime-washed wall of my old bedroom. The printing press was shrouded in a dust sheet and stood beneath it like a hidden dragon, waiting to come out and roar words. But which ones would be safe in this new England where even the Bible was being taken back from the parish churches so that people could only hear from the priest and not read for themselves? If the very word of God was forbidden, then what books could be allowed? I looked along my father's long shelves of books and pamphlets; half of them would now be called heresy, and it was a crime to store them, as we were doing here.

I felt a sense of great weariness and fear. For our own safety I should either spend a day here and burn my father's books, or never come back here again. While they had cords of wood and torches stacked in great stores at Smithfield, a girl with a past like mine should not be in a room of books such as these. But these were our fortune, my father had amassed them over his years in Spain, collected them during his time in England. They were the fruit of hundreds of years of study by learned men and I was not merely their owner, I was their custodian. I would be a poor guardian if I burned them to save my own skin.

There was a tap at the door and I gasped in fright; I was a very timid guardian. I went into the shop, closing the door of the printing room with the incriminating titles behind me, but it was only our neighbour.

'I thought I saw you come in,' he said cheerfully. 'Father not back yet? France too good to him?'

'Seems so,' I said, trying to recover my breath.

'I have a letter for you,' he said. 'Is it an order? Should you hand it on to me?'

I glanced at the paper. It bore the Dudley seal of the bear and staff. I kept my face blandly indifferent. 'I'll read it, sir,' I said politely. 'I'll bring it to you if it is anything you would have in stock.'

'Or I can get manuscripts, you know,' he said eagerly. 'As long as they are allowed. No theology, of course, no science, no astrology, no studies of the planets and planet rays, or the tides. Nothing of the new sciences, nothing that questions the Bible. But everything else.'

'I wouldn't think there was much else, after you have refused to stock all that,' I said sourly, thinking of John Dee's long years of inquiry which took in everything.

'Entertaining books,' he explained. 'And the writings of the Holy Fathers as approved by the church. But only in Latin. I could take orders from the ladies and gentlemen of the court if you were to mention my name.'

'Yes,' I said. 'But they don't ask a fool for the wisdom of books.'

'No. But if they do . . .'

'If they do, I will pass them on to you,' I said, anxious for him to leave.

He nodded and went to the door. 'Send my best wishes to your father when you see him,' he said. 'The landlord says he can go on storing the press here until he can find another tenant. Business is so poor still . . .' He shook his head. 'No-one has any money, no-one has the confidence to set up business while we wait for an heir and hope for better times. She's well is she, God bless her? The queen? Looking well and carrying the baby high, is she?'

'Yes,' I said. 'And only a few months to go now.'

'God preserve him, the little prince,' our neighbour said and devoutly crossed himself. Immediately I followed suit and then held the door for him as he went out.

As soon as I had the door barred I opened my letter.

> *Dear Mistress Boy*
>
> *If you can spare a moment for an old friend he would be very pleased to see you. I need some paper for drawing and some good pens and pencils, having turned to the consolation of poetry as the times are too troubled for anything but beauty. If you have such things in your shop please bring them, at your convenience, Robt. Dudley. (You will find me, at home to visitors, in the Tower, every day, there is no need to make an appointment.)*

He was looking out of the window to the green, his desk drawn close to it to catch the light. His back was turned to me and I was across the room and beside him as he turned around. I was in his arms at once, he hugged me as a man would hug a child, a beloved little girl. But when I felt his arms come around me I longed for him as a woman desires a man.

He sensed it at once. He had been a philanderer for too many years not to know when he had a willing woman in his arms. At once he let me go and stepped back, as if he feared his own desire rising up to meet mine.

'Mistress Boy, I am shocked! You have become a woman grown.'

'I didn't know it,' I said. 'I have been thinking of other things.'

He nodded, his quick mind chasing after any allusion. 'World changing very fast,' he observed.

'Yes,' I said. I glanced at the door which was safely closed.

'New king, new laws, new head of the church. Is Elizabeth well?'

'She's been sick,' I said. 'But she's better now. She's at Hampton Court, with the queen. I just came with her from Woodstock.'

He nodded. 'Has she seen Dee yet?'

'No. I don't think so.'

'Have you seen him?'

'I thought he was in Venice.'

'He was, Mistress Boy. And he has sent a package from Venice to your father in Calais, which your father will send on to the shop in London for you to deliver to him, if you please.'

'A package?' I asked anxiously.

'A book merely.'

I said nothing. We both knew that the wrong sort of book was enough to get me hanged.

'Is Kat Ashley still with the princess?'

'Of course.'

'Tell Kat from me, in secret, that if she is offered some ribbons she should certainly buy them.'

I recoiled at once. 'My lord . . .'

Robert Dudley stretched out a peremptory hand to me. 'Have I ever led you into danger?'

I hesitated, thinking of the Wyatt plot when I had carried treasonous messages that I had not understood. 'No, my lord.'

'Then take this message but take no others from anyone else, and carry none for Kat, whatever she asks you. Once you have told her to buy her ribbons and once you have given John Dee his book, it is nothing more to do with you. The book is innocent and ribbons are ribbons.'

'You are weaving a plot,' I said unhappily. 'And weaving me into it.'

'Mistress Boy, I have to do something, I cannot write poetry all day.'

'The queen will forgive you in time, and then you can go home . . .'

'She will never forgive me,' he said flatly. 'I have to wait until there is a change, a deep sea change; and while I wait, I shall protect my interests. Elizabeth knows that she is not to go to Hungary, or anywhere else, does she?'

I nodded. 'She is quite determined neither to leave nor marry.'

'King Philip will keep her at court now, and make her his friend, I should think.'

'Why?'

'One baby, as yet unborn, is not enough to secure the throne,' he pointed out. 'And next in line is Elizabeth. If the queen were to die in childbirth he would be in a most dangerous position: trapped in England and the new queen and all her people his enemies.'

I nodded.

'And if he were to disinherit Elizabeth then the next heir would be Mary, married to the Prince of France. D'you not think that our Spanish King Philip would rather see the devil incarnate on the English throne than the King of France's son?'

'Oh,' I said.

'Exactly,' he said with quiet satisfaction. 'You can remind Elizabeth that she is in a stronger position now that Philip is on the queen's council. There's not many of them that can think straight there; but he certainly can. Is Gardiner still trying to persuade the queen to declare Elizabeth a bastard and disinherit her?'

I shook my head. 'I don't know.'

Robert Dudley smiled. 'I warrant he is. Actually, I know he is.'

'You're very well informed for a friendless prisoner without news or visitors,' I observed tartly.

He smiled his dark seductive smile. 'No friends as dear to me as you, sweetheart.'

I tried not to smile back but I could feel my face warming at his attention.

'You have grown into a young woman indeed,' he said. 'Time you were out of your pageboy clothes, my bird. Time you were wed.'

I flushed quickly at the thought of Daniel and what he would make of Lord Robert calling me 'sweetheart' and 'my bird'.

'And how is the swain?' Lord Robert asked, dropping into the chair at his desk and putting his boots up on the scattered papers. 'Pressing his suit? Passionate? Urgent?'

'Busy in Padua,' I said with quiet pride. 'Studying medicine at the university.'

'And when does he come home to claim his virgin bride?'

'When I am released from Elizabeth's service,' I said. 'Then I will join him in France.'

He nodded, thoughtful. 'You know that you are a desirable woman now, Mistress Boy? I would not have known you for the little half-lad that you were.'

I could feel my cheeks burning scarlet but I did not drop my eyes like some pretty servant, overwhelmed by the master's smile. I kept my head up and I felt his look flicker over me like a lick.

'I would never have taken you while you were a child,' he said. 'It's a sin not to my taste.'

I nodded, waiting for what was coming next.

'And not while you were scrying for my tutor,' he said. 'I would not have robbed either of you of your gift.'

I stayed silent.

'But when you are a woman grown and another man's wife you can come to me, if you desire me,' he said. His voice was low, warm, infinitely tempting. 'I would like to love you, Hannah. I would like to hold you in my arms and feel your heart beat fast, as I think it is doing now.' He paused. 'Am I right? Heart thudding, throat dry, knees weak, desire rising?'

Silently, honestly, I nodded.

He smiled. 'So I shall stay this side of the table and you shall stay that, and you shall remember when you are a virgin and a girl no longer, that I desire you, and you shall come to me.'

I should have protested my genuine love and respect for Daniel, I should have raged at Lord Robert's arrogance. Instead I smiled at him as if I agreed, and stepped slowly backwards, one step after another, from the desk until I reached the door.

'Can I bring you anything when I come again?' I asked.

He shook his head. 'Don't come until I send for you,' he ordered coolly, very far from my own state of arousal. 'And stay clear of Kat Ashley and Elizabeth for your own sake, my bird, after you have given your message. Don't come to me unless I send for you by name.'

I nodded, felt the wood of the door behind me, and tapped on it with fingers which trembled.

'But you *will* send for me?' I persisted in a small voice. 'You won't just forget about me?'

He put his fingers to his lips and blew me a kiss. 'Mistress Boy, look around, do you see a court of men and women who adore me? I have no visitors but my wife and you. Everyone else has slipped away but the two women that love me. I do not send for you often because I do not choose to endanger you. I doubt that you want the attention of the court directed to who you are, and where you come from, and where your loyalties lie, even now. I send for you when I have work for you, or when I cannot go another day without seeing you.'

The soldier swung open the door behind me but I could not move.

'You like to see me?' I whispered. 'Did you say that sometimes you cannot go another day without seeing me?'

His smile was as warm as a caress and as lightly given. 'The sight of you is one of my greatest pleasures,' he said sweetly. Then the soldier gently put a hand under my elbow, and I went out.

Spring–Summer 1555

At Hampton Court they made the room ready for the queen's confinement. The privy chamber behind her bedroom was hung with the richest of tapestries especially chosen for their holy and encouraging scenes. The windows were bolted shut so that not a breath of air should come into the room. They tied the posts of the bed with formidable and frightening straps that she might cling to, while her labour tore her thirty-nine-year-old body apart. The bed was dressed with a magnificent pillow cover and counterpane which the queen and her ladies had been embroidering since her wedding day. There were great log piles beside the stone fireplace so that the room could be heated to fever pitch. They shrouded the floors with carpets so that every sound should be muffled and they brought in the magnificent royal cradle with a two-hundred-and-forty-piece layette for the boy who would be born within the next six weeks.

At the head of the magnificent cradle was carved a couplet to welcome the prince:

> *The child which Thou to Mary, oh Lord of Might, does send*
> *To England's joy: in health preserve, keep, and defend*

In the rooms outside the privy chambers were midwives, rockers, nurses, apothecaries and doctors in a constant stream of coming and going, and everywhere the nursemaids ran with piles of freshly laundered linen to store in the birthing chamber.

Elizabeth, now free to walk in the palace, stood on the threshold of the confinement room with me. 'All those weeks in there,' she said in utter horror. 'It would be like being walled up alive.'

'She needs to rest,' I said. Secretly I was afraid for the queen in that dark room. I thought that she would be ill if she were to be kept from the light and the sunshine for so long. She would not be allowed to see the king, nor to have any company or music or singing or dancing. She would be like a prisoner in her own chamber. And in less than two months' time, when the baby would come, it would be unendurably hot, locked into that room, curtained in darkness and shrouded in cloth.

Elizabeth stepped back from the doorway with an ostentatiously virginal shudder, and led the way through the presence chamber and into the gallery. Long solemn portraits of Spanish grandees and princes now lined the walls. Elizabeth went past them without turning her head, as if by ignoring them she could make them disappear.

'Funny to think of her releasing me from prison just as she goes into her confinement,' she said, hiding her glee as best she could. 'If she knew what it was like being trapped inside four walls she would change the tradition. I will never be locked up again.'

'She will do her duty for the baby,' I said firmly.

Elizabeth smiled, holding to her own opinion with serene self-confidence. 'I hear you went to see Lord Robert in the Tower.' She took my arm and drew me close to her, so that she could whisper.

'He wanted some writing paper from my father's old shop,' I replied steadily.

'He gave you a message for Kat,' Elizabeth pursued. 'She told me herself.'

'I delivered it to her, herself. About ribbons,' I said dampeningly. 'He is accustomed to use me as his haberdasher and stationer. It is where he first saw me, at my father's shop.'

She paused and looked at me. 'So you know nothing about anything, Hannah?'

'Exactly so,' I said.

'You won't see this then,' she said smartly, and released her hold on me to turn and smile over her shoulder at a gentleman in a dark suit, who had come out of a side room behind us and was following us, walking slowly in our wake.

To my amazement I recognised the king. I pressed myself back against the wall and bowed, but he did not even notice me, his eyes were fixed on Elizabeth. His pace quickened as he saw the momentary hesitation in Elizabeth's step, as she paused and smiled at him; but she did not turn and curtsey as she should have done. She walked serenely down the length of the gallery, her hips slightly swaying. Her every pace was an invitation to any man to follow her. When she reached the end of the gallery at the panelled door she paused, her hand on the handle, and turned to glance over her shoulder, an open challenge to him to follow, then she slipped through the door and in a second she was gone, leaving him staring after her.

The weather grew warmer and the queen lost some of her glow. In the first week of May, having left it as late as she could, she said farewell to the court and went through the doors of her privy chamber to the darkened interior where she must stay until the birth of her boy, and for six weeks after that, before being churched. The only people to see her would be her ladies; the queen's council would have to take their orders from the king, acting in her stead. Messages would be passed into the chamber by her ladies, though it was already being whispered that the queen had asked the king to visit her privately. She could not tolerate the thought of not seeing him for three months, however improper it was that he should come to her at such a time.

Thinking of the look that Elizabeth had shot the king, and how he had followed her swaying hips down the long gallery like a hungry dog, I thought that the queen was well advised to ask him to visit, whatever the tradition of royal births. Elizabeth was not a girl that anyone should trust with their husband, especially when the wife was locked away for a full quarter of the year.

The baby was a little late, the weeks came and went with no sign of him. The midwives predicted a stronger baby for taking his own time and an easier labour when it started, which it must do, any day now. But as May went by they started to remark that it was an exceptionally late baby. The nursemaids rolled their swaddling bandages and started to talk about getting fresh herbs for strewing. The doctors smiled and tactfully suggested that a lady as spiritual and otherworldly as the queen might have mistaken the date of conception; we might have to wait till the end of the month.

While the long hot dull weeks of waiting dragged on there was an embarrassing moment when some rumour set the city of London alight with the news that the queen had given birth to a son. The city went wild, ringing bells and singing in the streets, and the revellers roistered all the way to Hampton Court to learn that nothing had happened, that we were all still waiting, that there was nothing to do but wait.

I sat with Queen Mary every day in the shrouded room. Sometimes I read to her from the Bible in Spanish, sometimes I gave her little pieces of news about the court, or told her Will's latest nonsense. I took flowers in for her, hedgerow flowers like daisies, and then the little roses in bud, anything to give her a sense that there was still an outside world which she would rejoin soon. She took them with a smile of pleasure. 'What, are the roses in bud already?'

'Yes, Your Grace.'

'I shall be sorry to miss the sight of them this year.'

As I had feared, the darkness and quietness of the room was preying on her spirits. With the curtains drawn and the candles lit, it was too dark to sew for very long without gaining a splitting headache, it was a chore to read. The doctors had ruled that she should not have music, and the ladies soon ran out of conversation. The air grew stale and heavy, filled with woodsmoke from the hot fire, and the sighs of her imprisoned companions. After a morning spent with her I found I was coming out of the doors at a run, desperate to be out again in the fresh air and sunshine.

The queen had started the confinement with a serene expectation of giving birth soon. Like any woman facing a first labour she was a little afraid, the more so since she was really too old to have a first child. But she had been borne up by her conviction that God had given her this child, that the baby had quickened when the Papal legate had returned to England, that this conception was a sign of divine favour. Mary, as God's handmaiden, had been confident. But as the days wore on into weeks, her contentment was undermined by the delay. The good wishes that came pouring in from all around the country were like a string of demands for a son. The letters from her father-in-law, the emperor, inquiring as to the delay, read like a reproach. The doctors said that all the signs showed that the baby was coming soon, but still he did not come.

Jane Dormer went around with a face like thunder. Anyone who dared to ask after the health of the queen was stared out of countenance for their impertinence. 'Do I look like some village witch?' she demanded of one woman in my hearing. 'Do I look like an astrologer, casting spells, guessing birth dates? No? The Queen's Grace will take to her bed when she thinks fit and not before, and we shall have a prince when God grants it and not before.'

It was a staunch defence and it could hold off the courtiers, but it could not protect the queen from her own painful growing unease. I had seen her unhappy and fearful before and I recognised the gauntness of her face as the shine was rubbed off her.

Elizabeth, in contrast, now free to go where she would, ride where she liked, boat, walk, play at sports, grew more and more confident as the summer drew on. She had lost the fleshiness that had come with her illness, she was filled with energy and zest for life. The Spanish adored her – her colouring alone was fascinating to them. When she rode her great grey hunter in her green riding habit with her copper hair spread out on her shoulders they called her Enchantress, and Beautiful Brass-head. Elizabeth would smile and protest at the fuss they made, and so encourage them even more.

King Philip never checked them, though a more careful brother-in-law would have guarded against Elizabeth's head being turned by the flattery of his court. But he never said anything to rein in her growing vanity. Nor did he speak now of her marrying and going away from England, nor of her visit to his aunt in Hungary. Indeed, he made it clear that Elizabeth was an honoured permanent member of the court and heir to the throne.

I thought this was mostly policy on his part; but then one day I was looking from the palace window to a sheltered lawn on the south side of the palace and I saw a couple walking, heads close together, down the yew tree *allée*, half-hidden and then half-revealed by the dark strong trees. I smiled as I watched, thinking at first that it was one of the queen's ladies with a Spanish courtier, and the queen would laugh when I told her of this clandestine courtship.

But then the girl turned her head and I saw a flash from under her dark hood, the unmistakable glint of copper hair. The girl was Elizabeth, and the man walking beside her, close enough to touch but not touching, was Prince Philip: Mary's husband. Elizabeth had a book open in her hands, her head was bowed over it, she was the very picture of the devout student, but her walk was the gliding hip-swaying stroll of a woman with a man matching his step to hers.

All at once, I was reminded of the first time I had seen Elizabeth, when she had teased Tom Seymour, her stepmother's husband, to chase her in the garden at Chelsea. This might be seven years later, but it was the same aroused hot-blooded girl who slid a dark sideways glance at another woman's husband and invited him to come a little closer.

The king looked back at the palace, wondering how many people might be watching from the windows, and I expected him to weigh the danger of being seen, and take the Spanish way, the cautious way. But instead he gave a reckless shrug of his shoulders and fell into step a little closer to Elizabeth, who gave a start of innocent surprise, and put her long index finger under the word in her book so that she should not lose her place. I saw her look up at him, the colour rising in her cheeks, her eyes wide with innocence, but the sly smile on her lips. He slipped his arm around her waist so that he could walk with her, looking over her shoulder at the passage in her book as if they both could see the words, as if they cared for anything but the other's touch, as if they were not utterly absorbed in the sound of their own rapid breathing.

I put myself outside Elizabeth's door that night and waited for her and her ladies to go to dinner.

'Ah, fool,' she said pleasantly as she came out of her rooms. 'Are you dining with me?'

'If you wish, Princess,' I said politely, falling into her train. 'I saw a curious thing today in the garden.'

'In which garden?' she asked.

'The summer garden,' I said. 'I saw two lovers walking side by side and reading a book.'

'Not lovers,' she said easily. 'You lack the Sight if you saw lovers, my fool. That was the king and I, walking and reading together.'

'You looked like lovers,' I said flatly. 'From where I was standing. You looked like a courting couple.'

She gave a little gurgle of delighted laughter. 'Oh well,' she said negligently. 'Who can say how they appear to others?'

'Princess, you cannot want to be sent back to Woodstock,' I said to her urgently. We were approaching the great double doors of the dining hall at Hampton Court and I was anxious to warn her before we had to enter and all eyes would be on her.

'How would I be sent back to Woodstock?' she demanded. 'The queen herself released me from arrest and accusation before she locked herself up, and I know that I am innocent of any plot. The king is my friend and my brother-in-law, and an honourable man. I am waiting, like the rest of England, to rejoice at the birth of my sister's baby. How might I offend?'

I leaned towards her. 'Princess, if the queen had seen you and her husband today, as I saw you, she would banish you to Woodstock in a moment.'

Elizabeth gave a dizzy laugh. 'Oh no, for he would not let her.'

'He? He does not give the orders here.'

'He is king,' she pointed out. 'He told her I should be treated with respect, and I am. He told her that I should be free to come and go as I wish, and I am. He will tell her that I am to stay at court, and I will. And, he will tell her that I am not to be coerced or ill-treated or accused of anything at all. I shall be free to meet who I choose, and talk with who I choose, and, in short, do anything at all that I choose.'

I gasped that she could leap so far in her confidence. 'You will always be under suspicion.'

'Not I,' she said. 'Not any more. I could be caught with a dozen pikes in my laundry basket tomorrow, and I would not be charged. He will protect me.'

I was stunned into silence.

'And he is a handsome man.' She almost purred with pleasure. 'The most powerful man in Christendom.'

'Princess, this is the most dangerous game you are playing,' I warned her. 'I have never heard you so reckless before. Where is your caution gone?'

'If he loves me then nothing can touch me,' she said, her voice very low. 'And I can make him love me.'

'He cannot intend anything but your dishonour, and her heartbreak,' I said fiercely.

'Oh, he intends nothing at all.' She was gleaming with pleasure. 'He is far beyond intentions. I have him on the run. He intends nothing, he thinks nothing, I daresay he can barely eat or sleep. D'you not know the pleasure of turning a man's head, Hannah? Let me tell you it is better than anything. And when the man is the most powerful man in Christendom, the King of England and Prince of Spain, and the husband of your icy, arrogant, tyrannical ugly old sister, then it is the greatest joy that can be had!'

A few days later I was out riding. I had outgrown the pony that the Dudleys had given me, and I now rode one of the queen's own beautiful hunters from the royal stables. I was desperate to be out. Hampton Court, for all its beauty, for all its healthful position, was like a prison this summer, and when I rode out in the morning I always had a sense of escape on parole. The queen's anxiety and the waiting for the baby preyed on everyone till we were all like bitches penned up in the kennel, ready to snap at our own paws.

I usually rode west along the river, with the bright morning sunshine on my back, past the gardens and the little farms and on to where the countryside became more wild and the farmhouses more infrequent. I could set the hunter to jump the low hedges, and she would splash through streams in a headlong canter. I would ride for more than an hour and I always turned for home reluctantly.

This warm morning I was glad to be out early, it would be too hot for riding later. I could feel the heat of the sun on my face and pulled my cap down lower to shield my face from the burning light. I turned back towards the palace and saw another horseman on the road ahead of me. If he had headed for the stable-yard or stayed on the high road, I would hardly have noticed him; but he turned off the road towards the palace and took a little lane which ran alongside the walls of the garden. His discreet approach alerted me, and I turned to look more closely.

At once I recognised the scholarly stoop of his shoulders. I called out, without thinking: 'Mr Dee.'

He reined in his horse and turned and smiled at me, quite composed. 'How glad I am to see you, Hannah Verde,' he said. 'I hoped that we might meet. Are you well?'

I nodded. 'Very well, I thank you. I thought you were in Italy. My betrothed wrote to me that he heard you lecture in Venice.'

He nodded. 'I have been home for some time. I am working on a map of the coastline, and I needed to be in London for the maps and sailors' charts. Have you received a book for me? I had it delivered to your father in Calais for safety, and he said he would send it on.'

'I have not been to the shop for some days, sir,' I said.

'When it comes I shall be glad of it,' he said casually.

'Has the queen summoned you, sir?'

He shook his head. 'No, I am here privately to visit the Princess Elizabeth. She asked me to bring her some manuscripts. She is studying Italian and I have brought some very interesting old texts from Venice.'

Still I was not warned. 'Shall I take you to her?' I offered. 'This is not the way to the palace. We can go to the stable-yard by the high road.'

Even as he was about to reply, the little gate in the wall opened silently, and Kat Ashley stood in the doorway.

'Ah, the fool,' she said pleasantly. 'And the magician.'

'You miscall us both,' he said with quiet dignity, and got down from his saddle. A pageboy ducked out from under Kat Ashley's arm to hold John Dee's horse. I realised that he was expected, that they had planned he should enter the palace in secrecy, and – sometimes I was a fool indeed – I realised that it would have been better for me if I had not seen him or, if I had, better to have turned my head and ridden blindly past.

'Take her horse too,' Kat Ashley told the lad.

'I'll take her back to the stable,' I said. 'And go about my business.'

'This is your business,' she said bluntly. 'Now you are here you will have to come with us.'

'I don't have to do anything but what the queen commands me,' I said abruptly.

John Dee put his hand gently on my arm. 'Hannah, I could use your

280

gift in the work I have to do here. And your lord would want you to help me.'

I hesitated, and while I paused, Kat took hold of my hand and fairly dragged me into the walled garden. 'Come in now,' she said. 'You can scurry off once you're inside, but you are putting Mr Dee and me in danger while you argue out here in the open. Come now, and leave later if you must.'

As ever, the thought of being watched frightened me. I tossed my reins to the lad and followed Kat, who went to a little doorway, hidden by ivy, which despite all my time in the palace I had never noticed before. She led us up a winding stair, and came out through another hidden doorway, shielded by a tapestry, opposite the princess's rooms.

She knocked on the door with a special rhythm and it opened at once. John Dee and I went quickly inside. No-one had seen us.

Elizabeth was seated on a stool in the window, a lute across her knees, her new Italian lute master a few paces away setting out music on a stand. They looked as innocent as stage players enacting innocence. Indeed they looked so very innocent that the short hairs on the back of my cropped neck prickled as if I were a frightened dog.

Elizabeth looked up and saw me. 'Oh, Hannah.'

'Kat dragged me in,' I said. 'I think I should go.'

'Wait a moment,' she replied.

Kat Ashley planted her big bottom against the wooden door and leaned back.

'Would you see better if Hannah were to help you?' Elizabeth demanded of John Dee.

'I cannot see without her,' he said frankly. 'I don't have the gift. I was only going to prepare the astrological tables for you; that is all I can do without a seer. I did not know that Hannah would be here today.'

'If she would look for you, what might we see?'

He shrugged. 'Everything. Nothing. How would I know? But we might be able to tell the date of the birth of the queen's baby. We might be able to know if it is a boy or a girl, and how healthy, and what its future might hold.'

Elizabeth came towards me, her eyes very bright. 'Do this for us, Hannah,' she whispered, almost pleading with me. 'We all want to know. You, as much as anybody.'

I said nothing. My knowledge of the queen's growing despair in that darkened room was not one that I wanted to share with her flirtatious half-sister.

'I dare not do it,' I said flatly. 'Mr Dee, I am afraid. These are forbidden studies.'

'It is all forbidden now,' he said simply. 'The world is forming into two bands of people. Those who ask questions and need answers, and those who think the answers are given to us. Her ladyship is one who asks questions, the queen is one who thinks that everything is already known. I am in the world of those who ask: ask about everything. You too. Lord Robert as well. It is breath of life to question, it is like being dead when one has to accept an answer which comes with the dust of the tomb on it and one cannot even ask "why?" You like to ask, don't you, Hannah?'

'I was brought up to it,' I said, as if excusing a sin. 'But I have learned the price. I have seen the price that scholars sometimes have to pay.'

'You will pay no price for asking questions in my rooms,' Elizabeth assured me. 'I am under the protection of the king. We can do as we wish. I am safe now.'

'But I am never safe!' burst from me.

'Come, child,' John Dee urged me. 'You are among friends. Do you not have the courage to exercise your God-given gift, in the sight of your Maker and in the company of your friends, child?'

'No,' I said frankly. I was thinking of the faggots of wood that had been piled up in the town square of Aragon, of the stakes at Smithfield, of the determination of the Inquisition to know only what it feared and see only what it suspected.

'And yet you live here, in the very heart of the court,' he observed.

'I am here to serve the queen because I love her, and because I can't leave her now, not while she is waiting for her baby to be born. And I serve the Princess Elizabeth because ... because she is like no other woman I have ever met.'

Elizabeth laughed. 'You study me as if I were your book,' she said. 'I have seen you do it. I know you do. You watch me as if you would learn how to be a woman.'

I nodded, granting her nothing. 'Perhaps.'

She smiled. 'You love my sister, don't you?'

I faced her without fear. 'I do. Who could not?'

'Then would you not ease her burden by telling her when this slow baby will come? It is a month late, Hannah. People are laughing at her. If she has mistaken her dates, would you not want to tell her that the baby in her belly is growing well and due this very week, or the next?'

I hesitated. 'How could I tell her I knew such a thing?'

'Your gift! Your gift!' she exclaimed irritably. 'You can tell her you just saw it in a vision. You don't have to say the vision was conjured in my rooms.'

I thought for a moment.

'And when you go to see Lord Robert again you could advise him,' Elizabeth said quietly. 'You could tell him that he must make his peace with her for she will put her son on the throne of England, and England will be a Catholic and Spanish power forever. You could tell him to give up waiting and hoping for anything else. You could tell him that the cause is lost and he must convert, plead for clemency and set himself free. That news would mean that he could plead for his freedom. You could set him free.'

I said nothing but she understood the rise of colour in my cheeks. 'I don't know how he can bear it,' she said, her voice low, weaving a spell around me. 'Poor Robert, waiting and waiting in the Tower and never knowing what the future will bring. If he knew that Mary would be on the throne for the next twenty years and her son after her, don't you think he would sue for his freedom and set himself at liberty again? His lands want him, his people need him, he's a man that needs the earth under his boots and the wind in his face. He's not a man to be mewed up like a hooded hawk for half of his life.'

'If he knew for certain that the queen would have a son, would he be able to get free?'

'If a prince was born to her she would release most of them in the Tower for she would know that she was safe on the throne. We would all give up.'

I hesitated no longer. 'I'll do it,' I said.

Elizabeth nodded calmly. 'You need an inner room, don't you?' she asked John Dee.

'Lit with candles,' he said. 'And a mirror, and a table covered with a linen cloth. There should be more, but we'll do what we can.'

Elizabeth went into her privy chamber beyond the audience room and we heard her drawing the curtains and pulling a table before the fireplace. John Dee set out his astronomical charts on her desk; when she came back he had drawn a line through the queen's date of birth and the date of birth of the king.

'Their marriage was in Libra,' he said. 'It is a partnership of deep love.'

I looked quickly at Elizabeth's face but she was not scoffing, thinking of her triumph over her sister in her flirtation with Philip, she was too serious for her petty triumphs now.

'Will it be fruitful?' she asked.

He drew a line across the thin columns of dizzying numbers. He drew another downward, and where the lines intersected he leaned forward to read the number.

'I don't think so,' he said. 'But I can't be sure. There will be two pregnancies.'

Elizabeth drew a little gasp like the hiss of a cat. 'Two? Live births?'

John Dee consulted the number again and then another set of numbers at the foot of the scroll. 'It is very obscure.'

Elizabeth held herself very still, there was no outward sign of her desperation to know.

'So who will inherit the throne?' she asked tightly.

John Dee drew another line, this time horizontally, across the columns. 'It should be you,' he said.

'Yes, I know it *should* be me,' Elizabeth said, reining in her impatience. 'I am the heir now, if I am not overthrown. But *will* it be me?'

He leaned back, away from the pages. 'I am sorry, Princess. It is too unclear. The love that she bears him and her desire for a child obscures everything. I have never seen a woman love a man more, I have never seen a woman long more intensely for a child. Her desire is in every symbol of the table, it is almost as if she could wish a child into being.'

Elizabeth, her face like a beautiful mask, nodded. 'I see. Would you be able to see more if Hannah would scry for you?'

John Dee turned to me. 'Will you try, Hannah? And see what we can learn? It is God's work, remember, we will be seeking the advice of angels.'

'I'll try,' I said. I was not very eager to enter the darkened room, and look in the shadowy mirror. But the thought of bringing Lord Robert the news that might release him, of bringing the queen the news that might give her the greatest joy since her coming to the throne, was a great temptation for me.

I went into the room. The candleflames were bobbing either side of a golden mirror. The table was covered with a white linen cloth. As I watched, John Dee drew a five-sided star on the linen with a dark spluttery pen, and then symbols of power at each corner.

'Keep the door shut,' he said to Elizabeth. 'I don't know how long we will be.'

'Can't I be inside?' she said. 'I won't speak.'

He shook his head. 'Princess, you don't have to speak, you have all the presence of a queen. This has to be just Hannah and me, and the angels if they will come to us.'

'But you will tell me everything,' she urged him. 'Not just the things you think I should know. You will tell me all that there is?'

He nodded and shut the door on her eager face and then turned back to me. He pulled a stool before the mirror and seated me gently, looking over my head to my reflection in the mirror. 'You are willing?' he confirmed.

'I am,' I said seriously.

'It is a great gift that you have,' he said quietly. 'I would give all my learning to be able to do it.'

'I just wish there could be a resolution,' I said. 'I wish Elizabeth might have her throne and yet the queen keep it. I wish the queen might have her son and Elizabeth not be disinherited. I wish with all my heart that Lord Robert might be free and yet not plot against the queen. I wish I could be here and yet be with my father.'

He smiled. 'You and I are the most unhelpful of conspirators,' he said gently. 'For I don't mind which queen is on the throne as long as she will allow the people to follow their faith. And I want the libraries restored and learning allowed, and for this country to explore the seas and spread outward and outward to the new lands to the west.'

'But how will this work bring it about?' I asked.

'We will know what the angels advise,' he said quietly. 'There could be no better guide for us.'

John Dee stepped back from the mirror and I heard his quiet voice pray in Latin that we should do the work of God and that the angels would come to us. I said 'Amen,' heart-felt, and then waited.

It seemed to take a very long time. I saw the candles reflected in the mirror, the darkness around them became darker and they seemed to grow more bright. Then I saw that at the core of every candle there was a halo of darkness, and inside the halo of darkness there was the black wick of the candle and a little haze around it. I grew so fascinated with this anatomy of flame that I could not remember what I should be doing, I just stared and stared into the moving lights until I felt that I had fallen asleep, and then John Dee's hand was gentle on my shoulder and I heard his voice in my ear saying: 'Drink this, child.'

It was a cup of warm ale and I sat back on my stool and sipped it, conscious of a heaviness behind my eyes and weariness, as if I were ill.

'I am sorry,' I said. 'I must have fallen asleep.'

'D'you remember nothing?' he asked curiously.

I shook my head. 'I just watched the flame and then fell asleep.'

'You spoke,' he said quietly. 'You spoke in a language I could not understand, but I think it was the language of angels. God be praised, I think you spoke to them in their language. I copied it down as best I could, I will try to translate it . . . if it is the key to speaking to God!' He broke off.

'Did I say nothing that you could understand now?' I asked, still bemused.

'I questioned you in English and you answered in Spanish,' he said. He saw the alarm in my face. 'It's all right,' he said. 'Whatever secrets you have, they are safe. You said nothing that could not be heard by anyone. But you told me about the queen and the princess.'

'What did I say?' I demanded.

He hesitated. 'Child, if the angel who guides you wanted you to know what words were spoken then he would have let you speak them in your waking state.'

I nodded.

'He did not. Perhaps it is better that you do not know.'

'But what am I to tell Lord Robert when I see him?' I demanded. 'And what can I say to the queen about her baby?'

'You can tell Lord Robert that he will be free within two years,' John

Dee said firmly. 'And there will be a moment when he thinks everything is lost, once more, at the very moment everything is just starting for him. He must not despair then. And you must bid the queen to hope. If any woman in the world could be granted a baby because she would be a good mother, because she loved the father, and because she desired a child, it would be this queen. But whether she will have a son in her womb as well as her heart, I cannot tell you. Whether she will have a child from this birth or not, I cannot tell you.'

I got to my feet. 'I shall go then,' I said. 'I have to take the horse back. But, Mr Dee –'

'Yes?'

'What about the Princess Elizabeth? Will she inherit the throne as her own?'

He smiled at me. 'Do you remember what we saw when we first scried?'

I nodded.

'You said that there will be a child but no child, I think that is the queen's first baby which should have been born but still has not come. You said that there will be a king, but no king – I think that is this Philip of Spain whom we call king but who is not and never will be king of England. Then you said there will be a virgin queen all-forgotten, and a queen but no virgin.'

'Is that Queen Jane, who was a virgin queen and now everyone has forgotten her, and now Mary who called herself a virgin and is now a married queen?' I asked.

He nodded. 'Perhaps. I think the princess's hour will come. There was more, but I cannot reveal it to you. Go now.'

I nodded and went from the room. As I closed the door behind me I saw his dark absorbed face in the mirror as he leaned forward to blow out the candles and I wondered what else he had heard me say when I had been in my tranced sleep.

'What did you see?' Elizabeth demanded impatiently the moment I closed the door.

'Nothing!' I said. I could almost have laughed at the expression on her face. 'You will have to ask Mr Dee. I saw nothing, it was just like falling asleep.'

'But did you speak, or did he see anything?'

'Princess, I cannot tell,' I said, moving towards the door and pausing only to drop her a little bow. 'I have to take my horse back to the stable or they will miss her, and start to look for me.'

Elizabeth nodded my dismissal and just as I was about to open the door there was a knock on it from the outside, in the same rhythm that Kat Ashley had used earlier. In a moment Kat was at the door and had opened it. A man swung into the room and she shut the door smartly behind him. I shrank back as I recognised Sir William Pickering, Elizabeth's friend of old, and fellow-conspirator from the time of the Wyatt rebellion. I had not even known that Sir William was forgiven and back at court – then I realised that he was probably neither forgiven, nor allowed at court. This was a secret visit.

'My lady, I must go,' I said firmly.

Kat Ashley stopped me. 'You will be asked to take some books to Mr Dee. He will have some papers for you to take to Sir William at a house I will tell you,' she said. 'Take a look at him now so that he remembers you again. Sir William, this is the queen's fool, she will bring you the papers you need.'

If it had not come from Kat Ashley, I might not have remembered Lord Robert's warning; but my lord had been very clear with me, and his words confirmed my own sense of terror at whatever they were brewing here.

'I am sorry,' I said simply to Kat Ashley, avoiding even looking at Sir William, and wishing that he had never seen me. 'But my Lord Robert told me to take no messages for anyone. It was his order. I was to tell you about the ribbons and to run no errands after that. You must excuse me, Princess, sir, Mrs Ashley, I cannot assist you.'

I went quickly to the door and let myself out before they could protest. When I was safely away and down the corridor I drew breath and realised then that my heart was pounding as if I had run from some danger. When I saw that the door stayed shut and I heard the quiet shooting of the well-oiled bolt and the thud of Kat Ashley's bottom on the wooden panels, I knew that there was danger there indeed.

It was June and Queen Mary's baby was more than a month overdue, a time when anyone might start to worry; and the petals falling from the hawthorn in the hedgerows blew across the roads like snow. The meadows were rich with flowers, their perfume heady in the warm air. Still we lingered at Hampton Court, though usually the royal court would have moved on by now to another palace. We waited though the roses came into bloom in the gardens, and every bird in England had a baby in the nest but the queen.

The king went around with a face like thunder, exposed to sharp wit in the English court and to danger in the English countryside. He had guards posted night and day on the roads to the palace, and soldiers at every pier on the river. It was thought that if the queen died in childbirth there would be a thousand men at the gate of the palace to tear the Spanish apart. The only thing that could keep him safe then would be the goodwill of the new queen, Elizabeth. No wonder the princess swished around the court in her dark gown as if she were a black cat, the favoured resident of a dairy, over-fed on cream.

The Spanish noblemen of the king's court grew more irritable, as if their own manhood had been impugned by the slowness of this baby. They were frightened of the ill-will of the people of England. They were a small band under siege with no hope of relief. Only the arrival of the baby would have guaranteed their safety, and the baby was dangerously late in coming.

The ladies in the queen's train became sulky; they felt as if they were being made to look like fools, sitting around with little pieces of sewing in their hands, making napkins and bibs and gowns for a baby that did not come. The younger girls, who had been hoping for a merry spring at court with May balls and picnics and masques and hunting, begrudged sitting with the queen in the stuffiness of a darkened room while she prayed for long hours in silence. They emerged from her confinement chamber with faces like spoiled children to say that nothing had happened again today, all day; and the queen seemed no nearer to her time than when she had entered her confinement two months ago.

Only Elizabeth seemed unaffected by the anxious atmosphere of the palace as she walked briskly around the gardens with her long stride, her copper hair flying behind her, a book in her hands. No-one walked with her, no-one publicly befriended her, no-one risked being closely identified with this most problematic princess, but everyone was more aware than ever that as matters now stood, she was the heir to the throne. The birth of a son, would mean that Elizabeth was again unwanted, a threat to everyone's peace. But while there was no son, then she was the next queen. And whether she was the next monarch, or whether she was an unwanted princess, the king could not take his eyes off her.

At dinner every night, King Philip bowed his head to her before he closed his eyes for grace, in the morning he smiled at her and wished her good day. Sometimes, when there was dancing, she took to the floor with the young ladies of the court, and he sat back in his chair and watched her, his eyes veiled, his face revealing nothing of his thoughts. She never returned his look directly these days, she shot him a cool dark gaze from under lowered eyelids and moved carefully in the paces of the dance, her neck poised, her slim waist shifting from side to side, in time to the music. When she curtsied towards the empty throne of her sister at the end of the dance she kept her face down but her smile was one of absolute triumph. Elizabeth knew that Philip could not take his eyes from her, however guarded his expression. She knew that Mary, tired, despairing of her son, was hardly a rival worth vanquishing; but Elizabeth's young glad pride leaped up to the challenge of humiliating her older sister by filling her brother-in-law with baffled desire.

I was going to my dinner in the great hall on a cool evening in the first days of June when I felt a touch on my hand. It was a little pageboy, servant to Sir William Pickering, and I threw a quick glance up the stairway to see who else might have seen him before I bent my head to his whisper.

'Lord Robert says to tell you that John Dee is arrested for casting the queen's horoscope,' he said, his breath tickling my ear. 'He said to burn any books or letters of his.'

In the next second he was gone and all my peace of mind gone with him. I turned and walked into dinner, my face a mask, my heart hammering, the back of my hand rubbing feverishly at my cheek, thinking of nothing but the book that John Dee had sent to my father and which he had forwarded, like an arrow to our door.

That night I lay in bed, unsleeping, my heart pounding with terror. I could not think what I should do to protect myself, to protect my father's fortune which was still stored in the dusty shop off Fleet Street. And what if John Dee told them that I had scryed for him? What if some spy had reported on the afternoon in Princess Elizabeth's rooms when he had drawn up the astrological charts on the queen herself? What if they knew about handsome Sir William, leaning against the door and being assured that I would run errands for him and for Elizabeth?

I watched the dawn turn my little window pale with light, and by five in the morning I was on the steps at the river gate, scanning the water for a passing wherry boat which might take me into the city.

I was lucky. An old boatman, starting his day's work, came across at my hail and took me on board. The soldier sleepily guarding the pier did not even see that I was not a real lad in livery.

'Lechery?' he asked with a wink, guessing from the hour that I had been with some palace kitchen-maid.

'Oh aye, most vile,' I said cheerfully, and jumped into the boat.

I paid my fare and scrambled ashore at the Fleet stairs. I approached the street carefully, trying to see if the door of our shop had been forced. It was too early for our intrusive neighbour to spot me, only a few dairymaids were calling their cows out of the back yards to take them to the meadows for their grass, there was no-one to pay any attention to me.

Even so, I hesitated in the opposite doorway for long moments, watching the street and making sure that no-one was watching me before I crossed the dirty cobblestones and let myself into the shop and closed our door quickly behind me.

It was dark and dusty inside the shop with the shutters closed. I could see that nothing had been disturbed, nobody had come here yet, I was in time. The package labelled 'for Mr John Dee' in my father's hand had been taken in by our neighbour and left on the counter, as incriminating as a brand for the burning.

I untied the string and broke my father's seal. Inside were two books; one was a set of tables which showed, as far as I could tell, the positions of the planets and stars, the other was a guide to astrology in Latin. The two of them in our shop, addressed to John Dee, a man arrested for casting the date of the queen's death, was enough to have both my father and me hanged for treason.

I took them to the empty fireplace and crumpled up the wrapping paper, ready to burn them, my hands shaking in my haste. I rubbed at the tinder box for long minutes before it caught, my fear rising at every moment. Then the flint sparked, and lit the tinder, and I could light a candle and take the flame to the paper in the grate. I held it under the corner of the wrapping paper and watched the flame lick it until it was blazing bright yellow.

I took up the books, planning to tear out a handful of pages at a time and burn each one. The first book, the one written in Latin, fluttered open in my hand. I took a fat handful of soft paper pages. They yielded to my fingers as if they had no power, as if they were not the most dangerous thing in the world. I tried to tear them from the fragile spine, but then I hesitated.

I could not do it. I would not do it. I sat back on my heels with the book in my hand with the light of the fire flickering and dying down and realised that not even when I was in mortal danger could I bring myself to burn a book.

It went against the grain of me. I had seen my father carry some of these books across Christendom, strapped to his heart, knowing that the secrets they contained were newly named as heretical. I had seen him buy books and sell books and, more than that, lend and borrow them just for the joy of seeing their learning go onward, spread outward. I had seen his delight in finding a missing volume, I had seen him welcome a lost folio back to his shelves as if it were the son he had never had. Books were my brothers and sisters; I could not turn against them now. I could not become one of those that see something they cannot understand, and destroy it.

When Daniel's joy in the scholarship of Venice and Padua made my own heart leap with enthusiasm, it was because I too thought that some day everything could be known, nothing need be hidden. And either of these two books might contain the secret of the whole world, might hold the key to understanding everything. John Dee was a great scholar, if he took so much trouble to get hold of these volumes and send them in secret, they would be precious indeed. I could not bring myself to destroy them. If I burned them I was no better than the Inquisition which had killed my mother. If I burned them, I became as one of those who think that ideas are dangerous and should be destroyed.

I was not one of those. Even at risk to my life, I could not become one of those. I was a young woman living at the very heart of a world that was starting to ask questions, living at a time when men and women thought that questions were the most important thing. And who could say where these questions might take us? The tables that had come from my father for John Dee might contain a drug which would cure the plague, they might contain the secret of how to determine where a ship is at sea, they might tell us how to fly, they might tell us how to live forever. I did not know what I held in my hands. I could no more have destroyed it than I could have killed a new-born child: precious in itself, and full of unknowable promise.

With a heavy heart I took the two books and tucked them behind the more innocuous titles on my father's shelf. I supposed that if the house was searched I could claim ignorance. I had destroyed the most dangerous part of the package: the wrapping, John Dee's name written in my father's hand. My father was far away in Calais and there was nothing directly to link us to Mr Dee.

I shook my head, weary of lying in order to reassure myself. In truth, there were a dozen connections between me and Mr Dee if anyone wanted to examine them. There were a dozen connections between my father and the scholar. I was known as Lord Robert's fool, as the queen's fool, as the princess's fool, I was connected with everyone whose name was danger. All I could hope for was that the fool's motley hid me, that the sea between England and Calais shielded my father, and that Mr Dee's angels guided him, and would protect him even when he was on the rack, even if his gaolers gave him his faggot of kindling and made him carry it to the stake.

It was scant consolation for a girl who had spent her girlhood on the run, hiding her faith, hiding her sex, hiding herself. But there was nothing I could do now except to go on the run again, and my horror of running from England was greater than my terror of being caught. When my father had promised me that this would be my home, that I would be safe here, I had believed him. When the queen had put my head in her lap and twisted my hair into curls around her fingers, I had trusted her as I had trusted my mother. I did not want to leave England, I did not want to leave the queen. I brushed the dust off my jerkin, straightened my cap, and slipped out again to the street.

I got back to Hampton Court in time for breakfast. I ran up the deserted garden from the river and entered the palace by the stable door. Anyone seeing me would have thought that I had been riding in the early morning, as I so often did.

'Good day,' one of the pages said and I turned on him the pleasant smile of the habitual liar.

'Good day,' I replied.

'And how is the queen this morning?'

'Merry indeed.'

Like the curtains at the windows of her confinement chamber, shutting out the summer sun, the queen grew paler and faded through every day of the tenth month of her waiting. In contrast, as Elizabeth's confidence grew her very presence, her hair, her skin, seemed to shine more brightly. When she swept into the confinement chamber, taking a stool to talk lightly, sing to her lute, or stitch incredibly fine baby clothes, the queen seemed to shrink into invisibility. The girl was a radiant sparkling beauty, even as she sat over her sewing and demurely bowed her flaming head. Beside her, hand on her belly, always waiting in case the child should move, Mary was becoming little more than a shadow. As the days wore on, through the long long month of June, she became like a shadow waiting for the birth of a shadow. She seemed hardly to be there at all, her baby seemed hardly to be there at all. They were both melting away.

The king was a driven man. Everything directed him towards a steady fidelity to his wife: her love for him, her vulnerable condition, the need to appease the English nobility and keep the council favourably disposed towards Spanish policy as the country sneered at the sterile Spanish king. He knew this, he was a brilliant politician and diplomat; but he could not help himself. Where Elizabeth walked, there he followed. When she rode, he called for his horse and galloped after her. When she danced, he watched her and called for them to play the music again. When she studied, he loaned her books and corrected her pronunciation like a disinterested schoolmaster, while all the time his eyes were on her lips, on the neck of her gown, on her hands clasped lightly in her lap.

'Princess, this is a dangerous game,' I warned her.

'Hannah, this is my life,' she said simply. 'With the king on my side I need fear nothing. And if he were to be free to marry, then I could look to no better match.'

'Your sister's husband? While she is confined with his child?' I demanded, scandalised.

Her downcast eyes were slits of jet. 'I might think, as she did, that an alliance between Spain and England would dominate all of Christendom,' she said sweetly.

'Yes, the queen thought that, and yet all that has happened is that she has brought the heresy laws on the heads of her subjects,' I said tartly. 'And brought herself to solitude in a darkened room with her heart breaking and her sister outside in the sunshine flirting with her husband.'

'The queen fell in love with a husband who married for policy,' Elizabeth decreed. 'I would never be such a fool. If he married me it would be quite the reverse. I would be the one marrying for policy and he would be the one marrying for love. And we would see whose heart broke first.'

'Has he told you he loves you?' I whispered, aghast, thinking of the queen lost in her loneliness of the enclosed room. 'Has he said he would marry you, if she died?'

'He adores me,' Elizabeth said with quiet pleasure. 'I could make him say anything.'

It was hard to get news of John Dee without seeming overly curious. He had simply gone, as if he had never been, disappeared into the terrible dungeons of the Inquisition in England at St Paul's, supervised by Bishop Bonner, whose resolute questioning was feeding the fires of Smithfield at the rate of half a dozen poor men and women every week.

'What news of John Dee?' I asked Will Somers quietly, one morning when I found him recumbent on a bench, basking like a lizard in the summer sunshine.

'He's not dead yet,' he said, barely opening an eye. 'Hush.'

'Are you sleeping?' I asked, wanting to know more.

'*I'm* not dead yet,' he said. 'In that, he and I have something in common. But I am not being stretched on the rack, nor being pressed with a hundred rocks on my chest, nor being taken for questioning at midnight, at dawn, and as a rough alternative to breakfast. So not that much in common.'

'Has he confessed?' I asked, my voice a little breath.

'Can't have done,' Will said pragmatically. 'Because if he had confessed he would be dead, and there his similarity to me would be ended, since I am not dead but merely asleep.'

'Will . . .'

'Fast asleep and dreaming, and not talking at all.'

I went to find Elizabeth. I had thought of speaking to Kat Ashley but I knew she despised me for my mixed allegiances, and I doubted her discretion. I heard the blast of the hunting horns and I knew that Elizabeth would have been riding. I hurried down to the stable-yard and was there as the hounds came streaming in, with the riders behind them. Elizabeth was riding a new black hunter, a gift from the king, her cap askew, her face glowing. The court was all dismounting and shouting for their grooms. I sprang forward to hold her horse and said quietly to her, unheard in the general noise, 'Princess, do you have any news of John Dee?'

She turned her back to me and patted her horse's shoulder. 'There, Sunburst,' she said loudly, speaking to the horse. 'You did well.' To me in an undertone she said: 'They are holding him for conjuring and calculating.'

'What?' I asked, horrified.

She was absolutely calm. 'They say that he attempted to cast the queen's astrology chart, and that he summoned up spirits to foretell the future.'

'Will he speak of any others, doing this with him?' I breathed.

'If they charge him with heresy you should expect him to sing like a little blinded thrush,' she said, turning to me and smiling radiantly, as if it were not her life at stake as well as mine. 'They'll rack him, you know. No-one can stand that pain. He will be bound to talk.'

'Heresy?'

'So I'm told.'

She tossed her reins to her groom and walked towards the palace, leaning on my shoulder.

'They'll burn him?'

'Undoubtedly.'

'Princess, what shall we do?'

She dropped her arm around my shoulder and gripped it hard, as if she were holding me to my senses. I could feel that her hand did not tremble for a moment. 'We will wait. And hope to survive this. Same as always, Hannah. Wait, and hope to survive.'

'*You* will survive,' I said with sudden bitterness.

Elizabeth turned her bright face to me, her smile merry but her eyes were like chips of coal. 'Oh yes,' she said. 'I have done so, thus far.'

In mid-June the queen, still pregnant, broke with convention to release herself from the confinement chamber. The physicians could not say that she would be any worse for being outside, and they thought walking in the air might give her an appetite for her meals. They were afraid that she was not eating enough to keep herself and her baby alive. In the cool of the morning or in the shadowy evening she would stroll slowly in her private garden attended only by her ladies and the members of her household. She was changing before my eyes from the deliciously infatuated woman that Prince Philip of Spain had wedded and bedded, and loved into joy, back to the anxious prematurely aged woman that I had first met. Her new confidence in love and happiness was draining away from her, with the pink of her cheeks and the blue of her eyes, and I could see her drawn back to the loneliness and fearfulness of her childhood, almost like an invalid slipping towards death.

'Your Grace.' I dropped to one knee as I met her in the privy garden one day. She had been looking at the fast flow of the river past the boat pier, looking, and yet not seeing. A brood of ducklings was playing in the current, their mother watchful nearby, surveying the little bundles of fluff as they paddled and bobbed. Even the ducks on the Thames had young; but England's cradle, with that hopeful poem at the bed-head, was still empty.

She turned an unseeing dark gaze to me. 'Oh, Hannah.'

'Are you well, Your Grace?'

She tried to smile at me but I saw her lips twist down.

'No, Hannah, my child. I am not very well.'

'Are you in pain?'

She shook her head. 'I should be glad of pain, of labour pains. No, Hannah. I feel nothing, not in my body, not in my heart.'

I drew a little closer. 'Perhaps these are the fancies that come before birth,' I said soothingly. 'Like when they say women have a craving for eating raw fruit or coal.'

She shook her head. 'No, I don't think so.' She held out her hands to me, as patient as a sick child. 'Can't you see, Hannah? With your gift? Can you see, and tell me the truth?'

Almost unwillingly I took her hands and at her touch I felt a rush of despair as dark and as cold as if I had fallen into the river which flowed beneath the pier. She saw the shock in my face, and read it rightly at once.

'He's gone, hasn't he?' she whispered. 'I have somehow lost him.'

'I wouldn't know, Your Grace,' I stumbled. 'I'm no physician, I wouldn't have the skill to judge . . .'

She shook her head, the bright sunlight glinting on the rich embroidery of her hood, on the gold hoops in her ears, all this worldly wealth encasing heartbreak. 'I knew it,' she said. 'I had a son in my belly and now he is gone. I feel an emptiness where I used to feel a life.'

I still had hold of her icy hands, I found I was chafing them, as people will chafe the hands of a corpse.

'Oh, Your Grace!' I cried out. 'There can be another child. Where one has been made you can make another. You had a child and lost him, hundreds of women do that, and go on to have another child. You can do that too.'

She did not even seem to hear me, she let her hands lie in mine and she looked towards the river as if she would want it to wash her away.

'Your Grace?' I whispered, very quietly. 'Queen Mary? Dearest Mary?'

When she turned her face to me her eyes were filled with tears. 'It's all wrong,' she said, and her voice was low and utterly desolate. 'It has been going wrong since Elizabeth's mother took my father from us and broke my mother's heart, and nothing can put it right again. It's been going wrong since Elizabeth's mother won my father to sin and led him from his faith so that he lived and died in torment. It's all wrong, Hannah, and I cannot put it right though I have tried and tried. It is too much for me. There is too much sadness and sin and loss in this story for me to put right. It is beyond me. And now Elizabeth has taken my husband from me, my husband who was the greatest joy of my life – the only joy of my life – the only man who ever loved me, the only person I have ever loved since I lost my mother. She has taken him from me. And now my son has gone from me too.'

Her darkness flowed through me like a draught of the deepest despair. I gripped her hands as if she were a drowning woman, swept away in a night flood.

'Mary!'

Gently she pulled her hands from me, and walked away, alone again, as she always had been, as now she thought she always must be. I ran behind her, and though she heard my footsteps she did not pause or turn her head.

'You could have another child,' I repeated. 'And you could win your husband back.'

She did not pause or shake her head. I knew that she was walking with her chin up and the tears streaming down her cheeks. She could not ask for help, she could not receive help. The pain in her heart was that of loss. She had lost the love of her father, she had lost her mother. Now she had lost her child and every day, in full view of the court, she was losing her husband to her pretty younger sister. I fell back and let her go.

For the long hot month of July the queen said nothing to explain why her baby was not coming. Elizabeth inquired after her health every morning with the most sisterly concern, and remarked every day in her sweet clear voice:

'Gracious, what a long long time this babe is taking to be born!'

Every day people came out from London to say Masses for the

queen's safe delivery, and we all stood up in church three times a day to say 'amen'. The news they brought from London was that of a city of horrors. The queen's belief that her baby would not come until England was cleansed of heresy had taken a vicious turn. In the hands of her Inquisitors, Bishop Bonner and the rest of them, there was a savage policy of secret arrests and cruel tortures. There were rumours of unjust trials of heretics, of maidservants being taken up in their ignorance and when they swore that they would not surrender their Bible, being taken to the stake and burned for their faith. There was a vile story of a woman pregnant with her first child who was accused of heresy and charged before a court. When she would not bow her head to the dictates of the Roman Catholic priest they put her on a stake and lighted the pyre. In her terror she gave birth to the child then and there, and dropped it on to the faggots. When the baby slithered from her shaking thighs to the ground, crying loud enough to be heard over the crackle of the flames, the executioner forked the naked child back into the fire with a pitchfork, as if he were a crying bundle of kindling.

They made sure that these stories did not reach the queen but I was certain that if she knew she would put a stop to the cruelty. A woman waiting for her own child to be born does not send another pregnant woman to the stake. I took my chance one morning, when she was walking.

'Your Grace, may I speak with you?'

She turned and smiled. 'Yes, Hannah, of course.'

'It is a matter of state and I am not qualified to judge,' I said cautiously. 'And I am a young woman, and perhaps I don't understand.'

'Understand what?' she asked.

'The news from London is very cruel,' I said, taking the plunge. 'I am sorry if I speak out of turn, but there is much cruelty being done in your name and your advisors do not tell you of it.'

There was a little ripple at my temerity. At the back of the group of ladies I saw Will Somers roll his eyes at me.

'Why, what do you mean, Hannah?'

'Your Grace, you know that many of the great Protestants of the land have gone quietly to Mass and their priests have put away their wives and become obedient to the new laws. It is only their servants and the foolish people in the villages who do not have the wit to tell a lie when they are examined. Surely you would not want the simple people of your country to be burned for their faith? Surely, you would want to show them mercy?'

I expected her smile of acknowledgement, but the face she turned to me was scowling. 'If there are families who have turned their coat and not their faith then I want their names,' she said, her voice hard. 'You are right: I don't seek to burn servants, I want them all, masters and men, to turn again to the church. I would be a sorry Queen of England if I did not insist on the same law for rich and for poor. If you know the name of a priest with a wife in hiding, Hannah, then you had better tell me now or you will be risking your own immortal soul.'

I had never seen her so cold.

'Your Grace!'

It was as if she did not hear me. She put her hand on her heart and she cried out: 'Before God, Hannah, I will save this country from sin even though it cost life after life. We have to turn back to God and from heresy and if it takes a dozen fires, if it takes a hundred fires, we will do it. And if you, even you, are hiding a name then I will have it from you, Hannah. There will be no exceptions made. Even you shall be questioned. If you will not tell, I shall have you questioned . . .'

I could feel the colour draining from my face and my heart start to race. After surviving so long, to put myself into danger, to step up to the rack! 'Your Grace!' I stammered. 'I am innocent . . .'

There was a scream from the back of the court and we all turned to look. A lady in waiting was running, holding her skirts away from her pounding feet, towards the queen. 'Your Grace!' she whimpered. 'Save me! It is the fool! He is run mad!'

Will Somers was bent down in a squat, his great long legs folded up. Beside him in the grass was a frog, emerald green, blinking his fat eyes. Will blinked too, mirroring his actions.

'We are racing,' he said with dignity. 'Monsieur le Frog and I have a wager that I shall get to the end of the orchard before him. But he is playing a long game. He is trying to out-strategy me. I would wish someone to tickle him with a stick.'

The court was convulsed, the woman who had screamed had turned and was laughing too. Will, squatting like a frog, knees up around his ears, goggle-eyes blinking, was inescapably funny. Even the queen was smiling. Someone fetched a stick and stood behind the frog and gave it a little poke.

At once the frightened thing leaped forward. Will leaped too in a great unexpected bound. Will was clearly in the lead with his first hop. With a roar the courtiers ran into two lines to form a track, and someone prodded the frog once more. This time he was more alarmed and took three great bounds and started to crawl as well. The ladies flapped their skirts to keep him on course as Will bounded behind him, but the frog was clearly gaining. Another touch of the stick and he was off again, Will in hot pursuit, people shouting odds and bets, the Spaniards shaking their heads at the folly of the English but then laughing despite themselves and throwing down a purse of coins on the frog.

'Someone tickle Will!' came a shout. 'He's lagging back.'

One of the men found a stick and went behind Will who leaped a little faster, to keep out of the way. 'I'll do it!' I said and snatched the stick from him and mimed a great beating when the stick hit the ground behind Will and never so much as touched his breeches.

He went as fast as he could have done, but the frog was thoroughly frightened and seemed to know that the thick thorn hedge threaded with bean flowers at the end of the orchard was a safe haven. He bounded towards it and Will arrived a mere toad's nose behind. There was a great roar of applause and a chink of coins being exchanged. The queen held her belly and laughed out loud, and Jane Dormer slipped an arm around her waist to support her, and smiled to see her mistress so happy for once.

Will unfolded himself from the ground, his gangling legs stretching out at last, his face creased with a smile as he took his bow. The whole court moved on, talking and laughing about Will Somers' race with a frog, but I delayed him, a hand on his arm.

'Thank you,' I said.

He looked at me steadily, no trace of the fool about either of us. 'Child, you cannot change a king, you can only make him laugh. Sometimes, if you are a very great fool, you can make him laugh at himself, and then you may make him a better man and a better king.'

'I was clumsy,' I confessed. 'But Will, I spoke to a woman today and the things that she told me would have made you weep!'

'Far worse in France,' he said quickly. 'Worse in Italy. You of all people should know, child, that it is worse in Spain.'

That checked me. 'I came to England thinking that this was a country that would be more merciful. Surely the queen is not a woman to burn a priest's wife.'

He dropped an arm over my shoulders. 'Child, you are a fool indeed,' he said gently. 'The queen has no mother to advise her, no husband who loves her, and no child to distract her. She wants to do right and she is told by everyone around her that the best way to bring this country to heel is to burn a few nobodies who are destined for hell already. Her heart might ache for them but she will sacrifice them to save the rest, just as she would sacrifice herself for her own immortal soul. Your skill, my skill, is to make sure that it never occurs to her to sacrifice us.'

I turned a face to him which was as grave as he would have wished. 'Will, I have trusted her. I would trust her with my life.'

'You do rightly,' he said in mock approbation. 'You are a very true fool. It is only a fool who trusts a king.'

In July the court should have been on progress, travelling round the great houses of England, enjoying the hunting and the parties and the pleasures of the English summer, but still the queen said nothing about when we might leave. Our setting out had been delayed day after day waiting for the birth of the prince, and now, twelve weeks late, nobody truly believed that the prince would come.

Nobody said anything to the queen – that was the worst of it. Nobody asked her how she was feeling, whether she was ill, if she was bleeding or sick. She had lost a child which meant more to her than the world itself, and nobody asked her how she did, or if they could comfort her. She was surrounded by a wall of polite silence, but they smiled when she had gone by, and some of them laughed behind their hands and said that she was an old and foolish woman and that she had mistaken the drying-up of her courses for a pregnancy! and what a fool she was! and what a fool she had made of the king! and how he must hate her for making him the laughing-stock of Christendom!

She must have known how they spoke of her, and the bitter twist of her mouth showed her hurt; but she walked with her head high through a summertime court which was buzzing with malice and gossip, and she still said nothing. At the end of July, still without a public word from the queen, the midwives packed up their dozens of bandages, put away the embroidered white silk layette, packed away the bonnets, the little bootees, the petticoats and the swaddling bands and finally carried the magnificent wooden cradle from the birthing room. The servants took down the tapestries from the windows and the walls, the thick Turkish rugs from the floor, the straps and the rich bedding from the bed. Without any word of explanation from the doctors, from the midwives or from the queen herself, everyone realised that now there was no baby, now there was no pregnancy, and the matter was closed. The court moved in an almost silent procession to Oatlands Palace and took up residence so quietly that you would have thought that someone had died in hiding, of shame.

John Dee, charged with heresy, conjuring and calculating, disappeared into the terrible maw of the Bishop's Palace in London. It was said that the coalhouses, the woodstores, the cellars, even the drains below the palace were serving as cells for the hundreds of suspected heretics waiting to be questioned by Bishop Bonner. In the neighbouring St Paul's Cathedral, the bell tower was crammed with prisoners who scarcely had place to sit, let alone lie down, deafened by the ringing of the bells in the arches over their heads, exhausted by brutal interrogation, broken by torture and waiting, with dreadful certainty, to be taken out and burned.

I could hear nothing of Mr Dee, not from Princess Elizabeth, nor from any of the gossips around court. Not even Will Somers, who usually knew everything, had heard of what had happened to John Dee. He scowled at me when I asked him and said, 'Fool, keep your own foolish counsel. There are some names better not mentioned between friends, even if they are both fools.'

'I need to know how he fares,' I said urgently. 'It is a matter of some . . . importance to me.'

'He has disappeared,' Will said darkly. 'Turns out he was a magician indeed that he could vanish so completely.'

'Dead?' My voice was so low that Will could not have heard the word, he guessed the meaning from my aghast face.

'Lost,' he said. 'Disappeared. Which is probably worse.'

Since I did not know what a lost man might say before he disappeared I never slept more than a few hours every night, waking up with a start at every sound outside the door, thinking that they had come for me. I started to dream of the day they had come for my mother, and between my childhood terror for her and my own fears for myself I was in a sorry state.

Not so the Princess Elizabeth. She might never have heard of John Dee. She lived her life at the court with all the Tudor glamour she could exploit, walking in the garden, eating her dinner in the hall, attending Mass sitting one place behind her sister, and always, always, meeting the glance of the king with an unspoken promise.

Their desire for each other lit up the court. It was an almost palpable heat. When she walked into the room everyone could see him tense like a hound when he hears the hunting horn. When he walked behind her chair she would give a little involuntary shiver, as if the very air between them had caressed the nape of her neck. When they met by accident in the gallery they stood three feet apart, as if neither of them dared to go within arm's length, and they skirted each other, moving one way and then another as if in a dance to music that only they could hear. If she turned her head to one side he would look at her neck, at the pearl swinging from her earlobe, as if he had never seen such a thing before. When he turned his head she would covertly steal a glance at his profile, and her lips would part in a little sigh as she looked at him. When he helped her down from the saddle of her horse, he held her against him after her feet had touched the ground and the two of them were shaking by the time he released her.

There was not a word spoken between them that the queen could not have heard, there was no caress that anyone could see. The simple proximity of day-to-day life was enough to set them both aflame, his hands on her waist, her hands on his shoulder in a dance, the moment when they stood close, eyes locked. There was no doubt that this woman would escape any punishment while this king was ruling the country. He could barely let her out of his sight, he was not likely to send her to the Tower.

The queen had to watch all this. The queen, worn thin to gauntness, with a flat belly, had to watch her younger sister summon the king by merely raising her plucked eyebrow. The queen had to watch the man she still passionately loved at another woman's beck and call, and that woman, Elizabeth, the unwanted sister who had stolen Mary's father, was now seducing her husband.

Queen Mary never showed a flicker of emotion. Not when she leaned from her chair and made a smiling remark to Philip and then realised that he had not even heard her, he was so absorbed in watching Elizabeth dance. Not when Elizabeth brought him a book she was reading and composed a Latin motto for the dedication, extempore before the whole court. Not when Elizabeth sang him a tune which she had written for him, not when Elizabeth challenged him to a race while out hunting, and the two of them outstripped the court and were missing for half an hour. Mary had all the dignity of her mother, Katherine of Aragon, who had seen her own husband besotted by another woman for six long years and for the first three of them had sat on her throne and smiled at them both. Just as her mother had done, Mary smiled at Philip with love and understanding, and smiled at Elizabeth with courtesy; and only I, and the few people who really loved her, would have known that her heart was breaking.

I had a letter from my father in August, asking me when I would join them at Calais. Indeed, I was anxious to go. I could not sleep in England now, the place that I had sought as my home was no longer a haven. I wanted to be with my own people, I wanted to be with my father. I wanted to be far from Bishop Bonner and the smoke of Smithfield.

I went to Elizabeth first. 'Princess, my father asks me to join him in Calais, do I have your permission to go?'

Her pretty face scowled at once. Elizabeth was a great collector of servants, she never liked anyone to leave. 'Hannah, I have need of you.'

'God bless you, Princess, but I think you are well served,' I said with a smile. 'And you did not give me a very warm welcome when I came to you at Woodstock.'

'I was ill then,' she said irritably. 'And you were Mary's spy.'

'I have never spied on anyone,' I said, conveniently forgetting my work for Lord Robert. 'The queen sent me to you, as I told you. Now I see that you are respected and well-treated at court, I can leave you, you don't need me.'

'I shall decide what service I need and what I can do without,' she said at once. 'Not you.'

I made my little pageboy bow. 'Please, Princess, let me go to my father and my betrothed.'

She was diverted by the thought of my marriage, as I knew she would be. She smiled at me, the true Tudor charm shining through her irritability. 'Is that what you are after? Ready to put off your motley and go to find your lover? Do you think you are ready to be a woman, little fool? Have you studied me enough?'

'You would not be my study if I wanted to be a good wife,' I said sharply.

She gave a ripple of laughter. 'Thank God, no. But what have you learned from me?'

'How to torment a man to madness, how to make a man follow you without even turning your head, and how to get down from your horse so you press against every inch of him.'

She threw back her head and laughed, a loud genuine laugh. 'You've learned well,' she said. 'I only hope you get as much joy from these skills as I do.'

'But what profit?' I asked.

The glance Elizabeth shot me was one of acute calculation. 'Some amusement,' she conceded. 'And real profit. You and I have slept safer in our beds because the king is in love with me, Hannah. And my path to the throne has been a little clearer since the most powerful man in the world swore he would support me.'

'You have his promise?' I asked, amazed at her.

She nodded. 'Oh, yes. My sister is betrayed more deeply than she knows. Half her country is in love with me, and now her husband too. My advice to you, as you go to your husband, is never to trust him and never love him more than he loves you.'

I shook my head, smiling. 'I mean to be a good wife,' I said. 'He is a good man. I mean to leave this court and go to him and become a good and steady wife to him.'

'Ah, you can't be that,' she said bluntly. 'You're not a woman grown yet. You're afraid of your own power. You're afraid of his desire. You're afraid of your own desire. You're afraid of being a woman.'

I said nothing, though it was the truth.

'Oh, go then, little fool. But when you are bored, and you will be bored, you can come back to me again. I like having you in my service.'

I bowed and took myself off to the queen's rooms.

The moment I opened the door I knew that there was something wrong. My first thought was that Queen Mary was ill, somehow fatally ill and yet not attended. The room was empty of her women, she was all but alone. The room was gloomy; with the shutters closed, it was cold, as the summer heat did not penetrate the thick walls. She was crouched on the floor, doubled-up, folded over her knees, her forehead pressed on the cold hearthstone at the empty fireside. Only Jane Dormer was with her, seated in the shadows behind her, in stubborn silence. When I went to the queen and knelt before her I saw her face was wet with tears.

'Your Grace!'

'Hannah, he is leaving me,' she said.

I shot a bemused look at Jane and she scowled at me, as if I were to blame.

'Leaving you?'

'He is going to the Low Countries. Hannah, he is leaving me . . . leaving me.'

I took her hands. 'Your Grace . . .'

Her eyes were sightless, filled with tears, fixed on the empty hearth. 'He is leaving me,' she said.

I went over to Jane Dormer, stabbing her needle into a linen shirt in the window-seat. 'How long has she been like this?'

'Since he told her his news, this morning,' she said coldly. 'He sent her ladies away when she started screaming that her heart would break, then, when he could not stop her weeping, he left too. He has not come back, and they have not come back.'

'Has she not eaten? Have you brought her nothing?'

She glared at me. 'He has broken her heart, as you predicted,' she said flatly. 'Don't you remember it? I do. When I brought her the portrait and I was so hopeful and she was so taken with him. You said he would break her heart and he has done so. Him with his baby that was there and then gone, him with his Spanish lords longing to go and fight the French, and forever complaining about England. Now he has told her he is going to war against the French, but not when he will come back; and she can say nothing but that he is leaving, leaving her. And she cries as if she would die of grief.'

'Shouldn't we get her to bed?'

'Why?' she demanded. 'He won't come to her in bed for lust, if he won't come here for pity, and his presence is the only thing that will help her.'

'Mistress Jane, we cannot just sit here and see her cry and cry like this.'

'What would you have us do?' she asked. 'Her happiness is given over to a man who does not care enough for her to stay when she has lost his baby and has lost the love of her people for him. A man who does not have enough common pity to give her a word of comfort. We cannot heal this hurt with a cup of warm ale and a brick beneath her feet.'

'Well let's get her that, at least,' I said, falling on the suggestion.

'You get it,' she said. 'I'm not leaving her alone. This is a woman who could die of loneliness.'

I went to the queen and knelt beside her where she keened, soundlessly, her forehead knocking against the hearthstone as she rocked forward and back. 'Your Grace, I'm going down to the kitchen, can I bring you anything to eat or drink?'

She sat back on her heels but did not look at me. Her forehead was bloody where she had grazed it against the stone. Her gaze remained fixed on the empty hearth; but she put out her cold little hand and took mine. 'Don't leave me,' she said. 'Not you as well. He's leaving me, you know, Hannah. He just told me. He's leaving me, and I don't know how I can bear to live.'

Dear Father,

Thank you for your blessing in your letter to me. I am glad that you are well and that the shop in Calais is doing so well. I should have been glad to obey your command and come to you at once but when I went to the queen for permission to leave her service I found her so ill that I cannot leave her, at least for this month. The king has set sail for the Lowlands, and she cannot be happy without him, she is quite desolate. We have come to Greenwich and it is like a court in mourning. I will stay with her until he returns which he has promised, on his word of honour, will be very soon. When he comes back I shall come to you without delay. I hope this is agreeable to you, Father, and that you will explain to Daniel and to his mother that I would prefer to be with them, but that I feel it is my duty to stay with the queen at this time of her great unhappiness.

I send you my love and duty and hope to see you soon –
Your Hannah

Dear Daniel,

Forgive me, I cannot come yet. The queen is in a despair so great that I dare not leave her. The king has left and she is clinging to all her other friends. She is so bereft that I fear for her mind. Forgive me, love, I will come as soon as I can. He has sworn it is a brief absence, merely to protect his interests in the Low Countries and so we expect him back within the month. September or October at the latest, I will be able to come to you. I want to be your wife, indeed I do.

Hannah

Autumn 1555

The queen retreated into a private world of silent misery in the palace that had been the happiest of them all: Greenwich. Parting with the king had been an agony for her. Like a man, he had hidden from her despair in the elaborate formality of leave-taking, he had made sure they were always attended so she could not cry over him in private. He engineered it so that she said goodbye to him like a doll queen: one whose hands and feet and mouth were worked by an indifferent puppet-master. When he was finally gone it was as if the strings were cut and she dropped to the floor, all disjointed.

Elizabeth had slid away from him with a smile which suggested to some that she had a better idea of when he would come back to England than his own wife, and was reassured by his plans. He had the decency not to hold her close on parting, but when he boarded ship and leaned over the side and waved, he kissed his hand and it was a gesture directed ambiguously: towards the princess, and the heartbroken queen.

The queen kept to her darkened rooms and would be served only by Jane Dormer or me, and the court became a place of ghosts, haunted by her unhappiness. The few Spanish courtiers left behind by their king were desperate to join him, their anxiety to leave made us all feel that the English marriage had been nothing but an interlude in their real lives, and a mistake, at that. When they applied to the queen for permission to join him she flew into a frenzy of jealousy, swearing that they were going because they secretly knew that there was no point waiting for him in England. She screamed at them, and they bowed and fled from her fury. Her ladies scuttled from the room or pressed themselves back against their seats, trying to hear and see nothing, and only Jane and I went to her, begging her to be calm. She was beside herself, while the storm lasted Jane and I had to cling to her arms to stop her beating her head against the panelled walls of her privy chamber. She was a woman deranged by her passion for him, driven by her conviction that she had lost him forever.

When the queen's rage subsided it was worse, because she slumped to the floor and hugged her knees to her chest and buried her face, like a little girl after a beating. We could not make her stand up or even open her eyes for hours. She hid her face from us, deep in despair and filled with shame at how low she had been brought by love. Sitting beside her on the cold wooden floor, with nothing to say that could help her in her pain, I saw the skirt of her gown slowly darken as her tears soaked into the velvet, and she never made a sound.

She did not speak for a night and a day, and the day after she was stony-faced like a statue of despair. When she emerged to sit on her throne in the empty room it was to find that the Spaniards were openly rebelling against being forced to stay, and all the English men and women of the court were angry too. Life in the queen's service was not what it had been when the king had arrived and taken her with love; not what a court should be. Instead of literature and music, sport and dancing, it was like a nunnery ruled by a mortally sick abbess. No-one spoke above a whisper, no feasts ever took place, there were no entertainments or gaiety, and the queen sat on her throne with a face of blank misery and retired to her rooms to be on her own whenever she could. Life at court had become long days of hopeless waiting for the king to return. We all knew that he never would.

With no man to torment, and no chance of making the queen more miserable than she was already, Princess Elizabeth took the opportunity to leave the court at Greenwich and go to her palace at Hatfield. The queen let her go, without a word of affection. Any love she had felt for Elizabeth the child had been worn out by the disloyalty of Elizabeth the young woman. Elizabeth's flirtation with the king while Mary had been enduring the last weeks of a failed pregnancy had been the final act of wilful unkindness that would ever hurt her sister. In her heart Mary saw this as the final proof that Elizabeth was the daughter of a whore and a lute player. What other girl would treat her sister as Elizabeth had done?

In her heart she denied kinship with Elizabeth, she denied her as her sister, she denied her as her heir. She took back the love that she had constantly offered the younger woman, and she excluded her from her heart. She was glad to let her go and would not have cared if she had never seen her again.

I went down to the great gate to bid the princess farewell. She was wearing her solemn black-and-white gown, the livery of the Protestant princess, since her way took her through London and the London citizens would turn out for her and cheer. She gave me a roguish wink as she put her boot in a stable lad's cupped hands and let him throw her up into the saddle.

'I wager you'd rather come with me,' she said wickedly. 'I don't see you having a very merry Christmas here, Hannah.'

'I will serve my mistress in good times and bad,' I said steadily.

'You're sure your young man will wait for you?' she teased me.

I shrugged my shoulders. 'He says he will.' I was not going to tell Elizabeth that watching Mary destroyed by her love for her husband was not a great incentive for me to marry. 'I am promised to him when I can leave the queen.'

'Well, you can come to me, at any time, if you wish,' she said.

'Thank you, Princess,' I said and was surprised by my pleasure in her invitation, but nobody could resist Elizabeth's charm. Even in the shadow of a darkened court Elizabeth was a sparkle of sunshine, her smile utterly undimmed by her sister's loss.

'Don't leave it too late,' she warned me with mock seriousness.

I went closer to her horse's neck so that I could look up at her. 'Too late?'

'When I am queen they will all be rushing to serve me, you want to be at the head of that queue,' she said frankly.

'It could be years yet,' I rejoined.

She shook her head, she was supremely confident on this crisp autumn morning. 'Oh, I don't think so,' she said. 'The queen is not a strong woman and she is not a happy woman. D'you think King Philip is going to come running home to her at the first opportunity, and make a son and heir on her? No. And in his absence I think my poor sister will just fade away of grief. And when that happens they will find me, studying my Bible, and I will say –' She broke off for a moment. 'What did my sister plan to say when they told her she was queen?'

313

I hesitated. I could remember very vividly her words in those optimistic days when Mary had promised she would be the virgin queen and restore the England of her mother to its true faith and happiness. 'She was going to say: "This is the Lord's doing; it is marvellous in our eyes", but in the end they told her when we were on the run and she had to fight on her own for her throne, rather than be granted it.'

'I say, that's good,' Elizabeth said with appreciation. '"This is the Lord's doing; it is marvellous in our eyes". That's excellent. I'll say that. You'll want to be with me when that happens, won't you?'

I glanced around to make sure we were not overheard but Elizabeth knew there was no-one in earshot. In all the time I had known her she had never put herself at risk – it was always her friends who ended up in the Tower.

The small cavalcade was ready to go. Elizabeth looked down at me, her smiling face bright under her black velvet hat. 'So you'd better come to me soon,' she reminded me.

'If I can come, I will. God keep you, Princess.'

She leaned down and patted my hand as a gesture of farewell. 'I shall wait,' she said, her eyes dancing. 'I shall survive.'

King Philip wrote frequently but his letters were no reply to Mary's tender promises of love and demands that he should come back to her. They were brisk letters of business and orders to his wife as to what she should do in her kingdom. He did not respond to her pleading with him to come home, not even to tell her, at the very least, when he would come home, nor would he allow her to join him. At first he wrote warmly, bidding her to find things with which to distract herself, to look forward to the days when he would be with her again; but then, as every day he received another letter begging him to come back, warning him that she was ill from unhappiness, sick from the loss of him, he became more businesslike. His letters were merely instructions as to how the council should decide one matter or another, and the queen was forced to go to council meetings with his letter in her hands and lay before them the orders of a man who was king only in name, and force them through on her own authority. They did not welcome her as she came red-eyed into the chamber, and they were openly doubtful that a prince of

Spain, fighting his own wars, had English interests at heart. Cardinal Pole was her only friend and companion; but he had been exiled from England so long, and was so suspicious of so many Englishmen, that Mary came to feel like an exiled queen among enemies instead of the commander of English hearts as she once had been.

In October I was looking for Jane Dormer before dinner, and failing everywhere else I put my head around the door to the queen's chapel in case the lady in waiting had taken a few moments for prayer. To my surprise I saw Will Somers, kneeling before a statue of Our Lady, lighting a candle at her feet, his head bowed, his fool's peaked hat crumpled in his hand, his fist clenched over the little bell to keep it silent.

I had never thought of Will as a devout man. I stepped back and waited for him at the doorway. I watched him as he bowed his head low, and then crossed himself. With a heavy sigh, he got to his feet and came down the aisle a little stooped, and looking older than his thirty-five years.

'Will?' I said, coming to meet him.

'Child.' His habitual sweet smile came readily to his lips but his eyes were still dark.

'Are you in trouble?'

'Ah, I wasn't praying for me,' he said shortly.

'Then who?'

He glanced around the empty chapel and then drew me into a pew. 'D'you have any influence with Her Grace, d'you think, Hannah?'

I thought for a moment, then honestly, regretfully, I shook my head. 'She listens only to Cardinal Pole and to the king,' I said. 'And before everyone, to her own conscience.'

'If you spoke from your gift, would she listen to you?'

'She might,' I said cautiously. 'But I cannot command it to serve me, Will, you know that.'

'I thought you might pretend,' he said bluntly.

I recoiled. 'It's a holy gift! It would be blasphemy to pretend!!'

'Child, this month there are three men of God in prison charged with heresy, and if I am not mistaken they will be taken out and burned to death: poor Archbishop Cranmer, Bishop Latimer, and Bishop Ridley.'

I waited.

'The queen cannot burn good men who are ordained bishops of her father's church,' the fool said flatly. 'This must not happen.'

He looked at me and he put his arm around my shoulder and hugged me. 'Tell her that you have had a gift of Sight and that they must be sent into exile,' he urged me. 'Hannah, if these men die then the queen will make an enemy of every man of compassion. These are good men, honourable men, her father's own appointments. They have not changed their faith, the world has changed around them. They must not die on the queen's order, she will be shamed forever if she does this. History will remember nothing but that she was the queen who burned bishops.'

I hesitated. 'I dare not, Will.'

'If you will do it, I will be there,' he promised me. 'I'll help you. We'll get through it somehow.'

'You told me yourself never to meddle,' I whispered urgently. 'You told me yourself never to try to change the mind of the king. Your master beheaded two wives, never mind bishops, and you didn't stop him.'

'And he'll be remembered as a wife-killer,' Will predicted. 'And everything else about him that was so brave and loyal and true will be forgot. They will forget that he brought peace and prosperity to the country, that he made an England that we could all love. All they will remember of him will be that he had six wives and beheaded two of them.

'And all they will remember of this queen is that she brought the country floods and famine and fire. She will be remembered as England's curse when she was to have been our virgin queen, England's saviour.'

'She won't listen to me . . .'

'She must listen,' he insisted. 'Or she will be despised and forgotten and they will remember – God knows who! Elizabeth! Mary Stuart! – some wanton girl instead of this true-hearted queen.'

'She has done nothing but follow her conscience,' I defended her.

'She must follow her tender heart,' he said. 'Her conscience is not a good advisor these days. She must follow her tender heart instead. And you must do your duty to your love for her, and tell her that.'

I rose up from the pew, I found my knees were shaking. 'I am afraid, Will,' I said in a small voice. 'I am too afraid. You saw what she was like when I spoke out before . . . I cannot have her accusing me. I cannot have anyone asking where I came from, who my family is . . .'

He fell silent. 'Jane Dormer will not speak with her,' he said. 'I already tried her. The queen has no other friend but you.'

I paused, I could feel his will and my conscience pressing against my head, forcing me to do the right thing despite my fears. 'All right. I'll speak with her,' I burst out. 'But I'll do it alone. I'll do the best I can.'

He stopped me with a hand on mine, and pulled my hand out to see it. I was trembling, my fingers shook. 'Child, are you so afraid?'

I looked at him for a moment and I saw that we were both afraid. The queen had made a country where every man and woman was afraid of saying or doing the wrong thing, which would lead to a stake in the market place and a pile of green kindling that would burn smokily and slow.

'Yes,' I said honestly, pulling my hand from him to brush a smut off my cheek. 'I have spent my life running from this fear and now it seems that I have to walk towards it.'

I waited till the queen was going to bed that evening and was kneeling before her prie-dieu in the corner of her bedroom. I knelt beside her but I did not pray. I was going over in my mind what I could say to persuade her not to do this dreadful thing. For a full hour she was on her knees and when I peeped through my half-closed eyelids I could see that her face was turned up to the statue of the crucified Christ and the tears were pouring down her cheeks.

Finally she rose from her knees and went to her chair at the fireside. I drew the poker from the embers where it had been heating, and thrust it into the mug of ale to warm it for her. When I put it in her hands her fingers were icy-cold.

'Your Grace, I have something to ask you,' I said very quietly.

She looked at me as if she hardly saw me. 'What is it, Hannah?'

'I have never asked you for anything in the years I have been with you,' I reminded her.

She frowned slightly. 'No, you haven't. What is it you want now?'

'Your Grace, I have heard that your prisons are holding three good men on charges of heresy. Bishop Latimer and Bishop Ridley and Archbishop Cranmer.'

She turned her face to the small fire in the hearth so I could not see her expression, but her voice was flat.

'Yes. It is true that those men are charged.'

'I want to ask you to show mercy,' I said simply. 'It is an awful thing to put a good man to death. And everyone says that these are good men. Just mistaken men . . . just disagreeing with the church's teaching. But they were good bishops to your brother, Your Grace, and they are ordained bishops in the Church of England.'

She said nothing for a long time. I did not know whether to press the case or to leave it. The silence started to frighten me a little, I sat back on my heels and waited for her to speak and I could hear my own breathing coming too quickly, too lightly for an innocent person. I could feel my own danger coming towards me, like a dog on a scent, and the scent it was following was the sweat of my fear which was prickling me in the armpits and growing cold and damp down my spine.

When she turned to me, she was not like the Mary I loved at all. Her face was like a mask of snow. 'They are *not* good men, for they deny the word of God and the rule of God, and they win others to their sin,' she hissed at me. 'They can repent their sins and be forgiven, or they can die. It is to them you should be speaking, Hannah, not me. This is the law: not a human law, not any law, not my law, but the law of the church. If they do not want to be punished by the church then they should not sin. I do not set myself up as judge here, it is the church that decides and they must obey it, as I do.'

She paused for a moment, but I could say nothing against her conviction.

'It is men like them that have brought down the wrath of God on England,' she said. 'Not a good harvest, not a wealthy year since my father turned against the church and not a healthy child born into the cradle of England since he put my mother aside.'

I could see her hands trembling and her voice shook with her rising passion. 'Do you not see it?' she asked. 'You of all people? Do you not see that he put my mother aside and never again got another healthy legitimate child?'

'Princess Elizabeth?' I breathed.

The queen laughed a loud harsh laugh. 'She's not his,' she said derisively. 'Look at her. She is a Smeaton, every inch of her. Her mother tried to pass off her bastard as the king's own child, but now she is grown and behaves like the child of a lute-player and a whore, everyone can see her parentage. God gave my father only one healthy child: me; and then my poor father was turned against me and my mother. Since that day there has not been a moment's good fortune for this country. They persuaded him to destroy the word of God, the abbeys and the nunneries, and then my brother took England deeper into sin. See the price we have paid? Hunger in the country and sickness in the towns.

'God must be appeased. Only when this sin is rooted out of the country will I be able to conceive a child and be able to give birth. No holy prince could come to a country such as this. The wrong that my father started, which my brother continued, has to be reversed. It all has to be turned back.'

She broke off, panting. I said nothing, I was stunned by her passion.

'You know, sometimes I don't think I have the strength to do it,' she went on. 'But God gives me the strength. He gives me the resolution to order these dreadful judgements, to say that they shall continue. God gives me the strength to do His work, to send sinners to the fires so that the land may be cleansed. And then you – who I have trusted! – you come here to me when I am praying, to tempt me to error, into weakness, asking me to deny God and my holy work for Him.'

'Your Grace . . .' My voice caught in my throat. She rose to her feet and I jumped up. I had cramp in my right leg from kneeling for so long and it gave way beneath me so I sprawled down. I was half on the floor looking up at her and she looked at me as if God himself had struck me down.

'Hannah, my child, you are halfway to mortal sin yourself to ask this of me. Don't take one step further, or I shall send for the priests to wrestle with your soul.'

I could smell the smoke, I tried to tell myself it was from the fire in the grate, but I knew it was the smoke of my mother burning, the smoke of the other English men and women burning in the market places up and down the countryside, and soon they would take out Bishop Latimer and Bishop Ridley and the crowd would watch them as Dr Ridley would tell his friend to be of good heart as they would light such a candle in England that would never be put out. I scrabbled at the queen's feet like a cripple and she pulled her skirts away from me as if she could not bear me to touch her, and she went from the room without another word, leaving me on the floor, smelling smoke and crying for sheer terror.

Winter 1555

Christmas was celebrated at court with much weighty ceremony but no joy, just as Elizabeth had predicted. Everyone remembered that last year Queen Mary had swirled around the court with her stomacher unlaced and her big belly carried proudly before her. Last year we had been waiting for our prince. This year we knew that there could not be one, for the king had left the queen's bed and her red eyes and thin body attested to the fact that she was sterile and alone. All autumn there had been rumours of plots and counter-plots, it was said that the English people could not tolerate to be ruled by a Spanish king. Philip's father was going to hand over the empire to his son and then most of Christendom would be under his command. People muttered that England was an outlying island to him, that he would rule it through the barren queen who did not cease to adore him though everyone knew he had taken a mistress and would never come home to her again.

The queen must have heard at least half of this gossip, the council kept her informed of the threats that were made against her husband, against herself, against her throne. She grew very quiet and withdrawn and determined. She held to her vision of a peaceful religious country where men and women would be safe in the church of their fathers, and she tried to believe that she could bring this about if she did not waver from her duty, however much it might cost her. The queen's council passed a new law which said that a heretic who repented on the stake had changed his mind too late – he should still be burned to death. Also, anyone who sympathised with his fate would be burned too.

320

Spring 1556

The cold wet winter turned to a wetter spring. The queen waited for letters which came more and more infrequently and brought her little joy.

One evening in early May she announced her intention of spending the whole night in prayer and sent me and all her ladies away. I was glad to be excused from yet another long silent evening when we sewed by the fireside and tried not to notice when the queen's tears drenched the linen shirt that she was stitching for the king.

I was walking briskly to the chamber that I shared with three of the other maids when I saw a shadow by a doorway in the gallery. I did not hesitate, I would never pause for someone waiting to speak to me, and he had to fall into step beside me and keep to my rapid pace.

'You must come with me, Hannah Verde,' he said.

Even at the sound of my full name I did not pause.

'I only obey the queen.'

Like a slow flag unfurling he held before me a rolled scroll and dropped one end to let it fall open. Almost despite myself I felt my feet slow and stop. I saw the seals at the bottom and my name at the top, Hannah Verde, alias Hannah Green, alias Hannah the Fool.

'What is this?' I asked, though I knew.

'A warrant,' he said.

'A warrant for what?' I asked, though I knew.

'For your arrest, for heresy,' he said.

'Heresy?' I breathed, as if I had never heard the word before, as if I had not been waiting for this moment every day since they had taken my mother.

'Yes, maid, heresy,' he said.

'I will see the queen about this.' I half-turned back to run to her.

'You will come with me,' he said and took my arm and waist in a grip which I could not have fought even if my strength had not been bleeding away in my terror.

'The queen will intercede for me!' I whimpered, hearing my voice as weak as a child's.

'This is a royal warrant,' he said simply. 'You are to be arrested for questioning and she has given her authority.'

They took me to St Paul's in the city and they kept me overnight in a prison room with a woman who had been racked so badly that she lay like a rag doll in the corner of the cell, her arm bones and leg bones broken, her spine disjointed, her feet pointing outwards like the hands of a clock showing a quarter to three. From her bloodied lips came a moan like the sigh of the wind. All night she breathed out her pain like a breeze in springtime. With us also was a woman whose nails had been pulled from her fingers. She nursed her broken hands in her lap and did not look up when they turned the key in the door and thrust me inside. She had her mouth pursed in a funny little grimace, then I realised they had cut out her tongue as well.

I hunkered down like a beggar on the threshold, my back to the door. They said nothing to me: the broken moaner and the dumb one without fingernails. In my terror, I said nothing to them. I watched the moonlight stroll across the floor, illuminating first the woman whose body was twisted like a dolly, and then shining on the fingers of the woman who cupped her hands in her lap and pursed her lips. In the silver light her fingertips looked as black as nibs dipped in printers' ink.

The night passed in the end, though I thought that it would last forever.

In the morning the door swung open and neither woman raised her head. The stillness of the racked woman made her look as if she were dead, perhaps she was. 'Hannah Verde,' the voice outside said.

I tried to rise to my feet in obedience but my legs buckled beneath me from sheer terror. I knew that I could not have my fingernails torn out without screaming for mercy, telling everything I knew. I could not be tied to the rack without betraying my lord, Elizabeth, John Dee, every name I had ever heard whispered, names that had never even been mentioned. Since I could not even stand on my own two feet when they summoned me, how would I ever defy them?

The guard scooped me up in his arms, dragged me along, my feet scrabbling like a drunkard's on the stones behind us. He stank of ale, and a worse smell, smoke and burning fat which clung to his woollen cape. I realised that the smell was from the fires, the smoke from the kindling and the brands, the fat from the bubbling skin of dying men and women. As the realisation came to me I felt my stomach rebel and I choked on vomit.

'Here, watch out!' he said irritably, and thrust my head away from him so he banged my face against the stone wall.

He dragged me up some steps, and then across a courtyard.

'Where?' I said faintly.

'Bishop Bonner,' he said shortly. 'God help you.'

'Amen,' I said promptly, as if accurate observation now would save me. 'Dear God, amen.'

I knew I was lost. I could not speak, let alone defend myself. I thought what a fool of a girl I had been not to go with Daniel when he would have saved me. What an arrogant child I had been to think that I could weave my way through these plots and not attract notice. Me, with olive skin and dark eyes, and a name like Hannah?

We came to a panelled door, monstrous with hammered nails. He tapped on it, opened it at a call from within, and walked in, arms tight around me as if we were mismatched lovers.

The bishop was sitting at a table facing the door; his clerk had his back to the door. A chair was set at a distance facing both table and bishop. The gaoler dumped me roughly into it and stood back, closed the door and set himself before it.

'Name?' the bishop asked wearily.

'Hannah Verde,' the gaoler answered, while I searched for my voice and found it was lost in terror.

'Age?'

He reached forward and prodded my shoulder.

'Seventeen,' I whispered.

'What?'

'Seventeen,' I said, a little louder. I had forgotten the meticulous record-keeping of the Inquisition, the bureaucracy of terror. First they would take my name, my age, my address, my occupation, the name of my father and my mother, their address, their occupations, the names of my grandparents and their address and occupations, and then, and only then, when they had everything named and labelled, they would torture me until I spilled out everything I knew, everything I could imagine, and everything that I thought they might want to know.

'Occupation?'

'Fool to the queen,' I said.

There was a splashing noise in the room, a childish damp warmth in my breeches, and a shameful stable smell. I had pissed myself for fear. I bowed my head, mortification overlaying my terror.

The clerk raised his head as if alerted by the warm sharp smell. He turned and observed me. 'Oh, I can vouch for this girl,' he said as if it were a matter of very little interest.

It was John Dee.

I was beyond recognising him, beyond wondering how he came to be the bishop's clerk having been the bishop's prisoner. I just met his neutral look with the blank eyes of a girl too frightened to think for herself.

'Can you?' asked the bishop doubtfully.

John Dee nodded. 'She is a holy fool,' he said. 'She once saw an angel in Fleet Street.'

'That must be heretical,' the bishop maintained.

John Dee considered it for a moment, as if it were not a matter of life and death to me. 'No, a true vision I think, and Queen Mary thinks the same. She will not be best pleased when she discovers we have arrested her fool.'

That gave the bishop pause. I could see him hesitate. 'The queen's orders to me are to root out heresy wherever I find it, in her household, in the streets, and to show no favour. The girl was arrested with a royal warrant.'

'Oh well, as you wish,' John Dee said negligently.

I opened my mouth to speak but no words came. I could not

believe that he would defend me so half-heartedly. Yet here he was, turning his back to me once more and copying my name into the Inquisition's ledger.

'Details,' Bishop Bonner said.

'Subject was seen to look away at the elevation of the Host on the morning of 27 December,' John Dee read in a clerkly mutter. 'Subject asked the queen to show mercy to heretics before the court. Subject is a familiar to Princess Elizabeth. Subject has a knowledge of learning and languages unbecoming in a woman.'

'How d'you plead?' Bishop Bonner asked me.

'I did not look from the elevation of the Host . . .' I started, my voice weary and hopeless. If John Dee was not going to support me then I was a dead woman on this one charge alone. And once they started to investigate my journey across Europe and the family of my betrothed, I would be identified as a Jew and that would mean the death of me, of my father, of Daniel, of his family, and of their friends, men and women I did not even know, families in London, in Bristol, in York.

'Oh! This is nothing but malice,' John Dee exclaimed impatiently.

'Eh?' the bishop said.

'Malicious complaint,' John Dee said briskly and pushed the ledger away. 'Do they really think we have the time for maids' gossip? We are supposed to be rooting out heresy here, and they bring us the quarrels of waiting maids.'

The bishop glanced at the paper. 'Sympathy with heretics?' he queried. 'That's enough for burning.'

John Dee raised his head and smiled confidently at his master. 'She's a holy fool,' he said, laughter in his voice. 'It's her task in life to ask the questions that no sane man would ask. She talks nonsense, she is *supposed* to talk nonsense, shall we ask her to account for singing fiddle-dee-dee? Billycock sat on billycock hill? I think we should send out a very stiff letter to say that we will not be mocked by nonsensical accusations. We will not be used for the settling of servants' rivalries. We are hunting out enemies of the faith, not tormenting half-wit girls.'

'Let her go?' the bishop asked, his eyebrows raised.

'Sign here,' John Dee said, sliding a paper across the desk. 'Let's get rid of her and get on with our work. The child is a fool, we would be fools to question her.'

I held my breath.

The bishop signed.

'Take her away,' John Dee said wearily. He swung round in his seat to face me. 'Hannah Verde, also known as Hannah the Fool, we are releasing you from an inquiry into heresy. No charge to answer. D'you have wit enough to understand that, child?'

'Yes, sir,' I said very quietly.

John Dee nodded to the gaoler. 'Release her.'

I pushed myself up from the chair, my legs were still too weak to hold me. The guard slid a hand around my waist and kept me on my feet. 'The women in my cell,' I said quietly to John Dee. 'One is dying, and the other has had her fingernails ripped out.'

John Dee burst into a crack of laughter as if I had told him the most delightfully bawdy jest, and Bishop Bonner gave forth a great bellow.

'She is priceless!' the bishop shouted. 'Anything else I can do for you, fool? Any complaints about your breakfast? About your bed?'

I looked from the red roaring face of the bishop to the twinkling smile of his clerk and shook my head. I bowed my head to the bishop, and to the man I had once been honoured to know, and I left them with their bloodstained hands to interrogate innocent people and send them out to be burned.

I did not see how to get back to the court at Greenwich. When they turned me roughly out into the dirty street I wandered around at the back of St Paul's and stumbled blindly until I felt I had put a safe distance between the tower's ominous reaching shadow and my frightened weaving steps. Then I slumped in a doorway like a vagrant and shook, as if I had the ague. A householder shouted at me to clear off and take the plague with me, and I moved on one doorway and collapsed again.

The bright sunshine burned into my face and showed me that it was past midday. After a long time on the cold step, I pushed myself up and walked a short way. I found I was crying like a baby and had to stop once more. Step by step I went on, pausing when my legs buckled underneath me until I found my way to our little shop off Fleet Street and hammered on our neighbour's door.

'Dear God, what has become of you?'

I managed a twisted smile. 'I have a fever,' I said. 'I forgot my key, and lost my way. Would you let me in?'

He stepped back from me. In these times of hardship everyone was afraid of infection. 'Do you need food?'

'Yes,' I said, too low for pride.

'I will leave you something on the doorstep,' he said. 'Here's the key.'

I took it wordlessly, and staggered to the shop. It turned in the lock and I stepped into the shuttered room. At once the precious scent of printers' ink and dry paper surrounded me. I stood, inhaling it, the very perfume of heresy, the familiar beloved odour of home.

I heard the scrape and clink of a dish on the doorstep and went to fetch a pie and a little mug of ale. I ate sitting on the floor behind the counter, hidden from the shuttered windows, my back against the warm folios, smelling the perfume of the cured-leather binding.

As soon as I had eaten, I put the bowl back on the doorstep and locked the door. Then I went into my father's print shop and store room and cleared the volumes from the bottom shelf. I did not want to sleep in my own little trestle bed. I did not even want to sleep in my father's bed. I wanted to be closer to him than that. I had a superstitious terror that if I went to bed I would be dragged from sleep by Bishop Bonner again, but if I was in hiding with my father's beloved books then they would keep me safe.

I put myself to sleep on the bottom shelf of his books collection. I tucked a couple of folio volumes under my cheek for a pillow and gathered some French quarto volumes to hold me into the shelf. Like a lost text myself, I curled up in the shape of a G and closed my eyes and slept.

In the morning, when I woke, I was determined on my future. I found a piece of manuscript paper and wrote a letter to Daniel, a letter I thought I would never write.

Dear Daniel,

It is time for me to leave the court and England. Please come for me and the printing press at once. If this letter miscarries or I do not see you within a week, I shall come on my own.

Hannah

When I sealed it up I was certain, as I had known in my heart for the last few months, that there was no safety for anyone in Queen Mary's England any more.

There was a tap at the door. My heart plunged with the familiar terror, but then I could see, through the shutters, the silhouette of our next-door neighbour.

I opened the door to him. 'Slept well?' he demanded.

'Yes,' I said.

'Ate well? They are a good baker's?'

'Yes. Thank you.'

'Better now?'

'Yes. I am well.'

'Are you going back to court today?'

For a moment I hesitated, then I realised that there was nowhere else for me to go. If I went missing from court it was tantamount to a confession of guilt. I had to go back and act the part of an innocent woman rightly freed, until Daniel should come for me and then I could get away.

'Yes, today,' I said brightly.

'Would you see this gets to the queen?' he asked, abashed but determined. He offered me a trade card, an illustrated label which assured the reader that he could supply all the books that were moral and improving and approved by the church. I took it, and thought wryly that at my last visit to the shop I had made a comment about the paucity of reading that the church permitted. Now I would not speak a word against it.

'I will put it in her hands,' I lied to him. 'You can depend upon it.'

I came back to a subdued court. The maids in waiting that I slept with had thought that I had gone to my father's shop. The queen had not missed me. Only Will Somers cocked an inquiring eyebrow at me when I came into dinner and made his way over to my bench. I shifted up, and he sat down beside me.

'Are you well, child? You're white as a sheet.'

'I've just got back,' I said shortly. 'I was arrested.'

Any other person in the court would have found an excuse to move elsewhere to take his dinner. Will planted both elbows on the table. 'Never!' he said. 'How come you got out again?'

A little unwilling giggle escaped me. 'They said I was a fool, and could not be held responsible.'

His crack of laughter made all the neighbouring tables turn their heads and smile. 'You! Well that's good news for me. I shall know what to plead. And that's what they truly said?'

'Yes. But, Will, it is no laughing matter. There were two women in there, one half-dead from the rack and the other with her fingernails torn out of her hands. The whole house was packed from cellar to attic with men waiting their trial.'

His face grew sombre. 'Hush, child, there is nothing you can do about it now. You did what you could, and speaking out is perhaps what led you there.'

'Will, I was most afraid,' I said quietly.

His warm big hand took my cold fingers in a gentle grasp. 'Child, we are all of us afraid. Better times coming, eh?'

'When will they come?' I whispered.

He shook his head without saying anything; but I knew that he was thinking of Elizabeth and when her reign might begin. And if Will Somers was thinking of Elizabeth with hope, then the queen had lost the love of a man who had been a true friend indeed.

I counted the days, waiting for Daniel's arrival. Before I had gone downriver to Greenwich, I had put the letter in the hand of a shipmaster who was sailing to Calais that morning. I recited to myself his progress. 'Say: it takes a day to Calais, then say a day to find the house, then say Daniel understands, and leaves at once, he should be with me inside a week.'

I decided that if I heard nothing from him within seven days that I would go to the shop, pack the most precious books and manuscripts in as large a box as I could manage, and take a passage to Calais on my own.

In the meantime I had to wait. I attended Mass in the queen's train, I read the Bible to her in Spanish in her room every day after dinner, I prayed with her at her bedtime. I watched her unhappiness turn to a solid-seated misery, a state that I thought she would live and die in. She was in despair, I had never seen a woman in such despair before. It was worse than death, it was a constant longing for death and a constant rejection of life. She lived like darkness in her own day. It was clear that nothing could be done to lift the shadow which was on her; and so I, and everyone else, said and did nothing.

One morning, as we were coming out of Mass, the queen leading the way, her ladies behind her, one of the queen's newest maids in waiting fell into step beside me. I was watching the queen. She was walking slowly, her head drooped, her shoulders bowed as if grief were a weight that she had to carry.

'Have you heard? Have you heard?' the girl whispered to me as we turned into the queen's presence chamber. The gallery was crowded with people who had come to see the queen, most of them to ask for clemency for people on trial for heresy.

'Heard what?' I said crossly. I pulled my sleeve from the grip of an old lady who was trying to waylay me. 'Dame, I can do nothing for you.'

'It is not for me, it is my son,' she said. 'My boy.'

Despite myself, I paused.

'I have money saved, he could go abroad if the queen would be so good as to send him into exile.'

'You are pleading for exile for your son?'

'Bishop Bonner has him.' She needed to say nothing more.

I pulled back from her as if she had the plague. 'I am sorry,' I said. 'I can do nothing.'

'If you would intercede for him? His name is Joseph Woods?'

'Dame, if I asked for mercy for him my own life would be forfeit,' I told her. 'You are at risk in even speaking to me. Go home and pray for his soul.'

She looked at me as if I were a savage. 'You tell a mother to pray for her son's soul when he is innocent of anything?'

'Yes,' I said bleakly.

The maid in waiting drew me away impatiently. 'The news!' she reminded me.

'Yes, what?' I turned from the uncomprehending pain on the old woman's face, knowing that the best advice to her would be to take the money she had saved for her son's release and buy instead a purse of gunpowder to hang around his neck so that he did not suffer for hours in the fire but blew up as soon as the flames were lit.

'The Princess Elizabeth is accused of treason!' the maid in waiting hissed at me, desperate to tell her news. 'Her servants are all arrested. They're tearing her London house apart, searching it.'

Despite the heat of the crowd, I felt myself freeze, right down to my toes in my boots. 'Elizabeth? What treason?' I whispered.

'A plot to kill the queen,' the girl said in a breath of ice.

'Who else with her?'

'I don't know! Nobody knows! Kat Ashley, for certain, perhaps all of them.'

I nodded, I knew somebody who would know. I extricated myself from the train that was following the queen into her presence chamber. She would be in there for at least two hours, listening to one claim after another, people asking her for favours, for mercy, for places, for money. At every plea she would look more weary, older by far than her forty years. But she would not miss me while I ran down the gallery to the great hall.

Will was not there, a soldier directed me to the stable-yard and I found him in a loose box, playing with one of the deerhound puppies. The animal, all long legs and excitement, clambered all over him.

'Will, they're searching the Princess Elizabeth's London house.'

'Aye, I know,' he said, lifting his face away from the puppy, which was enthusiastically licking his neck.

'What are they looking for?'

'Doesn't matter what they were looking for, what matters is what they found.'

'What did they find?'

'What you would expect,' he said unhelpfully.

331

'I expect nothing,' I snapped. 'Just tell me. What did they find?'

'Letter and pamphlets and all sorts of seditious nonsense in Kat Ashley's box. A May-day plot cooked up between her and the princess's new Italian lute player and Dudley –' He broke off as he saw my aghast face. 'Oh, not your lord. His cousin, Sir Henry.'

'Lord Robert is not under suspicion?' I demanded.

'Should he be?'

'No,' I lied instantly. 'How could he do anything? And anyway, he is loyal to Queen Mary.'

'As are we all,' Will said smartly. 'Even Tobias the hound, here. Well, Tobias is more loyal because he can't say one thing and think another. He gives his love where he eats his dinner which is more than others I could mention.'

I flushed. 'If you mean me, I love the queen and I always have done.'

His face softened. 'I know you do. I meant her pretty little sister who has not the patience to wait her turn; but has been plotting again.'

'She's guilty of nothing,' I said at once, my loyalty to Elizabeth as reliable as my love of the queen.

Will laughed shortly. 'She's an heir in waiting. She'd attract trouble like a tall tree attracts lightning. And so Kat Ashley and Signor the lute player are for the Tower, half a dozen of the Dudley household with them. There's a warrant out for Sir William Pickering, her old ally. I didn't even know he was in England. Did you?'

I said nothing, my throat tightening with fear. 'No.'

'Better not to know.'

I nodded, then I felt my head nodding and nodding again, in trying to look normal I was looking ridiculous. I felt that my face was a folio of fear that anyone could read.

'What's the matter, child?' Will's tone was kindly. 'You're white as snow. Are you enmeshed in this, little one? Are you seeking a charge of treason to match your charge of heresy? Have you been a fool indeed?'

'No,' I said, my voice coming out harshly. 'I would not plot against the queen. I have not been well this last week. I am sick. A touch of fever.'

'Let's hope it doesn't spread,' Will said wryly.

I held to my lie of fever and took to my bed. I thought of Elizabeth who seemed to be able to summon ill health as an alibi when she needed one, and I knew the pangs of a terror which made me sweat so much that I would have passed for a sick girl indeed.

I heard the news from my room mates. Cardinal Pole headed the inquiry into the conspiracy and every day another man was arrested and taken for questioning. First Sir Henry Dudley, who had been betraying his own country to the French in return for their help. He had pockets full of French gold and the promise of a small army of mercenaries and French volunteers. From then they followed the trail to a traitor at the court of the Exchequer who had promised to steal money to pay for the army and the weapons. Under questioning he revealed that they were planning to send the queen to her husband in the Low Countries, and put Elizabeth on the throne. Then the cardinal discovered that Kat Ashley and William Pickering were old friends, and had met at the very heart of the court, Sir William had been smuggled into the country, into the Hampton Court itself.

Kat Ashley's box in Elizabeth's London house held the first draft of a pamphlet urging Englishmen to rise up against the Catholic queen and put the Protestant princess on the throne.

Cardinal Pole started to look around Elizabeth's friends and acquaintances for who might have a press that would have printed such a pamphlet in secret. I thought of the sheeted press in the printer's shop off Fleet Street and wondered how soon it would be before they came for me.

The cardinal, inspired by God, determined and intelligent, was following a trail which would take in many English Protestants, many friends and servants to Elizabeth, and would lead him inevitably to me, as to many others. Whenever one man was arrested and taken for questioning there was another man who might mention that the queen's fool was always with the princess. That someone had told someone that the queen's fool would run an errand or take a message, that she was known by sight to Sir William Pickering, that she was a trusted retainer of the Dudley family for all that she was said to serve the queen.

If Cardinal Pole took me to his quiet thickly curtained room and made me stand before his dark polished table and tell him of my history I knew he would pick it apart in a moment. Our flight from Spain, our arrival in England, my father's disappearance leaving his press behind: everything pointed to our guilt as Marranos, Jews trying to pass as Christians, and we could be burned for heresy in Smithfield as well as we could have been burned in Aragon. If he went to my father's shop he would find texts which were forbidden and heretical. Some of them were illegal because they questioned the word of God, even suggesting that the earth moved around the sun, or that animals now lived which had not been made by God in six days at the beginning of the world. Some of them were illegal because they challenged the translation of the Word of God, saying that the apple of knowledge was an apricot. And some of them were illegal simply because they could not be understood. They dealt in mysteries, and the cardinal's church was one that insisted on control of all the mysteries of the world.

The books in the shop would see us hanged for heresy, the printing press see us hanged for treason, and if ever the cardinal made a connection between my father's best customers, John Dee and Robert Dudley, and me, then I would be on the scaffold for treason with the noose around my neck in a moment.

I spent three days in bed, staring at the white ceiling, shivering with fear though the sunshine was bright on the lime-washed walls and bees bumbled against the glass of the window. Then in the evening of the third day, I got up from my bed. I knew the queen would be preparing to walk into the great hall and sit before a dinner that she could not bear to eat. I got myself to her rooms as she rose from her prie-dieu.

'Hannah, are you better now?' The words were kind but her eyes were dead, she was trapped in her own world of grief. One of her ladies bent and straightened the train behind her but she did not turn her head, it was as if she did not feel it.

'I am better, but I have been much distressed by a letter which came to me this day,' I said. The strain on my white face supported my story. 'My father is ill, near to death, and I would like to go to him.'

'Is he in London?'

'In Calais, Your Grace. He has a shop in Calais, and lives with my betrothed and his family.'

She nodded. 'You can go to him, of course. And come back when he is well again, Hannah. You can go to the Household Exchequer and get your wages to date, you will need money.'

'Thank you, Your Grace.' I felt my throat tighten at the thought of her kindness to me when I was running from her. But then I remembered the cinders which were always warm at Smithfield and the woman with the bloody hands in St Paul's, and I kept my eyes down, and held my peace.

She reached out to me and I knelt and kissed her fingers. For the last time, her gentle touch came on my head. 'God bless you, Hannah, and keep you safe,' she said warmly, not knowing that it was her own trusted cardinal and his inquiry which was making me tremble as I knelt before her.

The queen stepped back and I rose to my feet. 'Come back to me soon,' she commanded.

'As soon as I can.'

'When will you set out?' she asked.

'At dawn tomorrow,' I said.

'Then God speed and safe return,' she said with all her old sweetness. She gave me a weary little smile as she went to the double doors and they threw them open for her, and then she went out, her head high, her face drained, her eyes dark with sadness, to face the court which no longer respected her though they would bow as she walked in and eat well and drink deep at her cost.

I did not wait for dawn. As soon as I heard the court settle to their dinner, I put on my dark green livery, my new riding boots, my cape and my cap. I took my little knapsack from my box and put in it the missal the queen had once given me, and the wages I had from the Exchequer, in their little purse. I owned nothing else, not even after three years of service at court – I had not lined my pockets as I could have done.

I crept down the side stairs and hesitated at the entrance to the great hall. I could hear the familiar sound of the household at dinner, the buzz of conversation and the occasional shout of laughter, the higher voices of the women seated at the far end of the hall, the scrape of knife on trencher, the clink of bottle on cup. They were the sounds of my life for the past three years, I could not believe that this was no longer my home, my haven. I could not believe that this was increasingly the most dangerous place for me to be.

I closed my eyes for a moment, longing for the gift of Sight, that I might know what I should do for my own safety. But it was not the Sight that decided me, it was my oldest fear. Someone had burned something in the kitchen and the scent of scorched meat suddenly blew into the hall with a running servant. For a moment I was not at the queen's dinner hall, smelling roasted meat, I was in the town square of Aragon, and the scent of a burning woman was making the air stink as she screamed in horror at the sight of her own blackening legs.

I turned on my heel and dashed out of the door, careless of who saw me. I headed for the river, as my quickest and least noticeable route into the city. I went down to the landing stage and waited for a boat to come by.

I had forgotten the fears of Mary's court, now that the Spanish were openly hated and Mary had lost the love of her people. There were four soldiers on the landing stage and another dozen of them on guard along the river bank. I had to smile and pretend I was sneaking out for a secret meeting with a lover.

'But what's your fancy?' one of the young soldiers jeered. 'Dressed like a boy but a voice like a maid? How d'you choose, my pet? What sort of a thing d'you like?'

I was spared having to find an answer by a boat swinging across the current and bringing a group of London citizens to court.

'Are we too late? Is she still dining?' a fat woman at the front of the boat demanded as they helped her on to the landing stage.

'She's still dining,' I said.

'Under the canopy of state and all?' she specified.

'As she should be,' I confirmed.

She smiled with satisfaction. 'I've never seen it before, though I've often promised myself the pleasure of seeing her,' she said. 'Do we just walk in?'

'There is the entrance to the great hall,' I directed her. 'There are soldiers on the door but they will let you and your family pass. May I take your boat? I want to go to the city.'

She waved the boatman away. 'But come back for us,' she said to him.

I stepped into the rocking boat and waited till we were out of earshot before directing him to the steps at The Fleet. I did not want the court guards to know where I was going.

Once again I came down the road to our shop at a reluctant dawdle. I wanted to see that the place was untouched before I approached it. Suddenly, I came to an abrupt standstill. To my horror, as I turned the corner I could see that it had been broken and entered. The door was thrown wide open, the dark entrance was lit with a flickering light as two men, three men moved about inside. Outside waited a great wagon with two horses. The men were taking away great barrels of goods, I recognised the packed manuscripts that we had stored away when my father left, and I knew they would be evidence enough to hang me twice over.

I shrank back into a dark doorway and pulled my cap down low over my face. If they had found the barrels of manuscripts then they would also have found the boxes of forbidden books. We would be named as purveyors of heresy. There would be a price on our heads. I had better turn and head back for the river and get myself on a ship to Calais as soon as I could, for my father and I were baked meats if we were found in London.

I was just about to slide backwards into the alley when one of the shadows inside the shop came out with a big box and loaded it into the back of the wagon. I paused, waiting for him to go back into the shop and leave the street clear for me to make my escape when something about him made me pause. Something about the profile was familiar, the scholar's bend of the shoulders, the thinness of his frame below his worn cape.

I felt my heart thud with hope and fear but I did not step out until I was sure. Then the two other men came out, carrying a well-wrapped piece of the printing press. The man in front was our next-door neighbour, and the man carrying the other end was my betrothed, Daniel. At once I realised that they were packing up the shop and we were not yet discovered.

'Father! My father!' I cried out softly, and sprang from the dark doorway into the shadowy street.

His head jerked up at the sound of my voice and his arms opened wide. I was in his embrace in a moment, feeling his warm strong arms wrapped around me, hugging me as if he would never let me go again.

'Hannah, my daughter, my girl,' he said, kissing the top of my head. 'Hannah, my daughter, *mi querida!*'

I looked up into his face, worn and older than I remembered, and saw him too tracing my features. We both spoke at once:

'I got your letter, are you in danger?'

'Father, are you well? I am so glad . . .'

We laughed. 'Tell me first,' he said. 'Are you in danger? We have come for you.'

I shook my head. 'Thank God,' I said. 'They arrested me for heresy, but I was released.'

At my words, he glanced quickly around. I thought anyone in England would have known him for a Jew now, that furtive ever-guilty glance of the People with no home and no welcome among strangers.

Daniel crossed the cobbled street, strode over the drain and came to an abrupt halt before us.

'Hannah,' he said awkwardly.

I did not know what to reply. The last time we had met I had freed him from his betrothal to me with a burst of venom, and he had kissed me as if he wanted to bite me. Then he had written the most passionate letter imaginable and we were engaged to marry once more. I had summoned him to save me, by rights he should have something more from me than a down-turned face and a mumbled: 'Hello, Daniel.'

'Hello,' he said, equally inadequate.

'Let's go into the shop,' my father said, casting another cautious glance up and down the street. He led me over the threshold and shut the door behind us. 'We were packing up here and then Daniel was going to fetch you. Why are you here?'

'I was running away from court,' I said. 'I didn't dare wait for you to come. I was coming to you.'

'Why?' Daniel asked. 'What has happened?'

'They are arresting men for plotting to overthrow the queen,' I said. 'Cardinal Pole is making the inquiry and I am afraid of him. I thought he would discover where I had come from, or . . .' I broke off.

Daniel's glance at me was acute. 'Were you involved in the plot?' he asked abruptly.

338

'No,' I said. 'Not really.'

At his hard sceptical look I flushed red.

'I was involved enough,' I admitted.

'Thank God we are here then,' he said. 'Have you dined?'

'I'm not hungry,' I said. 'I can help to pack.'

'Good, for we have a ship that leaves on the one o'clock tide.'

I slipped off the printer's stool and set to work with Daniel, my father, and our next-door neighbour, carrying the boxes and barrels and pieces of the press to the wagon. The horses stood still and quiet. One woman threw up her window and asked us what we were doing and our neighbour went and told her that at last the shop was to be let and the old bookseller's rubbish was being cleared away.

It was near ten o'clock at night by the time we had finished and a late spring moon, all warm and yellow, had risen and was lighting the street. My father swung himself into the back of the wagon, Daniel and I rode on the box. Our neighbour shook hands all round and bade us farewell. Daniel signalled for the horses to start and they leaned against the traces and the wagon eased forward.

'This is like last time,' Daniel remarked. 'I hope you don't jump ship again.'

I shook my head. 'I won't.'

'No outstanding promises?' he smiled.

'No,' I said sadly. 'The queen does not need my company, she does not want anyone but the king and I think he will never come home to her. And though the Princess Elizabeth's household is charged with treason, she has the favour of the king. She might be imprisoned but she won't be killed now. She is determined to survive and wait.'

'She does not fear that the queen might pass her over and give the crown to another – Margaret Douglas or Mary Stuart, perhaps?'

'She had her future foretold,' I said to him in a tiny whisper. 'And she was assured that she will be the heir. She does not know how long she will have to wait but she is confident.'

'And who foretold her future?' he asked acutely.

At my guilty silence he nodded. 'I should think you do indeed need to come with me this time,' he said levelly.

'I was accused of heresy,' I said. 'But released. I have done nothing wrong.'

'You have done enough to be hanged for treason, strangled for a witch, and burned as a heretic three times over,' he said without a glimmer of a smile. 'By rights you should be on your knees to me, begging me to take you away.'

I was half a moment from outraged exclamation when I saw that he was teasing me and I broke into an unwilling laugh. At once he gleamed and took my hand and brought it to his lips. The touch of his mouth on my fingers was warm, I could feel his breath on my skin, and for a moment I could see nothing and hear nothing and think of nothing but his touch.

'You need not beg,' he said softly. 'I would have come for you anyway. I cannot go on living without you.'

Our road took us past the Tower. I felt, rather than saw, Daniel stiffen as the lowering shadow of Robert Dudley's prison fell on us.

'You know, I could not help loving him,' I said in a small voice. 'When I first saw him I was a child, and he was the most beautiful man I had ever seen in my life and the son of the greatest man in England.'

'Well, now you are a woman and he is a traitor,' Daniel said flatly. 'And you are mine.'

I shot a sideways smile at him. 'As you say, husband,' I said meekly. 'Whatever you say.'

The ship was waiting as Daniel had arranged and we had a few hours of hard work loading the pieces of the dismantled press and the barrels and boxes of books and papers before finally we were all aboard and the sailors cast off, the barges took us in tow, and the ship went slowly downriver, helped by the ebbing tide. My father had brought a hamper of food and we sat on the deck, sometimes shrinking from a passing sailor running to obey an order, and ate cold chicken and a strange strong-tasting cheese and a hard crunchy bread.

'You'll have to get used to this fare,' Daniel laughed at me. 'This is Calais food.'

'Shall we stay in Calais?' I asked.

He shook his head. 'It's not safe for us for ever,' he said. 'Soon Queen Mary will turn her attention there too. The place is riddled with runaway

Protestants and Lutherans and Erastians and all sorts of heretics, anxious to have a quick exit to France, or Flanders or Germany. Plotters too. And the kingdom of France has its own battle with the Huguenots or anyone who is not an orthodox son of the church. Between the two powers I think that people like us will be squeezed out.'

I felt the familiar sense of injustice. 'Squeezed out to where now?' I asked.

Daniel smiled at me and put his hand over my own. 'Peace, sweet-heart,' he said. 'I have found a home for us. We are going to go to Genoa.'

'Genoa?'

'They are making a community of Jews there,' he said, his voice very low. 'They are allowing the People to settle there. They want the trade contacts and the gold and trustworthy credit that the People bring with them. We'll go there. A doctor can always find work, and a bookseller can always sell books to the Jews.'

'And your mother and sisters?' I asked. I was hoping he would tell me that they would stay in Calais, that they had found husbands and homes in the town and we could visit them once every two years.

'Mary and my mother will come with us,' he said. 'The other two have good posts and want to stay in Calais, whatever the risks to them. Sarah is courting with a Gentile and may marry him.'

'Don't you mind?'

Daniel shook his head. 'When I was in Venice and Padua I learned much more than the new sciences,' he said. 'I changed my mind about our people. I think now that we are the yeast of Christendom. It is our task to go among the Christians and bring them our learning and our skills, our ability with trade and our honour. Perhaps some day we shall have a country of our own once more, Israel. Then we shall have to rule it kindly, we know what it is to be ruled with cruelty. But we were not born to be hidden and to be ashamed. We were born to be ourselves, and to be proud of being the chosen to lead. If my sister marries a Christian then she will bring her learning and her wisdom to her family and they will be the better Christians for it, even if they never know that she is a Jew.'

'And shall we live as Jews or Gentiles?' I asked.

His smile at me was infinitely warm. 'We shall live as suits us,' he said. 'I won't have the Christian rules that forbid my learning, I won't have Jewish rules that forbid my life. I shall read books that ask if the sun goes around the earth or the earth around the sun, and I shall eat pork when it is well reared and properly killed and well cooked. I shall accept no prohibitions on my thoughts or my actions except those that make sense to me.'

'And shall I?' I asked, wondering where this independence would take us.

'Yes,' he said simply. 'Your letters and everything you have ever said makes sense to me only if I see you as my partner in this venture. Yes. You shall find your own way and I hope we will agree. We shall find a new way to live and it will be one that honours our parents and their beliefs, but which gives us a chance to be ourselves, and not just their children.'

My father, seated a little away from us and carefully not listening to our conversation, enacted an unconvincing yawn. 'I'm for sleep,' he said. He put his hand on my head. 'Bless you, child, it is good to have you with me once more.' He wrapped his cape around himself and laid down on the cold deck.

Daniel stretched out his arm to me. 'Come here and I will keep you warm,' he said.

I was not in the least cold but I did not tell him that as I went into the circle of his arm and let myself stretch out against the mystery of his male body. I felt him gently kissing my cropped hair and then I felt and heard his breath against my ear.

'Oh, Hannah,' he whispered. 'I have dreamed of having you for so long I could cry like a girl for desire.'

I giggled. 'Daniel,' I said, trying the unfamiliar name on my lips. I turned my face up towards him and felt the warmth of his mouth on mine, a kiss which melted the very marrow of my bones so that I felt we were dissolving into one another like some alchemical mixture, an elixir of pleasure. Under his cape his hands caressed my back and then fumbled under my jerkin and linen and stroked my breasts, my throat, my belly, and I felt myself stretch out like a petted cat and whisper 'Daniel' once more and this time it was an invitation. Gently, his hands explored the contours of my body like a stranger in a new land. Shyly, but with gathering curiosity I let my fingers explore the soft fine hair of his chest, the warmth of his skin beneath his breeches, and then the extraordinary shape of his cock which rose and pulsed at my touch as Daniel groaned with desire.

The night was too long and the skies too dark for shamefulness. Under Daniel's cloak we slid our breeches down and coupled with an easy confident delight that started breathless and became ecstasy. I had not known that it could feel like that. Watching other women and men court, even trembling beneath Lord Robert's touch, I had not known that such pleasure was possible. We parted only to doze and within an hour we woke and moved together again. Only when we saw the sky lighten through the ropes to our left did I drift from arching desire and satisfaction into exhausted sleep.

I woke to a cold morning, and had to scramble into my clothes before the sailors could see what we had been about. At first I could see nothing but the dark outline of the land, and then slowly it became clearer to me. A stolid strong fort guarded the entrance to the harbour. 'Fort Risban,' Daniel said, standing behind me so that I could lean back against his warm chest. 'Do you see the port beyond?'

I raised myself up a little and giggled like a girl as I felt his body respond to my movement. 'Where?' I asked, innocently enough.

He shifted me away from him with a little grunt of discomfort. 'You are a coquette,' he said bluntly. 'There. Ahead of you. That is the main port and the canals flow from it all around the city, so it is a moated city as well as a walled one.'

As the ship came into port I stayed at the side, watching the features of this town with the sense – familiar to so many of my people – that I would have to start my life over again, and make my home here all over again. These red-tiled rooftops just showing over the strong thickness of the city walls would become familiar to me, the cobbled streets between the high houses would be my routes to and from the baker, from the market, to my house. This strange aroma, the smell of a working port: old fish, the tarry odour of drying nets, the fresh hint of newly sawn wood, the clean tang of salt wind, all this would become the familiar taste on my lips and the perfume of my woollen cape. Soon all this would mean home to me, and in a little while I would cease to wonder how the queen was this morning, whether better or worse, how Elizabeth was faring, waiting patiently as she must surely do, and how my lord was, watching the sun rise from the arrow-slit window of his prison. All of those thoughts and loves and loyalties I must put behind me and greet my new life. I had left the court, I had deserted the queen, I had abandoned Elizabeth and I had taken my leave of the man I adored: my lord. Now I would live for my husband and my father and I would learn to belong to this new family: a husband, three sisters and my mother-in-law.

'My mother is waiting for us.' Daniel's breath was warm against my hair as he leaned against me at the rail of the ship. I leaned back again and felt his cock stir inside his breeches at my touch and I pressed back, wanton and desiring him once more. I looked to where he was looking and saw her, formidable, arms folded across a broad chest, scrutinising the deck of the ship as if to see whether her reluctant daughter-in-law had done her duty and arrived this time.

When she saw Daniel she raised a hand in greeting, and I waved back. I was too far away to see her face, but I imagined her carefully schooling her expression.

'Welcome to Calais,' she said to me as we came down the gangplank. Daniel she wordlessly enfolded into an adoring embrace.

He struggled to be free. 'I have to see to them unloading the press,' he told her, and went back on board and swung down into the hold. Mrs Carpenter and I were left alone on the quayside, an island of awkward silence among the men and women bustling around us.

'He found you then,' she said, with no great pleasure.

'Yes,' I said.

'And are you ready to marry him now?'

'Yes.'

'You'll have to get out of those clothes,' she said. 'They're respectable people in Calais, they won't like the sight of you in breeches.'

'I know,' I said. 'I left in a hurry or I would have changed before I came.'

'That would have been better.'

We were silent again.

'Did you bring your wages?'

'Yes.' I was nettled by her tone. 'All of my wages for the last two quarters.'

'It will cost you all of that to buy stockings and gowns and shifts and caps, you will be surprised at the price.'

'It can't be more expensive than London.'

'Much more,' she said flatly. 'So much has to be shipped in from England.'

'Why do we not buy French?' I asked.

She made a little face. 'Hardly,' she said, but did not trouble to explain.

Daniel appeared and looked pleased that we were talking. 'I think I have everything unloaded,' he said. 'Your father is going to stay here with the things while I fetch a wagon.'

'I'll wait with him,' I said hastily.

'No,' he said. 'Go home with Mother, she can show you our house and you can get warm.'

He wanted to ensure that I was comfortable. He did not know that the last thing I wanted to do was to go home with his mother and sit with his sisters and wait for the men to finish their work and come home. 'I'll get the wagon with you then,' I said. 'I'm not cold.'

At a glance from his mother he hesitated. 'You can't go to the carter's yard dressed like that,' she said firmly. 'You will shame us all. Wrap your cloak around you and come home with me.'

Home was a pretty enough little house in London Street squashed in beside others in a row near the south gate of the town. The top floor was divided into three bedrooms; Daniel's three sisters shared the big bed in the room which faced the back of the house, his mother had a tiny room all to herself, and my father had the third. Daniel mostly lived with his tutor, but would sleep on a truckle bed in my father's room when he stayed overnight. The next floor served as a dining room and sitting room for the family, and the ground floor was my father's shop facing the street, and at the back a little kitchen and scullery. In the yard behind, Daniel and my father had built and thatched a roof, and the printing press would be re-assembled and set up in there.

All three of Daniel's sisters were waiting to greet us in the living room at the top of the stairs. I was acutely conscious of my travel-stained clothes and dirty face and hands, as I saw them look me up and down and then glance in silence at each other.

'Here are my girls,' their mother said. 'Mary, Sarah, and Anne.'

The three of them rose like a row of moppets and dipped a curtsey as one, and sat down again. In my pageboy livery I could not curtsey, I made a little bow to them and saw their eyes widen.

'I'll put the kettle on,' Mrs Carpenter said.

'I'll help,' Anne said and dived out of the room. The other two and I regarded each other with silent dislike.

'Did you have a good crossing?' Mary asked.

'Yes, thank you.' The tranced night on the deck and Daniel's insistent touch seemed to be a long way away now.

'And are you going to marry Daniel now?'

'Mary! Really!' her sister protested.

'I don't see why I shouldn't ask. It's been a long enough betrothal. And if she is to be our sister-in-law we have a right to know.'

'It's between her and Daniel.'

'It's a matter for all of us.'

'Yes, I am,' I said, to bring their wrangling to an end.

They turned their bright inquisitive faces towards me. 'Indeed,' said Mary. 'You've left court then?'

'Yes.'

'And will you not go back?' the other one, Sarah, asked.

'No,' I said, keeping the regret from my voice.

'Won't you find it awfully dull here, after living at court? Daniel said that you were the queen's companion and spent all the day with her.'

'I shall help my father in the shop, I expect,' I said.

They both looked aghast as if the thought of working with books and the printing press was more daunting than marrying Daniel and living with them.

'Where are you and Daniel going to sleep?' Mary asked.

'Mary! Really!'

'Well, they can hardly bed down on the truckle bed,' she pointed out reasonably. 'And Mother can't be asked to move. And we have always had the best back bedroom.'

'Daniel and I will decide,' I said with an edge to my voice. 'And if there is not enough room for us here we will set up our own house.'

Mary gave a little scream of shock as her mother came up the stairs.

'What is it, child?' she demanded.

'Hannah has not been in the house five minutes and already she says she and Daniel will live elsewhere!' Mary exclaimed, halfway to tears. 'Already she is taking Daniel away from us! Just as I knew she would! Just as I said – she will spoil everything!' She leaped to her feet, tore open the door and ran up the stairs leading to her room, leaving the wooden door to bang behind her. We heard the creak of the rope bed as she flung herself on to it.

'Oh, really!' her mother exclaimed in indignation. 'This is ridiculous!'

I was about to agree, and then I saw that she was looking accusingly at me.

'How could you upset Mary on your very first day?' she demanded. 'Everyone knows that she is easily upset, and she loves her brother. You will have to learn to mind your tongue, Miss Hannah. You are living with a family now. You have not the right to speak out like a fool any more.'

For one stunned moment I said nothing to defend myself. Then: 'I am sorry,' I said through my teeth.

Summer 1556

It was a long hot summer, that first summer in Calais. I greeted the sunshine as if I were a pagan ready to worship it, and when Daniel told me he was persuaded by the new theory that the earth revolved around the sun in the great vastness of space, and not the other way around, I had to acknowledge that it made perfect sense to me too, as I felt myself unfold into the heat.

I loitered in the squares, and dawdled at the fish quay to see the dazzle of sunlight on the ripples of the harbour. They called it *le Bassin du Paradis*, and in the bright sunlight I thought it was paradise indeed. Whenever I could, I made an excuse to leave the town and slip out through the gates where the casual sentries watched the townspeople coming and going and the country people arriving. I strolled in the little vegetable plots outside the city walls to sniff at the freshness of the growth in the warm earth, and I pined to go further, down to the beach to see the waves breaking on the shore, across the marshlands where the herons stood eyeing their own tall reflections, out to the country where I could see the darkness of the woods against the light green meadows.

It felt like a long summer and it was a breathtakingly tedious season for me. Daniel and I were under the same roof but we had to live as maid and suitor, we were hardly ever left alone together. I longed for his touch, for his kiss, and for the pleasure that he had given me on the night that we sailed to France. But he could hardly bear to come near me, knowing that he must always step back, knowing that he must never do more than kiss my lips or my hand. Even the scent of me, as

I passed him on the stairs or in the narrow rooms, would make him tremble, and when he touched my fingers as he passed me a plate or a glass I would long for his caress. Neither of us would show our desire to the bright curiosity of his sisters, but we could not wholly hide it, and I hated the way their gaze flicked from one of us to the other.

I was out of my breeches and into a gown in the first week and soon experiencing a constant tuition in how a young lady should behave. It seemed there was a tacit agreement between my father and Daniel's mother that she should coach me in the skills that a young woman should possess. Everything my mother had taught me of domestic skills I appeared to have left behind when we fled from Spain. And since then, no-one had taught me how to brew and bake, how to churn butter, how to squeeze the whey from cheese. No-one had taught me how to lay down linen in henbane and lavender in a linen chest, how to set a table, how to skim for cream. My father and I had lived, agreeably enough, as a working man and his apprentice. At court I had learned sword fighting, tumbling and wit from Will Somers, political caution and desire from Robert Dudley, mathematics from John Dee, espionage from Princess Elizabeth. Clearly, I had no useful skills for a young doctor's home. I was not much of a young woman and not much of a wife. Daniel's mother had awarded herself the task of 'taking me in hand'.

She found a sulky and unwilling pupil. I was not naturally gifted at housekeeping. I did not want to know how to scour a brass pan with sand so that it glittered. I did not want to take a scrubbing brush to the front step. I did not want to peel potatoes so that there was no waste at all, and feed the peelings to the hens that we kept in a little garden outside the city walls. I wanted to know none of these things, and I did not see why I should learn them.

'As my wife you will need to know how to do such things,' Daniel said reasonably enough. I had slipped out to waylay him where his road home from work crossed the market place before the great Staple Hall, so that I could speak with him before he entered the house and we both fell under his mother's rule.

'Why should I know? You don't do them.'

'Because I will be out at work and you will be caring for our children and preparing their food,' he said.

'I thought I would keep a printing shop, like my father.'

'And who would cook and clean for us?'

'Couldn't we have a maid?'

He choked on a laugh. 'Perhaps, later on. But I couldn't afford to pay wages for a maid at first, you know, Hannah. I am not a wealthy man. When I set up in practice on my own we will have only my fees to live on.'

'And will we have a house of our own then?'

He drew my hand through his elbow as if he were afraid that I might pull away at his answer.

'No,' he said simply. 'We will find a bigger house, perhaps in Genoa. But I will always offer a house to my sisters and to my mother; to your father too. Surely, you would want nothing less?'

I said nothing. To tell the truth, I did want to live with my father, and with Daniel. It was his mother and his sisters I found hard to bear. But I could hardly say to him that I would choose to live with my father but not with his mother.

'I thought we would be alone together,' I said mendaciously.

'I have to care for my mother and sisters,' he said. 'It is a sacred trust. You know that.'

I nodded. I did know it.

'Have they been unkind to you?'

I shook my head. I could not complain of their treatment of me. I slept every night in a truckle bed in the girls' room and every night as I fell asleep I heard them whispering in the big bed at my side, and I imagined they were talking about me. In the morning they drew the curtains of the bed so that I should not see them as they dressed. They emerged to comb and plait each other's hair before the little mirror and cast sideways glances at my growing mop of hair only half-covered by my cap. My dresses and linen were all new and were the focus of much silent envy, and occasional secret borrowing. They were, in short, as spiteful and as unkind as girls working in concert can be, and many nights I turned my face into my hay mattress and cried in silence for sheer frustrated anger.

Daniel's mother never said a word to me that could be cited against her to her son. She never said a thing that I could quote in a complaint. Insidiously, almost silently, she made me feel that I was not good enough for Daniel, not good enough for her family, an inadequate young woman in every domestic task, an awkward young woman in appearance, a faulty young woman in religious observation, and an undutiful daughter and potentially a disobedient wife. If she had ever spoken the truth she would have said that she did not like me; but it seemed to me that she was absolutely opposed to speaking the truth about anything.

'Then we surely can live happily together,' Daniel said. 'Safe at last. Together at last. You are happy, aren't you, my love?'

I hesitated. 'I don't get on very well with your sisters, and your mother does not approve of me,' I said quietly.

He nodded, I was telling him nothing he did not know. 'They'll come round,' he said warmly. 'They'll come round. We have to stay together. For our own safety and survival we have to stay together, and we will all learn to change our ways a little and to be happy.'

I nodded, hiding my many, very many, reservations. 'I hope so,' I said and watched him smile.

We were married in late June, as soon as all my gowns were made and my hair long enough for me to be – as Daniel's mother said – passable, at l'Eglise de Notre Dame, the great church of Calais, where the vaulting columns looked like those of a French cathedral but they ran up to a great English church tower set square on the top. It was a Christian wedding with a Mass afterwards and every one of us was meticulous in our observation of the rituals in church. Afterwards, in the privacy of the little house in London Street, Daniel's sisters held a shawl as a chuppah over our heads as my father repeated the seven blessings for a wedding, as far as he could remember them, and Daniel's mother put a wrapped glass at Daniel's feet for him to stamp on. Then we drew back the shutters, opened the doors and held a wedding feast for the neighbours with gifts and dancing.

The vexed question of where we would sleep as a married couple had been resolved by my father moving to a bunk alongside the printing press in the little room created by thatching the back yard. Daniel and I slept in Father's old room on the top floor, a thin plaster wall between us and his sleepless mother on one side, and his curious sisters, awake and listening, on the other side.

On our wedding night we fell upon each other as a pair of wanton lovers, longing for an experience too long denied. They put us to bed with much laughter and jokes and pretended embarrassment, and as soon as they were gone Daniel bolted the door, closed the shutters and drew me into the bed. Desperate for privacy we put the covers completely over our heads and kissed and caressed in the hot darkness, hoping that the blankets would muffle our whispers. But the pleasure of his touch overwhelmed me and I gave a breathy little cry. At once, I stopped short and clapped a hand over my mouth.

'It doesn't matter,' he said, prising my fingers from my lips to kiss them again.

'It does,' I said, speaking nothing but the truth.

'Kiss me,' he begged me.

'Well, very quietly . . .'

I kissed him and felt his mouth melt under mine. He rolled underneath me and guided me to mount him. At the first touch of his hardness between my legs I moaned with pleasure and bit the back of my hand, trying to teach myself to stay silent.

He turned me so that I was underneath him. 'Put your hand over my mouth,' I urged him.

He hesitated. 'It feels as if I am forcing you,' he said uncomfortably.

I gave a little breathy laugh. 'If you were forcing me I would be quieter,' I joked, but he could not laugh. He pulled away from me and dropped on to his back, and he pulled me to lie beside him, my head on his shoulder.

'We'll wait till they are all asleep,' he said. 'They cannot wake all night.'

We waited and waited but his mother's heavy tread did not come up the stairs until late, and then we heard, with embarrassing clarity, her sigh as she sat on the side of her bed, the 'clip, clop' as she dropped one wooden clog then another on the floor. Then we heard with a sharpness which showed us how thin the walls must be, the muted rustle of her undressing and then the creak of the ropes of the bed as she got under the covers.

After that it was impossible. If I even turned the bed creaked so loud that I knew she would hear it. I pressed my mouth to his ear and breathed, 'Let us make love tomorrow when they are all out,' and I felt the nod of his silent assent. Then we lay, burning up with desire, sleepless with lust, not touching, not even looking at each other, on our bridal night.

They came for the sheets in the morning, and would have flown them like a bloodstained flag from the window to prove the consummation of the marriage but Daniel stopped them. 'There's no need,' he said. 'And I don't like the old ways.'

The girls said nothing but they raised their eyebrows at me as if they well knew that we had not bedded together at all, and suspected that he could not feel desire for me. His mother, on the other hand, looked at me as if it proved to her that I was not a virgin and that her son had brought a whore into her home.

It was a bad wedding night and a sour wedding morning and, as it happened, they did not go out all day but stayed at home, and we could not make love that day, nor the next night, nor the next night either.

Within a few days I had learned to lie like a stone beneath my husband, and he had learned to take his pleasure as quickly as he could in silence. Within a few weeks we made love as seldom as possible. The early promise of our night of lovemaking on the boat that had left me dizzy with satisfied desire could not be explored or fulfilled in a bedroom with four nosy women listening.

I came to hate myself for the rise of my desire and then my embarrassment that they would hear us. I could not bear to know that every word I said, every snatched breath, even the sound of my kiss was audible to a critical and intent audience. I shrank from his sisters' knowledge that I loved him, I flinched from their intimacy with something that should be exclusive, just to us. On the first morning after we had finally made love, when Daniel came downstairs, I caught the glance his mother flickered over him. It was a look of utter possession, as a farmer might look at a healthy bull at stud. She had heard my cry of pleasure half-silenced the night before and she was delighted at his prowess. To her I was nothing more than a cow who should soon be in calf, the credit for it all was to her son, the prestige of founding a family would come to her.

After that I would not come downstairs at the same time as Daniel. I felt scorched by the bright glances of his sisters which flicked from his face to mine and back again, as if to read how we had been transformed into man and wife by the muffled exchanges of the night. I would either get up before the others, and be downstairs with the kindling laid on last night's embers, boiling the breakfast gruel before anyone else was up, or I would wait until he had eaten his breakfast and gone.

When I came down late, his sisters would nudge each other and whisper.

'I see you keep court hours still,' Mary said spitefully.

Her mother made a gesture with her hand to silence her. 'Leave her alone, she will need to rest,' she said.

I shot a quick glance at her, it was the first time she had defended me against Mary's acid tongue, and then I saw it was not me, Hannah, that she was defending. It was not even Daniel's wife – as though anything that belonged to Daniel was illuminated by the glow he cast in this household – it was because she hoped I was breeding. She wanted another boy, another boy for the House of Israel, another little d'Israeli to continue the line. And if I could produce him soon, while she was still young and active, she could bring him up as her own, in her own house, under her supervision and then it would be: 'my son's little boy, my son the doctor, you know.'

If I had not served for three years at court I would have fought like a cat with my mother-in-law and my three dear sisters-in-law; but I had seen worse and heard worse and endured worse than they could ever have dreamed. I knew that the moment I complained to Daniel about them I would bring down on my own head all his worry and all his love for them, for me, and for the family he was trying to make.

He was too young a man to take the responsibility of keeping a family safe in such difficult and dangerous times. He was studying his skill as a physician, every day he had to advise men and women who were staring death in the face. He did not want to come home at night to a coven of women torn apart by malice and envy.

So I held my tongue and when his sisters were witty at my expense, or even openly critical of the bread I had bought at market, of my wasteful kitchen practices, of the printers' ink on my hands, of my books on the kitchen table, I said nothing. I had been at court and seen the ladies in waiting vying for the attention of the queen. I knew all about female malice, I had just never thought that I would have to live with it at home.

My father saw some of it and tried to protect me. He found me translation work to do, and I would sit at the bookshop counter and work from Latin to English or from English to French while the smell of the ink from the press drifted in reassuringly from the yard outside. Sometimes I helped him to print, but the complaints from Mrs Carpenter if I got ink on my apron or, worse, on my gown, were so extreme that both my father and I tried to avoid arousing her indignation.

As the summer wore on and Daniel's mother gave me the pick of the food, the breast of the scrawny French chickens, the fattest sweetest peaches, I realised that she was waiting for me to speak to her. In the last days of August she could not bear to wait any longer.

'Have you got something to tell me, daughter?' she asked.

I felt myself stiffen. I always flinched when she called me 'daughter'. I never wanted another mother but the one who bore me. In truth, I thought it an impertinence of this unloveable woman to try to claim me for her own. I was my mother's child and not hers, and if I had wanted any other mother then I would have chosen the queen who had laid my head in her lap, and stroked my curls and told me that she trusted me.

Besides, I knew Daniel's mother now. I had not observed her for the whole of the summer without learning her particular route to things. If she called me 'daughter' or praised how I had combed my hair under my cap she was after something: information, a promise, some kind of intimacy. I looked at her without a glimmer of a smile, and waited.

'Something to tell me?' she prompted. 'A little news that would make an old woman very, very happy?'

I realised what she was after. 'No,' I said shortly.

'Not yet sure?'

'Sure I am not with child, if that is what you mean,' I said flatly. 'I had my course two weeks ago. Did you want to know anything more?'

She was so intent on what I was saying that she ignored my rudeness. 'Well, what is the matter with you?' she demanded. 'Daniel has had you at least twice a week ever since your wedding day. No-one can doubt him. Are you ill?'

'No,' I said through cold lips. She would, of course, know exactly how often we made love. She had listened without any sense of shame, she would go on listening. It would not even occur to her that I could take no pleasure in his touch or his kiss knowing that she was just the other side of the thinnest of walls, ears pricked. She would not have dreamed that I had hoped for pleasure. As far as she was concerned the matter was for Daniel's pleasure and for the making of a grandson for her.

'Then what is the matter?' she repeated. 'I have been waiting for you to tell me that you are with child any day these last two months.'

'Then sorry I am, to so disappoint you,' I said, as cold as Princess Elizabeth in one of her haughty moods.

In a sudden movement she snatched my wrist, and twisted it round so that I was forced to turn and face her, her grip biting into the skin. 'You're not taking something?' she hissed. 'You've not got some draught to take to stop a child coming? From your clever friends at court? Some slut's trick?'

'Of course not!' I said, roused to anger. 'Why would I?'

'God knows what you would or would not do!' she exclaimed in genuine distress, flinging me from her. 'Why would you go to court? Why would you not come with us to Calais? Why be so unnatural, so unwomanly, more like a boy than a girl? Why come now, too late, when Daniel could have had his pick of any girl in Calais? Why come at all if you're not going to breed?'

I was stunned by her anger, it knocked the words out of me. For a moment I said nothing. Then slowly I found the words. 'I was begged for a fool, it was not my choice,' I said. 'You should reproach my father if you dare with that, not me. I wore boy's clothes to protect me, as you well know. And I did not come with you because I had sworn to the Princess Elizabeth that I would be with her at her time of trial. Most women would think that showed a true heart, not a false one. And I came now because Daniel wanted me, and I wanted him. And I don't believe a word you say. He could not have the pick of the girls of Calais.'

'He could indeed!' she said, bridling. 'Pretty girls and fertile girls too. Girls who would come with a dowry and not in breeches, a girl who has a baby in the cradle this summer and knows her place, and would be glad enough to be in my house, and proud to call me mother.'

I felt very cold, like fear, like a dreadful uncertainty. 'I thought you were talking in general,' I said. 'D'you mean that there is a particular girl who likes Daniel?'

Mrs Carpenter would never tell the whole truth about anything. She turned away from me and went to the breakfast pot hanging beside the fireplace and took it off the hook as if she would go out with it and scour it again. 'D'you call this clean?' she demanded crossly.

'Daniel has a woman he likes, here in Calais?' I asked.

'He never offered her marriage,' she said grudgingly. 'He always said that you and he were betrothed and that he was promised.'

'Is she Jew, or Gentile?' I whispered.

'Gentile,' she said. 'But she would take our religion if Daniel married her.'

'Married her?' I exclaimed. 'But you just said he always said he was betrothed to me!'

She brought the pot to the kitchen table. 'It was nothing,' she said, trying to slide away from her own indiscretion. 'Only something she once said to me.'

'You spoke to her about Daniel marrying her?'

'I had to!' she flared up. 'She came to the house when he was in Padua, her belly before her, wanting to know what would be done for her.'

'Her belly?' I repeated numbly. 'She is with child?'

'She has his son,' Daniel's mother said. 'And a fine healthy boy, the very picture of him as a baby. Nobody could doubt whose child he is, not for a moment, even if she were not a lovely girl, a good girl, which she is.'

I sank to the stool at the table and looked up at her in bewilderment. 'Why did he not tell me?'

She shrugged. 'Why would he tell you? Did you tell him everything in all these long years when you made him wait for you?'

I thought of Lord Robert's dark eyes on me, and the touch of his mouth on my neck. 'I did not lie with another and conceive a child,' I said quietly.

'Daniel is a handsome young man,' she said. 'Did you think he would wait like a nun for you? Or did you not think of him at all, while you played the fool and dressed like a whore and ran after who knows who?'

I said nothing, listening to the resentment in her tone, observing the rage in her flushed cheeks and the spittle on her lips from her hissing speech.

'Does he see his child?'

'Every Sunday at church,' she said. I caught her quickly hidden smile of triumph. 'And twice a week, when he tells you he is working late, he goes to her house to dine with her and to see his child.'

I rose up from the table.

'Where are you going?' she asked, suddenly alarmed.

'I am going to meet him as he walks home,' I said. 'I want to talk with him.'

'Don't upset him,' she said eagerly. 'Don't tell him that you know of this woman. It will do you no good if you quarrel. He married you, remember. You should be a good wife and wink at this other. Better women than you have turned away and seen nothing.'

I thought of the look of blank pain on Queen Mary's face when she heard Elizabeth's lilting laugh at the king's whisper in her ear.

'Yes,' I said. 'But I don't care about being a good wife any longer. I don't know what to think or what to care for.'

I suddenly noticed the pot with the smear of gruel along the side and I snatched it up and threw it at the back door. It hit the wood with a resounding clang and bounced to the floor. 'And you can scour your own damned pot!' I shouted at her shocked face. 'And you can wait forever for a grandson from me.'

I stormed from the house and across the market place, not seeing the stalls and the usual traders. I made my way across the fish quay, not even hearing the cat calls of the fishermen at my rapid pace and my uncovered head. I came to the door of the physician's house in a rush and then realised that I could not hammer on it and demand to see Daniel. I would have to wait. I hitched myself up on to a low stone wall of the opposite house and settled down to wait for him. When passers-by smiled or winked at me I glared at them, brazen, as if I were in my lad's clothes again and had forgotten how to smooth down my skirts and cast down my eyes.

I did not consider what I would say to him, nor did I plan what I might do. I just waited like a dog waits for his master. I just waited in pain, as a dog will do with its paw caught in a trap and there is nothing to do but to wait; not understanding what the pain is, not knowing what can be done. Just enduring. Just waiting.

I heard the clock strike four and then half past before the side door opened and Daniel came out, calling a farewell and closing the door behind him. He had a flask of some green liquid in one hand, and when he came to the gate he started in the wrong direction, away from home. I was in a sudden terror that he was going to visit his lover, and that I, like some suspicious wife, would be caught spying on him. At once I crossed the road and ran up to him.

'Daniel!'

'Hannah!' His pleasure in seeing me was unfeigned. But after one glance at my white face he said: 'Is there something wrong? Are you ill?'

'No,' I said, my lip trembling. 'I just wanted to see you.'

'And now you do,' he said easily. He drew my hand through his arm. 'I have to take this to Widow Jerrin's house, will you come with me?'

I nodded, and fell into step beside him. I could not keep up. The fullness of my petticoats under my gown prevented me from striding out as I had done when I was a pageboy. I lifted my skirts out to one side but they still hobbled me as if I was a mare, hog-tied in the horse-breaking ring. Daniel slowed down and we walked in silence. He stole a glance at me and guessed from my grim expression that all was not well, but he decided to deal first with the delivery of the medicine.

The widow's house was one of the older buildings inside the criss-crossing streets of the old town. The houses were packed in under the sheltering bulk of the castle, all the little alleyways overshadowed by the jutting first storeys of the houses that lined them, running north and south and intersected by the next road going east–west.

'When we first came here, I thought I would never find my way round,' he said, making conversation. 'And then I learned the names of the taverns. This has been an English town for two hundred years, remember. Every street corner has a "Bush" or a "Pig and Whistle" or a "Travellers Rest". This street has a tavern called "The Hollybush". There it is.' He pointed to the building with a battered sign swinging outside it.

'I'll only be a moment.' He turned to a narrow doorway and tapped on the door.

'Ah, Dr Daniel!' came a woman's croaking voice from within. 'Come in, come in!'

'Ma'am, I cannot,' he said with his easy smile. 'My wife is waiting for me and I will walk home with her.'

There was a laugh from inside the house and a remark that she was a lucky girl to have him, and then Daniel emerged, pocketing a coin.

'Now,' he said. 'Shall I walk you home around the city walls, m'lady? Get a breath of sea air?'

I tried to smile at him but I was too heartsore. I let him lead me to the end of the street and then along a lane. At the very end of the lane was the towering wall of the town, shallow stone steps running up the inside. We climbed them, up and up, until we got to the ramparts and could look northwards towards the horizon where England lay. England, the queen, the princess, my lord: they all seemed a long way away. It seemed to me in that moment that I had known a better life as a fool to a queen than I had being a fool to Daniel and to his stone-hearted mother and his poisonous sisters.

'Now,' he said, matching his steps to mine as we walked along the wall, seagulls crying over our heads and the waves slapping at the stones. 'What is the matter, Hannah?'

I did not turn the conversation round and round like a woman would do. I went straight to the heart of it, as if I were still a troubled pageboy and not a betrayed wife. 'Your mother tells me that you have got a Calais woman with child,' I said bluntly. 'And that you see her and her child three times a week.'

I could feel his stride falter, and when I looked up at him he had lost the colour from his cheeks. 'Yes,' he said. 'That's true.'

'You should have told me.'

He nodded, marshalling his thoughts. 'I suppose I should have done. But if I had told you, would you have married me and come to live with me here?'

'I don't know. No, probably not.'

'Then you see why I did not tell you.'

'You cozened me and married me on a lie.'

'I told you that you were the one great love of my life, and you are. I told you that I thought we should marry to provide for my mother and for your father, and I still think that we did the right thing. I told you that we should marry so that we might live together, as the Children of Israel, and I could keep you safe.'

'Safe in a hovel!' I burst out.

Daniel recoiled at that: the first time that I had told him directly that

I despised his little house. 'I am sorry that is what you think of your home. I told you that I hope to provide better for us later.'

'You lied to me,' I said again.

'Yes,' he said simply. 'I had to.'

'Do you love her?' I asked. I could hear the pitiful note in my own voice and I pulled my hand from his arm, filled with resentment that love should have brought me so low that I was whimpering at betrayal. I took a step away from him so he could not wrap me close and console me. I did not want to be a girl in love any more.

'No,' he said bluntly. 'But when we first came to Calais, I was lonely and she was pretty and warm and good company. If I had any sense I would not have gone with her, but I did.'

'More than once?' I asked, wounding myself.

'More than once.'

'And I suppose you didn't make love to *her* with a hand over her mouth so your mother and sisters couldn't hear?'

'No,' he said shortly.

'And her son?'

His face warmed at once. 'He is a baby of about five months old,' he said. 'Strong, and lusty.'

'Does she take your name?'

'No. She keeps her own.'

'Does she live with her family?'

'She is in service.'

'They allow her to keep her child?'

'They have a kindness for her, and they are old. They like to have a child around the house.'

'They know that you are the father?'

He nodded his head.

I rocked with shock. 'Everyone knows? Your sisters, the priest? Your neighbours? The people who came to our wedding feast and wished me well? Everyone?'

Daniel hesitated. 'It's a small town, Hannah. Yes, I should think everyone knows of it.' He tried to smile. 'And now I should think everyone knows that you are rightly angry with me, and that I am begging your pardon. You have to get used to being part of a family, part of a town, part of the People. You are not Hannah on her own

361

any more. You are a daughter and a wife, and one day, I hope you will be a mother.'

'Never!' I said, the word wrung out of me by my anger and my disappointment in him. 'Never.'

He caught me to him and held me close. 'Don't say that,' he said. 'Not even in rage with me when you would say anything to hurt me back. Not even when I deserve punishment. You know I waited for you and loved you and trusted you even when I thought you were in love with another man and might never come to me. Now you are here and we are married, and I thank God for it. And now you are here we shall make a life, however difficult it has been for us to be together. I shall be your husband and your lover and you will forgive me.'

I wrenched myself from his grip and faced him. I swear if I had had a sword I would have run him through. 'No,' I said. 'I will never lie with you again. You are false, Daniel, and you called on me to trust you with lies in your mouth. You are no better than any man and I thought you were. You told me that you were.'

He would have interrupted me but the words were pouring out of my mouth like a shower of stones. 'And I *am* Hannah on my own. I don't belong in this town, I don't belong with the People, I don't belong with your mother or your family and you have showed me that I don't belong with you. I deny you, Daniel. I deny your family, and I deny your people. I will belong to no-one and I will be alone.'

I turned on my heel and marched away from him, the tears running hot down my cold cheeks. I was expecting to hear him hurrying after me but he did not come. He let me go and I strode away as if I would walk home across the foam-crested grey waves to England, all the way to Robert Dudley, and tell him that I would be his mistress this very night if he desired it, since I had nothing left to lose. I had tried an honourable love and it had been nothing but lies and dishonesty: a hard road and paid with a false coin at the end.

I strode furiously along the walls until I had done a whole circuit of the town and found myself back overlooking the sea once more at the spot where we had quarrelled. Daniel had gone, I had not expected to find him where I had left him. He would have gone home to his supper, and appeared to his family as composed and in control of his feelings as always. Or perhaps he would have gone to dine with his other woman, the mother of his child, as his mother had told me he did, twice a week, in the evenings, when I had stood at the window to watch for him coming and felt sorry for him, working late.

My feet, in the stupid high-heeled girls' shoes that I now had to wear, were aching from my forced march around the town walls and I limped down the narrow stone stairs to the sally port, through the little gate to the quayside. A handful of fishing boats was making ready to set sail on the evening tide, one of the many small traders who regularly crossed the sea between France and England was loading up with goods: a cart filled with household goods for a family returning to England, barrels of wine for London vintners, baskets of late peaches, early plums, currants, great parcels of finished cloth. A woman at the quayside was parting with her mother, the woman embraced her daughter, pulling her hood up over the girl's head, as if to keep her warm until they could be together again. The girl had to tear herself away and run up the gangplank and then she leaned over the side of the ship to kiss her hand and wave. The girl might be going into service in England, she might be leaving home to marry. I thought self-pityingly that I had not been sent out into the world with a mother's blessing. No-one had planned my wedding thinking of my preferences. My husband had been chosen by the matchmaker to make a safe home for my father and for me, and to give Daniel's mother a grandson. But no home could be safe for us, and she already had a grandson of five months old.

I had a moment's impulse to run to the ship's master and ask him what he would take for my passage. If he would let me owe him the fare I could pay when I reached London. I had a desire, like a knife in the belly, to run to Robert Dudley, to return to the queen, to get back to the court where I was valued by many, and desired by my lord, and where nobody could ever betray me and shame me, where I could be the mistress of myself. I had been a fool: a servant, lower than a lady in waiting, less than a musician, on a par perhaps with a favoured lap dog; but even as that I had been freer and prouder than I was, standing on the quayside with no money in my pocket, with nowhere to go but

Daniel's home, knowing that he had been unfaithful to me in the past and could be again.

It was dusk by the time I opened the door and stepped over the threshold of our house. Daniel was in the act of swinging on his cape as I came into the shop, my father waiting for him.

'Hannah!' my father exclaimed, and Daniel crossed the room in two strides and took me into his arms. I let him hold me but I looked past him to my father.

'We were coming out to look for you. You're so late!' my father exclaimed.

'I am sorry,' I said. 'I didn't think you would be worried about me.'

'Of course we were worried.' Daniel's mother came halfway down the stairs and leaned over the rail to scold me. 'A young lady can't go running around town at dusk. You should have come home at once.'

I shot her a thoughtful look, but I said nothing.

'I am sorry,' Daniel said, his mouth close to my ear. 'Let me talk with you. Don't be distressed, Hannah.'

I glanced up at him, his dark face was scowling with anxiety.

'Are you all right?' my father asked.

'Of course,' I said. 'Of course I am.'

Daniel took his cape from his shoulders. 'You say, "of course",' he complained. 'But the town is full of the roughest of soldiers, and you are dressed as a woman now, you don't have the protection of the queen and you don't even know your way around.'

I disengaged myself from Daniel's arms and pulled out a stool from the shop counter. 'I survived crossing half of Christendom,' I said mildly. 'I should think I could manage for two hours in Calais.'

'You're a young lady now,' my father reminded me. 'Not a child passing as a boy. You shouldn't even be out on your own in the evening.'

'Shouldn't be out at all except to go to market or church,' Daniel's mother supplemented robustly from her perch on the stairs.

'Hush,' Daniel said gently to her. 'Hannah is safe, that's the main thing. And hungry, I'm sure. What do we have left for her, Mother?'

364

'It's all gone,' she said unhelpfully. 'You had the last of the potage yourself, Daniel.'

'I didn't know that was all there was!' he exclaimed. 'Why didn't we save some for Hannah?'

'Well, who knew when she would come home?' his mother asked limpidly. 'Or whether she was dining out somewhere?'

'Come on,' Daniel said impatiently to me, pulling at my hand.

'Where to?' I asked, slipping from the stool.

'I am taking you to the tavern to get dinner.'

'I can find her some bread and a slice of beef,' his mother offered at once at the prospect of the two of us going out alone together to dine.

'No,' Daniel said. 'She's to have a proper hot dinner and I'll take a mug of ale. Don't wait up for us, Mother, nor you, sir.' He slung his cloak around my shoulders and swept me out of the door before his mother could suggest that she came too, and we were out in the street before his sisters had time to remark that I was not properly dressed for an evening out.

We walked in silence to the tavern at the end of the road. There was a tap room at the front of the building but a good parlour for travellers at the back. Daniel ordered some broth and some bread, a plate of meats and two mugs of small ale, and we sat down in one of the high-backed settles, and for the first time since I had come to Calais I felt that we might talk alone and uninterrupted for more than a snatched moment.

'Hannah, I am so sorry,' he said as soon as the maid had put our drinks before us, and gone. 'I am deeply, deeply sorry for what I have done.'

'Does she know you are married?'

'Yes, she knew I was betrothed when we first met, and I told her I was going to England to fetch you and we would be married when we returned.'

'Does she not mind?'

'Not now,' he said. 'She has become accustomed.'

I said nothing. I thought it most unlikely that a woman who had fallen in love with a man and borne his child would become accustomed within a year to him marrying someone else.

'Did you not want to marry her when you knew she was carrying your child?'

He hesitated. The landlord came with the broth and bread and meat and fussed around the table, which gave us a chance for silence. Then he left and I took a spoonful of broth and a mouthful of bread. It was thick in my mouth but I was not going to look as if I had lost my appetite through heartache.

'She is not one of the People,' Daniel said simply. 'And, in any case, I wanted to marry you. When I knew she was with child I was ashamed of what I had done; but she knew I did not love her, and that I was promised to you. She did not expect me to marry her. So I gave her a sum of money for a dowry and I pay her every month for the boy's keep.'

'You wanted to marry me, but not enough to stay away from other women,' I remarked bitterly.

'Yes,' he admitted. He did not flinch from the truth even when it was told baldly out of the mouth of an angry woman. 'I wanted to marry you, but I did not stay away from another woman. But what about you? Is your conscience utterly clear, Hannah?'

I let it go, though it was a fair accusation. 'What's the child named?'

He took a breath. 'Daniel,' he said and saw me flinch.

I took a mouthful of broth and crammed the bread down on top of it and chewed, though I wanted to spit it at him.

'Hannah,' he said very gently.

I bit into a piece of meat.

'I am sorry,' he said again. 'But we can overcome this. She makes no claims against me. I will support the child but I need not go and see her. I shall miss the boy, I hoped to see him grow up, but I will understand if you cannot tolerate me seeing her. I will give him up. You and I are young. You will forgive me, we will have a child of our own, we will find a better house. We will be happy.'

I finished my mouthful and washed it down with a swig of ale. 'No,' I said shortly.

'What?'

'I said, "No". Tomorrow I shall buy a boy's suit and my father and I will find new premises for the bookshop. I shall work as his apprentice again. I shall never wear high-heeled shoes again, as long as I live. They pinch my feet. I shall never trust a man again, as long as I live. You have hurt me, Daniel, and lied to me and betrayed me and I will never forgive you.'

He went very white. 'You cannot leave me,' he said. 'We are married in the sight of God, our God. You cannot break an oath to God. You cannot break your pledge to me.'

I rose to it as if it were a challenge. 'I care nothing for your God, nor for you. I shall leave you tomorrow.'

We spent a sleepless night. There was nowhere to go but home and we had to lie side by side, stiff as bodkins in the darkness of the bedroom with his mother alert behind one wall, and his sisters agog on the other side. In the morning I took my father out of the house and told him that my mind was made up and that I would not live with Daniel as his wife.

He responded to me as if I had grown a head from beneath my shoulders, become a monstrous strange being from a faraway island. 'Hannah, what will you do with your life?' he said anxiously. 'I cannot be always with you, who will protect you when I am gone?'

'I shall go back to royal service, I shall go to the princess or to my lord,' I said.

'Your lord is a known traitor and the princess will be married to one of the Spanish princes within the month.'

'Not her! She's not a fool. She would not marry a man and trust him! She knows better than to put her heart into a man's keeping.'

'She cannot live alone any more than you can live alone.'

'Father, my husband has betrayed me and shamed me. I cannot take him back as if nothing had happened. I cannot live with his sisters and his mother all whispering behind their hands every time he comes home late. I cannot live as if I belonged here.'

'My child, where do you belong if not here? If not with me? If not with your husband?'

I had my answer: 'I belong nowhere.'

My father shook his head. A young woman always had to be placed somewhere, she could not live unless she was bolted down in one service or another.

367

'Father, please let us set up a little business on our own, as we did in London. Let me help you in the printing shop. Let me live with you and we can be at peace and make our living here.'

He hesitated for a long moment, and suddenly I saw him as a stranger might see him. He was an old man and I was taking him from a home where he had become comfortable.

'What will you wear?' he asked finally.

I could have laughed out loud, it mattered so little to me. But I realised that it signified to him whether he had a daughter who could appear to fit into this world or whether I would be, eternally, out of step with it.

'I will wear a gown if you wish,' I said to please him. 'But I will wear boots underneath it. I will wear a jerkin and a jacket on top.'

'And your wedding ring,' he stipulated. 'You will not deny your marriage.'

'Father, he has denied it every day.'

'Daughter, he is your husband.'

I sighed. 'Very well. But we can go, can we? And at once?'

He rested his hand on my face. 'Child, I thought that you had a good husband who loved you and you would be happy.'

I gritted my teeth so the tears did not come to my eyes and make him think that I might soften, that I might still be a young woman with a chance of love. 'No,' I said simply.

It was not an easy matter, stripping down the press again and moving it from the yard. I had only my new gowns and linen to take with me, Father had a small box of his clothes, but we had to move the entire stock of books and manuscripts and all the printing equipment: the clean paper, the barrels of ink, the baskets of bookbinding thread. It took a week before the porters had finished carrying everything from the Carpenters' house to the new shop, and for every day of that week my father and I had to eat our dinner at a table in silence while Daniel's sisters glared at me with aghast horror, and Daniel's mother slammed down the plates with utter contempt as if she were feeding a pair of stray dogs.

Daniel stayed away, sleeping at his tutor's house, coming home only for a change of clothes. At those times I made sure that I was busy with my father out the back, or packing up books under the shop counter. He did not try to argue with me or plead with me and, wilfully, I felt it proved that I was right to leave him. I felt that if he had loved me he would have come after me, asked me again, begged me to stay. I willed myself to forget his stubbornness and his pride, and I made very sure to keep my thoughts from the life we had promised ourselves when we had said we would become the people we wanted to be and not be tied by the rules of Jew, or Gentile, or the world.

I had found a little shop at the south city gate: an excellent site for travellers about to leave Calais and travel through the English Pale to venture into France. It was the last chance they would have to buy books in their own language, and for those who wanted maps or advice about travelling in France or in the Spanish Netherlands we carried a good selection of travellers' tales, mostly fabulous, it must be said, but good reading for the credulous. My father already had a reputation inside the city and his established customers soon found their way to the new premises. Most days he would sit in the sun outside the shop on one of the stools and I would work inside, bending over the press and setting type, now that there was no-one to scold me for getting ink on my apron.

My father was tired, his move to Calais and then the disappointment of my failed marriage had wearied him. I was glad that he should sit and rest while I worked for the two of us. I relearned the skill of reading backwards, I relearned the skill of the sweep of the ink ball, the flick of the clean sheet and the smooth heave on the handle of the press so that the typeface just kissed the whiteness of the paper and it came away clean.

My father worried desperately about me, about my ill-starred marriage, and about my future life, but when he saw that I had inherited all of his skill, and all of his love of books, he began to believe that even if he were to die tomorrow, I might yet survive on the business. 'But we must save money, *querida*,' he would say. 'You must be provided for.'

Autumn 1556

The first month in our little shop, I absolutely rejoiced in my escape from the Carpenter household. A couple of times I saw Daniel's mother or two of his sisters in the market, or at the fish quay, and his mother looked away as if she could not see me, and his sisters pointed and nudged each other and stared as if I were a visiting leper and freedom was a disease that they might catch if they came too close. Every night in bed I spread myself out like a starfish, hands and feet pointing to each corner, rejoicing in the space, and thanked God that I might call myself a single woman once more with all the bed to myself. Every morning I awoke with an utter exultation that I need not fit myself to someone else's pattern. I could put on my sound walking boots underneath the concealing hem of my gown, I could set print, I could go to the bakehouse for our breakfast, I could go with my father to the tavern for our dinner, I could do what I pleased; and not what a young married woman, trying to please a critical mother-in-law, had to do.

I did not see Daniel until midway through the second month and then I literally ran into him as I was coming out of church. I had to sit at the back now; as a deserting wife I was in a state of sin which nothing would remove but full penitence and a return to my husband if he would be kind enough to have me. The priest himself had told me that I was as bad as an adulteress, worse, since I was in a state of sin of my own making and not even at another's urging. He set me a list of penances that would take me until Christmas next year to complete. I was as determined as ever to appear devout and so I spent many evenings on my knees in the church and always attended Mass, head shrouded in a black shawl, seated at the back. So it was from the darkness of the meanest pew that I stepped into the light of the church door and, half-dazzled, bumped into Daniel Carpenter.

'Hannah!' he said, and put out a hand to steady me.

'Oh, Daniel.'

For a moment we stood, very close, our eyes meeting. In that second I felt a jolt of absolute desire and knew that I wanted him and that he wanted me, and then I stepped to one side and looked down and muttered: 'Excuse me.'

'No, stop,' he said urgently. 'Are you well? Is your father well?'

I looked up at that with an irrepressible giggle. Of course he knew the answers to both questions. With spies like his mother and sisters he probably knew, to the last letter, what pages I had on the press, what dinner we had in the cupboard.

'Yes,' I replied. 'Both of us. Thank you.'

'I have missed you sorely,' he said, quickly trying to detain me. 'I have been wanting to speak with you.'

'I am sorry,' I said coldly. 'But I have nothing to say, Daniel, excuse me, please.'

I wanted to get away from him before he led me into talking, before he made me feel angry, or grieved, or jealous all over again. I did not want to feel anything for him, not desire, not resentment. I wanted to be cold to him, so I turned on my heel and started to walk away.

In two strides he was beside me, his hand on my arm. 'Hannah, we cannot live apart like this. It is wrong.'

'Daniel, we should never have married. It is that which was wrong; not our separation. Now let me go.'

His hand dropped to his side but he still held my gaze. 'I shall come to your shop this afternoon at two,' he said firmly. 'And I shall talk with you in private. If you go out I shall wait for your return. I will not leave things like this, Hannah. I have the right to talk with you.'

There were people coming out of the church porch, and others waiting to enter. I did not want to attract any more attention than I had already earned by being the deserting bride of Calais.

'At two o'clock, then,' I said, and dipped him a tiny curtsey and went down the path. His mother and his sisters, coming into church behind

371

him, drew their skirts back from the very paving slabs of the path where I was walking, as if they were afraid they would get the hems dirty by being brushed by me. I smiled at them, brazening it out. 'Good morning, Miss Carpenters,' I said cheerily. 'Good morning, Mrs Carpenter.' And when I was out of earshot I said: 'And God rot the lot of you.'

Daniel came at two o'clock and I drew him out of the house and up the stone stairs beside our house that went up to the roof of the gateway of the city walls that overlooked the English Pale and then south towards France. In the lee of the city walls, just outside, were new houses, built to accommodate the growing English population. If the French were ever to come against us these new householders would have to abandon their hearths and skip inside the gates. But before the French could come close, there were the canals which would be flooded from the sea gates, the eight great forts, the earth ramparts, and a stubborn defence plan. If they could get through that, they would have to face the fortified town of Calais itself and everyone knew that it was impregnable. The English themselves had only won it, two centuries ago, after a siege lasting eleven months and then the Calais burghers had surrendered, starved out. The walls of this city had never been breached. They never would be breached, it was a citadel that was famous for being impossible to take either by land or sea.

I leaned against the wall and looked south to France, and waited.

'I have made an agreement with her and I will not see her again,' Daniel said steadily, his voice low. 'I have paid her a sum of money and when I set up in practice on my own I will pay her another. Then I will never see her or her child again.'

I nodded but I said nothing.

'She has released me from any obligation to her, and the master of her house and his wife have said they will adopt her child and bring him up as if he were their grandson. She will see no more of me and he will not want for anything. He will grow up without a father. He will not even remember me.'

He waited for me to respond. Still I said nothing.

'She is young and . . .' He hesitated, searching for a word which would not offend me. 'Personable. She is almost certain to marry another man and then she will forget me as completely as I have forgotten her.' He paused. 'So there is no reason why you and I should live apart,' he said persuasively. 'I have no pre-contract, I have no obligation, I am yours and yours alone.'

I turned to him. 'No,' I said. 'I set you free, Daniel. I do not want a husband, I do not want any man. I will not return to you, whatever agreement you and she have made. That part of my life is over.'

'You are my wedded wife,' he said. 'Married by the laws of the land and in the sight of God.'

'Oh! God!' I said dismissively. 'Not our God, so what does that mean to us?'

'Your father himself said the Jewish prayers.'

'Daniel!' I exclaimed. 'He could not remember them all, not even he and your mother racking their brains together could remember all the words of the blessings. We had no rabbi, we had no synagogue, we did not even have two witnesses. All that bound us was such faith that we could bring to it – there was nothing else. I came to it with my faith and trust in you, and you came to it with a lie in your mouth, a woman hidden behind you and your child in her cradle. Whatever God we invoked – it was meaningless.'

He was ashen. 'You speak like an alchemist,' he said. 'We swore binding oaths.'

'You were not free to make them,' I snapped.

'You are following reason to its end and coming to madness,' he said desperately. 'Whatever the rights or wrongs of the wedding, I am asking you to make a marriage now. I am asking you to forgive me and love me, like a woman, not anatomise me like a scholar. Love me from your heart, not from your head.'

'I am sorry,' I said. 'I will not. My head and my heart are indivisible. I will not cut myself up into parts so that my heart can have its way and my head think it wrong. Whatever this decision costs me I take it entire, as a whole woman. I shall pay the price but I will not return to you and to that house.'

'If it is my mother and my sisters . . .' he started.

I raised my hand. 'Peace, Daniel,' I said gently. 'They are what they are and I don't like them; but if you had kept faith with me I would have found some way to live with them. Without our love, it all means nothing.'

'So what will you do?' he asked, and I could hear the despair in his voice.

'I shall stay here with my father, and when the time serves, we shall return to England.'

'You mean when the false princess comes to the throne and the traitor that you love comes out of the Tower,' he accused me.

I turned my head away from him. 'Whatever happens, it will be no concern of yours what I do,' I said quietly. 'Now, I want to go.'

Daniel put his hand on my arm, I could feel the heat of his palm through the thin linen of my sleeve. He was hot with torment. 'Hannah, I love you,' he said. 'It is death to me, if you will not see me.'

I turned back to him and met his gaze straight, like a lad, not like a woman meeting her husband's eyes. 'Daniel, you have no-one but yourself to blame,' I said flatly. 'I am not a woman to be played with. You were false to me and I have cut my love for you out of my heart and out of my mind and nothing, *nothing* will restore it. You are a stranger to me now and for always. It is over. Go your way and I will go mine. It is finished.'

He gave a hoarse raw-throated sob and turned on his heel and plunged away. I went as quietly and as quickly as I could back to the shop, I went up the stairs to the little empty bedroom in which I had celebrated being free, and I put myself face down on the little bed, pulled a pillow over my head and cried silently for the love I had lost.

That was not the last I saw of him, but we did not speak intimately again. Most Sundays at church I would glimpse him, meticulously opening his missal and saying his prayers, observant to every movement of the Mass, never taking his eyes from the Host and the priest, as all of us always did. In their pew his mother and his sisters stole little glances at me, and once I saw them with a pretty vapid-looking fair-haired young woman with a baby on her hip and I guessed that she was the mother of Daniel's child and that Daniel's mother had taken it upon herself to bring her grandson to church.

I turned my head away from their curious glances but I felt an odd swimmy feeling that I had not known for years. I leaned forward and gripped the smooth time-worn wood of the pew and waited for the sensation to pass but it grew stronger. The Sight was coming to me.

I would have given anything for it to pass me by. The last thing I wanted was to make a spectacle of myself in church, especially when the woman was there with her child; but the waves of darkness seemed to wash down from the rood screen, from the priest behind it, from the candles in the stone arched windows, wash down and engulf me so that I could not even see my knuckles whiten as I gripped the pew. Then I could only see the skirt of my gown as I dropped to my knees and then I could see nothing but darkness.

I could hear the sound of a battle and someone screaming: 'Not my baby! Take him! Take him!' and I felt myself say: 'I can't take him.' And the insistent voice cried again: 'Take him! Take him!' and at that moment there was a dreadful crash like a forest falling, and a rush of horses and men and danger, and I wanted to run but there was nowhere to run, and I cried out with fear.

'You're all right now,' came a voice and it was Daniel's beloved voice and I was in his arms, and the sun was shining warmly on my face, and there was no darkness, nor terror, nor that terrible crash of falling wood and the clatter of hooves on stones.

'I fainted,' I said. 'Did I say anything?'

'Only "I can't take him",' he said. 'Was it the Sight, Hannah?'

I nodded. I should have sat up and pulled away from him but I rested against his shoulder and felt the seductive sense of safety that he always gave me.

'A warning?' he asked.

'Something awful,' I said. 'My God, an awful vision. But I don't know what. That's what it's like, I see enough to feel terror but not enough to know.'

'I had thought you would lose the Sight,' he said quietly.

'It seems not. It's not a vision I would want.'

'Hush then,' he soothed. He turned his face to one side and said, 'I will take her home. You can leave us. She needs nothing.'

At once I realised that behind him was a small circle of people who had gathered for curiosity to see the woman who had cried out and fainted in church.

'She's a seer,' someone said. 'She was the queen's holy fool.'

'She didn't foresee much then . . .' someone said with a snicker and made a joke about me coming from England to marry a man and then leave him within three months.

I saw Daniel flush with anger and I struggled to sit up. At once his arm tightened around me. 'Be still,' he said. 'I am going to help you home and then I am going to bleed you. You are hot and feverish.'

'I am not,' I contradicted him at once. 'And it is nothing.'

My father appeared beside Daniel. 'Could you walk if we both helped you?' he asked. 'Or shall I fetch a litter?'

'I can walk,' I said. 'I am not ill.'

The two of them helped me to my feet and we went down the narrow path to the lane that led to the city gate and our shop. At the corner I saw a knot of women waiting, Daniel's mother, his three sisters, and the woman with a baby on her hip. She was staring at me just as I stared at her, each of us measuring the other, examining, judging, comparing. She was a broad-hipped pink milk-fed young woman, ripe as a peach, with pink smiling lips and fair hair, a broad face which denied deception, blue slightly protruding eyes. She gave me a smile, a shy smile, half-apologetic, half-hopeful. The baby she held against her was a true Jewish boy, dark-haired, dark-eyed, solemn-faced, with sweet olive skin. I would have known him for Daniel's child the moment I had seen him, even if Mrs Carpenter had not betrayed the secret.

As I looked at her I saw a shadow behind her, a shadow that was gone as quickly as I turned my gaze to it. I had seen something like a horseman, riding behind her, bending low towards her. I blinked, there was nothing there but this young woman, her baby held close, and Daniel's womenfolk looking at me, looking at them.

'Come on, Father,' I said, very weary. 'Get me home.'

Winter 1556–57

Of course within days the word was out that I had fainted in church because I was pregnant, and for the next weeks I had women coming into the printing shop and asking for volumes which were stored on high shelves so that I would have to come out from behind the counter and stretch up, so that they could see my belly.

By winter they had to acknowledge that they were wrong and that the bookseller's daughter, the odd changeling woman, had not yet received her comeuppance. By Christmas it was all but forgotten and by the long cold spring I was almost accepted as yet another eccentric in this town of runaways, vagabonds, ex-pirates, camp followers, and chancers.

Besides, there were greater interests for the most inveterate gossips that year. King Philip's long desire to drag his wife's country into war against France had finally triumphed over her better sense, and England and France were declared enemies. Even sheltered as we were behind the stout walls of Calais it was terrifying to think that the French army could ride up to the bastions which encircled the Pale. The opinion of our customers was divided between those who thought the queen a fool ruled by her husband and mad to take on the might of France, and those who thought that this was a great chance for England and Spain to defeat the French as they had done once before, and this time to divide the spoils.

Spring 1557

The spring storms kept ships in port and made news from England late and unreliable. I was not the only person who waited every day on the quayside and called to incoming ships: 'What's the news? What's the news in England?' The spring gales threw rain and salt water against the tiles and windows of the house and chilled my father to his very bones. Some days he was too cold and weary to get out of bed at all and I would kindle a little fire in the grate in his bedroom and sit by his bed and read to him from the precious scraps of our Bible. On our own, and quietly, lit only by candlelight, I would read to him in the rolling sonorous language of our race. I read to him in Hebrew and he lay back on his pillows and smiled to hear the old words that promised the land to the People, and safety at last. I hid from him as best as I could the news that the country we had chosen for our refuge was now at war with one of the strongest kingdoms in Christendom, and when he asked I emphasised that at least we were inside the town walls and that whatever might happen elsewhere to the English in France, or to the Spanish just down the road at Gravelines, at least we knew that Calais would never fall.

In March, as the town went mad for King Philip who travelled through the port on his way to Gravesend, I paid little attention to the rumours of his plans for war and his intentions towards the Princess Elizabeth. I was growing very anxious for my father, who did not seem to be getting any stronger. After two weeks of worry, I swallowed my pride and sent for the newly licensed Dr Daniel Carpenter, who had set up an independent practice at a little shop on the far side of the quay. He came the moment that the street urchin delivered my message, and he came very quietly and gently as if he did not want to disturb me.

'How long has he been ill?' he asked me, shaking the sea fret off his thick dark cape.

'He is not really ill. He seems tired more than anything else,' I said, taking the cape from him and spreading it before the little fire to dry. 'He doesn't eat much, he will take soup and dried fruit but nothing else. He sleeps by day and night.'

'His urine?' Daniel asked.

I fetched the flask that I had kept for his diagnosis and he took it to the window and looked at the colour in the daylight.

'Is he upstairs?'

'In the back bedroom,' I said and followed on my lost husband's heels up the stairs.

I waited outside while Daniel took my father's pulses and laid his cool hands on my father's forehead, and asked him gently how he did. I heard their low-voiced exchange, the rumble of male communion, saying everything by speaking words which said nothing, a code which women can never understand.

Then Daniel came out, his face grave and tender. He ushered me downstairs and did not speak until we were in the shop once more, with the wooden door to the staircase closed behind us.

'Hannah, I could cup him, and physic him, and torment him a dozen different ways but I don't think I, or any other doctor, could cure him.'

'Cure him?' I repeated stupidly. 'He's just tired.'

'He is dying,' my husband said gently.

For a moment I could not take it in. 'But Daniel, that's not possible! There's nothing wrong with him!'

'He has a growth in his belly which is pressing against his lungs and his heart,' Daniel said quietly. 'He can feel it himself, he knows it.'

'He is just tired,' I protested.

'And if he feels any worse than tired, if he feels pain, then we will give him physic to take the pain away,' Daniel assured me. 'Thank God he feels nothing but tired now.'

I went to the shop door and opened it, as if I wanted a customer.

What I wanted was to run away from these awful words, to run from this grief which was unfolding steadily before me. The rain, dripping from the eaves of all the houses down the streets, was running through the cobbles to the gutter in little rivulets of mud. 'I thought he was just tired,' I said again, stupidly.

'I know,' Daniel said.

I closed the door and came back into the shop. 'How long d'you think?'

I thought he would say months, perhaps a year.

'Days,' he said quietly. 'Perhaps weeks. But no more, I don't think.'

'Days?' I said uncomprehendingly. 'How can it be days?'

He shook his head, his eyes compassionate. 'I am sorry, Hannah. It will not be long.'

'Should I ask someone else to look at him?' I demanded. 'Perhaps your tutor?'

He took no offence. 'If you wish. But anyone would say the same thing. You can feel the lump in his belly, Hannah, this is no mystery. It is pressing against his belly, his heart and his lungs. It is squeezing the life out of him.'

I threw up my hands. 'Stop,' I said unhappily. 'Stop.'

He checked at once. 'I am sorry,' he said. 'But he is in no pain. And he is not afraid. He is prepared for his death. He knows it is coming. He is only anxious about you.'

'Me!' I exclaimed.

'Yes,' he said steadily. 'You should assure him that you are provided for, that you are safe.'

I hesitated.

'I myself have sworn to him that if you are in any difficulty or in any danger that I will care for you before any other. I will protect you as my wife for as long as you live.'

I held on to the handle of the door so that I did not pitch myself into his arms and wail like a bereaved child. 'That was kind of you,' I managed to say. 'I don't need your protection, but it was kind of you to reassure him.'

'You have my protection whether you need it or not,' Daniel said. 'I am your husband, and I do not forget it.'

He took up his cape from the stool before the fire and swung it around his shoulders. 'I shall come tomorrow, and every day at noon,' he said. 'And I shall find a good woman to sit with him so that you can rest.'

'I will care for him,' I fired up. 'I don't need any help.'

He paused in the doorway. 'You do need help,' he said gently. 'This is not something you can do well on your own. And you shall have help. I shall help you, whether you like it or not. And you will be glad of it when this is all over, even if you resist it now. I shall be kind to you, Hannah, whether you want me or not.'

I nodded; I could not trust myself to speak. Then he went out of the door into the rain and I went upstairs to my father and took up the Bible in Hebrew and read to him some more.

As Daniel had predicted, my father slipped away very quickly. True to his word, Daniel brought a night nurse so that my father was never alone, never without a candle burning in his room and the quiet murmur of the words he loved to hear. The woman, Marie, was a stocky French peasant girl from devout parents and she could recite all the psalms, one after another. At night my father would sleep, lulled by the rolling cadences of the Ile de France. In the day I found a lad to mind the shop while I sat with him and read to him in Hebrew. Only in April did I find a new volume which had a small surviving snippet of the prayers for the dead. I saw his smile of acknowledgement. He raised his hand, I fell silent.

'Yes, it is time,' was all he said. His voice was a thread. 'You will be well, my child?'

I put the book on the seat of my chair and knelt at his bedside. Effortfully he put his hand on my head for a blessing. 'Don't worry about me,' I whispered. 'I will be all right. I have the shop and the press, I can earn a living, and Daniel will always look after me.'

He nodded. Already he was drifting away, too far to give advice, too far to remonstrate. 'I bless you, *querida*,' he said gently.

'Father!' My eyes were filled with tears. I dropped my head to his bed.

'Bless you,' he said again and lay quietly.

I levered myself back to my chair and blinked my eyes. Through the blur of tears I could hardly see the words. Then I started to read. 'Magnified and sanctified be the name of God throughout the world which He has created according to His will. May He establish His kingdom during the days of your life and during the life of all of the house of Israel, speedily, yea soon; and say ye, Amen.'

In the night when the nurse knocked on my door I was dressed, seated on my bed, and waiting for her to call me. I went to his bedside and saw his face, smiling, illuminated and without fear. I knew he was thinking of my mother and if there was any truth in his faith, or even in the faith of the Christians, then he would be greeting her soon in heaven. I said quietly to the nurse, 'You can go and fetch the doctor Daniel Carpenter,' and heard her patter down the stairs.

I sat beside his bed and took his hand in mine and felt the slow pulse flutter like the heart of a small bird under my fingers. Downstairs, the door quietly opened and shut and I heard two pairs of footsteps come in.

Daniel's mother stood in the bedroom doorway. 'I don't intrude,' she said quietly. 'But you won't know how things should be done.'

'I don't,' I said. 'I have read the prayers.'

'That's right,' she said. 'You've done it right, and I can do the rest. You can watch, and learn, so you know how it is done. So that you can do it for me, or for another, when my time comes.'

Quietly she approached the bed. 'How now, old friend?' she said. 'I have come to bid you farewell.'

My father said nothing but he smiled at her. Gently she slid her arm under his shoulders and raised him up, turned him on his side so that he could face the wall, his back to the room. Then she sat by his side and recited all the prayers for the dying that she could remember.

'Goodbye, Father,' I said softly. 'Goodbye, Father. Goodbye.'

Daniel cared for me as he had promised he would. As son-in-law, all my father's goods became his by right; but he signed them over to me in the same day. He came to the house and helped me to clear the few possessions that my father had kept through our long travels, and he asked Marie to stay on for the next few months. She could sleep downstairs in the kitchen, and would keep me company, and keep me safe at nights. Mrs Carpenter frowned her disapproval at my unfeminine independence; but she managed to hold her peace.

She made the preparations for the Requiem Mass and then the secret Jewish ceremony, done the same day, behind our closed door. When I thanked her she waved me away. 'These are the ways of our People,' she said. 'We have to remember them. We have to perform them. If we forget them, we forget ourselves. Your father was a great scholar among our People, he had books that had been all but forgotten and he had the courage to keep them safe. If it were not for men like him then we would not know the prayers that I said at his bedside. And now you know how it is done, and you can teach your children, and the way of our People can be handed down.'

'It must be forgotten,' I said. 'In time.'

'No, why?' she said. 'We remembered Zion by the rivers of Babylon, we remember Zion in the gates of Calais. Why should we ever forget?'

Daniel did not ask me if I would forgive him and if we could start again as man and wife. He did not ask me if I was longing for a touch, for a kiss, longing to feel alive like a young woman in springtime and not always like a girl fighting against the world. He did not ask me if I felt, since my father was dead, that I was terribly alone in the world, and that I would always be Hannah alone, neither of the People, nor a wife, and now, not even a daughter. He did not ask me these things, I did not volunteer them, and so we parted kindly on my doorstep, with a sense of sadness and regret, and I imagine he went home and called on the way at the house of the plump fair-haired mother of his son, and I went into my house and closed my door and sat in darkness for a long time.

The cold months were always hard for me, my Spanish blood was still too thin for the damp days of a northern coastal winter, and Calais was little better than London had been under driving rain and grey skies. Without my father I felt as if some of the chill of the sea and the skies had crept into the very blood of my veins, and into my eyes, since I wept unaccountably for no reason. I gave up dining properly, but ate like a printer's lad with a hacked-off slice of bread in one hand and a cup of milk in the other. I did not observe the dietary restrictions as my father liked us to do, I did not light the candle for the Sabbath. I worked on the Sabbath, and I printed secular books and jest books and texts of plays and poems as if learning did not matter any more. I let my faith drift away with my hopes of happiness.

I could not sleep well at night but during the day I could hardly set type for yawning. Trade in the shop was slow; when the times were so uncertain no-one cared for any books except prayer books. Many times I went down to the harbour and greeted travellers coming from London and asked them for news, thinking that perhaps I should go back to England and see if the queen would forgive me and welcome me back to her service.

The news they brought from England was as dark as the afternoon skies. King Philip was visiting his wife in London but he had brought her little joy, and everyone said he had only gone home to see what he could have from her. There was some vile gossip that he had taken his mistress with him and they danced every day under the queen's tortured gaze. She would have had to sit on her throne and see him laughing and dancing with another woman, and then endure him raging against her council who were dragging their heels in the war against France.

I wanted to go to her. I thought that she must feel desperately friendless in a court that had become all Spanish and wickedly joyful once more, headed by a new mistress of the king's and laughing at the English lack of sophistication. But the other news from England was that the burning of heretics was continuing without mercy, and I knew there was no safety for me in England – nor anywhere, come to that.

I resolved to stay in Calais, despite the cold, despite my loneliness, stay and wait, and hope that some day soon I should feel more able to decide, that some day soon I should recover my optimism, that some day, one day, I should find once more my sense of joy.

Summer 1557

By early summer the streets were filled with the sound of recruiting officers marching along, drumming and whistling for lads to volunteer for the English army to fight the French. The harbour was a continual bustle of ships coming and going, unloading weapons and gunpowder and horses. In the fields outside the city a little camp had sprung up and soldiers were marched here and there, and bawled at, and marched back again. All I knew was that the extra traffic through the city gate did not bring much extra trade. The officers and men of this ramshackle hastily recruited army were not great scholars, and I was afraid of their bright acquisitive gaze. The town became unruly with the hundreds of extra men coming through and I took to wearing a pair of dark breeches, tucked my hair up under my cap, and donned a thick jerkin, despite the summer heat. I carried a dagger in my boot and I would have used it if anyone had come against me or broken into the shop. I kept Marie, my father's nurse, as my lodger and she and I bolted the door at six o'clock every night and did not open it until the morning, blowing out our candles if we heard brawling in the street.

The harbour was almost blocked by incoming ships; as soon as the men marched from the fields outside the town towards the outlying forts, the camp immediately filled with more soldiers. The day the cavalry troops clattered through the town I thought that our chimney pot would be shaken from the roof by the noise. Other women of my age lined the streets, cheering and waving as the men went by, throwing flowers and eyeing the officers; but I kept my head down. I had seen enough death; my heart did not leap to the whistle of the pipes and the urgent rattle of the drums. I saw Daniel's sisters walking arm-in-arm on the ramparts in their best dresses, managing to look modestly down and all around them at the same time, desperate for some attention from any passing English officer. I could not imagine feeling desire. I could not imagine the excitement that seemed to have gripped everyone but me. All I felt was worry about my stock if the men ran out of control, and gratitude that I had chosen by luck a house which was one yard inside the city gate instead of one yard outside.

By midsummer the English army, marshalled, half-trained and wholly wild for a fight, moved out of Calais, led by King Philip himself. They launched an attack on St Quentin, and in August stormed the town and won it from the French. It was a resounding victory against a hated enemy. The citizens of Calais, ambitious to reclaim the whole of the lost English lands in France, went mad with joy at this first sign, and every returning soldier was laden with flowers and had a horn of wine pressed into his willing hand and was blessed as the saviour of his nation.

I saw Daniel at church on Sunday when the priest preached the victory of God's chosen people over the treacherous French, and then, to my amazement, he prayed for the safe delivery of the queen of a son and heir to the throne. For me, it was better news even than the taking of St Quentin, and for the first time in long months I felt my heart lift. When I thought of her carrying a child in her womb again I felt my down-turned face lift up and smile. I knew how glad she must be, how this must bring her back to the joy she had felt in early marriage, how she must think now that God had forgiven the English and she might become a gentle queen and a good mother.

When Daniel came up to me as we all left church he saw the happiness on my face and smiled. 'You did not know of the queen's condition?'

'How could I know?' I said. 'I see nobody. I hear only the most general of gossip.'

'There is news of your old lord too,' he said levelly. 'Have you heard?'

'Robert Dudley?' I could feel myself sway against the shock of his name. 'What news?'

Daniel put a hand under my elbow to steady me. 'Good news,' he said quietly though I could see it brought little joy for him. 'Good news, Hannah, be calm.'

'Is he released?'

'He and half a dozen other men accused of treason were released some time ago and fought with the king.' The twist of Daniel's mouth indicated that he thought Lord Robert would serve his own cause first. 'Your lord raised his own company of horse a month ago ...'

'He came through the town? And I didn't know?'

'He fought at St Quentin and was mentioned in dispatches for bravery,' Daniel said shortly.

I felt myself glow with pleasure. 'Oh! How wonderful!'

'Yes,' Daniel said without enthusiasm. 'You won't try to find him, Hannah? The countryside is unsafe.'

'He'll go home through Calais, won't he? When the French sue for peace?'

'I should think so.'

'I will try to see him then. Perhaps he'll help me return to England.'

Daniel went pale, his face even graver than before. 'You cannot risk going back while the rules against heresy are so strong,' he said quietly. 'They would be bound to examine you.'

'If I were under my lord's protection I would be safe,' I said with simple confidence.

It cost him a good deal to acknowledge Lord Robert's power. 'I suppose so. But please, talk to me before you take a decision. His credit may not be so very good, you know, it is only one act of bravery in a long life of treason.'

I let the criticism go.

'Can I walk you to your door?' He offered me his arm and I took it and fell into step beside him. For the first time in months I felt a little of my own darkness lift and dissolve. The queen was with child, Lord Robert was free and honoured for his bravery, England and Spain in alliance had defeated the French army. Surely, things would start coming right for me too.

'Mother tells me that she saw you in the market place in breeches,' Daniel remarked.

'Yes,' I said carelessly. 'When there are so many soldiers and rough men and women on the streets I feel safer like that.'

'Would you come back to my house?' Daniel asked. 'I would like to keep you safe. You could keep the shop on.'

'It's making no money,' I conceded honestly. 'I don't stay away from you for the sake of the shop. I can't come back to you, Daniel. I have made up my mind and I will not change it.'

We had reached my door. 'But if you were in trouble or danger you would send for me,' he pressed me.

'Yes.'

'And you wouldn't leave for England, or meet with Lord Robert, without telling me?'

I shrugged. 'I have no plans, except I should like to see the queen again. She must be so happy, I should like to see her now, expecting her child. I should so like to see her in her joy.'

'Perhaps when the peace treaty is signed,' he suggested. 'I could take you to London for a visit and bring you back, if you would like that.'

I looked at him attentively. 'Daniel, that would be kind indeed.'

'I would do anything to please you, anything that would make you happy,' he said gently.

I opened my door. 'Thank you,' I said quietly and slipped away from him before I should make the mistake of stepping forward into his arms.

Winter 1557–58

There were rumours that the defeated French army had turned around and was regrouping on the borders of the English Pale and every stranger who came into Calais for the Christmas market was regarded as a spy. The French must come against Calais in revenge for St Quentin, but the French must know, as we all knew, that the town could not be taken. Everyone was afraid that the ramparts outside the town would be mined, that even now the skilled French miners were burrowing like worms through the very fabric of English earth. Everyone was afraid that the guards would be suborned, that the fort would fall through treachery. But over all of this was a sort of blithe confidence that the French could not succeed. Philip of Spain was a brilliant commander, he had the flower of the English army in the field, what could the French do with an army like ours harassing their own borders, and an impregnable castle like ours behind them?

Then the rumours of a French advance became more detailed. A woman coming into my shop warned Marie that we should hide our books and bury our treasure.

'Why?' I demanded of Marie.

She was white-faced. 'I am English,' she said to me. 'My grandmother was pure English.'

'I don't doubt your loyalty,' I said, incredulous that someone should be trying to prove their provenance to me, a mongrel by birth, education, religion and choice.

'The French are coming,' she said. 'That woman is from my village and she was warned by her friend. She has come to hide in Calais.'

She was the first of many. A steady flow of people from the countryside outside the gates in the English Pale decided that their best safety lay inside the untouchable town.

The Company of Merchants who all but ran the town organised a great dormitory in Staple Hall, bought in food ahead of the French advance, warned all the fit young men and women of Calais that they must prepare for a siege. The French were coming, but the English and Spanish army would be hard behind them. We need fear nothing, but we should prepare.

Then in the night, without warning, Fort Nieulay fell. It was one of the eight forts that guarded Calais, and as such was only a small loss. But Nieulay was the fort on the River Hames which controlled the sea gates, which were supposed to flood the canals around the town so that no army could cross. With Nieulay in French hands we had nothing to defend us but the other forts and the great walls. We had lost the first line of defence.

The very next day we heard the roar of cannon and then a rumour swept through the town. Fort Risban, the fort which guarded the inner harbour of Calais, had fallen too, even though it was newly built and newly fortified. Now the harbour itself lay open to French shipping, and the brave English boats which bobbed at anchor in the port could be taken at any moment.

'What shall we do?' Marie asked me.

'It's only two forts,' I said stoutly, trying to hide my fear. 'The English army will know we are under siege and come to rescue us. You'll see, within three days they will be here.'

But it was the French army which drew up in lines before the walls of Calais and it was the French arquebusiers who flung a storm of arrows which arched over the top of the walls and killed at random people running in the streets, desperate to get inside their houses.

'The English will come,' I said. 'Lord Robert will come and attack the French from the rear.'

We bolted the shutters on the shop and shrank inside to the back room, in a terror that the great gates, so close to our little shop, would be a focus for attack. The French brought up siege engines. Even hidden as we were in the back room of the shop I could hear the pounding of the great ram against the barred gates. Our men on the ramparts above were firing down, desperately trying to pick off the men who were pounding the defences, and I heard a roar and a hiss as a great vat of boiling tar was tipped over the walls and showered on the attackers below, I heard their screams as they were scalded and burned, their upturned faces getting the brunt of the pain. Marie and I, desperate with fear, crouched behind the shop door as if the thin planks of wood would shield us. I did not know what to do, or where to go for safety. For a moment I thought of running through the streets to Daniel's house but I was too afraid to unbolt the front door, and besides the streets were in turmoil with cannon shot overarching the city walls and falling within the streets, burning arrows raining down on the straw roofs and our reinforcements running up through the narrow streets to the walls.

Then the clatter of hundreds of horses' hooves was in the street outside our door and I realised that the English army, garrisoned inside the town, was gathering for a counter attack. They must think that if they could dislodge the French from the gates of the city, that the surrounding countryside could be retaken and the pressure relieved from the town defences.

We could hear the horses go by and then the silence while they assembled at the gate. I realised that for them to get out, the gate would have to be thrown open, and for that time my little shop would be right in the centre of the battle.

It was enough. I whispered to Marie in French, 'We have to get out of here. I am going to Daniel, d'you want to come with me?'

'I'll go to my cousins, they live near the harbour.'

I crept to the door and opened it a crack. The sight as I peered through was terrifying. The street outside was absolute chaos, with soldiers running up the stone steps to the ramparts laden with weapons, wounded men being helped down. Another great vat of tar was being heated over an open fire only yards from the thatch of a neighbouring house. And from the other side of the gate came the dreadful clamour of an army beating against the door, scaling the walls, firing upwards, pulling cannon into place and firing shot, determined to breach the walls and get into the town.

I threw open the door and almost at once heard a most dreadful cry from the walls immediately above the shop as a hail of arrows found an unprotected band of men. Marie and I fled into the street. Behind us, and then all around us, came a dreadful crash. The French siege engine had catapulted a great load of stone and rubble over the wall. It rained down on our street like a falling mountain. Tiled roofs shed their load like a pack of cards spilling to the floor, stones plunged through thatch, knocked chimney pots askew, and they rolled down the steeply canted roofs and plunged to the cobblestones to smash around us with a sound like gunfire. It was as if the very skies were raining rocks and fires, as if we would be engulfed in terror.

'I'm off!' Marie shouted to me, plunging away down a lane which led towards the fish quay.

I could not even shout a blessing, the smell of the smoke from burning buildings caught in the back of my throat like the stab of a knife and choked me into silence. The smell of smoke – the very scent of my nightmares – filled the air, filled my nostrils, my lungs, even my eyes, so that I could not breathe and my eyes were filled with tears so that I could not see.

From the ramparts above me I heard a high shriek of terror and I looked up to see a man on fire, the burning arrow still caught in his clothing, as he dived to the floor and rolled, trying to extinguish the flames, screaming like a heretic as his body burned.

I ducked from the doorway and started to run, anywhere to get away from the smell of a man burning. I wanted to find Daniel. He seemed like the only safe haven in a world turned into a nightmare. I knew I would have to fight my way through the chaotic streets, filled with frightened people rushing to the harbour, with soldiers pounding in the opposite direction to the ramparts, and somehow get through the cavalry, their horses wheeling and pushing in the narrow streets, waiting to charge out of the gates and push back the French army.

I pressed myself back against the walls of the houses as a company of horse mustered in the street. The big haunches of the animals pushed one against the other and I shrank back into the doorways, fearing that they would knock me over and I would be crushed.

I waited for my chance to get by, watching other people darting among the big hooves of the horses, seeing Daniel's street at the other side of the square, hearing the men shout and the horses neigh and the bugler blasting out the call to arms, and I thought, not of my mother – who had faced death like a saint, but of the queen – who had faced death like a fighter. The queen – who had got her own horse and ridden out in the darkness to stand up for her own. And thinking of her, I found the courage to plunge out of the doorway and dart around the dangerous heels of the big horses and duck into a refuge further down the street when a great charge of horsemen came thundering by. Then I looked up and saw the standard they were carrying before them, smirched with mud and bloodied by an earlier battle, and I saw the bear and staff embroidered on the bright ground and I called out: 'Robert Dudley!'

A man looked over at me. 'At the head, where he always is.'

I pushed my way back, afraid of nothing now, turning horses' heads to one side, sliding between their big flanks. 'Let me by, let me by, sir. I am going to Robert Dudley.'

It became like a dream. The great horses with the men mounted as high as centaurs above me. Their great heavy armour shining in the sunshine, clashing when they brushed one against another, sounding like cymbals when they hammered their halberds on their shields, hearing their great raw bellow above the clatter of the horses on the cobbles, louder than a storm.

I found myself at the head of the square and there was his standard bearer, and beside him . . .

'My lord!' I yelled.

Slowly, the helmeted head turned towards me, the visor down so he could not see me. I pulled off the cap from my head, and my hair tumbled down and I lifted my face up towards the dark knight, high on his great horse.

'My lord! It's me! Hannah the Fool.'

His gauntleted hand lifted the false face of metal, but the shadow of the helmet left his face in darkness and still I could not see him. The horse shifted, held in powerful control by his other hand. His head was turned towards me, I could feel his eyes on me, sharp under the sharp points of the helmet.

'Mistress Boy?'

It was his voice, coming from the mouth of this great man-god, this great man of metal. But it was his voice, as intimate and warm and familiar as if he had come from dancing at King Edward's summer feast.

The horse sidled, I stepped back on a doorstep, it raised me up four inches, nothing more. 'My lord, it is me!'

'Mistress Boy, what the devil are you doing here?'

'I live here,' I said, half-laughing and half-crying at seeing him again. 'What of you?'

'Released, fighting, winning – perhaps losing at the moment. Are you safe here?'

'I don't think so,' I said honestly. 'Can we hold the town?'

He pulled the gauntlet from his right hand, twisted a ring from his finger, threw it towards me, careless if I caught it or not. 'Take this to the *Windflight*,' he said. 'My ship. I will see you aboard if we need to sail. Go now, get aboard. We are to make a charge.'

'Fort Risban is lost!' I shouted above the noise. 'You can't sail away, they will turn the guns on the harbour.'

Robert Dudley laughed aloud as if death itself were a joke. 'Mistress Boy, I don't expect to survive this charge! But you might be lucky and slip away. Go now.'

'My lord . . .'

'It's an order!' he shouted at me. 'Go!'

I gasped, pushing the ring on my finger. It had been on his little finger, it fitted my third, just above my wedding ring: Dudley's ring on my finger.

'My lord!' I cried out again. 'Come back safe.'

The bugle played so loud that no-one could be heard. They were about to charge. He dropped his visor over his face, pulled his gauntlet back on his hand, lifted his lance from its place, tipped it to his helmet in a salute to me, and wheeled his horse around to face his company.

'A Dudley!' he shouted. 'For God and the queen!'

'For God and the queen!' they roared back at him. 'For God and the queen! Dudley! Dudley!'

They moved towards the city walls, out of the square, and like a camp follower, disobedient to his order, I moved after them. To my left were the lanes running down to the harbour but I was drawn by the jingle of the bits and the deafening clatter of the metalled hooves on the cobbles. The roar of the siege grew louder as they got near to the gate, and at the sound of French rage I hesitated, shrank back, looked behind for the way to the harbour.

Then I saw her. Daniel's woman, bedraggled with her pretty dress half-dragged from her shoulder, exposing her breast. Her child was on her hip, clinging to her, his dark eyes wide, her hair was tumbling down, her eye blacked, her face anguished, running like a hunted deer, skipping and stumbling on the cobbles of the street.

She recognised me at once. She had watched me, as I had watched her, every Sunday at Mass. Both of us confined to the poor pews at the back of church. Both of us trapped into shame by the other's determination.

'Hannah,' she called out to me. 'Hannah!'

'What is it?' I shouted irritably. 'What d'you want with me?'

She showed me her child. 'Take him!'

At once I remembered the intensity of my vision in church, the first time I had seen her. Then as now there was a screaming and a thundering noise. Then, in my nightmare, she had called out 'Take him!' As she cried out the sky suddenly grew dark with a hail of missiles and I ducked into a doorway but on the other side of the street she came on, dodging through the falling rocks. 'Hannah! Hannah! I need your help.'

'Go home,' I shouted unhelpfully. 'Go to a cellar or somewhere.'

The last of the horses was moving out of the square, we heard the groan of the counterweights as they pulled back the great gates for Lord Robert and his cavalry to charge out, and the great roar of rage as they thundered out to meet the French army.

'They are leaving us?' she screamed in horror. 'Running away?'

'No, going out to fight. Find yourself a refuge . . .' I yelled impatiently.

'God save us, they need not go out to fight them, they are in already! They must turn to fight! The French are here! They are in the town! We are lost!' Daniel's woman shouted. 'It was them . . .'

Her words suddenly penetrated my mind, and I whirled around to look at her again. At once I realised the significance of her black eye and her torn gown. The French were in the city, and they had raped her.

'They came in through the harbour! Ten minutes ago!' she screamed at me, and as she shouted the words I saw coming down the street behind her a tide of mounted horsemen, the French cavalry, in the streets and behind my lord, cutting off him and his men from the harbour, their horses foaming at the mouth, their lances down for a charge, their visors fixed so that they seemed to have faces of iron, their spurs tearing blood from their horses' sides, the scream of hooves on cobbles, the absolute horror of a cavalry charge in an enclosed space. The first rank was on us in a moment, a lance plunging down towards me and without thinking I snatched the dagger from my boot and with the short blade I parried the thrust. The shock of the blow jarred my blade from my hand, but saved my life as it threw me back against the door of the house behind me. I felt it yield and I fell back into the darkness of an unknown house as I heard Daniel's woman scream: 'Save my baby! Take him! Take him!'

Even as she ran towards me with him held out before her, even as she thrust him into my hands, and he came all warm and soft and heavy, I heard myself say: 'I can't take him.'

I saw the lance run her through, spearing her spine, as she cried out again: 'Take him! Take him!' and at that moment there was a dreadful crash like a forest falling down all at once and a rush of horses and men and danger, and I stumbled back into the dark interior of the house with the boy held tight against me, and the door swung shut on the street with a bang like a thunderclap.

I turned to thank whoever had saved me but before I could speak there was a roar of flames and a sudden blast of hot smoke, and someone pushed past me and threw open the door again.

The thatched roof of this temporary refuge was alight, burning like a pyre, blazing up like kindling in seconds. Everyone who had been hidden in the house was pushing past me to the street outside, more willing to face the merciless cavalry charge than death by burning; and I, smelling smoke like a frightened rat, dashed out after them, the child gripping to me, tight against my shoulder.

Mercifully, the streets were clear for the moment. The French horsemen had chased after Lord Robert's troop in one mad dangerous dash. But Daniel's woman was where they had left her with two great lance thrusts through her body. She lay in a deep puddle of her own blood, dead.

At the sight I snatched her child closer to me and started to run down the street, away from the gate, down the stone steps to the harbour, my feet thudding out a rhythm of fear. I could not wait to look for Daniel, I could not do anything but take the chance I had been given with Lord Robert's ring. I fled to the harbour like a criminal with the hue and cry at my heels, and I was conscious all around me that everyone else was racing too, some carrying bundles of goods, others clutching their children, desperate to get out of the town before the French turned their horses and came back through again.

The boats were tied by just one rope, all sails furled ready to go at a moment's notice. I looked desperately around for Lord Robert's standard and saw it, at the prime position, at the very end of the pier where it would be easiest to slip away. I ran down the pier, my feet thudding on the wooden boards, and skidded to a halt when a sailor leaped from the ship and stood before the gangplank with a shining cutlass out of its scabbard, pointing at my throat. 'No further, lad,' he said.

'Lord Robert sent me,' I panted.

He shook his head. 'We could all say that. What's happening in town?'

'Lord Robert led his company out in a charge but the French are in the town already, at his back.'

'Can he turn?'

'I don't know. I didn't see it.'

He shouted an order over his shoulder. The men on deck stood by the ropes for the sails and two men vaulted ashore and held the rope ready to cast off.

I held out my hand to show his ring gripped tight on my finger, above my wedding ring.

The sailor looked at it once, and then looked again more carefully. 'His ring,' he said.

'His own. He gave it me himself. He saw me before he led them out. I am his vassal. I was Hannah the Fool before I came here.'

He stepped back and raked me with a quick glare. 'I'd not have recognised you,' he said. 'And this? Your son?'

'Yes.' The lie was said and gone before I had time to think, and then I would not have recalled it. 'Let me aboard. It is my lord's order that I go to England.'

He stepped to one side and nodded me up the narrow gangplank and then positioned himself square at the foot again. 'But you're the last,' he said decidedly. 'Even if they come with a lock of his hair or a love knot.'

We waited for a long hour while others poured down from the town to the quayside. The sailor had to call for other men to come to push the refugees away from Lord Robert's pier, and curse them for cowards, while the winter afternoon grew dark and no-one could tell us whether Lord Robert had broken the French ranks or whether they had entered the town behind his back and cut him down. Then we saw the town lit up from one point to another as the French besieging army broke through the walls and fired one thatched roof and then another.

The sailor on guard at the gangplank snapped out orders and the crew made ready. I sat very quietly on deck, rocking the child against my shoulder, terrified that it would cry and that they would decide that an extra passenger was not worth the extra risk, especially if my lord was not coming.

Then there was a rush of men and horses down to the quayside and a check and a flurry as they flung themselves from the saddle, threw off their armour and hared up to the waiting ships.

'Steady, boys, steady,' came the stentorian shout from the sailor on guard at the gangplank. Six guards stood behind him, shoulder to shoulder with naked blades at the ready, and they checked every man who tried to come aboard for a password, and turned away a good few who raced back down the pier looking for another boat that would take them in. All the time from the town came the explosion of burning gunpowder and the crack of breaking roof tiles and the roar of buildings fired.

'This is not a defeat, it is a rout,' I said in bewilderment in the baby's tiny ear and he turned and yawned with his little rosebud mouth in a perfect 'ooo' as if he were in utter safety and need fear nothing.

Then I saw my lord. I would have recognised him in any crowd. He was walking, broadsword in one hand, helmet in the other, trailing his feet like a defeated man. Behind him came a train of men limping, bleeding, heads bowed. He led them to the ship and stood aside as they went up the gangplank and threw themselves down with a clatter of dented armour on the deck.

'That's enough, sir,' the sailor said to him quietly when we were fully loaded and my lord looked up, like a man newly wakened from sleep, and said: 'But we have to take the rest. I promised they would serve me and I would take them to victory. I can't leave them here now.'

'We'll come back for them,' the sailor said gently. He put one strong arm around my lord's shoulders and drew him firmly up the gangplank.

Lord Robert went slowly, like a sleepwalker, his eyes open but seeing nothing.

'Or they'll get another passage. Cast off!' the sailor shouted to the man at the stern rope. The man flung the rope on shore and the others unfurled the sails. Slowly we moved from the quayside.

'I can't leave them!' Robert, suddenly fully alert, turned to the widening gulf of water between ship and land. 'I can't leave them here.'

The men left ashore let out a pitiful cry. 'A Dudley! A Dudley!'

The sailor caught up Lord Robert in a great bear hug, holding him away from the rail of the ship, preventing him jumping ashore.

'We'll come back for them,' he assured him. 'They'll get safe passage in other ships, and if the worst comes to the worst then the French will ransom them.'

'I can't leave them!' Robert Dudley fought to be free. 'Hey! You! Sailors! Turn for port. Get to the quayside again!'

The wind was catching the sails, they flapped and then as they trimmed the ropes, the sails went taut and started to pull. Behind us in Calais there was a resounding crash as the doors of the citadel yielded and the French army spilled into the very centre of English power in France. Robert turned, anguished, towards the land. 'We should regroup!' he cried. 'We are about to lose Calais if we go now. Think of it! Calais! We have to go back and regroup and fight.'

Still the sailor did not release him, but now his hold was less to restrain the young lord and more to hold him in his grief. 'We'll come back,' he said and rocked him from one foot to another. 'We'll come back for the rest of them and then we'll retake Calais. Never doubt it, sir. Never doubt it.'

Lord Robert went to the stern of the boat, scanning the harbour, seeing the disorderly retreat. We could smell the smoke drifting in a pall across the water from the burning buildings. We could hear people screaming, the French were avenging the insult of the starving burghers of Calais who had surrendered to the English all that long time ago. Lord Robert looked half-minded to throw himself in the water and swim back to take charge of the evacuation of the harbour, but even he, in his rage, could see that it was hopeless. We had lost, the English had lost. It was as simple and as brutal as that and the path of a true man was not to risk his life in some mummer's piece of overacting, but to consider how to win the next battle.

He spent the voyage gazing over the stern to the receding coast of France, long after the formidable profile of the fortress had sunk below the horizon. As the light drained early from the grey January sky he remained standing, looking back, and when the small cold moon came up he was still there, trying to discern some hope on the black horizon. I knew, because I was watching him, as I sat on a coil of rope at the mast, just behind him. His fool, his vassal, wakeful because he was wakeful, anxious because he was anxious, sick with fear for him, for myself, and for whatever the future would bring when we made land in England, an odd trio: a renegade Jew with a Gentile bastard on her hip, and a newly released traitor who had led his men to defeat.

I had not expected his wife Amy at the quayside, but she was there, hand over her eyes, scanning the deck for him. I saw her before she saw him and said, 'Your wife,' in his ear.

He went quickly down the gangplank to her, he did not take her in his arms nor greet her with any sign of affection, but he listened intently to her and then he turned to me.

'I have to go to court, I have to explain to the queen what has happened at Calais,' he said briefly. 'Heads will have to roll for this, perhaps mine.'

'My lord,' I breathed.

'Yes,' he said savagely. 'I don't seem to have done much to advance my family. Hannah, you go with Amy, she is staying with friends in Sussex. I shall send for you there.'

'My lord.' I went a little closer. 'I don't want to live in the country,' was all I could say.

Robert Dudley grinned at me. 'I am sure, sweetheart. I cannot stand it myself. But you must endure it for a month or two. If the queen beheads me for incompetence, then you can make your own way where you please. All right? But if I survive this, I will open my London house and you shall come back to my service. Whatever you wish. How old is the child?'

I hesitated, realising I did not know. 'He's nearly two,' I said.

'You married his father?' he asked.

I looked him in the face. 'Yes.'

'And named him?'

'Daniel, for his father.'

He nodded. 'Amy will take care of you,' he said. 'She likes children.' A snap of his fingers summoned his wife to his side. I saw her shake her head in disagreement, and then lower her eyes when she was over-ruled. When she shot me a look of pure hatred I guessed that he had ordered her to care for me and my son, when she would rather have gone with him to the queen's court.

She had brought his horse. I watched him swing up into his saddle, his men mount up around him. 'London,' he said succinctly and rode his horse north towards whatever fate had for him.

I could not get the measure of Amy Dudley as we rode through the icy countryside of England in those cold days of January 1558. She was a good rider but she seemed to take little pleasure in it, not even on the days when the sun rose like a red disc on the horizon and when a few robins hopped and hid in the leafless hedgerows, and the frost in the morning made the blood sing. I thought it was the absence of her husband that made her so sulky; but her companion, Mrs Oddingsell, did not try to cheer her, they did not even speak of him. They rode in silence, as women accustomed to it.

I had to ride behind them, all the way from Gravesend to Chichester, with the baby strapped on my back and every evening I was aching from my buttocks to my neck with the strain. The extraordinary child had barely made a noise from the moment that his mother had half-flung him at me as the French cavalry rode her down. I had changed his clout with some linen lent to me on board ship, and wrapped him in a sailor's woollen knitted vest and generally lugged him around as if he were a box that someone had insisted I carry against my will. He had not uttered one word of inquiry or protest. Sleeping, he had rested against me, nestled in as if he were my own; awake, he sat on my lap or on the floor at my feet, or stood, one hand holding firmly on to my breeches. He said not one word, not in French, the language of his mother, nor in English. He regarded me with solemn dark eyes and said nothing.

He seemed to have a certainty that he should be with me. He would not fall asleep unless I was watching him, and if I tried to put him down and move away from him he would raise himself up and toddle after me, still silent, still uncomplaining, but with a little face which became more and more crumpled with distress as he got left behind.

I was not a naturally maternal woman, I had not been a girl for dolls, and of course there had been no baby brother or sister for me to nurse. Yet I could not help but admire this small person's tenacity. I had suddenly come into his life as his protector, and he would ensure that he stayed by my side. I started to like the feeling of his fat little hand stretching trustfully up for mine, I started to sleep well with him nestled against my side.

Lady Amy Dudley did nothing to help me with him in the long cold ride. There was no reason that she should, she did not want me nor him. But it would have been kind of her to order one of the men to take me on a pillion saddle behind him, so that I might have held the child in my arms and eased my aching back. She must have seen that at the end of a long day in the saddle I was so exhausted that I could barely stand. It would have been kind of her to see me housed quickly, to have made sure that there was gruel for the baby. But she did nothing for me, nothing for him. She eyed us both with a glaring suspicion and said not one word to me, other than an order to be ready to leave at the appointed time.

I felt the universal smugness of women with children and reminded myself that she was barren. I thought too that she suspected her husband of being the father of my child, and that she was punishing the two of us for her jealousy. I decided that I must make clear to her soon that I had not seen his lordship for years, and that I was now a married woman. But Amy Dudley gave me no chance to speak with her, she treated me as she treated the men who rode with her, as part of the cold landscape, as one of the ice-trimmed trees. She paid no attention to me at all.

I had plenty of time to think as we went slowly south and west on the frozen roads, winding through villages and past fields where it was clear that hunger had hold of the land. The great barn doors stood open, there was neither hay nor straw to keep. The villages were often in darkness, the cottages empty. Some small hamlets were utterly deserted, the people despairing of making a living on the poor land in the continuously bad weather.

I went down the empty roads with my eyes on the country which was bleak and so cursed; but my mind was on my husband and the town I had left. Now that our flight was over and we had arrived in a comparative safe haven, I was sick with fear for Daniel. Now I had time to realise that Daniel and I had lost each other again, and we had lost each other so finally that we might never meet. I did not even know if he was alive. We were trapped in countries at war with each other, and we had parted during the most bitter fighting that Christendom had ever seen. It would be impossible for me to return to him at Calais and for all I knew he could have been killed in that first vicious charge into the city, or he could be ill with the many contagious diseases that a wounded army would bring. I knew that he would think it his duty to go out to help the injured and the sick, and I could only pray for the unlikely hope that the French would show mercy to an enemy doctor in the town which had been a thorn in their side for two centuries.

The arrival of the army would be followed by the French Catholic church, alert for heresy in a town which had once been proudly Protestant. If Daniel had escaped death during the fighting, if he had escaped disease from the soldiers, he might still be taken as a heretic if someone accused him of being a Jew.

I knew that worrying about him helped neither of us, at all; but it was impossible to stop myself, as I rode along the cold hard roads. I could not get a letter into Calais until some sort of peace was declared and that would not be for months. Worse, I could not expect to hear from him, he would have no idea where I had gone or even if I were alive. When he went to my shop in the city wall to look for me, as he surely would do, he would find the place sacked or burned out, and not even Marie, supposing she had survived, would be able to tell him where I was. And then he would find that little Daniel's mother was dead and that the boy was missing too. He would have no reason to guess that I and his son were together in safety in

England. He would think that he had lost his wife and his child in one dreadful battle.

I could not enjoy my safety when I knew that he might still be in danger, there could be no happiness for me until I knew that he was alive. I could not settle in England, I did not think I could settle anywhere until I knew that Daniel was safe. I rode along the cold roads, the weight of his son strapped awkwardly on my back, and I started to wonder at my own discomfort. Somewhere on the road – in Kent, I think – it came to me with the simple brightness of the wintry sun lying on the horizon and shining blindingly into my eyes. I could not settle without Daniel, because I loved him. I had loved him perhaps from the moment I had seen him at the gates of Whitehall Palace where we had quarrelled at our meeting, and I had loved his steadiness and his fidelity and his patience with me ever since. I felt as if I had grown up with him. He had seen me begged as a fool to the king, devoted to the queen and entranced by the Princess Elizabeth. He had seen my schoolchild adoration of my master, and he had seen me struggle with myself to become the woman I now was. The only thing he had not seen, the only thing I had never let him guess, was the resolution of this inner battle: the moment when I could say, 'Yes, I am a woman, and I love this man.'

Everything that had happened in Calais melted away before this one fact. The intrusion of his mother, the malice of his sisters, his own innocent stupidity in thinking that we could all live happily under one small roof. Nothing seemed to matter but that I knew now that I loved him, and that I had to acknowledge that it might be too late for me ever to tell him. He could be dead.

If he were dead then it did not seem to matter very much that he had laid with another girl; the greater loss quite concealed the smaller betrayal. As I mounted my horse in the morning and dismounted wearily at night I realised that I was indeed the widow I announced myself to be. I had lost Daniel, and only now did I have the sense to find that I had loved him all along.

We were to stay in a great house, north of Chichester, and I was glad to clatter into the stable-yard at midday and hand over my tired horse to one of the grooms. I was weary as I followed Lady Dudley up the steps to the great hall, and apprehensive – I did not know these people, and being on my lady's charity was not a position any woman would freely choose. I was too independent in my own mind, and she was too distant and cold to make anyone feel welcome.

Lady Dudley led the way into the great hall, I followed Mrs Oddingsell with Danny on my hip, and there was our hostess, Lady Philips, with a hand held out for Lady Dudley, and a deep curtsey. 'You shall have your usual room overlooking the park,' she said, and then she turned to Mrs Oddingsell and me with a smile.

'This is Mrs Carpenter. She can share with your housekeeper,' Lady Dudley said abruptly. 'She is a woman known to my lord, that he rescued from Calais. I daresay he will let me know what she is to do, shortly.'

Lady Philips raised an eyebrow at Amy's abrupt tone, which all but named me as Robert Dudley's whore. Mrs Oddingsell curtseyed and went to the stairs but I did not immediately follow her. 'I need some things for the child,' I said uncomfortably.

'Mrs Oddingsell will help you,' Robert Dudley's wife said icily.

'There are some baby clothes in the paupers' cupboard,' Lady Philips said.

I curtseyed. 'It was very kind of his lordship to give me a place on his ship from Calais,' I said clearly. 'The more so since he had not seen me for so long, since I had been in royal service to the queen. But I am a married woman now, my husband a doctor in Calais, and this is my husband's son.'

I saw that they both understood me and had heard the reference to royal service.

'My lord is always good to his servants, however lowly,' Amy Dudley said unpleasantly, and waved me away.

'And I need proper clothes for my son,' I said, standing my ground. 'Not from the paupers' cupboard.'

Both women looked at me with renewed attention. 'I need clothes for a gentleman's son,' I said simply. 'I will sew him his linen as soon as I can.'

Lady Philips, not at all sure now what cuckoo she had welcomed into her house, gave me a cautious smile. 'I have some things put by,' she said carefully. 'My sister's boy wore them.'

'I am sure they will suit the purpose excellently,' I said with a pleasant smile. 'And I thank you, your ladyship.'

Within a week I was desperate to leave, the bleak countryside of Sussex in winter seemed to press on my face like a pane of cold glass. The Downs leaned over the little castle as if they would crush us into the unresponsive chalky earth. The sky above the hills was iron grey, filled with snow. Within two weeks I had developed a headache which plagued me all the hours of daylight and would only leave me at night when I would fall into a sleep so deep that it could have been death.

Amy Dudley was a welcome and regular guest here. There was some debt between Sir John Philips and my lord which was repaid by his hospitality to Lady Dudley. Her stay was indefinite, no-one remarked when she might leave, or where she might go next.

'Does she not have a house of her own?' I demanded of Mrs Oddingsell in frustration.

'Not one that she chooses to use,' she said shortly and closed her lips tight on gossip.

I could not understand it. My lord had lost most of his great lands and fortune on his arrest for treason, but surely his wife must have had family and friends who would have kept at least a small estate for him?

'Where did she live when he was in the Tower?' I demanded.

'With her father,' Mrs Oddingsell replied.

'Where is he now?'

'Dead, God rest his soul.'

Without a house to command or lands to farm, Lady Dudley was a woman of complete idleness. I never saw her with a book in her hand, I never saw her even write a letter. She rode out in the morning with only a groom for company on a long ride which lasted until dinner. At dinner she ate little and with no appetite. In the afternoon she would sit with Lady Philips and the two of them would gossip and sew. No detail of the Philips household, neighbours and friends was too small for their comment. When Mrs Oddingsell and I sat with them I nearly fainted from sheer boredom as Lady Philips retold the story of Sophie's disgrace, and Amelia's remark, and what Peter had said about it all for the third time in three days.

Mrs Oddingsell caught me yawning. 'What ails you?' she demanded without sympathy.

'I am so bored,' I said frankly. 'She gossips like a farmer's wife. Why would she be interested in the lives of dairymaids?'

Mrs Oddingsell gave me a quizzical look but said nothing.

'Does she have no friends at court, does she have no news from my lord, if she must tittle-tattle all afternoon?'

The woman shook her head.

We went to bed early, which was just as well for me, and Amy Dudley rose early in the morning. Ordinary days, ordinary to the point of boredom, but she went through them with an air of cold detachment, as if it were not her own precious life utterly wasted in nothings. She lived her life like a woman performing in a long pointless tableau. She went through her days like an automaton – like those I had seen in the treasure cases at Greenwich. A little golden toy soldier which could beat a drum or bend and straighten to fire a cannon. Everything she did, she did as if she were ticking along to do it on invisible wheels and her head turned and she spoke only when the cogs clicked inside her. There was nothing that brought her alive. She was in a state of obedient waiting. Then I realised what she was waiting for. She was waiting for a sign from him.

But there was no sign of Robert though January went into February. No sign of Robert though she told me he would come soon and set me to work, no sign of Robert though he clearly had not been arrested by the queen; whatever the blame for the loss of Calais, it was not to be laid at his door.

Amy Dudley was accustomed to his absence, of course. But when she had slept alone for all those years he had been in the Tower, she had known why she was alone in her marital bed. To everyone – to her father, to his adherents and kin – she was a martyr to her love for him, and they had all prayed for his return and her happiness. But now, it slowly must dawn on her, on everyone, that Lord Robert did not come home to his wife because he did not choose to do so. For some reason, he was in no hurry to be in her bed, in her company.

Freedom from the Tower did not mean a return to the tiny scale of his wife's existence. Freedom for Lord Robert meant the court, meant the queen, meant battlefields, politics, power: a wider world of which Lady Dudley had no knowledge. Worse than ignorance, she felt dread. She thought of the wider world with nothing but fear.

The greater world which was Lord Robert's natural element was to her a place of continuous threat and danger. She saw his ambition, his natural God-given ambition, as a danger, she saw his opportunities all as risk. She was, in every sense of the word, a hopeless wife to him.

Finally, in the second week in February, she sent for him. One of his men was told to ride to the court at Richmond where the queen had entered her confinement chamber to have her child. Her ladyship told the servant to tell his lordship that she needed him at Chichester, and to wait to accompany him home.

'Why would she not write to him?' I asked Mrs Oddingsell, surprised that Lady Dudley would broadcast to the world her desire that he should come home.

She hesitated. 'She can do as she chooses, I suppose,' she said rudely.

It was her discomfiture that revealed the truth to me. 'Can she not write?' I asked.

Mrs Oddingsell scowled at me. 'Not well,' she conceded reluctantly.

'Why not?' I demanded, a bookseller's daughter to whom reading and writing was a skill like eating and walking.

'When would she learn?' Mrs Oddingsell countered. 'She was just a girl when she married him, and nothing more than a bride when he was in the Tower. Her father did not think a woman needed to know more than to sign her name, and her husband never spared the time to teach her. She can write, but slowly, and she can read if she has to.'

'You don't need a man to teach you to read and write,' I said. 'It is a skill a woman can get on her own. I could teach her, if she wanted it.'

Mrs Oddingsell turned her head. 'She wouldn't demean herself to learn from you,' she said rudely. 'She would only ever learn for him. And he does not trouble himself.'

The messenger did not wait, but came home straight away, and told her that his lordship had said he would come to us for a visit shortly and in the meantime to assure her ladyship that all was well with him.

'I told you to wait for an answer,' she said irritably.

'My lady, he said he would see you soon. And the princess . . .'

Her head snapped up. 'The princess? Which princess? Elizabeth?'

'Yes, the Princess Elizabeth swore that he could not go while they were all waiting for the queen's child to be born. She said they could not endure another confinement which might go on for years. She could not abide it without him. And my lord said yes, he would leave, even a lady such as her, for he had not seen you since he came to England, and you had bidden him to come to you.'

She blushed a little at that, her vanity kindled like a flame. 'And what more?' she asked.

The messenger looked a little awkward. 'Just some jesting between my lord and the princess,' he said.

'What jesting?'

'The princess was witty about him liking court better than the country,' he said, fumbling for words. 'Witty about the charms of the court. Said he would not bury himself in the fields with wife.'

The smile was quite wiped from her face. 'And he said?'

'More jests,' he said. 'I cannot remember them, my lady. His lordship is a witty man, and he and the princess . . .' He broke off at the look on her face.

'He and the princess: what?' she spat at him.

The messenger shuffled his feet and turned his hat in his hands. 'She is a witty woman,' he said doltishly. 'The words flew so fast between them I could not make out what they said. Something about the country, something about promises. Some of the time they spoke another language so it was secret between themselves . . . Certainly, she likes him well. He is a very gallant man.'

Amy Dudley jumped from her chair and strode to the bay window. 'He is a very faithless man,' she said, very low. Then she turned to the messenger. 'Very well, you can go. But next time when I order you to wait for him, I don't want to see you back here without him.'

He threw a look at me which said very plainly that a servant could hardly command his master to return to his wife in the middle of a flirtation with the Princess of England. I waited till he had left the room and then excused myself and hared down the gallery after him, Danny bouncing along on my hip, clinging to my shoulder, his little legs gripped around my waist, as I ran.

'Stop! Stop!' I called. 'Tell me about the court. Are all the physicians there for the queen? And the midwives? Is everything ready?'

'Aye,' he said. 'She is expected to have the child in the middle of March, next month, God willing.'

'And do they say that she is well?'

He shook his head. 'They say she is sick to her heart at the loss of Calais and the absence of her husband,' he said. 'The king has not said he will come to England for the birth of his son, so she has to face the travail of childbed all alone. And she is poorly served. All her fortune has been thrown away on her army and her servants have not even been paid and cannot buy food in the market. It is like a ghost court, and now she has gone into confinement there is no-one to watch over the courtiers at all.'

I felt a dreadful pang at the thought of her ill-served and me kicking my heels with Lady Amy Dudley, and doing nothing. 'Who is with her?'

'Only a handful of her ladies. No-one wants to be at court now.'

'And the Princess Elizabeth?'

'She rode in looking very grand,' the messenger said. 'Very taken with my lord.'

'Who says so?'

'Nobody needs to say so. It is known to everyone. She does not trouble to hide it. She shows it.'

'How does she show it?'

'Rides with him every morning, dines at his right hand, dances with him, her eyes fixed on his face, reads his letters at his elbow, smiles at him as if they had a secret jest, walks with him in the gallery and talks low, walks away from him, but always looks back over her shoulder, so that any man would want to chase her and catch her. You know.'

I nodded. I had seen Elizabeth when she had someone's husband marked down for her own. 'I know well enough. And he?'

'Very taken with her.'

'Will he come here, d'you think?'

The messenger chuckled. 'Not until the princess lets him. He was at her beck and call. I don't think he could force himself away from her.'

'He's not a greensick boy,' I said with sudden irritation. 'He could decide for himself, I should hope.'

'And she is not a greensick girl,' he said. 'This is the next Queen of England and she cannot take her eyes from our lord. So what d'you think might come of that?'

In the absence of any work to do in the household, I found that I spent all my time with the child, Danny, and all my thoughts were with his father. I decided to write to Daniel and address the letter to my father's old shop in London. If Daniel came looking for me, or sent anyone to seek me, that would be one of the places he would visit first. I would send a copy of it to my lord and ask him to forward it to Calais. Surely there must be emissaries going to the city?

> *Dear husband,*
>
> *It is strange that after all we have been through we should once more be separated, and once again I am in England and you in Calais, but this time I think you are in greater danger than me. I pray every night that you are safe and well.*
>
> *I had the good fortune to be offered a place on the English ship belonging to Lord Robert and in the hurry of battle I thought it best to take it. I wish now I had found my way to you, but Daniel, I did not know what to do. Also, I had another life to consider. The mother of your child was killed by a French horseman before me, and her last act was to put your son in my hands. I have him with me now and I am caring for him as my own. He is safe and well though he does not speak yet. If you can reply to me you might tell me what should I do? Did he used to talk? And what language does he know?*
>
> *He is eating well and growing well, and learning to walk more strongly. We are living at Chichester in Sussex with Lord Dudley's*

wife until I can find myself a place. I am thinking of going to court or to the Princess Elizabeth, if she will have me.

I wish very much that I could ask you what you think would be the best thing for me to do. I wish very much that you were with me here, or that I were with you. I pray that you are safe, Daniel, and I tell you now, as I should have told you before, that I never stopped loving you even when I left your home. I loved you then, I love you now. I wish we had stayed together then, I wish we were together now. If God ever grants me another chance with you, Daniel, I would want to be your wife once more.

Your wife (if you will let me call myself that)
Hannah Carpenter.

I sent the letter to my lord, with a covering note.

My lord,
Your wife has been very kind to me but I am trespassing on her hospitality here. Please give me permission to come to court or to see if the Princess Elizabeth will take me into her service.
Hannah Green

I heard nothing from Daniel, and I had hardly hoped for it, though I could not tell if it was the silence of distance or the silence of death. In his silence I did not know if I was a widow, an errant wife, or just lost to him. I also waited for a message from my lord and heard nothing.

Waiting to hear from Lord Robert, I was able to recognise that his wife was waiting for him too. Both of us would look up eagerly when we heard a horseman cantering up the lane towards the house. Both of us would gaze out of the window when the early wintry evenings swept down around the castle and another day was gone with no word from him. As each day went by I saw her hopes of him die away. Amy Dudley was slowly but surely being forced to acknowledge that whatever love he had felt for her, when he was a young man and she a young woman, had been worn out by his years of ambition when he had followed his father's train and left her behind, and then eroded completely by his years in the Tower when his first thought had been to keep himself alive. In those years, when he had fought to keep his wits together and not go mad under the loneliness of imprisonment and the fear of his death sentence, his wife was the very last thing he considered.

I was waiting for him, but not like a resentful woman in love. I was waiting for him as the man who could set me free from this sleeping daze of domestic boredom. I was accustomed to running my own shop, to paying my own way, to earning my own money. To live off another person's reluctant charity was very galling to me. And I was used to living in the world; even the tiny dull world of English Calais was more exciting than life in this country house where nothing changed but the weather and the seasons and, God knew, they moved as slowly as years, as decades. And I wanted news of the queen, of her confinement, of the long-waited coming of her child. If she had a son now, the English people would forgive her the loss of Calais, the awful winter that England had suffered this year, even the illness which was plaguing the country in this season of cold weather and rain.

At last a note came from court.

I shall be with you next week. RD

Amy Dudley reacted coolly, with great dignity. She did not ask them to turn the house upside down to prepare for his arrival, she did not summon tenants and neighbours for a feast. She saw that the silver plate and the pewter trenchers were given an extra polish, and that the best linen was laid out for her bed, but other than that, she made no special provision for the return of the lord. Only I saw that she was waiting like a dog waits for his master's step on the threshold; no-one else would have noticed the tension in her body every day, from daybreak, when he might come early, till dusk, when he might arrive late. She took to going to bed as soon as it grew dark, as if the days of waiting were so unbearable that she wanted to sleep through the hours when he was not likely to arrive.

Finally, on Friday, when there was nothing to put before him but carp from the moat, we saw his train coming down the lane, his standard at the head of a trotting column of riders, smartly in step, two by two, all bright and smart in his livery, and Robert before them all, like a young king; and riding behind him – I squinted my eyes against the low winter sun shining towards me – was John Dee, the reverend and respected Catholic chaplain to Bishop Bonner.

I stepped up to the window of the upper gallery where I had been playing with Danny, so that I could see Robert Dudley's welcome. The front door of the house was torn open and Amy Dudley was on the top step, her hands clasped before her, the picture of demure self-control, but I knew she was raging to be with him. I could hear the rest of the household flinging themselves down the stairs and skidding on the polished floorboards to be in their places when the honoured guest walked into the hall.

Lord Robert pulled up his horse, jumped from the saddle, threw the reins to a waiting groom, tossed some remark over his shoulder to John Dee and bowed and kissed his wife's hand as if he had been away for a couple of nights and not for most of their married life.

She dropped a cool curtsey and then turned to Mr Dee and nodded her head, wasting little politeness on the bishop's curate. I smiled, I did not think Robert would like to see his friend slighted, she was a fool to snub him.

I picked up Danny, who came to me eagerly with his beaming smile, but saying nothing, and made my way down the great stairs to the hall. The household was assembled, lined up as if they were an army for inspection, Sir John Philips and his lady at the head. My lord stood illuminated in the doorway, his broad shoulders brushing the doorframe, his smile confident.

As always his sheer glamour amazed me. The years of imprisonment had scarred him with nothing worse than a deep groove on either side of his mouth and a hardness at the back of his eyes. He looked like a man who had taken a beating and learned to live with the knowledge of defeat. Apart from that shadow, he was the same young man whom I had seen walking with an angel in Fleet Street five years ago. His hair was still dark and thick and curling, his look still challenging and bright, his mouth ready to grin, and his whole bearing like that of the prince he might have been.

'I'm very glad to be with you,' he said to them all. 'And I thank you all for the good service you have done to me and mine while I have been away.' He paused. 'You will be anxious for news of the queen,' he said. He glanced up the stairs and saw me dressed as a woman, for the first time ever. His amazed stare took in the cut-down gown which I had sewn with the help of Mrs Oddingsell, my dark hair smoothed back under my hood, the dark-headed child on my hip. Comically, he looked and then looked again at the sight of me, recognised me despite the gown, and then shook a baffled head; but continued his speech.

'The queen is in her confinement chamber and expecting to give birth to a son. The king will return to England when the baby is born; in the meantime he is protecting the borders of his Spanish lands in the Low Countries, and has sworn to retake Calais for England. The Princess Elizabeth has visited her sister and wished her well. The princess is in good health, good spirits and great beauty, praise God. She has told the queen that she will not marry any Spanish prince, nor anyone of the king's choosing. She will remain a bride of England.'

I thought it an odd way to give news of the queen, but the servants were glad to hear it and there was a murmur of interest at the princess's name. Here, as in the rest of the country, the mood against the queen was very strong. Losing Calais was blamed on her, since she had taken us into war with the French against the tradition of her family, and against the advice of her council. They blamed her for the hunger in the country and for the bad weather, they blamed her for not having a child earlier, they blamed her for the deaths of the heretics.

A healthy son was the only thing that would redeem her in their eyes, and some of them did not want even him. Some of them, perhaps most of them now, would have her die childless and the crown go straight to the Princess Elizabeth – another woman, and though they were sick of queens, this was a good Protestant princess and one who had already refused to marry a Spanish prince and who now swore that she had no inclination to marry at all.

There was a little murmur at the news and they began to disperse. Robert shook John Philips warmly by the hand, kissed Lady Philips on her cheek and then turned to me.

'Hannah? Is that really you?'

I came down the stairs slowly, conscious of his wife behind him, still standing in the doorway.

'My lord,' I said. I reached the bottom step and dropped him a curtsey.

'I would never have known you,' he said incredulously. 'You are more than a girl, Hannah. You are a woman grown, and out of your breeches at last! Did you have to learn how to walk all over again? Show me your shoes! Go on! Are you in high heels? And a babe in your arms? This is a transformation!'

I smiled but I could feel Amy's eyes boring into me. 'This is my son,' I said. 'I thank you for saving us from Calais.'

His face clouded over for a moment. 'I wish I could have saved them all.'

'Have you any news from the town?' I asked him. 'My husband and his family may still be there. Did you send my letter onward?'

He shook his head. 'I gave it to my pageboy and told him to give it to a fisherman who goes out deep into the French seas, and asked him to pass it to a French ship if he met with one, but I could do no more for you. We have heard nothing of the men who were captured. We have not even begun peace proposals. King Philip will keep us at war with France for as long as he can, and the queen is in no position to argue. There will be some exchange of prisoners, and men sent home, but God knows when.' He shook his head as if to dislodge the memories of the fall of the infallible castle. 'You know, I have never seen you in a gown before. You are transformed!'

I tried to laugh but I could see Amy coming to claim her husband.

'You will want to wash and change out of your riding clothes,' she said firmly.

Robert bowed to her.

'There is hot water in your bed chamber,' she said.

'Then I'll go up.' He glanced over his shoulder. 'And someone must show Dee where he is to lodge.' I shrank back, but my lord did not notice. He called out: 'Here, John – look at who we have here!'

John Dee came forward and I saw that he was more changed than Robert. His hair was greying at the temples, his eyes were dark with fatigue. But his air of confidence and his inner peace were as strong as ever.

'Who is this lady?' he asked.

'I am Hannah Carpenter, Mr Dee,' I said guardedly. I did not know whether he was going to acknowledge that we had last met in the most terrible place in England when I was on trial for my life and he was my judge. 'I was Hannah Green. The queen's fool.'

He looked quickly at me again and then a slow sweet smile spread from his eyes to his lips. 'Ah, Hannah, I would not have known you in your gown.'

'And he is Dr Dee now,' my lord said casually. 'Bishop Bonner's chaplain.'

'Oh,' I said guardedly.

'And is this your son?' John Dee asked.

'Yes. This is Daniel Carpenter,' I said proudly, and John Dee reached forward and touched my little boy's fingers with his own. Comically, Danny turned his head away and pressed his face into my shoulder.

'How old is he?'

'Nearly two.'

'And his father?'

I frowned. 'I parted from my husband at Calais, I don't know if he is safe,' I said.

'You have no . . . sense of him?' John Dee asked me, his voice low.

I shook my head.

'Dr Dee, Hannah will show you to your chamber,' Amy's voice broke in abruptly, speaking of me as if I were her servant.

I led the way up the stairs to one of the small bedchambers on the first floor, John Dee following me. Lord Robert sprang up the stairs two at a time behind us, we heard the door bang as he went into his room.

I had barely showed John Dee where he was to sleep, the cupboard where he could put his clothes, and poured hot water for him to wash, when the chamber door opened and Lord Robert came in.

'Hannah, don't go,' he said. 'I want to hear your news.'

'I have none,' I said coolly. 'I have been here, as you know, all this long while, with your wife, doing nothing.'

He gave a short laugh. 'Have you been bored, Mistress Boy? It cannot be worse than married life, surely?'

I smiled. I was not going to tell Lord Robert that I had parted from my husband within a year of our marriage.

'And have you kept your gift?' John Dee asked quietly. 'I always thought that the angels would only come to a virgin.'

I thought for a moment, I could not forget that the last time I had seen him he had been advising Bishop Bonner. I remembered the woman who had cupped her torn fingers in her lap. I remembered the smell of urine in the little room and the wet warmth in my breeches, and my shame. 'I don't know, sir,' I said, my voice very small.

Robert Dudley heard the constraint in my tone and looked quickly from me to his friend. 'How now?' he asked sharply. 'What's this?'

Dr Dee and I exchanged an odd complicit glance: that of the secret torturer to his unproclaimed victim, that of a horror shared. He said nothing.

'Nothing,' I said.

'Odd sort of nothing,' Lord Robert said, his tone hardening. 'You tell me, John.'

'She was brought before Bonner,' John Dee said briefly. 'Heresy. I was there. The charges were dismissed. She was released.'

'My God, you must have pissed yourself, Hannah!' Robert exclaimed.

He hit the mark so precisely that my cheeks burned red and I gripped Daniel's son against me.

John Dee shot a brief apologetic look at me. 'We were all afraid,' he said. 'But in this world, we all do what we have to do, Robert. We all do the best we can. Sometimes we wear masks, sometimes we can be ourselves, sometimes the masks are truer than the faces. Hannah betrayed no-one and was clearly innocent herself. She was released. That's all.'

Lord Robert leaned over and gripped Bishop Bonner's most orthodox, most rigorous chaplain by the hand. 'That's all indeed. I would not have wanted her racked, she knows much too much. I am glad you were there.'

John Dee did not glow in return. 'No-one was there by choice,' he said. 'There were more innocents than this one that went to be scourged and burned.'

I looked from one man to the other, wondering where the allegiances truly lay. At least now I knew enough not to ask, and not to trust any answer.

Lord Robert turned back to me. 'And so *do* you have your gift still, even though you have lost your virginity?'

'It comes so rarely that it is hard to tell. But I had a true seeing in

Calais, after my wedding: I foresaw the horsemen riding through the streets.' I shut my eyes against the memory.

'You saw the French coming into Calais?' Lord Robert asked incredulously. 'Dear God, why didn't you warn me?'

'I would have done if I had known what it was,' I replied. 'Don't doubt me. I would have come at once if I could have understood what I was seeing. But it was so unclear. It was a woman being cut down as she ran from them and calling out . . .' I broke off. I would not tell even these trusted men that she called me to take her son. Danny was mine now. 'God knows I would have warned that woman . . . even though . . . I would not want anyone to suffer that death.'

Robert shook his head and turned to look out of the window. 'I wish to God I had been warned,' he said moodily.

'Will you scry for me again?' John Dee asked. 'So that we can see if your gift remains true?'

I looked at him in utter disbelief. 'Are you seeking the advice of angels?' I asked the Inquisitor's chaplain. 'You? Of all men?'

John Dee was not at all perturbed by the sharpness of my tone. 'I do not change my beliefs. And we need guidance all the more, in these troubled times. But we must ask discreetly. There is always danger for those who seek knowledge. But if we could know that the queen will give birth to a healthy child we would be better able to plan for the future. If she is to be blessed with a son, then Princess Elizabeth should change her plans.'

'And I should change mine,' Lord Robert remarked wryly.

'Anyway, I don't know if I can do it,' I said. 'I have only seen the future just once, in all the time I was in Calais.'

'Shall we try this evening?' Lord Robert asked. 'Will you try and see if it comes easily, Hannah? For old times' sake?'

My gaze slid past him to John Dee. 'No,' I said flatly.

John Dee looked directly at me, his dark eyes meeting mine with honesty. 'Hannah, I do not pretend that my ways are not dark and tortuous,' he said simply. 'But you for one should be glad that I was there at St Paul's when you were arraigned to answer.'

'I was glad that my innocence was recognised,' I said staunchly. 'And I don't want to go in there again.'

'You will not,' he said simply. 'My word on it.'

'So will you scry for us?' my lord pressed me.

I hesitated. 'If you will ask a question for me,' I bargained with them.

'What is it?' John Dee asked.

'If my husband is alive or dead,' I said. 'It's all I want to know. I don't even ask the future, if I shall see him again. I would be happy just to know that he is alive.'

'You love him so much?' Lord Robert asked sceptically. 'Your young man?'

'I do,' I said simply. 'I cannot rest until I know that he is safe.'

'I shall ask the angels and you shall scry for me,' John Dee promised. 'Tonight?'

'When Danny is asleep,' I said. 'I couldn't do it while I was listening for him.'

'At eight o'clock?' Lord Robert asked. 'Here?'

John Dee glanced around. 'I will ask the men to bring up my table and my books.'

Lord Robert noticed the smallness of the room and made an impatient noise. 'She always does this,' he said irritably. 'She never puts my friends in the best chambers. She is sick with envy of them, I shall tell her . . .'

'There is plenty of room,' Dee said pacifically. 'And she is bound to resent you coming with a great train when she will have wanted you to herself. Should you not go to her now?'

Lord Robert went reluctantly to the door. 'Come with me,' he said. 'Come, both of you, and we'll take a glass of ale to wash down the dust from the road.'

I hung back. 'I cannot come,' I said when he held the door for me.

'What?'

'She does not receive me,' I said awkwardly. 'I am not invited to sit with her.'

Robert's dark eyebrows snapped together. 'I told her that she was to keep you with her as her companion until we decided where you should live,' he said. 'Where do you dine?'

'At the table for the maids. I am not seated with your wife.'

He took a rapid step towards the stairs and then he checked himself and came back. 'Come,' he said, holding out his hand to me. 'I am master here, I do not have to argue to see my wishes done. Just come, and you shall dine with me now. She is a stupid woman who does not reward her husband's loyal servants. And a jealous woman who thinks that a pretty face is safer seen from afar.'

I did not go to his outstretched hand. I smiled at him steadily, keeping my place in the window-seat. 'My lord,' I said. 'I imagine you are going back to court within a few days?'

'Yes,' he said. 'What of it?'

'Shall you take me with you?'

He looked surprised. 'I don't know. I hadn't thought.'

I felt my smile turn into a giggle. 'I thought not,' I said. 'So I may have to stay here for some weeks yet?'

'Yes. And so?'

'And so I would rather not spur your wife's irritation into rage if you are going to blow in and out again like a spring wind that spoils the peace of the orchard.'

He laughed. 'Are you at peace, my little orchard?'

'We are in a state of quiet enmity,' I said frankly. 'But I would rather that, than the open warfare you would bring. Go and sit with her now, and I will meet you back here tonight.'

Robert patted me on the cheek. 'God bless your caution, Hannah. I think I should never have given you to the king. I would be a better man today if I had kept your counsel.'

Then he ran downstairs whistling, and it made me shiver when I heard the wind at the castle windows whistle back at him.

I watched Amy at dinner. She never took her eyes off her husband throughout the prolonged meal. She ached to be the centre of her husband's attention but she had no skills to fascinate him. She knew nothing of the gossip of the court, she had not even heard of half of the names that he mentioned. I, seated below the salt, kept my eyes on my plate to prevent myself from looking up and laughing at a story about a woman I knew, or interrupting to ask him what had become of one young courtier or another.

Lady Amy did not even have the native wit to invite him to talk, even if she knew nothing herself. She pursed her lips whenever he spoke of a woman, she looked down in disapproval when he laughingly mentioned the queen. She was downright rude to John Dee whom she clearly regarded as a turncoat from the defeated Protestant cause. But she was no enthusiast for news of the Princess Elizabeth either.

I thought that when my lord had first met her he must have loved the unspoiled freshness of her, when she was a young girl who knew nothing of the court or of his father's sly progress to power. When she was a simple squire's daughter in Norfolk with big blue eyes and large breasts pressing against the neck of her gown, she must have seemed to be everything that the ladies of court were not: honest, unsophisticated, true. But now all those virtues were disadvantages to him. He needed a wife who could watch the direction of change, could trim her speech and style to the prevailing tides, and could watch and caution him. He needed a wife who was quick in understanding and skilled in any company, a wife he could take to court, and know he had a spy and an ally among the ladies.

Instead he was burdened with a woman who, in her vanity, was prepared to insult the chaplain of one of the most powerful priests in the country, who had no interest in the doings of the court and the wider world, and who resented his interest.

'We'll never have another Dudley if she does not make more effort with him,' one of the upper maids whispered indiscreetly to me.

'What ails her?' I demanded. 'I'd have thought she would be all over him.'

'She can never forgive him for going to court in his father's train. She thought his imprisonment would teach him a lesson. Teach him not to over-reach himself.'

'He's a Dudley,' I said. 'They're born to over-reach themselves. They're from the greediest most ambitious line in the world. Only a Spaniard likes gold better than a Dudley, only an Irishman desires more land.'

I looked down the table at Amy. She was eating a sweetmeat, the sugared plum distending her mouth as she sucked on it. She was staring straight ahead, ignoring her husband's intense conversation with John Dee. 'You know her well?'

The older woman nodded. 'Yes, and I've come to pity her. She likes a small station in life and she wants him to be small too.'

'She'd have done better to have chosen a country squire then,' I said.

'For Robert Dudley is a man with a great future, not a small one, and he will never allow her to stand in his way.'

'She will pull him down if she can,' the woman warned.

I shook my head. 'Not her.'

Amy had hoped to sit up late with her husband, or to go to bed early together, but at eight o'clock he made excuses and he and John Dee and I gathered in John Dee's room with the door closed, the shutters across the window and only one candle lit and glowing in the mirror.

'Are you happy to do this?' John Dee asked.

'What are you going to ask?'

'If the queen will have a boy child,' Robert said. 'There is nothing more important to know than this. And if we can win back Calais.'

I looked towards John Dee. 'And if my husband lives,' I reminded him.

'We will see what is given us,' he said gently. 'Let us pray.'

I closed my eyes and at the rolling gentle sounds of the Latin I felt myself restored, returned. I was at home again, at home with my gift, with my lord, and with myself. When I opened my eyes the candle flame was warm as well as bright on my face and I smiled at John Dee.

'You still have your gift?' he asked.

'I am sure of it,' I said quietly.

'Watch the flame and tell us what you hear or what you see.'

The candle flame bobbed in a little draught, its brightness filled my mind. It was like the summer sunshine of Spain, and I thought I heard my mother calling me, her voice happy and filled with confidence that nothing would ever go wrong. Then abruptly I heard a tremendous banging that made me gasp and leap to my feet, jolted out of my dream with my heart thudding in fear of arrest.

John Dee was white-faced. We were discovered and ruined. Lord Robert had his sword from his belt and a knife from his boot.

'Open up!' came the shout from the barred door and there was a great blow against the wood which made it rock inward. I was certain that it was the Inquisition. I crossed the room to Lord Robert. 'Please, my lord,' I said rapidly. 'Don't let them burn me. Run me through, before they take me, and save my son.'

In one fluid movement he was up on the window-seat, pulled me up beside him and kicked out the window pane. 'Jump out,' he advised me. 'And run if you can. I'll hold them for a moment.' There was another terrible blow on the door. He nodded at John Dee. 'Open up,' he said.

John Dee flung open the door and Lady Amy Dudley fell into the room. 'You!' she exclaimed as soon as she saw me, half out of the window. 'As I thought! Whore!'

A servant behind her raised a mace in a half-apologetic gesture. The Philipses' elegant linenfold door panels were splintered beyond repair. Robert slammed his sword back into the scabbard, and gestured to John Dee. 'Please, John, do shut what is left of the door,' he said wearily. 'This will be half way round the county by dawn.'

'What are you doing here?' Amy demanded, striding into the room, her eyes taking in the table, the candles, their flames guttering in the draught from the window, the holy symbols. 'What foul lechery?'

'Nothing,' Robert said wearily.

'What is she doing here with you? And him?'

He stepped forward and took her hands. 'My lady, this is my friend and this my loyal servant. We were praying together for my prosperity.'

She broke from his grasp and struck at him, her hands clenched into fists, pounding against his chest. 'She is a whore and he is a dealer in black arts!' she cried. 'And you are a false deceiver who has broken my heart too many times to count!'

Robert caught her hands. 'She is a good servant of mine and a respectable married woman,' he said quietly. 'And Dr Dee is chaplain to one of the most important churchmen in the land. Madam, I beg you to compose yourself.'

'I will see him hanged for this!' she shouted into his face. 'I will name him as a dealer with the devil, and she is nothing more than a witch and a whore.'

'You will do nothing but make yourself a laughing stock,' he said steadily. 'Amy, you know what you are like. Be calm.'

'How can I be calm when you shame me before your own friends?'

'You are not shamed . . .' he started.

'I hate you!' she suddenly screamed.

John Dee and I shrank back against the wall and glanced longingly at the door, wishing to be away from this uproar.

With a wail she tore herself from his grip and threw herself face down on the bed. She was screaming with grief, quite beside herself. John Dee and my lord exchanged an aghast look. There was a little tearing noise and I realised she had bitten the counterpane and was ripping it with her teeth.

'Oh, for the sake of God!' Robert took her shoulders and pulled her up from the bed. At once she went for his face with her nails, her hands clenched like a cat's unsheathed claws. Robert grabbed her hands and bore her down till she fell on the floor, kneeling at his feet, her wrists in his grip.

'I know you!' she swore up at him. 'If it is not her, then it is another. There is nothing about you but pride and lust.'

His face, suffused with temper, slowly calmed, but he kept a tight hold of her hands. 'I am a sinner indeed,' he said. 'But thank God, *I* at least am not crazed.'

Her mouth trembled and then she let out a wail, looking up into his flinty face, the tears pouring from her eyes, her mouth drooling sobs. 'I am not crazed, I am ill, Robert,' she said despairingly. 'I am sick of grief.'

He met my eyes over her head. 'Fetch Mrs Oddingsell,' he said briefly. 'She knows what to do.'

I was transfixed for the moment, watching Amy Dudley grinding her teeth, scrabbling at her husband's feet. 'What?'

'Get Mrs Oddingsell.'

I nodded and went from the room. Half the household was busy on the landing outside the chamber. 'Go to your work!' I said abruptly, and then I ran down the long gallery to find Mrs Oddingsell seated before a mean fire at the cold end of the chamber.

'Her ladyship is crying, and his lordship sent for you,' I said baldly.

She got to her feet at once, without surprise, and went quickly down the room. I half-ran beside her. 'Has this happened before?' I asked.

She nodded.

'Is she ill?'

'Easily distressed by him.'

I took that in, made allowances for a servant's loyal lies. 'Was she always like this?'

'When they were young and in love it passed for passion. But she was only at peace when he was in the Tower – except for when the princess was imprisoned too.'

'What?'

'She was ill with jealousy, then.'

'They were prisoners!' I exclaimed. 'They were hardly dancing in masques together.'

Mrs Oddingsell nodded. 'In her mind they were lovers. And now, he is free to come and go. And she knows that he is seeing the princess. He will break her heart. It is no figure of speech. She will die of this.'

We were at Dr Dee's door. I put a hand on her arm. 'Are you her nurse?' I asked.

'More like her keeper,' she said and quietly went in.

The scrying was abandoned for the night, but the next day, when Lady Dudley kept to her room and was not to be seen, Dr Dee asked for my help in translating a prophecy that he thought might apply to the queen. I had to read a set of apparently disconnected Greek words to him which he carefully wrote down, each one having a numerical value. We met in the library, a room cold with disuse. Robert called for a fire to be lit in the grate and a servant came in and threw open the shutters.

'It looks like code,' I observed when they had finished and we were alone again.

'It is the code of the ancients,' he said. 'Perhaps they even knew the code for life.'

'A code for life?'

'What if everything was made of the same things?' he asked me suddenly. 'Sand and cheese, milk and earth? What if beyond the illusion of difference, beyond their clothes as it were, there was only one form in the world, and one could see it, draw it, even re-create it?'

I shook my head. 'What then?'

'That form would be the code of everything,' he said. 'That would be the poem at the heart of the world.'

Danny, who had been sleeping on the broad footstool beside me as I wrote, stirred in his sleep and sat up, smiling around him. His beam widened when he saw my face. 'Hello, my boy,' I said gently.

He slid down and toddled towards me, keeping a cautious hand on his chair, and then mine, to hold himself steady. He took hold of a fold of my gown and looked up attentively into my face.

'He's very quiet,' John Dee said softly.

'He does not speak,' I said, smiling down at his upturned face. 'But he is no fool. I know he understands everything. He will fetch things, and he knows their names. He knows his own name – don't you, Danny? But he will not speak.'

'Was he always like this?'

The fear clenched at my heart: that I did not know what this child was like, and that if I admitted I did not know, someone might take him away from me. He was not my child, not born of my body, but his mother had put him into my arms and his father was my husband, and whatever I owed to my husband Daniel in terms of love and duty might be redeemed by my care for his son.

'I don't know, he was with his wet nurse in Calais,' I lied. 'She brought him to me when the city was under siege.'

'He might be frightened,' John Dee suggested. 'Did he see the fighting?'

My heart contracted, I could feel it like a pain. I looked at him incredulously. 'Frightened? But he is only a little baby. How would he know when he was in danger?'

'Who knows what he might think or understand?' John Dee said. 'I don't believe that children know nothing but what is taught them, as if they were empty pots for the filling. He will have known one home and one woman caring for him, and then he might have been afraid, running through the streets to look for you. Children know more than we allow, I think. He might be afraid to speak now.'

I leaned over him, and his bright dark eyes looked back at me, like the liquid eyes of a little deer. 'Daniel?' I asked.

For the first time I thought of him as a real person, someone who might think and feel, someone who had been in the arms of his mother and felt himself thrust violently from her, into the arms of a stranger. Someone who had seen his mother ridden down by a horse and gored by a lance, who had seen his mother die in the gutter and then felt himself carried like an unwanted parcel on a boat, unloaded without explanation in England, jolted and jogged on the back of a horse to some cold house in the middle of nowhere, with no-one he knew.

This was a child who had seen his mother die. This was a child without a mother. I leaned over him, I could feel the prickle of hot tears underneath my eyelids. This was a child whose grief and fear I, of all people, could understand. I had hidden my own childhood fear behind all the languages of Christendom, in becoming fluent in every tongue. He, so much smaller, so much more afraid, had gone mute.

'Danny,' I said gently. 'I will be your mother. You will be safe with me.'

'Is he not your child?' John Dee asked. 'He looks so like you.'

I looked up at him and I was tempted to trust him with the truth but fear kept me silent.

'Is he one of the Chosen People?' John Dee asked quietly.

Silently, I nodded my head.

'Circumcised?' he asked.

'No,' I said. 'Not in Calais, and here it is impossible.'

'He might need the outward sign of being one of the People,' Dee suggested. 'He might need to be among his people before he can speak.'

I looked at him in bewilderment. 'How would he know?'

He smiled. 'This little one has just come from the angels,' he said. 'He would know more than all of us put together.'

Lady Amy Dudley kept to her room for the next three days while Robert and John Dee rode out hunting, read in the library, gambled small sums of money, and talked, night and day, riding and walking, at dinner and at play as to what the future of the country might be, what shape the nobility and the parliament should take, how far the borders might extend overseas, what chance the small island kingdom of England had against the great continental powers, and – John Dee's great obsession –

how England was uniquely placed to send out ships the world over and create a new form of kingdom, one which extended overseas, an empire. An empire which might dominate the unknown places of the world. He had calculated how big the world might be and he was convinced that there were great lands we had not yet touched. 'Christopher Columbus,' he said to my lord. 'A brave man but no mathematician. It is obvious that you cannot have a passage to China that you can broach within weeks. If you make the proper calculation you can show that the world is round but far, far greater than Columbus thought. And in that great extra quarter must be land. And how would it be if that land were to be English?'

Often I walked or rode or dined with them and often they would ask me how things were done in Spain, what I had seen in Portugal, or what I thought might be the success of such a scheme. We were cautious not to discuss what sort of monarch might be on the throne to launch such confident and ambitious schemes. While the queen was waiting to give birth to a son and heir, nothing could be certain.

On the evening of the third day of their visit my lord had a message from Dover, and left me and John Dee alone in the library. John Dee had drawn a map of the world after the model of his friend Gerard Mercator and tried to explain to me that I must think of the world as round, and think of this map as the skin of the world peeled off, like the skin peeled off an orange and laid flat.

He struggled to make me see it until he laughed and said that I must be content to see angels, I clearly could not see longitude. He took up his maps and went with them to his room as Lord Robert came into the library with a piece of paper in his hand. 'At last I have news of your husband, he is safe,' he said.

I jumped to my feet and found I was trembling. 'My lord?'

'He was taken by the French who suspected him as a spy, but they are holding him with other English soldiers,' he told me. 'I daresay I can arrange for him to be exchanged for other prisoners of war, or ransomed, or something.'

'He is safe?' I asked.

He nodded.

'Safe?' I asked incredulously.

He nodded again.

'Not sick, nor injured?'

'See for yourself,' he said, handing over the three scrawled lines on the sheet of paper. 'Held in the castle. If you were to write to him I could get it sent on.'

'Thank you,' I said. I read and re-read the letter. It said nothing more than he had already told me but somehow in words of black ink on travel-stained paper it seemed more true. 'Thank God.'

'Thank God indeed,' said my lord with a smile.

Impulsively I took his hand. 'And thank you, my lord,' I said fervently. 'You are kind to take the trouble for me. I know it. I am grateful.'

Gently he drew me in, put a warm hand on my waist. 'Sweetheart, you know I would do anything in my power to make you happy.'

I hesitated. His hand was light, I could feel the heat of his palm through the fabric of my gown. I felt myself lean towards him. He stole a quick glance up and down the empty gallery and then his mouth came down towards mine. He hesitated, he was such a practised seducer that he knew the power of delay to increase desire. Then he bent a little lower and he kissed me, tenderly and then with increasing passion until my arms were around his neck and he had me pressed against a wall, my head tipped back, my eyes closed, quite given up to the delicious sensation of his touch.

'Lord Robert,' I whispered.

'I'm for bed. Come with me, sweetheart-mine.'

I did not hesitate. 'I am sorry my lord, no.'

'You are sorry, my lord, no?' he repeated comically. 'What d'you mean, Mistress Boy?'

'I shall not lie with you,' I said steadily.

'Why not? Don't tell me it is not your desire; for I shan't believe you. I can taste it on your lips. You want me as much as I want you. And that is a good deal, tonight.'

'It is my desire,' I admitted. 'And if I were not a married woman I would be glad to be your lover.'

'Oh, Hannah, a husband such a long way away and safely in prison need not concern you. A word from you to me, and he can stay there until there is a general amnesty. For all I care he can stay there forever. Come to bed with me, now.'

Steadfastly I shook my head. 'No, my lord. I am sorry.'

'Not sorry enough,' he said crossly. 'What ails you, child?'

'It is not that he might catch me,' I said. 'It is that I do not want to betray him.'

'You betray him in your heart,' Robert said cheerfully. 'You lean back against my arm, you tip your head, you open your mouth for my kisses. He is betrayed already, Mistress Boy. The rest is just enacting the desire. It is no worse than what you have done already.'

I smiled at his persuasive, self-serving logic. 'Perhaps, but it is wrong. My lord, I tell you true, I have adored you since the day I first saw you. But I love Daniel with a true and honourable love, and I want to be good wife to him, and faithful to him.'

'This is nothing to do with true love between us, sweetheart,' he said with his simple rake's brutality.

'I know,' I said. 'And now I want love. Lust is no good for me. I want love. His love.'

He looked at me, his dark eyes brimming with laughter. 'Ah, Hannah, this is a big mistake for a woman like you, with everything to play for and nothing to lose. You are the closest thing to a free woman I have ever known. A girl educated far beyond her sex, a wife with a husband miles away, a woman with gifts, ambition, the sense to use them and the body of a beautiful whore. For God's sake, girl, be my mistress. You don't have to descend to being a wife.'

I could not help but laugh. 'I thank you,' I said. 'But I want to be a wife without descending. I want to choose Daniel when I find him again, and love him from my heart and with faithfulness.'

'But you would so enjoy a night with me, you know,' he said, partly from vanity, partly as a final attempt.

'I am very sure of it,' I said, as shameless as he. 'And if I cared for nothing but pleasure then I would be begging you for tonight and every night after. But I have fallen in love, my lord, and no-one but my lover will do for me.'

He stepped back and swept me a beautiful courtly bow, as low as if for a queen. 'Mistress Boy, you always exceed my expectations. I knew you would make a wonderful woman but I never expected you would make a surprising and honourable woman. I hope your husband is worthy of you, I do indeed. And if he is not . . .'

I laughed. 'If he breaks my heart a second time then I will come back to you as heartless as you are yourself, my lord,' I said.

'Oh well, it is agreed,' he said with a laugh, and went to his bed alone.

Within a few days his lordship and John Dee were ready to return to court. John Dee would go back to Bishop Bonner and would note the detail of the charges and the words of the interrogation of hundreds of men and women charged with heresy. He would see them sent for torture, and then when they confessed, he would see them sent for burning.

We walked to the stables together to check that the horses were ready for the journey, and an awkward silence fell between us. I would never ask him how he could bear to leave these innocent days in the country and go back to his work as hangman.

He spoke first. 'Hannah, you know, it is better that it is me there, advising, than any other.'

For a moment I did not understand him, then I realised that it was a plot, another plot, within a plot, within the great plots. Better that John Dee was examining Princess Elizabeth's supporters and friends than a man whose loyalties were solid to the queen and who desired to see them all burn.

'I don't know how you can bear it,' I said simply. 'The woman I saw, without her fingernails . . .'

He nodded. 'God forgive us,' he said quietly. 'I am sorry that you were taken up, Hannah.'

'I thank you for saving me, if that is what you did,' I said unwillingly.

'Did you not know that I interceded for you?'

'I did not quite understand it, at the time,' I said carefully.

John Dee took my hand and patted it. 'You are right. I had a greater aim in view than your life. But I am glad that you were only brushed, and not broken, by this.'

We walked into the stable-yard and there was Lord Robert, watching a wagon being loaded with goods that he wanted for his rooms at

Richmond: a beautiful tapestry and some fine carpets. I went up and spoke to him privately.

'Will you write and tell me how the queen does?' I asked.

'You are taking an interest in the succession?'

'I take an interest in the queen,' I said. 'I had no truer friend when I first came to her service.'

'And then you ran off and left her,' he observed.

'My lord, as you know, they were dangerous times. I was safer away from court then.'

'And now?'

'I don't expect safety. But I have to find some way to make my living and to raise my son.'

He nodded. 'Hannah, I would have you stay here for the time being, but by the summer I shall want you to meet me at court. I want you to see the queen again and enter her service.'

'My lord, I am a fool no more. I have a child to care for and I am waiting for my husband.'

'My child, you are a fool indeed if you think you can argue with me.'

That checked me. 'I do not mean to argue,' I said pacifically. 'But I don't want to be parted from my son, and I cannot go back into breeches.'

'You can send him to a nurse. And you can be a fool in petticoats as well as breeches. There are many fools in petticoats, after all. You will not be an exception.'

I bit the inside of my lip to keep myself calm despite my sense of danger. 'My lord, he is only a baby still, and he does not speak. He is in a strange country and we neither of us know anybody. Please let him stay with me. Please let me keep him.'

'If you insist on staying with him then you will have to remain here in the country with Amy,' he warned me.

I measured the price I must pay to be Danny's mother and to my own surprise, I found it worth paying. I would not leave him, whatever it cost me.

'Very well,' I said. I stepped back against the wall, out of the way of the porters carrying two great chairs and a table to the back of the wagon.

Lord Robert scowled at me, he had not thought I would put the child

before my own ambition. 'Oh, Hannah, you are not the woman I hoped
you would be. A faithful wife and a devoted mother is not much use to
me! Very well! I will send for you when I need you, probably May. You
can bring the boy,' he forestalled me. 'But come as soon as I send for
you. I will need your ears and your eyes at court.'

Lord Robert rode out at noon, a cold March day, and his wife got up
from her sick bed to see him go. She stood, silent again, like a woman
made of snow, in the hall of the house as he clapped his hat on his head
and swung his cape around his shoulders.

'I am sorry that you have been ill for all of my visit,' he said brightly,
as if speaking to a little-known host. 'I have not seen you since dinner
that first night.'

She hardly seemed to hear him. She managed a blank smile, more
like a grimace.

'I will hope that you are in better health and spirits when I come
again.'

'When will that be?' she asked quietly.

'I cannot say. I will send you a message.'

It was as if his refusal to make a promise was a spell that made her
come to life. She stirred, and glared at him. 'If you do not come soon,
I shall write to the queen and complain of you,' she threatened, her
voice low and angry. 'She knows what it is like to be abandoned by a
false husband who runs after every pretty face. She knows what sort of
woman her sister is. She has suffered from Elizabeth's ways as I have
suffered. I know about that, you see. I know what you and the princess
are to each other.'

'It is treason to say such a thing,' he remarked quietly, in a pleasant
tone. 'And such a letter would be evidence of your treason. We have
just got this family out of the Tower, Amy, don't plunge us back
in again.'

She bit her lip and the colour flooded into her cheeks. 'At any rate
your whore shall not stay here with me!'

Robert sighed and looked across the hall towards me. 'I have no
whore here,' he said with elaborate patience. 'I barely have a wife here,

as you well know. The honourable lady, Mrs Carpenter, will stay here until I send for her to work for me at court.'

Amy Dudley let out a little shriek of rage and then clapped her hand over her mouth. 'You call what she does "work"?'

'Yes,' he said quietly. 'As I say. And I will send for her. And I will come to visit you again.' He lowered his voice and his tone was gentle. 'And I shall pray, for your sake and for mine, that when I see you again you are composed. This is no way for us, Amy. You must not behave like a mad woman.'

'I am not mad,' she hissed at him. 'I am angry. I am angry with you.'

He nodded, he would not argue with her, and clearly it mattered to him very little one way or the other what she chose to call it. 'Then I shall pray for you to recover your temper rather than your wits,' he said. He turned for the front door where his horse was waiting.

Lady Dudley completely ignored John Dee as he went past, though he paused and bowed, as calm as ever. When they were both gone she suddenly seemed to realise that in a moment she would be too late and she hurried out after them to the top of the steps. She flung open the big double doors and the wintry sunshine poured into the dark hall. I was dazzled and half-closed my eyes, seeing her as a shadow at the top of the steps. For a moment it seemed to me that she was not on a broad stone step but on a very knife edge of life and death, and I stepped forward and put out my hand to steady her. At my touch she whirled around and she would have fallen down the stone steps if John Dee had not caught her arm and held her.

'Don't touch me!' she spat at me. 'Don't you dare to touch me!'

'I thought I saw . . .'

John Dee released her and looked carefully at me. 'What did you see, Hannah?'

I shook my head. Even when he drew me quickly to one side, almost out of earshot, I did not speak. 'It is too vague,' I said. 'I am sorry. It was as if she was balanced on the very edge of something, and she might fall, and then she nearly did fall. It is nothing.'

He nodded. 'When you come to court we will try again,' he said. 'I think you still have your gift, Hannah. I think the angels are still speaking to you. It is just our dull mortal senses that cannot hear them.'

'You are delaying my lord,' Lady Dudley said sharply to him.

John Dee looked down the steps to where Lord Robert was swinging into his saddle. 'He will forgive me,' he said. He took her hand and was going to bow over it, but she pulled it away from him.

'Thank you for my visit,' he said.

'Any friend of my lord's is always welcome,' she said through lips that hardly moved. 'Whatever sorts of company he chooses to keep.'

John Dee went down the steps, mounted his horse, raised his hat to her ladyship, smiled at me, and the two men rode away.

As she watched them go I could feel the anger and resentment towards him bleeding out of her like a wound until all that was left was the hurt and the injury. She stood straight until they rounded the corner of the park and then she buckled at the knees and Mrs Oddingsell took her arm to lead her inside and up the stairs to her chamber.

'What now?' I asked when Mrs Oddingsell came out, carefully shutting the door behind her.

'Now she will weep and sleep for a few days and then she will get up and be like a woman half-dead: cold and empty inside, no tears to shed, no anger, no love to give. And then she will be like a hound on a short leash until he comes back, and then her anger will spill out again.'

'Over and over?' I asked, inwardly horrified at this cycle of pain and anger.

'Over and over again,' she said. 'The only time she was at peace was when she thought they would behead him. Then she could grieve for him and for herself and for the love they had shared when they were young.'

'She wanted him to die?' I asked incredulously.

'She is not afraid of death,' Mrs Oddingsell said sadly. 'I think she longs for it, for them both. What other release can there be for them?'

Spring 1558

I waited for news from court, but I could hear nothing except common gossip. The baby which was due in March was late, and by April people were starting to say that the queen had made a mistake again, and there was no child. I found myself on my knees in the Philipses' little chapel every morning and evening, praying before a statue of Our Lady that the queen might be with child and that she might be, even now, in childbirth. I could not imagine how she would be able to bear it if she were to be once more disappointed. I knew her for a courageous woman, no woman braver in the world, but to come out of the confinement chamber for the second time and tell the world that once again it had been a ten-month mistake and there was no baby – I could not see how any woman could bear the humiliation of it, least of all the Queen of England with every eye in Europe on her.

The gossip about her was all malice. People said that she had pretended to be pregnant on purpose to try to bring her husband home, people said that she had plans to smuggle in a secret baby and pass him off as a Roman Catholic prince for England. I did not even defend her against the spiteful whispers that I heard every day. I knew her, as none of them did, and I knew that she was utterly incapable of lying to her husband, or lying to her people. She was utterly determined to do right by her God, and that would always come first for her. The queen adored Philip and would have done almost anything in the world to have him by her side. But she would never have sinned for him nor for any man. She would never deny her God.

But as the weather warmed, and the baby did not come, I thought that her God must be a harsh deity indeed if he could take the prayers and the suffering of such a queen and not give her a child to love.

> *Mistress Boy,*
> *The queen is to come out of her confinement soon, and I need you here to advise me. You may bring me my blue velvet missal which I left in the chapel at my seat and come at once. Robt.*

I went to the chapel, with Danny walking before me. I had to stoop low so that he could hold my fingers with both his hands, and walk with my support. My back ached by the time we got to the chapel and I sat in Robert's chair and let Danny make his way down one of the pews, steadying himself on the seat. I would never have believed that I would have stooped till my back ached for the amusement of a small boy, and yet when I had the missal and we walked back to our chamber I bent low again to let Danny hold on to my fingers. I prayed in silence that perhaps even now, the queen might have a son and might know joy like this, such a strange, unexpected joy – the happiness of caring for a child whose whole life was in my hands.

He was not an ordinary child. Even I, who knew so little about children, could tell that. Like a house with shuttered windows the child had shielded himself, and in closing doors and windows, had shut himself away from the life of the world outside. I felt that I was standing outside, calling for a response that might never come. But I was determined to go on calling to him.

The court was at Richmond and the moment I arrived I knew that something had happened. There was an air of suppressed excitement in the stables, everyone was gossiping in corners and there was no-one to take our horses, not even the Dudley grooms.

I threw the reins to the nearest young man, and with Danny on my hip strode up the flagged path to the garden entrance of the palace. There were more people whispering in groups and I felt a clutch of fear at my heart. What if one of Elizabeth's many plots had brought a rebellion right here to the heart of a royal palace and she had the queen under arrest? Or what if the queen had gone into labour with this late-conceived baby, and it had been the death of her as so many people had warned her that it would be?

I did not dare to ask a stranger, for fear of the reply I might get, so I pushed on, walking faster and faster, through the entrance to the inner hall, looking for a friendly face. Looking for someone to ask, someone that I could trust. At the back of the hall was Will Somers, sitting all alone, very isolated from the other whispering groups of people. I went up to him and touched him gently on the shoulder.

His dull gaze went first to Danny and then to me. He did not recognise me. 'Mistress, I can do nothing for you,' he said shortly, and turned his head away. 'I have no spirits for jests today, I could only manage the lowest of humour, for I am very low myself.'

'Will, it's me.'

At my voice he paused and looked at me more closely. 'Hannah? Hannah the Fool? Hannah, the Invisible Fool?'

I nodded at the implied reproach. 'Will, what has happened?'

He did not remark on my clothes, on my child, on anything. 'It's the queen,' he said.

'Oh, Will, she's not dead?'

He shook his head. 'Not yet. But it can only be a matter of time.'

'The baby?' I asked with a swift sure painful knowledge.

'It's happened again,' he said. 'There was no baby. Again. And again she is the laughing stock of Europe and the mistress of her own humiliation.'

Without thinking I stretched out my hands to him for comfort and he gripped them tightly.

'Is she ill?' I whispered after a moment.

'Her women say that she will not rise up from the floor,' he said. 'She sits, hunched on the floorboards, more like a beggar woman than a queen. I don't know how it can have happened, Hannah. I don't know how it can have come about. When I think of her as a child, so bright and bonny, when I think of the care her mother gave her, and her father adoring her and calling her his own, his best Princess of Wales, and now this miserable ending . . . what will happen next?'

'Why? What will happen next?' I repeated, aghast.

439

He hunched a shoulder and gave me a crooked sad smile. 'Nothing much here,' he said dismissively. 'It's at Hatfield that it will all happen. There is the heir, clearly, we can't make one here. We've had two tries at an heir here and all we get is wind. Not the right sort of air at all. But at Hatfield – why, there is half her court already, and the rest rushing to join them. *She'll* have her speech ready, I don't doubt. She'll be all prepared for the day when they tell her that the queen is dead and she is the new queen. She'll have it all planned, where she will sit and what she will say.'

'You're right.' I shared his bitterness. 'And she has her speech ready. She's going to say: "This is the Lord's doing; it is marvellous in our eyes".'

Will gave a bitter crow of laughter. 'Good God! She is a marvellous princess. How d'you know that? How d'you know she's going to say that?'

I could feel a gurgle of laughter in my throat. 'Oh, Will! She asked me what the queen was going to say at her accession, and when I told her she thought it so good she would use it herself.'

'Well, why not?' he asked, suddenly bitter again. 'She will have taken everything else. Queen Mary's own husband, the people's love, the throne, and now the very words out of her sister's mouth.'

I nodded. 'Do you think I can see the queen?'

He smiled. 'She won't recognise you. You have become a beautiful woman, Hannah. Is it just the gown? You should pay your dressmaker well. Was it her that transformed you?'

I shook my head. 'Love, I think.'

'For your husband? You found him, did you?'

'I found him, and then I lost him almost at once, Will, because I was a fool, filled with pride and jealousy. But I have his son, and he has taught me to love without thinking of myself. I love him more than I thought possible. More than I knew I could love anyone. This is my son, Danny. And if we ever see his father again I will be able to tell him that I am a woman grown at last, and ready for love.'

Will smiled at Danny, who shyly dipped his head and then looked into Will's kindly creased face and smiled back.

'Can you hold him for me, while I ask at her door if I may see the queen?'

Will held out his arms and Danny went to him with the easy trust that Will inspired in everyone. I went up the sweep of stairs to the queen's presence chamber and then to the closed door of her private rooms. My name got me as far as her privy chamber and then I saw Jane Dormer standing at the closed door.

'Jane, it is me,' I said. 'Hannah.'

It was a sign of the depth of the queen's grief and Jane's despair that she did not remark on my unexpected return, nor on my new costume.

'Perhaps she'll speak to you,' she said very quietly, alert for eavesdroppers. 'Be careful what you say. Don't mention the king, nor the baby.'

I felt my courage evaporate. 'Jane, I don't know that she would want to see me, can you ask?'

Her hands were in the small of my back pushing me forward. 'And don't mention Calais,' she said. 'Nor the burnings. Nor the cardinal.'

'Why not the cardinal?' I demanded, trying to wriggle away. 'D'you mean Cardinal Pole?'

'He is sick,' she said. 'And disgraced. He's recalled to Rome. If he dies or if he goes to Rome for punishment, she will be utterly alone.'

'Jane, I can't go in there and comfort her. There is nothing I can say to comfort her. She has lost everything.'

'There is nothing anyone can say,' she said brutally. 'She is as low down as a woman can be driven, and yet she has to rise up. She is still queen. She has to rise up and rule this country, or Elizabeth will push her off the throne within a week. If she does not sit on her throne, Elizabeth will push her into her grave.'

Jane opened the door for me with one hand and thrust me into the room with the other. I stumbled in and dropped to a curtsey and heard the door close softly behind me.

The room was in deep shade, still shuttered for confinement. I looked around. The queen was not seated on any of the looming chairs nor crumpled in the great bed. She was not on her knees before her prie-dieu. I could not see her anywhere.

Then I heard a little noise, a tiny sound, like a child catching her breath after a bout of sobbing. A sound so small and so thin and so poignant that it was like a child who has cried for so long that she has forgotten to cry, and despaired of the grief ever going away.

'Mary,' I whispered. 'Where are you?'

As my eyes grew accustomed to the darkness I finally made her out. She was lying on the floor amid the rushes, face turned towards the skirting board, hunched like a starving woman will hunch over her empty belly. I crawled on my hands and knees across the floor towards her, sweeping aside the strewing herbs as I went, their scent billowing around me as I approached her and gently touched her shoulders.

She did not respond. I don't think she even knew I was there. She was locked in a grief so deep and so impenetrable that I thought she would be trapped in that inner darkness for the rest of her life.

I stroked her shoulder as one might stroke a dying animal. Since words could do nothing, a gentle touch might help; but I did not know if she could even feel that. Then, I lifted her shoulders gently from the floor, put her head in my lap and took her hood from her poor weary head and wiped the tears as they poured from her closed eyelids down her tired lined face. I sat with her in silence until her deeper breathing told me that she had fallen asleep. Even in her sleep the tears still welled up from her closed eyelids and ran down her wet cheeks.

When I came out of the queen's rooms, Lord Robert was there.

'You,' I said, without much pleasure.

'Aye, me,' he said. 'And no need to look so sour. I am not to blame.'

'You're a man,' I observed. 'And men are mostly to blame for the sorrow that women suffer.'

He gave a short laugh. 'I am guilty of being a man, I admit it. You can come and dine in my rooms. I had them make you some broth and some bread and some fruit. Your boy is there too. Will has him.'

I went with him, his arm around my waist.

'Is she ill?' he asked, his mouth to my ear.

'I have never seen anyone in a worse state,' I said.

'Bleeding? Sick?'

'Broken-hearted,' I said shortly.

He nodded at that and swept me into his rooms. They were not the grand Dudley rooms that he used to command at court. They were a modest set of three rooms but he had them arranged very neat with a couple of beds for his servants, and a privy chamber for himself and a fire with a pot of broth sitting beside it, and a table laid for the three of us. As we went in Danny looked up from Will's lap and made a little crow, the greatest noise he ever made, and stretched up for me. I took him in my arms.

'Thank you,' I said to Will.

'He was a comfort to me,' he said frankly.

'You can stay, Will,' Robert said. 'Hannah is going to dine with me.'

'I have no appetite,' Will said. 'I have seen so much sorrow in this country that my belly is full of it. I am sick of sorrow. I wish I could have a little joy for seasoning.'

'Times will change,' Robert said encouragingly. 'Changing already.'

'You'd be ready for new times, for one,' Will said, his spirit rising up. 'Since in the last reign you were one of the greatest lords and in this one you were a traitor waiting for the axe. I imagine change would be very welcome to you. What d'you hope from the next, my lord? What has the next queen promised you?'

I felt a little shiver sweep over me. It was the very question that Robert Dudley's servant had posed, the very question that everyone was asking. What might not come to Robert, if Elizabeth adored him?

'Nothing but good for the country,' Robert said easily with a pleasant smile. 'Come and dine with us, Will. You're among friends.'

'All right,' he said, seating himself at the table and drawing a bowl towards him. I hitched Danny on to the chair beside me so that he could eat from my bowl and I took a glass of wine that Lord Robert poured for me.

'Here's to us,' Robert said, raising his glass in an ironic toast. 'A heartbroken queen, an absent king, a lost baby, a queen in waiting and two fools and a reformed traitor. Here's health.'

'Two fools and an old traitor,' Will said, raising his glass. 'Three fools together.'

Summer 1558

Almost by default, I found myself back in the queen's service. She was so anxious and suspicious of everyone around her that she would be served only by people who had been with her from the earliest days. She hardly seemed to notice that I had been away from her for more than two years, and was now a woman grown, and dressed like a woman. She liked to hear me read to her in Spanish, and she liked me to sit by her bed while she slept. The deep sadness that had invaded her with the failure of her second pregnancy meant that she had no curiosity about me. I told her that my father had died, that I had married my betrothed, and that we had a child. She was interested only that my husband and I were separated – he in France, safe, I hoped, while I was in England. I did not name the town of Calais, she was as mortified by the loss of the town, England's glory, as she was shamed by the loss of the baby.

'How can you bear not to be with your husband?' she asked suddenly, after three long hours of silence one grey afternoon.

'I miss him,' I said, startled at her suddenly speaking to me. 'But I hope to find him again. I will go to France as soon as it is possible, I will go and look for him. Or I hope he will come to me. If you would help me send a message it would ease my heart.'

She turned towards the window and looked out at the river. 'I keep a fleet of ships ready for the king to come to me,' she said. 'And horses and lodgings all along the road from Dover to London. They are all waiting for him. They spend their lives, they earn their livings in waiting for him. A small army of men does nothing but wait for

444

him. I, the Queen of England, his own wife, waits for him. Why does he not come?'

There was no answer that I could give her. There was no answer that anyone could give her. When she asked the Spanish ambassador he bowed low and murmured that the king had to be with his army – she must understand the need of that – the French were still threatening his lands. It satisfied her for a day, but the next day, when she looked for him, the Spanish ambassador had gone.

'Where is he?' the queen asked. I was holding her hood, waiting for her maid to finish arranging her hair. Her beautiful chestnut hair had gone grey and thin now, when it was brushed out it looked sparse and dry. The lines on her face and the weariness in her eyes made her seem far older than her forty-two years.

'Where is who, Your Grace?' I asked.

'The Spanish ambassador, Count Feria?'

I stepped forward and handed her hood to her maid, wishing that I could think of something clever to divert her. I glanced at Jane Dormer who was close friends with the Spanish count and saw a swift look of consternation cross her face. There would be no help from her. I gritted my teeth and told her the truth. 'I believe he has gone to see the princess.'

The queen turned around to look at me, her eyes shocked. 'Why? Hannah? Why would he do that?'

I shook my head. 'How would I know, Your Grace? Does he not go to present his compliments to the princess now and then?'

'No. He does not. For most of his time in England she has been under house arrest, a suspected traitor, and he himself urged me to execute her. Why would he go to pay his compliments now?'

None of us answered. She took the hood from the waiting woman's hands and put it on, meeting her own honest eyes in the mirror. 'The king will have ordered him to go. I know Feria, he is not a man to plot wilfully. The king will have ordered him to go.'

She was silent for a moment, thinking what she should do. I kept my gaze down, I could not bear to look up and see her, facing the knowledge that her own husband was sending messages to her heir, to her rival, to his mistress.

When she turned back to us her expression was calm. 'Hannah, a word with you, please,' she said, extending her hand.

I went to her side and she took my arm and leaned on me slightly as we walked from the room to her presence chamber. 'I want you to go to Elizabeth,' she said quietly, as they opened the doors. There was hardly anyone outside waiting to see her. They were all at Hatfield. 'Just go as if for a visit. Tell her you have recently come back from Calais and wanted to see how she did. Can you do that?'

'I would have to take my son,' I temporised.

'Take him,' she nodded. 'And see if you can find out from Elizabeth herself, or from her ladies, what Count Feria wanted with her.'

'They may tell me nothing,' I said uncomfortably. 'Surely, they will know I serve you.'

'You can ask,' she said. 'And you are the only friend that I can trust who will gain admission to Elizabeth. You have always passed between us. She likes you.'

'Perhaps the ambassador was making nothing more than a courtesy visit.'

'Perhaps,' she said. 'But it may be that the king is pressing her to marry the Prince of Savoy. She has sworn to me that she will not have him but Elizabeth has no principles, she has only appearances. If the king promised to support her claim to be my heir, she might think it worth her while to marry his cousin. I have to know.'

'When d'you want me to go?' I asked unwillingly.

'At first light tomorrow,' she said. 'And don't write to me, I am surrounded by spies. I will wait for you to tell me what she is planning when you come back to me.'

Queen Mary released my arm and went on alone into dinner. As the noblemen and the gentry rose to their feet as she walked towards the high table in the great hall I noticed how small she seemed: a diminutive woman overwhelmed by her duties in a hostile world. I watched her step up to her throne, seat herself and look around her depleted court with her tight determined smile and thought – not for the first time – that she was the most courageous woman I had ever known. A woman with the worst luck in the world.

It was a merry ride to Hatfield for Danny and me. He rode the horse astride before me until he grew too tired, and then I strapped him to my back and he slept, rocked by the jolting. I had an escort of two men to keep me safe; since the epidemic of illness of the winter, and the hardship of one bad harvest after another, the roads were continually threatened by highwaymen, bandits, or just vagrants and beggars who would shout for money and threaten violence. But with the two men trotting behind us, Daniel and I were light-hearted. The weather was fine, the rain had stopped at last, and the sun was so hot by midday that we were pleased to break our fast in a field, sheltering in a wood, or sometimes by a river or stream. I let Danny paddle his feet, or sit bare-arsed in the water while it splashed around him. He was steady on his feet now, he made little rushes forward and back to me, and he continually demanded to be lifted upward to see more, to touch things, or simply to pat my face and turn my gaze this way and that.

As we rode I sang to him, the Spanish songs of my childhood, and I was certain that he heard me. His little hand would wave in time to the music, he would give a little wriggle of pleasure when I started singing, but he never joined in the tune. He remained as silent as a leveret in hiding, as a fawn in the bracken.

The old palace at Hatfield had been the royal nursery for generations, chosen for its clean air and proximity to London. It was an old building, small-windowed and dark-beamed, and the men led the way to the front door so that Danny and I might dismount and go inside while they took the horses away to the ramshackle stable block at a little distance from the house.

There was no-one in the hall to greet us but a boy bringing in logs for the fire which was kept going, even in midsummer. 'They're all in the garden,' he said. 'Acting a play.'

His gesture directed me to a door at the rear of the hall and with Danny in my arms I opened it, followed the stone corridor to another door and then stepped out into the sunshine.

What play-acting there had been was clearly over, and what was left was a romp. Veils of cloth of gold and silver and overturned chairs were scattered around the orchard, and Elizabeth's ladies were running in all directions from a man in the centre of the circle with a dark scarf over his face to blindfold him. As I watched he caught a flying skirt and drew a girl to him but she wriggled free and ran away laughing. They

447

gathered around him and with much giggling and cooing they turned him round and round until he was dizzy and then they retreated. Again he dashed and lunged, while they ran this way and that, giggling with that heady mixture of girlish playfulness and female arousal. Among them, her red hair flying loose, her hood cast away, her face flushed and laughing, was the princess. She was not the Elizabeth I had seen white-faced with terror. She was not the princess I had seen bloated on her bed, sick to her very bones with fear. She was a princess coming into the midsummer of her life, coming into her womanhood, coming to the throne. She was a fairytale princess, beautiful, powerful, wilful, infallible.

'Well, glory be,' I whispered to myself, as sceptical as any fool.

As I watched she tapped the blindfolded man on the shoulder and made to run back again. This time he was too quick for her. His hand flashed out, she sprang back just too slowly, he snatched her at the waist and though she struggled he held her close. He must have felt her panting against him. He must have smelled the perfume in her hair. He must have known her at once.

'I have caught you!' he called out. 'Who is it?'

'You have to guess! You have to guess!' the ladies cried.

He ran his hand over her forehead, her hair, her nose, her lips. 'A beauty,' he said certainly. He was rewarded by a gale of shocked laughter.

Impertinently, he let his hand stray down over her chin, down her neck, he took her throat in his hand. I saw the colour flame into Elizabeth's cheeks and I realised she was on fire with desire at his touch. She did not step back from him, she did not move to check him. She was ready to stand before him and let him finger her all over, watched by all her court.

I moved a little forward to see this man better, but the blindfold covered all of his face, I could see only his thick dark hair and the strong square shoulders. I thought I knew who this man was.

He held her firmly, and there was a little whisper almost of dismay from her ladies as he gripped her with one hand at the waist, and with the other traced the border of the neck of her gown, his fingertips brushing the tops of her breasts. Slowly, tantalisingly, he slid his hand down the front of her gown over the embroidered stomacher, past the

448

girdle at her waist, over the thick skirt of her gown at the front as if he would pat her sex, shielded by petticoats, as if he would touch her like a whore. Still the princess did not stop him, still she did not step back from him. She stood stock still pressed against this man with his one hand around her waist, pulling her close to him as if she were a loose-lived maid who would offer a squeeze and a kiss. She did not resist even when his hand went down the front of her gown, to her very crotch beneath her petticoats, and then round her back to take hold of her buttocks in his hand, then he slid his other hand down from her waist, so that he was embracing her, so that he had her arse in both hands, as if she were his own woman.

Elizabeth gave a little soft moan and twisted from his grip, almost falling back amongst her ladies. 'Who was it? Who was it?' they chanted, relieved that she had freed herself from his embrace.

'I give up,' he said. 'I cannot play some foolish game. I have touched the very curves of heaven.'

He pulled the blindfold from his eyes and I saw his face. His eyes met Elizabeth's. He knew exactly who it had been in his arms, he had known from the moment he had caught her, as he had intended to do; as she had intended him to do. He had caressed her in front of all the court, caressed her as an accepted lover, and she had let him stroke her as if she were a whore. She smiled at him, her knowing desirous smile, and he smiled back.

Of course, the man was my lord Robert Dudley.

'And what are you doing here, child?' he asked me before dinner, walking on the terrace, the ladies of Elizabeth's little court observing our progress while pretending not to watch.

'Queen Mary sent me to pay her compliments to Elizabeth.'

'Oho, my little spy, are you at work again?'

'Yes, and most unwillingly.'

'And what does the queen want to know?' He paused for a moment. 'Anything about William Pickering? About me?'

I shook my head. 'Nothing that I know of.'

He drew me to a stone seat. There was honeysuckle growing on the wall behind me and the smell was very sweet. He reached over and plucked a flower. The petals, scarlet and honey, lolled like the tongue of a snake. He brushed my neck with it. 'So what does the queen want?'

'She wants to know what Count Feria was doing here,' I said simply. 'Is he here?'

'Left yesterday.'

'What did he want?'

'He brought a message from the king. Queen Mary's own beloved husband. A faithless dog, isn't he, the randy old Spaniard?'

'Why d'you say that?'

'Mistress Boy, I have a wife who does me no service, and shows me no kindness, but not even I would court her own sister under her nose and shame her while she was still living.'

I swayed in my seat and took hold of his hand which was still playing with the flower. 'He is courting Elizabeth?'

'The Pope has been approached to give permission for their marriage,' he said flatly. 'How is that for Spanish punctilio for you? If the queen lives then it's my guess that Philip will apply for an annulment of their marriage and marry Elizabeth. If the queen dies, then Elizabeth is heir to the throne and an even richer plum for the picking. He will snap her up within the year.'

I looked at him, my face quite blank with horror. 'This cannot be,' I said, appalled. 'It's a betrayal. It's the worst thing he could do to her. The worst thing he could do to her in all the world.'

'It's an unexpected move,' he said. 'Disagreeable for a loving wife.'

'The queen would die of grief and shame. To be put aside, as her mother was put aside? And for Anne Boleyn's daughter?'

He nodded. 'As I said, a faithless Spanish dog.'

'And Elizabeth?'

He glanced over my shoulder and he rose to his feet. 'You can ask her yourself.'

I slid into a curtsey, and then came up. Elizabeth's black eyes snapped at me. She did not like to see me seated beside Robert Dudley with him stroking my neck with honeysuckle flowers.

'Princess.'

'I heard you were back. My lord said that you had become a woman. I did not expect to see you quite so . . .'

450

I waited.

'Fat,' she said.

Instead of being insulted, as she intended, I giggled out loud at the childish jealous rudeness of her.

At once her eyes danced too. Elizabeth never sulked.

'Whereas you, Princess, are more beautiful than ever,' I said smoothly.

'I hope so. And what were you talking about with your heads so close together?'

'About you,' I said simply. 'The queen sent me to find out how you did. And I was glad to come and see you.'

'I warned you not to leave it too late,' she said, her gesture taking in the waiting women, the lounging handsome men, the courtiers from London who saw me recognise them and looked a little abashed. A couple of members of the queen's council stepped back from my scrutiny; with them was an envoy of France, and a minor prince or two.

'I see your ladyship keeps a merry court,' I said evenly. 'As you should. And I cannot join you, even if you would condescend to have me. I have to serve your sister. She does not have a merry court, she has few friends. I would not leave her now.'

'Then you must be the only person in England who has not deserted her,' she said cheerfully. 'I took on her cook last week. Does she get anything to eat at all?'

'She manages,' I said drily. 'And even the Spanish ambassador, Count Feria, her greatest friend and trusted councillor, was missing from court when I left.'

She shot a quick look at Robert Dudley and I saw him nod permission for her to speak.

'I refused his request,' she said gently. 'I have no plans to marry anyone. You can assure the queen of that, for it is true.'

I gave her a little curtsey. 'I am glad not to have to take her any news which would make her yet more unhappy.'

'I wish she would feel some distress for the people of the country,' Elizabeth said sharply. 'The burning of heretics goes on, Hannah, the agony of innocent people. You should tell the queen that her sadness at the loss of a child who never was is nothing compared with the grief of a woman who sees her son go to the stake. And there are hundreds of women who have been forced to watch that.'

Robert Dudley came to my rescue. 'Shall we dine?' he asked lightly. 'And there will be music after dinner. I demand a dance.'

'Only one?' she queried, her mood lifting at once.

'Only one,' he said.

She made a little flirtatious pouting face.

'The one that starts when the music starts after dinner and ends when the sun comes up and no-one can dance another step,' he said. 'That one.'

'And what shall we do then, when we have danced ourselves to a standstill?' she asked provocatively.

I looked from her to him, I could hardly believe the intimacy of their tone. Anyone who heard them would have thought them to be lovers in the very first days of their desire.

'We will do whatever you wish, of course,' he said, his voice like silk. 'But I know what I would wish.'

'What?' she breathed.

'To lie with . . .'

'With?'

'The morning sun on my face,' he finished.

Elizabeth stepped a little closer to him and whispered a phrase in Latin. I kept my expression deliberately blank. I had understood the Latin as readily as Lord Robert, she had whispered that she wanted kisses in the morning . . . From the sun, of course.

She turned to her court. 'We will dine,' she announced out loud. She walked alone, head up, towards the doors to the great hall. As she went into the dark interior she paused and threw a glance at Lord Robert over her shoulder. I saw the invitation in her look, and almost like a moment of dizziness, I recognised that look. I had seen that very same look before, to the queen's husband King Philip. And I had seen that look before then, when she had been a girl and I had been a child: to Lord Thomas Seymour, her stepmother's husband. It was the same look, it was the invitation of the same desire. Elizabeth liked to choose her lovers from the husbands of other women, she liked to arouse desire from a man whose hands were tied, she liked to triumph over a woman who could not keep her husband, and more than anything in the world, she liked to throw that look over her shoulder and see a man start forward to go to her side – as Lord Robert started now.

Elizabeth's court was a young merry optimistic court. It was the court of a young woman waiting for her fortune, waiting for her throne, certain, now, that it would come to her. It hardly mattered that the queen had not named her as heir; all the time-serving, self-serving men of the queen's court and council had already pledged their allegiance to this rising star. Half of them had sons and daughters in her service already. The visit from Count Feria was nothing more than another straw in the wind which was blowing smoothly and sweetly towards Hatfield. It told everyone that the queen's power, like her happiness, like her health, had waned. Even the queen's husband had transferred to her rival.

It was a merry, joyful summertime court and I spent the afternoon and night in that happy company. It left me sick and chilled to the bone. I slept in a little bed with my arms tight around my child, and the next day we rode back to the queen.

I made sure I did not count how many great men and women we passed on the road to Hatfield, going in the opposite direction. I did not need to add to the sour taste of sickness in my mouth. Long before this day, I had seen the court move from a sick king to a waiting heir and I knew how light is the fidelity of courtiers. But even so, even though I had known it, there was something about the turn of this tide that felt more like the dishonourable turning of a coat.

I found the queen walking by the river, no more than a handful of courtiers behind her. I marked who they were; half of them at least were the dourest most solid Catholics whose faith would never change whoever was on the throne, a couple of Spanish noblemen, hired by the king to stay at court and bear his wife company, and Will Somers, faithful Will Somers, who called himself a fool but had never, in my hearing, said a foolish word.

'Your Grace,' I said, and swept her my curtsey.

The queen took in my appearance, the mud on my cloak, the child at my side.

'You have come straight from Hatfield?'

'As you commanded.'

'Can someone take the child?'

Will stepped forward and Danny beamed. I set him down and he gave his quiet little gurgle of pleasure and toddled towards Will.

'I am sorry to bring him to Your Grace, I thought you might like to see him,' I said awkwardly.

She shook her head. 'No, Hannah, I do not ever want to see him.' She gestured for me to walk beside her. 'Did you see Elizabeth?'

'Yes.'

'And what did she say of the ambassador?'

'I spoke to one of her women.' I was anxious not to identify Lord Robert as the favourite at this treacherous alternative court. 'She said that the ambassador had visited to pay his compliments.'

'And what else?'

I hesitated. My duty to be honest to the queen and my desire not to hurt her seemed to be in utter conflict. I had puzzled about this for all of the ride back to court and I had decided that I should be as faithless as the rest of them. I could not bring myself to tell her that her own husband was proposing marriage to her own sister.

'He was pressing the suit of the Duke of Savoy,' I said. 'Elizabeth herself assured me that she would not marry him.'

'The Duke of Savoy?' she asked.

I nodded.

The queen reached out her hand and I took it and waited, not knowing what she would say to me. 'Hannah, you have been my friend for many years, and a true friend, I think.'

'Yes, Your Grace.'

She lowered her voice to a whisper. 'Hannah, sometimes I think I have run mad, quite mad, with jealousy and unhappiness.'

Her dark eyes filled with tears. I held tightly to her hand. 'What is it?'

'I am doubting him. I am doubting my own husband. I am doubting our marriage vows. If I doubt this then my world will fall apart, and yet I do doubt.'

454

I did not know what to say. Her grip on my hand was painful but I did not flinch. 'Queen Mary?'

'Hannah, answer me a question and then I will never think of this again. But answer me truly, and tell no-one.'

I gulped, wondering what terror was opening up beneath my feet. 'I will, Your Grace.' Inwardly I promised myself that if the question endangered me, or Danny, or my lord; I would allow myself to lie. The familiar tremor of fear of court life was making my heart flutter, I could hear it pounding in my ears. The queen was white as a shroud, her eyes madly intent.

'Was there any suggestion that the king was pressing his own suit?' she whispered, so low that I could hardly hear her. 'Even though he is my husband, even though he is forsworn before God, the Pope, and our two kingdoms? Please tell me, Hannah. I know that it is the question of a madwoman. I know that I am his wife and he could not be doing this. But I have become filled with the thought that he is courting her, not as a pastime, not as a flirtation: but for his wife. I have to know. I am tortured by this fear.'

I bit my lip, and she needed nothing more. With the quick apprehension of a woman seeing her worst fear, she knew it at once.

'Dear God, it *is* so,' she said slowly. 'I thought that my suspicion of him was part of my illness, but it is not. I can see it on your face. He is courting my sister for marriage. My own sister? And my own husband?'

I clasped her cold hand between my own. 'Your Grace, this is a matter of policy for the king,' I said. 'Like making a will to provide for the future. He has to provide in the case of your accident or death. He is trying to secure England for Spain. It is his duty to keep England safe, and in the true faith. And if you were to die, sometime in the future, if he were to marry Elizabeth after your death then England would remain Roman Catholic – and that is what you and he wanted to secure.'

She shook her head, as if she were trying to hear my rapid words but none of them made any sense to her. 'Dearest God, this is the very worst thing that could ever have happened to me,' she said quietly. 'I saw my mother pushed from her throne and shamed by a younger woman who took the king from her and laughed as she did it. And now this woman's daughter, the very same bastard daughter, does just the same thing to me.'

She broke off and looked at me. 'No wonder I couldn't believe it. No wonder I thought it was my own mad suspicion,' she said. 'It is the thing I have feared all my life. Ending up like my own mother, neglected, abandoned, with a Boleyn whore in triumph on the throne. When will this wickedness stop? When will the witchcraft of the Boleyns be defeated? They cut off her head and yet here is her daughter rising up like a serpent with the same poison in her mouth!'

I gave her hand a little tug. 'Your Grace, don't give way. Not here. Not here before all these people.'

I was thinking of her, and I was thinking of Elizabeth's court who would laugh till they cried if they heard that the queen had broken down because she had heard at last what all of Europe had known for months – that her husband had betrayed her.

She shook from head to toe with the effort; but she drew herself up, she blinked back the tears. 'You are right,' she said. 'I will not be shamed. I will say nothing more. I will think nothing more. Walk with me, Hannah.'

I glanced back at Danny. Will was seated on the ground with the boy astride his knees, showing him how he could wiggle his ears. Danny's chuckle was delighted. I took the queen's arm and matched my stride to her slow pace. The court fell in behind us, yawning.

The queen looked out over the swiftly moving water. There were few ships coming and going, trade was bad for England, at war with France and with the fields yielding less and less each year.

'You know,' the queen whispered to me, 'you know, Hannah, I loved him from the moment I first saw his portrait. D'you remember?'

'Yes,' I said, also remembering my warning that he would break her heart.

'I adored him when I met him, d'you remember our wedding day, when he looked so handsome and we were so happy?'

I nodded again.

'I worshipped him when he took me to bed and lay with me. He gave me the only joy I had ever known in all my life. Nobody knows what he was to me, Hannah. Nobody will ever know how much I have loved him. And now you tell me that he is planning to marry my worst enemy when I am dead. He is looking forward to my death and his life after it.'

She stood quietly for a few moments as her court halted aimlessly behind her, looking from her to me and wondering what fresh bad news I had brought. Then I saw her stiffen, and her hand went to her eyes, as if she had a sudden pain. 'Unless he does not wait for my death,' she said quietly.

A quick glance at my white face told her the rest of the story. She shook her head. 'No, never,' she whispered. 'Not this. He would never divorce me? Not as my father did to my mother? With no grounds except lust for another woman? And she a whore, and the daughter of a whore?'

I said nothing.

She did not cry. She was Queen Mary who had been Princess Mary, who had learned as a little girl to keep her head up and her tears back and if her lips were bitten to ribbons and her mouth was filled with blood then what did it matter, as long as she did not cry where anyone could see her?

She just nodded, as if she had taken a hard knock to the head. Then she beckoned to Will Somers and he came forward, Daniel at his side, and gently took her outstretched hand.

'You know, Will,' she said softly, 'it's a funny thing, worthy of your wit, but it seems to me that the greatest terror of my life, which I would have done anything to avoid, would have been to end my life as my mother ended hers: abandoned by my husband, childless, and with a whore in my place.' She looked at him and smiled though her eyes were dark with tears. 'And now look, Will, isn't it ridiculous? Here I am, and it has come to me. Can you make a joke about that?'

Will shook his head. 'No,' he said shortly. 'I can find no joke in that. Some things are not funny.'

She nodded.

'And, in any case, women have no sense of humour,' he said staunchly.

She could not hear him. I could see that she was still taking in the horror that her nightmare had come true. She would be like her mother, abandoned by the king, living out her life in heart-break.

'I suppose one can see why that might be,' Will remarked. 'Women's lack of humour. Given the present circumstances.'

The queen released him and turned to me. 'I am sorry I was unkind about your boy,' she said. 'He is a fine boy, I am sure. What is his name?'

Will Somers took Daniel's hand and drew him towards her.

'Daniel Carpenter, Your Grace.' I could see she was holding herself together by a thread of will.

'Daniel.' She smiled at him. 'You be a good boy when you grow up and a faithful man.' Her voice quavered for only a moment. She rested her beringed hand on his head. 'God bless you,' she said gently.

That night as I waited for Danny to fall asleep I took a page of pressed notepaper and wrote to his father.

> *Dear Husband,*
> *Living here, in the saddest court in Christendom with a queen who has never done anything but what she believed to be right and yet has been betrayed by everyone in the world that she loved, even those who were sworn before God to love her, I think of you and your long years of faithfulness to me. And I pray that one day we can be together again and you will see that I have learned to value love and to value fidelity; and to love and be faithful in return.*
> *Your wife*
> *Hannah Carpenter.*

Then I took the page, kissed his name at the top, and dropped it in the fire.

The court was due to leave for Whitehall Palace in August. The usual progress had been abandoned for the queen's pregnancy, and now that there was no child it was almost as if she had abandoned the summer as well. Certainly there was no good weather to invite the court into the country. It was cold and raining every day, the harvest would be bad again and there would be starvation up and down the land. It would be another bad year of Mary's reign, another year when God did not smile on England.

There was less fuss about moving than usual; there were fewer people travelling with the queen this year, fewer than ever before, and they had fewer goods, and hangers-on. The court was shrinking.

'Where is everybody?' I asked Will, bringing my horse beside his as we rode into the city at the head of the court train, just behind the queen in her litter.

'Hatfield,' he growled crossly.

The change of air did nothing for the queen, who complained that very night of a fever. She did not dine in the great hall of Whitehall Palace but took to her room and had two or three dishes brought to her. She hardly ate at all. I went past the great hall on my way to her chambers and stopped to glance in the door. For a moment I had a sudden powerful picture in my mind, almost as bright as a seeing: the empty throne, the greedily eating court, the ladies unsupervised, the servants kneeling to the empty throne and serving the royal dinner to the absent monarch on plates that would never be touched. It had been like this when I had first come to court, five years ago. But then it had been King Edward, sick and neglected in his rooms while the court made merry. Now it was my Queen Mary.

I stepped back and bumped into a man walking behind me. I turned with an apology. It was John Dee.

'Dr Dee!' My heart thudded with fright. I dropped him a curtsey.

'Hannah Green,' he said, bowing over my hand. 'How are you? And how is the queen?'

I glanced around to see that no-one was in earshot. 'Ill,' I said. 'Very hot, aching in all her bones, weeping eyes and running nose. Sad.'

He nodded. 'Half the city is sick,' he said. 'I don't think we've had one day of clear sunshine in the whole of this summer. How is your son?'

'Well, and I thank God for it,' I said.

'Has he spoken a word yet?'

'No.'

'I have been thinking of him and of our talk about him. There is a scholar I know, who might advise you. A physician.'

'In London?' I asked.

He took out a piece of paper. 'I wrote down his direction, in case I should meet you today. You can trust him with anything that you wish to tell him.'

I took the piece of paper with some trepidation. No-one would ever know all of John Dee's business, all of his friends.

'Are you here to see my lord?' I asked. 'We expect him tonight from Hatfield.'

'Then I shall wait in his rooms,' he said. 'I don't like to dine in the hall without the queen at its head. I don't like to see an empty throne for England.'

'No,' I said, warming to him despite my fear, as I always did. 'I was thinking that myself.'

He put his hand on mine. 'You can trust this physician,' he said. 'Tell him who you are, and what your child needs, and I know he will help you.'

Next day I took Danny on my hip and I walked towards the city to find the house of the physician. He had one of the tall narrow houses by the Inns of Court, and a pleasant girl to answer the door. She said he would see me at once if I would wait a moment in his front room, and Danny and I sat among the shelves which were filled with odd lumps of rock and stone.

He came quietly into the room and saw me examining a piece of marble, a lovely piece of rock, the colour of honey.

'Do you have an interest in stones, Mistress Carpenter?' he asked.

Gently, I put the piece down. 'No. But I read somewhere that there are different rocks occurring all over the world, some side by side, some on top of another, and no man has ever yet explained why.'

He nodded. 'Nor why some carry coal and some gold. Your friend Mr Dee and I were considering this the other day.'

I looked at him a little more closely, and I thought I recognised one of the Chosen People. He had skin that was the same colour as mine, his eyes were as dark as mine, as dark as Daniel's. He had a strong long nose and the arched eyebrows and high cheekbones that I knew and loved.

I took a breath and I took my courage and started without hesitation. 'My name was Hannah Verde. I came from Spain with my father when

I was a child. Look at the colour of my skin, look at my eyes. I am one of the People.' I turned my head and stroked my finger down my nose. 'See? This is my child, my son, he is two, he needs your help.'

The man looked at me as if he would deny everything. 'I don't know your family,' he said cautiously. 'I don't know what you mean by the People.'

'My father was a Verde in Aragon,' I said. 'An old Jewish family. We changed our name so long ago I don't know what it should have been. My cousins are the Gaston family in Paris. My husband has taken the name of Carpenter now, but he comes from the d'Israeli family. He is in Calais.' I checked when I found that my voice shook slightly at his name. 'He *was* in Calais when the town was taken. I believe he is a prisoner now. I have no recent news of him. This is his son. He has not spoken since we left Calais, he is afraid, I think. But he is Daniel d'Israeli's son, and he needs his birthright.'

'I understand you,' he said gently. 'Is there any proof you can give me of your race and your sincerity?'

I whispered very low. 'When my father died, we turned his face to the wall and we said: "Magnified and sanctified be the name of God throughout the world which He has created according to His will. May He establish His kingdom during the days of your life and during the life of all of the house of Israel, speedily, yea soon; and say ye, Amen."'

The man closed his eyes. 'Amen.' And then opened them again. 'What do you want with me, Hannah d'Israeli?'

'My son will not speak,' I said.

'He is mute?'

'He saw his wet nurse die in Calais. He has not spoken since that day.'

He nodded and took Daniel on to his knee. With great care he touched his face, his ears, his eyes. I thought of my husband learning his skill to care for the children of others, and I wondered if he would ever again see his own son, and if I could teach this child to say his father's name.

'I can see no physical reason that he should not speak,' he said.

I nodded. 'He can laugh, and he can make sounds. But he does not say words.'

'You want him circumcised?' he asked very quietly. 'It is to mark him for life. He will be known as a Jew then. He will know himself as a Jew.'

'I keep my faith in my heart now,' I said, my voice little more than a whisper. 'When I was a young woman I thought of nothing, I knew nothing. I just missed my mother. Now that I am older and I have a child of my own I know that there is more than the bond of a mother and her child. There is the People and our faith. Our little family lives within our kin. And that goes on. Whether his father is alive or dead, whether I am alive or dead, the People go on. Even though I have lost my father and my mother and now my husband, I acknowledge the People, I know there is a God, I know his name is Elohim. I still know there is a faith. And Daniel is part of it. I cannot deny it for him. I should not.'

He nodded. 'Give him to me for a moment.'

He took Daniel into an inner room. I saw the dark eyes of my son look a little apprehensively over the strange man's shoulder, and I tried to smile at him reassuringly as he was carried away. I went to the window and held on to the window latch. I clutched it so tightly that it marked my palms and I was not aware of it until my fingers had cramped tight. I heard a little cry from the inner room and I knew it was done, and Daniel was his father's son in every way.

The rabbi brought my son out to me and handed him over. 'I think he will speak,' was all he said.

'Thank you,' I replied.

He walked to the front door with me. There was no need for him to caution me, nor for me to promise him of my discretion. We both knew that on the other side of the door was a country where we were despised and hated for our race and for our faith, even though our race was the most lost and dispersed people in the world, and our faith was almost forgotten: nothing left but a few half-remembered prayers and some tenacious rituals.

'Shalom,' he said gently. 'Go in peace.'

'Shalom,' I replied.

There was no joy at the court in Whitehall, and the city, which had once marched out for Mary, now hated her. The pall of smoke from the burnings at Smithfield poisoned the air for half a mile in every direction; in truth it poisoned the air for all of England.

She did not relent. She knew with absolute certainty that those men and women who would not accept the holy sacraments of the church were doomed to burn in hell. Torture on earth was nothing compared with the pains they would suffer hereafter. And so anything that might persuade their families, their friends, the mutinous crowds who gathered at Smithfield and jeered the executioners and cursed the priests, was worth doing. There were souls to be saved despite themselves and Mary would be a good mother to her people. She would save them despite themselves. She would not listen to those who begged her to forgive rather than punish. She would not even listen to Bishop Bonner who said that he feared for the safety of the city and wanted to burn the heretics early in the morning before many people were about. She said that whatever the risk to her and to her rule, God's will must be done and be seen to be done. They must burn and they must be seen to burn. She said that pain was the lot of man and woman and was there any man who would dare to come to her, and ask her to let her people avoid the pain of sin?

Autumn 1558

In September we moved to Hampton Court in the hopes that the fresh air would clear the queen's breathing, which was hoarse and sore. The doctors offered her a mixture of oils and drinks but nothing seemed to do her any good. She was reluctant to see them, and often refused to take her medicine. I thought she was remembering how her little brother had been all but poisoned by the physicians who tried one thing and then another, and then another; but then I realised that she could not be troubled with physic, she no longer cared for anything, not even her health.

I rode to Hampton Court with Danny in a pillion saddle behind me for the first time. He was old enough and strong enough to ride astride and to hold tightly on to my waist for the short journey. He was still mute, but the wound had healed up, and he was as peaceful and as smiling as he had always been. I could tell by the tight grip on my waist that he was excited at the journey and at riding properly for the first time. The horse was gentle and steady and we ambled along beside the queen's litter down the damp dirty lanes between the fields where they were trying to harvest the wet rye crop.

Danny looked around him, never missing a moment of this, his first proper ride. He waved at the people in the field, he waved at the villagers who stood at their doorways to watch as we went by. I thought it spoke volumes for the state of the country that a woman would not wave in reply to a little boy, since he was riding in the queen's train. The country, like the town, had turned against Mary and would not forgive her.

She rode with the curtains of the litter drawn, in rocking darkness, and when we got to Hampton Court she went straight to her rooms and had the shutters closed so that she was plunged into dusk.

Danny and I rode into the stable-yard, and a groom lifted me down from the saddle. I turned and reached up for Danny. For a moment I thought he would cling and insist on staying on horseback.

'Do you want to pat the horse?' I tempted him.

His face lit up at once and he reached out his little arms for me and came tumbling down. I held him to the horse's neck and let him pat the warm sweet-smelling skin. The horse, a handsome big-boned bay, turned its head to look at him. Danny, very little, and horse, very big, stared quite transfixed by each other, and then Danny gave a deep sigh of pleasure and said: 'Good.'

It was so natural and easy that for a moment I did not realise he had spoken; and when I did realise, I hardly dared to take a breath in case I prevented him speaking again.

'He *was* a good horse, wasn't he?' I said with affected nonchalance. 'Shall we ride him again tomorrow?'

Danny looked from the horse to me. ''es,' he said decidedly.

I held him close to me and kissed his silky head. 'We'll do that then,' I said gently. 'And we'll let him go to bed now.'

My legs were weak beneath me as we walked from the stable-yard, Danny at my side, his little hand reaching up to hold mine. I could feel myself smiling, though tears were running down my cheeks. Danny would speak, Danny would grow up as a normal child. I had saved him from death in Calais, and I had brought him to life in England. I had justified the trust of his mother, and perhaps one day I would be able to tell his father that I had kept his son safe for love of him, and for love of the child. It seemed wonderful to me that his first word should be: 'good'. Perhaps it was a foreseeing. Perhaps life would be good for my son Danny.

For a little while the queen seemed better, away from the city. She walked by the river with me in the mornings or in the evenings; she could not tolerate the brightness of midday. But Hampton Court was

465

filled with ghosts. It was on these paths and in these gardens where she had walked with Philip when they were newly married and Cardinal Pole newly come from Rome and the whole of Christendom stretched before them. It was here that she had whispered to him that she was with child, and gone into her first confinement, certain of her happiness, confident of having a son. And it was here that she came out from her confinement, childless and ill, and saw Elizabeth growing in beauty and exulting in her triumph, another step closer to the throne.

'I feel no better here at all,' she said to me one day as Jane Dormer and I came in to say goodnight. She had gone to bed early again, almost doubled-up with pain from the ache in her belly and feverishly hot. 'We will go to St James' Palace next week. We will spend Christmas there. The king likes St James'.'

Jane Dormer and I exchanged one silent glance. We did not think that King Philip would come home to his wife for Christmas when he had not come home when she had lost their child, when he had not come home when she wrote to him that she was so sick that she did not see how to bear to live.

As we had feared it was a depleted court at St James' Palace. My Lord Robert had bigger and better rooms not because his star was rising, but simply because there were fewer men at court. I saw him at dinner on some days but generally he was at Hatfield, where the princess kept a merry circle about her and a constant stream of visitors flocked to her door.

They were not always playing games at the old palace either. They were planning how the country would be ruled by the princess when she came to her throne. And if I knew Elizabeth, and my Lord Robert, they would be wondering how soon it might be.

Lord Robert saw me only rarely; but he had not forgotten me. He came looking for me, one day in September. 'I have done you a great favour, I think,' he said with his charming smile. 'Are you still in love with your husband, Mrs Carpenter? Or shall we abandon him in Calais?'

'You have news of him?' I asked. I put my hand down and felt Danny's hand creep into my own.

'I might have,' he said provocatively. 'But you have not answered my question. Do you want him home in England, or shall we forget all about him?'

'I cannot jest about this, and especially not before his son,' I said. 'I want him home, my lord. Please tell me, do you have news of him?'

'His name is on this list.' He flicked the paper at me. 'Soldiers to be ransomed, townspeople who are to be returned to England. The whole of the English Pale outside Calais is to come home. If the queen can find some money in the treasury we can get them all back where they belong.'

I could feel my heart thudding. 'There is no money in the treasury,' I said. 'The country is all but ruined.'

He shrugged. 'There is money to keep the fleet waiting to escort the king home. There is money for his adventures abroad. Mention it to her as she dresses for dinner tonight, and I will speak with her after dinner.'

I waited until the queen had dragged herself up from her bed and was seated before her mirror, her maid behind her brushing her hair. Jane Dormer, who was usually such a fierce guardian of the queen's privacy, had taken the fever herself, and was lying down. It was just the queen and I and some unimportant girl from the Norfolk family.

'Your Grace,' I said simply. 'I have had news of my husband.'

She turned her dull gaze on me. 'I had forgotten you are married. Is he alive?'

'Yes,' I said. 'He is among the English men and women hoping to be ransomed out of Calais.'

She was only slightly more interested. 'Who is arranging this?'

'Lord Robert. His men have been held captive too.'

The queen sighed and turned her head away. 'Are they asking very much?'

'I don't know,' I said frankly.

'I will speak with Lord Robert,' she said, as if she were very weary. 'I will do what I can for you and your husband, Hannah.'

I knelt before her. 'Thank you, Your Grace.'

467

When I looked up I saw that she was exhausted. 'I wish I could bring my husband home so easily,' she said. 'But I don't believe he will ever come home to me again.'

The queen was too ill to transact the business herself, the fever was always worse after dinner and she could barely breathe for coughing; but she scrawled an assent on a bill on the Treasury for money and Lord Robert assured me that the business would go through. We met in the stable-yard, he was riding to Hatfield and in a hurry to be off.

'Will he come to you here at court?' he asked casually.

I hesitated, I had not thought of the details of our meeting. 'I suppose so,' I said. 'I should leave a message for him at his old house, and at my old shop in Fleet Street.'

I said nothing more, but a deeper worry was starting to dawn on me. What if Daniel's love for me had not grown, like mine, in absence? What if he had decided that I was dead and that he should make a new life elsewhere in Italy or France as he had so often said? Worse than that: what if he thought I had run away with Lord Robert and chosen a life of shame without him? What if he had cast me off?

'Can I get a message to him as he is released?' I asked.

Lord Robert shook his head. 'You will have to trust that he will come and find you,' he said cheerfully. 'Is he the faithful type of man?'

I thought of his years of steady waiting for me, and how he had watched me come to my love of him, and how he had let me go and return to him. 'Yes,' I said shortly.

Lord Robert sprang up into the saddle. 'If you see John Dee would you tell him that Princess Elizabeth wants that map of his,' he said.

'Why would she want a map?' I asked, immediately suspicious.

Lord Robert winked at me. He leaned from his horse and spoke very low. 'If the queen dies without naming Elizabeth as her heir then we may have a battle on our hands.'

His horse shifted and I stepped back quickly. 'Oh no,' I said. 'Not again.'

'No fight with the people of England,' he assured me. 'They want the Protestant princess. But with the Spanish king. D'you think he'd let such a prize slip away if he thought he could come over and claim it for himself?'

'You are arming and planning for war *again*?' I asked, dreading the answer.

'Why else would I want my soldiers back?' he demanded. 'Thank you for your help with that, Hannah.'

I choked on my shock. 'My lord!'

He patted the horse's neck and tightened the rein. 'It's always a coil,' he said simply. 'And you are always in it, Hannah. You cannot live with a queen and not be enmeshed in a dozen plots. You live in a snake pit and I tell you frankly, you have not the aptitude for it. Now go to her. I hear she is worse.'

'Not at all,' I said stoutly. 'You can tell the princess that the queen has rallied and is better today.'

He nodded, he did not believe me at all. 'Well, God bless her anyway,' he said kindly. 'For whether she lives or dies she has lost Calais, she has lost her babies, she has lost her husband and lost the throne and lost everything.'

Lord Robert was gone for more than a week and so I could have no news of the release of the English captives. I went to our old print shop and pinned a note on the door. The times were so bad and rents so poor in London that still no-one had taken the shop, and many of my father's books and papers would still be stacked, untouched, in the cellar. I thought that if Daniel did not come to me, and if the queen did not recover, then this might be my refuge once again. I might set up as a bookseller once again, and hope for better times.

I went to Daniel's old house which was at Newgate, just past St Paul's. The neighbours there had not heard of the Carpenter family, they were new in the city. They had come hoping to find work after their farm in Sussex had failed. I looked at their cold pinched faces and wished them well. They promised to tell Daniel, if he should come, that his wife had been seeking him and was waiting for him at court.

'What a handsome boy,' the woman said, looking down at Danny who was holding my hand and standing at my side. 'What's your name?'

'Dan'l,' he said, thumping his chest with his fist.

She smiled at me. 'A forward child,' she said. 'His father won't recognise him.'

'I hope he will,' I said a little breathlessly. If he had not received my letter, Daniel would not even know that I had his son safely with me. If he came to me on his release, our whole life as a family could start again. 'I certainly hope he will,' I repeated.

When I got back to court there was a scurry around the queen's apartments. She had collapsed while dressing for dinner and been put to bed. The doctors had been called and were bleeding her. Quietly, I handed Danny to Will Somers who was in the privy chamber, and I went inside the guarded doors to the queen's bedchamber.

Jane Dormer, white as a sheet and visibly ill herself, was at the head of the bed, holding the queen's hand as the physicians were picking fat leeches off her legs and dropping them back into their glass jar. The queen's thin legs were bruised where their vile mouths had been fixed on her, the maid twitched down the sheet. The queen's eyes were closed in shame at being so exposed, her head turned away from the anxious faces of her physicians. The doctors bowed and got themselves out of the room.

'Go to bed, Jane,' the queen said weakly, 'You are as sick as I am.'

'Not until I have seen Your Grace take some soup.'

The queen shook her head and waved her hand to the door. Jane curtseyed and went out, leaving the queen and I alone.

'Is that you, Hannah?' she asked without opening her eyes.

'Yes, Your Grace.'

'Will you write a letter for me, in Spanish? And send it to the king without showing it to anyone?'

'Yes, Your Grace.'

I took some paper and a pen from the table, drew up a little stool and sat beside her bed. She dictated to me in English and I translated it into Spanish as I wrote. The sentences were long and fluent, I knew that she had been waiting a long time to send him this letter. In all the nights when she had wept for him, she had composed this letter to be sent from her deathbed, knowing that he was far away, joyously living his life in the Netherlands, courted by women, fawned on by men, and planning marriage with her sister. She wrote him a letter like the one her mother wrote to her father from her deathbed: a letter of love and constancy to a man who had offered nothing but heartache.

> *Dearest Husband,*
>
> *Since it has pleased you to stay far from me in my illness and my sorrow, I write to you these words which I wish I might have said to your beloved face.*
>
> *You could not have had and never will have a more loving and faithful wife. The sight of you gladdened my heart every day that we were together, my only regret is that we spent so much time apart.*
>
> *It seems very hard to me that I should face death as I have faced life: alone and without the one I love. I pray that you will never know the loneliness that has walked step by step with me every day of my life. You still have a loving parent to advise you, you have a loving wife who wanted nothing more than to be at your side. No-one will ever love you more.*
>
> *They will not tell me, but I know that I am near to death. This may be my last chance to bid you farewell and to send you my love. May we meet in heaven, though we could not be together on earth, prays*
> *Your wife*
> *Mary R.*

The tears were running down my cheeks by the time I had written this to her dictation but she was calm.

'You will get better, Your Grace,' I assured her. 'Jane told me that you are often ill with autumn sickness. When the first frosts come, you will be better and we will see in Christmas together.'

'No,' she said simply. There was not a trace of self-pity in her tone. It was as if she were weary of the world. 'No. Not this time. I don't think so.'

Winter 1558

Lord Robert came to court with the queen's council to press her to sign her will and name her heir. Every man in the council had been at Hatfield the previous month, all their advice for Queen Mary had been dictated by the queen in waiting.

'She is too sick to see anyone,' Jane Dormer said truculently.

She and I stood shoulder to shoulder in the doorway to the queen's apartments. Lord Robert winked at me but I did not smile back.

'This is her duty,' said the Lord Chancellor gently. 'She has to make a will.'

'She made one,' Jane said abruptly. 'Before she went into confinement last time.'

He shook his head and looked embarrassed. 'She named her child as heir, and the king as regent,' he said. 'But there was no child. She has to name the Princess Elizabeth now, and no regent.'

Jane hesitated, but I stood firm. 'She is too ill,' I maintained. It was true, the queen was coughing up black bile, unable to lie down as her mouth filled with the stuff. Also, I did not want them to see her on her sickbed, still weeping for her husband, for the ruin that Elizabeth had made of her hopes.

Lord Robert smiled at me, as if he understood all of this. 'Mistress Carpenter,' he said. 'You know. She is queen. She cannot have the peace and seclusion of a normal woman. She knows that, we know that. She has a duty to her country and you should not stand in her way.'

I wavered, and they saw it. 'Stand aside,' said the duke, and Jane and I stood unwillingly back and let them walk in to the queen.

They did not take very long, and when they were gone I went in to see her. She was lying propped up on her pillows, a bowl at her side to catch the black bile which spewed from her mouth when she coughed, a jug of squeezed lemons and sugar to take the taste from her lips, a maid in attendance but no-one else. She was as lonely as any beggar coughing out her life on a stranger's doorstep.

'Your Grace, I sent your letter to your husband,' I said quietly. 'Pray God he reads it and comes home to you and you have a merry Christmas with him after all.'

Queen Mary did not even smile at the picture I painted. 'He will not,' she said dully. 'And I would rather not see him ride past me to Hatfield.' She coughed and held a cloth to her mouth. The maid stepped forward and took it from her, offered her the bowl, and then took it away.

'I have another task for you,' she said when she could speak again. 'I want you to go with Jane Dormer to Hatfield.'

I waited.

'Ask Elizabeth to swear on her immortal soul that if she inherits the kingdom she will keep the true faith,' she said, her voice a tiny thread but the conviction behind the words as strong as ever.

I hesitated. 'She will not swear,' I said, knowing Elizabeth.

'Then I will not name her my heir,' she said flatly. 'Mary Stuart in France would claim the throne with French blessing. Elizabeth has the choice. She can fight her way to the throne if she can find enough fools to follow her, or she can come to it with my blessing. But she has to swear to uphold the faith. And she has to mean it.'

'How will I know that she means it?' I asked.

She was too weary to turn her head to me. 'Look at her with your gift, Hannah,' she said. 'This is the last time I will ask you to see for me. Look at her with your gift and tell me what is the best thing for my England.'

I would have argued but simple pity for her made me hold my tongue. This was a woman clinging on to life by the thinnest thread. Only her

473

desire to do her duty to God, to her mother's God, and to her father's country was keeping her alive. If she could secure Elizabeth's promise then she could die knowing that she had done the best she could to keep England safe inside the Holy See.

I bowed and went from the room.

Jane Dormer, still recovering from her own fever and exhausted from nursing the queen, riding in a litter, and I, with Danny astride before me, made our way north to Hatfield and noted sourly the number of fine horses who were going in the same direction as us, from the ailing queen to the thriving heir.

The old palace was ablaze with lights. There was some sort of banquet in progress as we arrived. 'I cannot break bread with her,' Jane said shortly. 'Let us ask to see her, and leave.'

'Of course we can dine,' I said practically. 'You must be starving, I am, and Danny needs to eat.'

She was white-faced and trembling with emotion. 'I will not eat with that woman,' she hissed. 'Who d'you think is in there? Half the nobility of England clamouring for a place, her greatest friends now, the very ones who sneered at her and despised her and named her as a bastard when our queen was in her power.'

'Yes,' I said flatly. 'And the man you love, Count Feria, the Spanish ambassador, who once demanded her death, among them. Now he brings love letters from the queen's own husband. Betrayal is no new thing in England. If you won't break bread with men with false hearts you will starve to death, Jane.'

She shook her head. 'You have no sense of what is right and wrong, Hannah. You are faithless.'

'I don't think faith can be measured in what you eat,' I said, thinking of the bacon and shellfish I had eaten contrary to my people's law. 'I think faith is in your heart. And I love the queen and I admire the princess, and as for the rest, these false men and women, they will have to find their own ways to their own truths. You go and eat in the kitchen if it pleases you. I am going in to dine.'

I could have laughed at her astounded face. I lifted Danny up on to my hip and, braced against his weight, I walked into the dining hall at Hatfield.

Elizabeth had the trappings of queenship already, as if she were an actor practising a part in the full costume. She had a gold canopy over a wooden chair so thickly carved and heavy that it might almost have been a throne. On her right hand she had the Spanish ambassador, as if to flaunt that connection; on her left hand was seated the most favoured lord at this court, my Lord Robert. Beside him was the right-hand man of the Grand Inquisitor of London, the scourge of Protestantism, Dr John Dee, on the other side of the Spanish ambassador was the princess's cousin, who had once arrested her, now dearly beloved to his kin. Beyond him was a quietly ambitious man, a staunch Protestant: William Cecil. I looked at Elizabeth's table and smiled. Nobody would be able to guess which way this cat might jump judging by those honoured with seats beside her. She had put Spanish and English, Catholic and Protestant advisors side by side, who could deduce what was in her mind?

John Dee, looking down the hall, caught my smile and raised his hand to me in greeting. Lord Robert followed the direction of his gaze, saw me, and beckoned me forward. I threaded my way through the court and dropped a curtsey to the princess, who shot me a gleaming smile from her eyes like a jet arrow.

'Ah, it is the girl who was so afraid of being a woman that she first became a fool, and then became a widow,' she said acidly.

'Princess Elizabeth,' I said, curtseying as the words hit home.

'Have you come to see me?'

'Yes, Princess.'

'Have you a message for me from the queen?'

'Yes, Princess.'

There was a little ripple of attention all along the table.

'Is Her Majesty in good health?' The Spanish ambassador, Count Feria, leaned forward, taking the heat from the exchange.

'You would surely know better than I,' I said with a sourness which came easily to me, seeing him at Elizabeth's table. 'Since she writes intimately to only one person, since she loves one man in all the world, and he is your master.'

Elizabeth and my lord exchanged a hidden smile at my rudeness. The count turned his head away.

'You may take a seat with my ladies and see me privately after dinner,' the princess ruled. 'Did you come alone with your son?'

I shook my head. 'Jane Dormer came with me, and we were escorted by two gentlemen from the queen's household.'

The count turned quickly back. 'Mistress Dormer is here?'

'She is dining alone,' I said, my face insolently blank. 'She did not want to keep this company.'

Elizabeth bit her lip to hide another smile, and waved me to the table. 'I see you are not so choosy,' she taunted me.

I met her bright black gaze without shrinking. 'Dinner is dinner, Princess. And both of us have gone hungry in the past.'

She laughed at that and nodded at them to make a space for me. 'She has become a witty fool,' she said to Lord Robert. 'I am glad of it. I never had much faith in seeings and predictions.'

'Once she told me a pretty vision,' he said, his voice very low, his eyes on me but his smile for her.

'Oh?'

'She told me I would be adored by a queen.'

They both laughed, that low-voiced chuckle of conspiring lovers, and he smiled down the hall at me. I met his gaze with a face like flint.

'What *is* the matter with you?' Elizabeth demanded of me after dinner. We were standing in an alcove in the gallery at Hatfield. Elizabeth's court was at a distance, our words hidden by the playing of a lute nearby.

'I don't like Count Feria,' I said bluntly.

'You made that clear enough. Do you really think I will allow you to come into my dinner and insult my guests? You took off a fool's livery, you will have to behave like a lady.'

I smiled. 'Since I carry a message that you want to hear I think you will listen to it before you have me thrown out of the gates, whether I am a fool or a lady.'

She laughed at my impertinence.

'And I doubt that you like him either,' I said boldly. 'First he was your enemy, now he is your friend. There are many such as him around you now, I should imagine.'

476

'Most of this court. And you among them.'

I shook my head. 'I have always admired you both.'

'You love her more than you love me,' she insisted jealously.

I laughed aloud at her childishness; and Lord Robert, standing near, turned to look at me with a smile. 'But Princess, she loves me, and you have never done anything but abuse me and accuse me of being her spy.'

Elizabeth laughed too. 'Yes. But I don't forget that you came to serve me in the Tower. And I don't forget that you brought me a true vision. When you smelled the smoke from the burnings I knew then that I must become queen and bring peace to this country.'

'Well, amen to that,' I said.

'And what is your message?' she asked more soberly.

'Can we talk in your privy chamber? And can I bring Jane Dormer to you?'

'With Lord Robert,' she stipulated. 'And John Dee.'

I bowed my head and followed her as she walked down the gallery to her chamber. The court billowed into bows as she went past as if she were queen already. I smiled, remembering a day when she had limped with her shoe in her hand and no-one had offered her an arm. Now they would lay down their cloaks in the mud to keep her feet dry.

We went into her chamber and Elizabeth took a small wooden chair by the fireside. She gestured that I could pull up a stool and I took it to the other side of the fire, put Danny on my knee, and leaned back against the wooden panelling. I had a sense that I should be quiet and listen. The queen wanted me to advise her if Elizabeth would keep the true faith. I had to listen through the words to the meaning behind them. I had to look through the mask of her smiling face and into her heart.

The door opened, and Jane came into the room. She swept Elizabeth the scantest of curtseys and stood before her. Elizabeth gestured her to sit.

'I will stand, if it please you,' Jane said stiffly.

'You have business with me.' Elizabeth invited her to begin.

'The queen has asked Hannah and me to come to you and put a question to you. The queen requires you to make your answer in very truth. She would want you to swear on your soul that the answer you give is the truth and the whole truth.'

'And what is this question?'

Danny squirmed in my lap and I shifted him in a little closer, putting his small head against my cheek, so that I could look over him to the princess's pale face.

'The queen bid me tell you that she will name you as her heir, her one true heir, and you will be queen on the throne of England without a word of dissent if you will promise her that you will cleave to the true faith,' Jane said quietly.

John Dee drew in a sharp breath, but the princess was absolutely still. 'And if I do not?'

'Then she will name another heir.'

'Mary Stuart?'

'I do not know and I will not speculate,' Jane replied.

The princess nodded. 'Am I to swear on a Bible?' she asked.

'On your soul,' Jane said. 'On your immortal soul before God.'

It was a solemn moment. Elizabeth glanced towards Lord Robert and he took a little step towards her, as if he would protect her.

'And does she swear to name me as heir in return?'

Jane Dormer nodded. 'If you are of the true faith.'

Elizabeth took a deep breath. 'I will swear,' she said.

She rose to her feet. Robert Dudley started forward as if he would stop her but she did not even look at him. I did not rise as I should have done, I stayed completely still, my eyes fixed on her pale face as if I would read her like a clean page of text, fresh off the press, with the ink still drying.

Elizabeth raised her hand. 'I swear, on my immortal soul, that I shall keep this country in the true faith,' she said. Her hand trembled slightly. She brought it down and clasped her hands together before her, and turned to Jane Dormer.

'Did she ask for anything more?'

'No more,' Jane said, her voice very thin.

'So you can tell her I have done it?'

Jane's eyes slid towards me, and the princess was on to her at once.

'Ah, so that is what you are here for.' She rounded on me. 'My little seer-spy. You are to make a window into my soul and see into my heart and tell the queen what you think you know, what you imagine you saw.'

I said nothing.

'You will tell her that I raised my hand and I swore her oath,' she commanded me. 'You will tell her that I am her true heir.'

I rose to my feet, Danny's little head lolled sleepily against my shoulder. 'If we may, we will stay here tonight, and return to the queen tomorrow,' I said, avoiding answering.

'There was one other thing,' Jane Dormer said. 'Her Grace requires you to pay her debts and take care of her trusted servants.'

Elizabeth nodded. 'Of course. Assure my sister that I will honour her wishes as any true heir would do.'

I think only I could have heard the ripple of Elizabeth's joy under her grave voice. I did not condemn her for it. Like Mary she had waited all her life for the moment when she might hear the news that she was queen, and now she thought that it would come to her, without dissent, tomorrow, or the day after.

'We will leave at dawn,' I said, thinking of the frailty of the queen's health. I knew she would be hanging on to hear that England was safe within the true faith, that whatever else was lost, she had restored England into grace.

'Then I will bid you goodnight and God speed now,' Elizabeth said sweetly.

She let us get to the door and Jane Dormer to go through ahead of me, before she said, so quietly that only I, listening for her summons, could have heard it: 'Hannah.'

I turned.

'I know you are her loyal friend as well as mine,' she said gently. 'Do this last service for your mistress and take my word as true, and let her go to her God with some comfort. Give her peace, and give peace to our country.'

I bowed to her and went out.

I thought we would leave Hatfield without another farewell but when I went for my horse on a frosty cold morning with the sun burning red like an ember on the white horizon, there was Lord Robert looking handsome and smiling, wrapped in a dark red velvet cloak with John Dee at his side.

'Is your boy warm enough for the journey?' he asked me. 'It's been a hard frost and the air is bitter.'

I pointed behind me. Danny was labouring along under an extra-thick jerkin of wool, carrying a shawl that I had insisted he bring. He peeped at me from under a heavy woollen cap. 'The poor boy is half-drowned in clothes,' I said. 'He will sweat rather than freeze.'

Robert nodded. 'The men are to be released from Calais within a week,' he said. 'They will be collected by a ship which will bring them into Gravesend.'

I felt my heart beat a little faster.

'You are blushing like a girl,' Lord Robert said, gently mocking.

'Do you think he will have had my letter, that I sent when I first came home?' I asked.

Lord Robert shrugged. 'He may have done. But you can tell him yourself, soon enough.'

I drew a little closer to him. 'You see, if he did not receive it then he will not know that I escaped out of Calais. He might think I am dead. He might not come to England, he might go to Italy or somewhere.'

'On the off-chance that you are dead?' Lord Robert asked critically. 'With no-one ever mentioning it to him? With no proof? And his son?'

'In the confusion of the battle,' I said weakly.

'Someone would have looked for you,' he said. 'If you had been killed they would have found your body.'

I shifted awkwardly. Daniel came to me and stretched out his arms 'Dan'l up!' he commanded.

'Wait a moment,' I said absently. I turned back to Lord Robert. 'You see, if someone told him that I left with you . . .'

'Then he would know that you are alive, and where to find you,' he said logically. Then he checked and slapped his forehead. 'Mistress Boy, you have played me for an idiot all along. You are estranged from him, aren't you? And you fear that he will think you ran away with me? And he won't come for you because he has cast you off? And now you don't want me; but you've lost him, and all you've got is his son . . .' He broke off, struck with sudden doubt. 'He *is* your husband's son, isn't he?'

'Yes,' I said staunchly.

'Is he yours?' he said, some sense warning him that there was a lie hidden away somewhere near.

'Yes,' I said without wavering.

Lord Robert laughed aloud. 'My God, girl, you are a fool indeed. You did not love him till you lost him.'

'Yes,' I admitted through gritted teeth.

'Well, more a woman than a fool,' he said fairly. 'I would say women love men most when they have lost them, or cannot get them. Well-a-day, my pretty fool. You had best get a ship and set sail for your Daniel as soon as you can. Otherwise he will be out of prison and free as a bird flying away, and you will never find him at all.'

'Can I get a ship to Calais?' I asked blankly.

He thought for a moment. 'Not very readily; but you could go over with the ship that is going to fetch my soldiers home. I'll write you a note.'

He snapped his fingers to a stable boy and sent him running for a clerk with pen and paper. When the lad came he dictated three lines to give me a free pass on the boat for myself and my son.

I curtseyed low to him in genuine gratitude. 'Thank you, my lord,' I said. 'I do thank you very deeply.'

He smiled his heart-turning smile. 'My pleasure, dearest little fool. But the ship sails within a week. Will you be able to leave the queen?'

'She's sinking fast,' I said slowly. 'That's why I was in such a hurry to leave at once. She was holding on for Elizabeth's answer.'

'Well, thank you for that information, which you denied me earlier,' he said.

I bit my lip as I realised that to tell him, was to tell Elizabeth, and those planning her campaign, when she should be ready to call out her army to claim her throne.

'No harm done,' he said. 'Half of her doctors are paid by us to let us know how she is.'

John Dee drew closer. 'And could you see into the princess' heart?' he asked gently. 'Could you tell if she was sincere in her oath for keeping the true faith? Do you believe she will be a Catholic queen?'

'I don't know,' I said simply. 'I shall pray for guidance on the way home.'

Robert would have said something but John Dee put a hand on his arm. 'Hannah will say the right thing to the queen,' he said. 'She knows that it is not one queen or another that matters, it is not one name of

481

God or another, what matters most is to bring peace to this country so that a man or woman in danger of cruelty or persecution can come here and be certain of a fair hearing.' He paused, and I thought of my father and I, coming to this England and hoping for a safe haven.

'What matters is that a man or woman can believe what they wish, and worship how they wish, to a God whom they name as they wish. What matters is that we make a strong country here which can be a force for good in the world, where men and women can question and learn freely. This country's destiny is to be a place where men and women can know that they are free.'

He stopped. Lord Robert was smiling down at me.

'I know what she will do,' Lord Robert said sweetly. 'Because she is my tender-hearted Mistress Boy still. She will say whatever she has to say to comfort the queen in her final hours, God bless her, the poor lady. No queen ever came to the throne with higher hopes and died in such sadness.'

I leaned down and scooped Daniel up into my arms. The grooms brought my horse from the stables and Jane Dormer came from the house and got into the litter without a word to either man.

'Good luck in Calais,' Robert Dudley said, smiling. 'Few women succeed in finding the love of their life. I hope you do, little Mistress Boy.'

Then he waved and stepped back, and let me go.

It was a cold long ride back to St James's palace but Danny's little body was warm as he rode before me, and every now and then I could hear a delighted little carol of song from him.

I rode in silence, thoughtful. The end of my journey when I would see the queen loomed very large ahead of me. I did not yet know what I would say to her. I did not yet know what I had seen, nor what to report. Elizabeth raised her right hand and took the oath she had been asked to do, her part was done. Now it was for me to judge whether or not she meant it.

When we got to the palace the hall was subdued, the few guards playing cards, the firelight flickering, the torches burning low. Will Somers was in the queen's presence chamber, with half a dozen others, mostly paid court officials and physicians. There were no friends or beloved kin waiting to see the queen, praying for her in her illness. She was not England's darling any more, and the chamber rang with emptiness.

Danny spotted Will and sprang towards him. 'You go in,' Will said. 'She has been asking for you.'

'Is she any better?' I asked hopefully.

He shook his head. 'No.'

Cautiously I opened the door to her privy chamber and went in. Two of her women were seated at the fireside, enjoying a gossip when they should have been watching her. They jumped up guiltily as we came in. 'She did not want company,' one of them said defensively to Jane Dormer. 'And she would not stop weeping.'

'Well, I hope you lie alone weeping and unwatched one day,' Jane snapped at her, and the two of us went past them and into the queen's bedchamber.

She had curled up in the bed like a little girl, her hair in a cloud around her face. She did not turn her head at the sound of the opening door, she was deep in her grief.

'Your Grace?' Jane Dormer said, her voice cracking.

The queen did not move, but we heard the quiet occasional sob go on, as regular as a heartbeat, as if weeping had become a sign of life, like a pulse.

'It is I,' Jane said. 'And Hannah the Fool. We have come back from Princess Elizabeth.'

The queen sighed very deeply and turned her head wearily towards us.

'She took the oath,' Jane said. 'She swore she would keep the country in the true faith.'

I stepped to the bedside and took Queen Mary's hand. It was as small and as light as a child's, there was nothing left of her. Sadness had worn her away to dust that could blow away on the wind. I thought of her riding into London in her shabby red costume, her face bright with hope, and her courage when she took on the great men of the kingdom and beat them at their own game. I thought of her joy in her husband and her longing for a child to love, a son for England. I thought of her absolute devotion to the memory of her mother and her love of God.

Her little hand fluttered in mine like a dying bird.

'I saw Elizabeth take the oath,' I started. I was about to tell her the kindest lie that I could form. But gently, irresistibly, I told her the truth, as if the Sight was speaking the truth through me. 'Mary, she will not keep it. But she will do better than keep it, I hope you can understand that now. She will become a better queen than she is a woman. She will teach the people of this country that each man and woman must consider his or her own conscience, must find their own way to God. And she will bring this country to peace and prosperity. You did the very best that you could do for the people of this country, and you have a good successor. Elizabeth will never be the woman that you have been; but she will be a good queen to England, I know it.'

She raised her head a little and her eyelids fluttered open. She looked at me with her straight honest gaze once more, and then she closed her eyes and lay still.

I did not stay to watch the rush of servants to Hatfield. I packed my bag and took Danny by the hand and took a boat down the river to Gravesend. I had my lord's letter to show to the ship's captain and he promised me a berth as soon as they sailed. We waited a day or two and then Danny and I boarded the little ship and set sail for Calais.

Danny was delighted by the ship, the moving deck beneath his feet, the slap and rush of the waves, the creaking of the sails and the cry of the seagulls. 'Sea!' he exclaimed, over and over again. He took my face in both of his little hands and gazed at me with his enormous dark eyes, desperate to tell me the significance of his delight. 'Sea. Mamma! Sea!'

'What did you say?' I said, taken aback. He had never spoken my name before, I had expected him to call me Hannah. I had not thought, I suppose I should have thought, but I had never thought he would call me mother.

'Sea,' he repeated obediently, and wriggled to be put down.

Calais was a different place with the walls breached and the sides of the castle smeared with black oil from the siege, the stones darkened with smoke from the fire. The captain's face was grim when we came into the harbour and saw the English ships, which had been fired where they were moored, at the harbour wall, like so many heretics at the stake. He tied up with military smartness and slapped down the gangplank like a challenge. I took Danny in my arms and walked down the gangplank into the town.

It was dream-like, to go into the ruins of my old home. I saw streets and houses that I knew; but some of them were missing walls or roofs, and there had been a terrible toll paid by the thatched houses, they were all but destroyed.

I did not want to go down the street where my husband and I once lived, I was afraid of what I might find. If our house was still standing, and his mother and sisters were still there, I did not know how to reconcile with them. If I met his mother and she was angry with me and wanted to take Danny away from me I did not know what I would do or say. But if she was dead, and his house destroyed, it would be even worse.

Instead I went with the captain and the armed guard up to the castle under our white pennant of truce. We were expected; the commander came out civilly enough and spoke to the captain in rapid French. The captain bridled, understanding perhaps one word in three, and then leaned forward and said very loudly and slowly: 'I have come for the English men, as has been agreed, as per the terms, and I expect them forthwith.'

When he had no response, he said it again, pitched a little higher.

'Captain, would you like me to speak for you, I can speak French?' I offered.

He turned to me with relief. 'Can you? That might help. Why doesn't the fool answer me?'

I stepped forward a little and said to the commander in French: 'Captain Gatting offers his apologies but he cannot speak French. I can translate for you. I am Madame Carpenter. I have come for my husband who has been ransomed and the captain has come for the other men. We have a ship waiting in the harbour.'

He bowed slightly. 'Madam, I am obliged to you. The men are mustered and ready. The civilians are to be released first and then the soldiers will march down to the harbour. Their weapons will not be returned. It is agreed?'

I translated for the captain and he scowled at me. 'We ought to get the weapons back,' he said.

I shrugged. All I could think of was Daniel, waiting somewhere inside the castle for his release. 'We can't.'

'Tell him very well; but tell him that I'm not best pleased,' the captain said sourly.

'Captain Gatting agrees,' I said smoothly in French.

'Please come inside.' The commander led us over the drawbridge and into the inner courtyard. Another thick curtain wall with a portcullis doorway led to the central courtyard where about two hundred men were mustered, the soldiers in one block, the civilians in another. I raked the ranks for Daniel but I could not see him.

'Commandant, I am seeking my husband, Daniel Carpenter, a civilian,' I said. 'I cannot see him, and I am afraid of missing him in the crowd.'

'Daniel Carpenter?' he asked. He turned and snapped an order at the man guarding the civilians.

'Daniel Carpenter!' the man bawled out.

In the middle of one of the ranks a man came forward. 'Who asks for him?' said Daniel, my husband.

I closed my eyes for a moment as the world seemed to shift all around me.

'I am Daniel Carpenter,' Daniel said again, not a quaver in his voice, stepping forward on the very brink of freedom, greeting whatever new danger might threaten him without a moment's hesitation.

The commander beckoned him to come forward and moved to one side so that I could see him. Daniel saw me for the first time and I saw him go very pale. He was older-looking, a little weary, he was thinner, but nothing worse than winter-pale and winter-thin. He was the same. He was my beloved Daniel with his dark curling hair and his dark eyes and his kissable mouth and that particular smile which was my smile; it only ever shone on me, it was at once desiring, steadfast, and amused.

'Daniel,' I whispered. 'My Daniel!'

'Ah, Hannah,' he said quietly. 'You.'

Behind us, the civilians were signing their names and marching out to freedom. I did not hear the shouted orders or the tramp of their feet. All I could see, all I could know, was Daniel.

'I ran away,' I said. 'I am sorry. I was afraid and I did not know what to do. Lord Robert gave me safe passage to England and I went back to Queen Mary. I wrote to you at once. I would not have gone without you if there had been any time to think.'

Gently, he stepped forward and took my hand. 'I have dreamed and dreamed of you,' he said quietly. 'I thought you had left me for Lord Robert when you had the chance.'

'No! Never. I knew at once that I wanted to be with you. I have been trying to get a letter to you. I have been trying to reach you. I swear it, Daniel. I have thought of nothing and no-one but you, ever since I left.'

'Have you come back to be my wife?' he asked simply.

I nodded. At this most important moment I found I lost all my fluency. I could not speak. I could not argue my case, I could not persuade him in any one of my many languages. I could not even whisper. I just nodded emphatically, and Danny on my hip, his arms around my neck, gave a gurgle of laughter and nodded too, copying me.

I had hoped Daniel would be glad and snatch me up into his arms, but he was sombre. 'I will take you back,' he said solemnly. 'And I will not question you, and we will say no more about this time apart. You will never have a word of reproach from me, I swear it; and I will bring this boy up as my son.'

For a moment, I did not understand what he meant, and then I gasped. 'Daniel, he *is* your son! This is your son by your woman. This is her son. We were running from the French horsemen and she fell, she gave him to me as she went down. I am sorry, Daniel. She died at once. And this is your boy, I passed him off as mine. He is my boy now. He is my boy too.'

'He is mine?' he asked wonderingly. He looked at the child for the first time and saw, as anyone would have to see, the dark eyes which were his own, and the brave little smile.

'He is mine too,' I said jealously. 'He knows that he is my boy.'

Daniel gave a little half-laugh, almost a sob, and put his arms out. Danny reached for his father and went confidingly to him, put his plump little arms around his neck, looked him in the face and leaned back so he could scrutinise him. Then he thumped his little fist on his own chest and said, by way of introduction: 'Dan'l.'

Daniel nodded, and pointed to his own chest. 'Father,' he said. Danny's little half-moon eyebrows raised in interest.

'*Your* father,' Daniel said.

He took my hand and tucked it firmly under his arm, as he held his son tightly with the other. He walked to the dispatching officer and gave his name and was ticked off their list. Then together we walked towards the open portcullis.

'Where are we going?' I asked, although I did not care. As long as I was with him and Danny, we could go anywhere in the world, be it flat or round, be it the centre of the heavens or wildly circling around the sun.

'We are going to make a home,' he said firmly. 'For you and me and Daniel. We are going to live as the People, you are going to be my wife, and his mother, and one of the Children of Israel.'

'I agree,' I said, surprising him again.

He stopped in his tracks. 'You agree?' he repeated comically.

I nodded.

'And Daniel is to be brought up as one of the People?' he confirmed.

I nodded. 'He is one already,' I said. 'I had him circumcised. You must instruct him, and when he is older he will learn from my father's Hebrew Bible.'

He drew a breath. 'Hannah, in all my dreams, I did not dream of this.'

I pressed against his side. 'Daniel, I did not know what I wanted when I was a girl. And then I was a fool in every sense of the word. And now that I am a woman grown, I know that I love you and I want this son of yours, and our other children who will come. I have seen a woman break her heart for love: my Queen Mary. I have seen another break her soul to avoid it: my Princess Elizabeth. I don't want to be Mary or Elizabeth, I want to be me: Hannah Carpenter.'

'And we shall live somewhere that we can follow our beliefs without danger,' he insisted.

'Yes,' I said, 'in the England that Elizabeth will make.'

Author's Note

The characters of Hannah and her family are invented, but there were Jewish families concealing their faith in London as elsewhere in Europe, throughout this period. I am indebted to Cecil Roth's moving history and to the broadcaster and film-maker Naomi Gryn for giving me a small insight into these courageous lives. Most of the other characters in this novel are real, created by me in this fiction to match the historical record as I understand it. Below is a list of some of my sources, and for the history of Calais I am also indebted to the French historian Georges Fauquet who was generous with his time and his knowledge.

Billington, Sandra, *A Social History of the Fool*, 1984

Braggard, Philippe, Termote, Johan, Williams, John (ed), *Walking the Walls, Historic Town Defences in Kent, Côte d'Opale and West Flanders*, Kent County Council, 1999

Brigden, Susan, *New Worlds, Lost Worlds, The rule of the Tudors 1485–1603*, 2000

Cressy, David, *Birth, Marriage and Death, Ritual, Religions and the Life Cycle in Tudor and Stuart England*, 1977

Darby, H.C., *A New Historical Geography of England before 1600*, 1976

Doran, John, *A History of Court Fools*, 1858

Fontaine, Raymond, *Calais, ville d'histoire et de tourisme*, Syndicat d'initiative de France, (P.d.C.) 2002

Green, Dominic, *The Double Life of Doctor Lopez*, 2003

Guy, John, *Tudor England*, 1988

Haynes, Alan, *Sex in Elizabethan England*, 1997

Hibbert, Christopher, *The Virgin Queen*, 1992

Lenoir, Laurent, *Á la decouverté des anciennes fortifications de Calais*, Nord Patrimonie Editions, 2002

Loades, David, *The Tudor Court*, 1986

Marshall, Peter, *The Philosopher's Stone, A quest for the secrets of alchemy*, 2001

Neale, J.E., *Queen Elizabeth*, 1934

Plowden, Alison, *Elizabeth: Marriage with my Kingdom*, 1999

Plowden, Alison, *The Young Elizabeth*, 1999

Plowden, Alison, *Tudor Queens and Commoners*, 1998

Ridley, Jasper, *Elizabeth I*, 1987

Roth, Cecil, *A History of the Marranos*, The Jewish Publication Society of America, Philadelphia, USA, 1932

Somerset, Anne, *Elizabeth I*, 1997

Starkey, David, *Elizabeth*, 2001

Turner, Robert, *Elizabethan Magic. The art and the Magus*, 1989

Weir, Alison, *Children of England*, 1997

Weir, Alison, *Elizabeth the Queen*, 1999

Welsford, Enid, *The Fool: His social and literary history*, 1935

Woolley, Benjamin, *The Queen's Conjuror*, 2001

Yates, Frances, *The Occult Philosophy in the Elizabethan Age*, 1979